4P: Part Particle Porta

Book 1 Series 1 Episode

By Steve Baglow

To Dad

UncleBaggy, Uncle Baggy, Uncle-Baggy, Uncle_Baggy, unclebaggy (c)

25/12/17

Copyright (c) 2017 by Steven Baglow

All rights reserved

Cover design by Steve Baglow
Book design by Steve Baglow

No part of this book may be reproduced in any form or by any electronic or mechanical means, including information storage and retrieval systems, without permission in writing from the author. The only exception is by a reviewer, who may quote short excerpts in a review.

This book is a work of fiction. Any names, characters, places and incidents are products of the authors imagination or are used fictitiously. Any resemblance to any actual persons, creatures, living or dead, events or locals are entirely coincidental.

Steve Baglow
First seen on Amazon August 2017

Dedicated to

Mum

Preface.

This book you are potentially about to read, is something I personally refer to as the thing. Writing was something I had always wanted to attempt but really never got around to starting, mainly due to the annoyance of life getting in the way.
Then one day (after being single again had sunk in) on the 18/September/2010 I found a little Writer program for my smart phone, this served me very well as I always had my phone on me, until I reached the text limit which was somewhere around ten thousand characters. As it started to slow, stop, pause and generally be a bit useless, I had finally saved up enough money to buy a cheap small laptop and downloaded a free open office program. It was somewhere at this point that I realized that I might actually be writing a thing, something book sized, I worried that it was not going to be good enough and would actually be pointless.
Then I realized why I was writing and who I was writing for.
The answer was simple, I had always wanted to write something in the science fiction vein that was all mine and I would enjoy myself if I was to read, so I persevered.

This book thing might be awfully badly written, have errors the size of the Universe in it but rather than keep going back over and over changing, altering things. I have decided to leave it as something to measure myself by. After all I hopefully could not get any worse writing another book thing could I.
I have heard other writers say that you do not stop editing and they are right, there is always a thing to alter, something to improve and for me it is the same. So my final edit was on the 17/August/2017 and may all who read the thing, enjoy it.

Ps I have started a second book, sorry...

Prologue.

Jack has been charged with saving the Earth, by something he has apparently known for years, who he has just met. The problems with this are the actual lack of Earth, should he bother and a normal hero may be required.
Here lies one of the many issues, Jack is most definitely not a hero, let alone normal.

Then there is the fact he has been informed he needs to win a surf competition, one that happens between Universes! What exactly he surfs on or with, whilst someone attempts to remove him from the living, is anyone's guess?

Chapter 1 : Rubble Me This.

Jack woke up with a typical Monday morning headache. The type that you know is going to last beyond three coffees, especially on the long journey of fourteen stops on the train.

He still had not moved but something felt a little out of sync. First of all he could feel the wind ruffling his short dark hair, which considering his bedroom window had been painted shut by a very reasonable decorator a little over a year ago. This was a tad odd. No it was not that, maybe it was the lack of traffic sounds. That was always a possibility if he got his days wrong again. Still thinking about it, that was not it either. Now he thought about it the bed did feel like it was at an odd angle. Jack opened one eye, gave a little moan after the sun shining directly onto his face nearly blinded him. Jack sat bolt upright in his bed, promptly fell off the bed and then fell an additional thirty feet on to his sofa on the ground floor. Landing on his back this came as a bit of a shock, considering his bed was on the second floor, which made him take a closer look at the sofa. Yes, yes it was his sofa. A rather nice burgundy velour finish, although it did seem a little damp and oddly shaded in places through the dust.

Still in his black pyjamas Jack had that feeling of wrongness as he looked round what used to be his lounge. Everything was either stained, covered in some white dusty powder or blown apart by unknown sources. This did not include the hole in his ceiling, that went right though to the early morning clear blue sky.

Feeling shocked and a little overwhelmed that some possible plane had crashed into his house, he sat for several minutes awaiting the sound of sirens. When they were not very forthcoming he decided to climb back up to his room via the dubious looking stair case. Glancing about before he began his climbing expedition, he noticed no lights on the television, radio or even the lava lamp.   After slipping, sliding and with minor splinters now in his feet, Jack made it too his room. Knowing he left his mobile phone on the bedside table, he was quite surprised to find no wall next to his table and the middle of his bedroom floor missing. His phone still sat there flashing with a message, but it was the view across his room into the city that had now captured his eyes.

There did not appear to be anything taller than about twenty feet, it was as if a great scythe had followed the lay of the land and chopped everything down in a several really big circles to the same height. In little patches buildings and even some streets had survived the scything by the simple fact they had been next to some trees, which had not been touched.

Jack carefully lined up a loose floorboard across the gaping hole in his floor and gingerly crawled to his bed, which was angled slightly into the hole. He rolled across his bed, careful not to take the quick route to the ground floor again and disconnected his phone from the charger. No service flashed across the top of the screen as he swiped at it. Typical thought Jack and it had not charged fully either.

Jack then checked his text message, it was from an unknown number and read: 'The Banks have been hoarding your money for years!

So isn't it about time you got it back, with a PPI claim from Payment Protection Insurance Smith Solvency. Just reply YES to this text and PPISS will take care of the rest!'

Well at least emergency calls should work he thought. Nope, nothing available after tapping at the screen. Now that was a might odd, there was always something, somewhere. Then the shock of the view finally hit home 'what the hell had happened and what was going on?' he thought.

Jack sat for several moments on the corner of his bed, in his black pyjamas with blacker skull motifs, just staring across the battered city. This really cannot be he thought, there has to be a logical explanation and one that did involve him having a really bad dream. Jack pinched himself on the inner thigh "ouch!" that really hurt he said.

After sitting on his bed for several more minutes Jack decided it was time to wash, dress and judging by the hair on his face, have a shave. There another thing was wrong, Jack hated shaving and remembered doing it the night before, so he should not be doing it in the morning just before work. But now he seemed to have several inches of scraggly beard, growing all over his face.

Deep in relentless worrying thought, Jack wandered through to his bathroom, which quite surprisingly had survived the incident with only cracks in the walls. After having washed himself and shaved in the sink, Jack meandered back to his room, opened the closet and put on blue jeans, white t-shirt and a cream cardigan. The socks were white of course as were his trainers. No point in putting his suit on for work if there was no work he thought. Still he mused, he should try and get to the office and see if everyone was okay, whatever day of the week it was.

A dark thought crossed his mind in the form of his immediate boss having been decapitated by the event. Jack smiled a bit, well quite a lot actually and then tried without much effect to clear the mildly evil thought from his head. Whatever the event was? Still he should go in, especially as Jenny would be there. Jack picked up his wallet, phone and door keys and climbed gingerly down the wobbly staircase.

His front door still needed to be unlocked, but when he put the key in and turned the latch, the whole frame fell outwards, door and all. Jack wondered about insurance at this point and as he stepped outside through the cloud of dust into the exceptionally bright morning, he paused.
"It must be morning he thought?" out loud.

As he stepped cautiously further outside he could see rubble everywhere, some buildings had completely collapsed and others simply had windows broken, mostly inward but a few had been smashed out. Jack just gazed around the reality of the day still sinking in. He pinched himself for good measure to test his dream state and boy did that hurt.

Then he heard what can only be described as the sound of a bear roaring into a bucket, admittedly a very large bucket. Jack had watched enough wildlife programs to know the sound of a bear and had been often enough to the zoo to see them. 'Still it must have escaped from the zoo' he thought 'along with some of its friends?' he added slightly worriedly.

Jack wandered further from his fallen front door, maneuvering around what he thought of as his pavement oak tree, then stepping carefully over bricks and the occasional fallen lamppost or sign. As he looked about he had the feeling that something was tickling his ears, occasionally he felt the need to swipe at some tingling invisible strands of nothing. It was like a multitude of tiny furry things rubbing gently against his skin, not unpleasant but mildly annoying and uncatchable.

Jack slowly ambled about the rubble strewn street like a tourist shocked by the lack of cleanliness from the authorities, he heard the scrape of metal on metal but could not see where the sound was coming from, he looked first one way and then the other.

"Psst" something said somewhere from the centre of the rubble strewn street. Jack turned round slowly and eventually some fingers could be seen waving at him from a man-hole in the centre of the road. As he wandered over he glanced around and the thought occurred to him that since waking up, in his rather damaged house, he had seen not one sign of actual people. Oh he had heard some wildlife that should be in the zoo, but he had not seen or heard any local animals and now some fingers were waving at him. Presumably they belonged to the 'psst ' sound effect.

Jack looked into the man-hole, cautiously and with just one eye peering over the edge.
"What the sod are you doing wandering around up there?" came the whispered question from the hole, followed shortly by the person climbing sharply up the ladder, grabbing Jack by his T-shirt collar and tipping him into the man-hole head first. Jack didn't even have time to scream before he landed flat on his back on a mattress in the tunnel, which made a horribly wet squelchy noise as he landed on it.
"Your one lucky boy!" said his assailant as they climbed back in the hole and pulled the metal cover back over. Jack considered this for all of three seconds in the dim light, whilst his assailant climbed down the ladder. Warm comfortable bed, admittedly a leaning bed but his bed. He had woken up and fallen into his lounge, the city looked like a bomb had hit it and now he was lying in what was an actual sewer.

Jack could feel his assailant glaring at him, even in the gloom of the sewer and so he asked "I was just wondering, how I'm so lucky, to be here lying in a sewer with you?"
"You weren't seen!" came the curt reply from his assailant.
Jack stood up carefully, trying not to touch anything in the sewer more than he had too and looked at his clothes, which were now slightly mucky with unmentionable things.
"Come on, don't hang about" came the voice from down the tunnel. Jack turned and saw his supposed saviour beckoning for him to follow further down the tunnel. Jack had a few questions in mind, not least of which was why was everything so wrecked and who was he hiding from?

He kept trying too ask questions as he followed her further and further down the tunnels, getting all kinds of strange things washing over and in his trainers. After a few minutes Jack realized why he thought of his saviour as a her. The voice was muffled by some rubberized hat and coat, but if he listened to her incessant commands of "hurry up you idiot!"and "stop talking!" he could tell it was just about female. Finally it was the swaying of the hips and the other sexist give away being pink rubber Wellington boots, that had lead him to think of her as female. As to how old she was, while wearing an all covering seaman's long shore coat, he would not like to guess, especially out loud.

After only a few minutes but what felt like an age, Jack was still following this women down the surprisingly well lit sewer tunnel. She was using a pencil torch and running her brown gloved hand along the tunnel walls. Least he hoped it was brown in colour and not stained by unmentionables. She must have some eye issues he thought, as she again stumbled over some tunnel debris, which Jack stepped over easily.

She finally stopped and turned to him and asked "where's your torch then?"

Jack looked at her and very calmly replied "what do I need a torch for?" The lady, well he was being polite in thinking of her as a lady, because he could not really see or hear her with her dark green rubber hat pulled down so far over her face, made an impolite sound in the back of her throat, waved her hands in the air, slapped them on her thighs and said "why me?" in an small desperate voice.

She then turned away down the tunnel, Jack watched her stumble along again, tripping over various drain paraphernalia and the odd bit of house, with its associated internal clutter.

Jack would have offered assistance as she banged along but he recognized a self sufficient women when he saw one. Not that there was anything wrong with self sufficient women but in the case of this one, he knew that any assistance offered would be taken as an insult, followed by a glare and even the possibility of violence upon his person.

Watching her walk down the sewer in front of him, Jack was actually enjoying the shape and shake of each of her steps, whilst admiring her behind from behind. Jack let his imagination wonder off to moonlit beaches and how her bottom might look in a bikini, as she turned sharply and caught him admiring her posterior with her torch. She opened her mouth in anger, which he could just see beneath her hood to presumably give him another verbal ear bashing. Jack was quite taken by the shape of her lips and all sorts of thoughts passed across his minds eye, including the one that said 'do I know her?'

Before either of them could say a word, they were both suddenly surprised to be bathed in dusty sunlight, as a four foot diameter hole appeared in the sewer roof above there heads. Looking up Jack could see the hole had been made by some form of soundless explosion, he watched as bits of tunnel sailed away into the air. As he shaded his eyes from the sudden light, he could just make out bits of tunnel fly up and not stop, like gravity had been apparently reversed and was not giving up now it had a grip.

For all of a few seconds the blast of light lasted, until it was blanked out by what looked like an obscenely large vacuum nozzle. Then the sound started, a sort of low gurgling, which very quickly turned into a deep sounding high pitched whine.

The hooded women turned to run, as she did so she tripped and her legs were swiped from under her and sucked up towards the hole. She grabbed at some broken metal pipe sticking out from the hole and hung on with her legs dangling into the nozzle.
She turned her head towards Jack and said "pull me out you idiot!"

Jack stood staring up into the black nozzle vacuum thing, feeling lost as to what was going on, thinking to himself that he must still be dreaming and brushed a shoulder clear of nothing in particular.

With jaw open he turned his head slightly to look at the women hanging upside down in front of him, he could not help but wonder what was underneath that ridiculous green coat and rubberized hat.

With her continuing to shout at him about rescuing her and with no little personal abuse, he reached his hand out to help her. Jack thought he was moving quickly but it seemed like he was sliding his hand through treacle to reach her.
"Will you hurry up and pull me out and stop being a prat!" she screamed at him.

Jack stopped moving his hand towards her, he was only inches away and so far all she had done was abuse him in various forms. This had included pulling him into a sewer full of over␣whelming smells and debris.
'This has got to be a dream' he thought 'or some reality television show, and it better be because I'm definitely gonna need new trainers after this!'
'Still, better to play along' he thought.

Jack reached for her outstretched hand and as soon as he touched her glove his feet started to swing up towards the black hole. It was strange, there was no suction effect, just the slow reversal of gravity. It was like the feeling of falling but slower and up, towards the black hole in the ceiling.
"Well that was well done you nit!" said the annoyed sounding women as he started to float past.
"You ever had one of those days?" asked Jack as he floated level, kicking his legs around into the hole and grabbing at a piece of broken pipe on the opposite side of the opening.
He gripped her free hand, just as the machine started to increase the level of noise and apparent suction. Upside down, Jack still kicking his legs caught the edge of the large nozzle, which being a little way into the hole, swung about dangerously.

A couple of things happened shortly afterwards, the machine banged to one side, twisted and struck a wall on the surface.
Presumably the red button on the side was an emergency cut off switch, because as soon as it struck the wall, gravity was returned to normal in the sewer. This had the effect of reversing the pull to push, Jack was thrown out first and landed flat on his back with a splash.
Just as he raised himself up on his elbows in the damp sewer, the

women was forced to let go of her jagged pipe in the hole and landed bum first on his nether regions. She turned to look at her groaning soft landing, the look of anguish on Jack's face nearly made up for his simpleness she thought.

As she gathered herself Jack began rolling about in the fluid of the sewer, moaning like a little boy kicked by a playful mule for stroking its behind. The women turned her face to the hole in the roof of the sewer, listening she heard the clicking and whistling of annoyed sounding conversation.

"Right Brian, what happened and why are you lying down covering your eyes?"
"Will you stop calling me Brian, George!"
"I've told you before to not call me that, I look nothing like a George and your still covering your eye holes!"
"Well, I'm waiting for the explosion!" there was a pause, a considerable amount of shuffling and finally the first voice said "yes, I remember now, something got wedged inside didn't it and destroyed everything over twenty feet for miles on several occasions?"
Another considerable pause followed "well I'm uncovering my eye holes now, it looks like we'll live" said the Brian named voice in a relieved tone of clicks and whistles.

All this was lost on the two humans, bounding like rabbits after the last carrot in the field down the tunnel, with one moving with a limp that gradually lessened. They would not have understood it anyway, being that the conversation occurred in universal four and they were running and hopping really fast with there hearts pounding in there ears.

Twenty minutes later after there mad dash down the sewer tunnels, with so many junctions and turnings that Jack really had absolutely no idea where they were, the women stopped. She leant heavily against a mildly slimy bricked sewer wall and Jack looked about, wondering if they were still even in the city?
She stood leaning, gasping for breath, looking at Jack like he was something she had trodden in along a dog walkers lane.
"Why are you looking at me like that" he asked "it's not as if I wasn't being shanghaied by a vacuum cleaner as well you know?"

While catching her breath and trying hard not to smile too much, she asked him "yes I realize this Jack but I'm surprised your not the least bit breathless though, after sprinting for the last twenty minutes?"

"I'm really fit!" in all honesty Jack did think that he was the fittest of all his friends, maybe not the fastest but he had stamina. The fact he had a small keg for a six pack, where his stomach muscles should be and smoked and drank once a month was not relevant in his book. Jack then turned and started patting his pockets, seeming to get a little more desperate as the seconds wore on. Finally he made a small begrudging sound as he realized the only things in his pockets were his phone, wallet and a bunch of keys. No lighter, no cigarettes, he would have to find a shop he thought.

As he held the objects in his hands the women snatched his phone and threw it across the sewer to smash in the opposite wall. It disintegrated in to many small parts, with little sparks flying off and then vanishing as the many pieces landed in the brown water of the sewer. Jack stood completely shocked, the rage inside slowly building up, making his face turn red and him to clench his now empty hand.

"You absolute idiot, numb nuts, tool and not forgetting plank. No wonder they found us ten feet underground!" she shouted this with such anger at him that Jack decided not to slap her for destroying his phone, not just yet.

His whole life, his work, his social life, his planning, everything was on his now ex-phone. "Couldn't I have just put it in air-plane mode or even just turned it off?" he asked quietly through clenched teeth, he stared angrily at the murky water where some of the bits had landed.

Much as he wanted his phone back, searching through a used sewer for the component parts was not high on his options list and what could he do with them if he found them.

'If I could find the contacts card, maybe something could be saved?' he thought, whilst looking hopefully at the slowly gurgling mess by his feet.

The women moved forward off the sewer wall and clipped him across the back of his head "you know damn well the Aliens track the precious metals in our electronic devices, you twit!"

Jack was properly shocked now, having your phone destroyed was one thing, being slapped because he did not believe in aliens was quite another thing.

"Aliens now is it? Where did they come from then, Mars I suppose?" Jack saw her jaw tighten, as she raised her hand he quickly took a step back. 'This women must be nuts' he thought, and remembered something about playing along with the fantasy to mollify the patient.

'Yeah that's it she's an escaped patient from some mental hospital or something and I've banged my head really, really hard this morning. Yeah that's it' he thought 'I must have, because I'm seeing the same things too'.

The woman sighed, turned and started to gently jog down another tunnel before Jack could ask or argue with anything. Left with few options, Jack decided to follow her, giving a forlorn look over his shoulder at where his phone had died, he jogged after her.

Finally sometime later after many tunnels and turnings, she stopped in front of a rusty metal latched door halfway down a tunnel, with a dim yellow light hanging above it from the sewer ceiling. There had been more and more light in the sewer tunnels as they had jogged along, with eventually the debris, water and most importantly the smell decreasing.
"This it Jack, this is where you explain why your being more of an idiot than normal?"
Jack stood dumb founded, not sure that he had told this annoying female his name. Then realization struck, this women must be from the office but what was her name, because it certainly was not Jenny whom he had always wanted on many levels and knew he would probably never have?

Jack started to say "well I know who ..." a squeak stopped him talking, the rusted metal door had a small slide hatch which opened, letting both of them be bathed in blinding light.
"Claire ... thank god!" came an female voice through the hatch, with that the door swung out into the tunnel bathing them in brighter yellow light.

Jack opened his mouth in surprise at the name, looking closely at the rubberized and green coated women in front of him. He remembered Claire as being a pretty, quiet blonde lady, who wore very big glasses and would not even give him the time of day, let alone let him pass her security desk without the obligatory frown. It was not really a security desk she sat at, rather it was a secretarial desk. It may as well of been a security desk as far as Jack was concerned, with an truncheon and tazer hidden away within easy reach no doubt, he always thought. It was the way she stared at Jack each morning as he passed, giving him the impression that she was running possible ways to disable and maim him through her head, that sent chills through him every morning. It was the continuous and hot thermic lance like stare that got him, as if he, Jack, was bringing illicit contraband into work every day. Admittedly this was technically true, various films and music he had copied and was handing out to work colleagues. It was the only way he knew how too make friends and keep them at work, so he did it more and more.

Claire stepped through and briefly hugged the door opener. Jack after his brief flash of memory was a little bemused, he stepped through the door and only then noticed that the lady inside the door was quite scantily clad, wearing white short shorts and a red tucked up t-shirt. Being male Jack just stared, stopping halfway through the door with various thoughts running across his mind, which had the effect of also making his jaw drop open.
"Stop mucking about and give us a hug you idiot" Jack unable to move was dragged from the doorway and roughly bear hugged by the nearly naked women, if it could of his jaw would have dropped open even further.

What had made Jack stare so hard at her, was not her long brown hair tied in a pony tail running down her back, nor her nearly black coloured eyes, neither her shapely angled face. It was her physique. She looked like a female body builder with muscles sprouting out of places Jack did not even know women had muscles to sprout out of. She also moved like Jack imagined a ballet dancer might move that was performing a show about cats. She was all lithe and agile but when she held Jack, he felt like she could crush him with her little finger and here he was being pressed against her ample chest.

Claire looking on sighed and said "this is Jack Mel, he and I used to work in the office together and currently he is the biggest fool on the planet."

Mel then pushed Jack away from her and spun him around so he was splayed against the bone dry and slightly yellowy crumbling wall.

She ran her hands up and down his back and then finally spun him around, Jack was wearing a very shocked big grin when he faced her. Ignoring his smile Mel looked him up and down and asked "well he's real, which is a bonus, but are you trying to tell me he's been wiped?"

"What do you mean wiped?" both Claire and Jack said together.

Mel turned and marched off down the corridor with Claire and Jack following along behind.

As the three of them walked down the tunnel, Mel stopped in a cubby hole and put on a very thick woollen jumper and jeans. It was only when they stopped Jack realized he had been sweating an awful lot in the last corridor and now the temperature in this corridor was easily twenty degrees cooler.

"Over the last couple months we've found people wandering round up top, with no idea what's going on. Some of them must have been interrogated and then had their minds blanked of the last three months!" said Mel as they meandered down yet another corridor and through various junctions.

"About one in every five were also some form of machine, the only way to tell is to hug every new comer and feel their spine. Being partially clothed also helps as real people look everywhere, plus its damn hot at the door."

Claire and Jack looked at one another both thinking similar thoughts though not quite the same about him.

'That's why he's more of an idiot than normal.'

'That's why I've no idea what the hell is going on?'

Claire asked "so you feel the spine, because?"

Mel replied "humans only have one ha ha ha."

Just around the next bend they met another young lady coming the other way, Mel made a comment about needing sun tan lotion whilst guarding the door. In return she got a very descriptive hand gesture with regards to where she could stick guard door duty as they passed by.

Jack following behind the two women, who were walking far too quickly for his liking, noticed as they were getting closer to wherever the centre was, that every person he had seen so far had been female. He pondered this as they passed through what amounted to various checkpoints. In each case they were either hugged or some handheld scan device was swiped over them by a female guard.

Finally they came to a much wider corridor and at the end stood guards in what looked like black military issue clothing, the sort you might find in some evil cackling master criminals lair.

These guards also had black matching helmets to go with there black uniforms, with the clothing seeming to absorb the light, making each one look like a shadow rather than an actual person.

The guards were standing on either side of what looked like a bank safe door, all bars and wheels and over the top heavy metals. Jack slowed his walking pace as he looked at the door. It must have been one hundred meters or more from when they had come round the corner and the door looked big from back there. Now as he stood in front of the door, he thought it must be four or five times taller than him.

Mel and Claire stood just too one side of Jack as a small metal pole raised itself out of the floor in front of them. A panel opened near the top of the pole and a yellow laser light scanned the two women up and down in turn. As the beam started to scan from Jacks feet, it started to change colour, until when it got to his chest it turned a luminous red. A small static electric sound went off behind him and before Jack could say a word, everything in his world went blank.

Jack woke up with a monumental headache and after rubbing his palms across his face several times, properly opened his eyes. This took several attempts as it seemed like they'd been strung shut by an overly enthusiastic spider. Still feeling woozy and with a lump on the back of his head the size of a boiled egg, Jack sat up and looked around. It was a cell, there was no other way to describe it. All the hall marks were there, no windows, no doors and the size of the room was about six foot by eight foot. The mattress he woke up on in it, well lets be polite, it had seen better days after being used in an incontinent clinic. There was a light that was just about a candles worth, hanging from the ceiling, which appeared to be over twelve feet above him. Jack looked around, eventually finding found the door, it was actually quite small and he would have to stoop to get in or out and it was only about two feet wide. Jack looked closer at the door, noticing that not only was it only five foot or so tall but appeared to be made of some plastic, come to that so did the cell walls. They were a very good stone brick effect, giving the impression of being a 'yea olde prison' cell. Jack rubbed his hand across the surface and felt a vibration from the fake stone. He pulled back a little surprised and then a link of some very thin metal bracelet type thing fell off his wrist to the floor. When it hit the floor it bounced and then shattered, then Jack noticed the chains in the floor. There were four chains, which came from a hole in each corner of the box room and ran to the ill looking mattress where he had woken up. They were obviously there to worry the occupant, which judging by how his bladder felt, it was working. It was then he noticed that someone had changed his trousers for him, which were now pyjama like bottoms and by the feel of it his underwear too!

Looking down through a tinted glass slit in the ceiling, Mel turned to the dark leather clad figure stood beside her, both stood with arms folded and Mel said "he's human in here, well so say the scanners." The women dressed in black turned to Mel and shrugged "nothings full proof now and all the scans whilst he slept, show him to be a man of about twenty years old ... and yet the chains seemed to fall off his wrists within seconds of him waking?" she mused.
They both turned to look at Jack "he looks so normal, if not a little lost and confused" said Mel, as they watched Jack walked slowly around his tiny cell, shaking his head and flapping his hands at invisible fleas.
"I would have put that down to him being wiped, but he also failed the nano scan at the main vault door and the chains are no longer chains. He also saw the door within a few seconds, which even I know is there, but would take me time to feel round the edge to find it in that dim light" said the leather clad figure.
Mel asked "so what do you think then boss, is he a new form of bot or some random bloke who swallowed some metal and eats chains for breakfast?"

"Hmm, I'm hoping he could have something we need and those chains were brittle to start with anyway" the dark figure paused before answering Mel's questioning look "but put some newer chains in please for our next guest."
Mel smiled with a certain viscousness, she got some guilty pleasure from restraining people and the Boss knew this, so she added "but don't chain him to them, just put them in the room, okay!"
Mel looked disappointed and then mused "psychological warfare. What do you want done with the old chains?"
The glossy dark hair moved for the first time on the leather clad women as she turned her head slightly and replied "throw them away of course!"

They stared down at Jack through the slit window, as he finally sat down on the mattress and looked straight up at them.
The Boss looked at Mel and in an resigned voice said "there's only one way to find out for sure if he's a bot and that's to give him a mind probe."
Mel looked sharply round at the Boss, her hands made some impressive waving affects round her head, pantomiming that it would make him a bit more nuts.
"Nuts he may end up but we've got to know if he's some new type of bot or something else entirely."
Mel paused in thought before speaking and replied "Claire seems too know him quite well but she did say he was a bit of a loser before everything went to hell."
"We'll see Mel, get him and the probe ready, if he resists give him another shock and this time don't build up to a million just give it too him okay. We don't want another seizure, the mess took ages to clear up and we all have to walk through that door!"
Mel remembered the smell, the mess and she had had to clean it up, this meant there visitor was also probably not a bot. Least not a normal one at any rate.

Jack now more or less, probably less, had nearly recovered from his assault, when not only the door but the wall slid open and up. He was feeling very angry and hard done by and had no real idea what was going on. Yet he still noticed that the door was not a door at all, it must have a been a test or trap he thought. Probably another shock if he had touched it and tried to open it too, but then why? Why all the scanning and tests on the way here? It was then Jack noticed the three guards stood in the now fully open wall. It must be a very well oiled wall jack thought. The guards appeared again to be all female and carrying some form of truncheon each, with electric crackling at the end.

The light from the corridor beyond was a very bright yellow, accentuating the figures of the women. They were all clothed in black and wore motor cycle style helmets, least at a glance they looked like motorbike helmets, with some round breathing filters built in on either side of where the jawline sat. The helmets were all oddly coloured, like you would find in the best bike shop that had been invaded by an angry bull, which had battered his way through the pottery shop, broken through a fluorescent paint shop and finally wrecked his way into and ended up licking the helmets of the bike shop to within an inch of there usefulness.

"Get up, turn around and put your hands behind your back" said the middle figure in a rasping voice. Jack stood up and opened his mouth to ask what was going on, one of the guards jumped forward and lightly touched his most personal place with her sparking stick. The shock from the electric truncheon touching him where no truncheon had ever been before and should never go again, caused him too hurl himself forward into a somersault and end up lying on his back. Curled up with both hands clutching his private man area, Jack let out a throat gurgle. His jaw was welded shut and he was just glad he had not had his tongue anywhere near his teeth, which were really aching from clamping shut so quickly.
The middle guard turned to her fellow enforcer and said "really! That's another mess you've made and this time your clearing it up."

Jack still rocking back and forth was turned over, had his hands pulled roughly behind his back and tied with plastic straps. Still moaning he was lifted to his feet and half dragged, half walked out of the cell and down numerous corridors, leaving a slightly wet trail behind him. They passed many rooms with women and children working on various shaped weapons and clothing. Jack would have been very interested in all these rooms, had he not still been contemplating the pain in his nether regions and being marched smartly towards who knows what?

Just as he was regaining some composure in his legs he realized his socks were wet, as he worked out why he groaned inwardly. The two black clad women turned him sharply into quite a large room. Before he could get a good look they spun him round, cut the plastic straps on his wrist and pushed him down into a padded, heavy set metal chair. They then tied leather straps around his wrists and legs, binding him to the chair. All this was done in a matter of seconds, in a very efficient fashion, leaving no chance to think and showing a great deal of practice.

Jack's head was then strapped into position, leaving just his eyes able to move and him to speak "under normal circumstances, I might find this a bit of fun ... if the roles were reversed, maybe."
Jack stifled a nervous laugh, which ended in a gurgle as all the heads he could see turned towards him and then turned away with little shakes. He sat waiting for something to happen or a comment of some kind, when none was forthcoming he started to look round the room.

There were two black clad guards stood either side of the door he came in, this time with just black helmets. Another guard to his left was holding his least favourite truncheon near his head, she was wearing the multicoloured helmet. Two more women in white coats with nose and mouth masks stood either side of him, they were punching keyboards and from what he could hear at least one more stomping around behind him.

The room itself was huge and reminded Jack of the inside of a concrete missile silo he had seen once on television. The floor was randomly painted a bright white, with little track marks from where the desks had been dragged around on there wheels. The metal desks sat in a half circle around him, with various keyboards, screens and even an old analogue cathode ray tube television sat on its own table.

From where he was tied down, Jack really could not see what was on the screens, the occasional ping he heard sounded like an ECG machine somewhere behind him. If they were monitoring his heart, then what was going to happen next could not be good for him he thought.

"Could I just ask please ... what the hell is going on and why couldn't you just question me over a nice cup of tea?" asked Jack hopefully.

Nobody said a word in the room, the truncheon holding guard must have pressed the electrical warm up on her tool, as it was now crackling and spitting charges out the end. Jack was getting mildly singed eyebrows and wondering why he got up this morning, when another female walked in the room.

She was dressed all in black and rather than being a shiny plastic, her suit appeared to be made of leather, which as she walked forward made a smooth sounding rasp. She was not wearing a helmet, her long dark glossy hair and attractive yet angular features reminded Jack of a very hot character from only the very best vampire feature film. As she waltzed in wearing her three inch heeled boots, also of the black variety, they made virtually no sound on the floor. Her skin was pale and obscenely smooth, like someone had troweled over all the cracks and lines with mortar.

With one hand swinging at her side as she paraded into the room, Jack wondered what she was holding in her other hand, held behind her back. He had a vision of some black leather whip being brought round and applied to his vulnerable bits until he talked. The only real problem he could see with this scenario, was that he had nothing he could actually tell them, about anything!

"Can you tell me what's going on please?" asked Jack still looking for the whip and after a moments pause added "I woke up this morning and found everything destroyed, got dragged into a sewer, attacked by a vacuum cleaner, assaulted twice, and now I'm strapped to a chair and no one will explain anything" after another moments thought he finished with "especially why I'm the only man I've seen?"

"Everything in time Jack, all your questions will be answered" she raised her finger and waved it in the air in a slow tick tock fashion as Jack made to object.

"You, need to be patient and the overriding question for us needs to be answered first."
"And that's what then?" he blurted out.
Turning and ignoring Jack's pleas for mercy, which turned to silent relief when he saw the hand behind her back was just clenched, she asked one of the white coated women "are we ready for the probe?"
"Yes Boss" said one of the white jacketed women.
"Well I'm not!" said Jack in panic, as he heard one of the women shuffling around behind him, then he felt part of the seat under his bottom move, giving the sensation of space, airy even.
"What are you doing back there?" Jack asked with a slight tremor to his voice.
Ignoring him another female put a sandy coloured child shaped dummy in his mouth, tied the attached strap around the back of his head with a lead going off somewhere else. At the same time Jack felt his pyjama bottoms and then his under garments pulled down, just enough to expose his rump. Then something only slightly warm and presumably dummy shaped was stuck up his bottom with alarming ease. He gave a small grimace as it was inserted and recited the old mantra, 'exit only.'

    Jack sat there for a few moments longer with his eyes screwed tightly shut since the insertion, when nothing else appeared to be forth coming he opened first one eye and then the other cautiously. Two women in white coats were having an urgent discussion over to his left, they both turned round to look at him, one smiled slowly at him with the fixed air hostess smile you get for not knowing something, whilst the other had a nurses frown when bad news is coming your way. At least that was what Jack imagined was behind there masks, it did not make him feel any better when the frowning one said "are you sure?" to her colleague.
The fake smiling one replied "yep, sorry, one day I'll get it right."
Both women stepped over to Jack and the two dummy's were removed without ceremony and surprisingly quickly.
"Thank you very much!" said Jack with a fair degree of relief, as the sandy coloured dummy was pulled from his mouth and the other one from the other end. Then he noticed that the dummy from 'back there' was coming his way from behind, so to speak and the other one was going below.
"Oh no!" mumbled Jack as tried to shake his head, with realization taking hold.
    When the dummy's had been reinserted into there now squirming victim the right way round, to the now full and beaming woman's satisfaction, the Boss turned to the women and said "now you've finished playing with the probes, can we get on please?"
'Yes do' thought Jack 'as quickly as feasibly possible'.

The probe in his mouth then started to expand, filling his mouth almost completely with an thin air hole down the centre. After twenty minutes or so Jack was unplugged, untied, pyjamas pulled back into there rightful place, his hands tied behind his back again and then he was dragged moaning down corridors. He then had his hands untied with a knife to the plastic straps on his wrists, and pushed into a bigger but still dark room. The door was slammed shut behind him and several bolts could be heard sliding into place. Jack started to rub the inside of his mouth furiously with his fingers, then he spotted a small tap on the wall over a toilet.

Back in the probe room the head prober could hear something tapping behind her, she turned her head away from the flickering cathode screen and could see the impatient fingers of the boss rapping on the desk top.
"Erm, sorry was there something you wanted?" this was directed at the black leather clad Boss.
"Yes actually, I was wondering when you were going to tell me what was wrong with him and what images you got from his memory?"
Turning around from the desk and now standing straight, the dark blonde haired prober said "well its going to take some time to analyse all the information."
"Surely you can tell me if he's normal or even at the very least whether he's been wiped and reprogrammed. That after all is what you built the machine for, at great cost and risk to us all?" the Boss said this with a degree of exasperation.
"Yes normally, we would be able to say within the first thirty seconds of the probing as to whether the subject is normal, but ..."
"Go on, is he normal then Jane?"
Jane shrugged and said "for all intensive purposes he's as normal as any of us."
The Boss turned to walk away muttering to herself "that's all I needed to know."
"Wait, that's the problem don't you see?"
Shaking her head the boss turned back "no I don't, you've just said he's normal!"
"Then why are the memory banks full?"
"What do you mean full? I thought over a hundred complete memories could be stored, from birth till death?"
Jane raised her hands and waved them about in a rocking fashion "yes, that's why we're at a bit of a loss really, as there was only four stored, and they've been overwritten! And then there's the images we're getting!"

The Boss looked at the nearest screen which showed an image of hundreds of black armoured figures, stood in what could only be described as rank and file. All were facing towards a raised dais, with what looked like a furry brown jelly trying too stand on it. What it actually reminded her of was a gingerbread man that had eaten all the vodka soaked and spiky jelly babies, it was slightly out of focus rather than the viewer. The room the armoured creatures stood in was cavernous and seemed to be made from a glossy black quartz. From the angle the image was taken from, presumably through the eyes of Jack, only half appeared to be human, the rest were various shapes ranging from coiled snake like things too huge multi legged crabs. All of which wore variations on the black armour. The oddest thing of all which gave an obscure look to everything, minus the obviousness of the hugely varied species, was the black armour itself. It was not really black, it was a black as if viewed from the other end of the spectrum. It seemed to absorb all light, to the point where the eye piercing spotlights facing out around the dais appeared to be struggling to provide any illumination, apart from straight at the viewers eyes.
"So your saying he's normal and yet these are some strange images?" Jane turned and pointed at the screen "strange isn't quite the word I'd use, I mean we've all seen some odd things recently and recorded some even more bizarre ones with my device."
The Boss shook her head "so what's the problem then?"
Jane pulled a plastic stool out from under the desk and with a sigh sat down "right okay first, he is human, the probe confirms that, his memory hasn't been tampered with either. But?" and here Jane paused to think how too explain the readings, which were still filing at a great speed down another screen.
"But what then?" asked the Boss, whom was getting more impatient by the second and knowing a thousand other things needed her attention before this man.
Jane caught the tightening of her jaw, a sure fire build up to an explosion "look Boss the final scan before he came in the base went nuts, because of the high metal content in his body. The automatic defence system cut in and told the guards to shock him till he passed out."
Another pause from Jane would drive the Boss mad and Jane hurriedly continued after seeing her jaw tighten further.
"So we ran the scan again here and he was normal, then we did the memory consistency test. Which again ran true but took a few minutes and not seconds as it would usually. Then the probe started the memory copy and that's where it all fell apart due to the sheer volume!"
"Volume?"
"Yes, because the flamin' thing is still compiling, we think he has about, approximately, close to, about, maybe nearer ... four hundred years worth of memory!"
The bosses jaw seemed to drop, showing some quite sharp white things, before she quickly closed her mouth with a sharp click of her teeth.

Then with a sigh the Boss asked "did you definitely have the probes the right way round this time?"

Back in the cell Jack was still vigorously washing out his mouth and spitting in the toilet, when he heard a deep chuckle somewhere behind him. Making very sure so as to not swallow, Jack turned his head round slowly from his kneeling position over the china seat and stared into the gloom of his new prison.

The room or jail cell as Jack thought of it, was easily the size of a village hall but with only about six and half feet head clearance. Again it was that very same fake rock and brick looking wall structure, both on the floor, ceiling and walls. The door he had been pushed through was not even visible, no outline, just brick work. Back in one of the corners Jack could just make out someone sat on a mattress, with the occasional glow of the tail end of a cigarette lighting up the corner.

"Hello?" said Jack trying to sound overly confident, the sound he actually made came out more like the squeak of a mouse stuck in one of those infernal mazes, while a scientist poked his nose and eyes over a wall to surprise the tiny rodent.

Jack tried again saying 'hello' and this time it came out as a deep rich manly baritone, which had the effect of making him sound even more nervous.

"Hello yourself" echoed from the other end of the room, followed by "I see you've had your first probing experience then ha ha ha" came the humorous reply.

The laughing continued for quite some time until a racking cough pulled him up short. Jack still kneeling down got up slowly, turned around and started to walk towards the sullen glow.

'This is the first bloke I've heard or seen today' thought Jack 'so let's go say hi.'

Walking to the other end of the cell took a bit longer than Jack anticipated, due to the enforced rearrangement of his under garments and the excessive size of the room. Chaffing was not a word Jack was overly familiar with but it perfectly suited what was going on down below and it needed to be sorted out. Rearranging himself as he walked towards his fellow incarcerate gave Jack the time to think. He still had no idea what was really going on, the possibility of the man at the other end of the cell knowing what was going on, was going to make him Jacks best friend, even if he did not to want be.

Jack crouched down and offered his hand in friendship to the man sat cross legged on the mattress.

"Hi, my names Jack, you have no idea how pleased I am to see you" said Jack pleasantly.

The man looked up at Jacks manically grinning face and said "why, you batting for the other team mate?"

Jacks grin stayed where it was but the rest of his face seemed to be trying to back away "no mate, I'm as straight as they come. I just meant your the first bloke I've seen, which I thought was a bit odd?"

The man looked at him over the top of his thin rimmed sunglasses and said in an mischievous tone "how was your probing?"
Jacks grin which had been straining to get away finally disappeared, he realized he was still rubbing his teeth with one hand and withdrew his other from the man.
"They've probed me several times to try and restore my memory but the first time was the worst" the man smiled and asked "I guess there still pulling the wrong probe in the hole trick?"
Jack nodded and sat down on the other end of the mattress, he then realized what this man in the penguin suit had just said "what do you mean the wrong hole trick?"

     Looking sidelong at Jack the man relaxed back against the wall and smiled a knowing smile. He flicked his depleted cigarette butt into the room, where it spun away leaving a heavy smoke trail, until it landed with a tiny explosion of vivid orange. The man then pulled another cigarette out of a pocket, lit it and put it in his mouth all in one smooth movement.

     Puffing away and ignoring Jack's frown of disapproval he replied "they actually have four probes, two brown and two blue and you should have been able to at least taste the slight citrus from the disinfectant?"
Realization dawned slowly across Jack's face and he smiled grimly at the dirty joke.
Then he started to scowl and asked "but why do it at all? Is it for there own bit of fun or some obscure torture method?" Jack was annoyed at this, thinking how did he not realize.
"Actually it's quite simple, it's so your mind is displaced and therefore the probe can work its magic."
"Whilst the victim panics about where the probe has last been and all they simply do is swap them over behind your back in the buckets" finished Jack, who had by now stopped rubbing his teeth and instead carried on flicking at errant and invisible spiders.
The man paused and tipped his head back "by the way my names Mark, I used to be a pilot."

Chapter 2 : Space Break.

High above the earth orbiting gently and serenely sits the international space station, the only known human manned object in the night sky. To the external observer it looked rather like a great number of large round metal dustbins carefully knitted together. On closer inspection scorch marks and various patches could be seen on the once white pristine shell. In the darkened interior two men and two women were floating around having an arm waving competition.
"Well what are we supposed to do about it then, we've got three days of food and water left and no one wants to talk or even listen?" said one of the women, whilst pointing and waving out the window.
The other women replied with "it was definitely some kind of electro magnetic signal, but it wasn't directed at us. It was too general and came from somewhere near London" she paused, looked at a panel with numbers scrolling across a small display and carried on to say "and we know our communications should come from Germany."
All four people looked at one another in the dim light, floating around despondently as that was really all they could do.
"If it wasn't for us, who was it for?" said one of the men.
The crew of the international space station, as one, looked out of the viewing window into the bright depths of space.
The first women said "well whoever it was has certainly got the attention of the Armada!"

Through the window could be seen thousands of vessels effectively blockading the earth, although blockading the Earth from what they had not yet discovered. The ships all varied hugely in colour and size, some only twenty meters long and half as wide, wore vivid base white and gold flamed streaks of artistic paint, dragged across there flanks. These angular small craft with bulging round rear ends, zipped around performing roles and sharp turns on there patrols. The other vessels ranged from a couple of hundred meters, to the biggest at well over a kilometer long and half again as wide. They were also white but with red flakes streaked across there hulls, they also appeared to have various dents and patches all over there bodywork. The general shape of these mammoth vessels looked to be designed by someone who thought that bulbous television remote controls were all the rage, very large, ambitious and only the best streamlined design would do.

These space faring vessels generally just appeared to be milling about, right up until the signal suddenly emanated from Earth. The effect on the spaceships was like watching the paparazzi suddenly seeing a famous person in place they should not be, according to popular convention and there camera lenses, dishes and antennas turning to follow them like moths to a flame.
The darkened ships were by now all facing the Earth and there noses rather specifically tracking a point on England's south east coast.

On the bridge of the biggest ship by far, the Commander turned his centrally placed seat to look at his communication specialist. The internal lighting was at a bare minimum, leaving only shadows and the faint fairy light of floating images depicting the earth and the flow of communication.

In short squeaks, clicks and burps the Commander asked "well a twenty minute burst of high level electromagnetic emissions, which are always very concentrated, and, you can't tell me with any accuracy within thirty kilometers where they came from?"

With three furry fingers and a tail like thumb, the specialist manipulated the floating earth zooming back and forth across the image. Finally resting on a glowing orb just south of London. Spinning gently round on its seat, it was just possible to see the outline of a furry figure in a sleek dark green uniform.

"Commander" complained the specialist "the reason we can't get a positive or accurate fix on the signal is actually quite simple!"

The specialist whilst talking could not stop moving, it was as if it were continuously needing to move, too avoid being put in the cross hair of a rabbit hunters gun, what any human would call a fidget.

"The signal wasn't directed at anything outside of its sphere of influence and was underground. Probably several hundred feet underground and therefore the local rock has amplified and distorted the signal."

The Commander assumed it was one of there fallen satellites, turning back towards the helmsman he sniffed making a sound like a drowning burglar alarm "well take us out of reconnaissance mode and send a search squad."

The bridge lit up with a brief flare of orange light, blinding almost after the near dark of reconnaissance mode.

To the external floating human observers, the vessels all looked like pay-day had come and more coins had been shoved in the electric meter. The windows and running lights flickered on each vessel in turn, fanning out and across the armada, relighting the night sky.

Chapter 3 : Bunker Down.

Down on earth in the seemingly never ending bunker and its tunnels, stalked the Boss to Jack's cell. She was not a happy Boss, she had wanted control of her life but not control of others on such a scale. It seemed like everything stopped at her, not even the simplest problem could be solved by the discoverer of said problem. They came to her with the issue and expected her to have an instant solution, regardless that the majority of the time they already knew what had to be done. They just seemed to need reassurance that what they were going to do was correct. The worst thing of all was that as the unofficial leader, all problems came to her. If she were truly honest with herself she loved the attention and provided she kept making the apparently correct decisions, they ignored her quirks. There were no official leaders, as the official leaders had mostly been caught and either imprisoned or memory wiped. The fact they were mostly male was just a grave over-site the invaders made on day one. Whether by design or some freak of the x and y chromosome, most of the male population was rendered incompetent, impotent even, by a gas that wiped mainly the skilled part of the memory. Some ten percent of the female population were also affected, this just meant that a limited retaliation by automatic systems kicked in, firing various missiles randomly across the sky. Some did hit the invaders, others exploded causing more damage to the earth and its meagre defenses.
Most women tried to help there fallen and dumb struck male comrades, when the invaders finally landed and were met by some very angry women indeed, they simply applied a more virulent gas. They were then simply herded along, both male and female to what in effect were concentration camps. No excessive security was actually needed, people simply followed along and obeyed without question after being exposed to the gas. Fortunately for some even the extra strength gas made no difference to them, whether this was by mistake or just plain old fashioned genetic luck, it still had no effect. These people hid as best they could and eventually found there way to the resistance, somewhere underground.

Jack was having the attack explained to him by Mark in there dingy cell, while the Boss stood outside listening to recent history "so if nearly everyone has been wiped, why can you remember what's happened?" asked Jack with a tinge of worry, he did not like the idea of losing his memory and it all still seemed surreal.
"It wasn't a complete wipe, my memory wasn't completely blanked, it was sort of mixed up and out of order. There was no sequence to it, I could remember what I had for breakfast, but it would be a year ago or even two!" Mark sighed and continued with "so the ladies here started using the mind probe for information and too try and put some eventual order to my head. That's when I remembered the start of the war."

Mark started to shake a little with his hands grabbing at imaginary plane controls "you have no idea how brown my underwear was after the gas seeped into my air supply. Can you imagine flying a fighter jet and dodging and rolling across the sky, avoiding lasers and missiles that have instantly fried your friends. Then suddenly your sat holding a flight stick, you know what it is and where you are, but you have no idea what to do with it or how? It was the scariest moment of my life and then I blanked out and woke up here."

Jack sat bemused, he had no memory of the invasion. The last thing he remembered was going to bed on a Friday night and waking to find the world turned upside down. He was sure his own memory was fine, he just seemed to have misplaced an invasion from space somewhere. Then a small tap on his mental shoulder caused him to think. It was not like Jack to think, he had a picture in his head of small puffs of smoke leaving his ears, as some unused mental gears started to move without a good oiling first, preferably with alcohol of some description for oil he mused.

As he sat thinking he wondered if he had been wiped, he would of course have no memory of the invasion, at least not in any order but by the same reasoning, surely the gas would have affected other memories and skills. He just had no memories, mixed or otherwise of Martians invading his world.

The Boss walked back to her white splash painted concrete room, the paint on the walls looked like the result of a small stick of dynamite stuck in a paint tin and left with a bomb nut. They also had not bothered to move the small amount of furniture in the room before getting to work, or themselves judging by the slight shadowing by the door. The painted room gave the impression that the phantom paint bomber wanted to stick around, just to see what happened as it happened, there was even still the faint outline of a tin in the middle of the floor.

She closed the door behind her and stood leaning against it for several seconds with relief, then she looked at her paint splashed single bunk, chair and lonely metal table sat at the end. The room was not big but at least it was private and a chance to be herself, 'only the paint bomber would understand about that in here' she thought smiling to herself.

Just as she was thinking 'it's been a long day' and started towards her bunk, an alarm started to sound. She listened for a few seconds as it continued to 'wah wah' through several octaves and then start again, becoming so loud you could hardly hear yourself think, she groaned inwardly.
"We need a better sounding alarm" she said to herself "or a silent one."

Then her earbud buzzed in her ear, she briefly touched it and said "yes I heard the alarm and probably our visitors in orbit too, might I suggest turning it off or at the very least down?" she shouted the last bit to be heard over the alarm.

The alarm continued wah wahing for a few moments, then suddenly cut off and gurgled away like the sound of toad gulping a fly in a tunnel. "Now I'm assuming we have some unwelcome visitors in the tunnels?" asked the Boss, listening to the reply she opened her bunk room door and walked briskly down a corridor towards the command centre.

She turned a corner and could see command at the end, just before she got to the doorway Jane came rushing the other way and spun her round. She was bursting with energy and some might even say vim and vinegar 'like a horse with ginger up its bum' thought the Boss. Jane was talking at such a great rate of knots and in such excitement that it was completely unintelligible. The Boss grabbed her by the shoulders and kissed her on the lips, not a passionate kiss, just anything other than a smack to stop the babbling. Jane was so surprised she stopped dead and her mouth fell open.

The Boss held her away at arms length and said "it was either that or a slap" she said.

Jane calmed down with a slow sigh, still with much excitement in her voice she started again, much slower "Jack has four hundred years of memories, because he appears to be over four hundred years old. Before you ask, they aren't implanted memories either, he really has living memories for that long but they're all mixed up and out of sequence. The probe took longer because there were so many memories and something was trying to sort the memories into some sort of order, which it still hasn't managed!"

Jane paused for long enough that the Boss managed to ask "what about the blaring alarm?"

"Oh that was just the aliens finding one of our tunnels" Jane said this in such an off hand manner as if a pizza delivery person had just turned up, that the Boss was actually speechless.

Four hundred years of memory was a great deal, the fact there base had been found was far more urgent and so the Boss brushed Jane aside and stalked into command.

The room was massive, on the scale of another conical missile bunker in shape, it took twenty or more long paces to reach a large round tent pitched in the middle. The smooth concrete walls here were all slap dashed with white paint again, this time they must of used one really big paint tin and several sticks of dynamite.

As the Boss approached the white tent she could only see vague shadows within because of the three layers of canvas. The Boss pushed aside the flap of the tent and let it swing back behind her as she entered. Behind her was a sound like a leathery slap, as the triple layer of tent smacked into the face of Jane, who had been trying to keep up behind her. Jane pulled the flap aside rubbing her cheek, quite glad she had turned her face at the last second. She was expecting an apology or something at the very least, the Boss was already at the central desk looking at one of the screens.

Jane glanced around the inside of the tent, it really had not changed much since she was last inside, unless you count the look of panic on each face as they stared at various sized screens.

Three rings of wooden desks surrounded a central table with meter wide gaps between each, on each desk were various screens, keyboards and computers. In the middle of the tent sat a three meter tall pillar of complete confusion, made up of computer base units, wires, keyboards and several screens.   Each screen was displaying four cameras dotted around the base, on one Jack could be seen walking around banging on the walls of his cell with his fists and occasionally his head. The biggest screen showed one of the shadowy invaders, walking along carefully behind what could only be described as a metal dustbin on its side, plodding down the tunnel with three multi knee legs on either side. It also had three aerials sticking out like spikes about a meter long on its back, with orange glowing balls on the end of each. The invader seemed to be struggling to herd it a long with many squeaks and whistles, then the device stopped for apparently no reason, the alien raised its furry arms and shook them in apparent frustration. With the dim orange light of the antennas casting a strange wobbly glow over the alien, everyone in the tent watched closely.

The Boss looked interestedly at the biggest screen, a look of anger crossed her face and she then slammed her closed fist on the desk, sending a mug of coffee into the air and into a waste bin on the floor. Everyone who had been watching the screens jumped in there seats and turned to look at the now furious retreating Boss as she stormed out the tent.

Jane mumbled "good shot" looking at the bin.

The Boss was already out the tent, briskly walking out of the bunker door as Jane chased after her, more curious at her wild reaction at there first proper view of an shadowy alien invader than Jack's memory dump. She got to the bosses room, slowly pushed and knocked on the door which creaked open on metal hinges. The Boss was lying on her back on the bunk, just staring at the ceiling.

"Um, I was just wondering what's got you so upset?" Jane asked curiously.

The Boss turned her head towards Jane, just for a second her eyes appeared to flash with electric blue and then purple. She also, just for a second, appeared to have some awfully white fang like teeth flicker out over her lower lip.

"It's the wrong lot!" the Boss hissed quietly through her teeth.

Jane had been staring into the bosses eyes as they flickered from blue to purple and back again, in surprise Jane wiped a hand across her brow, finding a bead of worry.

She continued haltingly after a second or two, to be excited about the aliens "this is our first view, of the aliens, up until till now, we've only seen there machines!"

Jane would have been bouncing round the room like a toddler at a caffeine and sugar party, but the flashes of blue and purple in the bosses eyes, not to mention the flickering teeth too much, had unnerved her a bit. She was strangely not even sure she had actually seen anything, with the Boss now sat on the edge of her bunk with pursed lips and an expression of polite attention being applied in her direction.

Jane shook her head slowly to try and clear away the light fog that had clouded her memory of the last few moments. Suddenly she remembered why she was stood in front of the Boss and returned to being excited about having seen the invaders for the first time, forgetting something that she might or might have not seen.

From the bosses point of view it was like Jane had suddenly gone from a run down clockwork toy, to an overwound and recently released clockwork toy.

"It had a face like a brown fox, a thin gangly body, no tail and stood like a biped over six feet tall!"

"Huh" said the Boss.

"And did you see those hands, they only had three fingers and a really bendy thumb!"

The Boss still sat on her bunk felt a tear as it appeared in one of her eyes, she quickly wiped it away with a pale hand. Jane still trying not to bounce round the room, noticed that her boss was not overly happy but could not remember why.

"I'll just leave you with your thoughts then, oh and they haven't moved any further into the tunnel, they don't seem to like dark holes or collapsing tunnels using triggered explosives."

Jane skipped out of the door way and back to her lab, with a slightly puzzled expression on her sweet face.

The Boss sat still on the edge of her bunk for several minutes with her eyes closed, apparently resting until she suddenly sat up straight and said out loud "why?"

She quickly got up off the bed and walked quickly from her room to the command centre, with her boots clip clopping down the corridor. She burst into the tent, surprising the women stood and sat watching the screens of aliens milling about outside the tunnel with there machines.

"Why did they find us and how?" she asked of everyone in the tent, whilst standing stock still hands on her hips and head erect.

She looked at all present and was just about to ask again when Jane walked in and said "I think I know how they found us."

The Boss spun on her black heeled shoes, appearing to not actually move her legs in anyway.

With a glare that made Jane try and shrink behind her dark blonde fringe, the Boss asked "how then have we hidden for the last three months, with not a glimmer of alien attention and now we're being dug up?"

Jane looked a little sheepish and gave the appearance of melting under the thermic stare of the Boss.

The Boss always got answers with that ice cold blue stare, it was like being pinned to the spot with hot icicles. The stare was freezing cold but the effect was to heat you up, to the point where you had to give an answer of one description or another.

Jane shuffled her feet uncomfortably, replying a little hesitantly to start with "it, um, appears that with the probe being used for so long, meant a signal of some kind managed to leave the bunker. I'm assuming that being so far underground has meant it wasn't a clear signal, as the invaders are only at the far edge of the tunnel network."

The Boss shook her head and mumbled with a certain amount of relief "least it isn't my enemy I suppose."

Jane just about heard this comment and wondered not for the first time what enemy, other than the current one, the Boss was really waiting for? She did not really want to meet them, if the current invaders were only an apparent annoyance.

Looking at the screens it appeared to Jane that the invaders liked to mill about and argue with one another a lot, as well as wave there arms and other similar appendages at there machines. It made them look almost normal, from an human perspective but also meant Jane did not want to meet the bosses alternative enemy.

Chapter 4 : Back Once Again.

In his prison cell Jack sat rubbing his wrists from where the straps had been, bored now, more to the point he was being bored to death by Mark's incessant chattering. He had heard everything from birth to apparent near death in his plane and back again. It was like Mark wanted to intentionally point out all of Jack's short comings in society and the work place, by remembering that every event in his life had been amazingly significant for the world, whilst Jack's had been rubbish and boring in comparison.
What Jack did not realize was that by just his presence, he was encouraging Mark to remember and sort his memories, which was just what he actually needed to help him.
After hours of listening though Jack had heard enough, it felt like his brains were dribbling out of his ears. Jack put his hand to an ear, and yes there was something damp coming out, he just prayed it was not brain matter. He did not think he had that much to spare and judging by his treatment so far, neither did his captors.
Jack had tried interrupting Mark's monologue with little effect, he finally managed to stop Mark from talking by the use of his hand being slapped over his fellow prisoners mouth.
"Just stop all right, the only thing you haven't explained fully with all your talk, is why we're locked up?" asked Jack.
Jack took his hand slowly away from Mark's mouth, the look of outrage started to slip from Mark's face "no need to be rude mate and I thought it was obvious?"
"What was?"
"Repopulating the planet, obviously!"
"That's what you think we're here for?"
"What else is there?" asked Mark with mild excitement.
Admittedly Jack had not seen any male figures outside of the cell and from the way they had been treated, like collaborators, he could not really see what Mark was saying could possibly be true. Still it would not hurt to muse on it for a few moments at any rate. Jack had images of Amazonian styled ladies pandering to his every need, then for some reason Claire popped into his head and the blonde haired women ruined it all by pulling him into a sewer again, face first.
They both sat for several minutes, lost in there own thoughts and then Mark asked what the last thing Jack remembered was.
Jack sat back heavily on his backside, banging his head on the fake panelled cell wall, he turned to Mark and started to explain his waking up and eventual incarceration.
He finished with "they've worked out I'm not a robot and just think I've been wiped, but I remember everything right up to going to bed last night!"

Mark looked sidelong at Jack "so you don't have any jumbled memories? You know, out of sequence, almost like a dream you can't quite remember properly?"
Jack shook his head and leaned against the wall behind him. It was quite cold in the cell now, with water just starting to condense on the ceiling and drip down the walls, making intermittent drip and drop noises as each one splashed on the floor.
"Even if you had been wiped, you'd still have some memories from the wiping, you'd have jumbled images, sounds and smells that didn't quite fit. As to why we're locked up it's quite simple, some people are open to suggestion after the wipe and have been used as spies, not that many of them but enough that all new people have to be probed."
"Don't I know it!" murmured Jack.
"Then there's the robots they've occasionally used, which look and act really well but have that double spine thing. There memories are also very good, photographic you might even say" Mark smiled to himself, as some old memory washed over him.

Jack shook his head again and sighed, he was getting annoyed with Mark and his odd pauses, odder comments and even odder assumption that Jack should know all these things.
"I just remember going to bed and waking, that's it, no odd memory bits floating around" said Jack.
Mark with one final look at Jack's stony face turned the other way and shut his eyes, seeming to drop of to sleep.

Finally Mark started to snore and just as Jack was starting to relax a little himself, thankful that Mark had already dropped off and the drip drop of condensation was becoming regular, the door at the end opened with a high pitched squeak of metal on metal. Two fully black clad guards stepped through and gestured for Jack to get up and move towards the door. Jack just sat where he was, he really did not fancy another good probing, they would just have to come and get him and carry him out he thought.

Then a white coated women looked round the door "Jack what are you doing, will you get your fat ass out the door!" the tone used was annoyed and amused at the same time.
Jack recognized the voice from somewhere recently, the persistent head bobbing and waving eventually got through to him, it was Claire again. Jack inwardly groaned and replied "drag anyone through a sewer recently and probe them to your hearts content?"
Claire stared at him for a moment and was just about to reply when she saw his defiant look, instead she turned to the two guards and gestured with some degree of pantomime where they could stick there electric batons to get Jack to move. Having watched the explicit gestures with interest, Jack jumped up quickly and put his back against the wall as the guards stepped further into the cell.
"Jack will you please stop mucking about, we only want to help you remember" said Claire.
Jack had started to inch away into the furthest corner from the door, he stopped and asked "so, more probing?"

"No Jack, we think talking through your experience will help you remember, as well as helping us."
"Really, are you sure? Cos I distinctly remember something similar happening not too long ago, that ended up with me feeling the need to stand up for quite a while afterwards?"
Claire shook her head and said "Jack I promise you, your not getting probed today!" she then quickly checked the time was only a few minutes to midnight on some device in her pocket and under her breath muttered "today at any rate."
Suddenly smiling Claire turned and walked out the door.

Jack stood leaning against the wall for a few seconds weighing up his options, which admittedly were a mite limited, then cautiously and with a slightly exaggerated limp he walked towards the door.
The two guards now stood on either side of the exit, turned there visored heads to face Jack as he paused in the doorway. Then in one smooth movement shoved him through, paced through themselves and slammed the door shut behind them. Jack banged against the opposite wall, smacking his nose obscenely hard and slid down onto his knees. Sat rubbing his nose leaning his back against the concrete corridor wall, which of course was explosively painted white, Jack wondered what he had done wrong. Claire turned from walking down the corridor at the thump of Jack's head on the wall, walked back and dragged him to his feet by an elbow.

"Why are your guards so rough?" asked Jack as he carefully stood, slightly bent over rubbing his nose.
Claire still holding Jacks elbow breathed into his ear "there more than wiped I'm afraid."
Jack had not had a girl breath into his ear for years and started to get a little too excited, he turned is head to look at Claire, a question hanging in his expression.
Claire dragged Jack by his elbow down the corridor, he realized his excitement was unfounded as Claire still whispering said "some had an odd reaction to the gas used by the aliens and now only have a limited understanding of commands."
"You mean there dead from the neck up then, like politicians?"
"No, not quite, there more like drones really, buzzing round a Queen protecting her at all costs. And before you ask, the helmets and suits are more for us than them. Not that there disfigured in any way, its just the vacant eyes and the look of lost minds that's disturbing."
Claire watched Jack open his mouth and said "not like politicians Jack!" Claire pulled back from Jack a little, nudged him with an elbow and said with a knowing smile "a bit like you most Monday mornings, after your wild weekends down south, in Poole!"
Jack frowned at this comment, trying to think of some retort, but honestly she was right about him looking vacant, she thought he went out binge drinking most weekends with his mates down near Poole. Really he just turned on his game console, drank ridiculous volumes of caffeine based energy drinks and played near solid for forty eight hours online with people, probably from Poole.

They could have been from anywhere in the world, it was just Poole had sounded nice one Monday morning when he had wandered into the office with his sun glasses on to cover the bags under his eyes and had been questioned by a surly Claire.

The guards followed along behind as they walked at quite a brisk pace down several corridors and finally into what could only be described as the staff canteen. There were tables setup in an orderly fashion, so orderly that they were mirrored on either side of the room. At the top sat several large tables, two of which had some very large heated urns on them, these were bowing under the weight of the caffeine required to keep the rebellion awake.

Jack was finally thinking that his captors were not quite so much his foes, as they were more like mother goose protecting her young. This still did not make Jack feel any better, having been captured and tortured by this lot, still it was nice to be in a room that had lights and proper chairs to sit on.

Claire guided Jack to a table near the top left, there one person sat in the room all alone gently stroking her long dark hair, Claire then disappeared out of the door. One of the guards pulled out a chair opposite the lone occupant, whilst the other guard guided Jack with some force and the use of an ear to sit heavily down in the seat opposite. As he landed the women slowly raised her head from the small hand held screen she was watching, as Jack rubbed his ear with a grimace, he saw she took several seconds to focus on him.

The women appeared to be wearing one hell of a lot of makeup thought Jack, either that or she was some impossibly beautiful vampire. She stared at him for what felt like several minutes to Jack, seeming to pin him to the spot like a rabbit trapped in a cars headlights. Jack shuffled round in his seat getting more uncomfortable by the second. It was like sitting under the glare of an very upset kindergarten teacher, one who had caught him with his hand not only in the cookie jar but stealing the jar. It did not help that her eyes, though very attractive, were shifting and rotating through various shades of blue and purple as she continued to stare at Jack.

Finally Jack got fed up with the silent treatment and the thermic like stare of this women and asked "what do you want?"

The women jumped in her seat in shock, like her dog had just asked for sherbet instead of barking for sorbet. Normally within a few seconds of people being subjected to her hypnotic, rotating and phasing blue eyes, they would crumble and tell her everything she wanted to know and even some things she did not want to know. But no, not this one. He just looked a little uncomfortable and ragged around the edges. He was also often patting at himself, as if he were plucking away at tiny spiders that tickled him, she had first noticed this when watching Jack in his cell but he did not seem to notice the habit.

She put the tiny screen down on the table between them and spun it round so Jack could see the image displayed. The screen was showing the image copied from Jack's memory of the armoured black creatures in the massive black quartz cavern. Jack reached out, tilting the screen towards him, wondering what she was trying to show him and not knowing the image came from his memory.

Just then as the Boss was trying to work out Jack and Jack was worrying that this really might be reality, Jane pushed through the doors to the canteen. She walked briskly the first several meters from the doorway and then noticed the Boss was not alone. She paused obviously debating with herself whether to interrupt the conversation. After a few seconds of indecision she made the decision that what she had to say was more important than the bosses lunch, so she continued her walk, albeit in a round about fashion.

Because of Jane's circuitous route through the canteen, she had a better angle on the Boss as she reached her hand towards Jack. He was holding the small screen tablet on the table with his back to Jane as the bosses hand neared his. With only centimeters to spare the Boss suddenly froze in front of Jack and Jane stopped dead herself.

The Boss suddenly changed in front of Jane, her eyes had always been blue and known to change there shade, depending on her mood, now though they appeared to be flashing and gently spiraling into shades of purple that she never knew existed. Her skin, always quite a pale white, seemed to be getting lighter and more translucent, veins could be seen starting to throb and pulse quicker under her skin. The biggest surprise to Jane however were the bosses teeth; she had on occasion thought they were a bit too pointy and seemed to change there size, but here and now two of her canines were protruding, getting bigger and flashing a frosty white.

Suddenly realizing that she was being watched and not so much doing the watching herself. The Boss glanced up at Jane, who had just appeared in her vision and saw her shocked expression. Realization dawned that she had started a change and after a quick look at her hands, she shut her eyes and concentrated. Her skin lost its transparency and became almost tanned in colour, more slowly than she would have liked, everything went back to normal. Apart from Jane's face, which appeared to have frozen in an odd expression trying to show shock, awe and intrigue all at the same time.

What had started the change within herself was fairly obvious to the Boss, as to when and where Jack been to collect the unusual particles needed and how were they still hanging around him like a static field was anyone's guess. She could hazard a guess, which had started with the dis-solvable chains in his cell after all. She paused, well whatever the reason was, the Boss now needed to get to know Jack better, even if it (perish the thought) became intimate.

Jack looked up from the screen in his hand and noticed the women across from him looked decidedly different. She had more colour in her cheeks for one thing, another was the fact she was looking very embarrassed, like she had been caught stealing cookies as well. She was not looking at Jack though, she was staring over his shoulder at something or someone. He turned in his seat to see a white coated woman stood swaying slightly behind him, wiping one hand across her brow and juggling her glasses in her other hand with a clip board. On closer inspection they were not glasses, but some form of magnifying see through coloured screens on a spectacle frame. Jack could not help but stare at Jane, not only was she quite attractive, in a science geek ponytail wearing kind of way but the lens on her glasses appeared to be showing a video.

Still staring at Jane as she fumbled her way into a seat next to Jack, with a bump of her knees on the table on the way, he saw a brief flash of blue across her face and a briefly vacant look pass over her face. Her face first had the look of shock, like catching her parents doing something naughty in the bedroom and then the look of someone carefully having blanked the image from there mind.

Jack looked to the Boss who had a satisfied expression on her face, ignoring Jack's questioning look she asked "so what new problem do we have now Jane?" talking as if they were in the middle of a conversation and not the start.

Jane replied hesitantly "um" and then continued as if nothing had happened "we need to send out some scouts to asses the tunnel integrity and to see if the invaders have found a way in past the cameras and collapsed tunnels?"

The Boss sat for a moment assessing Jane, making sure that she had forgotten what had just happened. Then thinking not for that first time that something so obvious as arranging a scouting party should already be in motion said "so get the girls organized and send them out!"

"Yes, I've already put that into motion but there's a slight problem with how they found us and whether they'll find us again!"

As Jane was part way through the sentence, both of the women had turned there heads to look at Jack. Jack for his own part was still not sure he could accept all that he had been told and so muttered under his breath "I hate bad dreams!"

"This is not a dream Jack" said the Boss with some force and degree of impatience "all this you see and hear around you is really happening, the invasion happened, the wiping and destruction, everything" the Boss wiped her hand, still feeling the static discharge from Jack and finished with "for some reason your involved with this!"

"I'm not involved in anything!"

"Yes you are Jack" said Jane quietly, both Jack and the Boss looked at Jane with questions on there faces but for different reasons "you linked with the probe device, which sent out a signal to the armada in orbit, which in turn meant they've tracked us down."

Jack as usual when confronted with something he could not quite grasp, sat with his mouth opening and shutting like a goldfish gulping air having been flicked out of its fishbowl onto the lounge carpet by an enthusiastic kitten.

Before he could get control of his brain long enough to shut his mouth, Jane continued with "we don't think you did it intentionally, rather something else or possibly some coincidence coincided with you coincidentally. Some how though we think there tracking you and so we need to send you out along the tunnels to see if they will follow you."
"Away from us" finished the Boss looking rather sullen.

Jane looked at the Boss and nodded in agreement, although why the Boss appeared to be upset she could not tell. She had been quite happy to send him back to be probed earlier and possibly lose his mind, so why she was upset now when he might probably escape she could not quite fathom.

The Boss turned to Jane and said "you can have him in a few minutes, I just need a quick chat in private with him."
Jack mumbled in an angry tone "do I get a choice, sacrificial gerbil in a maze that I am?"

Ignoring his comment with a sharp look, Jane stood up from her seat and walked to the door and stood leaning against the frame. Occasionally she glanced at the pad she had pulled out of a pocket and stood tapping her fingers on it like a countdown, which in some respects it was.

Jack sat waiting to hear his fate in an uncertain amount of confusion. Here he was sat down in front of the Boss, with guards waiting to pounce on him with there electrified truncheons and he was not cuffed. Was he still a prisoner or as he had heard suggested they needed him for some reason, as a form of bait?

The option of escape briefly flashed across his mind but where was he escaping from, who was escaping from and to go where, maybe just escaping was the answer?

The Boss turned to face Jack, who was looking quite angry as he sat squirming in his seat, like a child filled with indecision or more probably, wee.
In a conspiratorial whisper and leaning forward the Boss said "I didn't want any of this you know. I just wanted a simple life, settle down, farm, then we were invaded and over run but through various means found a way to fight back."
She sighed sitting back "it took a long time for us to find a way to even start to make a difference against our invaders. But in the end we found a way, if not to beat them at every turn, at least to stall them by using there own technology against them."

The Boss looked at Jack's blank face intently and realized he either was not listening or did not care "so what do you say Jack, are you with the resistance or against the resistance?"
Jack shifted in his seat and replied "honestly I have no idea what your talking about."

He saw that she was getting angry and probably frustrated with him, but as to why he did not know. Her eyes also seemed to flash and flow through various blues.

Jack held his hands up in mock surrender "no really" said Jack "I genuinely have absolutely no idea what your talking about, I mean my fellow cell mate explained the invasion from his view. But from my point of view I just woke up to it this morning. It must be like you said, that I've been wiped."

The Boss sat shaking her head at Jack and wagging her finger in a no no your wrong fashion, almost under his nose "Jack the one thing we always check for first, above all others, is whether the subject has been wiped. In your case we found you hadn't been wiped or tampered with in any way."

"So why can't I remember the war then?"

"It wasn't a war Jack, it was a roll over! As to why you can't remember I think you may have suffered some form of trauma, which is why your memory is all mixed up."

Jack looked a little dubious and shook his head at this comment, the only trauma he could remember with any accuracy, involved him with his trousers pulled down without his consent.

The Boss then said "Jack I'm about to tell you something that no one else knows and I want you to be patient and here me all the way through."

Jack looked up and into her eyes, again they appeared to be to be changing colour, shifting from a pale blue to purple as she spoke "my real name is Sara Orin Shavan and I'm really not from anywhere near here."

She paused for a moment and continued "well I suppose technically you could say I'm from New York but not your New York. I come from a place much the same as yours, it just isn't any easy trip to get there, especially back!"

"Queens?" asked Jack trying to recall his limited knowledge of the rest of the world.

Raising her voice slightly Sara said "no Jack, well yes, actually Queens but not your Queens."

Then Jane who had been stood rather impatiently tapping at her screen, looked up and walked very quickly back to the Boss. She had an expression of concern on her face as she said "sorry to interrupt but they've found another tunnel, disabled the explosives and are only" quickly she looked back at hand held screen "only five hundred meters away from the nearest entrance. So do you want to setup a defence, evacuate or try moving Jack here?"

Jane said this with one hand on a hip, glasses on her head and her other hand swinging the screen between her and Jack, like she was attempting to fan herself with a brick.

Sara looked up at Jane with blue fire in her eyes and wondered not for the first time about her timing for things in general. She then looked back to Jack, who sat slouched in his chair with an air of unconcern.

"Both Jane, we'll move Jack and evacuate outside the city."
"Are we taking my lab?"
"No, we'll just take the data and destroy the rest with the timer. How long before they breach the inner markers?"
Jane looked down to her screen and her lips moved quite quickly as she worked out timings, after a few mumbled seconds she answered with "we'll have about ninety minutes give or take five either side."

Jack sat listening to this conversation asked "surely it doesn't take an hour and half to walk five hundred meters?"
Both women glanced at one another and smiled together, it was not an all together nice set of smiles, the sort you might find floating across the face of a snake, sat on a hill in a grassy valley, with a grass fire in the distance and a used match stuck to its tail.

"Jack" said Sara "think of the tunnels as almost continual booby traps. Different explosives used at different points. Different traps and trips used, some log related, some electric, some flour and water and others just plain old fashioned tar and feathers."
"Oh and don't forget the occasional bear trap for good measure" said Jane, still smiling while she started to tap again on her little screen. After a few taps she looked up and said "the evacuate alarm has been triggered and we'll be empty in thirty minutes. Everyone should be out in the tunnels to the West site in twelve hours. I just need to go empty and destroy my Lab now?"
She asked this because it had taken weeks for her and her team to adapt the fallen invaders technology, she really wanted to take it with them.
"As we discussed a long time ago" replied the Boss with a sigh in her voice "just the data. It may be your anti-wipe project, reverse engineered from that fallen probe thing that's the cause and not Jack at all!"
"This only started after Jack here turned up!" Jane whined.
"Yes, this is true, but it may very well have only occurred after he was plugged in the machine for a rather extended and prolonged length of time, hmm?"

Jane thought about answering back but if she were honest with herself the longest anyone else had been plugged in to the device had only been seven, maybe eight minutes, Jack had been in for just over twenty!

It was entirely possible what the Boss was saying was true, but really to destroy the only thing they had got that could near completely undo the memory wipe and disable the robots!
It was ridiculous to throw that away, then again the machinery did weigh just over forty tonnes and was the size of an average family car. She did have a plan to move it that involved a crane, a helicopter, a long lorry and a very dark overcast night, all of which was currently unavailable apart from the night.
Jane sighed and turned to Jack "right come on then, lets get you into some kit."

As Jane lead Jack out of the canteen, Sara sat on her own for several minutes contemplating her next move. Really she should head up and lead everyone to safety but she was getting tired of leading and very tired of being hungry.

Nodding her head to herself she made a decision, she tapped the side of a small earpiece and said "Jenny Norris."

She sat tap tapping her fingers on the table waiting for an answer and after a few seconds "hello Jen, it's time you took over as we discussed and yes I know the timings bad but when will it ever be good?"

She sat listening for a bit and continued "I'll catch up with the evac later but for now I need to go with Jack."

"What, he's not that special you know!" could be heard seeping out of the earpiece.

Sara winced a little at the volume "I know your not particularly fond of him but there is something about him that I need to follow up" to herself she thought 'he may help me last longer here'.

"So I'll leave everything to you and I better catch up before everyone has left" with that Sara tapped the earpiece again and stood up from the table, with the grace of a majestic feline on the hunt and made her way to the kit room.

As Sara walked down the couple of corridors to the kit room, she passed dozens of people making ready to leave. All had at least one back pack and a case with them, they also all without fail carried a variation on the guards gas mask, hanging loosely around there necks or perched atop there heads.

The masks were mostly made from a malleable but strong rubber, courtesy of the invaders, it could be moulded into a rough shape for the head and a filter made from what looked like a black sponge. Really that should have been her first clue that it was the wrong invaders, the invaders she wanted did not use that particular rubber as it was so easily altered with heat.

They evacuees were also pretty exclusively all female, apart from the occasional small child and baby, not forgetting the detainees. They wore plastic tie's around there wrists and electronic tags around there ankles for moving them about and keeping track of them. Nearly all had been processed through the probe at one time or another, with varying degrees of success on undoing the wipes or reprogramming. They still needed to be taken to safety, even if some were and possibly still might be enemy spies, just because if the resistance were to continue it might need its gene pool expanded.

Looking over the prisoners were the black clad drone guards, shepherding them as they ambled along with there electric truncheons and watching over the drone guards were the multicoloured sporting helmeted guards.

As Sara walked past they gave curt and precise salutes for her, in turn turn she gave an answering flick of her wrist and smiled to herself, she really liked there following of military signaling but not necessarily the command structure. It seemed like no one was capable of making there own decisions without her authority, that had ended now she hoped breathing a sigh of relief.

All she had to do now was swing by her bunk, collect her few possessions and she could join the diversion crew and of course Jack.

Chapter 5 : Kitted Out.

In the kit room Jack had been manhandled, there was no other way he could think of it. In the last few minutes he had had so many female hands run up, down and over him, more than he could ever imagined, that he was stood in a shocked daze swaying slightly. Only in his dreams had so many female hands fondled him, the main difference really were the layers of clothing and the brisk measuring, pushing and shoving between him and them as he was passed along the line.

Jack had followed along behind Jane after leaving the canteen and then been passed to Claire at some point, along one of the endless corridors. Dutifully he had followed behind, after only a few corridors did he realize that no one really was watching him or apparently cared where he went, he toyed with making his escape. It then hit him again that what would be the point and where would he go?

He was not exactly a prisoner any more but they were watching him because of some tracking thing inside him and they needed him. Whom was watching and who they were was a mystery to Jack, he guessed that in some way he did not really have a choice, it would appear that in some way he had brought the invaders to the resistance door. Although resistance to what, where and how exactly had not been explained fully. It was only now following Claire down the tunnel and corridors that he had time to think, clear his mind of a slight fogginess he had felt since waking yesterday. 'It must have been yesterday' he thought, some internal clock was telling him that it was now early morning of the following day.

If he did escape they would not mind, so long as he did not go in a westerly direction. The problem was quite simple, where exactly would and could he run to? The little he had seen of the outside had been a complete surprise and even though it was still there, although technically flatter and grubbier than normal, there did not appear to be anywhere to go. What if the whole of England was like that or even the world he mused. Then there had been the sewer tunnel chase and near abduction by an device unknown that had resembled a really big vacuum cleaner. Jack resigned himself to following along, maybe if they started to trust him he might be able to find out the answer to his questions.

Finally the fast walking Claire stopped at a door and waited for Jack a few paces behind to catch up "Jack, do not say anything on going in, just let them take hold of you and pass you along."

Jack quickly poked his head round the door frame and saw a very long wide corridor like room, it had once been army green but now was a splashed white, just like the concrete corridors. Along one wall there was shelving that ran from top to bottom and nearly the entire length of the room. Running down the centre of the room was a series of metal looking benches, with several attractive women stood behind to apparent attention. Oddly they all had different body shapes, hair colour and faces but were all similar in height.

With that quick glance done, Jack made to turn back but Claire pushed him into the room and shouted "new recruit, full outdoor kit!"

As he had fallen through the doorway, a women had grabbed him from inside the door he had not noticed and he had been passed along. Hands had briefly run over him, then clothes, boots, masks and all manner of kit had been thrust into his arms. By the time he had been pulled, twisted, pushed and had got to the other end, he felt a little hard done by and quite rushed, not to mention slightly miffed and hardly able to see over the bundle of kit in his arms.

Claire who had been following along behind Jack and the door women said "now you get changed Jack, we can't have you wearing civvies when your caught."

He was just about to object when he saw her smile and she continued with "just a joke Jack and it's just you and me going south, hopefully getting the aliens to follow us. And no, I have no plans to get caught tonight or any other night."

At the end of the benches the long room turned left and in the corner were five curtained off changing rooms. Claire pulled back one of the curtains and ushered Jack inside with an extravagant wave of her hand and a cheeky smile.

The cubicle was of the typical retail clothes shop fair, with a curtain that was too short, allowing easy access for animals and small children, a watchful eye therefore needing to be maintained at all times. The curtain also managed to be not quite wide enough, meaning you have to change in the precise centre of the tiny room to avoid a peep show for the general public. All of this while balancing on one foot in the changing room trying to get in or out of the item of clothing, it is also advisable to not lose your balance. Inevitably you will lose your balance and gravitate towards the curtain, away from the little rooms mirror, tiny chair and end up tugging on it. The curtain will then detach from the rail it is hanging from, flail uselessly to cover the floor and none of your private bits.

This happened to Jack now, sort of. Claire had been expecting Jack to lose his balance and plummet out the changing room, she was already half smiling when he had entered. As he had started to grab desperately at the curtain for balance, the women from the door had caught the material and held it up, whilst also at the same time supporting Jack and stopping him from falling over with her other arm.

Claire was slightly disappointed now, she had made sure Jack had gone in the changing room with the uneven floor. The little room had been deliberately set up to be used for any insufferable and annoying recruits, not by themselves of course but by the previous tenants, who were either captured or lost.

In a slightly aggrieved tone Claire asked the women from the door "why did you do that?" not expecting an answer she was very surprised when the women turned from putting the curtain back up and said in a neutral tone "to protect and serve."

A few moments later Jack had sorted himself out and was looking at the black on black uniform and boots he was now wearing, in the mirror. It was very comfortable, surprisingly light weight and very similar in colour, though not the same shape as the guards uniforms. He twitched the curtain aside, stepped out and was very surprised to see Claire in front of him pointing a very white gun at his chest. As he stood slightly shocked he noticed the gun was not quite pointed at him but off to his left a bit. Looking to his left he saw the women from the kit room door whom had dragged and guided him along the benches.

Jack looked back and forth at the two women a couple of times and was just about to ask what Claire was doing, when when she said sharply "step away from her Jack."
Jack dutifully ducked under Claire sighting down the muzzle of her gun and stepped to one side of her, licking and sucking his lips in curiosity he asked "what's going on Claire?"

Claire sighed, to Jack this did seem to be a near continual feature of her make up, ever since he had known her. She appeared to sigh nigh on all the time he was around her, whether or not she sighed in private he could not tell but guessed that she must have practiced quite a lot to get so good at it.

Claire then sternly looked at Jack and then straight back to the women from the door, the gun not wavering for one moment.

Jack then looked closer at the gun she was pointing. It was not really like any gun he had ever seen before, it was a brilliant waxy white colour apart from the grip, which was a velvety red colour with a fizzy drink can like attachment under the barrel, this was a dull silver and nearly touching the trigger finger guard. In her hand it looked quite light weight, not wavering and dipping whatsoever. Jack wondered if Claire had been packing the weapon when they had met outside his house.

Claire then said to him "I was just thinking what an idiot you are ... again, but you haven't been here long enough to know that these ladies." At this point she waved the gun down the length of the room, indicating the women stood patiently behind the benches and then realized it should be pointing at the women in front of her.
Snapping the gun back to face her captive she said "these ladies are robots we've caught and reprogrammed for our use. Most of the original program contained there main objective and had to go. This also contained the basics for speech, so they shouldn't be able to talk and definitely not answer back!"

Jack looked the women up and down, he really could not see how anyone could tell that she was not real. After all she was very attractive, with mousy brown hair that flowed down her back to just below her shoulder blades and she had green eyes. She had pale skin and a surprisingly clear complexion, given what was going on in the world, she was also wearing a plain green all in one jumpsuit affair.

Jack asked in a curios tone "hold on a minute, when you brought me in you hadn't heard about these robots either. So how do you now know so much and talk like they've been here for ages?"
"Selective memory wipe" came a voice from behind them.

Both Jack and Claire jumped, turning to see Sara walking in the room from the doorway at the other end.

"Selective memory wipe?" repeated Jack.

"Memory is only data after all Jack, which can be easily copied and then deleted. The hard part is putting it all back again and in the right order. Claire here." Sara touched Claire's shoulder with her hand in a sensuous fashion, gently sliding her hand around her neck and to the other shoulder as she lightly walked behind her. "Claire volunteered to have the mental surgery, so she could wander further above ground and if caught wouldn't be able to give away too many of our secrets. This she knew had been done to her with her consent, but she wouldn't get back her memories until she returned and went under the probe."

Sara then paused and looked at the women from the doorway "so this is the one that can now talk is it?"

Sara walked slowly towards her, she was only eight feet away and to Jack it seemed she was walking in slow motion.

Claire was looking around, up one corner of the L shaped room and then back over her shoulder at the other. Finally she had to ask the Boss, as she was nearing the half way point "where are the guards Boss?"

"The guards are needed elsewhere, so I cancelled the alarm and told them to carry on."

Jack looked around the corridor like room and twisted his head slightly trying to detect the alarm, then it occurred to him that Sara had just said she had turned it off but still he wondered why he had not heard it.

Claire looked at Jack for help, when none was forthcoming she looked back only to find the Boss standing with her back to her but also between her and the intended target.

"Boss, will you move out the way!" exclaimed Claire.

Not turning her head and still looking with a fair degree of curiosity at the door women, the Boss said "I'm no longer your boss."

"Then what are you?"

"Just Sara" said Sara formally the Boss.

Claire looked a little lost at suddenly having a real name for her former Boss, then she looked to Jack again who was smiling to himself and asked him "what are you smiling at?"

Jack opened his arms, which had been folded since Sara had appeared and said "Claire meet Sara, Sara meet Claire."

"Har har Jack that's not funny" replied Claire.

"Well that's what's she's called and I thought an introduction should be made" said Jack smiling, he was enjoying this a bit.

Since Claire had tumbled him off the street into the sewer, she seemed to have taken great pleasure in telling him things that in her book he should have known and usually with a sarcastic tone. This was the only time so far he had known something about her world which she did not, the bosses real name.

Shaking her head Claire stepped to one side to get a better view of the door women robot thing and pointed the gun back at her chest. She then put her hand in her pocket and took out a small piece of shiny black plastic, five centimeters by about three, and five millimeters thick. As she pushed her thumb into the middle, the display lit up and a green light flashed slowly from a top corner edge. She then put the shiny black plastic thing back in her pocket, put the gun up behind her back, there was a small click like noise and when her hands came back they were empty.

"So do you want to tell me why we don't need the guards then?"
Sara did not turn round but said to Claire "ask it for it's protocols."
Claire remembered she had been through this before at some point and so asked "name your primary protocols?"
The robot answered in a precise fashion "to protect and serve Jack Jonas Johnstone. To protect and serve humans, where possible if no contradiction with protocol one. To protect and serve oneself, where the protocol does not contradict protocol one and if possible two."

Claire's mouth was agape as the list of protocols, commands and instructions continued, she eventually realized her mouth was wide open and shut it, then she ordered the robot to stop listing its protocols. She then turned to look at Jack who was admiring the robot, looking her up and down in a very suggestive manner "yes Jack Jonas Johnstone it's a robot. It may look human but it's not and just so you know ... it has all the relevant bits in the relevant places."
Jack realized he had been staring and started to go a rather nice shade of red in his cheeks.
"And Jack I know what you were thinking, especially about the serve part of its protocols" Claire said this in the playground sing song tone that children use when saying 'we know who you fancy!'

Claire was beaming so much at Jack's discomfort that she nearly forgot how the Boss or Sara as she was now, had known about the change in protocols or even how they occurred. Claire stepped round to the side of her and asked "so how did you know about the change of protocols?"
Without saying a word and still looking at the robot, Sara handed Claire a black plastic screen that looked identical to the one she had just put back in her pocket. On the display though was a video on pause, Claire pressed play, then after a minute looked up with a blank expression and passed the black card to Jack.

Claire turned and questioned Sara "so it shows Jack getting his kit, so what?"
"If you'd looked a bit more carefully you might have noticed that this" she stopped and pointed at the door women "started walking Jack down the room in a jerky fashion, but by the end of the tables she was sashaying down the room. Look at her now she isn't standing to attention but leaning on her hip."
Looking closely at the robot, Claire could see that it appeared to be standing more naturally and she was starting to worry that it might revert to its old programming at any moment.

"Do you have a name?" asked Sara.
"Yes" came the polite but short reply.
Both of the women looked briefly at one another and had similar thoughts, along the lines that even the robots voice was sounding more sultry, although the answers were still robotic.
"So what's your name then?" asked Claire, not really expecting anything other than a number.
"Elizabeth ... though I remember being called Beth" came the hesitant reply.
"How did you know it'd have a name?" Claire asked this in an accusatory fashion turning to Sara.
Sara finally looked away from Beth and turned to face Claire "something happened when she was walking Jack down the room that enabled her old life to start to be remembered."
"Well that's worrying, we don't want a bunch of raving robots on our hands."
"No, not her old life as a robot, her previous life as a human."
"Are you saying that she used to be human!" Claire looked back down the room at the other robot women all lined up, awaiting instruction.
"Not entirely no, the body is an approximation with an edited copy of the original human brain inside."
"Edited?"
"The invaders added there own instructions."
Claire nodded slowly and said "so they could infiltrate us and provide information to the aliens or even stop us!"
"Yes and the gas they used wiped everyone's memories, which in turn helped get the robots inside any resistance group because they appeared to have memory issues like everyone else."

    Jack finally felt he could join in the conversation with a sensible question "so why aren't the others joining in the conversation then?" he said this indicating the other women down the line with a waved hand.
Sara gave Jack one of her questioning looks "why don't you tell us Jack, since we caught them and put them under the probe, not one has spoken anything other than there number until now?"
Sara had strong suspicions about Jack but was keeping them to herself, mainly because she did not want to scare Jack into doing something stupid.
Jack looked at Claire for help and received a cold angry stare, like he had just done something dangerous and reckless, like giving her the fright of her life, yet at the same time she was happy he had survived his stupid stunt and yet very annoyed.
Jack wondered, not for the first time, why he was always being quizzed for answers he could not give "how would I know, I've only been in this weird reality for all of a day?"

    Both women sighed together at Jack, then quickly reached into there respective pockets as something vibrated, they pulled out there shiny black cards and looked intensely at the screens. Claire looked up sharply from her screen and said "there at the half way point, I think its time we moved."

Sara just nodded as they walked briskly back towards the door she had come through, with Jack tagging along behind like a puppy with really short legs.

Claire got to the door first and pushed it open, walked through to the other side and held it open for Sara, she was going to let it swing back on Jack but then saw Beth following along only a few paces behind him.
"Stop, what do you think your doing?" she asked sharply of Beth.
Jack looked round at Beth and whilst Claire was still holding the door open stepped quickly through.
Beth managed to look slightly taken aback and replied "to protect and serve Jack Jonas Johnstone."
"What does that mean?" asked Claire.
"It means she will go wherever Jack goes I believe" answered Sara from further down the corridor.
"And your alright with that are you, having a potential alien explosive device wandering around with us. Not to mention it can probably be tracked once we're outside!"
"Explosive device or not I'd rather have her on our side as her memory comes back. And surely the whole point of our mission is to take Jack, who may be being tracked, away from the base with the invaders following. If he's not being tracked then Beth here will have the same effect, hopefully and since she's following Jack and we're escorting Jack, she goes along."

Claire stood in the doorway still holding the door, Beth walked through and Claire just opened and shut her mouth trying to get her objections straight. She could not fault Sara's logic, but it felt just plain wrong having an enemy tool following along, she looked at Jack as she thought this and smiled to herself. She picked up her old brown leather satchel from the floor in the corridor and swung it over her shoulder, following along carefully behind.

After a couple of minutes walking down now dark and emergency lit corridors, Jack had some questions. He was not sure he would get answers if they were asked of Sara or Claire, so decided to ask Beth an easy opener "are you really a robot?"
"Yes."
Jack paused as various thoughts ran through his head, the first thought being that questions asked of Beth would need to be better phrased for a start.
"Okay, so what type of robot are you and what are you made from, because you look human to me?" asked Jack.
"Our creators called us Hersatz, we are made from bio-plastics in a mould with a metal core and dynamic fluid for our operation and storage."
Jack looked a little lost for a minute and then realized it was not an embarrassment to ask what something meant, especially from a robot "so what is an Hersatz then?"
"Ersatz is a copy, typically inferior from the original, the first letter denotes the species. So I am Hersatz or a copy of human."

Both Claire and Sara were trying to listen quite closely to Jack's questions and Beth's answers, as a result of this they had started to walk slower. The corridor had also got quite narrow at this point, all four were brushing shoulders with one another or the walls, which were now curved like a tunnel and still explosively painted.

Before Jack could ask any further questions Sara picked up the pace as they walked round a bend in the concrete corridor and stopped opposite a door.

Jack thought about the doors he had seen so far, they had been almost all made of metal or the wall was the door, this door though appeared to be all wood, oak if he was any judge.

Sara rapped a complicated knuckle bashing code on the door and after a few seconds a counter code was heard being tapped out from the other side. She replied and then Jack realized they were playing some drum rhythm sequence from a song he knew, but could not quite remember.

Whilst the tapping and banging was going on, Jack waved his hand at Claire indicating the door and asked "why is this one made from wood and what's behind it?"

"This is the armoury" sighed Claire in a resigned tone, as if it were obvious to everybody but Jack.

Jack thought of saying 'really, well it ain't that obvious luv' but turned to look back at the door, just in case he had missed something obvious. As he looked above the door he saw the word 'Armoury' written in a faded blue ink. The lettering itself was not that visible on the splashed white walls, unless you were stood directly in front of the door and then it appeared that the letters were floating a few inches out from the surface.

"Yes I can read that it says armoury thank you, but I would have thought that an armoury would have an indestructible front door and not something made from something that burns quite easily as a rule!" said Jack with a hint of sarcasm.

Sara had looked round sharply at Jack as he said the word 'read', then before Claire noticed turned her head quickly and stared back at the door.

"No Jack it doesn't say 'armoury', but it is the only wooden door down here" said Claire.

Claire held her hand up at Jack as he made to object, not realizing he was going to say 'yes it does, in blue to!' Thinking he was going to interrupt about the wooden door she finished with "have you ever tried to bend, burn, break or even just dent a really old well seasoned bit of wood? It can be tougher than most metals and it's much easier to get hold of, plus this door only gives you access to the repair shop anyway."

As Claire finished explaining about the door, a fuzzy green four foot thinly lined square faded into view on the floor, Sara was stood already in the square as it formed and Claire stepped in soon after. Claire turned to Jack and waved him to join her in the square, looking doubtful he joined the women in the box and Beth stepped in behind him.

"All arms and legs inside the fuzzy green lines please!" said Claire.

"Yes, but why?" asked Jack.
Claire smiled one of those smiles at Jack that you would more commonly find on a cat, that not only had got the cream, but had planted the evidence in the dog's basket as well.

The square they were all standing on jerkily started to raise itself up towards the ceiling, the roof of the corridor had only been a few feet taller than Jack and now he was going to meet it with his head. Jack covered his arms over his head and tried to crouch on the square, there was an invisible barrier that stopped him from leaning outside the edge of the box, they then passed right through the ceiling without a sound or feeling of movement. The only indicators that they were moving at all was the rushing of air as they moved up, and the intermittent fuzzy green lights in the dark lift shaft itself.

In a voice full of mirth Claire said "you can uncurl your head out of your bum now Jack."
"A warning would have been nice!" he muttered as he straightened up.
"Where's the fun in that? Any-way's, just think of it as another test you've passed."
"Test?"
"Of your memory, your experience, your knowledge, your humanity."
Jack looked hard at Claire and said "my what of what's?"
Claire sighed, getting a little bit more annoyed each time she had to explain something that any other person would know.
"If you were a robot like Beth here, you would've been able to feel, if not see the entrance above the lift. If you'd experienced anything similar or at least have seen it, you'd know what to expect and wouldn't have reacted as you did!" Claire waved her hands around as she spoke, trying to indicate the world around them was full of tests.
"So you've been on one of these lifts before then?" queried Jack.
"Once before" replied Claire shortly, who then turned to look up the shaft, which appeared to have no end.
"As I remember you were quite ill afterwards" commented Sara also looking up the dimly sparkling shaft.
Claire ignored her comment, whilst Jack smiled to himself, feeling quite pleased she had not sighed at the end of her answer.

After a moment Jack thought Claire was also being quite rude, not seeing his point of view at all, she was assuming he had lost his memories but like Mark had said, he should at least have some fragments to pick from. Nothing came to mind though, everything he had seen so far, apart from one person he knew, were quite literally all new. He genuinely had not seen any of these things before, unless of course he had been successfully wiped clean he mused, a blank slate if you will.   Whilst thinking about this he decided not to mention the blank slate thought, as Claire was sure to say he had always been one, so instead asked "Mark made it out the base okay did he?"
Claire replied as if Jack were asking a stupid question again "yeah, of course he did!"

Slowly the pressure of the air gradually started to drop and the lighting started to flick past slower, as if there ascent were slowing down. Then they passed through a border of some kind and were in a bright room of the officious white variety, so bright after the darkened shaft, that it took several seconds for them all to adjust to how brash the room really was.

Claire and Jack both looked around in wonder as there eyes adjusted, not so much at the white room but at the panels in the walls. They both walked round the room which was twelve meters by twelve meters and three meters tall. The size of the room was of little interest to the pair, as depending on the angle you looked at a wall, you could see a weapon of one description or another floating inside.

"This is amazing!" said Jack "if you look straight at a wall you see nothing, but as you change the angle a gun or something appears in the wall."

"Whatever you do, do not touch anything in this room without express permission from the Armourist" warned Sara, who had not moved from the spot the lift had deposited them on.

"I'm sorry what did you say, the Armourist?" asked Claire while Sara ignored her.

Claire had just realized that her staring round the room in wonder was not something she wanted Jack to see, mainly because she wanted to appear more knowledgeable and valuable than Jack who was receiving deferential treatment.

Jack on the other hand had noticed her gawking at the room and then had caught her trying to look nonchalant at the whole thing. As to why he could not quite guess yet, but he assumed it was a female thing he was not supposed to know about anyway. At least until he was getting told off for something he should have noticed but did not and should forget unless he should remember, or when the other person required you to remember but not before or after. This was Jack's ground belief in relationships, which was probably why he was not in one.

Claire felt different in some way, uncomfortable, like something was missing. She reached around to check her old weapon, she realized she no longer had it on her and started to panic that she had lost it. Sara looking on at Claire's mounting worry said "weapons are not permitted in front of the Armourist" the irony of the sentence made her smile, which somehow was lost on Claire.

Sara looked around the room, after a few seconds she began tapping her right foot, which after several taps was really getting on Jack's nerves as it was starting to echo. The echo was not right though, it seemed that every other tap of Sara's booted toe on the polished white floor did not echo. It was as if the echo could not decide whether it should be heard or not, or even if it should be an echo at all.

"So what's this Armourist then?" asked Claire moodily, still thinking about her lost gun "and will she hurry up, we're a bit short on time you know."

Sara ignored Claire, who was not accustomed to being totally neglected herself. She was about to rephrase the question, beginning to pout in frustration, as a middle section of the white floor started to raise itself up, until it was three meters long, two meters wide and a meter tall. The rest of the room, the floor, walls and ceiling were also uniform blank white things, with no edges or lines whatsoever, including the border with the walls. It was like a very large sheet of very shiny paper had been folded around to make a box, without the actual folds being visible. The very shiny paper had no reflections, no lines could be seen, with only occasional shadows in the room. The only visible things had been the panels and there contents when you caught the angle right with your eyes, until the raised plinth started to appear. There was lighting in the room, it was just that the walls appeared to be doing the lighting, giving the strange impression that you were somehow stood in a light bulb.

All three were now looking at the box that had emerged from the floor, each on a different side, with Beth still stood behind Sara where the lift had deposited them. Jack and Claire exchanged a look over the top that said 'what's that then?' Sara had thankfully stopped tap tapping her boot, to Jack's relief. Beth stood like a naughty child, almost like she was in standby, head dropped forward and down. Then the top of the box in the precise centre started to change colour a few inches at a time, until a round sea green metallic circle could be seen forming.

As they looked at the new object forming, Jack turned his head slightly and realized that the circle was not a circle but a sphere or ball coming out from the box. He stepped back and when he looked round he saw both women transfixed by the sphere, the top of the box though was still perfectly flat with a greenish tint across the top. When he cautiously looked back in at the top of the box, he could see that the depth of field was all wrong, it was like the sphere was right in front of you and yet at the same time coming from a long way off. Then the sea green metallic sphere seemed to wobble slightly, as if it bounced over some sought of speed bump or boundary marker and started to come out of the box. All this took only a few seconds but seemed to take ages. Finally there it was, a perfect sphere about a meter in diameter floating a few inches above the box, which was now perfectly white again.

The sphere hung in the air, casting a green tinted shadow over the white box in the floor and appearing to sway slightly in some invisible breeze. The sea green coloured metal of the sphere gently seemed to move and flow with a mottling effect rolling across its surface, like wind blowing gently over the sea. Then a simple face started to meld together in front of each them, made up from the varying shades of green and blue on the sphere.

Sara looked quite relived and without turning her head said to Jack and Claire "meet the Armourist."
The sphere in a slightly metallic deep sounding male voice said "hello" seeming to bow to the two females.

The lips moved in perfect sync with the voice, no dubbed over sound, it seemed as if the green ball was actually talking to them thought Jack "hello yourself" he replied.
The Armourist seemed to frown, least Jack assumed it was a frown, then he saw Sara looking round the side of the ball at him, giving him a withering look, followed by a forcefully whispered "shut up Jack!"

Sara turned back to face the green ball, her features bathed in shades of green, giving the impression that she was looking over an oily lagoon "we have come for our coded weapons."
The Armourist spun round for several revolutions and then stopped suddenly, the facial features took a few seconds to drift back in to place, giving the impression of oil washing round on the surface of the sea. When the face was back to normal and Jack had finished feeling queasy, it asked "why?"

Sara looked a little confused to Jack, as if she were not expecting that particular question and then he noticed Claire was looking at her black quartz screen, starting to look worried.
"We have come for our coded weapons please!" Sara said this with exaggerated care and quite a lot of emphasis on the please.
"It is not yet time" came the metallic reply.
"The invaders have found our base and we need to distract them so others may escape" Sara almost seemed to be pleading with the sea coloured ball.
Jack was surprised when the three other faces from around the sphere suddenly swam round, like jelly octopuses, to form one detailed face in front of him.
He was even more surprised when the sphere asked of him "is this true?"

Jack was confused, as far as he had been aware so far, nobody of any description had asked his opinion on anything, now he was being addressed by a green floating metal football.
Hesitantly he replied "yes?"

The faces on the sea green ball moved back to face the three of them, then a brief blueish green light seeped from the sphere and played up and down there bodies. The green faces then appeared to nod to each of them and the metallic sphere started to sink into the white block it had come from.
"Was that it then?" asked Claire in a slightly peeved voice of Sara "we get to chat with a green ball and scanned by a blue light. It's like being arrested, so could we please make a run for it, before we are actually caught?"
Jack opened his mouth to ask when she had been arrested, because he never had and Claire quickly said before he could ask "once Jack and no it's not the time to chat about it."
The sphere halfway through entering the block replied "time isn't relevant here and you came to us not us to you!"

The sphere finished its passage into the block, making a cheeky noise like someone sticking their finger in their cheek and then flicking it out. To Jack Claire looked quite insulted by the sound the sphere had made and then the sea green metallic ball was gone.

With hands on her hips and an annoyed expression on her face, Claire asked of Sara "so now what, we've lost several minutes in here and no weapons to speak of at the Armourist's?"

"Be patient, the Armourist didn't say no and we haven't left yet" said Sara.

The white block, well thought Jack what other colour would it be in here, started to sink into the floor, he looked at Sara and asked "the weapons are so good then, there invisible to us and the aliens?"

Jack and Claire had been looking around the white walled room, the weapons in the walls were no longer visible.

Sara did not reply, she had questions of her own. On the occasions she had requested help from the spheres, they had given her answers and equipment, not always what she thought she needed though. The answers admittedly were not always complete but she had never been quizzed as to why she wanted them; the spheres seemed to be all knowing in the past but this one did not seem to know what was happening on the Earth.

Jack looked closer at the block, it was like water draining from a tank with no top or sides, only the water was very white and thick like gloopy paint. As the white block descended further into the floor, the top of it started to show some wave like distortions and three objects started to appear. As it finally drained out, it left no impression that it had ever been there before, apart from the three items floating just in front of each of them.

Jack looked at the three weapon like objects drifting in front of them, he was not really sure what he had been expecting and was quite pleased for everyone, up to a point.

In front of Claire floated a white gun, the shape of a revolver, admittedly a very big revolver that would probably require two hands to pick up and aim. The dangerous end had three exits, two large ones like a shotgun and then a smaller aperture one sat on top, protruding over the lower two by a few inches. Then a hand grip along the lower part, followed by what looked like a revolver style rotating ammunition chamber, with lots and lots of chambers. The red velvet grip and trigger were housed behind the chamber and on top was what looked like several white fins, presumably for aiming between thought Jack, like sitting on a Llama's back and aiming though its ears for chewed cud projectile launches.

In front of Sara hovered a far more elegant gun, something quite small, light and shaped quite simply like a purse gun designed by a perfumery bottle specialist. This was also white.

In front of Jack floated a long tube shaped thing in white, with small odd shaped black splodges printed intermittently around the middle, it was about eighteen inches long and just over an inch in diameter. All were of the same shiny but non reflective white as the room they stood in.

All three looked at the weapons floating in front of them, then Sara and Claire reached out hands and picked up there respective guns. Jack on the other hand just stood looking at what he would describe as a diseased log.

"Where's my gun?" moaned Jack looking at the two women admiring there guns, after all why should he get a twirling baton.

"Just pick it up Jack, for all you know it could be a gun and we really don't have time to muck about" said Claire turning the gun over in her hands with a sparkle in her eye and then she started to stroke it like it was some lost kitten needing a home.

Jack stepped forward to pick up the baton but as soon as he touched it the thing started to fall towards the floor. He ended up doing one of those juggling to catch a tumbling glass exercises, whilst dancing on the spot, thinking the whole time that it might be a bomb of some description and should not be allowed to strike the floor. Finally Jack got control of his hands and the baton and stood mildly surprised to find that it weighed virtually nothing. He examined it from one end to the other, carefully touching the splotchy bits in the middle, only after careful scrutiny did he find a small off white ring going around the baton an inch from one end. He then held it like a baseball bat in both hands, imagining he was on the field ready to smack a small innocent ball made of leather.   Other than the thing being used as a cudgel, Jack could not see what else it could be used for. As he gripped and rotated the baton he found the surface started to move under his fingers, it felt like it was trying to turn around in his hands. So he turned the baton up the other way and noticed that the small off white ring was now at the top of the shaft. As he moved the baton in his hands everything suddenly slipped into place, the baton no longer felt like a lump of diseased wood but more like a well balanced knife with a comfy handle.

Sara looked carefully at Jack and asked "you don't know what it is do you Jack?"

Jack looked up "it's a cudgel isn't it?"

Sara rolled her eyes "does it look like a cudgel? Actually don't answer that, instead put your thumb print on the bottom of the shaft."

After a few seconds of fumbling, Sara started tapping her foot on the floor and told Jack with a degree of exasperation "the other end!"

Before she could tell him to not be looking at the opposite end to where he was applying his thumb, he pressed his thumb on the base. A sliver of gold like coloured wire shot straight out the end to a length of four feet from the handle. The gold wire missed Jack's face by an inch "that was lucky ha ha" laughed Jack. He would have laughed further but the gold wire then ignited a red fuzzy colour to a diameter of an inch along its entire length. It made a crackling sound as it ignited, which fortunately surprised Jack enough to move it away from his face, in time to only get a singed eyebrow and drop the weapon on the floor. Once released from his hands the weapon recalled the gold thread and the red fizzing faded into the air, not before it had bounced with the handle on the floor and spun round leaving a three foot long gash in the floor. "Oh wow I'm really sorry, but shouldn't these things come with a warning?" asked Jack as he bent and carefully retrieved his weapon. As he picked it up he looked at the slice taken out of the floor, expecting to see burned or fried edges, instead it was a cool and clean slice with no trace of damage, apart from the obvious gash he had created in the floor.

Sara rolled her eyes again and was about to give Jack a verbal slap when Claire got there first "that is the coolest thing I've ever seen!" said Claire "it's like one of those sword things from a film. Can I have a go?"

Sara looked at her in surprise, she had been fully expecting Claire to have given Jack a verbal berating, but instead wanted to congratulate him on his clumsiness.

Sara quickly stepped in front of Claire and grabbed her hand as she reached to take the sword from Jack "no Claire it's Jack's, and anyway it wouldn't work for you. The same way your or my gun won't work for Jack, his Glade won't work for anyone but him."

Jack looked at Sara and then back at the weapon in his hand, rolling the still diseased looking log around in his hands "what's a Glade and why can't she use it?" asked Jack.

"I asked for coded weapons, because they are coded to our DNA so no one else can use them and Glade is the name for your type of sword."

"You mean there are other types of sword?" asked Claire.

"Yes several but only" Sara paused for a second, trying to reword the fact that Glades were only used by one race that she knew of "the Glade is quite rare" she finished.

Both Jack and Claire had noticed the pause and exchanged a look that said 'what's she not telling us?'

Then the green fuzzy square faded into view on the floor and started to flash, Claire said "finally, I was wondering how we were going to get out of this ridiculously white box."

Claire pulled out her Shiny black card again, tapped it and Jack asked "I've seen you both with those black credit card things, what are they?" As they stepped into the flickering square, Claire looked up from the light on the card and replied "there called Quellz and it's a tablet like communication device, that works everywhere but apparently doesn't work down here!"

Jack looked at Claire's troubled face as she started to bang the thing on her leg.

"Don't do that" said Sara "if you remember the Armourist said 'time isn't relevant here' so my guess is that it runs faster to the outside world here, or not at all."

Standing in the green lined square, Jack saw Sara place her gun on her hip and let go, a white belt flicked round her waist from the gun, round her back to her front and re-attach to the gun. The gun was now hanging from her hip, in easy reach. Jack did the same, as did Claire and they both felt a slight tingle as the belt was released from there new weapons, swung round there waists to clasped back into there respective weapons.

The square then started to move up again towards the ceiling, again they passed straight through and were in a dark lift shaft with the intermittent fuzzy green lights passing by. Jack turned to look at Beth and then back to Sara "so why didn't Beth get a gun?"
Sara looked round and replied in an offhand manner "probably because she doesn't need one."

Jack could tell from Sara's tone that he was not going to get any further answers so instead asked "okay, another question, why are we going up again, didn't we come up through the floor in the first place?"
Sara paused, she did not actually know why they were going up. She assumed they would be going back to where they had come from and not somewhere else. In fact the only thing above them was the railway or tube as far as she could remember. So it came as a surprise to them all, when they came up through the floor, right outside the wooden door Sara had tapped out her strange knocked code in the first place.

As the four of them stood looking at the solid door, Jack noticed once again the floating faded blue lettering above the door saying 'Armoury'. On closer inspection he also now noticed a symbol in the top left corner of the door, which looked like a 'P' and an 'S' written over the top of one another. On closer inspection they actually read as the letters 'tJi', they were written in italics and were a fuzzy faded green in colour, where they crossed over one another the colour briefly changed to a summer sky blue.

Sara then turned with Claire and started to walk down the corridor at quite a brisk pace for Jack, who was almost skipping without running to keep up. Jack looked at Beth stepping it out beside him, nearly tripped over his own feet when he saw how she had lengthened her stride to walk quicker, by rotating her hips rather than lifting or rolling them.
"Doesn't it hurt to do that?"
Beth looked at him "does what hurt?"
"Your sort of walking odd for a human ... copy."
"It is an efficient way of walking quickly and keeps the body level."
Jack up until this point had still thought of Beth as human in some way but the way she was walking was making him feel ill. So he stepped up the pace to keep in front of her and catch up to Sara and Claire, he then glanced back at Beth and a shudder ran through him.

Claire had her Quellz out again and smiling to herself Sara asked her "so, how long were we away?"
Claire looked sidelong at her "only a few seconds, but you knew about the whole time relevance thing, didn't you?"
Sara simply replied "yes."
"But how did you know?"
"I've met them before."
"The Armourist?"
"Yes."
"Where?"
"In another place."
"What other place?"

Sara took hold of Claire by the shoulder and they both stopped dead in the corridor, forcing Jack to sidestep quickly to avoid the pair of them, whilst performing this intricate maneuver for Jack, he tripped over his feet and bounced off the wall. Well he thought he should have bounced off the wall, instead he fell through the wall backwards, like it was made of paper and indeed it did make a noise like paper being ripped. Both Claire and Sara turned at the tearing sound and saw both of the souls of Jack's boots disappear into the wall, toes up.

Staring at the corridor wall, which showed no sign of Jack's recent departure, the ladies began running there hands over the wall where Jack had fallen through. After several tries neither of them could find any difference in the wall and Sara decided to call out "Jack, are you okay?"

Jack lying on his back gradually levered himself up on his elbows and let out a little "ooh" and "ow", more at the surprise of landing on his back and being winded than in any actual pain. He then looked at the doorway he had come through. The doorway was a standard size and showed the corridor perfectly as if it were just a normal opening, Claire and Sara could be seen running there hands over the doorway and there expressions said it all. Jack started to laugh as he watched them and there confused faces, as they mimed running there hands over an invisible wall. Jack then pulled himself upright and stood up. Looking round he realized it was pitch black everywhere but the doorway and the light coming through the opening. It was not just the absence of light anywhere else, the dark seemed to suck the light away completely, either that or the distance to the far wall was a really really long way off.

Somehow it was really funny to Jack to watch the two women in the corridor, knocking and waving, right up to the moment he heard the sounds behind him. The slithering, rustling and of course hissing noises were all the incentive he needed to exit quickly, before the light faded for any reason.

Turning back to the lighted doorway Jack saw Sara mouth something, as the door seemed to start to shrink, he was only a few feet from the doorway when she seemed to say it louder with some gusto a few moments later. Jack walked forward and reached through the doorway with his hand to Sara, as soon as his hand touched some border between the corridor and this room, he was pulled through the doorway like a cork escaping from a bottle of very fizzy champagne. He piled into Sara and Claire, all three ended up lying in a pile of entwined arms and legs.

After carefully untangling themselves the three stood up and brushed themselves down, Jack then asked of Sara "what was that then?"

Looking back at the corridor wall Sara mused "well I would have said it was a hologram, but as it felt solid from the outside I would guess it was a dologram."

"What's a dologram?"

"First Jack, what was on the other side?"

"Well there was a floor and nothing else."

"Nothing else?"

"Yep just black and blackness everywhere."

"No corridor, no light in the distance?"

"No nothing, just darkness, the doorway and the floor" he was not going to mention the sound of something or something's shuffling around in the dark bits of the room, avoiding the light from the corridor. It would effect his manly image if he talked about it in a squeaky voice.

Sara stood rubbing her hand over her face, lightly tapping her boot on the corridor floor and muttering something about 'bubble Universes being banned', as she tried to work out what this was doing here.

Jack asked again "what's a dologram?"

Still Sara seemed to be lost in her own world, so Claire turned to Beth and questioned her instead "do you know what a dologram is?"

"A dologram is a dimensional Universe hologram."

Both Claire and Jack stared at one another and in unison asked "what?"

"A hologram is a virtual representation of something in the real world, it can be made to look like real substances but is not solid. A dologram is a dimensional hologram, it has the state of appearing solid on one side and generally can only be entered with a certain pass or key, this can be electronic, touch, sound or any combination."

"So anything could open one then, but why is it here, who put it here and what's the point of one?" asked Claire.

Sara turned to the three of them "it really is time to go and before you ask, the point of a dologram is to hide something in plain sight in it's own little split bubble Universe. As to what this one was hiding we may never know, and no, I have no idea who put it here or why" she looked meaningfully at Jack.

"Why are you looking meaningfully at me? This is the first I've heard of any of this!" Jack waved his arms about to indicate the Universe in general, which would have worked better if he had been stood outside in a field and not in a concrete and white splashed tunnel.

Sara began walking quite quickly down the seemingly endless corridors with Jack, with Claire and Beth trailing along behind. After a few minutes, that felt like monotonous hours of the same corridors to Jack, the mad white painting on the walls suddenly stopped and the corridor turned into a concrete tunnel, sloping ever steeper uphill.

As the white paint had stopped, so had the strip lighting in the ceiling and now it was getting quite dark. Neither Sara nor Claire pulled out torches, they just walked along running there hands along the walls following the slight bend in the tunnel, until some light started to filter through from somewhere up ahead.

Jack felt he had to ask about the paint on the walls "what's with the slap dash painting I've seen everywhere but here?"
Claire replied in the infuriating tone she used whenever Jack asked what she considered to be another stupid question "it's slightly radioactive and no it won't have damaged you, much"

Jack's face had blanched and lost most of its colour on hearing the word radioactive, as well as an involuntary covering of his most dear private bits with his hands.
Claire smiling continued "it just confuses the enemies scan and if it were the same white paint everywhere it would look unnatural when there scans passed over us."

As they rounded a final bend in the tunnel Jack could see daylight ahead, about thirty meters or so away. As they walked closer his eyes started to adjust to the light in the tunnel and he could see there was a grill of sorts over there exit.

Sara had her Quellz out tapping at the screen as they walked forward, she then touched something in her ear and could be heard talking briefly to Jane.
"I've spoken to Jane, she got her precious data out and says she's the last to leave."
"So everyone is on there way west then?" asked Claire.
"Yes and she's set the timer in the lab for" Sara looked at her Quellz "for four minutes from now. I should also mention that the bread crumbs are working, according to Jane" Sara looked pointedly at Jack, who managed to look a bit shocked and started to involuntarily pat himself down looking for a tracking device. He stopped after a few seconds feeling slightly embarrassed, he had no idea what he was looking for and knowing his luck so far, probably his entire body was the bug.

Jack had hoped to escape from whatever was happening and just get some time to think, to work out what was going on and more importantly, what he Jack was going to do with his life. He had enjoyed his job, his house, his car, his phone and now that had all been taken away. In the case of his house it could still be repaired and his car was in the country still at a friends, hopefully. His office had probably been destroyed, which was no bad thing, unless Jenny was in it at the time he thought. His phone though, that had contained his life, realization now slowly dawned that Sara and Claire were using similar things right out in front of him. Jack was starting to get angry with Claire, flaunting her device in front of him, especially after she had so violently disassembled and destroyed his own phone in the sewers.

Anger started to build up in Jack and was then lightly dowsed with a cold drop of water down the back of his mental neck, as Claire asked something Jack had forgotten "does that mean they're actually following Jack then?"

As if in answer to that question, further back down the tunnel could be heard some banging and chattering of alien voices. All three cocked there heads towards the sounds and then looked at one another and promptly hurried to the grill.

When they got to the grill Jack could see it was made from very thick and very heavy black coated metal, set deep into the concrete. He tapped one of the bars with the handle of his Glade attached to his hip, it made a resounding and solid clang as he struck it.
With no apparent hinges and no way pushing or pulling the bars was going to move them, Jack said "well now what?"
Sara turned to him and whispered "shut up, we don't need them to know how close they are!"
"Well yes okay, but this grill ain't moving and we certainly aren't fitting between the bars" whispered Jack back to her.
"Who said anything about moving the whole grill?" asked Claire.

With that Claire and Sara took hold of one of the bars to the right of the centre of the grill, pulled it down and then lifted and twisted it into the ceiling. It made a little click noise that sounded like the cocking of a gun to Jack, as it was moved around and into the ceiling. Open mouthed in surprise, Jack finally realized this was an escape tunnel, as he was dragged and pushed through the gap in the grill by Sara and Claire.

As they exited Sara turned back to see Beth grab and twist the bar from the ceiling, lowering it back into place in the grill and twisting it with another gun cocking click to lock it.
Sara grabbed hold of a bar in the grill and asked through gritted teeth of Beth "why?"
Calmly Beth looked at Sara through the bars at her flashing blue eyes "they will assume I couldn't escape with you, or had been discovered and left behind. Either way Jack will escape with you and they will have me for information."
"But you know about the others going West?"

"In a moment I shall not, as a permanent delete program will be run once you leave."

"But if there tracking you and not Jack the whole point of this exercise was to mislead them from the resistance. And aren't you sworn to protect Jack?"

"They will only be able to track Jack for a few more hours as the residual effects of the probe wear off. This is protecting Jack, as I will be far more important for the information I carry about this base, which I will shortly be deleting and they will struggle to recover any data from."

Sara looked deep in thought as she mulled over what Beth had said, the only thing that bothered her was whether or not Beth was telling the truth about protecting Jack.

Beth then turned and walked back down the darkened tunnel, towards an unknown fate and Sara turned to see Jack meandering about like a holidaymaker without a care. Beth glanced back her shoulder, watching the escapees slowly walking away to the left of the tunnel exit.

Whilst Sara was talking to Beth, Jack was looking around. When they had first squeezed through the bars of the grill, he had only paid limited interest to the river and its banks. Now with Sara taking her time at the grill, Jack was looking around and feeling slightly confused. This he concluded was going to be his ground state of being for the rest of his life. In Claire's eyes it made him look stupid, but to Jack he was seeing new things all the time and was considering giving up being shocked any more.

Jack was stood just a little way down the bank from the recessed grill and was looking across two hundred meters of concrete to the vertical bank on the other side. As far as he could remember the city did not have any American style levy's running right through or around it. They were stood in a small valley on a steep bank of concrete, which then leveled out to a flat piece fifty meters wide running down the middle. The bank then restarted on the other side with trees poking over the top. There was a trickle of water running continually down the centre and when he looked left and right the whole system seemed to be in a long curve running round behind them.

Then some shouts and loud bangs echoed from the grill, the three of them quickly jogged around some rock and bushes protruding from near the grill exit and carried on jogging round until they had moved past several more protrusions. On closer inspection the rock protrusions were not rock but rubble from buildings, some even looked like they had once been metal of some description, all now wrecked and had bushes growing out of them.

As they stopped to catch there breaths, Jack turned to ask Claire about the levy they were stood in, as he did so his feet felt odd, heavy even as he tried to turn. Looking down at his feet Jack was quite surprised to see that he had sunk an inch into the concrete, which was everywhere even under the rubble and bushes. He quickly stepped to one side and his footprints gradually disappeared as the bank slowly returned to its former shape. Reaching down to touch the ground Jack found the concrete did in fact feel like a sponge.

Claire turned round to find Jack pawing at the ground and not for the first time thought what an idiot "what are you doing now Jack?" Jack looked up and replied curiously "it's a sponge?"
Claire was just opening her mouth to reply with another barb when Sara put her hand on her shoulder and said quietly "remember, before you call him anything, two things: he genuinely doesn't know what's happened and we need him on our side not there's."
"But he keeps making and asking stupid questions that'll get us caught and killed!" moaned Claire.
"I ... that is we, need him. He is special in some way."
"Oh Jack's special alright ha ha ha" laughed Claire.
When she had finished laughing she started to think about Sara's little slip of the tongue, why did Sara say 'I need Jack' and the only special things about Jack that she could see was his lack of supposed memory and being tracked?
Sara turned to Jack who was still bent down pressing at the ground and watching his fingers leave rude signs as indentations and said "Jack will you stop making indents on the floor please."
Jack looked up "it's a weird kind of concrete don't you think, to be so soft and spongy."
"That's because it's not concrete, it's a form of foam that surrounds the entire area for about a hundred square miles."
Jack looked a little confused and looked both ways at the gentle curve of the foam river bed before asking "so why's it here?"
"When they attacked, not long after, as people wandered round, they dropped the rings from orbit. As they fell they grew in size until they were big enough to cover any area they chose. There are four that we know of in England and before you ask what there for" looking at Jack's questioning face "in essence the foam ring we're in is a prison camp."
Jack looked at the foam river bank and asked "so why not just walk across and out the other side?"
Claire rolled her eyes and slapped her hands on her sides before turning to Sara to say "we really don't have time for all these explanations you know."
Sara looked round at Claire "if we don't explain it as we go along he'll get annoyed, go looking for answers himself and then we may definitely get caught."
Sara turned back towards Jack, whilst looking at him she picked up a piece of brick rubble and tossed it to the middle of the river. The brick stopped dead in the air and fell into the river like it had been caught and dropped all in one motion. The water was only an inch or so deep as it landed with a splash, but it did not bounce and was then sucked away like a bug down a plughole leaving no trace.
Jack gave a little whistle and said "so err, that's why no one has got out then."
"It looks safe but the closer to the middle you get the softer it gets, until you get sucked from view" said Sara.
"So what happens to people that disappear?" asked Jack
"We actually don't know, but you can assume it isn't good" replied Sara.

Jack looked up and down the foam river, turned to Claire who was stood with arms folded and an annoyed expression on her face and asked "so where to now then if were sealed in a foam ring?"
Claire unfolded her arms and simply replied "out!"
This time it was Sara's turn to roll her eyes at a silly answer that was deliberately toned to wind someone up. Before Jack could answer back to Claire and a further childish like argument start, Sara quickly put in "we find the shuttle and leave the area as quickly as possible and above all else silently."
"So how do the other escapees get out the ring? I assume they aren't flying out?" asked Jack whilst avoiding mentioning the word shuttle.
"No Jack, no one knows about the shuttle except myself and Claire here. The base personnel are going outside through long established tunnels, really more like old train tunnels really."
"And these lead outside the foam ring?"
"Yes" replied Sara "now it really is time to move, I would imagine Beth has been found by now and is probably on her way to the CPU to be analyzed."
Jack paused in the act of following the two women as they turned and started to walk away. The only CPU he new of was inside a computer called an Central Processing Unit and was the main, if not the central bit where all the main processes were carried out. He did not want to appear dumb again but could feel the question needing to be asked.
After a minute of walking briskly following the edge of the river he decided to ask "so what's CPU stand for? And before you accuse me of being stupid again Claire" this was said pointing an accusing finger at Claire and shaking it vigorously "I know it stands for Central Processing Unit in a computer, or at least it used too."
"CPU stands for the same thing here, just to a different scale. Inside each ring there is a central hub which has landing, defence capabilities and where people get processed, besides everything else you need in an invasion. So us and them call it a CPU for ease" replied Sara quickly trying to head off any hostilities between the two of them.
Jack mulled this information over as the three of them gently walked round the very long curve of a river. It was only after they had been walking for an hour or more with no one apparently giving chase, that Jack felt mentally at least at ease, even if the scenery had not changed.
He was having some thinking time and several questions were now clearly forming in his mind. Firstly 'what do the aliens want and why have they invaded?' and secondly asking out loud "ladies, I hate to be the one with all the silly questions but have you noticed the river?"
Both women stopped walking and looked at the river and then back to Jack, followed by Claire asking "it runs down the middle Jack!"
Jack stood smiling at the pair of them and finally before there expressions got too dark towards him Jack said "when we left the sewer grill the water was running left to right. We've passed no junctions, water falls or exits that I can see and yet the water..."
Sara interrupted with "it's running right to left!"

Jack stood looking on with a smug expression on his face and folded arms "would you care to explain this one, to somebody who isn't as all knowing as you then?" this was said by Jack who was looking quite pointedly at Claire.

Claire just shrugged her shoulders at Jack, not willingly to admit that Jack knew something she did not, realization then dawned on her face as she turned to carry on walking away and she quickly turned back, swinging her satchel around to her back. She watched Jack and Sara stood looking up and down the flow of the river.

"I've just realized something ladies" said Claire "our shuttle was parked near a river exit that we've obviously walked passed in the last hour somewhere?"

Sara turned from looking over the river to face Claire and said slightly confused "well yes, but no. The shuttle was by an exit and it should have been this one, it wasn't this far round as I remember?"

Whilst the women had been talking and he had been ignoring Claire's 'lady' comment, Jack had been lining up some rubble and a couple of twigs on the foam bank. He was now crouched down lining them up on an old radio relay mast outside the river walls, as something occurred to him.

"We had better get moving then" said Sara whom had started to walk off with Claire at her side. After only a few strides they realized Jack was not following them and Claire turned back to ask "are you trying to get us caught Jack? Or are you just wasting time thinking of more time wasting questions?"

Jack looked up at Claire with a puzzled expression and said "whilst you two were discussing how you've lost the exit, I've been wondering why the scenery hasn't changed, it looks like we haven't been getting anywhere in here!"

Jack still crouched over his rubble and twigs, pointed down at the arrow he had made out of them "we haven't moved in the last couple of minutes and neither has my arrow. But apparently the radio mast outside the wall is moving slowly around us!"

Sara came back to look down at the arrow, which was now pointing several degrees off to the right of the mast. As she watched, it was vaguely possible to see the mast move slowly away from the arrow, a little like watching clouds in the sky on a lazy summer day. Your never really sure if they are moving when your looking right at them, until you look away for a few moments and when you turn back the little fluffy thing has belted off across the sky.

Claire by now was also looking at the arrow, now not pointing at the tower "so what does it mean then?" this was asked of Sara.

"I would say that the outside appears to be rotating anti-clockwise, but more likely is that we're actually rotating clockwise and walking anti-clockwise" said Jack.

"You mean us don't you? That's not possible, is it?" asked Claire.

"Just by looking, Jack's discovered we're spinning slowly round inside this foam ring" said Sara slowly, as she finally started thinking how this knowledge could have been used earlier. It would have been difficult though to observe the effect, as the last few months had either been spent hiding underground or briefly dashing across the surface avoiding being shot at.

Jack was looking backwards and forwards between the mast and the rubbled bits of buildings and then a thought occurred to him "I know I'm not the quickest on the uptake and this really doesn't feel like my world as I remember it. But if we're spinning round, doesn't that mean we could be walking against the flow, like being on a treadmill or a giant merry-go-round and not going anywhere?"

"Not only that Jack, the shuttle will be in the same place but we won't, not without knowing where we've spun round to" said Sara.

Claire then covered her mouth with her hand in slight shock and said "the escape tunnels everyone else is using, if there spinning round too, they'll be walking into a dead end!"

"You know I really don't know how deep this ring goes, but if it's completely around and under us then we're pretty ..." Sara paused lost for words.

"Stuffed" filled in Jack.

"Yes pretty much, it might also explain why there hasn't been any help from the outside, they basically couldn't find a way in through the tunnels!"

"Or even a way out through the foam" said Claire.

The three of them stood in there little triangle, occasionally looking backwards and forwards forlornly between the arrow on the floor and the mast gradually moving further away.

Finally Jack had to ask "so how far down do you think the foam thing goes and why is it going round in a circle?"

Sara looked up and said "I think we've been stood here long enough and should carry on walking, at least to get away from the invaders."

Sara held her hand up as Jack started to speak again "I don't think it matters why it spins, just that it does. As to how far down, I would imagine its half of a sphere."

"That wasn't what I was going to ask again. What I was going to point out is that the aliens don't appear to be following us!"

Looking back the way they had already walked, the three could see there foot prints nearly fading completely from view in the foam and no sign of any chase.

Claire asked "do you think they've given up?"

Jack replied before Sara could say anything with "I very much doubt they've given up, more like they don't need to track us, we're already going in the direction they want or they've already caught all the fish they want."

"Don't say that Jack, the whole point of our running round outside was to get them to follow us and not the rest!" said Claire.

"Then why aren't they anywhere to be seen Claire?"

Sara said "maybe they don't need to follow us. The foam bank tracks our progress anyway and maybe there just waiting to see what we do and where we go."

"Or Beth has already told them our plan" said Claire.

All three looked quite glum as they contemplated the negative possibilities until Sara said "we should look on the positive side of this and assume that no one has been caught and try and find my shuttle. As I remember, it was parked in a small ravine directly South of our exit tunnel."

"Which will have moved won't it, due to the spinney thing we're all stood on!" said Claire.

Jack looked up at the sun and then started to rummage through his pockets, looking for his phone. Jack had stopped using a watch years ago and always relied on his phone for the time, now though he remembered that Claire had thoroughly destroyed it and its contents.

He turned to Claire and asked "have you got the time?"

Claire pulled back her sleeve and looked at her watch, it was one of those super expensive motion charged, diving contraptions that would have looked too big for an heavy weight boxer let alone an average build women.

She saw Jack's jaw open at the sight of her watch and said "don't worry I'll pay for it one day soon, maybe, if we get out of this."

Jack closed his mouth and realized she had miss took his expression and then further realized Claire had stolen the watch "you stole it!"

"No, not exactly."

"How not exactly?"

"If you must know I left an IOU."

Jack looked surprised first and then he started to laugh and wave his hands around pointing in every direction "do you really think there gonna care that you stole a watch and promised to pay for it later?"

After a few seconds his face dropped from a smile to annoyance and Claire continued to stare hard at him. Then Jack asked as casually as he could without too much anger he hoped in his voice "so why are you wearing the watch then?"

"I thought it would be obvious even to you, that I like to know the time and a watch is quite effective at giving this information" Claire replied in a sarcastic tone.

Jack was getting angry now and so was quite sharp with his reply "this I know but, and correct me if I'm wrong, isn't that watch made from rare Earth metals just like my murdered phone back in the sewers and therefore traceable? If it isn't then why destroy my phone, when I could have just turned it off?"

Claire sighed and rolled her eyes, annoying Jack further but before she replied Sara stepped in and said "everything we have ever brought back to the bunker is tested outside and before you start demanding why your phone wasn't tested before it was destroyed, every single phone we tested of any description and nearly any age failed. The trace test involved leaving the device in an outside area and watch the drones turn up to inspect it. The older analogue phones weren't traced by the drones until they connected to a cell tower or mast and then they were simply destroyed. The more modern phones were found straight away, whether they were connected to a network or not and were then destroyed."

Jack opened and shut his mouth a few times and then asked of Claire "why didn't you tell me that at the time, rather than disassembling it to it's component parts with your oversized throwing arm?"

"Honestly Jack we didn't have time for a discussion and we were nearly caught anyway, if you remember."

Jack shrugged and turned away, his anger was fading having been robbed of its target.

"What did you want a watch for anyway?" Sara asked of Jack. Jack looked up at the sun beating down relentlessly on there heads, sat down on the foam river bank next to his makeshift arrow, replying "I really wanted my phone because it had a built in compass, then I saw Claire's watch and remembered that using the sun's position and a clock you can tell which way is North."

Sara sat down next to Jack and quickly asked "so with Claire's watch you could tell which way South is then?"

Jack shook his head and looked up from staring at his crossed legs and said "you can but I can't remember how you do it and I don't think it would have helped find our way any way."

"Why not?"

"Cos I've been looking at the sun's position, as we've been walking round and the thing has been sat in the same bit of sky, it's not lost any height or moved at all!"

Claire looked up at the sun, trying to remember its position in the sky as they had exited the tunnel and asked "that's not possible, is it?"

"In this cage I guess anything is possible" replied Sara with a sigh.

"I vote we keep going till you recognize something Sara" said Jack "we can't go back, so as we're walking against the spin we'll just have to walk faster."

Claire nodded her head in agreement and waited for the other two to pull themselves out of the foam, which took considerably longer than anyone thought. The noise of there backsides finally departing the ground, was not too unlike the sound someone might make by sucking there lips over there teeth with a little pop to finish. The dents in the foam took much longer to fill in than just there feet making marks in the bank had. Sara looked back down at the two impressions she had left and wondered how big her bottom really was, she caught Jack doing exactly the same but looking at her impressions. Jack carefully avoided eye contact with Sara, as a slightly muted tapping sound started with one of her boots, with that he raised his head to look at something really interesting somewhere in the opposite direction entirely.

Then a thought occurred to Sara "let's not go to sleep anywhere near the foam, I think it'll suck you from view as you sleep."

They all nodded in agreement and started to walk further along the foam river bank at quite a brisk pace, trying to keep ahead of the spin.

After some time, with the sun not seeming to diminish in any way whatsoever, Sara finally let out a burst of a relieved sigh and said "if you look up ahead I recognize that great tree leaning over the bank from the outside. I remember there's a drain cover nearby that we can lift out and climb inside the tunnel to get outside to my shuttle."

Jack stopped along side Sara and said "not until the drain cover spins round into view on our side and we're gonna have to time it so we can get out the other end to."

Sara and Claire both looked round sharply at Jack, it was the first nearly sensible thing Jack had said all day. Jack watched both there faces look at him in surprise and continued with "I think we're spinning clockwise, but I suggest we keep walking until we find your drain cover and then sit on it till it's in the right place."

Both women just nodded in agreement, Jack then did a shooing motion with his hands to Sara, who looked at him blankly for a few seconds until he said "you'll have to go first Sara as I don't know what or which drain cover we're aiming for!"

Sara started walking briskly away, with the trees and river on her right and the bank on her left. Jack and Claire fell in behind and Jack started thinking for the first time in a long time. You could tell this by the strained expression on his face, like a small child faced with a sweet dilemma of eat this one now or wait and have two later.

Chapter 6 : Agent Exit.

"Agent forty eight, step away from the exit" came an echoey muffled voice from somewhere down the tunnel.

Beth carefully watched Jack, Claire and Sarah dive off to her left like naughty school children, she turned from looking out of the grill and turned to face the invaders, her captors, her creators? She was starting to question everything she was doing now, but only since she had touched Jack in the equipment room, which sounded wrong on many levels and would not be repeated outside of her own head. She could not explain it all to herself yet, it felt for the first time like she was becoming herself, finally remembering what and who she was.

As she turned and looked back down the dim tunnel toward the voices coaxing her away from the grill, she realized several things. Firstly she must not let on that she was regaining her memories, her sense of self. If they found out she would probably be disassembled and reused in the field to catch Jack.

Secondly she now knew she was a robot of sorts and was therefore wondering about how she got her memories in this body in the first place and where was her original body now? This body looked like hers, felt like hers but was tauter, fitter and so far no hint of cellulite or excess anything. She had actually never felt quite so perfect, which instinctively she knew was wrong but was going to enjoy it anyway.

Thirdly she was thinking much faster and clearer than normal, the voices calling her away from the grill did not sound like the invaders. In fact they actually sounded human and this was a worry now too, as the only things to call her by her creation name 'Agent forty eight' were the invaders themselves. Some of fellow humans must have joined the invasion team she thought, collaborators even and then she started to sigh, which she quickly stopped, realizing they would not expect her to sigh on being captured or retrieved. She should act pleased on being returned to the fold and yet not smile.

Beth's final task was to quickly delete and write new data over her memories, not all of them and not completely, just enough so that they would find her of use, giving her a chance to formulate a plan of escape and rescue Jack from the resistance women.

Beth started to walk back towards the voices and her eventual capture. She was thinking and processing things much quicker as the voices talked to her, but she was not really listening as she was still struggling with finding her sense of self.

Beth sat in the back of an army truck moving along a road somewhere, with the canvas surround of the truck billowing and booming in the wind, slapping her in the face like a plastic bag stuck on a flag pole in a thunderstorm. Beth realized then she was wide awake, but could not move a muscle and had no memory of leaving the tunnels or entering the truck. She could not move or react to the slapping, instinctively she felt her mind flinch every time the flap came near her and yet she was frozen solid with her eyes wide open. Then panic suddenly reared its ugly head as it dawned on her that not only was she wide awake and immobile but she was not breathing either!

'Do not worry, we need to talk and you are perfectly safe, for now.'

If she could of Beth would have jumped off the bench she was sat on in surprise, the words were being spoken directly to her but most disconcertingly by her own voice.

'That is not strictly true' came the other voice again.

The voice carried on reciting 'do not worry, you are perfectly safe' for what felt like an age, until finally Beth started to relax, well mentally at least she started to relax and then laugh slowly at her predicament.

After laughing internally at her position, she now at least felt happier, if not a little bit confused. Then it occurred to her that of the five pairs of feet she could see from her dipped head position, not one of them had moved when the words had been repeated. They had not heard the words she realized, because the words had been inside her head.

Beth mused 'great, not only am I a robot who shouldn't have human memories, but now I'm schizophrenic robot as well!'

Beth was unsure exactly what was going on, because if you were ever to hear your own voice played back to you from a recording, it sounds different from what you mentally picture your voice as sounding like. You can recognize it as your voice, it sounds unusual with you ending up in denial for a few moments, until realization dawns and then you either love or loath the sound of your own voice.

Now imagine the sound of your own voice in your head talking to you, along with your own voice discussing yourself, you might feel a bit left out.

If she could of Beth would have been looking wildly around the truck for a means of escape, since she could not move this was not an option. Instead she was being forced to listen to her mind having a conversation with its self to while away the time.

The internal voice came back 'we know this is strange for you, to be having a conversation with what feels like yourself, but it is necessary and important that you have some information regardless of the means of provision.'

'Am I going mad?' Beth felt she should have been shaking as she said this to herself but then added 'hold on a minute, if this is me talking to me why do I need to be told information, surely I already know what I need to know?'

'This is not you talking to yourself or imagining you talking to yourself. We need to explain some things to you before we get to the end of the line and using your own voice was the only way we could wake your mind and have a conversation.'
'So I'm not going mad, being that my mind isn't in the right body or even a real body right now?'
'No you are not mad.'
'So how did I get here?'
'When the invasion occurred, obviously some humans were captured for further experimentation and some of those experiments involved the creation of robotic copies. This was to aid there knowledge of humans and to infiltrate any hidden systems. A human near to death would have the contents of there brain copied and placed in a Master Editor Suite System, where it would be dissected, trimmed and where appropriate rewritten. The copy could then be placed back in to the environment, with the newly edited mind and simply tracked until the time came to do something about them. Before you say that's disgusting, it is a tried and tested technique that all sides in many wars use, it is both highly illegal and highly effective. There are many regulations governing copies and nearly all can be circumvented in some way by some means when required.'
'So my real body is dead then?' asked the real Beth.
'Yes, it was partially severed, you survived for three minutes before being discovered by the invaders and your brain essence copied to the Memory Editing Suite System.'
'Partially severed?' asked Beth with a slight choking of her mental voice, she had hoped that she might find her body one day and get back into it somehow.
'Basically from your sternum upwards you were okay, everything below had been dragged completely from your spinal column. We could show you some images that might better explain the trauma if you wish?'
'I really don't think that'll be necessary thank you very much.'
'This, is a good thing.'
   Beth paused as she started to think things through logically, then the inner voice came back 'now we've seen your finally thinking productively, it is time for you to understand your purpose as we help you.'
Before the voice could carry on any further Beth interrupted with 'I do have some more questions before we go any further.'
'We thought you might, so please ask away and we will answer what we can and then explain your much needed purpose.'
'Thank you and firstly I'm noticing that I'm not breathing?'
'This is a requirement for animals.'
'So what am I then and you didn't answer the question?'

'Your body was grown in a bio-mechanical laboratory, using your DNA in seven days. Then the complete but redacted copy of your brain essence was copied into your new body from the Memory Editing Suite System. Your skin will absorb any requirements from the atmosphere, so breathing is only required to push air over your vocal chords for external speech, which we are not currently using at the moment.'
'Okay that makes sense apart from the redacted bit?'
'Rather than delete bits of data from the host, which may be needed later, they blank the data by the use of a small electrical charge. The data can be retrieved by reversing the charge, but only over small sections at a time and with considerable pauses.'
If she could have frowned Beth would of, as she gradually absorbed or rather she now thought of herself as processing the information.
'So robot or not robot then?'
'It could be said that you were constructed and therefore your body is robotic or android like in nature, but your core being is an exact copy of your former human body.'
'With a double spine?'
'Single spines had in previous specie copies been found to be insufficient to support the body without excess modeling of musculature. Therefore species with single spines had an additional one added for stability.'
'But we got on with single spines, as a species!'
'This is true but to reconfigure an old system to make Hersatz is easier and much cheaper than building one from scratch.'
Beth mentally took a breath, as she realized that even in war there might be a financial budget 'your telling me the invaders were saving money, by using an old copy machine to copy us and make a copy with twin spines because they didn't want to exceed there copy budget.'
'Yes, it's the same everywhere. If it's not money, it's energy conservation.'
  Beth paused in her questioning, as she could not move her eyes they had been staring at the same set of army boots opposite her, she then realized that they were tapping out a really very slow dance beat. Her hearing was also working quite well and everything she was hearing was sounding very clear but slow, like watching a slow motion replay of some accident you might have seen.
  Beth could almost hear the mental sigh of the invading voice in her head, as it replied to her observation of time moving slowly 'time isn't moving slowly we are just conversing very quickly, giving the impression of time moving slowly and no you don't need any more information than that about it right now.'
Beth finally asked the one question that had been bothering her 'are you the invaders?'
'No we are not, we are here to help.'
To Beth this did not sound like a complete answer and they could be lying, at least it sounded like they were trying to help in some way. Then another question sprang to mind 'who or what are you and why are you offering to help me?'

'We are helping you help yourself, which in turn helps us. We have already uploaded to you a lot of information which is scrambled, so the invaders will think it junk. This information will be unscrambled as and when the data is required by you. Your ultimate task should you choose to help us, is to assist Jack in whatever way possible.'
Beth was a bit taken aback by that remark, helping Jack had been the last thing on her mind and yet he was always on her mind somehow. She had also assumed that she had no choice in the matter but 'your saying I have a choice of whether to obey you or not?'
'Yes.'
'So what happens if I say no?'
'We leave.'
'Okay, that sounds simple enough' she also thought to herself they either did not notice the word 'obey' used instead of join. Was that deliberate or merely an oversight on there part?
'Hold on, hold on, what happens to me personally if I say no and you leave?' asked Beth with a tinge of worry in her tone.
'We delete anything and everything to do with us and we leave.'
'Yes I guessed that, but what happens to me personally?'
'You are very persistent in your questioning, but as your aware within the eyes of the law because you do not have a body...'
'I cannot technically be classed as living and therefore do not have any rights? But I can think for myself and feel?'
'Only since we changed some aspects of the base code. If we were to leave, we would have to return them to there original state so the invaders would not find the changes. With us here we would change what needed to be changed and back again after there checks.'
'Another question then, how did you get in here with me?'
'We removed some of us from Jack when you touched him, allowing us to assist you.'
'From Jack! Is Jack a Hersatz too?'
'No.'
   Sensing she was not going to get any more answers, probably for security reasons. Beth returned to mulling over her choices, to be a robot thing with no control or a robot thing being controlled. Then would she be aware, awake and trapped in this body with no option but to obey her programming from someone else? The other option offered was almost as bad, except the voice was giving her an option, a choice, a decision to make on whether to help it or not. But was it her making the decision or something else?
'All we will say is not to over think the two options we have presented you with.'
'I choose myself ' hope of survival is wonderful thing and I feel better already 'one more thing though, in future can you not use my own voice to talk to me, it's the most infuriating thing.'
   Beth still with her head down, looking at those black army boots lightly bouncing up and down with the movement of the truck, watched as time sped up to normal and her vision gradually faded to black until the army boots were finally gone.

Chapter 7 : Going Out.

Jack sat cross legged with his back leaning against a raised concrete drain, with his head tipped back absorbing the blazing sun in the clear blue sky, even if it was altered in some way, when the ground beneath his buttocks gave several jumps. He tried to bound up but his feet were entangled in the weeds around the drain, the effect for Jack was like having his shoe laces tied together just at the point he needed balance for standing straight.
For Claire and Sara it was like watching the statue of an ageing rotund religious god try to stand cross legged, then at near to standing upright, simply to tip forward with a considerable amount of arm wind milling. This was followed by the inevitable planting of Jack's face into the ground, minus his arms for landing gear and a muffled cry. They were only slightly disappointed by the sound of his face hitting the ground, which sounded more like a lump of wet clay being thrown onto a potters wheel than a face thumping concrete.
"Damn the foam river bank!" mumbled Claire to Sara, both of them stood with slight smiles on there lips and hands ready to cover there faces if it got too much.
As Jack unstuck his face from the foam with a light pop noise, he heard the barely audible tinkle of female giggling somewhere in the air in front of him.
He rolled over onto his back to try and stop the mirth from getting any louder, glancing at his feet as he sat upright. The weeds and long grass his feet had been sat in, appeared at one point to have been tied in a knot around his boots. He was fairly certain there had been no loops and knots in the grass before he had started to relax against the drain cover, in fact he was pretty certain the green bits had been pointed straight up into the air.
"Was it really that funny to tie my boots to the ground then?" Jack asked of the women over his shoulder.
Between stifled giggles and struggling not to laugh too much, Sara answered with "honestly Jack we didn't do it, but what made you jump up so quickly anyway?"
"Didn't you feel the ground bounce up?" exclaimed Jack.
Sara and Claire exchanged a slightly puzzled look, then Sara's expression traveled from puzzlement to realization, she clicked her fingers and replied "the invaders, they must have tried to access one of the labs!"
"And what's that got to do with ground bouncing up and down like a colony of moles riding pogo sticks?" Jack asked this in a tired fashion, expecting Claire to jump down his throat with some sarcastic or barbed comment.

Jack stood up slowly and checked himself, facing the two women he was quite surprised to see Claire looking a little confused, not actually prepared to admit that she did not know something that Jack did not know either.

Sara walked forward to Jack and once she was standing on firmer ground, bent down on to her knees, touched the earth and said "gosh, you can still feel the ground shaking!"
"I know this, but from what exactly?" asked Jack.
"Bit bigger than we thought mind" mused Sara.
"What was a bit bigger than you thought?" asked Claire with a little bit of frustration in her voice.
Standing up and tapping her foot excitedly on the ground, almost like she was itching to perform a jig and a smile on her face, Sara replied "oh the Poly bomb."
Claire and Jack exchanged mildly baffled looks, then both turned to face Sara with questioning expressions.
"I guess it's safe to tell you now, as it's gone off" said Sara with a relieved sigh from keeping one too many secrets "Jane devised a booby trap based on the bunkers self destruct system."
"You mean a bomb then?" asked Claire moving further down the foam river bank and away from the drain cover.
"No not a bomb as such, more of a surprise really. The original explosive liquids were drained years ago, but the system for the self destruct on the base, was still in place. We had no explosives to put in it anyway and any we did have were going to be used in the fight against the invaders. Then one day on one of our forays into the city we found two lorries." Sara began to smile, but not in an overly nice way "these two lorries, at different ends of the city were labeled with all kinds of warning signs. Fortunately they were both radioed through at the same time and crossed Jane's desk at the same time. The normal procedure would have been to drain both vehicles of there chemical loads and get them back to a tunnel, where we could take them apart and re-purpose them."
Sara paused here for dramatic effect and a knowing look, but since neither Jack nor Claire had any idea what was in the lorries, they both just stood around looking a bit miffed.
"Okay" said Jack eventually "I'll bite, what was in the lorries?"
"Ethylene in one and Benzene in the other!" Sara said this with a little wonder in her voice and then after seeing there blank looks continued with "there's a bit more to the process than that, but when the two are mixed together you get a rather exciting expansion and end up with a lot of Polystyrene which, I'm sure you've heard of?"
Nodding Jack said "yeah I know the stuff, the white plastic packaging you find round your new TV in it's box."
"That's the stuff" said Sara with a smile.

As if on cue there was a creaking noise from the high banked wall behind them, as they turned to look, they could see something white pushing its way through some of the green vines halfway up the old looking stone wall.
"There must be some vents linked to the bunker up there" said Jack.

The three of them stood for several seconds just looking at the white stuff flowing and oozing out of the wall above them.
　　　After several minutes the white stuff had still not stopped dripping from between the vines on the wall, Jack asked of Sara "so this Poly explosion" waving his hand at the white stuff still flowing everywhere "the tunnels it's traveling down, are they connected to this drain we're about to dive in, to find the shuttle?"
Sara looked back from the wall to Jack and then at the drain "no Jack, I'm fairly certain there not connected. To be on the safe side though we should get in the drain now and make our way to the end."
　　　With that they levered open the rusted metal drain cover, climbed inside one after another and down the ladder into another wet outlet. Jack feeling he should be a gentleman went last, once all three were inside, he pulled the metal cover back into place. He then heard much cursing and abuse from Claire and Sarah, aimed towards the flaking rusted ladder. Jack wondered, as he clambered down the rusty rungs, if this was an entirely sensible course of action, mainly because of the possibility of being chased by the white stuff down an enclosed tube with potentially no exit?
Moments later could be heard the interesting sound of a metal ladder rung, detaching itself from a metal ladder. Followed shortly by a relatively quiet and surprised "uh oh!" from a male voice, then a double thud and finally a wet sticky splash echoing from the drain.

　　　Jane was feeling put upon, everybody and she meant everybody, had turned to her once the alarms had started to go off again. Now they were all asking questions of there faith in her, after turning the final bend in the corridor, in there bid to escape, and there was no more corridor to speak of, it just stopped in a blanked off concrete wall.
She had been so sure of the bunker plans and even had sent out Mel, one of her, if not her most trusted assistant, to check the escape route was clear.
　　　Jane turned to ask Mel if they had taken a wrong turn over the hubbub of disgruntled voices and found Mel stood with her mouth open and a shocked expression on her face, like a ghost seeing itself for the first time.
　　　Mel turned to look at Jane, her mouth opening and closing noiselessly, then she managed to stammer "I...I..I was here last week and I'm telling you, the tunnel went on for miles and miles."
Jane looked first at the solid wall in front them and then back to Mel "are you sure, 'cos it sure ain't here now?"
A light lit up on Mel's face for a second, thinking they could have taken a wrong turn somewhere, then she remembered "I walked back down this tunnel in the pitch black for several hundred feet, marking off points as you asked me to do and then I checked back a week later." Mel continued shaking her head in disbelief and mumbling something about cream not being taken orally.

Jane could see the black paint streaks on the wall every couple of meters or so, this last one though, where the tunnel ended, looked half complete. She walked over and tapped on the wall a few times, just to make sure it was real and there was the resounding thump thump of hand on concrete.

The people behind her had by now climbed out of the various cars, trucks and lorries and were forming a crowd stood behind her. They sounded like they were getting more agitated by the infuriating minute, like people stuck in a queue for a concert that has been cancelled but no one told them. Jane knew that as more people joined the crowd and time moved on, the chance of her being lynched and left as a crucifixion on the wall for the invaders was becoming more likely.

She looked down at her feet in dismay, glancing at the bottom of the wall there were scratches of some kind in the concrete. As she stood and watched, it seemed to Jane that the wall was moving, it was almost like trying to watch paint dry, giving the impression of nothing actually happening because it was happening so slowly, like continental drift. Jane picked up a stone from the ground, scratched a line in the middle of the floor straight up the blocked tunnel wall and sat down to wait.

After a few minutes Mel was getting worried, the crowd of people was nearly a mob now and Jane was sat cross legged on the floor, head resting on her hands just staring at the blocked tunnel wall.
Mel walked carefully up behind Jane, she wanted to walk with authority for the benefit of the crowd, but not so loud as to break Jane's concentration. Jane nearly always had a plan or solution, but she did need privacy to work things out.
"Um, Jane I'm sorry to interrupt but we really should be doing something don't you think?" asked Mel cautiously.
Jane nodded her head slowly, then turned to look up into Mel's earnest and concerned face, she started to laugh quietly. Mel frowned in worry at the cackling Jane.
Jane then raised her hand slowly, first she pointed to the scratched line she had made straight along the ground and up the wall. It was no longer connected, being that the line on the wall was off to the left, then she pointed to the right where the tunnel met the blank wall. Everyone including Mel looked to the right, following Jane's pointing finger and for several seconds they saw nothing.

Mel was just starting to think her friend had properly lost her mind this time, when she saw a change in colour appear in the wall to the right. Staring for several more seconds she thought she was seeing something that was not, then when she turned and looked back there really was something there.
Then behind her in the crowd someone asked "is the wall moving?"
Then someone else in the crowd replied "no it's not, don't be stupid, walls don't move, especially underground! It's all that weight above that stops them from moving about you know" said a knowledgeable female voice.

The inky dark green that had started to appear very slowly turned bright orange for a second and then again and again. It looked like the effect of an emergency orange light spinning slowly round and round behind the now small slit in the wall. As the seconds wore on, it was now obvious that not only was there a light on the other side but there actually was an other side to get too.

Mel asked of Jane "so what's going on then?"
Jane stood up, turned to face the now less angry crowd but still very agitated individuals and said "I'm only guessing, but it would appear that we're moving around."
Jane paused, putting a her hand to her chin in thought, then with her face lighting up as she paced up and down in front of the blanked off tunnel she said "so that's what the rings were for!"
"What rings were for? You mean the rings that fell from space?" asked Mel.
"Yes, as they fell they grew until they were big enough to cover large areas. They sort of landed like protective bubble domes" said Jane curving her hands in the air like she was caressing a football.
"Prisoner domes more like" somebody chimed in an knowledgeable tone from the crowd, with others mumbling in agreement.
"Yes, well, whatever you want to call them, the one thing we didn't know is how deep they went into the earth and it would appear for some reason they also move around."
"Why would they need to?" questioned Mel.
"Do you know, I have absolutely no idea" Jane looked quite pleased about not knowing something, that she was guessing would be obvious later. It was the discovery that she enjoyed, the working a problem through to a solution, although now looking at Mel's rather annoyed expression Jane asked "I'm guessing your not happy with that answer?"
"No, because the question is not so much why they do what they do but what are we going to do about it?"
"Well that's obvious!"
Mel gave Jane one of those looks that said 'give me a complete answer or I am liable to slap you very hard and I don't care who you are'.
"Meaning that even though I don't know why, we just sit down and wait for us to spin around until we can fit through the tunnel again."
Jane held up a hand as Mel started to ask another question "and I'm fairly certain that if we looked back in the logs, we'd find you were here several hours after now last week. Explaining why the tunnel was complete then but not right now."
"So we just sit and wait for the aliens to come and catch us, sat against a blank wall twiddling our thumbs?"
"Yes! Unless you can find another way to make several probable hundreds of thousands of tonnes of the Earth rotate quicker!"
"That's assuming we're moving and not the outside?" asked someone trying to sound knowledgeable in the crowd.

Mel looked into the crowd, looking for the questioner with a sharp look in her eye, Jane answered first "we saw four rings falling from the sky at the start of the invasion and I assume there were many more across the World. With that in mind why would we be the pivot for everything else and the other rings not? It's not like we're the centre of the Universe or anything!" The tone of Jane's reply kept everyone stone dead quiet, the sort of sound-less-ness you would expect to find in a classroom after a verbal bottom kicking from a strict teacher.

   Everyone was looking at one another now, the lack of noise was eerie and no one felt compelled to make any sound, even breathing too loud seemed wrong somehow.

It was the feeling of expectation that hung in the air, like waiting for an overenthusiastic stuntman to finish his or her motorbike jump. The sharp intake of breath as they zipped up the ramp, the slow release of breath as they left the jump to begin there flight in the air, a quick sucking of air through the teeth as they floated between ramps. The breath held in as it looked like they would land short of there final destination and the final release in relief as the tyres bounce raggedly on the landing.

   The crowd of escapees were all in the holding there breath in anticipation of the landing stage, as a series of small detonations shook the ground, followed by several muffled booms. There was a collective sigh, a nodding of knowing heads at the sounds coming from down the tunnel behind them.

"Found the booby traps then" commented Mel, pointing back down the long curved tunnel they had driven up, as she smiled from ear to ear.

Jane nodded in agreement without a smile on her face, in fact she even looked a little glum to Mel.

"Come on Jane, you should be happy the aliens set off the traps" said Mel.

"I would agree with you normally but it means getting the bunker back is nearly impossible now. The aliens aren't gonna be very happy stuck in polystyrene either, if they are stuck at all. The tunnels will soon be useless and we're stuck here..." Jane trailed off in finishing her sentence, almost as one the group first turned to look at the tunnel behind them and then back at the blocked tunnel in front of them.

"Why don't you finish what your saying" said Mel crossing her arms.

Jane slowly lowered herself to the floor and relaxed her back against the tunnel wall, whilst stretching one leg at a time out in front her.

Jane then asked "I don't think you all realize how much of a problem the Poly bomb really is?"

"You mix some chemicals together and you get a lot of Polystyrene, don't you?" asked someone with apparent knowledge from the crowd.

Jane snorted and covered her mouth with her hand, trying to control the laugh begging to be set free by the silly assumption.

Mel looked down at her, guessing that they had not been told the complete story about how the Poly bomb would work "so has the Poly bomb not worked then or the booby traps?"

"Oh they worked just fine, it's the chemical reaction, you might say it's a bit more enthusiastic than we told everyone."

"What are you saying?" asked Mel cautiously.

"Well not to put too finer point on it or to be too inaccurate, fifty square miles is the approximate coverage in a few minutes, possibly even seconds as it expands outwards and plugs in all the gaps."

Several jaws dropped as this information started to sink in, then slowly the crowd of people turned and looked back down the tunnel again. Imagining a foaming, churning mass of liquid Polystyrene barreling along all the corridors and tunnels, plugging up all the available spaces and orifices. This was to a fair degree of accuracy correct.

Mel turned back from looking down the tunnel and while tapping a foot on the concrete floor asked Jane "if it moves so quickly why hasn't it engulfed us yet?"

A frown of thought gradually crossed over Jane's face, she slowly stood up to stare thoughtfully down the tunnel "you can stop tap tapping your foot like Sara, you really have no idea how distracting that is. As to why we're not swimming up to our eyeballs in Polystyrene, I'm guessing someone ignored the command to open all the doors and shut at least one?"

Mel stopped tapping her foot "yes that was me, I shut and locked the two doors behind us."

With a look of horror and frustration at her commands being ignored playing across her face, Jane eventually started to smile and even laugh a little "well I hope the doors hold."

"What do you mean by that?" asked Mel in an irritated tone.

"The plan was to leave all the doors open, so the invaders wouldn't know which way we escaped. But if they had been left open, we would most definitely be not chatting, more muffling really."

Mel mused over this for a few seconds and then asked "but we're over ten kilometers from the base here?"

"And your point being?" asked Jane.

"It's miles for the Poly to cover, it couldn't reach us, could it?"

"Really when you think about it, we're under ground and the Poly can only follow the tunnels, it can't go straight up in the air can it? It just has to follow the tunnels until it runs out of energy, finds an exit or sets."

Everyone was by now looking back down the tunnel towards the last big metal door they had passed through, which was shut. The door was several hundred meters behind the last of the vehicles, just barely visible but that did not appear to be far enough. The door appeared to be bulging and creaking with the sound of tortured metal, which was clearly audible in the worried silence of the tunnel.

"I'm sorry, there's nothing we can do but wait for the tunnel to move round and hope that second door holds" said Jane in a resigned voice.

Mel did not look happy with Jane's final assessment and was thinking that she should be more positive, if not for herself then for everyone else, she could even have lied a little bit more positively. It was then that Mel remembered that she had shut the two doors, the first one must not have held for very long under the pressure of the white stuff.

Jane was still sat down leant against the tunnel wall, Mel sat down next to her and asked in a voice with a slight quiver in it "so how long have we got then?"

"Three maybe four hours before we can climb through the tunnel and maybe an hour before the door back there gives way" replied Jane quietly.

Looking a little more worried if that were possible Mel said "so not long then before we're stuffed, probably quite literally too. Is there nothing we can do?"

Jane suddenly jumped to her feet and ran pushing and shoving her way through the crowd of people to get to the nearest truck, clambering up on to the cab roof. The crowd of people after hearing about the impending engulfment, which had passed further back down the tunnel from mouth to mouth and presumably ear to ear too, were stood loosely together. The story of doom had only been marginally exaggerated.

Jane stood straining on a cab roof, trying to see and hear what was going on further down the tunnel at the big metal door in the distance. All she could hear from under her feet though was a boys pleading voice "look, we've only got five minutes to live, it won't take me that long, so please please please can I at least have a look?"

The reply came from a short surly sounding female voice, slightly muffled like it was underneath something thick "not even if you were the last man on Earth and we had three minutes to live!"

Jane bent down and banged on the ceiling of the cab with her clenched fist.

The boys voice answered sharply "whatever you want you can't have it" a little pause followed and then "life's too short you know."

Jane sighed and said "you can have your life for a bit longer, after I've finished listening for a minute" Jane then paused and said "I'm sure she'll keep, now shut up!"

After a minute Jane smiled to herself in satisfaction, turned and sat down with her legs crossed and gave a relieved sigh, she then knocked on the cab roof underneath her.

"What do you want now?" came the boys annoyed voice through a gap in the cabs steamy window.

"It's okay" replied Jane "you'll both live a while longer, we all will in fact."

"See, you lied again, that's the second time today!" said the short tempered young female voice.

There came an annoyed reply from the boy "thanks very much, for nothing" then directed at his young lady "and what was the first lie?"

"You said 'it'd be over quickly'?"

"And isn't it?"
"Yes, but you didn't say it would be over that quick!"
　　　Jane smiled to herself and relaxed back on the cab roof, like someone enjoying the lazy afternoon sun on a lush green hill. After a minute or so the only thing that was spoiling her mood was the continuous tap tap tap of someone's shoe on concrete. It was getting quite annoying after a while, then Jane sighed and guessed who it was "what is it Mel?"
With no reply forthcoming Jane leaned over the edge of the cab, looked down at Mel's frustrated expression, which did not soften on seeing Jane poke her head over the top, if anything her expression seemed to harden.
Eventually Mel opened her mouth and between tightly clenched teeth asked "how's the view?"
"Oh I didn't come up here to look, I came up here to listen."
"To what?"
"The door."
"And?"
"It's still there."
"We know this, otherwise we'd be swimming in Poly!" finished Mel.
Jane looked down at the people now gathering around Mel, with there serious expressions and thought to herself 'why do they look angry?'
After the staring had gone on for a moment, Jane finally worked out that they had not worked out what she had and an explanation might be required "I climbed up here to better hear the door."
"We know this, but why?"
"Because if the door back there" Jane pointed to the metal door down the tunnel "has stopped creaking, then chances are that the Polystyrene has set and we just have to wait to spin round to escape."
"Why didn't you say that then?" asked Mel.
"I thought it was blatantly obvious really, as we're not covered in anything but dust!"
　　　The looks of frustration from the crowd beneath her feet swept from anger to relief, as they realized they would all be safe for a little while longer. People gradually walked away and sat down in various places to wait for the tunnel to open, except Mel who stalked off.

Chapter 8 : Timed Exit.

Finally in the darkness of the round storm drain tunnel, after sitting for what seemed and probably was hours, there was a smidgen of light visible as the tunnel turned. An hour later there was nearly a gap big enough for Jack to consider squeezing through, past some vines to the outside world and who knew what. It would be a blessed relief to be in the open air again, after hours spent in a brick walled tunnel so old and cold that when you were sat leaning against the wall, barely big enough to stand in, the stones felt like they were sinking into your bones.

The company was also getting annoying, not only did Claire have the troubling habit of shooting down any observation or comment he made with surgical missile strike accuracy and volume, but Sara was near continually staring at him. It was getting to the point where Jack was going to have to say something to stop the staring or fall on his own sword for some peace and he just knew Claire was going to shoot him down again in either case.

It had all started as soon as he had taken out his Glade for an inspection, he did not know how long the torch and its batteries would last and wanted to see his sword up close and personal. He could only stand looking at it for a minute because of the stern looks he was getting as soon as he turned it on, he turned it off. The thing was his after all and how he had come by it was not only down right strange but the whole circumstance was weird. Everything still seemed a little out of kilter, off balance, to the extent that Jack still could not wholly believe that all this was still actually happening. After all here he was sat in a storm drain wearing black on black army like fatigues and boots, supplied by a very hot robot, which seemed able to absorb any light making them blacker than black. He had also been gifted a glowing sword in a room that existed in a corridor via a lift into a holographic ceiling, by a floating sea green mottled sphere and was being chased by supposed aliens from who knew where. All because for some reason he was transmitting something they could chase. All in all it was either the biggest trick ever or really happening and neither scenario was very pleasing to Jack. He had given up pinching himself to wake up because it was not working, but mainly because it was starting to really hurt and the bruising was going to be massive.

Jack finally felt that the time was right to question Sara about her staring at him, before they jumped out the drain exit. As he quickly looked up to catch her eye's staring at him, they were not staring at him at all, they appeared to be looking back down the tunnel over his shoulder.
Jack now felt a little silly having mentally accused Sara of glaring at him all this time, when she had more than likely just been checking back down the drain.

Neither women had been very pleasant to Jack after there entrance into the tunnel, mainly because he had landed on top of them at the base. The giving way of the ladder rung had not been Jack's fault, it was just that they had been in his way on the trip down and he had been on top of them at the bottom as they landed in a soggy mess. He was quite clean, having stopped on top he had only experienced minor splash back, while the two women's black on black uniforms were now coloured more brown on brown really. Maybe that was why Claire was so short with him, Sara still kept staring through him though back down the tunnel, maybe not at the lighting of the Glade at all?

Claire gave a relieved sigh, stretched, stood nearly up staying bent over in the small drain tunnel and said "finally, I can see some daylight!" she was facing the tunnel exit with a smile of relief playing across her face.

Jack had been watching the light filter round the edge for hours, he had been waiting for the hole to be big enough so he could escape Sara's blazing gaze and Claire's snorted retorts at him. The only thing really stopping him from diving forward and out the tunnel exit were the vines masking the hole. Jack swiped slowly at his shoulder like he was wiping away a loose cobweb.

"Those vines look pretty thick, don't you think?" said Sara ignoring Jack's umpteenth shoulder wave.

"That's why we have Jack and is sword" said Claire, also ignoring Jack's umpteenth swipe around his neck.

"Oh, so now I can turn it on then!" said Jack with instant regret that he had not kept his mouth shut, the frosty looks were akin to being stared at by glowing eyes from the forest in the dead of night.

"Don't worry we'll soon brush them aside" said Claire emphasizing 'brush'.

"We'll have to really, otherwise they'll know exactly where we came out and which direction we're going in if the vines have been burned away!" Jack paused "and the spiders of course" he finished quietly.

Both women turned back in Jack's direction, Sara stared harder than she had been and Claire stared around trying to see more clearly where he was sitting. Eventually after Jack gave a little wave of his hand to show where he was, Claire frowned at him and asked in an slightly exasperated tone "why's that then?"

"They are vines, aren't they?" replied Jack.

"Yes Jack I believe they are!" Claire rolled her eyes.

Jack pulled a hurt face for a few seconds and replied to Claire with "thick vines, very heavy and underused? Full of nesting spiders!" Jack shuddered at the thought of eight hairy legs scampering across his scalp as he pushed through the vines. He also chose not to mention the cobwebs that always stuck to only your face.

"What do you mean underused?" asked Sara quickly before Claire could make a wild comment.

"Obviously this tunnel hasn't been used recently or serviced, otherwise the vines wouldn't be here would they" said Jack.

"And your point is?" asked Claire.

"Nature" replied Jack simply.

Sara and Claire both took a breath, looked at one another with puzzled expressions and then back to Jack and said together "what?"

"Nature!" said Jack again.

"Jack if you keep saying that I really am going to have to bite you" said Sara.

"I will too, maybe not the bite thing but a slap across the chops at any rate if you don't explain what you mean by keep repeating 'nature'?" said Claire.

"I distrust nature at the best of times" Jack replied and held his hand up to stop the instant barbed reply he knew was coming from both the women.

Jack continued with "before you ask I've never liked nature, that's why I work in the city where's there less of it! Even here you get wiggly, crawling things and in my garden I don't go near the vines on my garden wall cos' of the spiders!" Jack actually shook in mild distaste at the thought of the creeping crawlies.

    Both of the women sat for a minute digesting this new information, then they started to giggle together as they worked out what Jack was scared of, until they looked at one another's faces and could not hold it in any longer, both burst out laughing.

    Jack sat leaning against the cold and slightly moist brick tunnel wall. The laughing had finally ebbed away down the tunnel after several minutes. For what seemed like an age both women sat looking much happier in themselves than they had any right to be in Jack's book. Jack crossed his arms with a stern expression on his face and looked at both of them, awaiting an explanation for the excessive mirth.

    Finally Sara looked up at Jack and wiped away a tear of laughter, still with a smile on her face she apologized "we're sorry Jack, for laughing at you so hard."

"You might be but I'm not" muttered Claire with a chocked back giggle on the end, this was heard through hands firmly planted over her mouth in case any more mirth should escape down the tunnel.

    Sara gave her a sharp look and looked away before she started to laugh again, she continued carefully talking to Jack while not acknowledging Claire "you have to understand Jack, we've been under immense stress recently. We haven't felt the need or even had the opportunity to laugh because of the fear of the invasion and the unknown. Until this morning none of us knew exactly who or what we were fighting. I mean, we knew they weren't human but we hadn't seen them walking about outside with out armour or vehicles of some description, so they could have been anything at all. As to why we were laughing? It was a form of release, a relief even, and you having a fear of spiders is just down right silly after all we've been through to worry about." Sara finished by waving her hands above her head and finally giving the vines a brush with her finger tips.

"I just don't like them" mumbled Jack to himself.

"It's okay Jack, I'll go through first and chase away any spiders" said Claire smiling.

"Terrorize, more like!" said Jack to himself, the angry look he got from Claire as she stood up, partially bent over in the drain tunnel, might have said 'I think I heard that you stupid boy'.

Wisely Jack kept any more wise cracks to himself, as Claire brushed past him towards the exit and her bottom blanked out all the light coming in the tunnel through the curtain of vines. Jack had heard the phrase 'hold your tongue' and up until now had not fully appreciated how hard that could actually be when someone was so annoying.

Sara pushed herself off from the wall, brushing past Jack as she turned back towards where they had come from down the tunnel, with curiosity written on her face. As she walked crouched over, back past Jack in the tunnel, he felt that she need not have stamped quite so hard in the freezing cold, almost ice melt temperature water running down the centre of the drain. It would be his own fault if he complained he assumed, for sitting with his legs slightly apart, that he now had a soaking wet and very chilled gentleman's area.

Jack rolled his eyes, starting to snuffle as he began searching around in his pockets, eventually coming up with a white handkerchief and proceeded to blow his nose with the sound like that of a sinking fog horn on an ocean liner.

"My God what was that?" exclaimed Claire turning round to face them, whilst holding the vines to one side with a look of fearful dread on her face, that gradually faded to a warm cheeked glare as Jack wiped his nose.

"I was just getting rid of the wobbly bits" came the slightly nasal reply.

"Ooh yuck" said Claire, who then paused for a moment and started searching round in her own pockets, when she came up empty she turned back to Jack and asked "where did you get the handkerchief from and come to that, one in nuclear white?"

Before Jack could answer 'my pocket', Sara looked back at them both and said "it is very bright Jack, appears to be glowing and I'm sure I haven't got one either. So the real question is where did you get the handkerchief from?"

"I don't know, I needed to clear the old nasal passage and dug out this here handkerchief!" said Jack sat on his heels, waving the cloth around in the tunnel to make a point, soon he noticed that both women were giving him withering looks.

With the time he had spent with Sara so far he was surprised he was not hearing the tap tap of her boot, he looked down at her feet. Sara looked down at her feet too, she was tapping her foot, because it was slowly being swamped with something of a muddy white nature, her foot was making tiny sucking noises instead, like a dribbling mouse with a giant gob stopper.

Jack pointed at Sara's feet as he walked past, which were nearly covered in dirty white Polystyrene balls and said "I believe it may be time to go?"

Sara performed a series of little hops, skips and with one final leap was stood next to the vine covered exit with Jack and Claire.

All three of them stood looking back into the gloom of the tunnel and Claire finally said "it's really time to go. I just wish this thing would turn faster!" indicating the round tunnel exit by pointing a thumb over her shoulder through the vines.

Jack frowned at Claire, pulled his Glade out from the case on his waist, twisted it round and placed his thumb on the base. The gold thread sprung out to a length of just over a meter and a half, then ignited itself a fuzzy red, it then flowed through various colours until it finally settled on an very bright white just in front of Jack's face.
"What are you gonna do with that Jack" asked Claire "clean your ears out?"
Jack knew it was childish but stuck his tongue out at Claire anyway, to stop any reply he raised his glowing, fizzing sword and twitched it through the vines dangling on the outside. The vines dropped with a sizzle as the Glade sliced through with no apparent effort on Jack's part, revealing that the tunnel exit was now uncovered enough for them all to squeeze through to the outside world, with only minor abrasions.

The light outside the drain exit was dusky, the setting sun could be just seen slowly dropping down casually behind a toppled building of some description. Jack poked his head briefly back into the drain, wondering why it had appeared so light looking out when in effect it was nearly night time.

When he had finished peering about he turned round and Sara asked "well?"
Jack shrugged and said "I don't know, but there's light seeping in from all round the edge of the hole, which I guess must be to do with the dome thing surrounding the prison camp."
"Yeah well the question really is, are we actually outside the ring thing?" Claire mused out loud.
All three stood looking around, trying to take in the level of destruction outside the walls of there ringed prison camp.

The drain tunnel they had all clambered out of was gradually becoming more whole, as it moved gently out from behind the tired stone walled bank, with the white flow gradually getting thicker by the second. The drain had for years been spewing its load down a man-made bank, carving a dirty brown mark all the way along the concrete trough that led to the small river. It was not this though that had captivated the three escapees, nor was it the slow addition of little white pellets to the river mix. It was the level of destruction that was now in front of them, as far as the eye could see, as they stood on the sides of the little trough.

Inside the gently spinning ring it had been bright if not airy and the destruction had been at various levels, like a massive swooping scythe had been dipping and bobbing in the sky, cutting some urban buildings down to a few feet and others at only roof level. From a good vantage point you could see this quite clearly, as housing was vaguely bounced over, offices and such like had been all but destroyed. Outside the prison dome, it was like the scythe had not raised itself much above four feet, apart from to avoid nature whilst culling the steel and concrete giants.

The three of them stood looking at the destruction off to there left down a small valley, directly in front of them and continuing around to there right, was a pleasant grassy green hill that lead up to a large oak tree towering over the landscape.

They stood staring at fallen buildings in the valley, some of which were near see through, the glass in the buildings and the inner walls had shattered on impact as the bottom was cut through. Buildings of business lay on there sides like beached Wales, with an occasional structure that had collapsed in on itself like it had been deflated. Then you were left with the trees, bushes and wildlife in general that lay untouched, the destruction looked very picky, careful even. Here and there the three of them pointed at tall bushes or trees still standing, next to buildings that had been sliced in half. It was like a great blade had scythed along the Earth's surface, destroying humanities creations and looping over nature to strike back at the pimples on creations bottom. Then in urban areas, like in the dome, the destruction was marginally less, as the great mowing down of homes had been more of a shaking up of the molecules holding them together, than a full slice and dice. The urban human had been left living in a property that an accidental sneeze might have collapsed, thus forcing them outside and into the prison camps.

In front of them the big oak tree stood atop of the grassy hill, standing lonely and proud against the burning sky. They would need to walk down the gully, step over the river and walk up the green hill to reach it. The tree towered over the fallen landscape, Jack guessed it was this tree that Sara had been aiming for from within the foam ringed dome.

After some time of just looking with bewilderment at the strange destruction and the poetic licensed landscape, they all came to there own conclusions about the invaders state of mind.
Jack turned to the two women and asked "time to go?"
Sara looked round and after a moment laughed and said "where to Jack?"
"I would have liked to check up on Jenny really" thought Jack but he had absolutely no idea where to start or even if he could.
Claire sharply turned to Jack and asked "how do you know Jenny?"
Jack then realized he had mused his thoughts out loud, rather than keeping them to himself and so he began to turn a rather nice shade of pink in embarrassment.

"Come on Jack, out with it, how do you know Jenny?" then Claire had a moment of clarity whilst Jack continued to try and control his ever increasing cheek rosiness.

"Yes that's right, I remember you having a thing for Jen, from the office upstairs."

"No I didn't!" denied Jack.

Claire laughed and said "oh Jack you did and still do" turning to Sara, Claire took up the in-confidence pose and continued at normal volume with "he worshiped the very ground she walked on, the air she breathed, his little eyes going all puppy dog and the non stop fawning at her very presence or even mention of her name. Everyone in the office knew and Jack didn't know we knew!"

Jack started to open and close his mouth to object but he honestly did not know how, or if objecting would be an admission of guilt or accuracy.

"Is this the same Jen we're talking about that took over and issues our orders?" asked Sara.

Claire stood leaning against Sara with her hand over her mouth, nodding her head and smiling at Jack's condition.

     Jack was feeling the discomfort and the heat, yet at the same time he felt relieved that it was all now out in the open, far too much out in the open really. Then a question raised its quivering hand in the back of his mind "does Jen know?" he asked.

Claire started to nod furiously, a tiny gerbil squeak like giggle escaped through her fingers.

"You know I'm not finding this funny don't you?" said Jack.

In quite a high pitched tone, even for Claire, came the answer "yes."

     Sara stood between the two of them, she could see Jack was wrestling some degree of control out of his careering emotional unicycle. While Claire on the other hand seemed determined to chase him down, high on caffeine at the wheel of an eighteen wheeler lorry with nitrous oxide flooding the cab. At this point Sara looking closely at Claire surmising that as much as Claire baited, shot down and criticized Jack, it was in effect to hide her own deep felt, if not love, then care for Jack.

     Claire caught a look in Sara's eyes, quickly looked away out towards the setting Sun and the oak tree, trying to choke back some returning giggles.

Jack had now worked something out and asked of Sara "so Jenny Norris from the office in legal, is running the resistance and alive?"

"Yes Jack, she's fine."

"Well um... can we check she's okay?"

"I did that just before we left and no I'm not trying her again with the Quellz, because as much we want them to follow us, we don't want them to follow us out here in the open do we?"

Jack shook his head, sighed and said "no I guess not."

"Good, then I think we should find somewhere to hole up for the night and look for my shuttle in the morning."

Claire looked up from staring at the ground and said to Sara "I thought it was near where the drain came out?"

"Yes it was, if you remember it was parked the other side of the big oak tree in the field" said Sara, Claire finished the sentence off in a dull tone "in the shadow of the satellite dish."

"Yes, I'm sorry. From the oak tree up there we should be able to see what remains of the dish but by the time we get down there, it'll be pitch black and unlikely we'll find the shuttle. So we should hide till first light and then go looking."

They walked slowly down over the rough ground surrounding the drain, with the Sun nearly settled in the horizon, crossed the river and up walked up the gentle hill to the big oak tree.

The tree stood on a slight rise all on its own, with its magnificent arms stretching in all directions. As Jack leant against its trunk, he felt something brush over his face and the back of his neck, making him feel ever so slightly lighter in the process. Stood next to the tree, Jack felt a tiny bit insignificant, as he looked up into the slowly darkening branches. He guessed it would take four people, at full stretch with there arms and finger tips barely touching, to reach all the way around the trees trunk.

Looking down past the two wandering female figures just in front of him, Jack could just make out the fallen remains of an huge grey satellite dish. It was easily a hundred meters across, or at least it had been before it had been "stamped on" mused Jack out loud.

"What?" asked Claire turning back.

"The dish, it doesn't look like its been chopped down, more like someone stomped on it really."

In the last of the summer evenings light, the dish was barely visible in the central gloom of the valley and to Claire it looked like Jack was right, it had been stamped on. To Sara the dish also looked like it had been stamped on, with a great deal of over enthusiasm, to the extent that some of the pieces of dish had been blown into and even through some of the surrounding trees. As far as Sara knew there was only one thing that could do this type of damage and pancake such a large object. It involved a "super gravity weapon", usually from a portal, which might be thought of as a tad excessive to use on such a primitive planet.

"What's 'super gravity'?" asked Jack innocently.

Sara and Claire had started there walk down in to the valley to find a hidey hole till morning, both turned very sharply to look back at Jack. Claire turned to Sara and asked curiously "what is super gravity?"

"Why do you ask?" asked Sara.

"Because you just mumbled something about super gravity weapons."

"No I didn't, did I? I must have been musing out loud, like Jack does all the time."

Jack held up his hands to calm the two women down, pushing himself away from the big tree, he then started to swipe at the invisible spiders and there cobwebs again.

"Jack will you stop waving your arms about" said Claire "you'll attract all sorts!"

As Claire replied to Jack he suddenly stopped moving, something buzzing and whirring shot past his ear, flew off into the dusk, glinting as it bent down into the valley towards the two women. Whatever it was skimmed over the top of Claire and then Sara's head, briefly tickling there scalps, forcing wavy hand signals from them both.

Another buzzing thing started to fly past but was obstructed by the great oak tree with a solid sounding thunk. Jack turned to look at the trunk of the tree, embedded in it was a twelve inch dart at about his neck level. Jack involuntarily gulped, eyeing up the projectile. The first thing to go through his mind, as he pulled it out of the bark, was how much something that big would hurt if it went through his mind, especially looking at the size of the attached needle and the depth it had been stuck in the tree. Jack pulled the dart out with difficulty.
The next thing to go through his head was that someone or something was shooting elephant darts at him, it was time to go and quickly or "the next dart might go right through" he worried out loud.

Jack hopped behind the oak trees hill, down the gently sloping valley and down through the long dark green grass towards Claire and Sara. As he approached them at a careful jog, because even though it was not a steep hill it was meadow like and could be deceptively slippery and oddly lumpy. He started to wave the dart at them as he flopped by and said "run, they've found us."

The first thing the two women thought, when they saw Jack gently jogging past down the hill was 'finally he's moving'. Since they had been with Jack he had seemed lazy, seeming like he had no purpose, no reason to be helpful and above all else he had no urgency. But here he was finally moving with some urgency, purpose and not a sign of lethargy.

After Jack had passed them, they both looked back up the hill to the tree and saw three, then six human shaped shadow like outlines appear next to the great oak tree. Within a second they had turned, accelerated and were catching up with Jack, who was veering away from the flattened dish.
As they carefully ran down the hill, between breaths Sara said "aim for the tree line on the right, then we'll make our way to the base of the dish."
Over his shoulder Jack said a little breathlessly "okay."

Looking back he saw why the two women were running quite so hard, the shadowy figures were holding large shadowy looking guns, with outlines of knives, spinning chainsaw things and glowing whip like laser wire dangling from there weapons.

From the big oak tree on the hill to the tree line the distance was several hundred meters, once the three of them had skipped, hopped and in Jack's case tripped over the low bushes at the tree border and landed damply amongst the foliage, they all felt much better. Apart from Jack, whom just felt wetter because he had tripped and rolled through something dark, soft and definitely farm related.

By the time Jack had wiped himself down a bit, finished groaning to himself about the colour and smell, the two women had caught there breaths.

Looking between some bushes back up the gently rolling hill trying to see there pursuers, Claire without turning said to Jack in a hoarse whisper "shut up, they haven't seen us yet but with all your moaning they might yet hear us!"

"Might not be a bad thing, he does need a shower" said Sara stepping further back into the trees whilst holding her nose.

The three of them stood for a moment, watching the human like figures gently sway down the hill vaguely towards them and Jack wondered something.

In a hushed voice Jack asked "not to sound stupid or anything but are they on our side" he said this while pointing at the dark figures on the hill "and if they are, why don't they just call out? If there working for the invaders or are the invaders, wouldn't they have specialist night vision stuff anyway to find us?"

Sara put a hand on Claire's arm and turned to Jack and said "okay first of all as you know some humans are actually robots, some people we've heard even joined the invaders and yes they could be allies but we've no way of knowing. Yes they do have specialist equipment but I'm hoping that the closer we are to the dish, the less likely there equipment will be to work."

"Ah, you mean that the super gravity thing might effect there equipment?" asked Claire after a moments thought.

"Yes and ours too Claire."

"But we don't have any equipment, unless you count the Guns you two have?" moaned Jack, flicking the baton hanging on his belt around like a set of jangling keys.

"He's right you know, we do have guns. We could take them out in a cross fire?" Claire said rather eagerly, feeling round to find her own gun.

Sara sighed and said "we don't know whether there friend or foe and we could be shooting at allies."

Jack pulled out the dart from his pocket, that he had removed from the oak tree, he flourished it like a street theatre magician in the dark of the wood and said "have you seen the size of this thing? I don't think there friendly you know!"

"It's okay Jack, they must have heard how thick headed you are" Claire said this whilst trying desperately not to laugh out loud.

"Stop it both of you!" hissed Sara "what I was really talking about was the shuttle, because if there tech isn't working why should our own? No, we make our way to the shuttle and see if it survived."

Jack moved from a crouch to a kneeling position and found he was suffering from pins and needles, he sighed and asked Sara, whilst rubbing some life back into his knees "why do you say survived?"

Sara took a little gulp, sat with her legs crossed she started to draw the dish and tree line in the damp mud with a finger "the shuttle is about forty feet into the tree line behind the satellite dish."

"So the opposite side to where we are then and maybe too close to the flattened dish?" asked Claire. Sara sat and nodded her head slowly, looking slightly defeated as she continued to nod slowly.

Claire saw for the first time that Sara looked depressed, in all the attacks and raids they had made and been subjected too, at no point had Sara looked quite as defeatist as she did now. If anything her continual positive outlook had been the glue that had held them through many battles, it was like she knew the final outcome of the war, that they would some how eventually win.

With Sara looking more depressed and pale with each passing second, Claire started to feel down trodden and lost herself, she looked over at Jack who was checking he was down wind by throwing leaves in the air. How that would actually help in anyway when they started firing at them again, she did not really know.

He really did not seem to fully understand there dire situation, so she was quite surprised when he said in a positive tone of voice "right you two, our hunters have spread themselves out in the long grass. I guess we've got maybe a few minutes before they reach the tree line, so it's time we circled around to the back of that dish and found your shuttle don't you think?"

Sara mumbled an 'okay' and all three of them slowly moved back into the trees, away from the bushy edge.

Chapter 9 : Logging Off.

It took a little over twenty minutes to circle round in the trees to the back of the dish, Jack found it strange that at no point had he seen or heard the 'hunters' as he thought of them, crashing through the foliage behind them. He kept turning back to check, even though the three of them were not the quietest animals in the forest and would be easy to track, he would have expected to see or hear there would be chasers. Jack being a 'townie' had no idea about subtlety when it came to walking through a wet, trip laden, clothe grabbing, snapping under foot and dark forest. Strangely the forest was not that dark under the yellowy moon lit forest canopy, it was actually quite bright, in the same way that looking at a camp fire makes the fire clear and everything else seem to flicker in and out.

Jack could here Sara mumbling to herself that it was too bright, looking about Jack eventually understood what she meant when he realized how far he could actually see in the moonlight, which also meant there pursuers could too. Then Sara slowly stopped and held up a hand to stop them walking any further, she pointed in front where bits of the dish could just be seen poking out of the grass, through the trees. The long grass had started to overcome the satellite dish, using it like a bag of fertilizer, full of minerals and miscellaneous chemicals to grow from. Sara then pointed off to her right, at a mound of moss laden logs and almost seemed to skip over towards them.

After walking around the entire log pile twice, Jack stopped following the two women wandering round in a circle. He sat down on a tree stump nearby, watched the pair of them for a few moments and began thinking. It was unusual for Jack to just stop and think about things, he was more of the put off things to think about type, until later, much later, usually after the fact or during the fact later.

Jack by now had several questions bubbling away inside his head and needed the space to think, to organize the questions into some form of sensible order. Otherwise Claire would launch another air barrage in his direction of abuse for asking silly things, he did not think he could take much more bashing of the ears, without blood being spilled and probably his.

So Jack just sat, thought and watched the two women wander around the log pile and strangely he felt himself unwind. It was quite relaxing to see the two women poking and pulling at the log pile, gradually getting more and more frantic as time went on. After a few minutes Jack had his questions all lined up, deciding after a moments thought this was not really the time to ask all of them. By now Sara and Claire had stopped running round the pile of logs and moss and were stood looking decidedly annoyed.

Jack asked the only question he felt was relative "not to be funny or anything …" he waited till he had there full glaring attentions "but is this the right pile of logs?"

"Why do you think we're looking at this pile of logs?" Claire almost shouted.

Sara then turned and said "Jack, there's only one pile of logs here. I just can't seem to find the marker I left?" she said this more questioning herself than anything else.

Jack swiveled his bottom round on the tree stump to face the opposite way, then over his shoulder asked "what does SHOT stand for then?"

Sara's instant reply was "Short Hop Orbital Transport" she slowly spun around as if on a turntable, then with an expression of mild anger on her face and through gritted teeth she asked "where did you see that Jack?"

Casually Jack pointed to the other big log pile, not more than twenty feet from his seat and said "in this other big log pile, I can just about see where a log has fallen down and the word SHO and maybe part of a T is visible?"

The mood of the two women flowed from angry frustration with not being able to find the shuttle, to annoyance with Jack, to the realization that they had now found the means for there escape.

Both women then walked briskly passed Jack, to the alternate log pile and Claire asked Jack with annoyance "at what point were you going to mention the other log pile?"

Jack looked a little hurt at the hidden accusation but replied as calmly as he could "well it's a wood, there's bound to be more than one log pile here and I didn't see this one till I spun around!"

Sara just the other side of the logs said "thank the Shaper, I've found the marker."

Jack stood up and walked round the log pile a few times, whilst Sara and Claire started to pull various green moss like netting from the top of the shuttle. The log pile was about three times the size of the previous one and rather than being round, was shaped more like a pear. This log pile was easily six, maybe even eight meters wide and fifteen or more meters long mused Jack as he wandered around it, waiting to be berated for not helping uncover the shuttle. Manual labour, in Jack's experience, should be avoided at all costs.

After three laps of the log pile, Jack stopped to look at the lettering he had seen on the side of the ship and where Sara had started to pull the last of the fake moss netting off. On closer inspection Jack could see that the netting mimicked the moss growing on the other log pile almost perfectly, the logs had only been piled up to two meters or so and then the netting thrown over the top to a height of four meters

As Sara stood back Jack could see that in front of the foot high acronym S.H.O.T. was another word "hot?" asked Jack.

Sara stepped back from uncovering the dark green shuttle and said "yeah, all the shuttles have names as well as numbers, apparently it's a human thing to do that and your invaders copied it. Least the wording is better than the first one's they produced!"

Jack was a little shocked at the thought of the aliens copying anything humans did 'I mean just imagine if they'd watched the internet before the invasion' thought Jack. Jack wondered briefly what Sara meant by 'your invaders', then he thought about the exclamation in Sara's sentence and asked "wording?"
"Oh yes the first ones were called Short Hop Interplanetary Transport's."

Claire finished pulling the last of the netting off, turned to look at Jack who was looking thoughtful, she herself was thinking about the abbreviation and after a second or two of mulling it over she started to smile at the same time as Jack. Looking at one another and then looking away quickly, they both realized that once they started laughing they would not be able to stop.

Jack innocently asked "the word 'hot' would work at both ends of that one, wouldn't it Claire?"
After covering her mouth for a few seconds, guffawing through her fingers, Claire finally got control and had to ask of Sara "at what point did they realize what it actually said?"

Sara leaning forward sighed, she placed her palm on a flat light blue panel just over a meter behind the name on the shuttle and replied "they didn't right away, they produced a thousand or more before someone pointed it out and they changed the letters on all the new ones, with a general recall being issued for the earlier ones."
"So what does SHOT stand for again then?" asked Claire.
"Short Hop Orbital Transport" replied Sara in an off hand tone, as she took her hand off the panel a door slid out to her left, obscuring some of the lettering on the side of the shuttle. Sara then stepped inside the doorway and motioned for them both to follow with a wave of her arm. Claire dutifully stepped in behind her, whilst Jack seemed to be stuck in indecision like a lady in a shoe emporium.

Jack had been staring thoughtfully at the lightly burnt dark green paint of the shuttles hull as it had been uncovered and the white name along its side. The word 'Hot' had been written across the top of the 'S' of shot, in italic lettering at an excessively jaunty angle.
There was something familiar bothering him about it, for the life of him he could not think what it was. Also there was a long number written underneath the letters S.H.O.T, which Jack assumed was something like a version number.

Sara and Claire kept beckoning him through the little doorway with mildly growing frustration, into what looked like an frosty grey ice cube that they were stood in. Jack felt that as soon as he took that step into the shuttle, he would be at the point of no return. The choice was simple; enter a world where there was going to be excitement and knew things or stay with the old things he knew.

Jack stood carrying on with his dilemma, ignoring the two women, who were by now almost shouting at him to get in the shuttle. His decision was made, he started to step back away from the shuttle, right up until he put his hand in his pocket and touched the excessively big, supposed tranquilizer dart. After wrapping his fingers around the main shaft of the dart, at first wondering what it was in his pocket, he shortly remembered and pulled is hand out with some speed and almost ran to the shuttle door. The things he remembered now included being shot at by armed men, firing darts the size of knives at him and sharp pointy ones too.

Jack looked inside the shuttle door, surprised to see quite how large the little room actually was, there was just enough room for eight adults to stand. What it reminded him of was a lift from some modern skyscraper, the main difference was the colour. From a distance it had looked like a frosty grey ice cube, standing this close the grey had raised its game and had become an almost reflective frosty white instead. The two women were still shouting at him, it was then that Jack realized something else that had been bothering and was also a blessing, he could not hear them.

As soon as touched the outer boundary of the doorway he was sucked inside, that was not what surprised him the most, it was the lack of sound from the forest as it was suddenly cut off, like dunking your ears in treacle. Jack could not believe that trees could be so noisy, right until the noise had been suddenly removed, the only sounds he could hear were breathing and the unfortunate tap tap of Sara's boot on the floor. If he listened really carefully, he could hear the vague background hum of the shuttle and just about feel it vibrating up his boots.

Jack turned to look out into the forest and said "you know, I never realized how noisy nature really was?"
"It's the Suspension Field Jack, it keeps the undesirable things like birds, beetles and disease from entering the shuttle and ruining internal systems, not to mention contaminants such as noisy lifeforms" said Sara as she gave Jack an irritated look. She pressed her hand to another panel on the inside of the shuttles airlock, about halfway down its length. The door to the outside world smoothly slid and 'whooshed' seamlessly back into place.
Out the corner of his mouth Jack asked Claire quietly "Suspension Field?"
"In here think of it as having a higher atmospheric pressure, because it's higher it also means that any time the door is opened to the outside, the lower pressure can't get inside" said Sara.
"But doesn't that mean that because it's higher, some of it escapes to the outside?" asked Jack curiously.
"Jack" said Sara wearily "I said it was like atmospheric pressure, not that it was!"

Jack jumped suddenly, a shiver ran through his entire body as the door made a final click as it locked itself in place. It was like every part of his anatomy at once had been caressed by the coldest hands ever, these hands had also been in the complimentary ice bucket beforehand for quite some time.

Jack had felt shivers before but not one through every atom of his being "you know, right up until this point, I would have still said that this was all a dream. Right up to the point where I've just had the weirdest feeling run through my entire body that I've never felt before. Ever!"

Sara stepped back from the panel and brushed passed Jack, Jack then noticed something weird about the whole room airlock thing and had to comment on it "there's only one door!"

On entering the shuttles airlock he had looked at the little room, but not actually looked at the little room he was stepping into. Additionally he had stayed facing the two women as they had looked over his shoulder at the closing door behind him. Now they were both stepping by, brushing passed him. When he turned he was quite surprised, actually massively shocked, to be looking through the now open doorway into the depths of the shuttle, through the door they had entered in the first place.

What had shocked Jack the most was the size of the room, it was genuinely bigger on the inside than the shuttle was on the outside and also looked surprisingly like a large lounge with a bar.

There were all types of seating designs visible, from six legged bean bag like chairs to apparently floating stools and a lush green corner sofa.

Jack was open mouthed as he stepped into "the lounge area Jack" said Sara "with a mini bar and all the other amenities you could think of".

Jack looked around with amazed wonder written all over his dribbling jaw, then he looked out the huge windows and found he genuinely had nothing to say. Jack was shocked into silence as the windows were easily two meters high and seemed to run the entire length of the lounge, about twenty meters or so he guessed on both sides, they were shaped like angled speed stripes that you might find on the most expensive trainers.

Both Sara and Claire stood looking at Jack's slack jawed expression, waiting for the inevitable question, Sara turned to Claire and said "nineteen eighty-two."

Claire had stood with a barely concealed smirk on her face, waiting for Jack's silliest question ever, therefore she was caught off guard by Sara's apparently random number, she frowned and asked "what?"

"The number you'll need to get the shuttle started."

"You mean your letting me fly the shuttle?"

"More letting you start the warm up process."

Claire stood open mouthed in indecision, wanting to get another one over on Jack and at the same time wanting to fly the shuttle, or at least start it up from the command seat.

Claire still was not moving, she was locked in uncertainty, until Sara said "if you think I'm going to let you wind Jack up any more than you have already in the last twenty four hours, then you've got another thing coming! So, go to the cockpit and start the engines please." Sullenly Claire replied "well, okay then" as she started to shuffle off to the front of the shuttle, which then turned into almost skipping in excitement as she neared the rectangular doorway to the cockpit.

Jack walked slowly round the room, poking at things, not quite believing that they were real and mumbling to himself about the colour white. For a start, he had never realized that there were so many shades of white possible before and apparently they were all inside this lounge. The walls were white but a sort of fluffy non reflective shade, the floor was an almost grey white, the ceiling was curved, blended white to the walls and so was nearly impossible to tell how high above it actually was. There was colour in the room in the form of overly ornate rugs of large proportions on the floor, with aliens and alien landscapes sewn or printed on them. The seating was of various shades of the rainbow, with some colours that were not even colours to Jack's eye. They seemed to shift through the known and in some cases unknown spectrum as he looked at them. There were coffee tables and loungers in creamy whites, Jack felt himself being pulled towards the bar at the back end of the lounge, or stern, 'gravitating towards mental freedom' he thought 'if it serves alcohol of course?'

Jack pulled a frosty glass looking single legged stool out from the under the bar without even thinking about it and sat down with a sigh on it.

He looked at the bar top, which was four meters long and of the scuffed used glacial white variety, on placing his hands on the frosty glass top it shifted its colour to an age old oak wooden design.   Jack pulled back his hands in surprise but carried on sitting on the stool at the bar and then slowly ran his hands over the bar top. It was still cool glass to the touch, as far as he could remember though, it looked just like the bar top from the pub round the corner from the office called the 'Drum Lugger'. Over various drunken nights out and quite a long time, the letters of the pub had been either moved, edited or scuffed out and now it read as something much ruder. The owners had seen the changes over time but were reluctant to replace the sign, as it would need to say 'Young Lovers Inn' and had a feeling this might be detrimental to there trade.

The bar top though had remained the same over the years, Jack had a vague memory of scratching his and hers initials inside a heart with his keys on one drunken occasion. Looking carefully at the bar top he was sure they would be at one end or the other and sure enough on the far right, there were was his little bit of light graffiti. Jack stared down at his marks in the wood 'T.J. 4 J.N.' and then realized it could not really be here, it must be a memory that the bar accessed some how. Jack shuffled back to his bar stool and sat down with a sigh again.

Jack leant back on the stool, still with his hands on the bar, when Sara sat down next to him on another stool which she pulled out from the side of the bar. Sara then touched a small pulsing line running down the middle of the bar top.

Jack had noticed the fading white and back to wood half inch wide line down the middle of the bar, but really had not given it a thought. Upon touching the line with a brush of her fingers, a friendly human female face materialized above the bar at forty five degree angle from the bar top and asked politely, in an American accent "which beverage can I supply please?"

Sara slid a glance at Jack and replied "he'll have a cider and black and I'll have a straight cider thank you."

Jack nodded his head in thanks, expecting the drinks to materialize from nowhere and was therefore only slightly disappointed when they appeared from behind the bar top, held by soft pincer like hands. The hands were of course white, the arms were black bendy tube things, which was a surprise considering how white everything else was Jack thought and the arms reminded him of ribbed plastic tubing but tubing that curled and twisted like a snake. The tube action was strange, the arms gave the impression of scooping the drinks into there final resting place in front of there recipients. Jack was more used to his drink being placed in front of him with care and precision and a grimace from the bar keep, which in his experience was standard practice wherever he went.

Jack honestly was not bothered in the slightest and was more than happy to collect his drink from the bar top. After he and Sara had a slurp each, they both twitched slightly and without a word or look swapped there drinks with one another.

After several seconds of contented slurping, almost matching one another gulp for gulp, they both put there respective glasses down, one half empty and one half full.

Sara turned to Jack, who was 'finally' she thought, looking around the shuttle in amazement, with his head tipped back and asked "so what do you think of my shuttle then?"

After drinking back his first cider in what felt like millennia, with black currant flavouring too! Jack on tipping his head back, had not only had his eyes open at the ceiling but had had his eyes opened. It felt like a fog clearing slowly from his head, meaning he felt like he was thinking clearer somehow, due to the alcohol. In general terms things always seem clearer after a few drinks, the problems arise when they become a bit too clear and you pass through to the other side. Then the morning after follows, which shows you how far through clear you had actually gone and the need to remove all the evidence from your room.

Without looking at Sara and staring into his half pint Jack replied "it's much bigger on the inside, isn't it!"

"No, it's not" Sara had always loved this conversation with newbies and had learned to answer the questions without rudeness or sarcasm entering her voice.

"Okay then, it's some kind of trans-dimensional space" looking at Sara shaking her head with a light smile on her face, Jack tried again "or we stepped through into another Universe which is within the shuttle?"
"Nope and I think you've watched far too many science fiction films."

Jack sat and looked round the interior of what was a very large room indeed, then looked out of the window, whilst at the same time finishing off his pint with a glad final sigh.
Spinning slowly back round on the stool, he put the empty pint glass carefully back on the bar, turned to Sara and asked "well if it's not 'another place' in here then I'd guess we've shrunk?"
Sara sat open mouthed for a moment and then asked "how did you work that out?"
"I haven't quite yet, I just looked out of the window and I knew the logs were big, but there absolutely gigantic out there!" replied Jack waving a hand at the giant logs leaning against the window. Outside the shuttle they had only been a maximum of two foot in diameter but in here they looked like they were twenty foot wide and gnarled for some reason.

Sara looked round at the windows and indeed the pile of logs left leaning against the windows were massive in comparison to the shuttle, in fact they were too big if you looked at them.
"So what is it then?" asked Jack.
"A Suspension Field" said Sara and held up her hand as Jack meant to object to such a simple answer, she continued after a few more slurps of her pint with "when I said it was like higher atmospheric pressure but wasn't, it was slightly misleading. There is a higher pressure in here that stops the outside from getting in and if you remember I called it a Suspension Field?"

Jack sat on his frosty white padded stool and nodded his head in agreement, whilst his hand involuntarily began searching for his pint glass on the bar top. After a little wandering round the bar with his fingers, like a drunken spider, they found the glass and much to his pleasant surprise he heard the light splash and glug of liquid filling it up. He looked round to the glass in his hand on the bar and found it being filled from the bottom up, as it neared the top of the glass an injection of black currant was shot in from the bottom in a forced cloud like swirl. Jack sat watching the black currant slowly mix in with the amber liquid, marveling at the strange shapes forming in the glass, until the end when eventually it was all one uniform light blackberry currant colour.

Jack raised the glass to his lips with a pleasurable sigh and caught Sara's eye "what?" he asked before drinking deeply. He then inspected the bottom of the glass expecting to find some hint of how it had been filled and then looked at the surface of the bar which was also spotless.

Sara sighed to herself and continued with "you do want to know why there's more stuff in here than there should be, don't you Jack, I mean Claire understood it right away?" 'well almost' thought Sara.
"Yes please."
"Right, it's all to do with space."
"Or the lack of it?" asked Jack.

"Quite the opposite actually. It's all down to the space inside you and me, the space that makes up most of everything. We are all made from atoms which are in turn made up of electrons, protons and neutrons, amongst other things. There is a lot of space between these component bits that the Suspension Field reduces" she then waved her hands around indicating the inside of the shuttle "by a factor of ten."
Jack frowned and questioned "smaller atoms then?"
Sara looked quite surprised when he answered with that, most people replied with 'a smaller ship then' she continued in a slightly surly tone "yes, but because the space within an atom is smaller, so any object subjected to the field is smaller."
"So anything brought in through the front door is shrunk then, by a factor of ten?"
"Yes and..."
"So where does the space go and where was the space to start with?"
"Most of the matter in our Universe is made up of space or vacuum, so using a Suspension Field to compress the excess space is the key."

  Jack now on his third pint leant back on his stool and started to pull at his trouser waist, attempting to investigate the shrink everything inside the shuttle policy. What eventually stopped him from analyzing the contents any further, was the tapping of boot on stool leg and the icy blue stare being applied to his forehead by Sara's eyes.

  It crossed Jack's mind that if the field failed it might hurt a bit "so um, if the suspension field fails and everything goes back to normal size, does the outside of the ship grow too?"
"No the outside of the shuttle stays the same size, the field can't fail until the end of all the Universes" replied Sara coolly.

  Sara then sat up straight and leaned to one side, pulling out her Quellz from a pocket, as it had started to vibrate with an incoming call.
"Hello?" she asked holding it to her ear like a normal phone.
"Oh hi, it's only me your long suffering non pilot. I just thought you should know that our hunters are nearly here and the engines are all warmed up and I've turned on the internal communication system" it was Claire, calling in a deprecating tone of voice that echoed throughout the shuttle as well as Sara's Quellz.
"Okay I'll be right with you Claire."
"But I could fly ..." Sara cut her off before Claire finished her echoing question.

  Sara then stood up and Jack watched those long legs of hers straighten, even in combat trousers and boots which appeared to have a high heel, she did have the most amazing legs.
Jack only actually watched her legs for a second, as his eyes were drawn to the stool she had been sat on. It quickly melted into the floor just like he would imagine a stool shaped wax candle might after having had a nuclear powered blow torch applied to it, then it reappeared on the side of the bar wall, like it was being poured in from the bottom up.

  Sara turned back to Jack, cocked her head to one side and asked him "do you want to come and watch the take off from the cockpit?"

Jack was staring at where the stool had been, which Sara mistook as staring down at her legs, ankles and feet, she thought then that there might be some chance of getting what she needed from him without any hassle. After all he was male and what males mostly think with could be described in a variation of four letter words that rhymed with 'lock' and 'tennis'.
The look he gave her when he lifted his head though, was more of wonderment than the lust she was looking for from him.
Jack nodded and answered vaguely "yes, okay that would be nice."
      Sara proffered her hand to Jack as he stood up from the stool. Jack took her hand, prepared to turn and marvel at his stool dribbling into the floor like Sara's had, but the frozen ice and vice like grip of her hand had surprised the 'staring round like an idiot' right out of his system.
As soon as her hand had held his Jack could not stop the incredibly sharp intake of breath whistling through his teeth at the sheer coldness of her hand. It was like immersing your hand in ice water or a lake on the verge of freezing over, it seemed to travel up his arm and across his chest making him shudder slightly, not in pain but the cold was an almost unbearable shock.
Within a few paces of being towed the long walk to the cockpit however, her hand no longer felt like it was sucking the heat from his very core, it seemed to have equalized with his normal temperature or he had with hers. After the initial freezing shock, Jack found holding her hand very pleasant, whether because it was something he had not done in a long, long long time or just because it was her, he was not sure.
      When they got to the cockpit door it had what Jack would have described now, as an old style keypad on the left, the only real difference he could see was the addition of six letters on the pad, A, B, C, D, E and F. The little bit of corridor they were stood in that led to the cockpit was only three meters or so long and just over two meters high and wide. It was also quite dim, almost black in comparison to the extreme whiteness of the rest of the shuttle. There was an outline of a door in front of them in faded white, with rounded corners. Sara tapped in a code on the pad, Jack watched the door very carefully as it simply faded from view, like it suddenly went from out of focus to crystal clear. They stepped through the doorway, no longer hand in hand.
      Sara strode forcefully forward, with Jack looking over her shoulder at Claire sat in the white leather looking central seat, reclining back so far in it that she may very well actually be classed as being upside down. Jack glanced back over his shoulder at the tiny dark corridor they had just walked down, the corridor lead back to the brightly lit lounge and bar. The cockpit door then 'swooshed' shut abruptly, it simply faded back into place and Jack turned his attention to the rest of the shuttle cockpit. Something bothered him about the door for some reason, not the look of the thing but maybe the sound. He was sure it had made a 'swoosh' like noise as it had closed but for the life of him he could not remember the thing making a noise when it had opened.

　　　　　Shaking his head Jack turned to scan the cockpit, his first impression was that it was pear shaped, this was not a comment on the whole invasion of Earth thing, although it was pretty darn close run thing. It was however the actual shape of the cockpit, with the pointy bit being at the front and whiteness everywhere again with metallic accents on the various controls and floating screens.

　　　　　There were three seats that looked more like recliners across the front of the viewing window, with Claire sat in the middle one and three more seats on either side at various control stations. The control stations themselves were moulded into the walls round the shuttle cockpit, sat in curved extensions of the walls jutting smoothly out into the cockpit, like sensuous fold out tables.　　　The bulbous front wall panels, under the viewing window, were just out of reach of all three front facing recliners. Unless the chairs could detach themselves from the floor somehow, Jack saw no way of operating the metallic coloured controls sat in front of them, without a pole and maybe a tennis ball to throw at them or really long arms and legs. The screens around the controls were all outlined in silver but were white everywhere else, until they were presumably turned on. The other visible lines were around the edges of the metal controls, where the panels met the moulds, with the metal controls themselves sat in yet more white.

　　　　　"You'd think a modern shuttle like this one, could be flown by one person really?" commented Jack.
Sara looked round and without thinking answered "yes it can Jack, but this one's been modified."
"To do what?" questioned Jack.
Sara opened and shut her mouth a few times as she just realized she had said too much, although Jack would not know that but Claire might unfortunately. She needed an answer and one that was not the truth, much to her surprise Claire came to her rescue "to help in the fight against the invaders, obviously Jack."
As Jack turned to survey the rest of the shuttle and stare out the front window at the trees and moss cover still present, Claire gave Sara a look that said 'you'd better explain to me later love.'

　　　　　Claire then climbed out of the central seat she was sat in and offered it to Sara, when she sat down the seat adjusted itself to her height and build almost immediately, then an holographic floating touch screen appeared just above her lap. The screen was black in sharp contrast to the white of everything else in the shuttle, the shapes on the screen were a mixture of bright colours but the ones that caught Jack's eye were the flashing red ones on a sixteen character pad, the same as on the door outside of the cockpit.
"1982?" hazarded Jack.
Quite obviously preoccupied Sara replied without moving her head in an irritated tone "I know the code Jack. Just go and sit down will you, this thing hasn't flown for a few years, so the take off might be a little rough!"

Jack and Claire stood just behind Sara exchanged a questioning look. As they both moved away back into the cockpit, Jack had to ask of Claire "I thought the war was only a few months old and she's just said this ships been sat here for years! How long has this war been going on then and how long has she been here with the ship?"

Claire paused trying to think of a way of switching the question round so Jack appeared to be silly once again but before she could think of anything Jack added to his question "and how much time have I really lost?"

Claire looked thoughtful for a moment and replied "you know Jack, the way you've been acting to things, makes me think you haven't had your memory wiped, you've simply not got the memories in the first place."

"Are you trying to say I've been on holiday?"

"No Jack, just that even with a memory wipe you'd still be able to remember bits and pieces and you can't. It's almost like you've been asleep through it all!"

"Or on holiday."

Claire ignored Jack's flippant remark and stood staring at him deep in apparent thought. Claire was thinking Jack could look quite intelligent in the right lighting, when he was was not actually doing any thinking. She caught herself gazing up and down his form and not for the first time wondered why she found him 'quite attractive, no no no annoying more like' she added quickly to her thought.

Jack watched Claire suddenly look up with a defiant look in her face, which he mistook to be Claire about to have another go at him but was actually Claire defying herself to go beetroot red with embarrassment at her own thoughts.

To quickly fend off another verbal attack on his good self, Jack quietly asked "so how long has the war been going on?"

Sara without turning round from her seat, whilst tapping at various floating holographic screens said "thirty seconds to launch, so I suggest you two get in some seats and strap in now, it might be a bit rough!"

Claire quietly whispered to Jack as they split and sat on either side, just behind Sara "four months."

She then almost jumped into her seat, it automatically adjusted itself to her body and selected a more upright position than the reclining position she had been seen in earlier.

Jack stood and looked at the chair in front of him, it was the same as the other two front seats in the cockpit, up until this point, when he was going to sit in one, he had not paid them much attention. To Jack it looked like it was going to be as uncomfortable as sitting on a bed of nails, being used as a saddle for the bucking bronco ride he was sure must still exist somewhere in the world.

The rear of the chair was gently curved, almost like an egg, the general shape from the side was of an lazy S. The floor mounting appeared to be of Egyptian pillar like design, almost as wide as the base of the seat but with all manner of shapes and wording in some form, curving and twisting around the base. Jack looked closer at the Egyptian like hieroglyphic pictogram's of animals, creatures, devices and general scenery spiraling up the pillar, all in various eye watering ambiguous positions that lead the observer to one conclusion. The designers were probably neutered and frustrated. The reason Jack noticed the pictures at all was because there were no other graphical design in the ship he had seen so far, everything was basically clean white, everywhere.

What had put Jack off jumping in the thing in the first place though, were the spikes. The bit he was supposed to sit on, or in, was more spiky than it had any right to be. It could not have been any more spiky than it already was, even a bed of nails he had seen someone lying on before, did not appear to be as spiky as this seat he was supposed to the sitting in. The pointy bits were at least ten centimeters long, at the tip they looked impossibly sharp and at the base they were a centimeter wide. There were thousands of the squared off things, covering the entire inside of the chair in a light matte grey finish, from where his ankles would be to the top of his head. Jack stood back and just looked at the seat sat there in its various shades of white, white metal and gun metal white colours.

"Jack!" shouted Claire across the back of Sara "just touch the arms on the side as you sit down and it'll mould to you."

Jack flicked one of the spiky grey things with his finger, it twanged like a piece of stiff foam, reminding him of the sound a wooden ruler made when twanged on the side of a school desk. Then he turned, put one hand on the seat arm and felt the chair growing smaller behind him. Jack would have jumped in the seat like Claire had, now though it had lowered itself to knee height, so he sat down still with half his pint left. Much to his surprise, after the briefest moment of discomfort, the seat was now moulded perfectly to his body, in such a complete way that at first he was not even sure he was in a seat any more, more a whole body glove.

Under his right hand a holder for his drink popped out of the side of the chair, which he then carefully placed his half pint of cider and black in. It still tasted like something he had not had for years, the taste sensation washing over his tongue and occasionally up his nose had been amazing. It was something he could not have explained, because he had no explanation as to why it tasted exactly the same but at the same time was completely magical to his senses.

Sara then started to count down from five to one, Jack could see her continually pressing virtual buttons on the floating screens in front of her, appearing to chew at the inside of her mouth every time something flashed up red on one of the screens or other and had to be dealt with. There were at least three screens of various sizes floating in front of Sara at any one time, he could see her frustration as she stabbed at the floating buttons and switches and finally swept all but one to the side.

By now her count down had long passed the final digit, although Jack was excited to be on his first jaunt on an alien shuttle, he was still more worried than excited, especially as there was a war going on, so in a trembling voice he asked "what are we waiting for?"

Sara looked over her shoulder at him and said "the shuttle has been in hibernation for years, so it's taking ages to warm up."

Then a little green light started to flash hesitantly on the final display, Sara reached forward and just before she touched it said "I hope this works."

As she lightly brushed the green flash there followed the brightest blue beam of light, it was over ten meters wide and splashed down just in front of the shuttle, then just as quickly turned off again leaving a large gap right through the leafy tree canopy to the stars. It also left a hole in the ground with an impossible depth, a considerable volume of steam and smoke was now billowing out of it, with several furry woodland creatures bounding full pelt in every direction from the hole.

"I think it's warmed up alright" said Jack, pointing at the flaming blue edges of the hole.

"That didn't come from us Jack" said Sara cautiously looking up through the hole in the trees.

"Warning shot, maybe?" asked Jack after a moment, also craning to see.

Sara looked over at one of the floating displays, showing shadowy figures approaching the shuttle, slowly by the age old method of walking with menace towards them.

"Hmm probably but I don't think we want to stay and find out. So, here goes" with that Sara touched the green flashing light again on the floating holographic panel.

In the forest, the log pile surrounding the shuttle seemed to start to bounce up and down, jerking about like a salmon fish trying to release itself from a net. Then an angry roar started, that sounded like the illegal offspring of a motorbike and an jet engine, being kicked into life for the first time by a giant.

Accompanying the sound, from the rear of the pear shaped log pile, was the intermittent firing of a piercing blue and white coned heat and light riot. It vaporized anything sat behind it into little dusty stars for several meters. Further from the back of the shuttle it knocked over and crisped logs, smaller trees and bushes, not to mention the four dark figures who had been sneaking up behind the shuttle. They had been within touching distance of the log pile and were now quite literally just four dark figures outlined on the furthest trees.

The four dark figures had had no time to react, the other dark figures, two on either side of the bouncing shuttle, were reacting, badly. They had been crouched furtively in the bushes, thinking the blue weapon warning shot would have forced any sensible people to surrender. Instead there colleagues were patterning a few trees.

One figure rose slowly to there feet, with shoulders hunched over and arms hanging despondently by there sides. The other was swearing and banging what looked like a Quellz communication device on a log, looking for all the world like a frustrated and angry caveman. The two on the other side of the rumbling shuttle, simply froze in there crouched approach, unsure what to do, whether moving was good or staying still was good.

A final jolt from the logs, another smaller but no less significant spurt of blue flame out of the back, followed by the revving sound of a jet-bike combination piercing the wooded silence and the shuttle was free of its log pile prison. It could now clearly be seen as a bulbous flattened pear shape, with a sharp front end and two angled tail fins sliding out and in to place at the rear. This was clearly visible to the two remaining non crouched figures. Something had been holding the shuttle back from launching and had caused the back of the thing to swing round towards the crouched figures. Where they had been crouched, there was now just a couple of blobby bubbling outlines on the forest floor, obviously freezing had not been a good idea.

Inside the shuttle the cockpit windows, which took up a two-thirds of the wall space in one grand swoop, showed the bucking and twisting of the world outside but no apparent sensation inside.
"Before either of you say you didn't feel a thing, look at the floor" said Sara.
Both Jack and Claire looked down at the cockpit floor, they watched lightly pinked ripple like waves but looking a very long way off, pass through the floor from one end to the other and back again.
"It's like watching the tide wash in" said Jack as he stretched out a foot to test the waving floor.
"Whatever you do, do not touch the floor until it's white again and ripple free!" said Sara quickly.
"Why?" asked Claire, who had also been in the process of stretching a toe towards the floor and now sat frozen in an odd twisted position, the same as Jack.
"Conservation of energy!" said Sara.
"Why are we conserving it?" asked Jack, mesmerized by the wavy flooring.
Sara sighed and said "basically the shuttle is bucking round and we're not because the excess energy is being converted and stored in the floor. Touching it would give it somewhere else to go and you really don't want that!"
Jack found the endless waves bounding up and down the floor fascinating, with great effort he dragged his eyes away and looked once again out the cockpit window. Turning his head to Sara he asked her "why are we still bucking around?"
"I forgot to detach the anchor" Sara said dully with another sigh.
"Why can't we detach that from the cockpit, that we're currently sat in?" said Claire with a hint of sarcasm.

Sara raised a hand to her mouth and replied with her own sarcastic reply "gosh, I never thought of that, you know maybe if we're quick we can skip over to the red flashing lever and pull it, all without dying horribly from the excess energy flooring!"

Sara pointed jerkily with her thumb over her right shoulder towards Jack. Jack looked over his right shoulder, just behind him was a distinct grey metal panel on the curved bench wall, with an L shaped curved lever sticking up, which was in itself flashing white to red.

"Ah I see, when you said a 'flashing red lever' you really meant a 'really flashing red lever' ha ha" laughed Jack lightly to himself.

Both women looked at him in mild disgust "what?" asked Jack innocently, followed in a slightly angry tone "I'm not the one with the bad floor design, with a lever out of reach across a deadly floor trap!" Jack dipped his head down and mumbled into his lap "you'd think with all this tech in here, they'd make seats you could move or panels you could reach."

    With his head dipped like it was, Jack could not be certain if it had been there all the time or it if had just appeared; on the foot rest, right between his feet, an orange coloured shaped half ball, roughly the size of a large orange, had appeared. Tentatively Jack rolled his foot over the top, much to his amusement found he that it was quite soft and moved the chair around the cockpit. The two women were arguing over who should test the floor first and who would be the most suitable martyr. If they had bothered to look behind them as they discussed and not argued, they would have seen Jack doing spins and figure of eights, until eventually he got bored and maneuvered himself and the chair to within easy reach of the lever.

    Jack placed his hand on the surprisingly warm metal feeling console and stopped himself in the act of pulling the pulsing red lever, on careful inspection the thing was standing upright in the middle of a cross with four possible directions.

Still looking at the lever and mulling over what to do next he asked curiously "so which direction do you need to pull the red lever then?" Without turning round Sara said "down."

    Jack still looking at the lever considered this to be, after a moments thought, an actually very unhelpful thing to say. Pulling the lever back towards him could be considered to be down, as the panel was angled and therefore the lever would be in the lowest position. On the other hand if he were to look at the lever as a flight joystick, then pushing forward could also be taken as down. It may also be possible to depress the lever into the panel or possibly even to pull it out and rest it somewhere else entirely. Then there was the left and right options, which considering he was sat in an alien craft, could actually mean that anything was possible in many directions. All he had to do was look at the foamy pink floor and that much was obvious.

    By this time Sara and Claire had exhausted there discussion and had turned to face the red lever, they found Jack hovering over it with a look of confusion on his face.

"How did you get over there?" asked Sara.

"What do you think your doing?" asked Claire at the same time as Sara. Jack looked up and said "right, I know I'm not the quickest person out the gate and I'm fully aware I still don't know what's going on around here, but your instruction 'down' makes little sense. I mean is that pull down, push down, squash down or something else entirely down?" Shacking her head and grinding her surprisingly long teeth, Sara replied "push it down into the cross, like a detonator plunger and do it now please!"

After Jack pushed the lever into the pad several things happened; first the cresting pink foamed waves all washed out to the rear of the cockpit floor, the central anchor on the underside of the shuttle released and recoiled and Jack for the first time felt his stomach become so heavy he thought it was made of lead. Now twenty feet above the ground, the shuttle angled itself up at thirty degrees, it would now be able fire not just the one engine but the two larger ones on either side at the rear.

The two remaining hunters outside the shuttle, dressed in there blacked out clothing, were in the process of putting together, what to the casual observer looked like a very large black whaling harpoon gun. Unexpectedly they had both found themselves hurling half mumbled curses at the escapees in there shuttle, they were still professionals themselves though and were therefore doing it quietly.

The mounted gun on its three legged pedestal was just being quite literally screwed to the ground, with some seriously long screws, when the black anchor cable connecting the centre of the shuttle to the middle of the log pile suddenly twanged. The two hunters looked up at the sound, then at one another briefly over screwing in the last screw, then back at the shuttle twenty feet above the pile of logs angling itself for launch.

The black anchor cable, being rewound slowly into the shuttle, was spinning wildly around underneath and had collected a very shiny and excessively long wood saw from somewhere. Both black clad hunters had moved when the tangled saw blade buzzed its way past, one with greater success than the other. One of the hunters rolled to there feet, looked at the quick-metal pedestal and the harpoon gun neatly sliced in half, watching it slowly slide apart with there colleague doing the same.

The last hunter gave a sigh and then touched the top of there helmet, which felt a bit odd, airy in fact, pulling it off in the dark they found that it now had an angled sliced air hole on the top. Whatever the buzzing blade was made from, it did not seem to matter, the sheer speed on the thing seemed to be able to cut through anything. The hunter put the damaged helmet back on, watching the cable gradually disappear into the shuttle, obviously the blade and anchor were not going to fit in the hole. When the tangled cable with its saw reached the tiny hole in the base of the shuttle, it simply snapped it in two after a few attempts and with a loud twanging noise sent both saw pieces, with considerable speed, back towards the lone hunter.

The three fingered claw on the end of the anchor cable folded itself up and disappeared into the shuttles bottom, leaving not one trace on the surface.
Looking on the hunter though was not surprised by the direction of travel of the two saw pieces. In some respects it was a relief, they had given up trying to stop the rebels and were of the opinion that whatever happened next was meant to happen.
It was with some surprise that they heard the musical like boing sound of high speed metal striking the ground, so quickly that it now could be heard bending back and forth, like the sound of a metal school ruler being flicked and pulled across a table edge.
The hunter opened both eyes slowly in there helmet, they had been shut since the saw left the underside of the shuttle, awaiting there fate. The two pieces of the log saw were between there legs, one in front and one behind, still vibrating slowly.

    The hunter stepped carefully sideways with a little three hop jig, starting to back away from the shuttle as its three piece rear engine system swung round to point in the only possible direction.   The previous clearance blast had come from the smaller central engine and had charcoaled the band; for launch the two much larger engines would be used. It was at this point the hunter realized that the shuttle might also have an illegal 'suspension field' technology and that was why the clear out blast had been so massive and so destructive. The few trees that were left behind the shuttle were etched with figure like shadows that were only visible at a certain angle, any other angle and they just looked like a stain.

    The hunter turned and started to run into the trees, hoping to find a nice hole they could jump into. Too shallow and only a few spoonfuls of soil would be required to cover the remains, too deep and they might not dig them self out again. Then they found an old hollowed out trunk, just in a slight drop in the woodland floor and quickly clambered inside.

    The hunter started musing that it really was the bands fault the escapees were using the quick boost method for escape. If they had not shown themselves earlier they might have got the tag on the shuttle and the quick boost take-off would not be being used. Trying to stall them with the a precision blue light satellite strike had not worked either and now the band had paid for it with there lives. Why they needed to be followed had not been explained, it had turned from following to a chase though, that was when things started to unravel and they would be the only one blamed. Well be fair, they were the only one left from the group.

    The hunter mused to themselves that the launch was not exactly going to be quiet in anyway, shape or form either but it was very quick at getting you into orbit. The only real down side was that anyone in orbit would be able to track the lift off.

The final hunter crouched in there hollowed out tree trunk, crossing as many parts of there anatomy as they could find for luck. As the shuttle blasted off all manner of woodland debris flew past the hunter from the crafts wake, not to mention several surprised and sleepy animals flying past with little whistles, hoots and tiny screams. The shuttle took to the sky in a blaze of fiery blue glory.

Sara was having similar thoughts about being tracked as they left the Earth. Hopefully the other rebels had made it out of the bunker, before the Poly bomb had been set off by the invaders and by now were 'home free' she thought. There own escape would now give the invaders something else to track, instead of the insurrectionists and hopefully give those down below an even cleaner escape.

This had apparently been bothering Jack too, because after several minutes of staring out the cockpit windows with no little amount of dribble escaping his slack jawed mouth, the first question out of him was "are we still being chased?"

Sara thought initially he was being thoughtful towards those left behind, after turning to face Jack and look him in the face, she could see he was more worried about himself than the others back on Earth. To be fair to Jack he looked properly at a loss, at a loss to what though? If Jack had been asked, the answer would currently be 'everything' thought Sara with a smile.

Chapter 10 : Space Flight.

The shuttle launch had been far smoother than Jack had expected, again the floor had had those pinkish crested waves forming and foaming from one end to other as they had taken flight. Again Sara had warned them about touching the floor when the pinkness was in view, again Jack and Claire had stared at the mesmerizing patterns formed by the waves, galloping from one end to the other. Again they had both mulled over the health and safety issues of this thing being in the cockpit, where the pilot was supposed to be flying the shuttle. Again they had asked why the floor appeared to move like it did and the answer they had got, to Jack's mind at least had been wholly unsatisfactory "excess force transfer, now leave me alone I'm flying here!"

After giving Jack a hard look, Sara turned back to the front of the shuttle and its floating controls, making little "tsk" noises as she turned away in disgust. Jack on the other hand was too busy looking round the cockpit and out the windows to notice.

The view was almost exactly as he had expected, there was the Earth and the moon, glowing away like some very radioactive lemon thing, with a considerable amount of debris floating in between. Even though he guessed Sara was angry with him, he had to ask some rather pointed questions about weightlessness and currently the lack of it, along with what was actually going on please? After quickly looking at Claire he realized something and his train of questioning was put on another track.

Jack for some reason had expected to be blasted into space but at the same time he had not expected to be in space and asked Claire "your first time in space too, only I thought you'd been up before?" Claire slowly moved back from staring slack jawed out the window in the cockpit and facing Jack answered "oh I've never been in space before but I've been in the shuttle before, when Sara had to move it a few months ago!"

"I thought she said it hadn't moved for years?"

"It was on a trailer before we hid it in the log pile, it never flew Jack. She gave me and Jenny the tour before we hid it a couple of months ago."

"Uh okay then. Another question then for you, with all this advanced technology around us, are you really sure we're in space and not in some simulation?" asked Jack.

"Through the door at the back, first door on your right, override code fourteen ninety two and you can find out via an airlock" said Sara sharply without turning round from apparently an arm bending match with one of her screens and then she gave it a little swipe slap.

"Well um thanks, that wasn't quite what I had in mind" said Jack "I do have one more question though, why is the moon yellow and what's with all the debris in between?"

Claire looked back out the window, she had to agree with Jack, the moon was an awful sick yellow colour, so she looked at Sara questioningly and raised an eyebrow.

Sara was wrestling the controls, that was the only way she could describe what was going on, the only problem being that without something physical to actually touch, the wrestling was all in her mind. The controls were wholly holographic, apart from the joysticks on the seat arms, with floating panels of light that looked real but were insubstantial and were at this current point in time, useless. The only button that appeared to be working correctly, was the autopilot on one of the floating panels in front of her. Every time she pressed it the shuttle leveled out and stopped its spinning, but she had neither set the autopilot, nor did she know where it was set for. She could not find out because the light button that she needed to press for 'Plot Auto Navigate Edit' was flashing amber and amber in this cockpit meant broken.

Finally in defeat she touched the light button indicating the autopilot and turned to answer Jack "the junk out there is mostly yours, from failed missiles hitting satellites and one very lucky shot that hit an intake port on an Admiral Class Cruiser. The moon on the other hand is now a yellowing phosphorous colour from the Cruisers engines blowing out as it passed too close, which also cracked it. The Cruiser blew up somewhere between the Earth and the moon, hence the debris."

All three looked out of the window of the cockpit and could see the shuttle was having no problem moving round the floating junk, mainly because they were such large bits of junk to avoid.

It then struck Jack that another question needed to be asked "where are we going?"

Claire opened her mouth to reply with a sharp comment but she did not have one, as she had no idea where they were going either, apart from away from Earth.

Sara replied "away from Earth."

Claire's only plan, up to this point, had been to lead the invaders away from her friends in the bunker by being a distraction. They were now in space having left with a slight bang and so she concluded that there plan thus far had been a success.

If she had followed the shuttles wake behind her back to Earth, she might have seen the hole in the forest, the now slower expanding blue cloudy circle leading up into the atmosphere and through the atmosphere following there shuttle launch. The fact they had been followed to the shuttle at all was just a bonus, after all the shuttle was to have been the main distractor. Which was probably in part thanks to Jack being a beacon of some kind, Claire begrudgingly admitted to herself that he had been quite useful in that respect. Now they had escaped what was next and where were they going?

"Sara, where are we going?" Claire asked curiously.

When no reply was forthcoming Claire turned from leaning on the curved wall control panel under the window and saw Sara looked very uncomfortable in her seat.

"Um, Sara are you okay?" asked Claire.

Sara looked up and replied "I don't know where we're going alright!"
"Sorry, how can you not know where we're going? Your the pilot!" said Jack.
"The only button that works now is the autopilot and I didn't set it!"
"So you have no idea where we're going then?" asked Claire.
Sara waved her hand out towards the window and mumbled something like "that way" under her breath.

Then one of the floating panels by her knees lit up and floated into Sara's field of view, some text scrolled quickly across its screen for her to read.
"Docking procedure initiated?" asked Sara to herself "with what, there's nothing out here?"
Jack who was stood on the opposite side of the cockpit window now said "yes there is and it looks like the International Space Station to me!"
"What's the point in docking with that old thing?" asked Claire.

Jack on the other hand did not think of the station as old, maybe unnecessary given what he was currently traveling in now, he suddenly felt a form of nostalgia for a bygone age. Still it would be nice to know why they were going there of all places, they could after all travel to anywhere in the solar system and maybe even the Universe with this shuttle.
"Why there though?" he asked.
Sara looked up from staring into her lap and said "for the last time I don't know why we're going to the Space Station and no I can't change course, everything is fuzzed up."
"Computer virus" said Jack in a knowing tone, whilst nodding his head slowly and looking at a display below the central console.
"Jack, how could you possibly know that and ..." Sara answering Jack brought herself up short as she saw what Jack was watching.
"The buttons are fuzzing in sequence and the central base screen is flashing up errors" said Jack. Turning to Jack, Sara asked "how did you notice the screen error, it would take a genius to glance at it and spot the error straight away?"
The base screen was another holographic screen, unsurprisingly it was situated at the base of the central console under the forward window, which Sara now called up to the forefront and was floating at her fingertips.
"Jack come on your no genius, how did you see it?" asked Claire whining slightly.
Smiling to himself Jack pointed to the ceiling just above Sara's head, there another floating screen sat with flashing words in amber 'Agent Infectious Detected: Please Select Action.'

Sara groaned noisily, reached up a hand and swiped the contents of the screen down to float in front of her. After reading for a few seconds she began to mumble expletives and naughty words that even Jack and Claire, supposed adults, did not fully understand.

When Sara eventually finished reading, prodding things on the screen and various impolite words uttered under her breath had faded away. The autopilot was still engaged, so Jack had to ask "we're still on autopilot to the Station then?"

"Yes Jack, we're still on autopilot to the Station" said Sara in a level tone of voice.

"Okay that's good to know but why are we on autopilot to the International Space Station?"

"Because there's nowhere else to go" Sara replied simply.

Claire and Jack glanced at one another briefly, frustration written lightly across there faces. Jack signaled that it was Claire's turn to ask the obvious question with a wave of his free hand, as he walked out of the cockpit with his empty pint glass, on the hunt for a refill. The only problem that Claire could see was that there were other places to go, just Sara did not want to visit them.

The original plan was to lead the invaders a merry chase, to distract them, that much was complete and they had at least delayed them with various traps. Now they had the opportunity to go wherever they liked, even back to Earth.

"We could rejoin Jane, at the base outskirts?" hazarded Claire to Sara. Sara sat in the central seat, arms folded and legs crossed, looking for all the world like the most annoyed and pouting cat.

Claire sat for a bit longer before asking the same question, half expecting a minor eruption of some description, instead she got a rather short and sullen answer "we can't."

Before she could ask another question Sara stood up quickly, flicking both joysticks on the seat arms with her hands and walked out the cockpit, saying to no one in particular "I think Jack might just have the right idea."

Left alone in the cockpit Claire sat with her own thoughts, gradually feeling her brain fermenting to the point of mild annoyance and then she suddenly worked out what Sara had meant. She ran from the cockpit to the lounge bar, hunting down her favourite drink before they drank all the alcohol.

After twenty minutes or so of slow gins and various cider flavours, all three felt far more relaxed about things if not a little merry too.

"I'm sorry" said Sara apologetically, indicating them both with a wave of her pint glass and a slight spillage in most directions.

Jack frowned and asked politely "for what?"

Sara burped gently, leaned back on her stool and said "sorry that there's nowhere else to go."

"Why is there nowhere else to go?" asked Claire.

"That virus was an old one, it had been with me for years, like a slow cold following you around. I hadn't removed it cos' it would tell them that I knew that they knew that I knew that they had found it and done something about it."

"Meaning what?"

"Well the virus went live when I removed it before launch."
"Um, I guess you didn't remove it then?" asked Jack.
"Oh I did, it was one of the first things I did, what I didn't know was that by doing that I activated the proper virus and once we were clear of Earth, it or they or probably both, took over the ships controls for some reason and rather than get rid of us. We're docking with the international space station!" Sara gulped for air "For whatever reason I have no idea before you ask?"
"So how long have we got?" asked Claire.
"Hopefully many, many years that are long and fruitful, filled with rainbows and free cider" said Jack and then wished he had not, as Claire glared at him like he had just trod on her puppies tail with intent.

Sara did not seem to notice or if she did, she was choosing to ignore it and instead replied "oh we've got about thirty minutes or so before we dock."
Jack sat and nodded, putting his third now empty pint glass down on the bar again, still marveling at the way it was filled from the bottom up. The two women did the same with there respective drinks and Jack watched them being filled from the bottom, suddenly he felt resigned to his fate, whatever that maybe.

After nearly thirty minutes of solid drinking, they were all neatly drunk and if not drunk then at least merry with a touch of the invincible. Then they retired to the large rounded, curved lozenge shaped sofa's, they either fell back or relaxed back into the soft furnishings.
In the case of Claire, whom would never admit to being merry in the presence of Jack, she tripped and flopped face first onto a sofa. She quickly spun herself round, making her world spin for several seconds, before she could check if Jack had noticed they all heard a little tinkle in the air.

Sara sat up sharply, waving a complex symbol with her hand in the air, then she appeared to tap some buttons in the air that only she could see. As Jack smiling leaned round to see what she was doing, he saw that at an certain angle the floating cockpit screen controls had appeared.
Jack stood up slowly and asked in a whiny tone "why couldn't you have done that earlier, saving us from uncertain death with the stupid pink floor waves? Although I will admit they looked absolutely amazing, out of this world even!"
Sara ignored his question and waved him to be seated "the docking procedure has started, we'll be connected in two minutes."

Jack looked down at the seats, surrounding what looked like a coffee table but in white and not made from wood, chose a comfy looking sofa opposite Claire, not too garish in colour and sat down again. He let out a little scream as his buttocks landed and jumped abruptly up again, so quickly that it looked like he was attempting to leap onto the coffee table. Instead he smacked both his shins on it with such force that the table shot over towards Claire. She sat bleary eyed as it slid across the floor towards her knees. Sara stuck out a foot and stopped the table from hitting her, not for the first time thinking 'did she really did need Jack?'

He stood for a moment rubbing his shins furiously, then began rummaging through his back pockets, like a teenager desperate to find his fake identification for there first night of potential passion. Finally in a rear leg pocket he pulled out the dart that had nearly pierced him, having stabbed the tree next to him instead.

Jack twisted the dart around in his fingers, looked at the two women carefully and said "it pricked me okay."

Sara could not help herself and started to laugh, whilst Claire was sat trying with absolutely no effect whatsoever to move the coffee table. The thing would just not budge no matter how she tried to move it, so how Jack had moved it or Sara stopped it she had no idea.

Sara could not believe that Claire had missed the opportunity to have a valid laugh at Jack's expense, instead she was pushing and pulling at the coffee table. Sara felt a little sorry for Jack, as he would probably have no idea what she had been laughing at and his hurt expression said volumes about his own insecurities. She waved her hand at Jack, in what she thought of as an apologetic manner, which he mistook as her wanting the dart.

Jack looked down at the dart in his hand, with its attached misty green vial, he rotated it briefly in his hand and then tossed it towards Sara. Being ever so slightly drunk, in his own mind he thought the dart would fly perfectly true. Instead the thing spun high into the air, with Jack asking himself as he watched it tumble, 'why he had thrown a pointy sharp object in the first place?'

As it flew from his hand Sara could see that it really was an oversized dart for anything smaller than an Elephant or Whale. It also appeared to be about to land on the coffee table, rather than anywhere near her and it was at this point, just before it landed on the table, Sara realized what it was.

"A Trojan hor ... zzz" Sara started to exclaim, bang, bonk and smash went the dart, as its main body shattered on the table and a green gas billowed out. All three were unconscious a second later, the shuttle then made a light tinkle noise as it completed docking with the Space Station.

"What do you think then?" asked one of the International Space Station occupant males.
"It's a shuttle of some kind" said the other male in the dark gloom.
"Really, you don't say!" replied the first one sarcastically.

The four astronauts were all looking out small windows that looked over the docking system, as this new and exciting, yet quite worrying possible rescue, came hurtling towards there home.

All four of the stations floating incumbents had at one point or another, in the last few months, started to give up hope of ever being rescued and seeing Earth again. Obviously they could see the Earth, what they actually meant if they had been asked, was to be able to walk, to breath and to drink unfiltered things that should never be filtered ever again thank you very much on Earth.

Impatiently and with growing excitement that nearly could not be contained by the station, they watched various jets stream out of the shuttle to line it up its side with the docking door and the Station's clamps. How it was going to seal or even be able to dock they had no idea, they were all quite surprised when the microwave oven like 'ping' sound played out in the Station.

Looking carefully through the docking windows, they could see the shuttle had attached itself safely and all the clamps appeared to have clamped themselves in place.

"Do you think it's safe to open the door?" asked the first man looking at all the green lights above the airlock door.

One of the women on board turned to look at him, stuck her tongue out and turned the unlock handle.

The other women looked back at the two men and said "no offense but after four months in this barge with three unshaven arses, no supplies and no showers we're chancing it thanks."

The two men looked at one another and the first one to speak said "she's talking about yours, I wax."

"Har har and I think we should stop them before they do something silly" said the second man.

"Like what exactly? The board shows all green for docking and we're most definitely running out of everything up here!"

Both the bobbing men looked down the actually quite long metallic docking tube, where the two women had just opened the final hatch out of the space station. Without realizing it the two men had bobbed inside the docking transfer tube and automatically shut the door behind them, which in turn had enabled one of the women to open the outer hatch. All four of the enforced exiles were so desperate to get off the station that they had ignored all but the most basic of safety features and protocols. Shutting the door behind them was not only polite but actually necessary to enable the door at the other end to open, what was not protocol or actually considered safe was having no person on the station itself whilst everyone else was going out.

As the two men pulled themselves along the docking tube, they were fairly certain it had not been this long when it had been installed. They were also not quite sure whether there had been windows in the original design, along its entire length, although they did give a fantastic view of there potential dark green saviour.

The two men floated gently up to the two women, with one of them of course doing the obligatory somersault, twist and possible pike before grabbing hold of the final handle on the slightly grubby white and metal interior door.

"What!" he said when he got three dirty looks.

Shaking her head one of the women turned back to look at the shuttle, trying to see a door handle of some description or maybe even 'a doorbell' she thought.

She drew back her hand and clenched her hand into a fist as if to knock, then stopped suddenly as the other women grabbed her wrist and said "really! Don't you think they already know we're here, they did dock with us after all?"

"Okay that's true, but if so, why haven't they come out yet?"

The other women opened and shut her mouth a few times, like a reality television pop star on stage, whom has just realized there song is no longer playing any more and its now really obvious they have been miming all along.

The first women turned back to the door and hesitated, before the non somersaulting man turned and said "go ahead and knock, I don't think it'll be problem anyway."

He was looking out the window at the name on the shuttle, embossed in white, reading it out loud to the other three he asked "Hot Shot?"

"You can read it?" asked the second women in mild surprise after a moments thought.

"Yep, it's written in English after all. It's not like its written in Alien or anything, so I guess it's one of ours some how?"

The first women turned back to the blank dark green shuttle body in front of her and knocked gently on the side. After several seconds nothing happened so she knocked again and again, all the time thinking 'you've docked with us, not the other way round'.

Then the four of them heard the docking pressure warning alarm start to whoop from the other end of the docking tube, with a countdown overlaid in the background of ten seconds and depleting. The women's voice reading out the countdown sounded bored, if the astronauts had been around Beth earlier they might have recognized her voice as now doing the counting down.   Exchanging quick looks almost as one they turned round and kicked off back down the tube towards the Space Station. They all knew that the chance of them making it to the other end was quite small before the tube failed, not to mention unlocking the Station door. So it came as a mixed relief or blessing when a doorway on the side of the shuttle appeared from nowhere, next to a hand sized light blue panel that appeared. All four scrambled inside, just as part of the tube disappeared into the black of space and the door 'swooshed' shut behind them.

They astronauts now lay on top of one another in a tangled web of feet, arms, legs, groans and hands in odd shapes and places. The one thing they had not expected, when they had pulled one another inside the shuttle door, was gravity. It had come as a bit of a shock, even with all the weight training and exercises done on the space station, nothing could really prepare you for the sudden application of attraction. There was a great deal of groaning going on and mumbles of 'help', 'get off', 'no not there' and 'you can stop touching that right now!'

After a minute or so of careful maneuvering and some pain, the four of them all were stood up, leaning at various angles against the inside of the shuttle airlock and taking deep fresh breaths of clean air. There were a few coughs, rubbing of gums and looks of embarrassment at one another. Then a green light lit up over the door they had just fallen through, the door then simply dissolved away in front of them to reveal a very large lounge and bar. Still shaking and shivering slightly from entering the airlock and not knowing quite why, the four of them cautiously entered the shuttle. After looking around like tourists gawping in a cathedral, they collapsed and rolled gently down the tiny slope leading out of the airlock, lying in another heap of twisted and interlocked limbs at the bottom. If they could have looked at one another's faces, they would have seen green crystals forming on there noses and around there mouths. If Jack could have seen there faces, he would have been reminded of a certain green puppet like frog.

The shuttle detached itself from the disintegrating docking system on the International Space Station and slowly pirouetted around to face the centre of the armada of alien vessels. The engines kicked in, the shuttle lazily swooped, dived and sashayed its way through the debris to the white coloured central cruiser, eventually encountering a massive door.

If Jack and the others had been awake, they might have seen the white ship grow bigger, with its large entrance. They would have also seen the door on closer inspection was not quite so perfect a pristine white as they would have expected. Grubby might have been a better word to describe it, like it had once been a white T-shirt but after many mud battles and pond dunking's by child, no matter what it was washed or bleached with it just needed a darn good replacement. Not the child the T-shirt, although some people would argue for both to be replaced or maybe not at all.

The door slowly pulled down underneath the ship as it approached and the shuttle flew inside, with the door banging gently shut behind it with a little bounce.

Chapter 11 : Really Stellar.

Jack woke up with a typical Monday morning headache. The type that you know is going to last beyond three coffees and especially on the long journey of fourteen stops on the train. He still had not moved but something felt a little out of sync. This time though it was not the wind ruffling his hair that had woken him, nor the incessant arguing and bickering going on somewhere in front of him. It was something cold, hard and very stiff sticking in the back of his neck, which was highly uncomfortable. In addition on trying to move he found that all parts of his body were restrained. He could not even see what it was exactly that was holding him in place, because he could not move his head one bit. The first thing that went through his mind was the thought of the probe being used again, the arguing around him though did not seem to be anything to do with him for a change, which was nice.

Jack tried to relax as best he could, slowly he opened his eyes and scanned them over the arguers. He was quite surprised to see two men in white astronaut jump suits and two women dressed the same, arguing with Claire and Sara. After listening to them for a minute he felt he should make there acquaintance and started by saying "hello everyone."

If looks could kill Jack felt that right now he would have four, no make that six swords sticking out of his torso, as to why though he was not sure. They carried on arguing, ignoring him, Jack carried on trying to move and found the table thing he was strapped too was made of some type of plastic. The restraints were plastic too, wrapped around almost every part of his body, including tightly round his throat and the top of his head. He struggled for a while longer going quite red in the face, after a while gave up and so made one of those throat noises to get peoples attention.

When he had it, he asked very politely he thought "hi I'm Jack and who are you guys?"
"They know who you are Jack, we told them hours ago" said Sara a might acidly for Jack's taste. Before he could mount a suitable reply along the lines of 'yes I know who I am but who are they?'
The slightly taller of the two men strode up to Jack, starting to poke him very hard in the chest and said "this is all your fault mate!"

Jack was strapped in a near standing position, he guessed that if his feet had been on the ground this man would have still towered over him by several inches, even if the chap was lying down, he was that well built. The expression brick outhouse came to mind very quickly.

Still Jack wanted to know some things, after being prodded several times, with a chance of bruising more than likely, he decided to ask a reel of questions first and then answer the question that was not a question "first off why am I tied up, where are we, why are we here and where is here, how did we get here and what do you mean several hours? Also, this is not my fault!"

"Yes it is!" came a sanitized voice from the doorway.
Jack's instant reply of 'no it's not' hovered on the edge of his tongue, whilst he looked for the target that had accused him of, well, everything. Floating through the door was a black cube with what looked like a miniature galaxy inside, all slowly swirling stars with the occasional mysterious flying object passing through it, just a bright streak that did not stop. The doorway disappeared behind the cube and became just another bit of wall again. The cube floated into the middle of the group of humans at waist height, giving them all a good chance to look inside. This was exactly what they were doing, just staring into the cube because it really was like just looking through a window at an galaxy with no apparent boundaries. There thoughts were all fairly similar along the lines of 'wow, how did they get that in there' and 'it's so pretty', apart from Sara and Jack. Jack because he was a little too far away to see properly and Sara because she had come across these things before.

The cube floated to within a meter of Jack and then raised itself to his eye level. Jack looked into the cube and the first thing that came to mind was how desperately he needed the men's room right now! Mistaking his strained expression, the cube asked in its strangely clean voice with no tone, no inflection and oddly neutral speech "are you not curious as to how you started this war?"
Forgetting his near urgent bathroom requirements, Jack looked back from moving his eyes around the room and said "no I didn't! Didn't I, what war?"

The cube gave its equivalent of what Jack assumed was a shrug, floated up to the ceiling and just sat there waiting. Jack looked back at the people in the room, they all seemed to be very angry and staring purposefully towards him.

Whilst Jack lay strapped up, he tried to relieve the worried boredom by glancing about the room they were in, it was light grey in colour and actually had corners and edges where the plain walls met the plain floor and ceiling. There were what looked like triangular lensed cameras in all eight corners of the long rectangular room, Jack could not even guess what the walls were made from, mainly because he could not touch them. Basically it was another prison room in Jack's opinion. Looking around the long rectangular room with his just his eyes was not having the desired effect either, he just had no way of avoiding the other people in the room now stood in front of him.
Sara was tapping her foot again and all of them were looking pointedly at Jack "what?" asked Jack defensively.

Claire said to the others in the group "I got this" and turned towards Jack.
"I'll start slow Jack, so you can understand every word and therefore give a straight answer okay?"
"Um, yes that's okay I can do that."
"Good good Jack, now lets begin with the first question: what the hell did you do to start a war with the aliens, I mean I know you can be annoying but to annoy a whole galaxy of them enough for them to invade our world. That's not just taking the biscuit but the whole tin?"

Jack looked around the other five faces in the room, there was no help available in there stares. He attempted to shrug, then he remembered that was not possible and replied "whatever happened it wasn't me. You've gotta believe me Claire, Sara? I really have no idea what's going you know."

Sara stopped tapping her foot, sighed for quite a long time and replied "I'm sorry Claire but I really don't think Jack could start a war. I mean I know he can be annoying but it would take far more effort than he has ever put in to anything to start all this" she said this waving her hands about to indicate there cell and everything outside.

Claire replied "knowing Jack, he probably just turned up somewhere and didn't do something he was supposed to be doing!"

Jack felt relieved and also slightly put out by there statements, it sounded like he had done something or not done something in the past to offend Claire, which he could not remember.

The black cube then floated back down to his eye level and in its sanitized voice asked "how does your neck feel?"

Jack rolled his eyes and replied "I've always had a bit of a crick in it and this seems to be working it out thank you very much. But it was fine, right up to now that you've reminded me that it hurts like hell!"

The six other people in the room all moved to look at the back of Jack's neck and made comments along the lines of 'I've seen that neck screw thing before in a film' and 'ooh that looks painful.'

For Jack it was very uncomfortable and did not help when the cube said "there is currently one thousand tonnes of pressure being applied through the neck screw."

Jack tried to swallow but the brace round his neck was making it difficult, Sara was now stood right in front of him with her mouth open in surprise. Claire was surprised to see that Sara was surprised, she had never seen Sara lost for words or even actions.

Jack tried one of his previous questions out on Sara "what?"

"You are a Wiimp, a free Wiimp!" Sara said this with such reverence that everyone even the cube turned to look at her.

Jack looked back at her and replied defensively, not noticing the tone of her voice "no I'm not. I'm quite manly I'll have you know, thank you."

Sara shook her head and said with a light smile playing across her face "oh this is nothing to be offended about and actually explains very nearly everything about you."

Jack made one of those 'huh' questioning noises which was lost in the mild commotion that the others were making, until finally the blonde space station women asked of Sara "if your not calling him a playground name, then are you talking about the dark matter Wimp's?"

Claire and Jack both made faces that clearly said neither of them understood what she was on about, the bigger of the two men saw there expressions and answered "we assume that dark matter is a form of 'Weakly Interacting Massive Particle' or Wimp for short."

"And that helps how?" asked Claire quietly by Jack's ear.

If Jack could have nodded he would have, he did try but his neck was hurting.

"No" said Sara "in this case it doesn't stand for that, it's the name given to..." at this point the cube made a loud belching type noise, that was more attuned to what film goers would have expected from a gigantic dinosaur with tummy trouble to make.

When Sara tried to speak over the last echoes of the belch, she found that her voice did not appear to work any more, at least no sound seemed to be coming out, although she knew she was talking. Jack was looking at her slightly stricken face, he then tried talking himself, all that came out of his mouth was the feeling of air moving, a light breeze billowing gently over his tongue and through his teeth but no speech to speak of. In Jack's case nothing coherent was ever going to come out anyway thought Claire, she was also struggling to make a noise, even with her feet stamping on the floor.

The cube moved itself above Jack's head, a long quite thin black cord lazily dropped out of its bottom, it attached just behind his shoulders on the restraining stand he was strapped to. It then moved up towards the ceiling, passing right through with a slight ripple effect in the grey matter and disappeared from view with Jack on his table in tow.

The people left in the room stood in a circle around where Jack had disappeared, they had tried talking to one another but to no avail. The sound was being muted or there ears had been neutralized in some way, because after several attempts at shouting at one another and one rude hand signal, nothing could be heard. One of the female Astronauts turned, slapped the big man right across his face, which left a ruddy glow on his skin and an angry expression but no sound.

Chapter 12 : A Proper Interrogation.

After what seemed like an ice-age in the dark, being bounced around like so much airport luggage. Jack found himself in a rather nice room, which almost resembled his lounge at home after he had floated up through the floor. From the limited bits of the room he could see, it did most definitely look like his lounge, only a couple of things were wrong though. First of all it was all in one piece, which given the world ending events that had happened recently, this was unlikely. Secondly this was not his lounge but rather the lounge of his parents, from when he had been twelve years old. Still strapped on the table, in the middle of the room, Jack could only see the one door that lead to the kitchen. He assumed there was another door over his shoulder, which lead outside, he could also just see a staircase out the corner of his eye going upstairs. He guessed there was a door over his shoulder, until they spun him round he would never know. Then the cube dropped down from above his head, floating in front of his face, seeming to scrutinize him by just slightly changing its shape and twisting about.

Then a female voice sounded from behind Jack's shoulder and in a very English aristocrat tone said "loosen the screw."
The cube moved around to the back of Jack's head, a black cord slowly extended out to touch and twist the handle behind the screw. Before turning the handle the cube asked in its emotionless voice "are you sure, nothing has been proven yet?"
"Yes but keep ready please" came the unseen female voice.

Jack strapped to his table started to feel the pressure in the back of his neck start to lessen, to the point where he could just feel something pressing but not hurting.
The female voice from behind him said "you are to be sent for interrogation in a few minutes and are entitled to one question, about anything you so desire?"
Jack caught himself from asking the obvious 'what, any question?' because that would obviously be a question and even asking about who was asking him the question would be a question.

Jack then heard the tick bock sound of feet walking up behind him, which on his parents lounge carpet should have been more of a shuffle like sound and not the clip clop of shoes on metal. That meant that this room was all some form of illusion, it was not real!

The creature then stood in front of him and it was definitely an alien, there was no other way to describe it. It walked on its hind legs but with the knee caps reversed to his, it had a face like a fox and two normal human looking arms. If Jack had seen it in a dark alley he may very well have assumed that it was a sassy human female, possibly wearing a fancy dress costume because of the pointed and tufted ears. Fur also covered all the bits he could see and just because of the furry face, he expected it to be on all fours probably pawing through his dustbins again thought Jack.

It was wearing a very sleek dark green uniform, it seemed padded like armour but as it was styled like shorts and a T-shirt, Jack was unsure how much protection it could actually manage. There was a high collar around the neck and a patch on her right breast, with some dribbling alien canine embossed on it. A wide lighter green belt ran around the waist, with various vertical coloured strips on it, what caught Jack's attention though and held it for quite some time, was the oversized gun clipped on the belt running most of the way down a shapely furry leg. On her feet she wore what Jack would describe as door knocker boots, in glossy black with a short Wellington boot look and heel.

Light relief came to Jack from the face of the alien, which had the cutest, softest facial features he had ever seen on any animal, he resisted the urge to try and reach out to stroke it. He guessed he would probably get bitten and end up with rabies or something if he tried, besides his entire body, including his hands, were still tied down.

The creature kept flicking its tongue nervously out of its mouth and across its nose and sharp teeth. This made Jack think she looked hungry for something, he guessed it was probably some natural automatic reaction of the species as it seemed to be near continuous, or alternatively Jack really was the appetizer for this foxy faced alien.

Jack stopped himself, he had gone in a few seconds from critically analyzing this creature as an alien, to now comparing it to a cute species he might recognize Jack mentally pulled himself up short, after all this must be one of the monsters who attacked Earth and laid it all to waste.

Jack's expression slowly changed from one of curiosity and pet love, to anger and frustration. To Jacks surprise the alien noticed this almost immediately and started to back away, looking panicked.

She then said, still stepping away carefully "no no no, it's okay we mean you no harm, you are safe and no harm will come to you … ever. Please believe me!"

Jack was now exceptionally curious about a lot of things, especially as he was still tied up and posed no danger to anyone really. Apart from himself if he did not get someone to scratch his nose, it had been irritating him since he had woken up strapped to this table. It had reached the point where waggling his nostrils was no longer sufficient and was in need of some serious rubbing quite soon.

The alien was now half crouched behind a sofa/settee/couch whatever you wanted to call it but it was not his parents furniture, that was for sure. For a start he could see the aliens three fingers and weird bendy thumb holding on but the fabric of the seat was not being depressed at all, almost like it was a cloth overlaid over something more solid.

To Jack it looked like a stand-off, as the alien was reluctant or possibly even unable to move and Jack did not want to say anything in case it was taken as a question, which he would then have wasted.

Eventually the alien seemed to recover some of its composure, Jack decided to listen carefully to what was said and try not to show any facial emotions. The alien stood up slowly from behind the furniture, realizing that Jack was waiting for it to do something and not the other way around. There was a visible sense of relief that seemed to sweep over the alien to Jack's eye, she looked like she was suddenly high on something. In Jack's imagination it looked like she had been thrown over the snake pit, round the spiky tree, through the minefield and finally come to rest against a sweet apple tree in full bloom.

Through waggling and snorting, to try and ease the itch on his nose, Jack was slowly aware of a sweet apple like aroma in the air. Where it had come from he had no idea but guessed, after looking again at the alien, that it was having an effect on someone at least.

She suddenly looked full of confidence, as if it was oozing from every hair follicle on her body. The alien swaggered around its make shift barricade and came round to lean against it like a teenager showing off to her friends.

The alien turned its soulful light brown eyes on Jack and said "you are safe here, as am I. As I said before, you are entitled to ask any single question you like, which I am required to answer, before you go to interrogation."

Jack at this point realized he was in a waiting room of some description, he would have asked for what but the alien had already mentioned interrogation several times. How the questioning would go or even work, he had no idea whatsoever and was strangely looking forward to it. Strapped to a table with no where to go, even if he did get free, Jack had worked out that the type of questions he was asked would let him know what they wanted to know and possibly even why?

Jack lifted his eyes up from looking at the floor and stared at the alien until it said "I assume you have many questions and being limited to one is a little, shall we say limiting? So I shall make your life a little easier by telling you my species is Raifoon and my name is Summer."

Listening intently to the words Jack surmised that 'Summer' here was definitely female, whether that was right or wrong he did not know and would not know unless he was to ask.

Jack looking her full in the face said "I do have one question for you and it is quite important."

Feeling relieved that she might actually be getting somewhere, Summer asked "please ask any question you like."

"I'm not really sure your gonna like it" replied Jack, looking about considering his circumstance.

"Really any question you ask I am required to answer."

Summer was expecting a question along the lines of 'why me' or 'why have you invaded us' or 'why am I here' or 'what do you want' or even 'why am I going to be interrogated, I ain't done nuffin, honest guv'. What she got stumped her as Jack asked "why are you speaking English?"

Summer looked at Jack with her mouth slowly opening in surprise, the gold flakes in her dusty brown eyes flashing briefly. When she realized her mouth was open she snapped her jaw shut, briefly trapping her tongue between her teeth, followed by an expression on her face that you would normally find on someone sucking sour fruits.

Jack looked on in vague surprise, not really sure whether to laugh at the fox thing bouncing around holding its muzzle or to pass on some sympathies.

After the Raifoon stood up straight, with only a mild wince on its face, Jack decided to settle for clarification "I mean most things I've seen signed or written down have been in that boxy square writing, but right underneath, its also been written in English in most places. So I'm guessing I don't have a translator in my ear, as my eyes won't work on alien words. So I'm going with the question, why are most things in English, after all you spoke to me in my native tongue as did the cube thing?"

Looking carefully at Summer, Jack surmised she was still in some pain with her mouth, possibly a little sympathy might not go amiss "how's your tongue feeling?" he asked.

Summer was taken aback slightly, given this humans situation, sympathy for her tongue was unexpected. Unless it was clever or trying to be clever by hoping an emotional attachment would form, stopping her from sending him for interrogation. Focusing on Jack she looked closely at him and then started to giggle at her own stupidity. She came to her senses quite quickly, which most women did with Jack misunderstanding him entirely, concluding that he was not intelligent enough to have thought about using her emotions against her.

"My tongue is fine thank you" she replied in an aloof tone.

"Okay, that's good, now, how or why are we all speaking English please?"

"Are you not more interested in your upcoming appointment?" she asked curiously.

Jack tried to shrug from under his restraints and replied "no question I ask is going to get me out of the hot poker poking, with optional screaming. So I thought I'd ask a question that's been bothering me since this morning when I saw an alien shuttle, with English words written on the outside and English controls and signs on the inside. It was only now, being forced to stare at the door behind you, that I finally realized what had been bothering me all day!"

Summer turned round to look over her shoulder at the door, then snapped her head back before she had got a proper look, she had expected Jack to have found some way to escape his restraints and be stood behind her. But there he was still lying strapped to the floating bed smiling at her, she turned back to look at the door and above it written in English was 'No Exit for Crystal Repeating Autonomic Plant-forms.'

It was her turn to shrug and turning back she said "there are signs like that everywhere, all over this vessel."

She could not see it thought Jack, maybe he was reading too much into things, it was starting to get on his nerves now, like she was wasting his time and seemed indifferent to his forthcoming torment.
"My point being, regardless of what it says, is, why is it written in English?" he asked again.
Having now sat down with her long legs folded back under her, Summer looked up at Jack through long eyelashes and answered "it's been written like that for years now" seeing Jack getting a little upset she finished with "it's only a fad, next year it could be Raifoo or Dairy or even Whale!"
Jack stared at her, realization slowly dawning that language was probably like clothes to these aliens, falling in and out of fashion as quickly as flares of any description.
He then commented thoughtfully "when the language is changed then, it must be a monumental challenge to alter all the signs in the galaxy?"
Frowning at Jack she replied "why? All they do at the Lib-Bar is flick a switch!" Jack would not have noticed but if he had tried to spell Lib-Bar, he would have spelt it Lie-bar, because that was how it sounded to his untrained ears.
"Then it must be a pain, learning a knew language every couple of years?"
"Try every few weeks when a new intelligence is discovered! Though I will say that English does seem to have lasted much longer than some others. Maybe because it's taught, as well as loaded now?" mused Summer half to herself.

     Jack was at a slight loss really, he had watched science fiction movies all his life and had only wondered a couple of times why they all spoke English. The main reason he assumed, was so that the yarn could be understood by the viewing audience. Now though here he was in his own science fiction story, where the aliens actually spoke English, the signs were in English, it did not smell half bad and therefore he was not entirely sure this all was not a dream.
"Loaded?" ask Jack in an hopeful tone.
Reaching behind her furry pointed ears Summer unclipped something, when she held it in her hands in front of Jack it appeared to change colour and wiggled like a desperate worm looking to escape the beady eyes of the circling birds.
"What is it?" asked Jack curiously trying to look closer.
Putting it back somewhere behind her ear, Summer turned and said "gult or G.U.L.T."
"Have I got one of those stuck behind my ear?" asked Jack with a worried tone in his voice.
"Not unless you requested one from supplies you haven't. But don't worry you'll get one just before your interrogation."
"But I don't want one!" replied Jack still reeling slightly from all the wiggiliness.
"You have to have it."
"Not out of choice I don't."
"Specially chosen sarp are questioned as a matter of course."

"Special I maybe, but having a worm stuck to my face isn't for me thank you!"

Sighing to herself Summer said to Jack "you can argue all you like but you are in no position to make demands."

"Apart from my one question, which you still haven't answered yet."

Summer stared at him slightly at a loss and it was then that Jack worked out he had been asking the question all wrong. Asking 'why do you speak English' with the obvious answer being 'I learnt it' and not 'how did English become popular?'

Having finally found the error in his question, Jack asked carefully of Summer "how, when and why is the English language now so popular?"

"The Gult enables us to understand any language and learn it over time."

Jack knew he was going to have to ask at some point and so he did "what does Gult stand for then?"

"Galactic Universe Language Translator, there is also a Guls, Galactic Universe Language Standard. These are all numbered languages, for example Guls one is binary, you know on and off. Guls seven is Noofars and Raifoo combined" she sounded very proud of this as if it were some great achievement for her races language, then she continued in a voice of mild annoyance "English may be confirmed as a Guls ten soon."

"That's nice but why?"

"By common usage mainly, no language has been added to the Guls for over a hundred thousand years!"

"Ah the nub of my question then is this, how did English become a common language?"

"Through the Gekk of course!"

Right Jack thought now were getting somewhere. Then a noise that sounded like 'bloing', the kind of sound you would expect a rubber jelly to make bouncing off the floor and then the ceiling, could be heard coming from some hidden speakers somewhere in the room.

Jack found himself spun around by the cube above his head and towed towards his parents front door in the lounge. Another question sprang too mind about where they had got his child hood lounge from, it must have been from his memory some how but where and when was yet another question. Straining to look out the frosted windows, Jack almost shouted as he was dragged from his old lounge said "you can't take me for interrogation yet, you haven't answered my one question!"

Behind him he heard Summer say in a casual tone "no, actually I answered lots of questions until your meeting was ready."

Then Jack was through the door, quite literally through the door as it did not open and Jack not for the first time wondered why they seemed so found of holograms 'they must be everywhere' he thought. Yet another question to be answered one day, he mused to himself.

After being dragged through his parents old front door, Jack was not surprised to be, once again, in an white coloured corridor that seemed to be very long, excessively so. As he was being towed face first this time, Jack could vaguely see the end of the corridor, it was surprisingly clear and an awful long way off, possibly several hundred or even thousand meters away and with no atmospheric haze to obscure the end it just looked like a dot. There did not appear to be any doors, windows or openings of any kind along the corridor whatsoever. The walls were entirely blank to Jack's eyes and after several minutes of being towed, Jack was amazingly bored. The walls and ceiling were never ending in there whiteness and the end of the corridor, which had appeared as a dot earlier, was still a dot after several minutes of bobbing along. He just wished he could look behind him, to see if the corridor had another end to it.

After what seemed like hours of being pulled along like an errant helium filled balloon, Jack finally noticed something that he had been observing but not seeing until now. There was an ever so slight curve in the corridor to his left, it had not been observable to start with because it was so subtle. It was only really because his position in the centre of the corridor was not changing, that he could now notice the slight bend. Then the cube, with its floating galaxy inside, stopped in the corridor and a door shaped hole faded into view. With Jack in careful tow they both floated through the doorway. As they did so Jack noticed there was a slight indent above the door, in a slightly different shade of white was some of the strange box text he had seen earlier, with English text underneath that he had no time to read.

On entering the room Jack heard the now familiar 'swoosh' noise, meaning the door behind him was now shut, why the things did not make a noise when they opened he had no idea. That was another question to be added to his now seemingly endless list of things he wanted to know.

Jack was gently spun round in the room, he was now finding the colour schemes relentless and incredibly boring. Nearly every room he had been in was a shade of white, it seemed the aliens had no concept of colour and what little he had seen of the room contained no alien or cube. The room was just a blank white box, with vague shadowing marking the edges, which he guessed meant he was in a cube shaped room about ten meters square.

Finally he felt actually alone for once, in the last couple of days it had felt like he had not had moment to himself but now he might get some peace for a moment of two.
Jack shut his eyes in quiet contentment.

"Are you ready?" came the sound of a calm female voice, over what sounded like a typical aged train platform tannoy system. The voice was made up of broken words and crackles, meaning that if there was a time and platform in the train message, you were obliged to guess at where and when you were supposed to be to catch the thing.

Jack went to shake his head, then he remembered that moving was not option due to the bands round his skull, the neck and additionally the screw poking in the base of his head.

He sighed and said "no, thank you" after all there was no point in being impolite to his would be torturers.

There was a very long pause made up of crackles, pops, hisses, mumblings and tapping through the invisible speakers and some half whispered words seeping through the sound system. 'As' was not so bad a word, until Jack heard 'probe' a few seconds later, that was when his ears really started straining to hear what was being said through the system.

Just as suddenly the noises stopped, then started again and the female announcer crackled at him slightly clearer, saying "we shall be with you shortly, we apologize for the delay."

Jack instantly replied with "no, please, take as long as you like. It's not as if I've got anywhere to be is it!"

Then on the wall facing Jack a very large, probably five meters wide, screen was turned on and in boxes on the screen appeared a dozen faces. The face in the top right corner slowly moved into the centre of the screen and tripled in size. Jack could see the other faces were not all the same species and the one now enlarged was a Raifoon face.

It opened its mouth to speak and Jack jumped in first with "hello Summer" he had recognized the facial markings, much to her surprise and his own.

"Um, yes hello Jack."

"Hi."

"First the charges" then before Jack could reply or argue "do not interrupt!" she said quickly and precisely.

Summer cleared her throat and began "you are hereby charged with the willful use, theft, misuse, damage and deprivation of one privately owned vessel. Just so you know Jack that's the easy one."

Summer then continued to list many things of which Jack had no idea about and most of which ended up being a blur of noise as far as Jack was concerned.

Jack hung by straps on his stand, let his mouth drop open in mind numbing boredom, as the charge sheet seemed to be never ending and going for far too long.

Eventually he had to stop her when she got to the bit where he was accused of starting a war on Earth "sorry, I've gotta stop you there. The only thing I might possibly be guilty of, is stopping the vacuum thing from sucking me up or in and out of the sewer?"

Summer seemed to look around the room she was in and then looked back at Jack and said "we weren't aware you were responsible for the willful damage to one of our recovery helpers, that will be added to the charge list in a moment."

Jack rolled his eyes, after what seemed an eternity of mind numbing monotony, Summer stopped reading and looked closely at Jack and asked "how do you plead?"

Jack woke from his half sleep and replied with enough thought to say "I would like representation, before I answer that please."
Not only was Summer shocked by his request but so was Jack for even thinking to ask.
Whilst he stood musing over where the thought had come from, Summer said under her breath "who advised you to ask that?"

The screen went blank in front of Jack and then disappeared completely after a few seconds. Followed shortly by a door way fading open in front of him and Summer walking through, the door then swooshed shut behind her by simply fading back to wall.
"Right Jack are you ready for some home truths?"
"Any truths would be amazing but only if you release me and let me use a loo please?" he said this with some degree of desperation in his voice and no little shaking.
Summer put her hand to her ear briefly, as if she were getting instructions, then she walked over to Jack and touched the centre of his forehead briefly with a short furred finger and stood back.

Almost immediately, once she had touched his forehead, the room he was in faded away like a heavy mist being attacked by a blazing sun. It was no longer a bland white room but more like what you would expect a mad alchemists office to look like. There were tables, benches, chairs and strange metal stands of various heights, shapes and colours all around the room. Various odd shaped bottles sat on tables, shelves and book cases. There did not seem to be any material that would not and could not be used for whatever purpose was required for mixing random chemicals. The room was no longer a uniform white either, instead it was a dirty and well used white, with what looked like burn marks, scorches and patches like band aids stuck across the walls. Where Summer had walked through the fading doorway, Jack could now see that it was a bent and blotchy stained white metal panel that was now stuck partially open.
Jack touched his forehead tentatively and Summer said "blinkers."
"For horses?" asked Jack feeling something like spectacles on his face.
"Yes I know what you mean but no. They were developed by the military to only display the sounds and pictures required in battle to stop distractions. Then someone discovered there virtual reality and overlay uses and now there used most everywhere, including interrogations where they are used as probes."

Jack felt a little sick inside at the mention of the word probe, especially multiples or the plural of, it was at this point he noticed he could finally move his head and the pressure on the back of his neck had gone. With some relief he raised his hands again to massage the back of his head and then realized he was free at last. Due to the blinkers though, superimposing some reality over the top of reality, he had no idea how tied or untied he had been.

Stepping down from the plastic panelled table he had been strapped to for what felt like hours, Jack turned with what Summer thought of as a threatening expression on his face.

Standing in a slightly twisted pose, Jack asked quickly "where's the Jon luv?"
Summer shook her head in confusion, not fully understanding his meaning, until Jack started to pantomime some form of relief of release of pressure.
Mainly she worked it out when her GULT (Galactic Universal Language Translator) earpiece, informed her he meant 'Water Closet' or 'Facilities' or 'toilet' or 'loo.'
She eventually pulled the worm thing out from behind her ear and gave it a look of anger, it continued to give further explanations of bodily functions attached to the names. If she knew she would not have looked quite so silly, she would have shook her finger at it and told it off verbally.

Shaking her head slightly, this time in frustration, she pointed behind him to a door set in the back corner of the room. Jack stomped off in the general direction she had indicated, not caring if he knocked anything over in his haste. As he got to the door he stopped in front of it and had a moment of despair as he looked closely at it, he could see no way of opening it. There was no handle to speak of and it looked a bit solid to try and walk through without a blow torch of some description. Then Summer came to his aid by saying "just give it a push in the middle."
Jack put his hand against the middle of the door where a slightly indented circle sat, with a light push he felt it start to open towards him, so he stepped back and then walked inside with the door 'whooshing' shut behind him.
Summer heard Jack sigh with relief, after mumbling over some of the instructions as to which parts in the toilet did what, followed by a long heavy tinkling sound.
Over the noise he asked "looks like there's been a few explosions around here?"
Summer looked up, paused and replied "sorry about that, I'll let the cleansers know."
Jack laughed to himself and said "I meant in the room in general!"
"There's been a few explosions everywhere Jack, after all we are at war!"
"I would have thought with your technology you'd have us beaten hands down by now?"
"We have, though there are other wars going on and this ship has been in many battles and many other wars, some it lost and some it won. Every battle has a cost!"

A minute or two later Jack came back out the corner door, looking much better in himself.
'Sharper and possibly even cleaner' thought Summer, he was certainly standing straighter, less stooped certainly.
"Amazing" was all he said on seeing her face.
"What is?"

"These glasses things I've been wearing" said Jack holding them carefully in his hands, to his eyes they looked quite delicate. They resembled the white top half of a frame of spectacles, with opaque lenses and extra pieces that folded into your ears. Jack put them back on, like he would a pair of glasses, he felt a slight tingle as they locked in behind his ears and in his ears. Then a polarized curtain slowly flowed down in front of his eyes, within a second he could no longer feel them and the room was white walled again.

Jack put a finger to the centre of his forehead, touching the Blinkers like Summer had done, the curtain rolled up in front of his eyes and the pieces in his ears popped out.

Jack slid them on top of his head and asked Summer "I take it they can display anything you want, forests to walk in, footpaths, parks and alien worlds. Instead of the mundane white ship or the damaged ship we're currently in?"

Summer was a little taken back and stood for a while wondering how he could be so stupid and yet so astute at the same time.

"So what's the home truths then?" asked Jack and after a moments thought added "and how long have I been wearing these specs?"

He was wondering at what point they had been applied to him, when he had woken in his house or in the underground base or when they had got here, on this ship?

Summer stood open mouthed again, which on an Raifoon made her look to Jack like an overly dopey but loving spaniel type dog.

Jack resisted the urge to pet her on the head, surmising that he would get a slap or bitten in the process. All of a sudden her jaw clicked shut, with the sound of teeth snapping together and the super fast recall of her lolling pink tongue.

Regaining her composure Summer answered "do you remember picking up the dart?"

"Yes" said Jack, recalling that he had not so much picked it up as forcibly removed it from a tree.

"From that moment, till just now, you were wearing the blinkers."

Jack shook his head and asked "was the shuttle ride real then?"

"The blinkers take anywhere from a few minutes to an hour for a new user before there're fully acclimatized In your case, the first thing they did was hide themselves."

Again Jack shook his head "to hide them, so we wouldn't see one another wearing them, that was the other darts flying past all three of us then running down the grassy hill! I guess there also used to hide the fact your ship ain't quite as special as you'd have us believe?" finished Jack waving a hand at the damaged looking room.

"Yes and an easier form of interrogation, we've been through some tough times together but she's held up well" she said this while gently tapping or stroking even, one of the wall panels, which on closer inspection was warped out of place slightly.

Jack was now leaning against one of the many tables in the alchemy like lab, just looking around gave want to several questions he wanted answers too "so why are we here then and I mean in somewhere that doesn't look like an interrogation room?"

"Simply all the cells are full at the moment and we need your criminal past to sort out our now problem!"

"My criminal past? Your problem? You invaded us, didn't you?"

Summer folded her arms with an air of disappointment, leaned a hip against a table and stared at Jack.

"Okay from the beginning please" said Jack resignedly.

"Firstly Jack, you did start the war between humans and the 'Tested Alliances of Species and Kindred' or TASK. Waving your hands around protesting your innocence will make no difference Jack, it is a matter of public record in the Lib-Bar that you were the first identified human seen and recorded attacking and destroying a Super Stellar Class Carrier. Again waving your hands about makes no difference, I can show you the footage if you wish and yes we're aware you have no real time memory of this event." Summer paused and looked carefully at Jack's face, she was now sure he had no knowledge, at least directly, of the assault. So she continued "the records show that you, in armour, attacked and destroyed a Super Stellar Class Carrier, therefore starting the hunt for the new species allied with the Furrykin. You were then caught and de-armoured by a race we call the Watchers, you went missing, presumably as an escaped war criminal. Now you've resurfaced on Earth, just as some white hideous explosion occurs in your rebel base. This is not a coincidence according to the TASK and must be dealt with accordingly. There is also the not so minor issue of the installation of an 'illegal' suspension field, on your shuttle!"

Summer was not sure what reaction she had been expecting from this human, but no reaction was not what she had been expecting, he was just stood leaning against a table fiddling with the various containers.

"No comment to make then? Like I'm sorry or it wasn't me?" said Summer with a tang of sarcasm in her voice.

Jack looked up from playing with the glass like container in his hand and said "the thing is I can't believe what your telling me, yet at the same time it has a ring of truth to it that I just can't shake. Honestly it's a bit like deejay-vu, only with the bits of memory, like someone else is telling you the story about how drunk you were the night before and the mad things you did!"

Jack stopped swishing round the clear liquids he had been mixing randomly in a glass, he put them down exceptionally carefully on the work table he was leaning on, mainly because all of a sudden they had started to fizz an awfully bright orange colour.

      He could remember quite a few mornings where he had woken up with the hangover from hell. Strictly speaking not a hangover, more of a headache-over but a lack of memory of what had transpired the night before included as standard. Then after careful research and the occasional angry message, he usually could piece together what had happened and where he had been. Even then though there would be whole blank sections from the night before, which after the Monday morning stories, he was probably glad he could not remember entirely and some sounded like they never would have ever happened to him at all. The trouble was the memories this alien was talking about, did feel like they had happened to him but they were more like a dream than as actually having happened. It was like watching someone else's view but only with glimpses of what happened rather than the entire event. It reminded Jack of playing a video game but without him being in control of the character on the screen performing all the actions. Jack was also only getting flashes of a second or two of action and there was no context to the images, like looking at a large picture from a few feet away but through a telescope, meaning you only saw a small part of the whole but in great detail.

Jack summed himself up as memory stumped.

Chapter 13 : The Selector.

Summer stood with her hands on her hips, continually moving in some small way, like she was itching to be off running somewhere. Jack leaning calmly against a table, slowly batting invisible butterflies from his shoulders, then asked something that was now obvious "we're not in interrogation are we or for that matter was I ever?"
Summer sighed and replied "we don't need an interrogation room any more with Blinkers. No Jack you were never in an interrogation room, after realizing what and who you were when the probe started relaying its information to us, we decided to be 'off the record' so to speak and offer you some form of redemption for your actions."
Jack looked hard at Summer and then in an exasperated tone of voice asked "redemption?"
"Because we need you to travel back in time and stop the invasion from ever happening."
"Great that's just great that is, aliens want me to travel back in time to stop an invasion they started, when time travel isn't even possible" Jack paused "well forward is, but back not so much! And why should I help you again?"
Summer started to shake her head in mock defeat but then staring quite hard at Jack said "I shall say this only once; time travel is possible through the use of other Universes. It is difficult, highly illegal and requires several things which we will be obtaining. We also need your willing support as a species in fighting the Furrykin and we aren't very likely to get it from you after we've just invaded your home planet are we?"
Jack had by now found a stool very similar to the one on the shuttle, the only difference really was the jaded metal colour and burn effects over the whole thing. Basically it looked like a crispy golf tee.
Still confused Jack asked on a subdued voice "why though, why invade at all, surely you could have sent out ambassadors or something before hand?"
"Ah yes, well, that's where our and your problems collide you see."
Summer stood with a last lost puppy in the shop window expression on her face, Jack started to calm down as he realized he had been leaning further and further forward with a fair degree of aggression. He then looked round the room one last time and the dawn of enlightenment finally crossed his mind, the aliens needed him more than he thought if they were showing him reality. To a fair degree he might be the only human in the world, okay scratch that, Universe who might nearly know what is going on.
"Problems?" asked Jack.
"Your system is in a green reservation" after seeing Jack's face screw up into one of the human expressions that would mean 'what' she continued with "what it means is that your planet resides in the centre of an area designated as inviolate or untouchable."

Looking at his lost face again, Summer made a little growl of frustration in the back of her throat, which sent involuntary prehensile chills up and down Jack's spine, as his body was remembering the need to run away from scary sounds like that.
Summer watched Jack jump slightly on his stool, then with some effort get some degree of self control and say "good job I went to the loo just now, phew!"
With a little satisfaction in her voice that she still had it, she continued with "only the green guards are allowed in the designated area, the point being to leave the area to natural selection and keep it away from the influence of the rest of the Universe."
"To see what could have happened if we were left alone in the Universe" asked Jack "bit like a game reserve then?"
"More of an test to see what happens under isolation conditions and anyway you aren't the only species in the reservation."
"So why are you invading us then?"
"We've already invaded, we're occupying."
"Point taken. But. You haven't explained why you invaded us?"
Summer sighed, realizing that a quick over view would probably never do for Jack and talking did not appear to be working quickly enough for her needs. She turned and walked to an random door in the room, which obligingly stuttered open, took a package from the dark inside and turned back to Jack.
"Hold out your hand Jack."
Jack looked levelly into her face sat on his stool and not for the first time thought 'you know, she is hot!'
   In her proffered hand sat a small, heavily engraved, metal cigarette lighter or large matchbox sized and shaped box. Jack nearly took it straight out of her hand without even thinking but managed to stop himself at the last moment and looked closer at the metal box. The metal was an almost silver finish but not quite as shiny, though uniform in shading and colour, the two things that had got his attention though was the fact he had almost grabbed it without thinking and the engravings. They looked almost tribal in there shaping and appeared to be layered, one on top the other, to give an almost three dimensional effect, the final thing he noticed which was probably why he had not picked it up straight away was the depth. The engraved markings at certain angles appeared to have no end, they had no bottom, crevasse like they went on "forever" said Jack aloud.
   Summer had not moved her hand from under his nose, until he spoke out loud and now she looked closer at the metal box. From her point of view it was just that, a not very shiny metal box that was completely plain and unadorned, apart from an engraved label on the top reading in Guls two 'year four basics.' If Jack could have seen the words on the case, he would have just seen a series of squares, triangles and odd shapes which made up the language.
With a fair degree of curiosity she put her hand back under his nose and she asked "so what do you see then?"

By now he was prepared for how mesmerizing the box was and answered "some tribal symbols that appear to be engraved by someone with a really deep set of tools."

Looking back into Summer's golden flecked soulful light brown eyes Jack asked "what's it for?"

"It's called a selector or memory box, you simply put your blinkers on and place the selector on your brow above where the blinkers sit and let go."

Taking the selector box from Summer, Jack turned it over in his hand and then asked again "what's it for?"

Summer slammed an hand down on one of the benches, sending various tubes and chemical containers briefly into the air and ground her teeth at Jack's stubborn stupidity. She then stood up straight, clenched her hands together, letting her tail like thumbs extend and wind round her clasped fingers.

Jack had nearly fallen off his perch on the stool when the alien had suddenly slapped the bench hard, he had watched with shock at first and then amazement as she had calmed down by standing straight. With her legs bending the other way at the knees, Jack had not really noticed how tall she was, until she straightened her legs and really stood up. With her towering over Jack sat on his stool, he guessed she was easily eight or so feet tall, two foot taller than he was. Then he had noticed her thumbs extending and twirling round her clasped hands, what this actually signified to Jack was nothing whatsoever, it just looked amazing.

Jack just could not stop staring at her thumbs, there was something about them that had him completely mesmerized and whenever they bent and twirled like excited snakes his eyes followed. He was surprised he had not noticed them before.

"Your thumbs are brilliant!" said Jack in wonderment.

Summer looked down at her hands and let her thumbs move around like two exotic dancers meeting for the first time on her palms.

"There like an elephants trunk mated with a worm" said Jack still in awe "I want my thumbs to be like yours, there amazing!"

"There are very useful and..."

"They extend, there not one length?" said Jack as he watched them grow from two inches to six, with no effort whatsoever.

"They are very similar to your own digits but they are much stronger. Where your monkeys have tails at the back" she said this with some disgust in her voice, at the thought of toilet arrangements and a wave of a hand at her posterior "we had more of an elegant evolution."

Eventually Summer had enough of Jack looking at her hands and put them behind her back, he then just sat there twirling the selector in his own hands staring at her legs. She stepped forward, pulled the blinkers off the top of his head and down on to his nose. At the same time she snatched the selector out of his hand, slapped it with some force on to his forehead, with the comedy like sound of a blancmange hitting a clown in the face.

Jack was so shocked with how quickly she moved towards him, that he only just had time to open his mouth in surprise and then his vision was suddenly filled with a women's face.
"Oops, sorry too close!" said the women in his sight briskly.

Chapter 14 : Facing Reality.

Summer looking on from the outside of Jack, could see he had the usual expression on his face that all first time users had when the learning tool was applied. First a look of shock, surprise and generally an open mouth, which slowly then shut. Then a smile of one form or another moving from the persons crown to there mouth and neck. It was like watching someone having a scalp massage, as realization dawns that it is not going to be all bad and in fact is, in some cases, better than the action and practice towards reproduction. Summer stopped herself, where in the Universe had that thought come from.

As she stood analyzing her thought process Jack was getting a lesson, well more of a case of you will learn this you have no choice lesson, quite a bit like life really, except there are not many do overs in life.
"Who are you?" said Jack looking around himself "and where am I?"

Jack was stood in an blue space, looking around wildly in every direction. The entire area was bright sky blue and was everywhere. There were no corners, no light source, no shadow and no point of reference. It was similar to being in a raft lost at sea with nothing on the horizon but more water and sky, albeit without the raft, water or sky. Then gradually Jack felt the urge to look down at his feet and in doing so noticed, quite worryingly, that not only did he not appear to be stood on anything but he had nothing to be stood on with.
"Where's my body?" asked Jack in a wavering voice.
The reply came from a very long way off, almost like the person talking was stood at shouting distance and could only just be heard. All Jack heard was a few unintelligible words along the lines of 'you', 'fudge' and 'far off.'
Jack spun round and found the source of the small voice a long way off and then the women was suddenly stood in front of him.
Jack looked her up and down and asked "Beth? What are you doing here?"
"Ah you've remembered, excellent."
Jack would have been staring at her, stood open mouthed but he currently he had no body and so said quite abruptly "why have you got a body?"
Beth tipped her head to one side, put a hand on her shapely hip and a finger to her mouth in thought, before waving her finger in an almost magical wand like gesture. Jack let out an huge sigh of relief as his body quite literally popped into existence, although only partially clothed.
"Thanks for the socks and trainers, but the rest of my clothes would have been nice too you know!" Jack said this whilst covering a small private part of himself with both hands, when really he only needed one.

Beth stood stock still was trying hard not to laugh, then eventually she could not hold it in any longer and started to giggle, burble and guffaw until she was just barely staggering around. As Jack looked at her with some disdain at his predicament, he noticed that he had his favourite shirt, jeans and other garments on his body, as if from nowhere.

There was also a slightly darker shade of blue on the floor that seemed to go on for forever and with some relief Jack asked of Beth "what's so funny?"

Beth looked up from being slightly bent over and said "give me a minute."

Jack looked on, getting more annoyed by the second until something appeared at the edge of his vision, looking up and to his left he saw something of a grassy green nature rolling towards him as Beth straightened up. As he looked on he saw that it really was rolling towards him, very much like the wording of some books he had read at school.

"Well I've heard of 'rolling hills' before, but this is new!" he commented.

Jack stood rooted to the spot and just watched, amazed at how the grass followed up and down the gently rolling curve of the approaching green hills. Now it was possible to see that the green was grass, well grass that was excessively green, as it rolled gently but continually towards them, following invisible dips and troughs in the landscape.

As the scenery ploughed its way towards Jack and Beth, Jack could see that the leading edge was leaving a trail of construction behind it. Clumps of bushes, little wooded areas and clouds in the bluer sky, appeared slowly but quickly behind the ever approaching gliding bird like leading edge of the grass.

Just before the edge touched Jack he very nearly died of a jumping heart as Beth landed an heavy hand on his shoulder, she lifted him up slightly as the grass zoomed passed with the deep resonant sound of a plucked cello bass string. Jack without blinking was now stood in his parents open plan log cabin that they had planned to stay in but never built.

The cabin looked just like he had envisioned when his parents had been talking about it and planning it many years ago, when he had just been a young teenager.

Looking round Jack instantly felt at home, it felt so right and yet it was so wrong because the place had never been built, the landscape outside the windows was also exactly how he had seen it in his minds eye.

Beth looked at Jack's confused face and said "this is all a composition, everything you see, hear and feel has been composed from your memories. Before you say it, looking at your face, I'm assuming this place we're stood in isn't a memory?"

Jack nodded and replied "it's what was planned and the hills are what I imagined. So where are we now?"

"Oh we're still on the cruiser in the lab. You've just had a memory selector box plugged into the blinkers your wearing. Basically it's downloading information directly to your brain and when you are asked a question or need that particular information it will become available much quicker via the Blinkers. This" Beth waved her hands around to indicate the world they were stood in "is a virtual world that has been created to make the memories easier to access."

She paused then and gave Jack a look that could only be described as apologetic and said "I'm sorry but due to our being here it has appeared to have selected an unreal memory. Probably because there is less detail in it than a real memory and therefore less processing required."

"Sorry maybe I'm not up to speed on all this but why am I here and why are you here?"

Beth had never been one to get frustrated in her passed life but she could feel the start of something now, she replied in a bad French accent with a slight smile on her lips "listen carefully Jack, I shall repeat this only once."

Jack sat down heavily on the sofa draped in a rug and relaxed in front of the open stone fireplace, resting his feet on the oak style table in front of him.

Beth sat in the rocking chair opposite, with a look of mild disappointment on her face and started by saying "the blinkers you put on earlier can be programmed to show the wearer anything. Be it real or not. They work best altering the real environment to match a preprogrammed plan. Originally they were designed for military purposes to enable the user to concentrate on just what was required and filter out the superfluous. Then they hit the market and were found to be perfect as a teaching tool. Think of them as teachers, a learning tool when the selector box is plugged in."

"Slapped in you mean" said Jack, rubbing his unreal forehead for no apparent reason he realized after a few seconds and stopped abruptly.

"Yes, well the Raifoons can be a tad impatient sometimes, which is why we're having this conversation now in your composition, where time can be quicker compared to the outside, where Summer would be asking questions all the time."

Beth held up a hand to Jack to stop him from asking anything else "don't worry Jack we are getting to some of your questions I promise."

Beth sat back in the rocking chair and gave a very contented sigh as she drank from a large mug, of what smelled to Jack like hot chocolate and then looking over the top of the mug, with a lovely frothy brown moustache now curling on her upper lip, she continued with Jack's lesson for the day.

"Right that's the blinkers out the way and I think its time you had a quick history lesson of the rest of the Universe."

Jack looked around the room apprehensively, expecting it at anytime to dissolve away and be replaced by some battle zone, like he had seen in various films. To some degree he was right as the wall in front if him containing the fireplace simply turned into a very large flat television screen and displayed various related images as Beth talked through them.
"Since the beginning of life in the Universe, billions of years ago, creatures have always coveted the possessions of others, be it there own species or another. After war upon war, eventually a truce was reached called the Special Accord of Planets and Species. Peace reigned for millennia, obviously there were minor fracases, some of which did last centuries, but as a rule of thumb it was generally peaceful in the Universe. Then ten thousand years ago or so, planets and sometimes entire systems started to disappear without a trace. These were generally unpopulated ones but eventually one was attacked which had a significant population and a fair degree of technology."
Pointing at the screen, Beth showed Jack various clips of black clad armoured aliens romping quite literally through the defenders and there equipment. What amazed Jack was the lack of future technology being used. As far as he could see they were all using swords and double bladed staffs to fight.
"Where are all the laser guns and explosions?"
"They didn't work on the invaders Jack."
Jack gave Beth a frown that said 'what!'
"Both sides fought with laser and projectile weapons to start with but it soon became apparent that this merely slowed them down and didn't actually stop them. The invaders preferred to use swords and beam weapons made of filament light, which can very nearly cut through anything and the defenders eventually had to use the same. In such combat the invaders nearly always won. There armour was nearly impregnable to all weapons, save one eventually."
Jack felt guilty all of a sudden, reached his hand round behind him to feel the handle of his Glade and then with a little panic on his face he stood up and started to pat himself down, growing ever more worried as he could not find his weapon anywhere.
Beth sighed and said "Jack, we're in a virtual world! There is no Glade here unless the blinkers allow it."
Jack stopped patting himself down and sat back slowly on the couch with an expression of stupidity written all over his face.
Then another question came to mind "what about space battles?" he asked.
"Battles in space are exciting, bright and deadly. Once your shield has been depleted then its usually game over."
"What I meant was, why don't they just bomb the planet from orbit or something?"

"Because if you bomb a planet from orbit then you end up with no planet. If all the sides kept on escalating there bombing, until it reaches a point where the planet is left uninhabitable, then you have no reason to want the planet and can't influence the locals because there not alive or not there any more! Basically space battles do take place with high powered weapons and similarly equipped counter measures, but most battles for a planet happen on the planet itself. No one wants a dead planet, us or them."

Beth stopped for a moment to sip some more hot chocolate and to give Jack time to think, she then continued with "then one day the invaders attacked a species that had existed in our Universe that no one had ever seen or only vaguely heard of before. They had wanted to stay out of the way of the various conflicts and traded only occasionally through third parties. They were basically unknown until the invaders attacked there region of space and they asked for help in there defence. It then came to light that they were descendants of what the other races call the Observers and called themselves Watchers, with basically the same task of collecting and interpreting the rest of the Universe, but from a point of non-interference. It was at this point the allied forces found out the true name of the invaders, the Furrykin!"

Jack looked around the cabin and wondered if he could have a succinct version of events, as surely his current outside capturer must be wondering what is taking so long.

"Right, you've explained nothing to me really that makes any real sense, so could I have the short version before my furry capturer gets suspicious?"

Beth sighed, there were so many things he needed to know but maybe right now was not the time, so she threw her mug in the air and it disappeared with a pop.

"As I mentioned earlier this is a virtual world and an hour in here equates to roughly a second in real time" she held up her hand as Jack meant to interrupt again "don't bother asking any more questions Jack until I'm finished."

"Summer your questioner is not your enemy or bad or evil, she is simply following the best path for you and her species. She will also expect you to have certain information downloaded, maybe not understood but available to you when you are asked a question or you require an answer yourself. That will become clearer when you take the blinkers off. What you need to know is why you!"

"That would be nice, because so far not a single person has told me why?"

Beth paused with her mouth open in telling Jack why, she was not sure whether he was fully prepared for all the reasons and especially not the how. Better she thought to give him a general clue rather than all the facts right now.

Crossing and uncrossing her long slender legs Beth leaned forward in her seat and said to Jack "you were ab...".

Jack opened his eyes, his heart skipped a beat as all he could see was the dripping jaws of some monster about to chew his face off, with exceptionally sharp and vicious teeth right in front of his eyes.

Then just as suddenly the jaws were pulled away and Summer was stood smiling at him, tossing the silver matchbox from one hand to the other "good, your back. Vowke who are the Furrykin?"

Unbidden to Jack he found his mouth open and the answer came pouring out "as far as is currently known, the Furrykin are an Alien species to this Universe, whose ultimate aim is to subdue each Universe in turn with an as yet unknown purpose. They are fuzzy brown or orange variants in colour, weigh an average two hundred kilograms and have multiple followers to there cause. There most effective and dangerous ally is a species called human and..." Jack interrupted himself by clamping his jaw shut. He then turned unbelieving eyes to Summer, who looked down in sympathy at him, she was expecting an intelligent question along the lines of 'is this accurate' or even 'how's this possible', what she actually got was "huh, what?"

Summer leaned further towards Jack's face and could see that was all she was going to get as a response "for a supposedly intelligent species, you must have been the runt that proves the litter."

Jack sat with a confused and slightly lost expression on his face, very much the sort of look you might expect to find on a curious puppy, that had followed and now climbed off a merry-go-round used by teenagers. It was a face of dizzy confusion, loss and had a sickly green caste to it.

Summer rolled her eyes in frustration and said "you know the phrase, the exception that proves the rule?"

For a moment Jack sat there saying nothing and then replied slowly "yes, I've heard the phrase but honestly it never made any sense the first, second or twentieth time I heard it."

Summer growled at Jack and bared her teeth, Jack's expression of helpful incompetence drifted off his face and was replaced with "anger, you look angry for a human?" said Summer.

"Wouldn't you be, if you were being accused of starting a galactic, Universe expanding war?"

Summer stroked her long snout in thought and paced around the room. The one thing Jack had noticed about his inquisitor was that no matter what she was doing, she really could not stop moving or twitching in some way. It was like she had to be continuously moving to prove to herself that she existed. With that in mind his next question was obvious, although to Summer it was darn right insulting "why do the Raifoon jiggle about so much?"

Summer opened her mouth to answer, then looked down at her hands and her thumbs twisting around themselves and growled at Jack from behind bared teeth.

"I'm guessing that isn't a smile then?"

"No Jack, this is my annoyed face!"

Summer turned away and stalked off round the room, getting rid of her nervous and angry energy, as much as she could before she bit his head off.

Jack watched her do several circuits of the room, as she did so he could see that she went from stomping with hunched shoulders to being almost lithe and breezy in her walking as she calmed down.

Jack pulled the blinkers off his forehead where Summer had pushed them, he slid them down round his neck and they hung there quite comfortably because of the strap holding them in place. He sat there for a moment longer waiting for Summer to ask another question and then realized he could ask himself a question.

"Why was Earth attacked?" he asked out loud, he waited for a few seconds and when nothing was forthcoming he asked the question of himself again and then again. After several attempts he turned to Summer, whom was now leaning easily against one of the table like benches and said "it's not working luv!"

"For Crote's sake did the Vowke teach you nothing!"

"Obviously not, otherwise I would have an answer to my next question which would be 'why am I not answering my own question'?"

Jack looked down at the floor for a moment, realizing how actually mad that sounded and then asked of no one in particular "I must be mad expecting answers from myself, when I don't really know the questions to ask anyway and I sound really stupid to anyone else listening!"

Summer waved her arms about in frustration and said to Jack with some force in her voice "don't you remember anything I've taught you? Doesn't the past register with your species?"

With a frown on his face Jack asked "when did you teach me anything?" Then a strange burbling ring like tone could be heard, Summer turned away placing a hand up to her furry pointed ear and said "go."

Whilst Summer answered her call, Jack sat wondering why he could not answer her question using the 'Vowke' phrase, the only answer he could come up with was that he needed to be using the blinkers. Which for some reason gave him a headache and were now turned off but did not Beth tell him the information was downloaded into his brain and all he had to was request the data? Whatever was going on was confusing Jack beyond measure, there were so many questions he wanted answers too and simply was not getting.

The main reason seemed to be that he was not asking the right questions and someone or something else seemed to have an agenda for him.

Ultimately what Jack was feeling could be described as following a path, although he was seeing it more like having been pushed into a raging river torrent heading to the sea. The only consolation he felt, was that currently he was not wet.

Chapter 15 : The Commander.

Jack sat on his own staring around the room, brushing his shoulders free of invisible dandruff and not for the first time wondered what had caused the mess. Everything in the room looked either repaired or about to be repaired, with various scorch marks and cracks in the walls.
Finally Summer finished her nodding and grunting session with whomever she was communicating, ending with a grunt and whistle, turning to Jack she said "follow me."
She quickly turned and walked to the door which stuttered open, power walked out and down the corridor. After only a few long strides she realized Jack was not following her, she stalked back to the room, where the door still had not quite finished opening yet and peered inside.
"What do you think your doing Jack, we have to go!"
Jack crossed his arms and said "why, where and just why really?" being dragged along this rivers event path was starting to get on his nerves. Especially as he had no idea where the rudder was to steer the thing, or even if there was a rudder or even a boat.
"Because I'm telling you to and we don't have much time."
"Time for what?"
Summer ground her teeth in frustration, she could not call the guards to drag him out, as she needed his help, if not now then later and he was unlikely to give it if he felt forced. It was his rebellious nature that could derail everything, even if it was the right thing to do for his own species. Slowly she calmed herself down by wrapping her flexible thumbs around her wrists and counting under her breath.
Finally after a few moments, she turned to Jack and said "because we need you to stop the invasion of Earth."
She was expecting Jack to say something along the lines of 'really, I'll be right with you' but as was becoming annoying with him he said "why, hasn't it already happened?"
"Yes but your going to undo it! Its either that or we can send you for interrogation after all and a good probing" at the word probing Jack jumped to his feet, feeling his behind. Summer carefully filed this bit of information for potential use later, if he did not do as he was told.
Jack for the first time actually looked interested she thought and replied "okay then, lets go."
He almost bounced across the room and swept past Summer out into the corridor.
Summer watched in surprise as he walked away down the damaged corridor and sighed to herself, he turned around and looked at her saying "it's not this way is it?"
Summer shook her head and walked calmly off in the opposite direction.

Thinking hard was not a phrase or action that normally occurred in Jack's world, which therefore meant he was struggling a bit, mentally. He was also thinking for a change that he might actually need some advice, other than some random alien telling him what to do. At the very least someone who seemed to know what was going on.

As they walked down another corridor Jack asked Summer "could one of my friends come with us please?"

He paused as a thought struck him "I say a friend, more of a leading accomplice really."

"Who do you want Jack?" replied Summer with another sigh.

Jack was tempted to ask for Claire but was not sure he could take the continuous sniggering, so instead he asked for "Sara I think" whilst staring absentmindedly in no particular direction.

Summer looked back over her shoulder quickly and caught Jack apparently staring at her "your looking at my rear again Jack hmm?"

Jack focused his eyes briefly, blinked in surprise and then quickly looked up at the ceiling, brushing his arms with his hands. It then occurred to him that this was the first time he could remember really looking at her, admittedly very attractive posterior and he had not taken any notice of it whatsoever. It had just been somewhere to rest his eyes as they walked along, the thought occurred to him then that he could be been done for sexual harassment or malicious eye lingering back on Earth. He wondered what offense it might cause here with aliens and on top of that inter species relations were probably really badly frowned upon. The punishments would probably be eye-watering and the pain would probably start with excruciating.

"Sorry I didn't know I was staring" and then to quickly change the subject he asked "are we on the way to collect Sara?"

"Oh I think you did Jack and yes."

Summer walked down various corridors with Jack at a brisk pace, with Jack looking around at the odd damage on the walls. The corridors had obviously once been a sort of white metal at some point, with some walls, floors and ceilings now a pristine white finish but these were rare. There were also twists, creases and apparent folds in the corridor itself, when Jack ran an experimental hand over the top of one it felt strangely smooth, like seeing a crease in a shirt but feeling nothing when he ran a hand over it. What was more common was the blast damage, looking like several fireballs had been fired down the passageway, followed by deep clawing talon marks from some huge angry bird. Or to Jack's mind a Dragon fighting and mincing its way down the corridor like an angry rhino in a leather goods shop.

Summer continued her swaying walk, ignoring Jack staring around like a tourist in a nuclear power plant trying not to touch anything, with her feet making the staccato sound of polished heels on stone. As they walked round another corner in the corridor, Jack could see his fellow humans in there locked room at the end. He glanced down at Summers furry brown shoe free feet, with streaks of golden blonde mixed in the fur.

"Must be the toenails" he thought out loud.

"What is?" asked Summer.

"The tap tap tap as we walked down the corridor."

Summer smiled at Jack, showing quite a lot of sharp teeth and said "do you know your one of the few people to notice" with that she lifted one of her feet towards his face. This made Jack feel a little ill, mainly because her knees bent the opposite way to his own.

After a moment of mental readjustment, Jack looked at the base of her foot, he could see that she had four very long toes. The forth one though, on the inside of her foot, seemed to be a fatter stronger version of her curly thumb. They were of course covered in a very fine fur and Jack found himself thinking he had seen them before somewhere. Frowning to himself he moved closer and could see that on the base of her foot was what appeared to be a sandal, made of some flexible light coloured metal. Jack reached out an hand to touch the metal and Summer slammed her foot down on the floor with a loud clang, saying quickly and quietly "your not doing that again Jack."

Summer stormed off into the prison cell to fetch Sara, whilst Jack stood muttering to himself "what does she mean again, that's, oh I don't know, maybe the third or fourth time she's made out that we've met before and I'm sure I would remember an alien like her?"

There was also the footwear issue, he was sure she had been wearing Wellington boots earlier, he was not one to register these things normally but when had she changed them? It might have been all to do with the Blinkers he thought, as he twisted the things hanging around his neck. Then he noticed a thick black rubber band, about halfway up her shapely calves, it was the same shiny colour as her boots had been. As Jack watched Summer collect Sara, the band dribbled quickly back down to her feet, coating her lower legs in shiny black Wellington boot or as he thought of them, door knocker boots.

A few short steps later and the sound of the door attempting to swoosh shut cleanly, stuttering behind them and failing could be heard. Sara was now stood in front of Jack in the corridor and she did not look well at all to Jack's eyes. She looked as pale as death, might be the best way to describe her, with blue lips, sunken eyes and an expression of hopelessness.

It was then that Jack remembered that not only were the blinkers used for teaching, that they were also an highly effective prison tool, as the wearer could be told that anything was around them, or in them or even happening or not happening to them at all.

Jack looked at Sara's Blinkers compared to his own and they were of similar design, looking for all the world like wrap around sunglasses but without the anti-glare bit. They lenses neatly covered the eyes and the ears were covered by the strap meaning they could fit anyone or anything's head. The curved lens on Jack's were opaque but on Sara's they were currently green.

Summer walked round in front of Sara, Sara stood in front of Jack looking like she was expecting to be shot by a firing squad. Summer slowly pinched the centre point between the lenses, the green colouring simply glugged out of each lens like water from a leaky glass. Sara started to blink as her eyes cleared, a look of surprise crossed her face, all of a sudden she could see she was stood in a mildly ravaged corridor and not in front of an firing squad.

Jack could now see her eyes with out the green haze in front of them, they looked even more haunted than they had done with the green filter over the top. They were all dark and brooding, like only the best Gothic make-up could achieve if it had been applied in a darkened room, at night, with no moon and an pencil torch.

Sara's first reaction on seeing Jack was a snarl coming out of her mouth, followed by some odd language that Summer, who was now stood to one side, did not understand either.

Jack asked carefully "are you okay?"

Sara leant heavily against the corridor wall and put her hand up to her Blinkers, slowly with exaggerated care she pulled them off and held them in her hand at arms length. She then turned them over cautiously, eyed them carefully, let her hand slump against her thigh and then let them dangle from her hand like rubber banded swimming goggles.

She then looked up and said to Jack "I'll be alright in a few minutes … but, I'm guessing we're fairly important to have been given Blankers?"

Jack looked over at Summer and asked "Blankers?"

Shrugging Summer replied "it's the old name given to them, mostly by prisoners. Although I will say that she isn't in the system as a criminal, so where she learned the name from I don't know?" Summer asked this looking at Sara carefully.

Sara gradually stood straighter, turned to face them both and said "I've used them before, but these look newer?"

"Yes they are" said Summer "and now we must go to see the Commander."

Jack offered a hand to Sara, the look of pure hatred he got from her as she looked at his hand, following on up to his face, made him quickly put it behind his back and step away with some haste.

Slowly at first but gradually picking up speed they followed Summer, who stood impatiently tapping her foot at a junction in the corridor further down.

Jack walking beside Sara leaned over and asked "do you know what's going on?"

Glancing at Jack she replied "not as such no, but I'll hazard a guess it's to do with you."

Jack looked annoyed "yes, I had worked that one out for myself thank you, otherwise I'd still be in a cell with you lot" Jack sighed and then asked "but do you know why?"

"No Jack I don't for sure but I think we'll find out shortly, as it's quite rare to meet the Commander of the fleet and not be in chains!"

Summer stopped in front of a pale blue panel on the wall, which she swiped a hand over, a glass fronted doorway then slid into view in the wall like it had simply rotated round from somewhere. When Jack looked inside it was quite a large white tube with a flat top and bottom, there was a black hand rail running around the inside.
Summer stepped impatiently forward, muttering to them both "it's a lift."
The glass door of the lift made a long zip like noise as it quickly opened for Summer to walk through.
Sara followed her into the lift, leaving Jack stood in the corridor still marveling strangely at the lift, there was something unusual about it that he could not quite put his finger on.

Both females, unbidden by whatever runs through there minds, waved at him quickly to get in the lift at precisely the same time and with slight frustrations in there waves. Jack almost jumped into the lift, he would not say he had jumped, just moved quickly to fend off any possibility of verbal abuse or allegations of lethargy that might prevail now or later.
Summer then said "lift, forty two, Commanders lounge."
The door swooshed with a zip sound cleanly shut behind Jack, with not a stutter or jerk whatsoever, this came as a slight surprise to Jack.

As the lift started to move Jack asked Summer "why do most doors only make sounds when they shut and this one made a zip noise when it opened like a men's trouser zipper?"
Summer and Sara gave Jack what could be called withering looks, trying to make him see he was asking ridiculous questions, when there were far more sensible questions he could be asking.
The two females exchanged a look and Sara said "Jack they make a click and a coo noise when they open, to let you know there opening and a similar click noise and a coo when they shut, maybe in reverse though" she added thoughtfully.
By the tone she had finished the sentence Jack guessed there would be no point in arguing with either of them, it would just have to be put down to another thing he would not get an satisfactory answer to.
Sighing Jack asked "so who are we going to see now?"
Summer answered "the mission Commander and before you ask anything stupid Jack, it was him who asked us to privately find out why your underground base had been so nearly thoroughly destroyed. It was after the data recovery that he asked us to find you."
Jack feeling incensed and frustrated folded his arms, from between gritted teeth asked in a semi-calm voice "okay, and again I'll ask, why me?"
"You'll find out in a minute Jack I promise, when you meet the Commander he'll explain everything."

They stopped talking as the obligatory lift music started, Jack listened for a moment to the music playing, cocking an ear in mild surprise. Obviously it was going to be the same the Universe over in every lift, the music being catchy in some way, so much so that you knew it was going to stay with you for at least a day and at the same time lightly annoying in the way it was absorbed into your skull, like a drill boring in.

The lift stopped with a slight bump, presumably to let you know it was time to escape the mind melting music and to wake you up. The doors opened and Jack stood fixed to the spot by the view like a dribbling child in front of sweet shop.

After several seconds the two women stood behind Jack had had enough, both together pushed Jack out of the lift with impatience expressions on there faces, there minds linked in solidarity against men folk in general in that one moment.

Jack stumbled forward out of the lift and would have landed flat on his face but for being saved by an large oval oak table, that stood in the centre of the foyer. He caught himself with his hands on the table edge, bending both of his thumbs in the process and smashing his knee on the table as he had tried to rescue himself, before his thumbs were bent back any more.

Jack stood back from the table, favouring his left leg, he would have been rubbing his knee in agony but instead was pressing both of his thumbs together in torture and trying not to swear.

Jack turned round to the two women, that had by now stepped out of the lift and said "thanks!" in an sarcastic groan.

Neither of them offered any sympathy or chose to reply, because Summer went striding off to the other end of the large room and Sara was looking around with look of wonder on her face.

Jack took stock of his injuries and deduced that given a few minutes and some walking off, he would be fine if a little limp. This gave him time to look properly around the room, without being pushed through it and he was mightily impressed with what he saw, why it was on an space ship though he had no idea.

The place looked like a cross between a grand central station and a Gothic church, with high vaults and cornucopia on almost every surface and of many descriptions. Surprisingly, given the nature of churches to be dark, this foyer area was incredibly light and airy. It was as if some parts of the design actually gave off there own light, the main thing that made it stand out was the fact it was not white in any way shape or form. Jack looked down at the floor and changed his mind, the floor was plain white, again!

Sara and Jack walked slowly around the big oak like polished dining table, one on either side, the table was easily over fifty meters long as Jack paced it out to the end. The table had no breaks in it, it was just one long and thick piece of wood, with knots and circles like any tree would have had.

"This tree must have been massive to start with!" said Jack looking underneath as they walked along its length. Not only did it appear to be very long but over four meters wide and at least four inches thick. Jack had been running his hand along its entire smooth shiny length, apart from the last few meters where he had stopped to look underneath at the ornate legs holding the thing up. The legs were in themselves like tree trunks but with claws, toes and in some cases snake like appendages.
"Who are you calling a tree?" said a woody voice.
Jack jumped and looked around wildly for the voice.
"I think he meant you?" said another woody voice too.
Jack looked around trying to find the other voice, with his eyes turning in his head for a moment.
"I thought he meant you" said the first woody voice.
"Actually I thought he meant you too, being that your so wooden ha ha" said the second woody voice.
"Now that's not very nice coming from someone who is a chip off the old block" said woody one.
"Your barking up the wrong twig, you know" said woody two.
"Oh just leaf it alone will you, can't you see he's a wearing animal?" replied woody one.
"Your one to talk, given what you ate earlier and your all cellulose anyway!" finished woody two.

If wood could talk this is exactly how Jack envisioned it, halfway between a rumble of heavy leaves and a bark, although how they were actually talking was another question entirely.
Jack looked on bewildered, trying to work out where the several different voices were coming from, it was difficult as they were all resonating from under the table. Eventually the wood jokes stopped and one of the voices asked "so what do you think?"

Jack leaned away carefully from the table and its many legs, Sara did the same on the opposite side and both backed up to the walls behind them. Jack knocked against something hard, cold and decidedly pointy behind him. Turning his head he saw the stone walls had various benches, tapestries, weapons and armour hanging up or leaning against them, like some vast show of historic warfare but without the human shapes or edge. The suits of armour were what really gave it away, they appeared to be made of metal, were of the shiny steel variety but no human, maybe an gymnast, would have been able to fit in most of them. They were to Jacks eyes the oddest shapes for armour but they were made for a different selection of species after all.

There were also no chairs visible for the table, Jack guessed that they probably came from another room somewhere. There was not really any space along the walls for anything else next to the metal collections, a chair might look out of place here unless it was made of iron and built by maidens.

The second voice spoke again, this time quite insistent and still buried under the table "look, what do you think alright?"

Jack looked back under the table and the second woody voice asked "am I asking this in English or what! Okay lets try again, what do you think?" this final part was said slowly and with the force of voice you might have expected from something that can brush aside buildings, concrete and even metal, given enough time.
Still open mouthed Jack said with some degree of uncertainty, mixed with curiosity "who are you?"
"I'm the one talking to you num nuts!" said the second woody voice.
"So what do I think of what exactly?" asked Jack slowly and with a tinge of worry.
"Our act?" said woody one.
"The voices?" asked Jack.
"The one liners and play on words of course."
Jack paused in answering, he believed it always paid to tell the truth, unless you were talking to a women, that never worked "it was a good act, although I 'wood' say it needs time to 'grow'."
      Summer walked back into the foyer with a look of frustration on her face, glanced around the room until she found Jack leaning down under the table and said brusquely "will you stop mucking about and get a move on, we haven't got all day!"
Jack stood up shaking his head and mumbled to himself "must be going mad, thinking I'm talking to a table!"
"Who said you were talking to a table?" came a resonant woody reply.
"Sounds like he banged his head" said the first woody voice.
"Hmm that'll be the root of the problem, heh heh" replied the second woody voice.
"Still with the twee jokes!" said the first woody voice.
"It's the trunk of our root bee-leaf" what followed could only be described as laughter, it sounded more like someone sawing a branch with a bendy saw and a lot of reverb.
Summer sighed knowing how sarp's struggle with things that did not sit right in there memory and with some steel in her voice said "show yourselves you lot!"
Nothing happened, so with some force but quietly she said "NOW!"
Jack and Sara looked on with open mouths, as the table and its legs before them simply split, cracked and creaked into hundreds of shady looking humans.

Chapter 16 : Newish Friends.

Since waking up a few days ago, Jack had seen several strange things but this was one of the best he had seen so far. Each one of the human shaped creatures, which were presumably male and female denoted by the tactful placement of leaves and vines, ranged in size from four inches in height to over twenty feet. They all looked human, if oddly shaped, shaded and distinctly earthy in appearance, unbidden to Jack came the words "Tree Pixies."
The Tree Pixies looked at one another briefly in slow surprise, then almost as one turned to face Jack with various grimace like expressions and one said in a low growl "get him!"
Jack started to back away muttering, as the crowd or even mob, started to ebb forwards like a woody tidal wave "w wh … why?"
"No one calls us Pixies."
Jack backed up, finding a wood panel wall behind him, "Elves?" hazarded Jack banging his head on some animal trophy hanging on the wall above him. Whatever the animal had been, it was made mostly of long burnt orange fur hanging from a protruding snout. Whether that was its natural colouring or the end result of being hung on the wall, he had no idea, either way the hairy fond's were now tickling his ears.
"No one calls us Elves either, of any description and keeps the ability to speak" said the woody voice.
"Or keeps the ability to breath" said not an Pixie or Elf.
"Or pee" said another.
"Pee?" squeaked Jack peaking through some orange fur.
"Yeah, imagine the back pressure after five minutes of just worry alone heh heh" said the first woody voice.
Jack's nerves were never very good, he got through a normal day mostly on denial; the worry as he looked around the Tree People advancing on him, was mentally starting to trickle unbidden from somewhere.

With each step the Tree Pixies took they creaked, it was the type of creak that only the best horror story castle door could manage after weeks of deliberate hinge mismanagement and a lack of oiling. With each step came a veiled threat, magnified a thousand fold by the many creatures flowing towards him.

Jack looked at Sara and then at Summer with panic on his face, Sara was by the door white faced and Summer was trying hard not to laugh by covering her quivering jaws.

When the shortest Pixies were within touching distance to Jacks knees, with the tallest leaning over obscuring the light, they stopped dead, creakily turned to one another and started to laugh in there bendy saw twanging way, slapping one another on the backs in good humour.

Jack looked up and down in confusion, unbidden he found he had covered his delicates with one hand, the other was waving around a finger in a 'no no' fashion.

Summer had by now recovered her composure and said with a slight smile in her voice "don't worry Jack, these 'Tree Pixies' like humans, after all your species gave them shape and meaning."

The one nearest Jacks knees made a 'so so' shrug and smiled a toothy white grin at Jack, it was only then that Jack, who had been looking round in blind panic, noticed for the first time that they were now clothed. There were still a few creatures with strategically placed flora and fauna, but as he watched they would step behind or through another tree and came out clothed, even the truly massive ones were wearing a large figure hugging suit. The clothes they were wearing were generally all woodland shades, coloured and shaped so that he did not notice the hats, coats, suits, dresses and many other items of clothing he would have thought of as human. Jack stared at them all in wonder, as he realized what a riot of colour there actually was, you just had to think in wood variants from black all the way through to white, all blended together in the forest. They also seemed to like hats, almost all of them were wearing a hat, with every conceivable design and fascination on display.

Jack asked "gave them shape and meaning?"

Summer replied "meet the 'Green Army'."

Jack stared and after a few seconds said "if you lot are the Green Army, protecting us from the rest of the Universe, why didn't you stop the invasion?"

"Ah well there's a bit of sticky sap there my boy" said an old sounding woody voice.

"Yep, what you might call a legal twisting of the vines" came the first woody voice.

"Or even a lost ring in time" finished the old voice.

Summer interrupted the tree pixies with a "grr, will you stop it with the woodland analogies!"

She turned to Jack and said "there's a great deal of politics involved, which we're hoping to undo shortly, as to your next question I can hear bubbling away in your brain. The Green Army have lived for centuries on your planet but recently have had to reduce there numbers, purely because of your species destruction of it and of course picture technology."

"You mean filming them" Jack paused in his reply and then asked "you're where the pixie and fairy stories come from?"

The Green Army managed to look guiltily at one another and then one of the suit wearing pixies strode forward saying "we apologize unreservedly for the ancestors and our own recent misinformation" came the first woody voice from a standing height of twelve inches.

Jack looked down at the foot tall well dressed man wearing a trilby and said "you guys are the reason people have seen fairies, pixies and elves?"

"Yes, we do most humbly apologize for the confusion thrown on your species."

Jack waved his hand in an jovial form of dismissal and replied "nah you really needn't worry, it's just great to meet the source of all those stories and just goes to show we aren't totally mad, as a species."

Jack could see a visible sense of relief gradually sway through the crowd of wooden people in front of him, like a gentle wave lapping over the sea shore or breeze brushing through a forest. His reply had been exactly what the 'Green Army' had wanted, needed for centuries. Since the stories and pictures had been recorded by humans, they had been worried that one day they would be held accountable for influencing a reservation planet and potentially making the experiment invalid. The volume of compensation payable would be immeasurable. Jacks offhand comment, though unknown to him, had just given humanity one of its greatest allies.

"Is it alright to call you Pixies though, I mean it sounds so much more friendly than the Green Army?" asked Jack.

The woody creatures turned to one another in some form of rustling conversation, eventually the suited knee high trilby wearing Army member turned to Jack and said "that is acceptable."

As they were talking Jack felt a wave of almost palpable relief from the Pixies, then he saw the colour of there clothing and even there skin or bark becoming brighter and more vivid. Jack stared as the colours changed, he was staring so hard that they actually noticed.

"What!" said the lead woody voice.

"Your clothes … your skin, there all changing colour that's what!"

Looking down at himself the Pixie shrugged and said "and?"

Jack shook his head and turned to Summer looking for an explanation. Summer sighed and said quickly "there clothes are made from bark, that means they can change the colour as and when they wish."

Summer then turned, prowling back towards the ornate church door that she had been walking backwards and forwards through. Jack turned to follow, as did Sara and it was only on the opposite side of the door, when it swooshed shut, that Jack realized that if they were wearing bark clothing, they were wearing there relatives!

Outside of the ornate church and station look, back in an white corridor again, Jack was feeling lost. The only thing was, he was not exactly lost as such, he just did not know where he was going or why? He could not properly describe the emotion to anyone, except to say he thought it might be like the feeling of meeting someone on an aeroplane and having a lovely conversation. Right up to the point where you mention how much your looking forward to reaching your destination and the person replying 'oh we're not going there.' With realization slowly dawning, like water running down your back and turning to ice, that your on the wrong flight.

As the three of them walked down the endlessly curving white corridor, Jack started to get more nervous by the second, as he realized the person they were going to meet was the leader of the attack on Earth.

Eventually Summer stopped, turned and walked through an open door in the corridor, Jack had started to shake in nervousness as the door 'swooshed' shut behind him. The three of them now stood in an oval chamber with double doors at either end that were shut and probably locked, the walls were an glassy white, with thick black lines where you would expect the corners and edges to be. Summer stepped forward onto a thick black outlined square, somewhere near the middle of the oval room. Then blue coloured laser lines scanned her up and down like she was stood in a flat tube, a light ding sounded and she stepped off to stand by the far door. Sara did the same, then turned and faced Jack, standing on the other side of the door, she then started to tap her foot in impatience, not nervous at all thought Jack smiling to himself.

Jack then reluctantly stepped up to the black outlined square on the floor, sighed to himself stepping into the box and waited for the scanner laser to pass up and down him. As soon as it touched his feet the laser light turned from a friendly blue, to orange, to red and then black, then every conceivable alarm sounded in the chamber. Jack had his hands in his pockets, he sighed deeper, waiting to be electrocuted was never fun but on passed experiences a shocking experience was to be experienced. Suddenly the alarms were cut off, sounding like they were not very happy about it, they seemed to grumble and fade away in the background like a teenager sent to there room without tea but secretly knowing they have a stash of digestives hidden away for a just such an eventuality.

The oval chamber doors opened in front of Jack, Summer and Sara stepped through followed by a smiling cautiously Jack. As he stepped through the bright light of the door, he could hear an awful lot of mumbling creature noises, the sort of sound you might expect from the hippopotamus annual general meeting of snorters and affiliates. These creatures were stood all around the room, appearing to grumble to one another, whilst aiming various pointy and non-pointy gun like weapons in Jack's direction. As Jack walked forward, each gun muzzle followed him like the extravagant weapon was an iron filing and Jack was the overly large magnet.

"Well don't worry Jack" came an jovial sounding voice at the far end of the room "come forward."

Jack glanced around the bright room, it looked like an Egyptian style chamber, all pillars made from marble and a sandstone floor. The sandy looking walls had every surface painted with pictures, in the style of Egyptian tombs Jack had seen on television. The only real difference was that the hieroglyph like words and pictures contained slightly more alien looking creatures than Jack had seen on television. They were admittedly also performing what looked like lewd acts in the paintings, with some appearing to wave and use hand signals to encourage the participants. It made Jack wonder how much television editing had gone on back home, to disguise how down right rude the ancients were.

Glancing backwards and forwards between the pictures and the gun totting aliens, Jack finally noticed that a great many of the surrounding creatures had some degree of resemblance to the creatures in the paintings on the walls here and the ones back on Earth.
"Well come forward, I promise they won't shoot" came the friendly sounding voice "much ha ha" it finished.

Jack realized then that he had stopped dead under the glare of alien gun muzzles, while only a few paces into the huge room. In the distance, nearly twenty-five or so meters away, he could just see Summer and Sara stood waiting for him, both apparently tapping there feet in impatience or was it nerves?

Jack started to walk down the avenue of weapons and there associated menace, feeling that at any moment he was going to have to run.
As he reached Summer and Sara, he saw there was a large oak like coffee table on a slightly raised dais, surrounded by several soft looking coloured blocks at the end of the Egyptian themed room.   Stood on the other side of the table was an Raifoon, he had very distinctive, almost glowing, white markings on his face, which stood out starkly against his nearly black fur. Like Summer he wore a jumpsuit with a utility belt around his middle and a sash running over one shoulder to the other. The main difference was that the sash was a dull golden in colour, both sash and belt had attached pouches, with a few knives and what looked like an hand gun in one.

Jack stopped as he approached the end of the table, resisting the urge to check underneath, he guessed that it was probably not a group of Pixies stuck together, it would pay to be more careful from now on though. It was then he noticed that involuntarily he had covered his vulnerable bits again and so quickly moved his hand behind his back. As he did so there was a lot of clicks and similar sounds that could be associated with various weapons being armed, cocked and readied. The sound most alarming though, appeared to be coming from right behind Jack. It involved a low buzzing noise that was getting louder and more high pitched, as it presumably charged itself, making his hair stand on end. Jack made a mental note to move slower in future, especially when weapons were pointed directly at him.

Jack said "hello" in a wavering voice and gave what he thought of as a friendly wave to include everybody around him. The effect of which generated some loud low reverberating noises and added some rather worrying smells to the air. Suddenly needing to hold his nose and gulping for fresh air, Jack turned to see if he could spot the culprit, somewhere in the gaggle of aliens came an mumbled "sorry."
"I should think so" mumbled Jack "that's worse than a skunk who ate a brussel sprout curry!"

For several seconds there was a stand off, with no one seeming to move or even able to breath, which was probably a good thing. A few seconds later a loud strained whine could be heard somewhere in the distance, as some form of air scrubber was suddenly working overtime to remove the impurities from the air.

The Raifoon with the gold like sash then indicated the soft blocks surrounding the oval oak table and Summer said "we should sit now."

Chapter 17 : New Old Friends.

The soft looking multi-coloured square blocks, surrounding the oval table, were a meter in width, height and depth, this was of no help to Jack whom had no idea whatsoever to do with them. He watched closely, as Sara stood next to him sat down in the middle of the top of her block, the cube simply shaped itself into some form of half upright lounger.

Jack having been brought up on Earth was not familiar with these type of seats, looking at Sara he thought she looked quite uncomfortable and so he hesitated. Not for very long though, as Summer, who had already guessed he would pause, pulled him backwards by the scruff of his neck over his cube.

There were several sharp intakes of breath from the surrounding aliens and a few choking noises, as they expected Jack to react differently. In Jack's mind his choice was to either sit down or try hurdling backwards, considering he was one of the few people whom athletics had happened to someone else, he sat down. After a second or two he was sat in a near identical seated position to Sara and was quite relieved at how comfortable it actually felt. It was the right side of comfort but without being so pleasant as to make you feel sleepy.

The group of creatures surrounding him let out an collective sigh of relief, followed by several more unfortunate sounds and smells emanating from somewhere. A small sounding voice choked "sorry, sorry!"

In the background a loud whirring noise of the scrubbers kicking in could be heard again; the golden sash wearing Raifoon sat down, with what looked like an annoyed frown on his face and a crinkled his nose back.

Jack was seated opposite the sash wearer, at the longest point of the oval table, with Sara and Summer sat on either side of him. They sat waiting this way for several seconds, with Jack looking around the room and trying to take the whole thing in. At the other end of the table the Raifoon tipped his head from one side to the other, seeming to be assessing Jack. Then he started to laugh gently and made a small wave of dismissal with an hand.

One of his aides stepped up from behind his seat, Jack heard him ask in an hoarse and nervous whisper "are you sure sir?" whilst his bendy thumbs made nervous shapes around one another.

Without moving his head the sash wearing Raifoon replied "well actually yes I am. If anything was going to happen, it would have done so by now don't you think?"

The aide stepped back cautiously, as did the alien horde, although not far enough in Jack's mind, being that two strides was not that far for some of these long limbed creatures surrounding them with there guns.

The head Raifoon sat forward slightly, looked intently at Jack with his blue eyes and said "well, I apologize for the excessive security measures, I had to be sure the dangerous creature wasn't here."
Jack stared at him questioningly, then checked either side of himself cautiously, looking for the dangerous creature he was on about. Apart from the aliens with there guns pointing at him, there was no other dangerous creatures lurking about that he could see and then something clicked in his head.
With a surprised expression on his face and a raised eyebrow Jack exclaimed "me?"
Sara sighed and smiled to herself, Summer put on her annoyed face and said "of course you Jack! Who else did you think he was talking about?"
In an whiny voice Jack replied "I don't know do I, so far the only explanations I've had have come from a deranged pilot and a robot!"
Summer and Sara exchanged a quick questioning look, before they could ask anything, the sash wearer at the top of the table said "well we don't have time for this. What I need to know from you" he said this pointing at Summer "is this the one we want?"
Summer looked directly at her leader and said with out quaver or hesitation "yes."

Jacks ears were prickling at this point, to such an extent that he thought they would be growing like some puppets excessive nose if he lied, so he jumped in before anyone else with "for what?"
At the head of the table the Raifoon sat straighter in his chair and said calmly "well, to save the Universe of course!"
Jack gulped, looked around the room at the aliens still holding weapons pointed at his head, shook his head and asked "really?"
Summer said "I forgot how thick headed you can be. Yes really you Jack!"
"Well I know your memory is a bit mixed up, but that will pass shortly" said the alien at the end of the table.
Jack turned to look at him and asked "who are you?"
"Well you really don't remember do you Jack? My name is Kraggoor and I am Commander of this mission, I am referred to as Commander, Sir, Master or you may remember me as Slick!" the Commander slipped out his final name with a small chortle, hinting at something that Jack did not understand. The Commander seemed to be laughing at himself for far too long for Jacks liking.

Jack leant forward slightly on his precarious feeling upright lounger to ask another question and felt himself suddenly restricted by hands pressing deeply on his shoulders. Jack did not look for fear of what type of hand, claw, tentacle or other scary appendage may be holding him in place.
It came as some relief when the Commander said "well let him be, we don't have time for all the security checks, just some, as there is a time limit of six weeks! And yes I'm aware there are protocols."

Summer, Jack and Sara all glanced at one another and then Summer asked "I know I'm not privy to all the information. I've brought Jack here and considering what I thought you had planned, I don't understand the time restriction?"

"Well no you won't and until security verify he isn't a threat, which should only take a few minutes, we shall have to sit and wait before we have a private audience."

For all his confidence and assurances, Jack finally noticed that the Gold sash wearing Raifoon was not quite as relaxed as he would have everyone believe. This was given away by the nervous tapping of his toes and the ticking of his bendy thumbs, almost seeming to fence with one another in his palms.

Jack relaxed back in his seat, waiting with the others in there block loungers. Drinks were being supplied to them on little silver trays carried backwards and forwards by, here Jack was reluctant to say it, but 'little green men' were carrying them above there heads because they were only just tall enough to reach the table. They waddled around the table and chairs like slightly plump green avocados, short arms and even shorter legs causing them to sway about, with just there toes visible under there wobbling bellies. The heads were part of there bodies, at least you would call it an head because that was where the ring of eyes were, but they had no neck, just a couple of holes at presumably the front of the little wobbling creatures for there mouths and ears. There eyes, or eye, was a band of coloured hexagonal interlocked pieces, continually running like an sweat band around there entire heads. Jack was reminded of close up pictures he had seen of bees eyes and had always wondered how they saw the world, probably in shades of pink if the eye colouration was to be believed he thought.

The silver trays were placed on little arms that extended out of the cube loungers they were all sat on. Jack looked at the other loungers and could see that the Commanders was gold in colour, with red flashes depending on the light. Summers was a light brown or dare it be called beige and Sara's was black with silver accents. Jack looked down at his own block lounger and was decidedly unsurprised to find it was of the yellow variety.

Jack sniffed his drink, which had been supplied in an foam like cup and was amazed to find that it smelled just like a cup of tea. He had a sip and a smile played over his face as memories of an long forgotten road side cafe came to mind. Jack then turned in his seat and tried to get the attention of one of the avocado looking aliens, eventually resorting to a tap on one of there heads as it ploughed passed.

The creature turned sharply to face Jack with a loud hiss and Jack completely unperturbed said "thank you very much, that has got to be the best cup of tea I've had in years."

The aliens surrounding Jack had all jumped slightly at the hissing noise, expecting some minor nuclear explosive event to occur, they were all surprised beyond there own capacities for speech when the avocado replied "you are most welcome sir."

"That's alright" replied Jack.

The Commander clapped his hands together and with a smile showing most of his teeth, which were very yellow compared to Summers white ones, said "well leave us now, security lock out required."

With a strange mixture of reluctance, relief and smells of worry, the surrounding various races stepped off the slightly raised platform they had been stood on surrounding Jack. They seemed to grumble there way off the dais, still managing to keep there weapons trained on Jack as they ambled away. The last to leave the immediate area were the little green men, each gave Jack a friendly wave, which Jack returned in turn. Then an fog like dome flowed up from the floor in an circle and sealed itself over there heads without a trace.

The Commander turned to Jack, twisted his fingers together in apparent excitement, which looked outstanding to Jack because of his bendy thumbs and said "well alright my little flicker, I know this all makes little or no sense to you at the moment. There will come a time later on when your memories will all fall into place, some of which haven't happened yet and some that have but you haven't happened to them yet and others that you can't remember but will when the puzzle pieces are put together. This will take time and no I don't know how much time, length or period it will take. Suffice to say we really don't have time to explain everything, because, frankly four hundred years worth of memories would take a while."

Sara interrupted with "he's the subject!"
Summer said "yes and the cure."
Sara sat back and with relief in her voice said "he could be the one thing in the Universe that could beat them then?"
The Commander looked at her and said "well he might be, but first we have to sort out the committees mess of an invasion."

Jack sat staggered, they all were talking and pointing at him but at no point had anyone asked his opinion and so he felt it was time to say something "NO?"
The Commander turned to face Jack properly, putting his elbows on his knees leaning forward and saying "well I'm afraid you don't have a choice my friend and yes, we are friends or have been or possibly may be friends in the future. You see either you've got the memory lost in there" the Commander tapped his own head "or it hasn't happened to you yet."
"Hasn't happened to me yet?"
"Argh come on Jack you must have at least have worked out some of what we're talking about?" moaned Sara.
Jack looked round the three faces in the domed room and said with a small gulp "time travel?"
Summer said "but that's impossible!"
Jack stared at Summer "your from the future, you should know nothings impossible!"
"No I'm not, I'm from the here and now and time travel isn't legally possible" Summer paused briefly before correcting herself "well forward is but not backwards!"

The Commander clapped his hands together again, this had started to annoy Jack now, the way every time someone solved something that he himself knew and someone else had only just worked out, he would clap. Although why he knew this and how, was yet another question?
The Commander began to speak in the tone of a story teller, as if he were letting you in on some great secret "well in our Universe traveling forward is easy, after all, we all do it everyday. To go further into the future, you just need to be going fast enough that time in effect moves slower for you than for what your passing" said the Commander wagging a finger in the air. He continued with "but, well, the trick is going back in time, that's the thing that has perplexed scientists for millennia. As far as we know it's impossible to travel back in time from, say now, to five minutes or even five years ago."
The Commander sat back in his seat with an uplifting smile on his face, as if he had just imparted some great universal truth on his subjects, folded his fingers together and just sat there with a grin on his face. Summer found this to be highly annoying, more so than even Jacks stupid comments, at least he had a good reason to be annoyed, as his memories appeared to be all mixed up.
"So what is Jacks mission, as I assume that's what we're here for?" asked a curious Summer.
If at all possible a bigger grin appeared across the Commanders face as he replied "well we are going to send him back in time, to stop the invasion of Earth."
Everyone took a gulp of some description or another and Summer was the first to say "you've just said that was impossible!"
Leaning forward the Commander said "in this Universe it is."

Chapter 18 : The Frost Of Time.

   Still sat in the frosted dome Jack looked down at the small magazine, or more accurately, comic book he had just been handed by Summer. Sara had quickly flicked through it after intercepting it before it got to Jack from the Commander, she had nodded, whistled and said 'ah, now I see!' a lot and passed it to Summer. She in turn had grumbled, 'oohed' and said 'no way' a lot, finally passing it with a look of awe on her face to an frustrated looking Jack.
The Commander leant forward in his seat and said to Jack as he took the booklet "well, read it carefully Jack, it is after all your life's story."
Jack turned it over in his hands, backwards and forwards, noticing that it was made of some kind of plastic that was quite durable and yet this copy was actually quite dog eared.
   The Commander could see Jack was reluctant to open it, after all who wants to read about there life and death story, which has not actually happened to them yet. A story that they knew nothing about and was written by someone else, probably picking out all the juicy bits to embarrass them with.
The Commander said "well don't worry Jack, it doesn't detail your death, mainly because it hasn't happened yet after all, it only covers the basics of your life so far" the Commander chuckled at the word basics.
Jack looked up and said "what basics?"
"Well you'll have to read it to find out won't you!"
Jack finished turning, what he was thinking of as a comic autobiography, over in his hands and looked closer at the cover art.
"Whose in the black armour?" asked Jack.
This time it was Sara's turn to smack her hands, not together but quite hard on the table in frustration and say "it doesn't matter Jack, you just need to look through the thing and do it now!"
   Dutifully Jack flicked through the booklet, not really paying attention but enjoying the artwork, until he got to the end and then he could hear some tut tutting going on somewhere.
Looking up Jack saw it was Sara making the noises "you didn't say I had to read it and anyway there are pages missing" he pointed out.
   The Commander jumped out of his seat and leapt across the table with such speed that Jack threw the comic at him to stop him from attacking him. The look of anger on his face was so fierce, Jack feared that brown trousers may not be enough to cover up the flow of panic.
The Commander scooped up the comic from the table, he seemed to calm down as he flicked through and said "well ah I see, humour, you find it funny to dismantle a Raifoon's faith!"
Jack who had nearly climbed out of his seat backwards, using his rear cheeks, replied cautiously "no, just the page numbers are out of sequence and there aren't enough of them!"

The Commander still standing on the table waved the comic about for a second and then had a slightly closer look. After a few moments of flicking backwards and forwards through the booklet, he turned with a snarl saying "well, open security lock out" he shouted. The frosted dome simply drained away, like a drunken man striking a window and sliding down with a squeaky sound into the floor. The Commander jumped off the table and shouted "well Second, where are you?"
One of the gun wielding aliens said "I'm sorry Commander, but as soon as the dome went up he said he had something important to attend to and walked out."

The Commander looked exceptionally angry, the crew and guards started to point there weapons at Jack again, as if he had anything to do with it. The Commander eventually calmed himself down, enough to notice his crew moving in on Jack, who was looking very worried and trying to sit further back into the seat, hoping the floor might swallow him up.

With great care the Commander turned and said "well Jack is not our enemy! Second is now a traitor and must be stopped at all costs. Third you are now Second and have full authority and benefits without delay."
The Commander paused for breath, as no one had moved and continued "well Second is now a full traitor and must be stopped. Don't stand around, do it and do it now!"

The various aliens quickly left the stage, pulling or unwrapping Quellz devices from themselves, followed by a large hubbub of voices and retreating steps reverberating all around the room.
The Commander slowly sat back down in his blocky box seat recliner and turned to Jack saying "well the pages he has stolen I remember very well, he did an excellent job of putting the book back together again after removing them. He just the made the mistake of not putting them back in didn't he?"
"Okay so it wasn't a test then?" asked Jack slowly.
"Well no Jack, it was a traitor. I expect that with some little investigation my new Second will find that he was bribed in some way."
"We don't take bribes!" bristled Summer.
"Well maybe not when you were trained, but now, it's a new age and he was the fastest promoted Second in history. A mixture of losing the war, meaning short staff, even shorter training and dubious pasts overlooked."

The Commander sighed, using an armrest to rest his jaw on an paw, he looked closely at Jack and asked "well I suppose I should give you the shortened version of your history?"
Jack sat back, for the first time he thought he might actually get his questioned answers, after all the last few days had been manic. Slowly some more blocks formed out of the floor, in various colours ranging from red to green and black.

"Well, ahh more guests, welcome, please take a seat and have some food and drink" said the Commander, standing up briefly to wave a welcome.

Jack turned his head and saw all the previous incumbents of the prison cell on the ship, they had walked in the room from a door somewhere. Slowly they eyed up there new surroundings, with there blinkers resting on there heads or just dangling on the rubber like chains around there necks. After Sara got up and hugged Claire, they all sat back down around the table with Mike, Brian, Sophie and Zoe sitting down very carefully, 'like they had been probed' thought Jack, chuckling to himself.

The little green men appeared, quickly running around the table, placing drinks in front of everyone on the frosted metal and glass oval table. Before running off with tiny slap effects from there feet and touching Jack as each one left.

The Commander said "well I have brought you all here to prove that we now know for sure that we are not all the enemies we thought we once were. Before anyone else makes a comment I will now tell Jack's story, which may make things clearer and yes it will be the short version."

The frosted dome flowed back up from the floor and surrounding them all in its comforting blanket.

Jack looked at the cover of the comic in the Commanders hand, he was holding it almost like a shield against his chest. Jack read the title '4p' again, thinking that it was not much of a title really. The Commander started to tell Jacks life story, in the way a professional story teller might, all rolls and thunders of the tongue to generate an atmosphere with additional suspense.

Jack himself knew very little about his birth or parents, after all he had been too small to remember when and why they got rid of him, he had then been adopted by an amazing couple who had thoroughly looked after him. Jack had never known who his biological parents really were, even after years of research! If he was completely honest with himself it had been a year of searching and all he had heard back, was that they were not interested in meeting him. That was fine by him but the Commander was saying something else entirely about how had he came to be.

"Well now two young humans met a little over thirty years ago whilst at University, they graduated together, got jobs near one another and eventually they decided to move in together. But only after an extended holiday, walking over moorland and digging up geology, did they decide that living together was possible. Whilst wandering through hill and dale, hand in hand, digging for rocks and history they found something. They weren't sure what it was and so took it to the local pub with them. No one knew there what it was either, so they took it to there room in the pub, where it sat on the dresser and watched them. In the morning it was gone and few months later Jack was born."

The Commander paused for dramatic effect, looked at his audience and was met by blank stares until finally Brian said "and? That only means two things really, Jacks parents got busy with it and they either lost it, forgot it or the thing was stolen!"
"That's more than two things Brian" said Zoe.
Brian gave Zoe a withering look and turned back to the Commander to stare at him.
Jack on the other hand had been looking around the table at this group of humans, they were not fazed at what was going on and that was more curious to him than his apparent life story at the moment. Sara caught his eye, with the arrival of the prisoners she had sat in the block next to him again, as the frosted dome had gone back up.
"Jack, your looking at them like you don't know who they are?" asked Sara.
"I don't really, and there talking as if none of this is unusual, as if they understand what's going on. I certainly don't!"
Sara turned to look at the Commander, whom she could see was getting angry and she said "be quiet for a moment and let the Commander finish his story" she said this just loud enough for everyone to hear.
The Commander nodded in Sara's direction and said "well as is usual with most humans, they jump to conclusions and get it wrong" he looked around the faces sat at the table.
"I said Jack was born a few months after there consummation, not nine months, as is usually the case I believe, or that they had any previous intimate moments. This obviously put a strain on there relationship, as neither parent could quite believe the other. So Jack was born and within a week his parents went missing."
"Your leaving things out!" complained Jack, whom had been told something similar.
"Well not much I'm afraid, as we only have the book to go by now, some of the pages are missing and I'm reciting from memory."
The Commander unfolded his legs, which because of the reverse knee joint system made Jack feel quite queasy and he even managed to turn a shade of green.
When he was more comfortable the Commander continued his story "well Jack was eventually adopted by a loving family and lived a relatively normal life, catching frogs, torturing spiders and the other usual child like behaviour that in modern society you would have been flayed alive for!"
Jack sat at the end of the table and shrugged, after all who had not as a child either deliberately or out of fear, ripped a spiders legs off. The other two men in the room were looking everywhere else but at one another, with Claire doing exactly the same curiously. 'Maybe little girls did something similar at some point' thought Jack 'but with dolls instead of animals?'
"Well eventually he got an education, a job and then he went on his first holiday, in how many years was that Jack?" asked the Commander.
"Ten" came the short reply, Jack could not for the life him see where this was going.

"Well ten years before you had a holiday, two weeks in Devon if I'm not mistaken?"

"Yeah so, I went back to visit some relatives."

"Well you told work you were off to the south east of England not the south west, now why would you do that?"

Before Jack could answer the Commander carried on with "well it doesn't matter Jack we know what happened next … you were taken for the first time!"

Jack let his eyes wander round the people at the table, sat in there in cube chair loungers, then he glanced up at the frosted dome surrounding them, all the while trying to find the right words.

Finally Jack admitted something to himself, then with a small sigh mumbled "yeah, it was my first time."

The Commander clapped his hands together in apparent glee, then metaphorically speaking put his Commander hat back on and said with an little iron in his voice "well what happened afterwards Jack?"

With a look of guilt to either side of him, Jack finally dipped his head and said in an small voice "when I got home, I found something where there shouldn't have been something and the Doctor froze it off, okay!"

The Commander sat confused, with his legs folding and unfolding in strange and contorted ways to human eyes. Then Claire started to laugh and after a few seconds so did the other humans. Eventually the thermic blue laser stare of Sara was enough to make Claire suck back her giggling. The problem being that as soon as she looked at Jacks guilt ridden face before answering Sara's stare, she could not control herself and started to laugh a little harder.

The Commander slammed the table with his feet, so hard that all the supplied drinks jumped slightly in the air, some spilled, others spun and Jack caught his before it hit the table again.

Almost shouting the Commander demanded "well, what is the meaning of all this?"

Claire carefully cleared her throat, trying not to laugh and said slowly "you asked if Jack was taken and he took that to mean something of an intimate nature, between two consenting adults, which by the way he left a bit late! It would also appear he didn't use protection and caught something that had to be removed at a later date" she finished with a giggle.

"Thanks, thanks very much!" said Jack mournfully.

"Your welcome" answered Claire.

The Commander sat there for a moment longer, until it dawned on him what Claire was talking about and asked of Sara, out of the side of his mouth "well, what's the normal age?"

"Seventeen, maybe eighteen."

"Well, he was how old?"

"Twenty ish."

The Commander sat back and said after a moments thought "well, he's more like us than you then. Right, back to the story."

"Well, when I said taken" the humans giggled again to themselves "I meant abducted. You Jack were the first human appropriated by aliens for Wiimp experimentation, probing and adjustment."

Instinctively Jack jumped up at the mention of a certain word beginning with 'p', and checked himself, especially the back of him.

The Commander sighed and said "well Jack, it was potentially four hundred years ago, I propose to you that whatever damage was done has either healed, or is there to stay."

Jack sat back down carefully, very carefully, testing the seat as he landed.

"How can it have been four hundred years ago, exactly, he doesn't look that old?" asked Zoe curiously.

"Well Jack has been dated at just over four hundred years old, he has somewhere around four hundred years of worth memory and there are pictures of him throughout the last four hundred years. He's lived a very full life has our Jack, he's just not been aware of most of it."

"So four hundred years for Jack, is last week for us?" asked Zoe sounding annoyed.

"Well as to when he was stolen from your home planet is up for debate, but he was the first to be tested and found that the armour worked for. It fitted him almost perfectly from the start, so they went back and collected more samples from the Earth. As each new piece of armour was updated they tested it on Jack. Jack as you might say was a guinea pig, he has been recorded in many battles laying waste to entire civilizations and planets throughout our history."

The Commander paused and took several sips of his drink, trying to gauge the reaction in the room, especially from Jack. Really Jack just looked confused, disbelieving and about to get angry.

"Well before you deny anything and say it's impossible, we have evidence from all manner of sources, be it video, audio and even genetic material!" said the Commander.

Mike spoke for the first time in an questioning tone "you say evidence, through out time and also you said time travel isn't really possible, is it?"

"Well our sworn enemy the Furrykin."

"And mine" said Sara under her breath.

The Commander glanced at Sara and continued "well they found a way to send combatants back to a battle, almost continuously, so instead of having a thousand different troops fighting, they could have a thousand of the same trooper fighting!"

After a moment of thinking about it Zoe said "so Jack's four hundred years has been sent going backwards and forwards in time then?"

Wiping his muzzle with a paw like hand the Commander continued "well yes, the war with the Furrykin has been going on for centuries, with there black armoured army taking slightly more wins than loses. Then Jack here appeared and the results changed, we have been losing ever since humans were involved. Eventually the Furrykin made the mistake of invading a planet that had an high enough technological level to counter the new armoured menace. They eventually captured Jack and administered a serum, but it took years to take effect, with Jack eventually being lost and then suddenly he appeared here on his own planet, just after the invasion."

Mike asked "time travel is impossible?"

"Well yes it is, only forward in the Universe your in" the Commander said this as if it were obvious.

Then Jack asked "so if I'm a destroyer of worlds, why can't I remember it and I certainly wouldn't have done it?"

The Commander replied "well, it was only recently we discovered that humans have a state that you call a 'coma.' In this state the Furrykin found that you were easily controlled and influenced, leaving you under there power without conscious decisions getting in the way. They could tell you to destroy something and you would do it without question!"

"You mean conscious and subconscious thoughts, don't you?" asked Zoe.

The Commander nodded slowly and then continued "well, if we'd known at the time that you were being controlled by the Furrykin, we would not have started this war with your home, but would have opened up negotiations to find a way of stopping them from using your species."

"So are they using us now?" asked Brian curiously.

"Well they probably have a monitoring ship or station GFG'ed somewhere nearby, there probably sat in there laughing right now, watching us flounder around looking for the enemy, when they've already done the damage by stealing humans from Earth for years. We think they may even have set up a breeding program!"

Sara shifted in her seat, rested an hand on her chin and said "let me get this straight. Jack here, was abducted and experimented on over many years. He has been sent backwards and possibly forwards in time, fighting you all the time, with no one on Earth any the wiser. Then some benevolent race finds a way to remove the armour. He wakes up in his own house with no knowledge of anything but his own normal life, which you've really messed up by the way and now you want him to help you in some way?"

The Commander looked thoughtful for a moment and then answered with "well, hmm yes pretty much, apart from the removal of the armour."

"You mean he's still wearing it?" Sara said in a panicked tone, whilst climbing backwards over her seat, like she was scrambling her way through a hedge backwards to escape the ravenous tiger that was Jack. Summer reacted quickly too, she jumped up from her seat, banging her shins on the oval glass table, which made Jack wince. Not because of the sound but because of the reverse knee action going on below her green shorts, down to her boots.

Jack sat watching there reactions quite calmly and then started to pat himself down with a curious expression on his face. If he was wearing any armour he certainly could not find it, then he brushed his arms and ears like he was being lightly tickled by feathers.

Claire then asked curiously of the Commander "so what's your great master plan then?"

"Well it's quite simple really, we're just going to send Jack back to stop the invasion" replied the Commander.

Brian then held an hand up and asked "if it's so simple, why are we being told this and not your actual crew, who are no doubt more capable of sorting this out than we are?"

"Because what he proposes is both illegal and dangerous" said Summer interrupting, whilst climbing back into her seat along with Sara. Both were eyeing up Jack carefully, like he was a delicate explosive that might go off at any time.

"Well unfortunately Summer is correct. As I have said before going forward is easy, but going back is currently not possible in our Universe, because you need to use another Universe with a different set of, shall we say rules."

"But you still haven't explained why it's Jack you need?" asked Claire.

"Well Jack has already traveled in time, to other Universes, to other plains of existence, to alternate places if you will. He will know how, when and where to be, the only problem we have is translation" sighed the Commander.

Sara had regained enough of her composure to ask "translation?"

"Well the armour is part of Jack, the serum that released his mind and woke him up separated the control that the Furrykin use on there subjects. We will need a certain crystal for Jacks armour to work properly and find the correct Universe to travel back using. We therefore need to find a crystal to fix things" the Commander paused in the sentence as if there was something more to add or something that needed to be adjusted, but then he closed his mouth very firmly lest something escape.

The Commander pulled a leaflet out from behind his back and let it float over the glass table top. The leaflet skimmed from one end to the other of the table, it moved like a floating skateboard being flicked about, finally it stopped in the middle and started to perform some funky dance routines.

Claire grabbed at it with apparent annoyance and read out loud "SUDS competition, open to all creatures great and small."

An awkward silence followed as the humans had no idea what the leaflet meant, each in turn had a look and read the leaflet until it got to Sara whom looked at the winners prize section.

She started to laugh and then read out loud "the winner of this years twenty fifth annual Split Universe Drive Surf Competition, will not only receive ten million crowns but get to keep the crystal trophy of light!"

"Let me guess, the trophy is the crystal?" asked Mike.

"Well no, not quite, the trophy contains the crystal and Jack needs to win it" said the Commander.

Jack leant back in his lounger, using his feet to push on the table to lift it slightly, which promptly meant the seat lost its point of balance and tipped over backwards, tipping Jack out with a loud thump. Without even looking round Claire said "it'd be easier to steal it."

Standing, lounging and pausing outside the frosted dome, the alien masses were still pointing there weapons at Jack's vague shadow, albeit in a dejected fashion. They were trying very hard not to appear to be listening, like children stood outside there parents bedroom door as they placed an order with Father Christmas.

The occasional word filtered out from the dome, as one enterprising alien had applied some pointy ear shaped metallic device to the frosty thing by the simple method of throwing it at the dome very hard.

When the dome suddenly flowed down it made a strange metallic boing sound, the pointy metal ear clanged off the floor, bouncing into some corner, making an wailing noise as it flew in the air. The aliens were left stood milling around in surprise, they then all tried pointing out interesting and strange shapes on the walls. Whilst all the time aiming to look completely innocent, like small children surprised by there parents sudden appearance at the bedroom door, where they had been trying listen to them order from Santa Claus.

Chapter 19 : Anger Factor.

The Commander stalked along the corridor to his bridge, he was angry with himself for getting drawn into such a long conversation with these other humans. Not only did they smell funny but they asked nigh on continuous questions of such obviousness that it was beyond annoying. Now they were following him to his bridge, to watch there departure to a Surf competition!
'This may take some explaining to the bridge crew' he thought but 'R&R' was so rare at this time that frankly he would be amazed if anyone objected to some time off. As to explaining the human representatives, he had already thought of that, so as they turned the final corner towards the bridge, four members of his most trusted crew jumped out and arrested the humans.
Suitably cuffed and blinkered he quietly murmured into his own blinker that was on an closed loop with there's "well, don't resist, it'll only be till we get to the SUDS and then you can mingle with your own kind and disappear."
    A few minutes later, after only struggling slightly, Jack found his blinkers taken off and he was stood on the bridge of the ship.
Jack looked round the oval room and found that bizarrely it was exactly as he had expected it to be. The Commander was obviously expecting an comment so Jack said "very nice, very clean and um very white?" with black taped edging, noted Jack.
    There was an large viewing window that took up the front three quarters of the room, from ceiling to floor it must have been twenty feet tall and seemed to bow away from the ship itself. The windows width must have been over seventy feet thought Jack. The rest of the oval shaped room had various panel like screens with the occasional hologram floating out or above it, usually with an Raifoon manipulating it in some way with there bendy thumbs. The only other alien in the room, apart from the humans, was an couple of plant like looking things that appeared to be trees stood around the edges.
    In the centre of the room sat a single chair on an slightly raised plinth that the Commander now surged forwards and sat in. All the time he was walking forward he was issuing commands and orders, until he sat down with an hefty sigh and turned to face Jack.
He said "well, white? That's all your going to say about my Stellar Attack Vessel?"
Jack looked around "it's actually quite big too."
"Well yes, there ain't no illegal suspension fields in here!" he said this nodding pointedly at Jack.
"It wasn't my ship!" proclaimed Jack, remembering the shuttle suddenly.
"Well I'm afraid it was registered to you, so therefore any after market alterations that were made without registered consent are null, void and prosecutable."

The Commander smiled "well what this actually means is that in the current circumstances I own you and your ship."

There was a cough from behind the Commander, the sort of embarrassed nature type cough that meant something was wrong and the bearer does not really want to bring it to there Commanders attention but knows it has to be done sooner rather than later.

The Commander swiveled in his seat to look at his new Second and asked "well, have we found the traitorous thief?" he said this with a small piece of angered phlegm dripping from his jaw.

Gulping slightly the new Second said "um no, not as yet, he seemed to have an exceptional escape plan, planned!"

"Well then why are you not out hunting him down?"

"Um, we have locked the ship down completely, but I thought I should mention we can't prosecute one Jack Jonas Johnstone..." The new Second did not get to finish his sentence, as the Commander leapt from his seat, picked him up by his long furry ears and asked quietly but with some force and no little spittle being sprayed in his face "well, why not?"

Shaking and with feet dangling over the plinth, the new Second thought that maybe this was why his predecessor had defected but answered slowly anyway "we no longer have his ship, or any records of its violations."

The Commander almost screamed "well what, how?"

The Commander suddenly realized that everyone and probably the rest of the Universe too, was watching him right about now, as they were no longer in an state of emergency on the bridge.

He carefully placed his new Second gently back on the floor and with an conspiratorial like whisper leant forward to say quietly "well I wanted to hold his law breaking over his head, as persuasion, so we could use him to get to the Furrykin, because as you are well aware his innocence of the Furrykin has just been released!"

"I'm sorry Commander but shortly after my predecessor stole the book, the ship simply disappeared" the new Second stood there holding his hands out in supplication. He then continued to say "we then checked and rechecked the records and there is a record of a vessel named Hot Shot, with a registration number, registered to one Jack Jonas Johnstone" he said this finally pointing at Jack "but there are no upgrades from the manufactures original state and we have no record of having the ship on board!"

The Commander shook his head, turned and pointed at what appeared to Jack to be a random member of the bridge crew and said "well, set course for the Sud See."

The crewman looked a little surprised and asked without thinking "but that's not part of our mission parameters?" and then saw the Commanders glare, turned and furiously waved his hands over his console screen.

"Well as point of fact we are on mission, it just so happens that I'm bending the rules somewhat" the Commander paused and looked round the room "we have not had some shore leave for some time! Anyone who disagrees may leave now and go hunting for the probably highly weaponized and concealed Furrykin spotter vessel somewhere in this solar system?"
The Commander turned to his new Second and said "well, I shall leave you in charge of my yacht here."
Gulping quickly the new Second replied "you want me to hunt for a hidden vessel in a system we haven't fully scanned yet and your taking the one ship that we know can destroy it to a Surf Competition?"
"Well yes and I'm leaving you with the keys for my personal drinks cabinet on the yacht too!"
In the act of opening his mouth to complain bitterly, the new Second thought out loud "what! THE drinks cabinet, the one with all the squirple containers in?"
"Well yes that's the one, but only to be used at your discretion and carefully mind."
   The look of happiness on the Commanders new Seconds face melted away, like ice-cream from a toddlers chin and was slowly replaced by the realization that he was not going to the one place, to the one event he had and probably never would now ever get to go too. It was a crushing thing to watch but the Commander softened the blow slightly by saying "well, you can of course pick the four other crew members who will assist you in your mission here."
   The looks of excitement and joy that had been on every member of the bridge crews face disappeared, like a lone snow flake that had decided it was the right time to fall from the sky on the hottest summers day in history in the desert. They each in turn looked carefully at there panelled screens, pulling there blinkers down over there eyes, trying to look inconspicuous and not too industrious. All of the crew would have given there right arms from there nan or other grandparent, to be going to the SUDSc. Tickets were so hard to come by that on the black market they had been known to sell for hundreds of thousands of Crowns.
"Well you don't have to pick your crew right this moment, you have an hour to decide whilst we prepare Jack for his imminent freedom!"
   To Jack this all meant nothing of course, a surf competition was a surf competition and anyway it was better to watch it on the telly. You did not get wet, you did not get sand in you sandwiches and above all else you did not get sand in other unmentionable and private places.
So Jack voiced his opinion "first I'm being hunted at home, just because I'm human. Then I'm bundled into a ship I've never seen before, which I'm now told I own and coincidentally you've managed to have lost for me. You've then accused me of starting a war, of which you've now proven I had no awareness of because of the coma like state I was supposedly put in. You've attacked and nearly destroyed my home, I've been drugged, mislead, threatened and now you want me to go to a surf competition?"

One of the crew sat just behind Jack began answering so quickly and excitedly, that he nearly could not understand what she was saying "this competition is the competition of all competitions to beat all competitions, everyone wants to participate and everyone in the Universe wants to go." She was actually bouncing with so much excitement that she could have powered a small village, if she were sat on an dynamo.
Jack looked at the Commander and asked "so why do you need me and why should I help you?"
The Commander replied "well, your not going to watch the surf competition Jack, your going to win the surf competition!"

Jack's jaw went slack, the last time he had surfed he had been drilled, dislocated his shoulder and ripped his wet suit around the backside. There was even some debate in Jacks mind as to where some of the wet suit he had been wearing had ended up, some of it was still missing.
"You still haven't answered my question, why me and why I should help you?"
They were now in a private room above the bridge, the raised plinth the Commander, Summer and Jack had been stood on had elevated itself into the ceiling and they were now in an clear bubble like dome sat atop the ship. Around the edge of the bridge plinth were various comfy looking sofas, when Jack thought comfy he actually meant soft looking. They were mainly a dark rich reflective red in colour and spaced between them were various pedestals, with stone statues of strange shaped creatures balanced on top. The statues varied in design from Raifoons with wings, to blobs which floated over the top of the meter tall pedestals.
Jack had wondered why there had been white railings around the plinth, now he could see why as he leaned on them and gazed awestruck at the view. Jack had been surprised by how amazingly clear every star looked, he was sure he could see everything on the yellowish moon too, even a flag fluttering in the solar breeze.
The top of the ship looked like it had seen better days, this close too he could see it was actually a dirty or dusty white colour. There were white ish gun turrets shaped like angled vases in strange positions littering the top, with massive silver cables everywhere and red ribbed panels stuck in odd places all over this part of the ship. Jack knew he would find out one day what the reason for all the white everywhere was but right now he wanted to find out why he was going to have to surf again.
The Commander really was getting annoyed by having to explain every detail to Jack, he passed a piece of what looked like paper to Summer, who carefully unfolded it, whilst the Commander turned and stared up at the stars.

Summer cleared her throat with an hack and spat out a small wet fur ball into her palm, which she then placed in an belt pouch without a seconds thought. Jack looked on in mild horror, he was reminded of an alley cat he had once seen doing something similar, but with far less finesse.

She then started to read out loud, with odd pauses "there are very many things in the Universe that are hard to explain and some even harder to do. Traveling back in time is one of these hard to safely do things. The Surf Trophy has a crystal that enables the changing of an event and this is the first time that they have offered it to the winner to keep. Normally your name is assigned on the base and the trophy is kept in a secure cabinet, available only to view."

"And so why me? I haven't surfed in years!"

"Well, we know your going to win" said the Commander.

"What you mean to say is your going to cheat" said Jack.

"You can't do that, it goes against everything we believe in!" exclaimed Summer, who after looking at the Commanders face realized what Jack was saying was true.

"Well we need that crystal and I don't know of another that's readily available!" said the Commander angrily.

Summer stalked off to the other side of the clear dome, throwing the piece of paper on the deck and leaving Jack leaning his back against the railings, still wondering "why me?" out loud.

"Well, I already know you and should see you regardless, you're also one of the few creatures in the Universe who can hold the trophy/crystal and therefore one of the few creatures we can send back in time to stop me, us, from invading Earth. By invading the Earth we stopped forever the chance of your species helping us in the battle against the Furrykin, yes we could force you but eventually you would rebel and then we would have another threat to the Universe" said the Commander.

"Okay I have another few questions: how come only I can touch the trophy, aren't there more crystals in the Universe, why can't someone else win the crystal and give it to me and why do I have to travel back in time?"

"Well, all our conversations are being recorded for me, so all you need do when you've traveled back, is find me and hand over the recordings. Preferably after I've assumed command of the mission, then hopefully that will be enough to persuade me to stop the invasion. There are other crystals in the Universe but I don't know where they are, do you?" Jack shook his head, as did Summer with a look of disbelief. The Commander continued "your armour also enables you to touch the trophy, without being dissolved and once the winner (you) is presented with the trophy on Hyperversal, you can use it to present me with the recordings, a few months back from now."

"So that's why they always where those gloves on the casts!" said Summer suddenly.

Nodding the Commander continued "well, there is footage of someone trying to steal the trophy available on the Hypernet, if you look hard enough and … well, it isn't pretty" finished the Commander slowly.

"So how will I survive handling the trophy, if I'm not the right one?" asked Jack.
"Well your armour will protect you, the organizers have said that the trophy is so delicate that only gloved hands can handle it."
"Clever!" said Summer.
"Okay so I can handle the trophy and some how travel back in time using it but, why should I help you after you've invaded my home?"
The dome on the ship had by now gently spun round to face the Earth and the Commander said "well I'm sorry Jack but this was already set in motion by the Council, as soon as we arrived in orbit."
Jack turned to face the Earth, he watched as suddenly jagged lined cracks appeared in the surface of his home planet, all starting where the domes had been. After a few moments Jack realized the cracks he could see must be hundreds of miles wide, for him to be able to view them from space. The cracks all contained bright white light with tinges of red firing off into space.
"Is anyone still down there?" Jack asked the Commander in an hushed voice.
Summer and the Commander chose not to answer, as Jack looked back at the Earth it suddenly started to spin faster and faster, until it simply separated itself out, like a balloon in a centrifuge exploding full of coloured paints. Gases could be seen flowing off in every direction, with rock, metals and to Jack's mind animals and humans being flung into the depths of space. He was so angry that whatever handcuffs had been put back on him before entering the bridge, he snapped them. There remains went pin wheeling off in several directions and smashed into the side of the dome, with such force that they cracked the shell. Air could be heard whispering away into space, Jack stomped forward lifting the Commander off his long legs with one hand and holding him there. He heard Summer fiddling to pull out her gun but Jack already had the Commanders in his hand and fired it at the roof of the dome where it simply bounced around the inside of the dome with little ping noises. Eventually it made a hole right through the forehead of some small winged statue just behind Summer.
"Why?" asked Jack angrily.
The Commander could not answer as Jack's grip was so tight around his neck that he could not breath. The Commander had never met anyone so angry or so strong and as his sight started to fade he heard Summer say "now you see why we need your help with the Council."

The Commander woke up slowly and massaged his throat, he pulled himself up and leant on his control seat, looking around he noticed that they were now back on the bridge. In front of him Jack was on his knees with head bowed and his new Second had a gun pointed at his head.
The Commander rather more hoarsely than he would have liked said "well release him."
"Are you sure?" came the cautious reply from his new Second.

"Well ha ha yes, he could have easily have killed us all if he so chose, but I think he now knows what he must do and anyway wouldn't you be angry if we had just blown up your planet?"
"Very" muttered Jack from between clenched teeth.
"Well, in addition there is a way to undo the faulty intelligence given to us."
"Faulty intelligence?" asked the new Second cautiously.
Sighing the Commander turned to his bridge crew, noticing for the first time the actual tension in the room and said "well, traitorous though my previous Second may appear, it was him who leaked the information to the news agencies, detailing that humans did not volunteer but were being coerced to fight for the Furrykin" the Commander made a point of looking at Jack.
Jack looked from side to side worriedly, like a small rodent looking for a means of escape from the tyrannical headlights that seemed to follow them wherever they ran too.
The Commander coughed slightly rubbing at his throat and continued "well, when Second discovered these facts, he did not believe them himself but presented them to the Council anyway."

The Commander paused again, making Jack think that there was more to the story then he was actually telling. The one thing Jack had noticed of the crew was that every time the word 'Council' was used, they pretty much all had guarded expressions on there faces. It was as if you were to talk of doing hostile and disapproving to there mothers, then they would jump on you, beat you to a pulp, both verbally and physically.

Massaging his neck again, presumably to garner some more sympathy from somewhere, the Commander continued "well, the only solution is to send an ally back, before we sent down the bores."
One of the bridge crew asked "why not send them back further and stop the massing of the fleet in the first place, or even stop the war entirely?"
"Well because the Furrykin are more adept at this time travel stuff than we are and there's only a window in six weeks time which drops someone back here four months ago" the Commander said this nodding towards Jack.
Everyone looked at Jack who just shrugged, the same crew member asked "but why him why not me, I could do it!"
"So could I" came another call and another from various members of the crew.
The Commander held his hands up for quiet and said "well admirable though you all are, stepping back in time is more dangerous than you may think. So dangerous that you could unmake yourself entirely, which is something Jack can't do because he has already been misused by the Furrykin."
Turning to his new Second the Commander asked "well have you picked your crew?"
Standing suddenly tall, new Second with chin erect and prominent, the Commander knew the answer was not going to be good.

The new Second paused briefly before saying "yes, I'm afraid I have. Due to circumstances beyond our control I must insist that you are confined to your yacht, pending an official enquiry into your current orders and actions, furthermore all rights and privileges of your command are to be revoked, with charges!"
"Well, what exactly are the charges?" asked the Commander calmly, as his whiskers twitched angrily. To Jack the Commander appeared to be too calm, almost as if he expected something like this to happen.
New Second stood his ground, although he did appear to have the shakes under the calm question issuing forth from the Commander. New Second stood then for a moment, as if he were reading from some internal board before replying "several, but the top of the list is the willful destruction of the peaceful planet locally known of as Earth, contravening the Council's earlier explicit orders."
Some of the bridge crew had been present when the Commander had received his orders all those months ago, you could tell who they were by the way they stood open mouthed, exchanging looks of incredulity, mixed with shock and confusion.
Summer whispered to the Commander "but it was part of the Councils original orders to destroy the planet in the first place!"

With head bowed Jack could see that the Commander had a smile on his face, right up to the point where he lifted his head to face his new Second and said "well, thank you acting Commander? For making an easy decision. My final request is that I may choose some colleagues to accompany me on my exile?"
"This precedent is covered and you may choose after transfer of command" said new Second with a slightly smug tone to his voice.

Chapter 20 : Controlled Escape.

Once again Jack was being walked down what seemed like endless corridors, this time though he knew he was wearing blinkers, after only a few minutes he had got control of the darn things. What he eventually could see was that they were walking around in a great big circle, in some conical shaped docking bay. They were walking on a slightly spongy metal looking circular gantry system, that resembled a really skilled knife peal of a pear or a helter skelter.

The docking bay was huge in all directions, down being the biggest. There was no real way Jack could explain how big it was to anybody, because it would take several hundred football stadiums to fill it and they no longer existed.

Jack stole a couple of glances about, he could see what looked like the only humans he knew and the two Raifoon, all suitably plasti-handcuffed like himself. There were Raifoon guards walking in front of them, additionally one for each prisoner and several more marching along behind. They appeared to be taking no chances with them, which Jack did find odd, after all where would and could the humans run to. The only worry for them was the Commander and he appeared to be quite calm.

After another circuit of the gantry, they were roughly guided onto a narrow walkway made of what looked to Jack like cobwebs. For the life of him Jack wished he had not glanced down.

Gravity was something he appreciated on a day to day basis, after all it kept you grounded, but seeing depth with only web support, was like trying to swim from England to France and then having the water replaced with ropes to swing from.

As Jacks knees started to buckle at all that elevation but mostly depth, one of the guards asked him "what do you think your doing?" "Not enjoying the swinging without water" came the short reply.
The guard made to alter something on Jacks blinkers but another one said "why bother, we're here."

Roughly the captives were pushed into an airlock, finding there hands suddenly free, they all removed there blinkers and then were left to there own devices as the door closed with an 'swoosh' sound behind them.

A second later Jack felt the ice cold bucket of cold water pass through every fibre of his being again and knew they had just entered another suspension field, or possibly left one. It still did not feel any better this time around but at least he was prepared for the tingling and the weird itching of his teeth.

By the time Jack had his blinkers in his hand he saw the Commander striding away into the ship, he turned to find Summer helping the others take off there blinkers and heard Jane say "these are fascinating, how do they work again?"

Jack chased after the Commander, through a surprisingly near identical version of his own first shuttle and eventually caught up with him in the cockpit and asked "why me, Summer, Jane, Claire, Brian, Mike, Zoe, Sophie and Sara?"

Jack had made a mental note of all there names and faces as they had been introduced. Not because he liked them, it was just that they were the only ones left; his friend list would be a whole lot simpler, shorter and maybe filled with actual people he knew now too.

The Commander ignored him, starting to press and prod buttons on various consoles in the cockpit, until some floating joystick like controls appeared in front of him.

Then with a relieved sigh he turned to Jack and asked "well, do I have your permission, granted?" the Commander paused before he said 'granted' and emphasized the word quite a lot.

Jack looked confused "granted?" he repeated.

"Well, granted then" said the Commander with a pointy smile, followed by a large rumble which started under Jack's feet.

Quickly guessing what was going to happen next, Jack jumped into the nearest seat by the door and tried keeping his eyes off the floor of the cockpit.

He watched through the window as the shuttle suddenly detached itself from the docking system, dived down through the bowels of the docking bay and swooped towards what looked like an grey blank floor at the bottom. All the while dodging and rolling around gantries, ships and small floating islands of workers, repairing and replacing everything you could ever imagine.

There were things that looked like fluffy, mildly surprised sheep, grass, metal objects and even balls of glowing green gloop that appeared to be bubbling inside there own invisible cauldron. All these things sat on islands waiting to be loaded, as the shuttle swung past with Jack staring out the window at them in wonder.

The Commander stood furiously swiping his hands up, down and across various holographic displays until suddenly one started to flash green to red. The holograms had all manner of shapes but were for the most part written in English, so the one flashing 'exit' caught Jacks eye.

"Why don't you press that one?" asked Jack.

The Commander glanced briefly across at the flashing 'exit' hologram and said "well, when they don't have time to cancel it, I will! You may have also noticed the lens flares, the pretty lights flashing across the window?"

Jack looked back out the window and said "yes, so?" just as the cockpit lit up with another brief orange glow, as something whizzed passed the window leaving a splatter residue like red wine on a cream carpet.

Rolling his eyes, which looked highly effective on his species, the Commander said with only slight sarcasm "well, it's called weapons fire!"

Jack sat upright in his seat and asked "what, why?"

"Well, because, obviously, we're trying to escape!"

"We are?" asked Jack "from where?"

The Commander gave Jack a glance and almost in despair said "well really, you as a human do ask some obvious and ludicrous questions at a time like this!"

As if to emphasis his point, as he waved his four fingered hand at the window, a green beam splashed itself across the window, briefly turning everything in the cockpit a sickly shade of dark green.

Not expecting a sensible answer the Commander was quite surprised when he heard a female voice reply "the questioning, it's a form of defence mechanism, hoping against against hope that what there seeing or experiencing may not be true and denying it on general principles, just because. In Jack's case it's probably all of the above!" replied Sara quietly.

The Commander turned round to find Sara sat in another console seat, swiping her hands across various holographic buttons and she finished by saying "allegedly" with a wink in his direction.

"Anyway, why are they firing on the Commanders yacht?" asked Jack cautiously as he slowly looked around the cockpit, then back through the hatch door leading to the lounge and finally to the bar. After a moments thought Jack answered his own question "this is my ship, isn't it?" he asked with a sinking feeling in his stomach.

"Well yes Jack I believe it is, I got my Second to swap the security tag from my yacht to your shuttle" said the Commander.

Jack looked back through the hatch, down the short corridor and over the lounge, to see the astronauts being supplied from his bar. They were looking happier by the minute.

Jack licked his lips in appreciation, but before he indulged there was the pressing concern of "why?" he asked.

"Well lots of reasons but the main one being is, it's smaller."

"And size matters, because?"

"Well, my yacht is more for pleasure cruising with the occasional fishing trip, whilst the shuttle is more for maneuvering around."

"Okay, but that still doesn't quite explain why there shooting at us?"

"Well, I am now officially a wanted criminal for the attempted genocide of your species and actual Planocide and we've just flown off without permission."

"Planocide?" asked Jack.

"Well, you know, blowing up your planet" the Commander looked and sounded guilty about the whole thing.

Over his shoulder he asked Sara "well, how long before we've got the exit lined up?"

Sara concentrating intently and looking at a screen said "we've thirty seconds to make the bottom and then another thirty seconds to make docking door twelve. We've then got a ten second window on it shutting when they realize where we're going!"

"Well, seventy seconds should be enough time then, and then Jack I'll tell you everything, but for the moment be quiet!"

Jack dutifully sat back in his seat, using the ball between his feet to move lazily about the cockpit, being careful to not look at the floor. He could see all the flashing and near misses happening across the window but was reluctant to move too close. Although it looked exciting it was also dangerous and appeared to involve a great deal of verticality, then something blue and many limbed bounced off the window.
Sara looked over briefly at Jack, who was doing another short circuit of the cockpit and said "the floors fixed Jack."
"Hmm, what?" asked Jack.
"You can touch the floor now and even look at it!" said Sara pointing at the floor and smiling.

Jack looked down carefully, remembering how addictive and cool looking the floor had appeared before when they had been doing some maneuvering away from Earth. The floor looked white, which was of no surprise, but underneath he could just see the same puffy pink clouded waves breaking back and forth, the only real difference was that they appeared further away and slightly less interesting.

Having decided the floor was no longer a problem, Jack cautiously stepped off his chair and walked up to the main window to have a proper look. The shuttle was diving, rolling and even appearing at some points to flip over; what it was flipping around were all manner of shape and sized vessels. There were also pipes, levered arms, gangways, metal ropes and all manner of metallic looking objects through out the entire area and the Commander was weaving a mad flight path straight down through the middle of it all.
"You wouldn't think there'd be this much junk in a docking bay" mused Jack.
"Well, everything has its purpose Jack, but having a ship this small makes it easier to fly through and loose our pursuers" said the Commander.
The Commander then pointed out one particular evil looking dart shaped ship, portrayed on the side of the viewing window, all pointy dangerous looking bits and an riotous colour scheme to match and said "well, that's what's currently chasing us and amazingly there having trouble hitting us!"
Jack gaped out of the window again and asked "are you that good a pilot?"
From behind Jack came the answer from Summer as she walked into the cockpit "yes he is but even the Sharks should have hit us by now, it's like there targeting systems are off!"
"Well hold your breaths!" said the Commander "here comes the bottom!" you could hear the strain, or was it worry thought Jack, in his voice.

Looking out of the window Jack watched the floor of the hangar coming to meet them, it was painted the shiniest green Jack had ever seen, with luminous yellow strips painted across it, making some pattern he did not recognize Although it did somehow resemble a squared off bullseye to Jack, which also appeared to be scarred all around the edges.

Then there was a small cackle from the Commander, Jack realized it sounded like someone determined to enjoy themselves no matter what there ex-partner did at there party. Before Jack could ask if he was okay, the shuttle made a sharp turn away from the floor of the hangar. It swung away to the left under some oddly coloured silvery netting, leaving behind a wing tip shaped scar in the middle of the docking bays green floor.

Watching the shuttle make its daring descent was a rather portly and excessively furry Raifoon, he had been stood open mouthed within meters of the now newly scratched hangar floor watching the sparks fly. This hairy raggedly dressed character now needed new undergarments, then the wash of air hit him, throwing him and his trolley of spare parts into an sign next to some rather tall blue boxes.
Each box had a door and on each door there was a sign reading 'for your convenience, be a sweety and hover.'

Then the Sharks arrived, trying to turn hard under the near invisible silver thread-netting the shuttle had just zipped through. They failed marginally as one by one they stuck into the floor like darts, apart from the last two, one of which managed to turn slightly, bounced, showering sparks everywhere and skidded up to the now standing old Raifoons feet. The sign the old Raifoon had landed on behind read 'no parking for conveniences.' The final Shark followed in slow pursuit of the shuttle, gently kissing the bay floor, dragging tendrils of feathery silver behind it, which shortly sprung back to thinly cover the bay floor.

The ejection or protection systems on the parked Sharks then activated. Normally the Computer Automated Protocol Ejection System or Capes on the Sharks, would detach the cockpit system in its entirety. Detecting being in an atmosphere of some description, the Capes dissolved the blacked and silvered out cockpit windows away, like melting ice faced with a blast furnace and ejected the pilots.

The pilot parked flat on the docking bay floor was simply fired straight up in the air, his seats jets kicking in for a gently controlled landing next to his Shark.

The other Shark pilots were not quite so lucky, although they did have softer landings. As there ships had landed nose first, sticking into the ground like thrown javelins, there canopies were left facing the blue boxes when they were ejected with quite some force. The noise as they hit the blue boxes was not so much a bang, but more of a thud and a squelch. This was followed shortly by the coughing wheeze of various jet seat packs failing to fire, due to presumably something damp and moist having been forced inside.

The portly Raifoon heard the squelching, as the pilots started to untangle themselves from the remains of the blue boxes and rushed forwards to help.
After only a few steps he stopped dead, as the used smells hit his rather refined nostrils and he asked quite loudly "are you guys okay?" as he backed away.

Various replies sullied forth but at least no one appeared to be injured. The five Shark pilots eventually came staggering out, dripping, dribbling and dragging themselves towards the light. They were muttering curses in various languages, whilst at the same time trying desperately not to breath too much. Then a white shiny lozenge shaped barge descended from above like a bright sun, a dark ramp lowered itself to the floor and the pilots splashed aboard. The final words the portly Raifoon heard emanating from the barge as the ramp closed was "you guys are so going to decontamination and no don't touch anything!"

The final Shark pilot realizing his controls were a bit dull for some reason, had decided to take it easier. As a result he did not need the conveniences as much as his colleagues and had managed a slow turn to follow the shuttle under the webbed shield. He chased the shuttle over and under various bits of fallen machinery, diving in and out of the silvery netting shield at its weakest points.

Although they lived in an specialist environment, Raifoons had a tendency like humans to toss things away, once out of sight out of mind. Hence why there was a silvery debris shield hanging over the hangar floor. There were also various species who had lived, bred and maybe never even been beyond the docking bay floor. It was like an entire city lived here, unseen and you just had to drop below the protective screen to see it. The Shark pilot knew it was here and had visited it on occasion for medicinal purposes of a personal nature. The one thing he had not done though, was try to fly through it at over hundred miles an hour. Eventually he had to pull out from following the shuttle under the protective shield and cruise above the shield netting waiting for them to pop out.

Looking down the Shark pilot had only one problem, it was like trying to look through glass made of stringy blancmange. Something hitting it would be slowed down and would then simply drift down the rest of the way to the floor.

Underneath it looking up you could see various tools, machinery and food slowly passing through, on its way to be recycled by the peoples underneath. Most of this bounty came from the Raifoons own carelessness. Sometimes you would get the police come down to look up and look for various stolen goods, suicide attempts (from non-locals, obviously) and attempted murders from creatures not knowing about the slow shield at the bottom. If you could hit it fast enough and at its weakest point though, you would pass right through as the Shark pilots had found out. Otherwise you could bob in and out if you were running with the netting and did not mind losing a bit of speed in the process.

In the shuttle Jack was staring out of the window at clothes lines, alleyways, food and even aliens occasionally bouncing of the windscreen like so much bug squash. There were flying down what amounted to the main street Jack guessed, with makeshift wooden looking buildings on both sides, winding a course across the hangar bay floor. Why it could not be in a straight line Jack could not guess, it was like flying down some long forgotten city backstreet, where the tops of the dark buildings looked like they were nearly touching, below a silvery sky. Then a set of wipers, like he would have expected from his own car, swiped across the windscreen, wiping away the debris and leaving a trail of soap suds.

Jack turned to the Commander and asked "where are we?"

Summer answered "hangar bottom, think of it as a slum collection point, hmm!"

Then Sara said "ten seconds."

The Commander slowly raised the shuttles nose, looking for a clear spot in the netted shield, when he found one he accelerated up through it and they found themselves flying along right behind the last Shark. The Shark was weaving slowly from side to side and the Commander followed him.

"Why are we following him?" asked Jack quietly.

"Well, because he's going in the right direction" said the Commander simply.

For several seconds they followed, until the Commander saw a floating sign flashing in amber 'E-12' on a far wall and banked sharply right towards it, accelerating as hard as possible.

Jack meanwhile had discovered that waving his hands at one of the consoles projected a three dimensional display of the area in front of him. Placing his hands inside it he found he could spin it around, enlarge it and shrink it. Then he flicked it with a finger expecting it to be turned off, instead it was applied to the entirety of the cockpit; projected onto the window was all kinds of flight path, speed and jiggle information. Jack then turned guiltily and said "sorry, I think that Shark is after us again."

The Commander made a 'harrumph' like noise, sounding slightly disgruntled, after all having the information displayed like this was far easier than comparing what was in front of him with what was happening out the cockpit window all the time.

Summer kicked her seat over to Jack and swept her paw over the consoles mini floating display, some numbers began counting down between the two ships and the edge of the hangar bay.

"Just so you know Jack, we're the blue blob in the middle and the countdown is to effective weapon range. That doesn't mean he won't fire, just that the damage will be worse" said Summer "the other counter is for exit bay twelve, which I've just locked us into Commander."

The Commander grunted and Jack had too ask "will we make it?"

"Well yes, of course" came the Commanders extremely quick reply.

"Then why is the distance counter getting bigger and not smaller, for both targets?" asked Jack.

"Because that is the computer calculating odds of success as well" replied Summer.

There was quite a lot of silence in the cockpit, which was at odds with the loud sounds of well fed and nearly drunk humans in the lounge bar.

Jack turned his head to look down the corridor at his fellow humans, they all may very well be the last humans in the Universe and they were enjoying themselves immensely, whilst Jack was stone cold sober.

Feeling somehow disappointed and yet hopeful, wishing he could be back there at the bar Jack asked "can't we go any faster?"

"Only if you were to get out and push!" came the sarcastic reply from Summer.

"Why can't we go any faster?" asked Jack still thinking of the bar and what a nice cold cider would taste like right about now.

"Well because we're having to skim the slow shield, so they'll find it harder to track us with there weapons" came the Commanders reply.

"So why not go a little higher and therefore faster?" asked Jack still thinking of the bar and its contents, which could be washing over his tired tongue.

Summer was just about to bite on Jack, when like the Commander she thought out loud "there's a sensor gap between the two, because of interference!"

Both Sara and Summer were now feverishly pressing, swiping switches and buttons that floated in the air above the consoles. An angled route projection appeared in green, floating in front of the window, which the Commander then dutifully followed.

Suddenly the shuttle flew forwards at such a rate that they nearly missed the turning to hangar bay door twelve, which was just starting to shut after releasing some other vessel into the depths of space. With the narrowest of margins they slipped through the horizontal lift like closing doors and out into the brightest and yet darkest place Jack had ever seen.

On one side was the Earths moon with the sun reflecting brightly off its yellow and broken surface, on the other was a debris field where the Earth used to be and the Admiral Class Cruiser sat quietly, smugly even in space thought Jack.

Jack felt his temper start rise at the thought of the destruction of his planet, quickly he checked he was not wearing his blinkers. No they were safely hanging around the back of his neck.

Jack was just about to ask for some more answers when the Commander said "well now, Summer take us as quickly and quietly to the asteroid belt, whilst I go and check on our engineer."

"What engineer?" asked Jack.

"Well, as it's your ship Jack I guess its your engineer now. Would you like to meet them?"

Jack nodded his head, following the Commander through the bar and lounge, where his fellow humans had now started to sing loudly about doing unmentionable things to things, forgetting the words and by the sound of it the tune.

Chapter 21 : Flingfar.

As they walked through the shuttles corridors Jack had not had time to visit when he was on board before, he noticed the Commander seemed to be walking with evermore spring in his step, as they neared there destination.
"How is this ship mine?" asked a slightly confused Jack, still with a tinge of anger in his voice.
"Well actually I don't really know, all I really know is that when we did the standard ship code scan, you popped up as the owner. Then when we needed a ship to escape on, we switched your ship code out and replaced it with my yacht code."
Jack walked along behind for a few seconds in some thought and then asked "so it looked like my ship had simply vanished and all the records on it too?"
"Well, the ship records didn't go missing, just no one could remember the ship code and so couldn't find the records. It was just like it disappeared, poof!" said the Commander, waving his paw like hand in the air.
Jack paced along behind the Commander for a bit longer before asking "maybe I'm a bit slow but isn't this ship much bigger on the inside. What I mean is, I was told it was shrunk in here by a factor of ten but we've been walking for ages?"
The Commander lifted something of his face and turned to Jack and said "ask your Vowke."
"Ask my what?"
It was then as the Commander turned towards Jack, that he noticed him lift something off of one of his eyes before talking to him. It looked like a monocle to Jack's untrained eye.
"Well, you know the Blinkers Summer showed you?"
Before the Commander put his tiny looking Blinker back over his eye, Jack asked "yes I know about the Blinkers but I have no idea about the evoke?"
"Well, didn't you learn anything from the Blinkers and the Selector box?" sighed the Commander.
Jack opened his mouth to say 'yes, Beth had appeared', he got the impression that was not the answer the Commander was looking for.
After a moments thought Jack said "I don't think its sunk in yet?"
The Commander completely missed the question, frowned at him, twisting his monocle like Blinker with his thumb as they walked slowly along and said "well this, is one of the most useful tools we've ever had and is easy to use. Simply put them over your eyes and ask any question you like, starting with Vowke, such as 'Vowke, direct me to engineering' and they'll show you the way."

The Commander put his single eye piece back on, Jack pulled his from around his neck and put them over his eyes. As usual it was an exceptional fit that you hardly noticed and so Jack asked "Vowke, direct me to engineering please."
The Commander started to laugh and then said "well you don't need to ask out loud Jack, that's the beauty of them. You can ask any question you like, whilst your talking to someone in your mind and get all kinds of information about them whilst your talking to them."
Jack felt a little stupid but at the same time was looking carefully at what was being displayed in front of his eyes. Beth he knew was to blame for his lack of knowledge of such a simple device, what was being displayed in front of his eyes though did not make complete sense to him.
"Um Commander, there's a flashing green arrow in front of me that's telling me to perform a U turn when possible?"
"Well ha, I'm no longer a Commander, just call me Kraggoor and mine are saying..." he stopped dead as now his Blinkers were also telling him to do a U turn.
He glanced sidelong at Jack and said "well alright, come on then this way" he suddenly did a complete about turn. This left Jack walking on his own for a moment, before sliding to an squeaky abrupt spin around. Jogging he caught back up with the Commander and watched the now little green arrow on his Blinkers direct them to a door in the corridor with a green outline. Jack lifted his Blinkers up, the green outline and the door disappeared, when he put them back down over his eyes they clearly showed the door outlined. Above the door was written 'Engineering' in two languages, one English and the other was unrecognizable without the Blinkers on.
"So they translate for you too?" asked Jack.
The Commander just nodded, swiped his hand across the door and it opened smoothly. Standing on the other side of the dark doorway was a Raifoon, holding what looked like a shotgun shaped glass laser gun to Jack, pointed directly at them. There were bright green pulsing lights inside the gun, it lit up only a small area around the carrier, making them appear ghostly and gruesome in the shadows, like a moss covered garden gnome decoration holding a small torch late at night.
After only a moments pause the Commander stepped forward and embraced his "that's your Second, isn't it, the one who ran off with pages from the book and disappeared, the traitor?" asked Jack worriedly.
Stood just outside the door Jack was ready to run, he hesitated because the two Raifoons were now licking and caressing one another in such a way that he actually felt quite ill to be witnessing something that should be carried out in private, in his mind.
"Oh get a room please!" said Jack looking away "one without any windows, and don't mind me I'll wait for the explanation shall I?"
Both of the Raifoons were smiling fondly at one another as they finished off there lick ritual.

"Well, we've known that there was a mole in my Command somewhere, passing on information to various sources. Your arrival enabled me to work out it was third, as soon as he was promoted to second every security level was opened immediately, like he was looking for something. I assumed it was battle plans and War data but as it turned out it was your autobiographical book!" answered the Commander.
"My book?"
"Well yes, your comic autobiography, but he didn't know that there was no digital copy. There was the copy I showed you, with pages missing and the original which..."
"I have it right here Jack" said Second, handing it over almost reverently from a back pack somewhere behind him.
It was sealed inside what looked like a clear vacuum bag, with no air bubbles whatsoever. Jack took it slowly and asked "why's it so important?"
The two Raifoons were not ignoring Jack, they were just looking at one another with adoration until Jack discovered the effect of slowly tapping his foot like Sara did.
The Commander coughed slightly and said "well I read it once many years ago, that was when we decided to make the dud copy so to speak and seal the original."
"But why?" pleaded Jack
"Well you'll have to open it yourself and find out Jack" reaching forward the Commander stopped Jack from ripping the seal open and said "but I don't think today is that day. You'll know when it's time to open it, when you'll need the information inside."
"Yes okay but what information and why?"

The two Raifoons ignored Jack, turned and walked back down the dark corridor into engineering. Jack looked up at there retreating figures from the cover of his life story, watching them walk away down the nearly black corridor. He then heard Second say something like 'the Shark's update didn't get you shot then?' and the door swooshed shut in front of Jack's face.

Jack rubbed his nose, feeling that a couple of layers of skin may very well have been removed by the door as it shut.
He then waved his hands in front of the door but it did not open, so he pulled his Blinkers down over his eyes and ordered "Vowke, open this door" nothing happened.
Jack tried a few more times, with ever growing frustration as he had no idea what he was supposed to be doing and then asked his Blinkers to take him back to the bridge.

On the way to the bridge, following the green floating arrow, Jack suddenly had a thought.
If it was his ship then presumably he had a room for himself, so he asked "Vowke, show me to my room."
A green arrow pointed behind him, as he turned around an outline of a doorway flashed a few feet back. The outline of the door was clearly flashing green as he turned, but Jack was certain there had been no door or frame when he had walked past no more than seconds before.

Jack swiped his hand across the door entrance and it opened immediately. Inside was a small foyer like room with bright pale yellow walls, a wall length mirror hanging up, a coat rack next to the mirror, a small wooden table with a draw and deep chocolate coloured shag pile carpet. Jack was standing on a doormat as the door swooshed shut behind him. He stepped off the mat, after carefully wiping his feet, took off his grey prison issue shoes and opened the closet door opposite the mirror, kicking off the shoes into the closet. As he went to shut the door he saw some slippers, which looked amazingly comfortable and burgundy in colour. So he slipped them on and at the same time he saw a little bin in the closet which he carefully opened and deposited the dirty prison shoes in.
The bin said in an pleasant male voice "thank you, yum yum" without a trace of sarcasm.
Jack stood stock still for a moment, looking at the bin. This little corridor like room and closet felt so comfortable, so familiar that a talking bin was the least of his worries.

Jack shut the closet door and looked back at the front door, it looked like any normal front door you would find in an apartment block, except that there was no door knob.

He turned and walked the ten meters to the other end and the door there, pausing briefly to look at the eight pictures hanging up on the walls along the way as he passed. They were basically all strangely shaped coloured landscapes of various seasonal vistas, with sun, snow and woodland views, all of which looked like windows rather than actual pictures. Jack somehow felt he recognized them all.

The door at the end looked like normal wood, it had a normal door handle and what felt like a normal mechanical latch. As he rested his hand on it deciding on whether to go in or not, he realized he was being stupid really, up to now everything was as he had expected it to be, apart from the talking bin and the slow-motion pictures. So what could possibly be on the other side that he would not be ready for? Jack took one last look around the foyer and realized it looked how he would have expected a New York apartment foyer to look like. It was just in his style, with a chocolate coloured and deep shag-pile carpet.

Jack slowly opened the door, peaking around the edge and on the other side found a room the size of an small bus depot. There was easily enough space to park several coaches inside, with the floor changing from chocolate carpet to an painted white wooden floor at about half way. At the end was a massive window, which ran from one wall to the other and from floor to ceiling without apparent pause. The room had definite width Jack felt and even then it did not end, as there were three doors to his left and right in the far walls. The floor space was also full of things, nearer the window was a gaggle of sofas surrounding an large oaken looking table, which in turn was stood on what looked like a giant black and white chess board painted on the floor. There were seats, tables, stands with paintings on, musical instruments and what looked like ornaments all over the floor space and even the walls.

Jack had involuntarily taken a few steps forward into the room, more in shock than anything else, when he heard the door swing shut and apparently lock behind him. Jack tried to turn and found the carpet had hold of his feet, he completely lost his balance and discovered what it was like to have your feet glued to the floor. He ended up flat on his back slightly winded, with his legs trying to twist themselves out from his hips. When the pain had cleared a little from the twisting, he opened his eyes and using his elbows levered himself up into an sitting position. Leaning forward with his elbows still on the floor, he found several gun like barrels pointing, not only at his face but one particularly large one pointing at his crotch as well.

"Um" said Jack.

A disembodied female voice said "ID confirmation required?"

"Um, hi I'm Jack. Pleased to meet you?" squeaked Jack a bit more than he would have liked.

The voice continued in a slightly peeved fashion "yes I know who you are, obviously, I am addressing the other occupant!"

Jack looked around slowly with his head and eyes, clearly there was no one else in the room, what he was dealing with here was a security system gone "nuts" he said out loud.

A few more gun like barrels appeared from the floor and ceiling with various clicks and whirs, the nether region barrel inched a little closer to Jack. Jack lay there for a moment longer berating himself "I've gotta stop thinking out loud" he said out loud and slapped a hand across his own face.

Then Jack's mouth opened, without his permission and said quite plainly in Beth's voice "19,20,15,16,27,13,21,3,11,9,14,7,27,1,2,15,21,20."

Jack looked horrified and then in his head Beth said 'we apologize for using you like that but she would have kept us tied up for hours otherwise!'

Jack then felt the carpet untie itself from around his ankles and feet and he stood up with a look of a man ready to bolt away.

"Welcome back Jack. I had to check you had not been compromised and I apologize" there was to Jacks ears the sound of an blown kiss at the end of the sentence.

Jack checked he was not wearing his Blinkers, some how they had slid round to the back of his neck with the rubber cord at the front, pulling on his Adam's apple. He pulled them off over his head and threw them forcibly onto a nearby quilted chair. Much as they may help with understanding this new world, at the back of his mind was the thought that they could be used for 'nefarious' means.

Jack flopped down in the nearest comfy looking chair and then almost stopped breathing as the word 'nefarious' flashed across his minds eye. As far as he could remember he had never used the word nefarious for any reason whatsoever, he was more likely to use 'dangerous' or 'dark'. So after what sounded like Beth taking over his mouth, did the word actually come from his own vocabulary or someone else's?

The room continued to talk to him, with Jack paying little attention until she mentioned food.

"Sorry did you say croissants?" asked Jack.

"Why yes, I believe I did and I also included coffee!"

Jack looked around the room and for the life of him could not see where, then the pleasant smell of freshly brewed coffee and the even more enticing smell of actually just cooked bread wafted across the room. Jack got up and followed his nose, it seemed to want to lead him over to what looked like a large bar area, off to the left of the ridiculous window. As he walked through the room, the room continued to talk to him about the weather outside and surf conditions. By the time Jack got to what he now recognized as an breakfast bar and a kitchen behind, he found he kept glancing towards the window. The glass was so clean for a start, outside the sky was a deep summer blue, with a few wispy clouds in the distance, with what looked like hills of pleasant green grass and maybe even water in the distance. He sat down, tossing his comic autobiography onto the worktop and started to tuck in to some absolutely perfect chocolate and butter croissants, with a perfectly sugared and white coffee.

After a while he had to ask of the room, which was still chatting away about anything and everything "err sorry to interrupt but what's your name?"

The room stopped talking and Jack felt like he was being scrutinized and examined by something very heavy, as he felt a pressure all over his entire body and even his brain.

After a few seconds the room said in a very stiff and school teacher like tone "I see we are at the broken memory stage today" the tone used was of the forgotten homework variety. Where there are no marks are based on it but the teacher feels hard done by, mainly because you have deliberately disobeyed them in front of the whole class and you will have it all done by tomorrow wont you!

Jack sat with half a croissant going in his mouth, frowned and asked "and?"

The room replied with a sigh in its tone "my name is Sarah."

Jack finished of his croissant and then asked "thank you for breakfast but where are you?"

There was a small titter like laugh from all around the room and then Sarah said "I'm all around you, I am everything Jack."

"A computer, room?"

"In the least accurate sense, I am a Self Aware Reactive Artificial Intelligence Hierarchy or Special Artificial RAM And Harmony Gel, depending on whose definition you want to use but Sarah will do thank you."

Jack nodded, he stood up from the stool and took his steaming coffee with him as he walked towards the window. He was deep in thought, with so many things having happened to him recently and no memory of people or things that apparently he should know, he was feeling mildly lost.

What he really needed was time to think and ask questions of someone not too sarcastic, the only real problem he had was that he did not seem to be able to ask the right questions.

Gazing out of the window at the perfect summer weather Jack asked "Sarah, do I really have four hundred years worth of memories up here?" he said this whilst tapping the side of his head.

The view really was magnificent he thought, he was about one hundred feet above a beach, looking down a rolling grass hill with near perfect waves breaking in an ideal manner for surfing just off shore. The water looked blue and clear, and there appeared to be some wooden steps off to the right going down to the beach. Jack then noticed that he had without thought stepped out of the window, onto an wooden balcony overlooking the entire bay. Jack leant on the wooden bar going around the balcony and could now see the balcony seemed to run around the entire glass front, with occasional gates leading off to somewhere. There were table and chairs made from tree stumps and what looked like a barbecue, it was quite a large one too. The green hills surrounding the bay slowly ran off into the sea, with what looked like great big oak trees at spaced intervals as far as his eyes could see. He turned back to look at the outside of the building, it seemed to be built directly into the side of the hill, with just the glass front and balcony sticking out, all with a slight curve to it.

At this point he heard Sarah say "yes."

"Memories" mumbled Jack to himself.

Jack then worked out what had been really bothering him, he started to stare about the landscape, first one way and then the other, until he got control of his vocal chords and finally asked Sarah with a gulp "how the hell does all this fit in the shuttle, I mean I know about suspension fields but this is a planet?"

"It doesn't" came the reply.

Jack said "huh?"

"We're not on the shuttle."

"But when I'm in my room" walking back indoors the glass window simply parted out of his way, like a beaded curtain "like this, I'm in the shuttle!"

"No your not".

"Then how did I get here?"

"You walked."

"Through what?"

"A doorway."

Looking around Jack asked "then where is here?"

"Flingfar."

Jack felt worried that he was not going to like the answer to the obvious question but asked it anyway "what far?"

"Flingfar".

"Where far?"

"It's not Farflung, that was already taken as was Dunroamin, Dundiggin and Dungiggin before you ask!"

Jack felt that he had been lost somewhere "are we talking about the house?"
"What house?"
"This house!" Jack almost shouted waving his hands about.
"No."
"Then what are we talking about?"
"The place name".
"Why's it called that?"
"I thought we just covered that with the other place names?"
"No, we haven't covered anything. So, please tell me why it's called..." Jack paused trying to remember what Sarah had called this place.
"Flingfar."
"Yes, Flingfar. Why is the planet called Flingfar?"
"That's what you named it and it's a Moon not a Planet."
"Okay then, when did I get to name a Moon?" Jack sounded a little confused and maybe a tad perplexed in his tone of question.
The answer he got back was both simple, annoying and did not really tell him anything "when you moved in you named it Flingfar as Farflung, Dunroamin, Dundiggin and Dungiggin were all taken when you got here."
Talking to Sarah was like talking to someone who assumed you had a base knowledge of something ridiculous, like quantum entangled chaos theory or something, and therefore assumed you knew what they were going on about when they gave you the answer.
Jack gave up at this point and sat down on one of the sofa's facing out over the balcony and the frankly brilliant view over the bay.
After his now empty coffee cup was nearly cold in his hand, he also recognized that Sarah had either dodged the question, cunningly avoided answering it or was sidestepping the whole issue and was going to need further prompting.
"Back to my original question then, the four hundred years of worth or memories, where did they come from?" asked Jack.
"There your memories" came the reply "so whatever you've been doing!"
"Alright but are you sure there my memories and not someone else's, implanted for example?" Jack asked this with a little hope in his voice and then thought for a second that no, no he did not want someone else's memories in his head.
"They are your memories, from the last four hundred years of your life" said Sarah with an audible sigh.
Jack almost gulped "are you saying I'm four hundred years old?"
"As you would say, yes and with change."
Jack stood up and patted himself down "I don't feel four hundred years old?" Jack turned to find a mirror in panic "or look that old, less dusty for certain" he finished in relief after bounding across the room to check his reflection in the glass window.
"That'll be the Nots."
Now he was really getting confused, this computer was talking to him like everything had already happened to him, which to be fair it might have done, but he had no recall of any of it.

"Could I have a basic explanation from you, and you assume I don't know what your talking about please?" whined Jack.
There was a long pause and then Sarah said "the Nots agree that it might be time for an explanation of your inner workings."
Jack placed his hands together in an prayer like fashion and said "thank you."
Sarah started with "you are in effect at your origin point in memories, the point where you were abducted from Earth."
"Okay?"
"The cause of this appears to be several things, the continual armour updates, the serum and the probe."
Jack shuddered a little, remembering the chair and the coloured probes "so this affects me how?"
"The Nots are trying to organize your memories, from the point of your abduction by the Furrykin." Jack again started to slowly swipe at little things tickling him, he had been lightly tickled for so long that he did not seem to notice the distraction.
"So why haven't they done it yet?" he asked.
"I don't think you appreciate how complicated a task this actually is?"
"Enlighten me?" Jack replied rudely.
"Okay, on average you see and record things roughly twenty frames a second, sometimes faster sometimes slower. As an example if you watched something for one second, you will have memories for twenty images, twenty smells, twenty touches, twenty things heard and twenty tastes... now multiply that by minutes, hours, days, weeks, months and years, and that's a lot of memories. The effect of all the Armour updates, the release serum and the probes have combined to mix every element of those memories up!" said Sarah.
"So I've no memories from after my supposed abduction?"
"There is no 'supposed' abduction Jack, you have the memories but not in an order anything can understand at the moment! Think of it as a reset, the system has restarted and is now calibrating."

Jack walked around for what seemed like ages, opening doors, pressing buttons in a place that apparently he should be calling home but could not quite remember.
There were things that felt familiar, in one of the many bedrooms there was a brown teddy bear on the bed that he felt he should know. On turning it face up he remembered, having forgotten, how damned scary the thing was, which was why he had bought it in the first place. In panic at the gnashing teeth, stitched face and glowing red eyes Jack had helped the bear exit via the bedroom window. The window had dutifully parted and the teddy bear thing was presumably now sailing its way to far off moon lands.

Eventually Jack got bored of just wandering around the house, in fairness he was not actually bored, more in a state of confusion. He had already worked out in his head that if people started telling and showing him everything he had done, it would probably come as shocked disbelief. Some of the things must have been pretty terrible, judging by the alien hordes first response to him, although he had been reliably informed that he had no influence over his actions. He would still have those memories but when and if they came back, could he tell the difference between his action and someone or something else's?

Wandering back to the main room Jack had a few more questions for Sarah and was therefore surprised to see Sara sat at the breakfast bar drinking coffee.
"Hi" she said.
"Um hi?" replied Jack.
"How are you feeling?"
"Mildly concussed by all this" said Jack waving a hand round vaguely.

He then walked outside through the curtain like glass wall and stood on the balcony, after a few seconds he realized Sara had not followed him and turned round. He could see her sat on a stool in front of the food bar, with her mouth hanging open facing the direction he had just walked out, then she moved her head as if she were listening to someone and nodded slowly.
Jack walked back through with the glass window, which parted like a river around a rock and asked "something wrong?"
Sara replied "you just waltzed through a solid looking wall is all!"
Jack looked over his shoulder at the window and thought 'no I didn't, did I?'
"It's okay Sarah explained it."
"Did she, that's nice" he said this whilst thinking at the same time 'I could do with an explanation myself really!'
"So what happens now?" asked Jack of Sara.
"Simply, we wait, the shuttle is on course for the asteroid belt but it is taking it slowly, so we'll be there in roughly twelve hours."
"Why are we going to the asteroid belt?" Jack asked.
"Actually it's one of the best places to hide because of all the interference."

Jack stood looking at Sara blankly, up till this point everything had been moving along at such a rate of knots that he had not really had time to examine things. Now here he was with time on his hands and he did not know what to do. Then it occurred to him that everything that had happened to him had actually been out of his control, he in effect had been on a leash and now he could actually do what he liked. Therefore he was now at a loss as to what to do and so without thinking turned to Sara and said "sleep?"
"Usually I like a nice meal, some drink, maybe a chat first?" and then she laughed as Jacks expression changed from a question to shock and panic.
"I..I...I'm sorry that's not..."

"Your saying I'm not attractive enough for you then?" asked Sara teasingly.
Jack stood open mouthed for a second, finally Sara asked "cat got your tongue?"
Jack shut his mouth and then said "you know I never actually understood that phrase, I mean I know it means 'lost for words' but what does a cat having my tongue actually do? Oh and no I chose not to answer, as any answer could be twisted to your own nefarious means" there was that word again and this time he had said it out loud 'nefarious.'

      Sara was actually smiling, she could see why women liked to hate Jack, it was because they hated to like Jack, there was just something about him they all liked but thought they should not.
"Don't worry Jack I actually know what you meant, so why don't you go have a lie down and Sarah will wake you when we're near the belt."
Nodding slowly Jack wandered off to one of the doors and slowly pulled it open. The last thing he remembered before waking was the sound of whispering.

Chapter 22 : Belting Up.

Jack woke up feeling incredibly refreshed, in fact he would even go so far as to say rejuvenated or maybe even reborn, he genuinely felt that good. The only downer on the whole waking up experience was looking out the window and being nearly blinded by an actual Sun, and reminded that even though he was daily annoyed with his fellow man, the destruction of the Earth was a little overboard.

As he rolled out of bed, shielding his eyes, he felt something odd on the side of his neck, turning he looked for a mirror in the room to have a look at what felt like divots.
After a quick look round he asked out loud "Sarah?"
Then suddenly the Sun was gone and was replaced by a view of space, it happened so quickly that Jack was not even sure that he had even seen the Sun blaring through the window.
"Yes Jack?" replied Sarah's voice from somewhere above his head.
"Is there a mirror in here somewhere?"
"Facing the end of the bed Jack."
Now standing, Jack looked in the direction he had been told and indeed there were three mirrors on the wall, each three meters tall by two meters wide and protruding slightly from the wall.

They had definitely not been there when he had awoken, at least he was fairly certain they had not been there when had woken, after all this still felt foreign. It was like staying in an hotel you had seen pictures of before booking, the place looked the same but was at the same time subtly different enough that you were not quite sure it was the right place. It was like the feeling of waking up and not recognizing the room your in, then a sense of relief sweep over you as you remembered painting it a different colour the day before. Although in Jacks case relief was not the word he would have used, it was more likely to be reluctance. Actually he was not sure what he was reluctant about, but in his own mind he was going to settle for being reluctant about everything!

Jack also found after looking in the mirrors that he was in pyjamas, pale blue ones with large pink stars embroidered front and back. They were comfy and warm he had to admit but at no time did he remember putting them on. Stood in front of the three mirrors, trying to remember what happened before he fell asleep, Jack waved at himself in the middle mirror, which then slowly swung open and on the other side was a clothing collectors nirvana. Here was another room, probably only a quarter the size of the main room, with round boxes like tins in front of him. As he looked at the room of tins, there actually appeared to be more of them than he had first guessed at, because they actually seemed to curve down and away from his field of vision, like they were following the curvature of a tiny planet or even a moon.

These containers were also quite large for your basic tin and Jack was just thinking he would never get through a Can of beans that big, when Sarah said "what would you like to wear today Jack?"
"Wear! I was thinking about how much ga…" Jack stopped himself from talking just in time.
"Gas you would expel from eating an entire Can of beans that size?" said Sarah with a slight lilt of sarcasm.
"Um how did you know?"
"What you were going to say?" he nodded "we've had this conversation before, twice in fact, this is the third time at least."
Jack shuffled his feet feeling a little embarrassed, then guessed that he had done this before and so stood straighter and said "jeans, please."
"What colour shade, material and style would you like?" asked Sarah.
He did not think it would be this difficult to find some clothes, so went with "blue, denim, straight cut and with a zip not poppers."
Nothing happened, Jack stood for a bit twiddling his thumbs and then added hopefully "please."

As he looked closer into the room, there were Cans on every available surface behind the mirror that Jack could see, with barely enough room for a gymnast to squeeze between them as they dropped from view. Each meter wide Can had pictures of the garments on there sides, in bright wraparound stop start animations like they were flying, walking or some other weird form of locomotion for clothing. Then came a slow whirring sound from deep at the rear and one of the many Tins started moving somewhere at the back of the room. For Jack watching from the doorway it looked like someone had parted the way, just like he had imagined the Sea had parted for that chap in a book he read once. The only real difference he could see was the lack of marooned fish he had pictured in his mind, from when he had read the book.

Then a canister came bundling towards him, with just the rushing screaming sound of ripping air to accompany its journey from the far reaches of the oversized closet. Jack started to back away from the closet, because at its current speed there was no way it was going to stop in time. The Tin stopped a foot in front of Jack with a wash of warm air and vibrated as it sat in front of him. The silvery coloured lid opened slightly with a rusty creak on some rear mounted hinge, Jack cringed back expecting something to jump out and surprise him.
Then a light and buoyant female computer generated voice said "happy to be here, which jeans did you want again?"
"Um, blue denim, straight and a zip" said Jack.
There was a shuffling in the meter and half tall canister, then the Can split open like bent western style saloon doors and a pair of jeans appeared on an pink metal arm.
Jack dutifully took the proffered item of clothing and carefully ordered the rest of his attire.

Standing back in his bedroom, Jack looked at himself in the mirror and wondered out loud "I look good!"
"You do, but several decades out of fashion" said Sarah in an advisory tone.

"Least I'm not a chirpy metal canister, why was she so happy by the way?"
"Did you not see that the canisters were all slightly different shades of metal under there decorations? That Jean canister hadn't been called for decades!"
"No wonder she sounded overly helpful."

Jack looked back in the mirror and wondered how he was out of fashion. As far as he was concerned Jeans would never be out of fashion, white t-shirts would always be cool and the red trainers were his favourite sort. The only thing he was not sure on was the black leather Jacket he was now putting on. The leather belt on the jeans was some brown cowboy buckled affair that he had no choice about, but it did look cool with its blazing horse-dragon design combo on the belt and buckle. The belt also had several fabric like pouches of various sizes, the large penknife sized one that sat on his right hip felt heavier than the others for some reason. As he started to investigate it Sarah informed him "that's where your Glade resides."

Jack frowned to himself, he remembered the Glade as being quite a bit bigger than a few inches long. When he opened the pouch and looked inside, there was a lot of depth involved and indeed there was his Glade nestled into a corner, right next to what looked like a cling-film wrapped cheese and cress sandwich. In the other corner sat a bottle of water and his incomplete autobiography, still in its wrapper.

Jack walked casually through his bedroom and lounge, he opened the foyer door and walked to what was in effect his front door. The front door had no door handle, which meant Jack eventually found out how to open it by the simple means of waving like a loon at it. As it smoothly opened Jack quickly stepped through and found himself stood on the 'shuttles bridge?' The door swooshed shut behind him and Jack turned to look at it suspiciously.

They were all here, everyone he had seen at various points since waking in his house, was stood or sat somewhere on the bridge. He had definitely decided to call it a bridge now, because frankly it was too large for a cockpit as Sara had called it and it had work stations with keyboards of light and seating arranged in half circles.

Actually looking at it, this bridge, this room was easily ten times as big as the shuttles and almost round, then the thought occurred to Jack that he might not be on the shuttle any more somehow.

Sara was the first to turn around from looking out of the wall window and gulped as she saw him, seeming to look specifically at his neck. She quickly rushed over to Jack, kissed him on the side of the neck and bounced back with a look of satisfaction on her face of a job well done.
"Welcome to your ship!" said Sara.
For the moment they had time to themselves and so Jack asked quickly "what happened to the cockpit?"
"Doesn't it look amazing!"

Jack had to admit it did look really good, it was a sort of mad cross-breeding between all his favourite science fiction television shows and films, but in white with metal accents the same as the shuttle.

"It's how I would have done it, apart from the excessive whiteness of it obviously!" he said.

Sara gave him an odd sidelong look and said "no Jack, this is your ship. Its been sat in the asteroid sphere that sits around your solar system. Summer over there nearly had heart failure when all of a sudden it loomed out of nowhere and she found she had no control over the shuttle. We docked an hour ago and Sarah has been giving everyone the tour."

Jack looked slightly wild around the eyes like someone had just told him he was on another planet.

"I walked here?" asked Jack.

"I assume so" laughed Sara.

"No I meant, I walked here, how did I walk here?"

"In the normal way I would imagine, you know one foot in front of the other!" that tone, that level of annoyance and sarcasm in so few words could only come from one person.

Jack turned and there behind him was "hello Claire" said Jack with resignation in his voice.

    Much to his surprise Claire jumped at him as he turned, she gave him one of the biggest hugs he had ever experienced. He was so surprised by her reaction that he did not even have time to move his arms and ended up in such a fierce embrace, with his arms trapped by his sides, that he could not move. After the hug went over the unspecified and complicated too long period, Jack nodded at Sara to help release him. Sara tapped Claire on the shoulder and they walked off to look at a console screen, with Claire winking at Jack over her shoulder as she walked away.

    The wink left Jack in a whole lot of confusion, then Summer was bouncing up and down in front of him, playfully punching him both physically and mentally by asking over and over "why didn't you tell me you had a ship out here?" and "where did you get it?" and "why's it so big" the questions kept spewing out of her mouth.

Jack was frankly dumbfounded, he had no answer for all the questions that were being asked and found himself surprisingly happy to see Claire again, which was annoying.

    Ignoring Summer was going to get him in trouble he knew, but he had no answers for her yet or himself.

    Whilst walking towards a central white table between the window and the central seats, he had to ask "did anyone else make it? I mean did anyone else get off Earth before it blew up?" Jack added quickly. Claire gave him a glance and in a small voice said "I'm sure she made it Jack."

Jack had not really been thinking of anyone in particular, but now he was thinking of Jenny "what makes you think I meant Jenny" and quickly trying to cover the hitch in his voice continued with "I mean others could have made it, couldn't they?"

"Yes but the first name that came to your mind was Jenny's" replied Claire who then walked away from the console she had been stood at, to the furthest part of the bridge.
Jack opened his mouth to reply with an sarcastic comment but had the wind poked out of him by a very sharp elbow in the ribs and the quick wit of Sara "stop acting like your both thirteen!"
He shut his mouth and looked down at the table in front of him.

On the table was an inky black floating hologram that slowly oozed its way out of the tables white surface and floated above it. Jack could not see through the black cloud to the other side, then little points of light started to appear and disappear within the cloud like torches in a slow tornado.

Then the Commander spoke "well now that we're all here!" he said this with a nod towards Jack "I shall tell you my plan for saving the Universe. But first I must apologize for the destruction of a your planet."
"Why do you need to apologize?" asked Jane.
"Well, because I gave the final order" replied the Commander.

The only human that did not react to this statement was Jack, everyone else took sharp intakes of breath, with flashes of anger and surprise written on there faces.
Jack looked around at the remains of the human race he knew of, circling the table. There was Mike, Brian, Sophie and Zoe from the International Space Station with Jane, Claire and Sara at the opposite end.
"Well, I was following orders which I thought were from the TASK Council directly, which I of course now know to be the wrong orders, which is why I have gathered you all here so I can try and undo my mistake."
"Why is it your mistake" asked Sara quietly "I mean surely you were given the orders in the first place?"
"Well I carried them out to the letter without hesitation or forethought, while being the Commander I should have verified there intelligence, rather than blindly obeying the orders to destroy a planet and its inhabitants!"
Everyone shuffled there feet trying to find something to say that would make him feel better, in the end Jack asked "I assume you military types always follow orders to the letter, with that in mind I don't blame you but I am curious to know what changed your mind?"
"Well, you did actually?"
"Me! How did I change your mind?"
"Well, whilst hunting down the last of the resistance on your planet..."
"If you were going to blow up the planet why were you hunting us down?" asked Mike interrupting angrily.
"Well, to block any escape" came the simple answer from the Commander.
They all paused for a moment and then Sophie said "you were trying to eliminate the threat."

The Commander nodded slowly and managed to look even more guilty, he then continued with "well, whilst we were making sure you couldn't escape we came across your compound" he waved a finger at Sara. "Well, by the way your trap was most ingenious, the techs absolutely loved it and were falling over themselves to investigate it further."
"Don't look at me" said Sara "it was Jane's idea for the Poly-bomb."
Jane looked surprised to be given praise from anyone, especially Sara whom she only knew as a cold and clinical leader.
"Well anyway, whilst we were searching for clues as to where your ships might be, we came across one of our satellite probes, which had been modified to help people with the memory gas. We then discovered that it held a vast store of information, which we were surprised to find came from one individual" with this the Commander pointed at Jack.

Jack put a finger to his chest and said "hey, don't look at me I didn't do it!"
"Well no you didn't Jack but the probe had copied the mixed up data and then had started to automatically sort the information with an algorithm. This algorithm gave the probe a head start to sort out your memories and also led to a signal being given off with enough strength that we picked it up from orbit. The memory layer it had sorted, pointed to the fact that the Furrykin were abducting your species and using you against your will to fight there war against us. It was by this time too late to stop the bores from destroying your planet, so I withdraw all our personnel from the planet in the hopes that someone would escape. Then with my Seconds help we carefully analyzed your memories, as much as we could without arousing suspicion in the computer system, that's when we found you were the subject and this was your home planet. We therefore knew we had to find you and that's when we came up with the idea of sending you back to stop the invasion, because you have already traveled in time. Which was the jolt I needed to remind me we had met before, although you do look very different in your armour."

Everyone turned to look at Jack, he was the one person that no one would ever look at and think he was the hero type, maybe an anti-hero. He just did not look the part at all stood in his eighties fashion Jeans, T-shirt, Jacket and trainers. Everyone else was stood dressed in light blue coloured trousers, with pockets in the legs, blue zipped jackets, that fitted near perfectly on everyone and what looked like chain metal T-shirts underneath in an silver and white blend. There feet were also wearing what looked to Jack's eye like thick sock shoes with laces painted on in black, which accentuated the white. The only real thing that set them apart were there blinkers. They were dangling from the rubber band around there necks, either down there front or over there back. The only one who was any different was Claire who wore hers on top of her head. Jack stood thinking she would be the one to lose them, go searching for hours not to find them, only to ask if he had seen them and when he carefully pointed out they were on her head already, he would be the one to get the abuse.

Jack felt something more was required of him and so answered in as plain a voice as he could manage "no I haven't!"

"You haven't what Jack?" asked Summer tiredly.
"Traveled in time, well obviously I'm traveling forward in time as we speak but I don't remember traveling back, ever!"
"Well Jack that's what your first probe managed to discover, then our Stellar Vessel probe managed to confirm it, fortunately just before we had to leave" said the Commander.

Claire had been thinking and could see by Jack's face that he was going to continue to argue that none of this was true regardless of whom was saying it. She walked round the table and took hold of his hand and asked "how long have you known me Jack?"
Jack was a little taken back by the familiar way she had hold of his hand, images came to mind of him being back in the cell unconscious after being electrocuted and her holding his hand as he slept.
"Come on Jack how long have you known me?"
"At least four years."
"And in that time have I ever lied to you?"
Jack was just about to answer with a quip along the lines of 'you never asked, you ordered' but on seeing her serious expression he thought back and said "no, no I don't think you've ever actually lied to me."
"Right, well I'm not lying to you now when I say that after all the stuff that I've seen on Earth the last few months, this, suggestion by the Commander."
"Kraggoor, I'm no longer a Commander of anything I'm afraid."
"Okay, but you are to us" Claire looked at the Commander, paused and turned back to face Jack continuing "the Commander here's suggestion that your the key to stopping the invasion of Earth and its destruction is not as far fetched as it sounds."
"Why though, why is it me?" complained Jack.
"Well because your the only willing WIIMP I know of, the only person I know that can travel in time safely and before you deny it we've samples of your memory to prove it."
Jack opened and closed his mouth and then the Commander continued with "nobody is forcing you to do this, we're all asking you to do this?"

Looking around the room at all the faces staring at him Jack did not feel important at all, in fact the looks he was getting were more of shock and dismay that he was the key to saving humanity. The only positive faces were on Claire, the Commander and Summer, even Sara looked a little confused.

Sara then with her expression of mild confusion on her face turned to the Commander and asked "if he is a Wimp then will he be able to help us, I mean won't the Furrykin be able to take control again?"
"Well it's a risk we'll have to take, but from the memory clips we've managed to see, it looks like he's had at least three shots of three different serums. He may also have inhaled some of the memory vapour whilst still under the influence of the serum, corrupting his memory in some way which his Wimp is trying to solve."
"What's a Wimp?" asked Jane.

"Well it stands for Warrior Intelligence Interrupt and Matter Phasing, or Phaser" replied the Commander.

"Yes well, that might be an explanation for some people but to me that sounds like gobbledygook" said Jane with everyone else nodding in support.

Looking carefully at the Commander, Summer had a question in her eyes and then the Commander nodded thinking that if it was not all out in the open now it would just waste time later.

Summer turned to face everyone and said "it's a body armour system, a suit of armour that sits in an alternate Universe somewhere that can be called in at any time to surround the occupant. As far as we know it was developed by an ancient race for exploration purposes and to protect the occupant from any possible external danger. The Furrykin one day found this races storage facility for the armour and after a period of time turned it to there own needs. The first time we encountered the armour it was against thousands of the Furrykins allies dressed in the armour, it was total devastation of the planet. After that the Furrykin needed only to put a hundred or so armoured troops on the ground to frighten the planets populace into surrender. Then one day they attacked another race whose technology was on a par with the race who made the armour, when they realized there mistake the Furrykin blockaded there system but not before they managed to release a serum. This was a great time for us as we were able to shoot the armoured aliens with the serum, who then in turn collapsed and had breakdowns. This of course angered the Furrykin who went searching for a solution, which they found in humans. As far as we knew at the time, humans were willingly helping the Furrykin and immune to the current serum, until we found Jack here's memory records and realized that he was in some form of sleep and unaware of his actions."

"So what does the serum do?" asked Claire who was looking at Jack carefully and taking a step away from him like everyone else in the room.

"We found the suits occupants were generally under some form of mind control, the serum helped release there minds from the control of the armour and the armour disappeared. There was always a small delay in there actions like they were trying to work out what to do, with humans in the armour though there was no delay, the reactions were instant and deadly. We always assumed this was because they chose to help the Furrykin, like a few races had before but now we know it's what you call a coma like state and a new serum is obviously out there and working otherwise Jack here wouldn't be talking to us" replied Summer.

"I get the feeling that isn't the whole story is it?" asked Sophie.

The Commander sighed and said "well no, I'm afraid not. The main reason we had to leave so quickly and unceremoniously was due to the book."

"What book?" asked Jane.

The Commander pulled it from under the white table and placed it on the top, blocking some of the floating star map and said "well some of you know that this graphic novel tells Jack here's life story, to a point. It hints quite heavily that humans were not under there own control whilst in the armour, which we took to believe was a sales pitch in defence of Jack, being that it's his biography. After some research we found our own Council for some reason already knew this, confirming Jacks innocence, knowing this fact they still ordered the destruction of Earth!"
"But why?" asked Claire and Sara together, Claire picked up the comic-book and the map reignited.
The Commander shrugged "well who knows, political power, bribery, persuasion but mostly we think for the benefit of the public, by showing they were doing something to be rid of the Furrykin menace."
"Benefit to themselves more like" mumbled Brian and then when everyone looked at him continued "its self preservation ain't it, they are I guess voted onto this Council and they want to stay on the Council, so I assume they must appear to be doing something to warrant there re-election?"
"By destroying a planet!" exclaimed Mike "doesn't that seem a little extreme, even to you?" he said this pointing at the Commander and Summer.
Summer looked at the Commander and said "the Galaxy elections are in two months, do you really think they would blow up a populated planet to stay in power?"
"Well I hadn't thought so, until yesterday I obeyed without question. I mean they've destroyed planets before that were unstable, but generally they were barren lifeless things."
"So what's the plan then?" asked Sara.
"Well the plan is quite simple: Jack travels back in time, uses a password only I will recognize and then I plug this" the Commander waved a purple memory selector box in the air "into my blinkers and it passes on all the information I have learned."

"Here's some more information to be added" Second had just walked into the room, striding forward with a great deal of haste, he then banged his hand on the table in a furious manner and waved his hand over the top of the table to select current news. The star map faded like a dawn mist being barraged by a blazing sun, to be replaced by a very furry grey coated otter like head floating up from the table, wearing a ridiculously flamboyant feathered cap and pink spectacles.

The otter head started to speak "today's leading Hypew story, is that formally renowned Commander Kraggoor of the Stellar Seventeenth, has been disgraced, after it emerges he willfully disobeyed orders and destroyed an inhabited allied planet."
Second paused the image by waving and holding his hand open and then said "there offering a reward for you now, fifty thousand crowns for information leading to your capture."
"Dead or alive?" asked Jack in what he thought of his best cowboy western impersonation.

After the filthy looks he received Jack asked "well, does it say either way?"

"Well, you were hoping to avoid that question weren't you?" said the Commander with a wry smile looking at Second "don't worry I think I know where this is going."

Second replied "I do hate humans, sometimes they are too direct" he paused and with a sigh said "fifty thousand for you in any condition, the only proviso is that QNA can still prove identity."

"QNA?" asked Jane curiously.

With a slight pause for thought Second replied "your species used DNA or Deoxyribonucleic Acid, to quantify something's genetic identification. QNA is the universal superior standard equivalent that covers all life that can be sequenced."

The mood on the bridge was not exactly what you would call positive, it was only as everybody started to move away from the table and into there own thoughts that Jack realized something. Walking back to the table he banged his hand on it and asked "why now? I mean if the Council were going to use the destruction of Earth to aid in there re-elections, why are they blaming you?"

Then he turned and pointed at the table top still displaying the otter's head "what's changed exactly, some piece of information must be missing?"

"Or something has leaked into the public domain?" asked Summer quietly but with a little hope in her voice.

"I'll check the Hypernet" said Second quickly, who sprang off like an ambitious kangaroo to a separate console and screen on the bridge.

After several minutes of tapping at an actual keyboard, Second turned round to find everyone stood behind him waiting expectantly for an answer. He swallowed hard and said slowly "you aren't going to like it."

"Just spit it out, will you" said Jack.

"All I'm saying is that we all, aren't going to like it."

"You'll like it even less in a minute, so stop it with the suspense and tell us why they've changed the story?" quizzed Summer.

"It would appear that some parts of Jack's life story book has been leaked onto the Hypernet, which in turn made it to the news sites, which meant the Council had to change there cover story. Originally the council were going with humans helping the Furrykin willingly, but since the biography came out explaining that humans had no choice..."

"They needed a different scapegoat for there planned re-elections" said Brian.

"Exactly and since the Commander gave the order to destroy the planet, therefore blaming him for killing billions of potential allies in the war against the Furrykin, was easy."

"I bet there twisting it in some way to make themselves innocent for this election business?" asked Brian.

"Oh there's all kinds of stories about how they ordered and begged him to stop, how a Furrykin supporter got so high up in command, that there will be a full investigation and heads will roll and so on and so forth."

Turning to the Commander Jack asked "so what happens now?" Putting a hand to his chin in thought the Commander replied "well we stick with the plan. But first we need a board and you need some practice" he said this looking very directly at Jack.

Chapter 23 : Bigger Is Better?

"This ship of yours is really impressive Jack" said Summer as they walked through the docking bay towards the shuttle in the distance.

Jack looked up from the metal catwalk they were strolling on, since leaving the bridge she had followed him everywhere he had wandered and up until now she had not said a word.

Jack was actually finally relieved to see something other than white everywhere too, the walls and indeed every surface in the docking bay actually appeared to be made from metal, which to Jack's mind was what things should look like in space. Not this carefully manicured white stuff everywhere and on every surface, admittedly there were different shades of white, he had never known that there were so many shades! Nonetheless it was a pleasant relief to find metal everywhere, he found it gave him more a sense, a feeling of reality.

"It doesn't feel like it's my ship, you know" replied Jack to Summer's question.

"Maybe you don't feel like it's your ship, but I've checked. It's registered in your name, although through a dummy company and it was very decent of you giving the Commander control of it."

"It seemed like a the right thing to do, mainly because I don't know where we're going to and without any idea of things from before, I don't have a clue what to do!" Jack paused "plus he looked so lost."

"Still it was very good of you to pass command over to him" Summer appeared distracted in some way.

"It was the right thing to do, besides Commander of a small planet sounds better than Kraggoor?" asked Jack.

Summer nodded her head in agreement, although she did prefer his real name "besides people will be hunting for someone called Kraggoor, so it's better we call him Commander anyway" surmised Jack.

Summer opened her toothy mouth in surprise and thought to herself that 'much as she found Jack's logic a bit skewed sometimes, this time he was actually right.'

Walking a few paces in silence together, Jack gave proper consideration to the docking bay, where something about it was bothering him.

Maybe it was the size of the thing? He knew the ship they were on was big, because the Commander had reliably informed him that on there approach, they had wondered how something that was ten times bigger than the Stellar Attack Vessel they had left, could be hidden out here and no one had found or detected it.

The docking bay though was huge, they were walking on the topmost catwalk that ran more or less down the middle, looking forward he could only just see the other end of the bay through what looked like a light mist, with flying white blobs in the air. Looking to his left or right he could see the edges of the bay were made from light coloured metal panels bolted onto the walls and then down below through a steamy cloudy haze was the metal bottom. Jack assumed that all the six foot tall looking wall panels in the bay were bolted metal panels and he would have been quite correct.

They carried on slowly walking towards the other side of the docking bay from the bridge, on looking over his shoulder Jack could see out into space through a hazy blue shield of some kind. The bridge room was somewhere above the docking bay entrance, presumably so they could monitor the lack of traffic easier.

    The internal size he supposed could be explained by a suspension field of some kind or even by the fact the ship was so enormous. They had started there walk across the gantry so Jack could see 'his' shuttle as they called it, he still felt that none of this was his, after all how could any of it be? At the bridge he had been offered some white floating disc like transport to stand on and be whisked across the expanse to the shuttle. On looking at its wafer thin depth and the drop to the deck below, Jack had decided on the swaying metal gantry to cross the gap.

    The main reason he had chosen to visit the shuttle was because it was the only place he felt he would feel comfortable at the moment, to this end he was blaming the bar on board.

As they approached the shuttle Jack had to ask "whose working on the shuttle?"

"Drickers probably" answered Summer.

"What are Drickers" Jack asked with exaggerated care.

"Oh they were the ones who served us drinks earlier in the War room."

"The little green pitted aliens?" asked Jack.

"No need to be rude about them, don't forget I'm an alien too you know!"

"But your so soft and furry" Jack jumped to one side expecting to be struck, when he was not he continued "okay but why are they crawling all over the shuttle, I mean I thought we were alone on this ship?"

"Obviously you thought wrong and they can turn there hands to anything!"

"Thanks, thanks very much but what about all the other ships in the docking bay?"

Summer looked around moving her head backwards and forwards, from side to side, trying to see what he was on about and finally asked "what other ships?"

Jack looked at her like she was blind and then replied "oh I don't know maybe the hundred or so I can see just by being stood right here!"

Summer managed to look offended and then with care said "Jack, the only ship I can see is the one we came in on. You know, the shuttle!"

Finally Jack worked out what had been bothering him about the contents of the docking bay, it was full of ships and Drickers working away on various vessels but there was apparently no one else moving about. Where were the passengers and crew, what were they doing?

Jack walked over to a metal pedestal with a floating animated horse and dragon image made of apparent fire, flickering on top and asked Summer "can you make this work please?"
Jack carefully watched her wave the back of her hand across the pedestal, whilst he fiddled with his own belt buckle, then the image flickered to a tJi logo and Jack asked "Sarah are you there?"
"I'm always here for you Jack."
"Okay that doesn't sound creepy in any way shape or form" he replied sarcastically, Jack then asked clearly "why can't Summer see the other ships in the docking bay?"
"She and her blinkers have not been authorized for that information."
"Could you authorize her please."
"Are you sure?"
Jack pulled a face of confusion, before replying in an carefully questioning tone "yes?"
After a few moments Sarah then chimed back in with "authorization permitted."

Summer slowly pulled her blinkers from hanging around her neck and placed them slowly over her eyes, she was curious how Jack could see them without blinkers and she was going to need them to see whatever he was seeing. As the Blinkers adjusted there settings Summer's mouth slowly opened in surprise, she turned to Jack, pulling off her Blinkers and accused him of being "your a Cloven Pirate!"
Jack started to laugh but after seeing Summer's expression of fury cross over her face quickly said "aw come on, you should know me by now, I have no memory of any of this" he waved his hands in the air, to indicate everything in the Universe "so how would I know if I'm a Clover Pirate?"
Jack paused and turned to face the pedestal and asked in a curious voice "Sarah, am I a Pirate?"
"No" came the short reply.

Summer sighed outwardly and groaned inwardly and then said to Jack angrily "of the hundreds of ships in here, even at a glance I can see several banned and illegal models. Even some that look like War Catchers, which are not supposed to exist and it's actually Cloven Hoofed Pirates, not the ones of the smelling nice variety but the ones with your symbols for the devil all over there hulls!"
"Why do I get the feeling your having a go at me when I have no idea what your talking about?"
"Because there's a very high probability that regardless of my criminal status I shall have to turn you in to the Pugs!" answered Summer back, whilst striking the folded arm 'what you gonna do about it' pose.

If she could of, she would have dragged Jack by the ear to stand in front of the Commander but as it was the Commander was waiting for them both as they reached the bridge. As Summer opened her mouth to complain that Jack had been hiding his piratical ways from everyone, the Commander waved her into silence.

He started by apologizing "well I'm sorry Summer but we're not turning Jack into anybody and before you point out the obviousness of the contents of the docking bay. I only just found out myself, as Jack was kind enough to give me full access to this ship."

Sighing heavily and sitting down in the bridge Captains seat, the Commander continued "well let me start by saying this is not a Cloven Hoofed Pirate vessel!"

Summer interrupted "are you sure, have you looked in the docking bay!"

"Well yes, yes I have and do you know what I saw?"

"No, do tell?" asked Summer angrily.

"Well us. Well more accurately my past. You see I've been on covert missions before and we were nearly always based on a ship that looked not to dissimilar from this one."

Summer looked shocked and before she could say anything the Commander continued with "well I think you've worked it out now, by the look on your face, yes this is called a Ghost Ship. This is one of many vessels across the Galaxy used for, ah, shall we say hidden objectives or covert missions!"

"Yes I've heard of them but I didn't actually think they really existed and the rumour is they are used by pirates?" said Summer.

"Well more like people trying to avoid being searched by customs."

Jack looked up at this point and asked "we're on board a smugglers ship?"

The Commander replied "well ah, not so much a ship more like a space station on the edge of a boundary."

"A smugglers cove or cave then?" asked Jack.

"Lets try not to be too accurate with definitions, as you own it shall we" said Summer.

Jack walked round the Captains chair and stood looking out the ridiculous window onto space. He had always wanted an uninterrupted view of the stars and here it was in all its glory, but now all he wanted to see was his grimy neighbours house directly opposite back on Earth.

Feeling slightly melancholy, maybe even a little depressed Jack turned to face the Commander and asked "so what do we do now?"

The Commander carefully looked at Jack and nodded guessing that he had finally realized that he had no real choice but to help.

"Well first, we get you a surfboard."

"I haven't surfed in years."

"Well I really don't think that'll be a problem."

Summer asked with some sarcasm in her voice "what will then? I mean what will be a problem, besides a planet sized Ghost ship turning up at the competition?"

"Well we aren't taking this ship" replied the Commander.

"We can't take the shuttle, it's doesn't have the range!"

"Well yes, I know" said the Commander with a smug smile playing over his face.
"Your not going to tell me are you?"
"Well no, I'll leave it as a surprise but we'll leave in an hour for Surphon."

An hour later the group met on one of the docking bays many catwalks, with Jack still wondering how the things were supported, after all the walk ways simply seemed to float from one place to another. As he stared about trying to follow the floating catwalks, he finally saw why he had not seen anyone else moving about the hundreds of ships. There appeared to be a system in place that moved the walk ways around, so they were just out of visual range. Then there was the white ball like blobs zipping from one place to another. These balls, Jack finally saw, started out as thin flat disc things, then as you stood on them they enveloped you into a balloon like white ball and moved quickly off to your destination.

Whilst Jack was looking over the side, trying to find little jets or wires holding everything together and moving the different things about, he over heard Mike talking to Claire.
"The four of us are going to stay here, Sarah has got some very well paid jobs arranged for us and the opportunities for travel are awesome."
"Your not coming along to save the Universe with me then?" asked Jack.
"Apparently we've done all we can but don't worry we'll be supporting you when you're surfing" replied Sophie.

The four International Space Station personnel almost skipped off the catwalk, off to do who knows what. In fact Jack was actually very curious about what possible skill set they had that anyone would actually want, surely they were under trained and crucially under educated. Jack asked Summer what possible jobs they could do and the reply he got was "imaginary ones."
"Meaning they don't exist?" questioned Jack.
"Meaning they aren't limited by excess knowledge and have already had some ideas that apparently one company has already put into production. Don't look so disappointed Jack that you weren't asked, after all if you succeed none of this will have happened" Summer laughed at the end of her comment.

If he had felt unhappy earlier, the fact that the only other four human beings he knew of were running away, was making him feel quite lonely as well. Then Sara appeared with the Commander, looking at her now as she sashayed towards them, Jack could not help feeling that he and Claire were the only two humans left in this endeavour. There was just something that was not quite sitting right with him when he looked at her walking. Sitting, standing even lying down was fine but when she walked, it was as if she was trying not to fly off, like she was trying to be careful not to let go of the ground and a stiff breeze might lift her off her feet.

Sara turned from talking to the Commander and her eyes blazed that strange blue for a moment and then she said "I see you two are getting along better now then."

Jack had no idea what she was talking about, until he followed her gaze to his hand on the guard rail and saw Claire's hand disappearing from the gap between his arm and the rail. In fact she had moved so quickly that he was not even sure it had actually happened, until he caught the daggers in Claire's eyes firing at Sara, who seemed oblivious to the anger she had caused.

Regardless of whether it was Jack's fault or not, he now knew that at some point Claire would have an metaphorical dig at him for Sara's little comment. Either that or she would just slap him.

The Commander then said "well I'm glad to see we're all here, in time to introduce you all to our new ship!" the Commander pointed into the distance, where something could be seen moving towards them.

Jack asked "what's wrong with our old ship?"

"It's a bit big to try and fly under the radar don't you think?" replied Sara.

Maybe he was the only one not understanding what she just said, it was only as there new ship got closer that Jack realized that she had meant the big one they were standing in and he had meant the shuttle they had arrived in.

"I meant the shuttle!"

Sara frowned at him and said in an frustrated tone "does it matter!" Claire grabbed at his arm to stop him from replying, she knew what Jack would do, but Jack did not know what Sara could do in return.

Then Summer let out an 'eek' sound, the type of noise you would expect from a small rodent just before being run over, the only thing missing was the squelchy noise cutting of the sound at the end. They all turned to look at her and after a few seconds she found her vocal chords and said in reverence "it is a War Catcher ... we're trying to be inconspicuous and we're going to fly in a War Catcher!"

Jack turned to look at the approaching ship and even he, who had seen quite a few space ships just today, had to admit it did stand out somewhat. For a start it was black but not one shade of black, it seemed to have many different layers of black, some angled together and others seeming to blend into one another. The other main difference to the all the white and light coloured ships in the docking bay, was the shape. This ship was more angled, more aggressive looking like a bird of prey about to strike on a small furry creature left out in the open. The front of the ship had one central prong where the cockpit appeared to be, underneath which was some figure and then there were prongs on either side of the cockpit as part of the wings. The rest of the ship was all angles and a bird like stature, until the back of the ship swung round into view and the three engine ports could be seen. The central rear one was rectangular and very large with two oval shaped large engine ports just off at an angle on either side, with what looked like a loading door underneath the central engine.

Jack had to ask "what's a War Catcher?"

Summer replied "I thought it would be obvious Jack" she pointed at the ship being connected to the catwalk and continued with "that's a War Catcher!"
Jack stood lost for words for a moment and then Claire said "what Jack meant was, how is it any more different than the rest of the ships in here?"
"It's a War Catcher!" said Summer in an 'isn't it obvious' tone whilst gesticulating at the ship.
"Yes we know that, but why are you so" Claire paused not wanting to say 'afraid' and was saved by Jack finishing the sentence with "in awe of it?"
Sara held a hand over her mouth and smiling mumbled "that was very diplomatic Jack"
The Commander then interrupted and said "well, it's time to board your ship Jack."
Jack looked up at the smooth, very black hull, now brooding over the catwalk and there heads and mumbled "my ship again?"
"Well yes your ship" came the Commanders short reply, Jack stretched up to slide his hand along the hull, he suddenly snatched his hand away as the thing felt alive to his touch. It was like the static jolt you might get, involving your clothing, some carpet and something metal, the only difference for Jack was that it appeared to happen in his head.
The others were all waiting by the loading ramp, an outer panel had levered itself from the top of the War Catchers loading bay, to put a ceiling against the central engine. Another panel like ramp had lowered itself from the lower portion of the loading bay, on another set of large black hinges and onto the deck.
   Jack paused as he went to follow the others to the stern of the ship, something about the large white painted name on the side of the vessel had caught his eye.
"Beth's W.C?" asked Jack looking at the name with his head cocked at a slight angle in thought.
   Claire had put a foot on the ramp, she then paused and walked back to where Jack stood looking at the ships name. Surrounding the name were several what could only be described as mischievous imps, these were painted on in shades of white on the black hull. They were lounging together, smoking, drinking and using there spare clawed hands to perform rude hand signals or hold various weapons in suggestive manners. The over all impression was that of naughty behaviour boarding on lewd, when Jack stood further back the whole image somehow resembled the horse-dragon image on his belt buckle.
   Claire read out the name on the hull again "Beth's W.C?"
Jack and Claire exchanged a look and then both started to laugh together, they did not stop even when the Commander walked over and asked "what's so funny?"
It took several large gulped intakes of breath to stem the laughter for both Jack and Claire, then Claire asked "who names these ships then, no that's wrong, who shortened the name to W.C?"
Both Jack and Claire giggled to themselves at this.

The Commander looked first at the name and then at Jack and Claire, they were both trying very hard not to laugh any more. He looked back at the name on the ship, at the imps painted in various positions of what could be called toilet humour and shook his head.

"Well I'm sorry I still don't get it?" asked the Commander.

Suddenly light dawned in Jack's mind, he had now got so used to the way the Commander looked, he had forgotten that he was alien and so replied "W.C. in England, is short for Water Closet or what some might call a loo or a toilet?"

The Commander looked back at the ships name "well, Beth's Water Closet?"

Smiling Jack said "you got it."

The Commander shook his head and walked towards the ramp, waving his hand over his shoulder for them both to follow.

As Jack walked up the ramp with Claire just behind him, he walked past Summer who was just stood staring up at the ship in an half step. Jack waved his hand in front of her face as he walked past, she involuntarily snapped her many toothed jaw at his hand, which seemed to wake her up and made Jack jump. She carried on slowly stepping forward, with a look of wonder on her fox like face.

The ship looked quite dark and spacious inside as Jack stepped through some frosty air, off the ramp and into the War Catcher hull. As soon as stepped through the frosty barrier all the external sounds of banging metal, talking, screaming and other associated sounds of the Ghost Ship's docking bay disappeared.

Sighing, Jack turned to Sara and asked "another suspension field then?" Sara standing with hand on hip just nodded, whilst tapping her foot on the floor and looking impatiently at Summer ambling up the ramp.

"Um, why don't you call her?" asked Jack.

"Because she can't hear us" answered Sara shortly.

Summer then looked forward at the four people stood in the loading bay of the ship and quickened her pace, when she stepped inside Sara said in a slightly acidic tone "so nice of you to join us."

For a moment Jack felt slightly confused, miffed might have been a better word, as something about the darkened innards of the ship and the outside looked wrong somehow.

Stood just inside the hatch, the Commander swiped a pawed hand over a panel by the side of the doorway. Jack watched the slight shimmer of frost across the doorway suddenly turn solid, like frost moving super quick across a cold window, in the fashion of a swirling ballroom dancer. Then the lights came on in the loading bay of the ship and Jack realized what had been bothering him. They had simply walked straight onto this ship, without having to go through any airlock device like contraption.

Jack steadied himself and stared into the loading bay of the ship, it contained various sized boxes made from some dull grey plastic and metal combination, with odd shaped logos and colours on them. The most common of all the logos was 'tJi', in its green fading to blue italic slant.

Jack felt like he had seen this logo everywhere since waking up, it was simply nearly on everything he had looked at, it was like an infection he thought.

Most of the boxes were sat on pallets, pallets admittedly that were massively varied in size, they appeared to be made of anything from plastic and wood to metal, but they were basically still sleek looking pallets to be moved by forklift.

Jack looked around, finding on a wall hanging dejectedly what looked like human shaped forklift armed robot, with some seriously off-road type wheels attached to its legs. It was of course painted a standard crusty yellow.

The walls of the loading bay were a mixture of metal looking greys, with the floor appearing to be some dark blue colour and very shiny in places.

The Commander stepped through the cargo bay first, followed by the rest of the group and then a large glossy black gun, shaped like a bowling pin with all manner of cabling and wires dangling from it, slipped out of a hole that appeared in the floor.

A voice then came out of nowhere and said "stop, halt and desist?"

"Why" asked Jack "its not like I'm gonna steal from my own ship is it?" he said this in the tone of disbelief and confusion, like someone who just been informed they are the long lost heir of some great family and cannot quite believe it.

"Ooh someone sounds a little testy today don't they" said the overhead voice.

Jack cocked his head on one side, paused and questioned "Beth is that you?"

"Why yes, yes I do believe it is, in the flesh, so to speak" came Beth's voice echoing through the loading bay.

The Commander looked at Jack and asked quietly "well, who's Beth?"

"Another human, well I say human, I mean she was human until she was made into some kind of robot" replied Claire, before Jack could even think of answering.

"An Hersatz then" said Summer.

"Well ah yes I remember now, we only made a hundred or so" mused the Commander.

Sara looked round sharply and said "that can't be right, we've caught hundreds of the things!"

The Commander looked round at her as they walked across the loading bay towards a ramp and said "well, to my knowledge we built one hundred and four Hersatz and might I add on a very short budget" the Commander looked pleased with himself.

The rest of the way they walked in silence, with the Commander beaming all the way and everyone else, including Summer, wondering who made the rest.

As they continued to walk through the ship, Jack got the impression the thing was actually too big and so he asked "how big is this ship then, inside and out?"

The Commander turned and said "well its over ten times the size of your shuttle but internally the field is rated at forty times, because the legality of it doesn't matter!"

"No, no your right the field isn't illegal, just the whole ship is!" moaned Summer.

"Well, the ships not technically illegal" answered the Commander defensively.

"Okay then, strictly speaking the ship has been missing for so long that its become legend, people will be so pleased to see such an unusual design of ship that they won't recognize it instantly and report it immediately!" said Summer sarcastically.

The Commander winked at Summer, which infuriated her somewhat, before she could explode in anyway he answered her glare of fury with "well we will be using a Ghost Field Generator though, to disguise the ship!"

"You know there not technically legal or dangerous? And unfortunately very portable."

"Your gonna explain that aren't you?" asked Jack interrupting Summer and then looking at the Commander, after all if everything were true so far, everything they were currently doing was illegal and dangerous.

"A GFG is a disguise, generally it's a projection of one thing over another" said Summer.

The Commander looked very pleased with himself as they walked onto the bridge and Summer knew she was going to have to ask, it did not appear that he was telling the complete truth "and?"

The Commander saw the look in her eye and sighing replied "well we're not actually going to use the Ghost Field Generator as such. More have it powered on that people will think we're using it!"

"So they'll think we're hiding inside something when we're not?" asked Jack.

"Even though we won't be hiding anything?" finished Summer nodding to herself.

"Well exactly!" said the Commander smiling, who then walked off to the central seat, he did not sit down but jumped back in shock, Beth was sat in it as he spun it around.

Looking directly at Jack, Beth said "we're ready whenever you are Captain."

Jack not for the first time felt a bit flustered and replied "you know what we're doing?"

"Yes" said Beth.

"How exactly" asked Jack cautiously curious "I mean the last time we saw you, you were standing at a gate to a sewer?"

"By various means I escaped, Sarah helped a great deal and I ended up here" Beth said this with an almost brittle smile on her face and a look that said she would answer no further questions.

Jack got the hint and still could not believe how real she looked, the fact she was not human but was once, was just weird as far as he was concerned, because she looked so normal, so human.

"There's more to it than that though, isn't there?" asked Jack carefully.

With a little droop in her head and a sigh, she stood, leant on the chair and replied "yes, but you don't need to hear it all now."

Sara walked forward and touched her shoulder saying with compassion "one day we will, but not today I think. Until that day would you take us out of here?"

With a smile Beth looked up into Sara's sapphire blue eyes and asked "where to?"

Sara turned to the Commander who said with a shrug "well, a board shop. Surphon."

    With eyes half closed Beth concentrated for a moment, the window in front of them all showed the ship already facing the blue hazy door into space, which they zipped through and out into space like a cork from a fizzy wine bottle. The blue hazed door seemed to follow them for a moment, being stretched out into the vacuum of space like a bubble. Then as it released the ship, it looked like a foam explosion from a shaken champagne bottle, before springing back into place like a trampoline after ejecting its bouncers. Once the exit had finished vibrating backwards and forwards, the entrance and even the ship were nearly invisible, just another oversized metallic looking asteroid milling around in the belt. There ship swung round and began a long fly past of the Ghost Ship.

    Everyone stood talking to one another on the bridge, except Jack who was stood looking around the ships bridge. He would never have believed he would ever go into space, after all it was a small child's dream that was eventually crushed by reality. Yet here he apparently was, stood looking out of his own ship, or was that ships now, as had been mentioned on numerous occasions that he owned a few. Musing to himself that this was his dream to go into space but at the same time not exactly in this way, it just was not how he had imagined or expected it to be.

    He stood looking out the bridge window at the hull of the asteroid like ship they had just left, as they zipped passed. The name flashed by and Jack laughed as he worked it out "Snnugglers Rest!" If the ship was registered under that name, then a human would see the joke but a computer would not.

    Jack was impressed by this ships bridge, more so than by any others he had seen, it was how he had wanted and expected a ships bridge to look like.

The room was pear shaped with various screens around the back half of the bridge and very comfortable looking beige coloured seating in front of each screen. The walls and floor that were visible were a shiny gun metal grey, with the edges and important bits outlined in a thick black line.

    Jack heard the Commander and Summer exchanging comments about how 'old' and 'tired' looking the ship looked, with the Commander finally saying "well it is Legendary."

Summer rolled her eyes at him, which made her thick hairy eyebrows move around like a searching caterpillar.

The one thing Jack loved above all else though was the viewing window, the thing took up what looked like over seventy percent of the bridge. The window encased the entire front section of the bridge, like it had been carefully dipped in a pail of chocolate, nose first, then where it had stuck was where the window was installed. It was not a clean edge where the glass met the hull, it was like it was an ever growing moss.

Stood looking down between his feet into space and leaning on the forward metal rail, Jack was thinking of chocolate, it was making Jack feel hungry, not hungry in general but hungry for something very specific. He turned round to find Beth walking up behind him and he asked "where can I get some chocolate from please?"
Before she could answer Summer who was walking along behind her asked "what's chocolate?"
"The only reason to save the Earth actually" quipped Claire from the side of the bridge window.
Jack looked at Beth questioningly and asked "how do you explain what chocolate is? I mean I know generally its dark brown, has sugar in it and cream, contains cocoa of one description or another, which can be mixed to varying degrees for a different taste. But until you've actually tasted it how do you explain the sensation?"
"You don't" replied Beth, who then stepped to the back of the bridge and a very orange coloured rectangular panelled postbox, hanging in the wall. There was an angled floating darker shade of orange coloured screen on the front, which Beth touched briefly, more of a swipe actually and said "dairy milk chocolate, two hundred grams."
The screen appeared to fold back inside the box, followed by a metallic 'bing' like sound, a bar of chocolate sat in the alcove behind, which Beth reached for and then passed to Jack with a look of longing on her face. He unwrapped it and carefully took a bite, savouring the taste with his eyes closed.

When Jack finally opened his eyes, everyone was looking at him "what?" he asked curiously.
Claire looked impatient and asked "well, how does it taste?"
Jack looked at the bar in his hand and took another bite, with his mouth full he mumbled "you really wouldn't like it."
Claire turned away and then turned back to the sounds of Jack munching happily away "if its not very nice why are you still eating the bar?"
Jacks answering grin was all the clue Claire needed, she walked over to the panelled screen and ordered some chocolate for herself. After a few mouthfuls she felt like she was being watched and even found her own eyes were shut.
On opening her eyes she found everyone really was staring at her and Summer asked "well, what's it like?"
"You wouldn't like it" she replied, then she caught Jacks eye and they both laughed.
Eventually they all had a bar of chocolate in there hands, in various stages of chomping, it was then Jack asked Beth "are we going to run out of this?" he asked waving the bar in the air.

"No Jack, fortunately we have several bars to copy from, so it would take a million years for one person to go through the ships supply, if they could eat a kilo a day."

"That's a lot of chocolate to store?" mused Jack.

"We don't need to store it all Jack, just to have a copy to work from, which a tiny piece is taken from to make a near exact copy of" said Beth.

Jack looked back at the screen on the postbox "will it produce something, anything I ask of it?" asked Jack.

"Within reason, a base to copy from is always required" replied Beth.

"So if I wanted a copy of, say, me?"

"You would need to be in the stasis chamber and not mind having a small portion of your body removed."

"How small?" asked Jack.

"That part of your anatomy would be too small Jack" laughed Claire, whilst covering her below belt bits and gesticulating.

"I just wondered that's all, because I'm no closer to remembering what happened to me and..."

"Well ah, I see, your wondering if your a copy?" remarked the Commander.

Jack shrugged and said "it does seem odd to me that my memories are lost, it felt familiar in my room but new at the same time. But no, I don't think I'm a copy, who would?"

Claire looked round at the faces in front of her "your all thinking Jack here could be a copy?" various nodding suggested yes to her "but how and why?"

"We're not saying he is a copy, just that it would be possible and might explain his memory confusion, as no copy is perfect. As to why, who knows?"

Jack turned to the orangey coloured screen on the postbox, walked forward with his hand outstretched and said "there's only one way to find out."

Before his hand could touch the screen Beth took hold of his wrist in a vice like grip, stopping him dead and said in an conspiratorial whisper "you aren't a copy and it wouldn't be good to ask for a copy of yourself."

"Why not?" hissed Jack in a little pain around the wrist area.

"You've seen the size of the dispenser, haven't you?"

"Yes?" said Jack looking at the foot high and nearly as wide dispenser.

"So how big do you actually think the copy will be, if there is one of you in storage somewhere to make a copy from in the first place?"

Jack looked back at the alcove, measuring himself against the foot tall orange device, he would guess that "I'd come out in bits?"

"Or possibly very small! Since I know there are no copies of you anywhere and copying of sentient life is illegal, the machine would return an error, hopefully" said Beth.

"Excluding your good self obviously" said Jack.

"Or Jack being sentient" mused Claire quietly in the background.

Ignoring Claire, Beth continued "I'm not a copy Jack ... when I say that, I am a copy but as the original is gone, now I'm the original" she finished sullenly.

Wisely Jack decided to leave the conversation at that and instead glanced back at the machine.

There was something that had been bothering him ever since he had boarded the shuttle back on Earth for there escape, he just could not quite put his finger on it and yet this tiny copying machine in the wall of a foreign ship felt familiar somehow. Like a lot things he had seen so far he had felt some form of recognition but not with everything. Jack decided to look closer at the machine and that was when he noticed the letters printed in an italic slant on the top left corner of it, 'tJi' in green fading to blue. Next to the three letters was, presumably, the name of the machine and a version number. Something tickled his ears as he bent over to look and he swiped at nothing again.

"I assume f-code nineteen is the name and version of the machine but what does t.J.i. stand for?" asked Jack of no one in particular.

"You know what f-code stands for but not t.J.i?" asked Summer.

Jack nodded and Summer continued "everybody knows t.J.i. its one of, if not, the biggest company in the galaxy, possibly even in the Universe!"

Jack looked around the assembled faces for some help and was even surprised to find Claire shaking her head at him "you know what it is?" asked Jack of Claire.

"Nearly every bit of tech we've ever seen had t.J.i. written on it somewhere, it took us a few days, but we eventually worked out that it was a company or a business of some description."

"Okay so everybody knows what it stands for but me?"

The Commander opened his mouth to explain but Beth waved her hand at him to shush and said "t.J.i. stands for Triple J Industries."

Claire looked curiously at Jack and asked "so what does f-code nineteen stand for then?"

Jack managed to look slightly embarrassed and said "it means an error code where I come from!"

"No it doesn't, it stands for From Copy of Duplicate Entropy and the machines version number" replied Beth. As soon as she explained the short code to everyone she realized what Jack was thinking the 'F' stood for, which was very rude, preferably an action that should only happen between two lovers and mostly in private.

With a look of actual surprise on her face she turned back to Jack, for the first time since she had been in her new body she could not help herself and started to laugh. It took nearly a full minute for her to stop laughing, she was so pleased with the fact that she could still laugh she had not noticed when everyone had walked off in an awkward silence.

Jack was stood leaning on the bar that ran round the inside of the viewing window. He was still marveling at the lack of joins in the glass, it was what he imagined standing in a bubble might be like. The only break in the bulging window was where it met the hull of the ship and to Jacks eye it still looked like it was dripping in some way. The glass or whatever it was they were looking out of was brilliantly clean, the only indication of where to put your feet were the reflections in the material, which gave the impression that you were stood on a footbridge or the glass under foot was very, very deep.
He turned from staring out of the window to find the Commander walking up to him "well, you should really be watching the next bit Jack" he said.
Jack turned to watch the last of the frozen rocks slide by under and over the ships hull and asked "why?"
"Well, we're going to use the SUD's in a moment."
"SUD's?"
"Well, Split Universe Drive!"
"Ah, okay."
The Commander sighed and said "well it's what we use to travel across the galaxy and you'll be surfing it, in the competition."
"Surfing it! That's nice and why didn't we just use it when we left the big ship?"
"Well because it leaves a wake. Before you ask anything else just watch it and you'll see what I mean."

They both stood for several seconds until Jack got to the point where he felt he should ask when this was all going to happen, then Sarah's voice came over the ships speaker system counting down from ten.

When she got to three, he saw the Commander take a firm grip on the bar and Jack quickly looked round to find everyone else making sure they had a hold of something.

Staring out the window as Sarah's counting reached zero, Jack was presented with the effect of all the stars he could see being stretched and elongated, like he was seeing heavy acceleration as the stars were pulled into spaghetti strings. His body felt like it was being made lighter and lighter, like he had a great weight being lifted off his shoulders. Then he went from feeling super light to mega heavy and everything in between in a matter of a second, the view out of the window though was what he would call odd.

After all the stars had been stretched into one continuous sequence of lines, they made a bright white cylinder which for some strange reason reminded Jack of the inside cardboard bit from a toilet roll. Once as a child he had removed all the superfluous cleaning material from three rolls, being left with the rolls he had painted them inside and out in white paint, stuck them together to make one long tube and shined a torch down the opposite end. It had looked amazing as he watched from one end and had waggled a torch around at the other end, afterwards he had found his eyes were nearly blind from the torch for hours. This light show was nearly exactly like that, with streaks of blue and red flashing past and without him being blinded by a torch to an much larger scale.

Then the top of the tube split slowly from somewhere behind the ship, opening along its length like tearing a piece of paper. Above there heads it was total darkness, they then seemed to float up and through the inky blackness. As the ship moved through the layer of total black something could be seen on the other side, it was like surfacing from underwater at sea and at night. There appeared to be waves and troughs as they continued to move slowly up from underneath, one second black and next crashing through a wave and into a dusky foamy white cloud. This went on for several waves until they seemed to be cresting from one wave top to another.

Jack could not help but stare at where they were, it was near identical to being on a power boat at night, traveling at immense speed out at sea, the main difference was the lack of sea. They seemed to almost bounce from one wave to another and the waves were very big from Jacks point of view.

Looking closer Jack could see that everything was not all black as he had first thought, the waves they crested up and down on below were all made of up what looked like stars and galaxies. Above there heads were a similar set of waves with odd coloured stars and galaxies compared to the ones below. The ceiling of waves were quite close, they looked almost close enough to touch. It was like sailing on the sea at night, with reflections below distorted from above.

Jack then looked forward to view there apparent destination and in the distance could see a green dot, after staring at the green dot for a minute or more Jack had to conclude that it was getting bigger. Without turning Jack asked in an awe struck voice "where are we, exactly?"

"Well, we're in the gap or split between Universes" said the Commander. Claire's voice then came from behind, making both of them jump "it's amazing!"

Turning round Jack could see everyone staring through the glass, looking down Jack watched a wave come up, or was it go down and strike the bottom of the ship before splashing against the glass.

"What happens if we …"

"Sink?" said Claire finishing off Jacks question whilst following his gaze to the window floor.

"Well simply, we drop back into our Universe" answered the Commander.

It was such a sight to watch the Universe, actually two Universes, sliding by that they were both pretty much lost for words.

Eventually Jack found his voice and asked in the tone of a small boy asking for some more "how long is it?"

"Well, to our destination?" asked the Commander, Jack nodded and he replied "a little under an hour."

Jack was silent for a bit longer and then a confused frown appeared on his face and he asked "how long is the distance, I mean how far away is it in miles?"

The Commander exchanged a look with Summer and they both started to laugh at Jack.

"Actually I thought his question was quite relevant!" said Claire in a tone that would be understood by most human males as 'don't you mess with me boy.'

Catching her breath Summer said "you measure distance in light years, and your galaxy is roughly one hundred thousand light years across."

"You know that actually doesn't mean anything, right?" interrupted Jack.

Summer looked at him frustratedly and then she looked at Claire who appeared to be doing some complicated maths with her fingers.

Claire then looked up and said "if you traveled at the speed of light Jack for one year, you would travel ninety seven billion, seven hundred and sixty one million and six hundred thousand miles!"

Jack stared and then asked with a slight tone of annoyance "you did that with a calculator function on your Quellz didn't you?"

Claire went from glowing smugness too anger and then guilt, quicker than a schoolboy caught looking at there teachers melons and then making out they were staring out the window all the time 'honest guv'.

"You have to know the speed of light first!" she hotly retorted.

"Well before you two get to actual fighting, you should know that when we're using a SUD drive we talk of distance in Gals or Galaxies" said the Commander.

"So how many galaxies is it then?" asked Jack.

"Well two but actually a one point two. The first number denotes the distance possible to travel and the second the time it will take with the drive."

"So that means we're traveling a galaxy of how long every 2 hours, years or centuries?" asked Jack.

"Well approximately two hundred thousand light years in two days or so."

"Why didn't you say that earlier!" complained Jack, the Commander just shrugged.

Facing forward again Jack noticed the green dot had gotten bigger and asked "is that green thing our destination?"

"It's a graphical overlay on the window to show our exit point" said Beth who was sat back in the central chair.

"So a yes then!"

Then Jack remembered what he had been told earlier and asked "how exactly do you surf this?"

"Well I thought you'd never ask" answered the Commander with a smile and strode off beckoning for Jack to follow.

Chapter 24 : 2p.

Jack almost had to run to keep up with the Commander as they walked down a metallic grey corridor and then he suddenly stopped in front of a slightly sunken doorway. There was an orange panel to the left of the door, about palm size and just above it was written '2p'.
"2p?" questioned Jack.
"Well hmm, oh yes the Picture Palace" said the Commander.
The Commander touched his hand to the panel and the door slide open, the pair stepped through into an almost dark room and the door swooshed shut behind them.

Jack did not like darkened places over much, ever since he had a misdemeanor of a moment with a surprisingly naughty older lady in an even older cinema. Here he was in his nightmare equivalent, staring around at a black room, when he turned back the Commander had vanished. Jack almost jumped in panic and then after a few seconds of wildly spinning around he saw a shadow moving away from him.
He called out "is that you?"
"Well yes!" came a slightly far off reply.

Jack started to worry ever so slightly more, just as he had decided to make his way back to the door somewhere behind him, he looked down to find his feet and saw an ever so slightly green glowing line. It was only just visible, it led off in the direction of where the Commanders voice had come from and appeared to be flowing like a river. Jack followed it and after a few bends in the green line, which he had to follow because of the walls he struck, he came out into a room that was golden.

Jack stood next the Commander in a room that was basically a great big golden foil glowing sphere, then there was a swoosh noise behind him and he watched the door slide slowly shut. In fact it was the only door he had ever seen that shut with style, it was almost like the little wave of acknowledgment one cool spy at the bar would give to another equally cool spy at the other end of the bar. How a door shutting managed to convey this to Jack was impossible to tell, it was more of a feeling mixed with the visible way the door shut.

Jack said out loud "cool" nodded to himself and then felt that he should not be saying anything but appreciate whatever happened next. The Commander had been looking at Jack the whole time since he had entered the room and said "well, this is one of the most amazing places you'll ever see."
"What is it?"

"Well it's called a Picture Palace or 2p but it's actually more than that, it can show you anything, like your blinkers, but it was designed and engineered to help you feel what's happening too. They used to be in all our ships for training, until the blinkers came along. I mean when you consider how expensive this room is, the blinkers were a massive boon to the financiers and they could do exactly the same thing individually. The only thing the blinkers miss is the emotion, knowledge is fine but without a point of reference or emotion to go with it, it can mean nothing at all."

Jack listened to the Commander whom sounded mildly bitter about the whole thing, but he was not prepared to listen to a lecture and so interrupted by asking "it's a training room then?"

Looking slightly hurt the Commander replied "well it's more of a virtual world in the real world, watch."

The Commander turned to face what looked like an old style radio microphone that hung from the ceiling and said into it "in-Vowke London, late nineteen eighty five, Nelson's Column, England, Earth, Milky End, Westward Spiral."

The Commander said England 'Ing-land' with an almost west country accent, which got Jack thinking that he must have spent some time in the South West of the country. Jack knew something had been bothering him about the Commander ever since he had first spoken, it was not the words he was saying but the accent he was using. Considering the size of England, there was an awful lot of local dialect to pick from and so why he had a Devon twang to his voice he had no idea. Jack also knew he was to going to have to find out why it was so fashionable and almost universal, from his point of view, to speak English at some point, just now was not that time.

Jack asked "London?"

"Well yes, so that I can show you what the 2p can do, to show you how real it is!"

Jack had experienced the Blinkers and good though they were, there was something not quite right with them, as a tool for learning he would imagine they were very good. They just did not feel natural in some way, the feeling was like being on an walking holiday and finding a local country pub at the end of a hot hilly day of rambling. From the outside there appeared to be music and happy voices but as soon as you entered the country pub all sound and movement had stopped. Then everyone's head would swivel and face the newcomers with nary a movement of any other body part. The awkward silence would only be broken upon leaving the establishment and that was the feeling Jack got when he used his Blinkers.

Then there was a loud 'ping' noise and the Commander turned his head to Jack and asked "well, ready?"

Jack replied "yes!" in a tone that suggested 'obviously, I'm standing right 'ere aren't I?'

The Commander raised his arm at the elbow to the upright position, then lowered it slowly palm facing down. As his hand neared the horizontal, the view quite simply defogged its way into view, it was as if a sudden wind had come from nowhere to forcibly blow away the foggy final remnants of the golden foiled sphere and replace it with reality.
Jack spun around wildly trying to take it all in "it's amazing, it really looks like we're here, in London I mean."
The Commander smiled and said "well walk about, tell me what you see?"
Jack was lost for words it genuinely looked real, Nelson's Column, the people walking and stood around feeding pigeons and dodging there liquid thank you gifts from above. The red double decker bus driving round Trafalgar, belching black smoke from its exhaust and the puffy clouds in the sky wheezing there way across the horizon. To Jack, above all else, he felt he could smell the place, feel it, actually sense it.
"The stone feels real!" said Jack leaning on a Lion "but why eighty five?"
"Well I liked it, anyway we're here for you to see and really feel what surfing is all about" to Jack there looked like there was an glint of excitement in the Commanders eye.
The Commander then turned to the microphone still hanging in the air and said "in-Vowke last years SUD's Competition, final race."

The scene of London was slowly brushed aside like a breeze blowing away heavy mist, then Jack found he and the Commander were stood in a crowd of screaming aliens stood on high benches that ranked up on either side of what looked like a tarmac road to Jack. The whole place reminded Jack of a stadium seating for a race track, the main difference was the amount of seating that actually rolled up either side of the track, almost completing a tube.
At either end of the straight Jack could just see the track flicking away round a bend and the curved seating appearing to carry on around the corner. Where he could see daylight through what looked like a small gap above, on closer inspection was actually about a hundred meter gap, the sky was a reddish pink with bright blue clouds dusting the air.

Jack had never seen anything like this before and the emotion, the excitement was almost palpable, he felt like shouting himself. The thing that stopped him shouting out was the unreality of it all, the fact he knew he had never been here, in addition to remembering they were stood inside a golden ball.

Looking up once again at the horde of aliens sitting above them Jack asked "where's the water?"
When he got no reply he looked first left, then right and finally started spinning around searching for the Commander. He was nowhere to be seen.

Then a brazen horn sounded and everyone fell silent, Jack felt a light tap on his shoulder and on turning round found the Commander proffering a drink of some description in the obligatory polystyrene like cup.

Jack sighed as he took it and said "you know these don't recycle, don't you?"

Stepping over the back of the bench and sitting down, the Commander replied "well hmm, err no, you simply press the green spot underneath, then the cup compresses down into a small sugar like cube, which you can then swallow!"

Jack looked underneath his cup and indeed there was a green spot on the bottom "but its not real, how am I holding it?"

"Well, Particle Phasing Fabar and it won't compress when it's full, before you try" the Commander said this as if everyone knew what he was talking about including Jack.

Before he could ask what he meant a roar went up from the crowd and everyone jumped, slithered, clambered or levitated to a standing position. A part of the black tarmac like track had lowered like a ramp, then walking, carrying or standing on various sized surfboards, were forty two aliens making there way up the slope. Jack found he was staring like everyone else in fascination at not only the variety in aliens, but that the boards were actually floating about a meter off the ground. It was the first time Jack had seen anything like it, he must have seen other floating devices on the ships he had been on, it was just that he had not registered it before.

They all trooped up the ramp and stood four abreast in golden boxes with numbers that appeared in the tarmac; when they had all made it to there various starting positions the ramp closed itself, leaving not a trace of where it had been. The aliens all wore outrageous coloured suits, some with obvious sponsorship emblazoned across there clothing. Some carried helmets under there arm, tentacle or other appendage, then a second horn sounded and a timer appeared in the air counting down from a hundred at the front of the grid. The aliens waved various bits of there bodies at there audience and put on there helmets, the ones without helmets either pressed a button or willed it, but the thick collars around there necks unfolded to engulf them in close fitting headgear. Each one of them attached or made sure they were attached to there boards, by a cord of varying colour and design but all were about three meters long.

Jack had too ask "why the cord?"

In an hushed expectant tone the Commander replied "well, in case they fall off."

Jack looked back at the aliens now standing or lying on there boards and said "there a meter off the ground."

"Well, at the moment they are!" came the curt reply.

"I'm sorry but I can't see what there surfing?"

"Well, just watch Jack and you'll see."

As the counter on the track approached zero, everyone in the stands started to quieten down to an almost hushed silence of expectation. A faint fuzzy blue line then slowly faded into view above the heads of the racers, with quietly expectant 'ahh's' and 'ooh's' from the crowd. The blue line followed the entire length of the track, creating a tube like effect with a radius of about fifty meters Jack noticed. That was it, no explanation given of the blue thing because none was needed apparently, maybe it was 'there to light the track' thought Jack. The crowd stared harder at the competitors waiting for the race to start, seeming to be willing the race to begin early.

Jack concentrated on the four competitors at the front of the grid and suddenly all four were superimposed almost directly in front of him. Jack jumped out of his seat with shock, only to have the Commander forcibly pull him back down onto the bench. When he glanced back at the track they were all still lying or standing on there boards at a safe distance. When he concentrated on the front four, they again became massively enlarged right in front of his face, like having three-dee television forced between your teeth.

"Well what you concentrate on is shown in detail" said the Commander with a sigh.

"A warning might have been nice!" remarked Jack sitting back, rubbing his eyes and pulling at his teeth, with the feeling that he had been violated in some way.

The Commander just sat smiling to himself, then as the countdown got to ten, a horn sounded off each second, until it got to the final three numbers and then it slowed, displaying a set of coloured lights, red then orange and finally blue.

The blue light hung there in the air in front of the competitors; the tension and excitement was electrifying through out the crowd, then after what seemed like an eternity, the light went out and a trumpet like sound played out. The surfers all shot forward like an escapee soap at a lather party. Each one left a different coloured vapour trail as they accelerated, with some even managing to display there sponsors name in the clouds that followed them.

Jack concentrated to follow them as they crossed the start line, he was surprised by several things as they thundered past his point of view. First of all the boards themselves were actually a lot thicker than he expected, each one had tailored grips at various points around the edge of the board. There were fins for steering in water underneath, which varied greatly in design, some looked like big square blocks and others like threads of silk, which made no sense to Jack at the moment. The back of each board had a lump or hump at the rear which housed the propulsion system, with some having fins on top. Exhaust jets could be seen spilling out the back, sides and even the front of the surfboards, presumably for thrust and balance. Across the boards there were various grabs and loops, which each one of the competitors held onto differently or not at all.

Some competitors even had more than one board under there feet, with only one engine between them, Jack could not see the point, apart from twice the advertising space. One advert on an board read 'Cloudboards', written in blazing ink across the bottom and top of the board, others had SkyBoard, CloudSurfer and other similar obvious choices but weirdly no water related ones Jack could immediately see. It was like they feared getting wet, by actually having a water related name emblazoned across there bows.

The underside of the front of the boards were like boat hulls, as far as Jack could see, as they floated, hovered or flew past. As a he watched the last one cross the line, he had unintentionally moved the camera view to show the face in the helmet.

"That ones human!" Jack almost shouted, jumping from his seat.

The Commander briefly turned to look up at Jack and said "well no, that ones a New-man."

"What do you mean Newman, that's another human if ever I've seen one?" said Jack pointing and then sitting down slowly as he felt embarrassed, which he then thought of as silly because they were in a simulation.

"Well no, she's from Nerth."

"How do you know where she's from?"

"Well if you follow a racer and Vowke about there bio, it'll be displayed."

Jack quickly found her again wanting to know everything, all that was displayed was her age, statistics of how she got to the final and where she was from. There was a slowly spinning image of her head and shoulders in the background of the statistics, which showed her as blonde, blue eyed and what Jack would have called buxom in black leather.

Her name seemed wrong to Jack and he just had to read it out loud "Samantha Orin Shavan?"

"Well that's what it says on the tin!" commented the Commander.

"What did you just say?"

"Well isn't it one of your phrases?"

"I suppose it is but I thought it was 'does what it says on the tin', and is generally used by someone on someone else who is asking a stupid question. Like asking 'what does this do?' whilst holding up a tin with a label reading 'sticky stuff' or 'black paint' maybe. But I don't see how that works for Sammy here" replied Jack whilst pointing at Samantha racing around the track.

The Commander dismissed Jack by the simple method of waving him to look back at the track and then pointed to a floating, partially see through image that had appeared on the side of the track. The massive moving images were tracking the racers like any good race cameraman would, with Jack wondering why it was even there if you could look at your own personal screen right in front of you. Then he worked it out, it was an atmosphere thing; because everyone was seeing the same image at the same time, they were not only watching but feeling and experiencing an event.

Jack had to admit that so far after starting in last place, Samantha Orin Shavan was still holding her own, in last place.

The circuit did seem to be a bit odd to Jack as he watched the broadcast, the tarmac looking track raced out of the stadium and disappeared, as the blue line then twisted and twirled up into the sky. Then it turned over, seeming to dive back through a city just outside the stadium, twisting between skyscrapers of all shapes and sizes, that in some cases actually looked like they were defying gravity. Then the track zipped out and along a beach, where it angled up into a loop and dived into the sea. It was like traveling through a blue lit tunnel sliding past at terrific speed, with various odd shaped sea dwellers lurking at the edges and pawing to get in on the race. The tube carried on twisting and turning down through the water, sliding through undersea canyons and great big crevasses. Then suddenly it swept up, almost vertically, the racers exited the sea and the track twisted over to head inland. The competitors briefly being once again were upside down, some appearing to change shape as the centrifugal force of the harsh turn pulled on there bodies.

Then they started to head back towards the stadium and Jack asked "I don't see why they need surfboards, if there just floating around on them?"

The Commander was staring intently at his own viewers choice, sighing he turned to Jack and said "well, you remember the waves in the gap we saw, just a short while ago on the bridge?"

"Yes?"

"Well, we're still in the gap and when we left the big ship you asked why we didn't use the SUD drive right away?"

"Yes?"

"Well the waves are relevant to the mass of the object and your proximity to other matter."

Jack looked confusedly at the Commander and made a face at him that read as 'what are you on about?'.

In a tone of voice he would have used for a young child, the Commander said "well, big ship near bigger object means very big waves and lots of them. Small ship near big object means smaller waves, but still lots of them."

"So what's that to do with this?" said Jack waving at everything around him.

"Well when they cross the line they'll turn on there Split Universe Drives and..."

"Hold on aren't they a bit small to have Split drives?" interrupted Jack "I mean I thought someone said something about the shuttle not being big enough to have one and yet these surfboards have got them?"

"Well, that's not strictly true. You need a SUD drive to power the suspension field, which made it illegal on your shuttle because the thing was so small and therefore unsafe. Anyway you'll see in a minute as they cross the line that they don't disappear into the split, there drives are modern versions of the very first SUD drives. The first drives created choppy and uncontrollable waves, which no one uses any more."

"Except the surfers here?" asked Jack with a sarcastic tone.
"Well, that's what the blue line is for, stability."

Jack called up the race position table which had altered many times, the only constant was the leader and the Newman in last place, there positions had not altered.

A musical horn then played out in the stadium, as the competitors entered the arena to come sweeping through the stands, as each of the racers crossed the line they pressed something. A bubble then seemed to form around them, some of the bubbles were round, others followed the contours of the rider and board, some of the bubbles looked to be angled for an attack on the air. The only part not within the bubble was the bottom of the surfboards. Then the bubble seemed to breach the surface of a multicoloured sea, board and rider slowly emerged to be crashing through waves of nearby foaming reality.

Everyone in the crowd gave a massive sigh of relief, even Jack had not realized that he along with everyone else, had been holding there breaths as the first riders came flying round the final bend and crossed the start line.

"Well that was the second most dangerous point in the race" said the Commander with the sound of relief in his voice.

Jack looked at him and said "but you know how it ends!"

The Commander shrugged and continued "well the rest of the race goes on for another hour or so, then for the final lap they turn off there SUDs."

Jack sat back watching as the Commander ordered the recording to fast forward to the start of the final lap.

Watching the racers come round the final bend Jack asked "what are they actually surfing on?"

"Well our reality, you remember, there in the gap made by the SUD drive, between our Universe and another. Just like this ship we're in now is."

Jack was staring at the surfers as they drew ever closer to the start line, watching intently as they shifted there boards to make there way up the back of one wave, trying to find another wave traveling faster than they currently were but in the same direction. Whilst all the time trying to maneuver around other boarders, obstacles of our Universe and wherever they were in the split. Each one was trying to ride the crest of a wave and find a way to reach the next wave in front, which as a viewer Jack could only see ten square meters of. When two surfers got close to one another the area of the split the spectators could see tripled, it was like watching a dark sea with streaks of coloured light and where the surfers boards touched the waves a white spray foamed up around them.

As they closed on the line the Commander said "well, this is the most dangerous point in the race, because as they properly re-enter our reality, the bubble becomes unstable."

Jack could see that all the racers were slowing down to what looked like a crawl, after the mad dash around the track with there SUD drives activated. As they crossed the line the board and surfer seemed to sink into the black waves like a diver in quicksand or even slow-sand. Each one bobbed slightly as they crossed the line, there bubbles shimmered like a million stars were washing over them from a great distance and simply faded away.

Then as one of the tentacled competitors crossed the line waving his or hers hairy limb, the angled bubble around them gave an unusual shake, almost like a hiccup or even an hiccough. Halfway between the start line and the end of the straight, most of the competitors had sunk out of the gap or split they had been racing in and were back fully in reality cruising above the tarmac. The hairy tentacled racers face had gone from deep concentration to panic, as they realized there reality bubble was not working properly. Jack watched as the bubble started to crack above the head of the alien, it took hold with all of its appendages on the board it was racing on, hugging it like a bear. The bubble then simply exploded like a mallet striking a glass vase from above, what looked like immense weight was then being pushed down on top of the racer and its board, forcing it out of the split and back into reality with a loud pop. The surfer and its board disappeared from view for a second in the waves, then they came rushing out of the split angled steeply downwards. When it came plunging through into our reality, it came through with such added speed that the board dug into the tarmac track like a dart and vibrated. The racer was flung off its board like it had been bouncing on a diving board, only to be catapulted back onto the board again by the elastic cord with a loud splat sound.

Then something could be seen shimmering like a heat haze all over the board, holding the floppy tentacled alien in place. The track seemed to squeeze the board from its surface like a teenager popping an angry spot, the board then floated over to one side of the track, where a team of white clad, presumably medical personnel, waited impatiently to flick a switch on the board releasing the alien. The creature flopped around like a jelly in a blender, before going stiff in every possible way and the white clad medics waved around a big net to catch it in as it fell off the board.

Jack asked "that looked weird, did that look weird to you?"

"Well, because the bubble failed on re-entry, some of the split rules got stuck in her body and on contact with another reality they dissipated, everywhere."

"Did it hurt?"

"Well I'm not sure, she's still in care."

"It looked kinda painful to me! And you want me to race in this?"

"Well not just race but win!"

"Thanks but no thanks" said Jack standing up to leave.

The Commander grabbed his arm and with some force and dragged him back down onto the bench "well, all this is your fault you know" he hissed at Jack trying to make him feel guilty.

"All what, I don't remember any of this stuff" replied Jack shaking his free hand and waving at everything in general.
"Well you may not remember what you've done."
"You know perfectly well I don't!"
"Well the point being, everyone else remembers!" said the Commander slowly, emphasizing each word with a poke on Jack's chest.
Jack paused in replying, which was unusual and then asked "what do they remember?"
"Well they remember several things Jack and your face is well known. The first human they saw on the news destroying an entire world and then a star system. The first human seen beating a fleet of stellar attack vessels single handed. The first human seen torturing for information."
"I know I couldn't do any of that, who could?"
"Well one day you'll remember, it may have been you seen committing the acts but you were under the influence of the Furrykin. The general public now know you weren't in full control of your faculties but it will take time for them to pass the blame."
"Are you saying some of the aliens that the Furrykin use, know what they're doing?"
"Well some of them yes, it's easy to tell when there under the influence as there is a delay between thought and action but in human cases there was no delay. So they assumed you were an ally of the Furrykin and not a comatose lump."
"Right, right I'm glad we've got that sorted out" said Jack with light relief.
"Well now on to the serious business of getting you ready to surf. We'll start with water and work up to reality waves!"

After an hour of surfing at various beaches around the Universe, Jack was now used to variable types of water and waves, the Commander stopped the simulation.
Jack was slowly lowered from the top of a wave to stand in the golden ball, as the water and surfboard slowly faded and drained from view. The Commander turned and said "well I think your ready for the black stuff, well at least a trial anyway."
Slightly out of breath and not the least bit wet Jack said between gulps of air "I told you I could surf. I admit not well, but I can at least stand up!"
"Well Jack you've been learning on normal hover-boards in various gravities with liquid of variable buoyancy, but when your in the gap between Universes, the board and the wave are your balance, buoyancy and thrust all rolled into one!"
"Yeah, I saw jets on the back of the boards in the race earlier?"

"Well, each board has identical SUDs drives, the exhaust-jet system is really the only thing that can be altered, besides the shape of the board itself. The fins underneath and on the back of the boards are used for braking, steering and even to hold onto when it all goes wrong. The faint blue line you saw running down the middle of the track, is in effect a magnetic tube for the SUDs to latch onto. Otherwise they'd be popping in and out of the split like a ball bobbing out at sea in a storm."
Jack gave the Commander a sidelong glance and asked thoughtfully "it's a jet ski then?"
"Well more of a surf ski ha ha. One thing you will need though is real practice."
Jack stood looking at the Commander and after a while when nothing more was forthcoming asked "are we practicing then?"
The Commander seemed preoccupied for a minute, after Jack got a little impatient and asked again, the Commander turned to him, pulled his hand away from his ear and said "well, hmm, oh sorry I was just listening to the latest results. It's you practicing, not us and not until you've got your own board!"
"Why my own board?"
"Well everybody is different and in the gap those small variations can have strange and magnificent outcomes to how things are handled in the split. You hear people say that the tools of there trade are an extension of themselves, well in the case of your board that is especially true in the gap, where everything is contrasting and exaggerated."
"So using a board in here would be a bad thing?" asked Jack pointing at the Golden foiled ball they were still standing in.
"Well if you weren't racing it would be fine, but once you pick up a habit on a board, it rarely lets go" said the Commander with a knowing nod.
Jack nodded his head in agreement, remembering when he had learned to surf; he had borrowed a board that was far too big for him and it took years of practice to get rid of the bad habit when he eventually got his own board.

      A ding-a-ling type chime played from somewhere above there heads and Beth announced through a speaker somewhere "five minutes until re-entry."
The Commander started to walk quickly to the small red dashed marks, that outlined the door in the Golden globe they were stood in. After he had palmed the door open and stepped through, again he noticed that Jack was not following, it was like he was trying to be deliberately obstinate.
In a slightly rough tone, which only a dog talking English could ever hope to manage, the Commander said "well come here boy!"
Jack actually jumped in his skin, he might have recognized the words but the gruff no nonsense growling tone of a wild wolf that the Commander had used, ran straight through his ears and down his spine to the bottom. It bypassed the logic part of his brain and spoke directly to the panicky bit, which without hesitation told his legs to obey the command given on pain of pain or else.

The look of surprise on Jack's face as he started to lurch towards the doorway was priceless 'it was just a shame Claire had not been here to see it' thought the Commander who then laughed quietly to himself.

Chapter 25 : Dodging The RUM.

The Commander and Jack walked onto the bridge, making there way to what Jack thought of as the chocolate dipped window, but obviously was not because he could see out of it. Then Claire and Sara joined them, Beth seemed to just suddenly appear sat in the Captains chair. Beth then started to count down the seconds till the start of re-entry and Jack looked out the window cautiously.
"You look worried Jack?" asked Claire.
Jack turned his head slightly and answered "I've seen what happens when a bubble fails."
"What bubble?" asked a puzzled Claire looking around the bridge.
"The one we're in!" said Jack.
Before Claire could retort Sara butted in and said "don't worry Claire I'll explain it later."
Through the window the ship gradually sunk lower into the black waves speckled with light, each wave seemed to be attacking the ship with more and more venom as they neared the exit back to there Universe. As they passed down through ever more violent white foamy waves, Jack could have sworn he saw worms, shapes, odd moving things and faces in the foam. Then they were briefly in the black foam topped waves, before a thin white bar came zipping up from below the ship to surround them in the white tunnel again. The bright white tunnel closed in above there heads, seconds later the tunnel was gone with a slight lurch and a smear of the speeding stars as they returned to normal space.
"Fireworks?" asked Claire pointing excitedly.
They all turned to look out the viewing windows top left corner, they stared trying to find the fireworks, suddenly they appeared as lines but only in the green part of the spectrum.
Summer and the Commander exchanged a look, they both turned to Beth who said sounding annoyed "yes, Rocket Under Mines!"
"Here! But why?" asked Summer.
"And what are Rocket Undermines?" asked Claire "and where's here as there's nothing here?"
Beth chose to ignore her for the moment, whilst she directed the ship away from the streaking towards them green lines.
"There looking very definite those green lines, aren't they?" commented Jack as no matter where Beth moved the ship the lines followed, seeming to move ever closer.
"There mobile mines Jack" said Summer with slight irritation in her voice.
"Very mobile by the look of it" said Sara who got a dirty look off Summer "it was just an observation" she answered defensively.
"Go and observe quietly somewhere else please" growled Summer.

Then Jack asked "can't we out fly them or even SUD off?" Jack was quite pleased with his play on words, possibly in another Universe, time line or situation the subtlety might have been noticed, not with this audience.
"Well no Jack, that's why there called Rocket Under Mines" replied the Commander.
"That's a RUM way to go" said Jack after a moments thought, whilst doing the whole nudge nudge wink wink thing, that people do when they think there being funny and either are not or do not understand the situation. Claire punched him, quite gently by her standards, on his upper arm, before he could react Sara grabbed the back of his collar and pulled him into a seat.

After several sharp turns, which would have caused nose bleeds and the flattening of bodies in a normal human space vehicle, Jack noticed something that the others seemed to have missed.
"Have you noticed that the green tail bits only appear when we're turning?" he asked.
"Yes Jack, they only fire there engines when they need to make a course correction or try to catch us up" replied Summer.
"So why don't we fly about a bit or use the SUD drive to escape?"
"They can follow us into the split and flying around to waste there fuel would take approximately fourteen hours" said Beth looking at some readouts that were floating above the armrest on her chair.
After several more minutes of nothing really happening, apart from little green boosts appearing out the window, Jack was curious "if we're looking out the front of the ship why are the green trails not getting any bigger as there coming towards us?"
"That part of the window has been designated for target viewing" came Beth's reply.
"Ah" said Jack "I get it now. One more question though, if we're here for a board shop, where is it, why are there mines here and where are we if we're not at the board shop?"
"Well, all valid questions" said the Commander "and the answer is, we try and avoid exiting from the gap too near or in a star system, because the closer to matter and the denser the matter does matter, making the waves in the gap more exciting!"
Jack remembered the Golden ball surf simulator and the Commander continued with "also if the system your planning on surfacing in has the right sensors, they can pick you up long before you exit and lie in wait. Think of it as the ships bow wave showing itself first, giving more time for the defence system to come online."
"Okay but where are we?" asked Claire.
"Twelve hours from our destination" replied Beth.
"Okay so why not travel straight there and let there defence system get rid of the rocket mines?" asked Claire.
"What makes you think they have a defence system?" asked Summer.
"Because we didn't pop out nearer there system and the Commander just said so!" replied Claire.

"Okay, so we make a bee-line straight for the board shop then and hope there defenses pick off the mines?" asked Jack, heading off an argument between Claire and Summer who looked quite tired for some reason.
The Commander turned to Beth and said "well that sounds like a plan to me."
Beth slipped as many levers as she could to maximum, with an expression of mild hope tinged with worry and then she leant back in her seat mumbling to herself "let's hope we can out run them."
"Let's all get some rest then before we get to the board shop" said Summer glancing at Beth.

Several hours later Jack walked back onto the bridge, he had only been in the lounge area drifting in and out of sleep on an exceptionally comfortable sofa, that looked a little like the one he used to own back on Earth. It was the regret that he may never see his own sofa again that had prompted him to fall asleep on it he felt, that and the probable fact that more than likely in his room there would be another world entirely. Much as it had been amazing to see it, it was also quite worrying and disconcerting to find an entire world outside your window, when you knew you were basically on a submarine in space.
When Jack had slept, he had slept like a baby and given that he normally only had a few hours of your basic nightly snoring, he felt incredibly refreshed for his brief sofa liaison.
When he saw Beth she had not moved, she was just sat in the central seat looking out the viewing window, which was showing the occasional green boost line of the Rocket Under Mines moving ever closer.
After a few seconds she shook her head and turned to Jack saying "I'm afraid it won't work, the mines will overtake us long before we reach the systems defence network."
Jack looked round behind him, because of the informative tone she had used, Jack was not sure she had actually been talking to him but replied anyway "what won't work?"
"Traveling straight to the board shop."
"Um, why not?"
Beth turned to Jack and gave him a look that could only be described as 'are you simple or what!'
She then answered a little testily "as I said the Rocket Under Mines will overtake us or hit us long before we reach the defence network, assuming they have one".
Jack put a hand on his chin in thought and then asked "why are the mines chasing us in the first place?"
"Because we entered the area they were guarding?"
"Okay, so what were they guarding and why did we come out of the split there, and not say the other side of the system?"

Beth paused, then she started to trip through the ships flight records, with her fingers on an floating screen that popped into the space in front of her. All Jack saw was lines of text scrolling past, in the obligatory green colouration, at a frightening speed, then he felt something brush the top of his head like a feather duster being wiped over his skull. Jack waved his hand over his head and found nothing there, but could have sworn he heard some high pitched giggling fading away, as well as the rustle of something that sounded like lots of spines brushing together. Jack shuddered, no matter how many times people told him that porcupines did not hunt people, he had still been scared rigid as a small child visiting a zoo with his school, when one had shaken its spiny porcupine bits at him. The sound and motion of the animal had scared him so much, that he had hid for the rest of the day in the public lavatories.

Shaking himself Jack asked with a slight quaver in his voice that slowly faded "so, erm, what's the verdict?"

"Well, verdict on what?" boomed the voice of the Commander as he strode onto the bridge with vigorous intent in his stride.

Jack looked at him closely, he seemed different some how, bigger, more confident and above all else a great deal taller.

The Commander stood next to Jack, he towered over him with Jack feeling a crick in his neck starting as he stared up at him "been on the rack have we?" asked Jack.

The Commander looked down at him and gave a frown before saying "well only the top row, and how did you know?"

"Because your so much taller!" replied Jack slightly awestruck.

"Well, oh that, give it an hour or so and my spine will have shrunk back to normal."

Jack looked him up and down noticing that he also appeared to have a really small waist at the current moment in time.

Jack was not sure they had been talking the same language either, he had been talking about a torture like device and by the sound of the Commanders reply, he had been talking about some form of sleeping arrangement from a boat.

The Commander faced Beth and asked again "well, the verdict?"

"We have been confused."

Jack pulled a face, raised a hand like any school teenager worryingly admitting being a part of the guilty party but not all of the parts at the party and said "count me into that one."

"Well explain" said the Commander.

"Checking the records someone or something altered our exit point from the gap. For some reason they wanted us to appear near the mines."

"Can I just ask, what are the mines protecting, I mean you don't normally get a random mine field in space do you?" asked Jack.

"Well we have occasionally come across them from wars that ended millennia ago and everyone forgot or thought they were gone" said the Commander thoughtfully.

"So are they part of some forgotten war then?" asked Jack.

"No, the data is just coming through now. They were RUM protectors!" said Beth in surprise.

The Commander had a look of shock on his face and after a few seconds of surprise asked "well what ship?"

"The one oh one Cascade" replied Beth.

"Well I'll be a Playtor's uncle. That ship was presumed destroyed in the Gelflar wars, it was the most powerful ship ever built in every way. The fastest, biggest, most technically advanced ship that ever just disappeared. We're all taught about her at school and many stories revolve around her, so many that the Captain of the ship has been almost forgotten and the ship itself is the story" the Commander spoke of it in absolute awe.

Jack on the other hand quite obviously had no idea of its cultural significance on the Commander and asked "where is it then?"

"Well that's the point, nobody knows" said the Commander.

"Until now and I reckon I do" replied Jack as the Commander turned to stare at him "its been wrapped up in one of your Ghost thingies, hasn't it Beth?"

Open mouthed showing nearly all of his teeth the Commander turned back to Beth and asked "well is this true, have we really found the one oh one?"

"Presumably" answered Beth.

"Well what do you mean presumably, surely its a yes or no answer?" exclaimed the Commander.

"It's not quite as easy as that, the mines have registration codes from that ship and there is a GFG like distortion from that area of space. But I can't detect anything else!"

"Well we have to go back" said the Commander.

"No we don't. Whatever or whomever dropped us out of the gap near the ship then managed to board the ship."

"Well which ship, this ship?" asked Jack and the Commander almost in sync.

"Well I presume so, as shortly after we turned to make our escape one of the left hatches was opened and the air was cycled in the lock."

"Well, we've got an intruder on board?" asked the Commander angrily.

"Presumably."

"Well there's that word again, why presumably?" sighed the Commander.

"Because the same number of lifeforms as boarded the ship are still on the ship" said Beth curtly.

"Unless there was an exchange" mused Jack "or they weren't people but robots or something or even that there hidden from your sensors, the same as the Ghost Ship thingy."

Beth and the Commander stared at Jack until the Commander found his tongue and said turning to Beth "well this is why I both hate and like humans at the same time. They tend to think of things we would not, which is both worrying and exciting at the same time."

"I know exactly what you mean as I used to be a one, it presents multiple ideas that could all currently be true as we have little information to go on" said Beth.

"Well still the question remains as to whether we should go back?" asked the Commander hopefully.

"By your own instructions we have little time to train and win the trophy, so an excursion back to the distortion would not be beneficial. I shall make a note of the coordinates and judging by your expression make them a priority hidden project?" asked Beth.

The Commander nodded his head in agreement and had a tiny sulk to himself, finally he shook himself and before he could ask anything Jack said brightly "I think I know how we can escape the mines."

"Well how Jack" asked the Commander.

"Simple really, we use our own Ghost thingy to match the distortion thingy."

"Well, do we have enough sensor information to copy the GFG from the other ship?" asked the Commander of Beth.

"Even if I don't, we have data for the One Oh One Cascade so I can mask our ship in that" replied Beth.

"Well, that should be enough to confuse the mines. Okay then use the Ghost Field Generator to turn us into the One Oh One Cascade please Beth."

After several minutes with nothing apparently happening Jack asked "did it work?"

"Oh yes" said Beth "didn't I say?"

Almost growling the Commander said "well no, you didn't" both he and Jack let out sighs of relief and the Commander walked off briskly.

Jack still stood on the bridge turned to Beth and asked "is it possible all this was a distraction?"

"A distraction from what?"

"I don't know something, anything. I mean there was the rockets, the airlock and the supposedly hidden ship."

Beth shrugged and said "I really can't comment but I shall file your observation under probable."

"Probable what?"

"Just probable" Beth turned back to staring out into space and then said through the ships general communication system "we're an hour from landing."

Jack kept checking out the window for green rocket trails, which had by now faded from view long ago, like the wake of a tiny ship in the sea.

He then wondered only briefly why it actually mattered anyway, because if this time travel thing was successful then none of this would have happened anyway.

The approach to the board shop was very exciting for Jack, having never seen a planetary system heave into view before, he just stood and watched with awe as moons and various planetary looking objects swung by over and under the ship. It was the kind of bright, multi-coloured star system Jack had always wanted to see, like he imagined the Earth and its planets might have looked if it were painted by a circus style painter and decorator.

Claire was stood next to Jack paying little interest to the show, mainly because Sara who was stood the other side of him, kept checking out his neck. Jack was too absorbed to notice but Claire did and she was thoroughly annoyed with herself for noticing Sara staring almost hypnotically at his neck. Claire felt a jealous pout forming on her face and quickly wiped it away by remembering how annoying Jack was. After all it could not be jealousy because that would mean she had feelings for Jack, which she definitely did not. In fact she could not imagine anyone having feelings for Jack, after all what would be the point as he was being sent back in time, but then why was Sara staring at him so intently, and why was it bothering her so much?
It then occurred to Claire that she would not remember this event, as Jack was going to be sent back before the invasion even occurred, meaning that anything she did now would not actually matter, unless Jack told her in the past. Which she of course would not and could not believe, after all who would.
She completely missed the point that Jack would remember.
Pleased with her reasoning and realizing that Jack was the only available human male, actually made him quite eligible. This was something she kept telling herself, silently repeating 'eligible' under her breath.
Claire's mumbling made Jack turn round and stare at her, like she was trying to be deliberately annoying by making strange noises as the majesty of the system flew by.
'The cheek' thought Claire, clenching her jaw shut and promptly resolving to get her revenge for him being so rude to her at her time of sensitivity and need. Forgetting of course that Jack knew nothing of what she was thinking and had his own problems to consider, whilst he was trying to enjoy the view.
Jack frowned, shrugged and looked back out the window, completely at a loss to explain the hostility that Claire was showing towards him. Behind his back, Claire stuck out her tongue at him and waved her hands on either side of her head like paper antlers.

After passing a dozen or more bald planets, they started to approach a planet that appeared to be mostly made of water, with a large band of land circling the middle. The planet looked like it was on some weight loss scheme, trying to sweat a few pounds off by wearing a belly band around its midriff that was a tad too tight.

As they approached, the ship placed itself in orbit around the planet and Jack asked whilst pointing at the planet "are we not landing then?"
"On what?" asked Summer.
"The planet!" said Jack.

Looking slightly confused Summer said "we want the board shop, not the planet!"
Jack looked back out the all encompassing window and asked "so where's the shop, if it's not on the planet?"
"It's on a facility that'll be round in an hour or so" said Beth.
"You mean a space station?" asked Jack with some excitement in his voice.
"Yes" sighed Beth, knowing that saying 'no' would take some explaining "we'll shuttle over, when it appears."

Chapter 26 : Bad Landings.

After what seemed like forever to Jack but was only really half an hour or so, the darkened space station spun round the edge of the planet and into view. As it drew closer Jack could see thousands of spots of light, in what looked like the biggest multitude of interconnected skyscrapers he had ever seen. The main difference between normal huge buildings and these, was the way they were all collected together at such ridiculous angles to one another. They looked like they had been thrown together to make a spiky ball, some were upside down, some twisted and screwed through others, with some leaning for support and others dangling out into space. The whole thing really made no sense to look at, it was like someone had built a city out of tower blocks and skyscrapers, then with admittedly very large hands, had screwed the whole thing up like someone would screw up a piece of paper and tossed it in the bin.
Jack could not help staring and asked "what happened to it?"
Summer replied "there planet below had a whole series of natural disasters, which turned it into what we are seeing today, in order to escape they launched there buildings into space. They had years to plan and execute, then one day they launched together in a mass panic to escape what they thought was the planets sudden, final death throws. Most of the buildings which launched were destroyed, the one percent we see here were deliberately coalesced together, around a tiny orbiting moon. There plan was to gently stick the buildings back together, to make one big orbiting space moon-city. They got the buildings right, the only thing they didn't allow for was the excessiveness of the moons core, which they hadn't enough time to measure properly. The moon has the same gravity as there home planet but not the same reach, so they didn't know how persuasive the moons gravity was going to be or inconsistent, until they tried to land. That's why it all looks like a ball of twigs wearing fairy lights and is also why we're shuttling in, as there are various gravity distortions across the entire surface."

As the moon city drew ever closer, Jack could not help but wonder "so where's the board shop?"
"Well, on the other side where the dock is, we'll be in orbit in a few minutes, so lets go to the shuttle bay" said the Commander.

The shuttle in the loading bay was exactly what Jack had expected a shuttle to look like, an angled box with an engine at the back and a tinted window at the front. What he had not expected when he climbed inside up the few steps, was that everywhere was a window. He climbed in and out several times looking at the outside hull and then back inside, then half in and out of the shuttles door he waved his hands first on one side and then the other.
"That's amazing, you can only see out but not in and everywhere out but nowhere in and when your halfway out but not in you can't see in!" said Jack in excitement.

Claire and Sara were sat inside the tiny shuttle, one either side at the back with the Commander sat at the controls near the front, all ignoring Jack. Summer was stood in the loading bay watching Jack bounding backwards and forwards in and out of the shuttle.
She sighed and then nearly jumped, as an gentle paw landed on her shoulder and Second said "he'll be fine, it will take time for him to adjust and get his memories back to be the man you once knew."
"I don't know what you mean?" came her sharp reply.
Nodding slowly Second continued "everyone knows how you feel and since his return you have been out of sorts, because he does not remember you. I am sorry but it will take time, but don't worry too much, as when we succeed this will never have happened. Keep reminding yourself of this."
Summer sighed and pushed Jack into the shuttle, with the kind of expression a mother would give to an errant child that they love dearly, but are really feeling quite annoyed by at the moment but still cannot help smiling at.

From the bay Second waved in an quite enthusiastic manner, that Jack thought was a bit over the top, like waving off a lover on a long journey whilst wiping away an errant tear. Beth and Jane meanwhile gave small salute like gestures from an screen angled in the cockpit, then it went blank with only a vague outline and showed an image of the shuttle from some external camera.

The shuttle then bounced gently off the floor of the bay and seemed to bound eagerly towards the wall in the loading bay, which was approaching far too quickly for Jack's liking. It did not help that it was painted with comedic red blood splats, five of them dragged by some unknown brusher into the shape of an large 'X'.
Before he could say anything they had passed straight through the wall, with a slight tingling throughout his whole body and the smell of raspberry's almost seeming to sing in his nostrils. Then they were into space and making there way to the mixed-up orbiting city, with Jack itching his teeth.

Still strapped in his seat, where Summer had tied him down, Jack was looking around wildly still trying to take everything in. Of all the technology he had seen so far, this almost all encompassing view of the outside had him the most excited.
The rear of the shuttle and several cabinets were not see through, when Jack asked the Commander about it, he simply flicked a switch and everything became see through, then he flicked the switch further and it was only possible to look out the window at the front.

Watching the approaching moon of jumbled buildings left Jack with a slack jaw and a sense of excitement. It would be hard to explain to anybody what exactly the thing looked like, as the buildings stuck out into space at all angles. It looked like a ball of spikes, at the same time it was all gently rotating, spinning on its axis and all in front of banded shiny blue water planet.

They slowly rounded the side of the moon-city and approached a skyscraper lying down and poking the furthest out into space. As they got closer Jack could see that the entire city was surrounded by a bubble of some description, the only thing in real space was the fallen tower. As they neared the sphere, various lights and bubbling flares could be seen quite clearly on and in the building guiding them in.

The city had looked dead and deserted in some respects, like someone forgot to turn the lights out when they left. From a distance everything had looked static, now as they approached the docking building, Jack could see that it was very much alive and exceptionally well lit inside. There were various shadows moving across the lights as the shuttle entered the tube of the fallen tower, the Commander sat back and watched with everyone else as the inside of the tower slid past. It was the most surreal thing Jack had ever seen. It looked exactly how you would expect a tower or skyscraper to look, if the middle had been been de-cored, like someone had just driven one of those large underground drills they use for making tunnels straight up the centre of the tower. Down the middle of the fallen skyscraper was a black tarmac landing field, with glowing white arrows directing there progress. Jack wondered why he thought of the thing as a field, as they neared the surface he saw why, the tarmac runway looked like it was made of long tightly fitted together black grass. The white arrows in the field were very white grass, tightly fitted together like a very tight thing, with only slight gaps as they waved about in some breeze.
Everything else that was in the building had simply been left where it was, chairs, tables the occasional alien body.
Jack asked "why?" as he pointed at the top of an odd shaped desk, as they moved down the length of the tower.
The Commander replied simply and reverently "well, to remember."

The shuttle landed with a gentle bump on the landing pad, the side door slid open and Jack stepped out with his crew mates. The walls in the distance were gloomy and shadowy, with silvery white things poking out into the dark all around the cavern like interior, several hundred of them in fact.

Looking around there was only one way for them to walk, as the landing pad was shaped like an flat spoon, quite a large flat spoon and they had landed on the rounded bit not the other way round. There were boxes of all descriptions, placed almost strategically thought Jack, arranged for an convenient game of hide and seek along the neck or bridge of the spoon.

When they were halfway across the bridge and moving between the large container boxes, at just over waist height, Jack saw at the other end a door open in the blank dull white wall and some figures came running out. Shortly these figures took up positions behind some more boxes at the other end, then Jack heard what sounded like a lion growling into the sound of a large budgie.
"What's that noise?" asked Jack.

Everyone cocked there ears towards the sound and the Commander suddenly jumped down behind a convenient box and shouted "well, you better get down, that's a pulse laser charging!" Then various coloured beams of light shot over head, disappearing into the dusty cavern in pulses and whistle like sound effects of predatory fireworks.

After several ricochets and near misses, Jack leant out towards the Commander and shouted over the racket "why, exactly, are they shooting at us?"

"Well, what?" shouted the Commander back.

"Why are they shooting at us?" repeated Jack.

"Well what do you mean?" came the reply from the Commander, whilst leaning his back against a box with his pistol held against his chest.

"What have we done exactly, that we need to be SHOT at for?" asked an impatient Jack.

The Commander went to answer and then said "well you know what, I really hadn't considered that!"

Jack then pulled a loose piece of white plastic from the top of the box he was cowering behind, he then gently started to wave it vaguely with just his fingers visible. Reasoning that with the technology he had seen so far, if he lost a finger it might hurt quite a lot but could be regrown. Jack shouted "stop, please stop!" whilst still waving the hand sized, nearly white plastic sheet.

A few more volleys whizzed and banged with inaccuracy overhead, then a distant voice could be heard shouting "why?"

Jack looked over at the Commander and shouted back "because you haven't told us why your shooting at us!"

A hasty discussion could be heard vaguely, with the occasional wild feathered hand movement seen over the top of the box barricades, followed by an eventual shouted message of "your trespassing."

"Well how are we trespassing, if we've come here to shop?" shouted the Commander back.

"Ah well that's easy, you didn't give us the password" this reply came in the know-it-all style tone of voice, as if you should know to present the password when you have not even been asked for it.

"You haven't asked for the password yet!" shouted Jack back, sounding a little peeved.

There was a mumbled discussion at the other end of the long platform, by the time the defenders had got there own stories straight, about who had and had not asked for the password, Jack had wandered down and was stood behind them tapping a foot.

Jack stared at the three aliens stood arguing in front of him, they were of the bird or avian variety of foreign being and very expressive with there movements. They all wore plumage of the vivid parrot type, with tool belts, sashes and backpacks hung on shoulders, legs and even on there wings. They had long strong legs like an ostrich, bulky bodies with a neck that curled around like a snake. They had pointed beaks that looked like three beaks stuck next to one another and there head was shaped like a ball. The wings appeared to be short and stumpy, as Jack looked closer they looked like they had been clipped off at some point, rather than born that way. Not only did they have stubby wings but two arms, one on either side, very similar to human arms in shaping and even size, these stuck out from just under either wing, covered in downy feathers.

When one finally turned to face Jack, he could see that they had one large eye just above the beak and really that was all you could fit on that head, it was that big an eye.

The bird started to lift and point its oversized weapon at Jack, who asked quickly "your supposed to ask for the password before you start shooting, not after and say they didn't know it!"

The muzzle of whatever type of gun this was, of course was now pointing at Jack and his precious region. The bird creature did not seem inclined to raise it to any point higher than Jacks waist either, which made him feel quite uncomfortable.

The thing about the gun that was making Jack sweat the most, apart from what it was pointing at, was the cleanliness of the metal casing. It was perfectly smooth and incredibly shiny, like it was taken care of because of the amount of use it was getting. It was also shaped like stretched pear, appeared to be half the size of the alien holding it and needed a grey strap to hold up the user carrying it.

Then the bird creature demanded "access password?"

Jack had been hoping to avoid speaking any passwords, especially as he did not know any, other than what you might call 'in case of emergency please stop what your doing' safety word.

His favourite had always been "apples" he said out loud.

"Huh, bummer, your right" said the avian at the back.

They then proceeded to have an argument about who keeps telling everyone the secret password and started to hit one another with there stumpy wings.

Jack turned and waved to the rest of his merry band to come forward, making a mental note to stop speaking his thoughts out loud, again.

"Well, Avacors, soldier class!" mumbled the Commander as they walked the final length of the landing arm.

"That's there species is it?" asked Jack.

"Well yes, for a supposedly intelligent race they argue like no ones business. The only time you need worry is when they all agree, that usually means someone somewhere is going to have a big problem!" answered the Commander.

The Commander then asked Jack "well, how did you know the password?"

"Isn't it always apples?" asked Jack back and then quickly walked away from the Commander before he could ask any further questions, mainly because it had been one of the luckiest answers he had ever given.

As they started to walk to the blank looking wall at the end of the bridge, Sara who had been loitering at the back said "if it's okay I'll stay with the shuttle."

Claire was torn with wanting to see what was ahead and staying with somebody whom she even now thought of as her Boss and friend.

Summer saw Claire's dilemma and said "I think I'll stay too."

The Commander raised a bushy eyebrow at her in question and Summer shook her head.

As the three of them walked towards the wall, one of the three Avacors made a small panicked chirp, they stopped arguing and hopped, skipped, flew and bounced past them towards the wall. There tiny off cut wings flapping like mad to try and help them move ahead of the visitors, they looked very much like chickens crossing a blustery and wind swept road, all commotion and little motion.

The Avacors arrived at the wall looking slightly disheveled, trying to rearrange there guns, tool belts and blinkers, which had all swung round to tangle up there legs and arms. One of the Avacors tried to salute quickly at the wall, in so doing lost its balance because one of its yellow banded legs had some how been tied up with its gun strap. As it slowly toppled over to one side, still saluting, it struggled to release its tied up leg, which was unfortunate because the talon on the back of its leg was sat in the trigger mechanism. There was the loud sound of a roaring lion being converted into budgie over a second, as the gun fired. Fortunately the barrel of the weapon was pointing at the floor, which had the effect of creating a large steamy dust cloud and a black scorch mark on the dusty white floor. The other effect was the launching of the bird out of the steam cloud, leaving a trail of feathers and the lonely scream of an eagle. The Avacor sailed over the edge of the platform and the other two bird creatures, after sorting out there various limbs from straps, hopped, bopped and ran to look over the platforms side.

Jack asked "will it be okay?"

Cocking his head to listen to the chirping the Commander replied "well yes, he's caught on a goblin."

"A goblin?" questioned Jack.

"Well look around Jack, this is there landing hall. This is where it all started and where they come to worship the builders, the original Lordarians!"

Jack had glanced around as they had exited the shuttle, after being shot at by the dumb birds he had not really paid much attention to the place. After the Commanders comment he looked around first in boredom and then in gradual surprise, as he realized that apart from the blank wall in front of them and the bridge they were stood on, every other surface was made up of faces. Through the dust like air, he had seen the other spoon like platforms sticking out into the space, with something on the walls. The something on the walls were alien faces, admittedly of every conceivable size and shape, some had bodies attached and others seemed to have lost there bodies. It was only on following where you would expect the lonely faces to be connected to the rest of the body, that you would see a similarly sized hand, claw, talon or paw poking out somewhere.

Some of the faces appeared to be screaming and others simply angry but they all seemed to tell a story, the Commander then said "well, the faces tell a story, if you follow them round from the exit to space."

Jack was lost for words, not only by the shear size of the place but it was like looking at the stained glass windows in a church and realizing for the first time, that if you followed them around they told a tale. Here the faces and bodies told the history of the species, trying to escape there planet before it was destroyed, all the faces and bodies were made or carved from the crashed buildings themselves. It was only after actually looking at the walls, that they worked out that several of the bodies and faces represented the catastrophe, whilst others represented love, war, faith and everything in between, all made from various buildings.

Jack asked "I didn't think there would be a need for religion, with so much technology?"

"Well why not? There's always something that can't be explained by technology and even some technology and science that works without any explanation!" said the Commander.

"Like what?" asked Jack.

"Well the Split Universe Drive for a start!"

"Surely that just means the science is too advanced for us too understand then?"

"Well ah, your talking about the magic of technology, where something looks so advanced technologically that it could only be magic?"

After a pause Jack asked in a questioning tone that he knew he would be blasted for "yes?"

"Well no" said the Commander and walked off to the blank wall which obediently slid up, with Jack and Claire rushing through to keep up.

The door swooshed shut behind them as they walked down a large dark metal but short corridor, it ended in an hugely tall metal door. After a few seconds of inaction, the door behind them opened again, the two Avacors stumbled through carrying there very plucked looking comrade and the smell of charcoaled chicken flavoured the air. The door swooshed shut behind the three birds, one of which gave Jack the filthiest look he had ever seen, as his stomach continued to growl at them in anticipation.

The door parted in front of them, with the metal panels sliding off to either side, on the other side was a very wide, long and metal gantry. The metal tubed concourse ran straight down the middle of the room, it was not so much a room as an entire building lying on its side or even a cavern, with every conceivable surface holding a shop. They were surrounded on every side with shops of any and every description you could possibly think of arching about them. Everything curved around them like they were stood in a tube, the walk way they were stood on was also a large tube with various rails, ladders, steps and even what were probably lifts feeding off from supports from the tube like gantry.
The inside of the tower appeared to be well over a kilometer or two long, from the narrow entrance they had walked through it widened to what looked like a kilometer or more across the base.
In every direction Jack looked, he was looking at the top of something, looking up, down, left or right, Jack was presented with the top of various shops and alien heads bobbing along the streets and alleys.
The designers obviously knew this and had placed the grey shop names as adverts on the roof of most buildings, with small twisted glowing neon like arrows pointing every which way. The shops and adverts were all so perfectly in focus, it was actually oddly distracting.

Jack took another look around and felt his old enemy vertigo coming to say 'hello', shortly to be followed by vertigo's close friend, vomit.

After taking one look at Jack's face slowly turning an odd colour, the Commander said "well don't worry Jack, the gravity in here works, wherever you walk."
"That's what worries me" came the muffled reply, as Jack covered his mouth and stared at his feet.

From above there heads an Avacor flapped and floated gently down, this one had proper wings and smaller arms, with a different set of coloured parrot stripes on its feathers, mostly pinks.
"Take this, it will help you adjust" it chirped in a higher pitch than the other Avacors Jack had met earlier, in its downy feathered hand it proffered a small bright green tablet.

Jack grabbed at it and put it in his mouth without thinking, where it dissolved near instantly on his tongue. The effect though was immediate, even the Commander who had tried to stop Jack from taking the pill by grabbing at his arm, was surprised when Jack stood up straight again and the colour flowed back into his cheeks.
"Thank you" said Jack with relief.
"That's okay, I am after all, here to serve" said the Avacor.
"Well, are you?" asked the Commander with surprise written all over his furry face.
Managing to look only slightly disgusted for the briefest moment in time, the Avacor said "I am Joan and I shall be your guide for today."
"Well, at what cost?" asked the Commander abruptly.
"I receive a small percentage from any purchases you make."

"Well, we don't need your services today thank you" said the Commander.
Jack interrupted, although he did trust the Commander in many things, shopping he felt was probably not his strongest point "I will though Joan."
This time it was the Commanders turn to look disgusted "well we don't need her help!"
"In all honesty when was the last time you were here?" asked Jack
"Well, several years ago?"
"I thought so, I saw the way you looked around in wonder when we walked in, which makes me think that the last time you were here it was a little different?"
"Well yes, they hadn't built this bit yet" said the Commander looking around at the shops on every surface.
Turning to the Avacor Jack asked "Joan will you be our guide please?"
"With honour, what is it you are looking for?" the bird like creature was almost preening with pleasure as it then listed the shops available.

The list was almost endless, only after a minute did Jack realize that every single shop it was listing had surfing connections somewhere. There were shops for hooks, wax, straps, food, glue, repairs, all manner of materials and propulsion.
In the end Jack had to interrupt and asked "I just need a board."
The bird then started to list all types of board for surfing on water, lava, sunspots and clouds until Jack interrupted again "cloud surfing?"
"Oh yes its becoming a very popular sport that we all hope will be included in the next Ulympics."
"Well we just need a board that's legal for the SUDS Competition" said the Commander.
"Are you sure, there are more exciting ways to surf?"
"Well yes, take us to a SUDS C shop" said the Commander, through only slightly gritted teeth and a low growl from his throat.
With a gulp of panic that was very obvious traveling down its slender neck, the Avacor said brusquely "follow me" and swept angrily away down the gantry.

After only a short walk along the gantry, the bird like creature took a flight of stairs which twisted and twirled as they climbed. By the time they could see the bottom, Jack felt that his stomach had experienced more gravity defying stunts in the last few seconds, than he would ever have enjoyed if he had been a roller coaster tester for the past twenty years. The thing that was really worrying him though, was that at some point they had been twisted around, so that now they were no longer climbing up the stairs but stepping down the stairs. As they all stepped off the last metal step Jack looked up, above his head was the metal gantry they had walked in on, only it was the wrong way up, or was it the right way up and they were the wrong way up. Jack decided not to think about it too hard, lest the green tablet stop working and he had no idea which way the liquid would go.

The bird caught him looking at the gantry over head and said "don't worry, gravity is relative here."

"That's easy for you to say, you've got wings and can fly off if it all goes wrong!" replied Jack.
The Commander then strode forward and said "well, we'll go in this shop first" and pointed at the shop front almost opposite the stairs they had walked down.

Standing on the little grass area Jack looked back at the stairs and there metal polished hand rails. The steps had finished by landing on a small grassy island in the middle of a busy road, without any apparent support the steps rolled back into the gloom above and below the gantry. There was floating traffic of all shapes, sizes and colours bobbing along above there heads or was that technically below there heads.

They crossed the small road buzzing with all manner of alien looking creatures, the only thing they had in common was that nearly all of them were on foot, paw, claw or tentacle and only a few had personal transport devices that looked like crate trucks. There was a device with a similar function back on Earth that Jack remembered, the main difference was that the step you stood on varied in size here, to cope with its varied passengers and the back rest plate became a seat and or luggage carrier.

The number of aliens going about there business was almost too much for Jack "don't worry there only here to shop" said Joan looking at Jack's shaking hands.
Jack replied sniffing "it's not the number really, it's the smell, it's bloomin' awful. It's like being stood nose deep in a manure farm."
"It wasn't like this on the other side of the road!" moaned Claire wiping away an errant tear.

Jack turned to look at the Commander, whom he assumed being a fox like creature would have an even more sensitive nose than his own. He could see Claire holding her nose and gulping air like a fish out of water, then there was the Commander who was stood looking across the street without his eyes watering or his nose wrinkling in terror.

As the Commander turned to face them, Jack saw he had bright pink nose plugs pushed inside his nostrils "where did you get those from?" asked Jack pointing first at the Commanders nose and then his own.
"Well, these?" said the Commander pointing at his nose and the pink protrusions, Jack nodded "I got them the last time I was here, they wear out pretty quickly in this toxic environment you know!"
"I wonder why that is?" said Jack sarcastically and a little nasally.
"Well it's the air here, there are so many different species interacting down here that the air becomes almost toxic towar …" the Commanders voice trailed off as he noticed the angry stares.
"A warning might have been nice" said Jack.
"Nose plugs might have been better" remarked Claire.
"Well I didn't know it would still be quite as strong an odour down here did I?"
"And yet, you still brought the nose plugs" said Claire.
"Well, just in case" whined the Commander.

"It feels like the inside of my nose is melting, peeling off from sunburn" moaned Jack.

"Well, oh that's only the membrane in your nose" said the Commander. Looking shocked Claire said "thank you, thank-you very much, your telling me my nose is melting!" with slight panic in her voice she spun around looking for something reflective to see her nose in. After a brief moment of twirling panic, she ducked a hand into a pocket and pulled out her Quellz and flipped it round in her hand to use as a mirror.

Jack looked over her shoulder at the screen on the Quellz, there was obviously a camera somewhere on the front. It was now showing her face and alternating nostrils as she pulled her nose first one way and then the other. It was like watching a donkey rub its snout on a window. Jack tried not to laugh and instead hunted for the camera on the front of the Quellz, which for the life of him he could not see.

"There are chemicals in the air that put a protective layer in your breathing system and in your bodies, to guard against infection" said Joan in a slightly pompous tone of voice.

Both Claire and Jack looked around at the bird like creature standing smugly on one leg spouting information like it was better than they were. The one thing that neither of the humans had even thought of was infection or transfer, here they were quite literally on an alien world or moon-skyscraper-base and at no point had anybody mentioned infections, bacteria, viruses or anything else they might die from.

"We're not infected with anything, are we?" asked Jack catching a breath between careful gulps of air.

"Well, no Jack" said the Commander "it's a legal requirement that all travelers be protected by the PIST system. Which means that you get immunized against any native systems, after all you wouldn't want any potential customers dying before they could buy anything would you?" he said in an level tone, followed by "anyway, it's more likely you would bring in some unknown contagion and wipe out the population before perishing from some local infection!"

Jack stood for a moment feeling slightly lost for words until he asked "so won't you get infected with just your nose plugs?"

"Well no, these are military grade PIST's the same as was on my ship."

"But it didn't smell like this on your ship?" whined Claire wiping away another watery tear.

"Well I did say they were military grade didn't I and you were on a military ship!"

Nodding in understanding Jack said "so the cheaper PIST's don't have a nice smell then."

"Well no, they smell the same as the military ones, the difference is the military ones don't react with other chemicals in the air!"

The Commander then strode forward towards the shop leaving Jack and Claire with the Avacor. They were both breathing carefully, knowing that eventually there noses would become overloaded with the environmental nasal extravaganza they were experiencing and either melt or simply shut down.

A minute or so later the nasal assault had finished and they both stood a little straighter; for the first time Jack could see the area they were in clearly without viewing it through a lens of tears.

It was an odd place to look around, apart from the aliens themselves and the glowing pointers, everything was shades of grey or black, the buildings, the shop fronts, the road and walkways. It was also strangely not dark, it was like all the whites, greys and blacks that made up everything gave off there own light, rather than having to wait for the normal lazy method of light reflection to reach the visitors eye.

Nothing was out of focus here, as Jack looked around all he could see was pin sharp as if he had been given super focus eyes. It was like looking at a painting with so much detail in it that it looked like it would never end, like you could keep zooming in and seeing more and more detail.

The shop directly in front of them where the Commander stood impatiently in the doorway, looked clear, sharp and glossy, like an image from a really expensive table top coffee magazine. The sort of magazine you might find in some supposedly upper class waiting room, like the proprietor was trying to impress whilst daring you to touch the magazine and therefore doubling there fees.

"Advertising nirvana" said Joan as they crossed the last few paces to the front door of the shop.

"I'm sorry what does that mean?" asked Claire sharply, feeling that somehow she had been manipulated without knowing it.

"It's the name given to the type of advertising allowed here!" said Joan.

"That's still not clear, you know?"

Sighing Joan started to walk across the street to the board shop talking the whole time "bright coloured advertising is banned here, because of the distractions it causes to pilots, drivers and creatures in general. Therefore an alternative was developed, which beams the advertisement straight to your eyes, called an Laser Identifying Camera Kit."

"Huh?" said Jack.

"You only see what is projected" said Joan simply.

"Can we turn it off?" asked Claire rubbing an eye.

"Blinkers or polarized lenses" said Joan "that'll stop the beams."

Claire pulled her Blinkers from a pocket secreted somewhere around her chest, Jack was reluctant to think that they were hanging between anything, otherwise he might get excited, so to his mind they must have come from an inside breast pocket and not have been dangling anywhere.

After putting on her Blinkers Claire turned to find Jack mulling over his fingers, twisting and turning them around like he was really worried about something.

"Are you okay Jack" asked Claire.

"Oh yes I'm fine" replied Jack quickly.

"Okay then but where are your Blinkers?"

Jack said "I left them on the ship."

Claire was carrying a satchel over shoulder, there was no other way to describe it really, it was the usual used brown colour, made of some leather with big chunky buckles and a battered strap that looked like it had been gnawed on by gerbils. Jack had some vague memory of seeing her carrying it on there escape from the tunnels on Earth.
She swung it around from her back and began to root around inside. After what felt like several minutes to Jack, with Claire almost seeming to jump in head first to her satchel and be lost forever in its embrace, she made an 'I've found it' noise.
Claire finally came up from diving in the bag, like a free diver returning from the ocean depths and said triumphantly "here you go."
She handed Jack a spectacle case. He opened it carefully and inside were his best sunglasses.
Cautiously Jack asked "are these mine?" just in case they were not.
"Oh yeah, I found them on the floor after you left the office one night" replied Claire quickly.

Jack looked down at the sunglasses in his hands, bizarrely they felt like the most precious thing he had in the Universe, mainly because they were the only thing he had in the Universe.
Jack mumbled "thank you" and then tried to remember where and when he had dropped them. After a few seconds he shook his head, unable to recall even wearing them into work.
"Well will you two hurry up!" said the Commander still stood in the doorway.

Jack and Claire both looked round now wearing there respective eye wear and were slightly disappointed to see how dull the place now looked. There also seemed to be a haze in the air, preventing them from seeing more than a hundred meters or so, like the entire area was shrouded in an heavy fog. Jack looked over the top of his sunglasses, as soon as he did so it was like a photo being continuously fed directly into his eyes. If you looked carefully you could see the edges between the bright shop fronts did not quite fit in there pin sharp greys, whites and blacks. The only real colour came from peoples clothing, the street lighting which appeared to be a series of floating orbs and the lights from vehicles that swung past overhead.
"Now you know why we don't wear our blinkers quite so much on Surphon" said Joan.
"It's like a smog you could walk on, or even a soup. Is it dangerous?" asked Jack.
Claire and Jack both put there eye wear away, safely stashing them somewhere about there person.
"Well no, it's the PIST reacting with the natural dust of the moon, which is so fine that it passes through most things, there's just an awful lot of it!" said the Commander.

Jack and Claire stepped into the shop doorway but the Avacor stopped outside and placed a card into something that resembled a time stamp machine from 'yea olde' shop floor. Jack and Claire walked into the shop following the Commander, leaving the door swing with a 'swoosh' shut behind them and Jack felt the now familiar chill as they changed environments.

Looking back over his shoulder Jack found looking out of the window that the view was "not on this planet?" he asked.

"Well more precisely 'not on this moon'. But you are correct it is the view on Surphonite" came a slightly muffled voice from somewhere at the back of the shop.

Jack looked at Claire whom shrugged and he then asked "where's that then?"

"Well, we're orbiting it!" replied the Commander shortly.

Jack knew the Commander could have a slightly short temper but for some reason he was being overly short, ever since they had met the Avacor. He was not sure whether it was the bird like creature stood outside balancing on one leg, the moon they were on or the shop they were now stood in that was making him angry.

There came some small bangs from the back of the shop and a slightly panicked voice mumbling "I'll be right with you, as soon as I un-glue myself grr!" the last part was said quietly but carried surprisingly well in the shop.

Whilst they were waiting for the shopkeeper to untangle themself from whatever they were doing at the back of the shop, which seemed to involve a great deal of productive language and the occasional tearing noise, Jack looked around. Externally the shop had been about thirty feet or so wide but in here the shop was at least three times that and it seemed to be a few hundred foot long.   Both Jack and Claire exchanged a look with Jack saying "suspension field" and Claire just nodded in agreement. The shop inside was exactly how Jack and Claire would have expected a shop to look like back on Earth, for some reason this felt and looked wrong to their eyes. It was laid out with various surfboards of all types, some standing in box like islands that would probably float about on request, some leaning against the walls and others hanging from the ceiling like a stuffed alligator prize. There were hanging racks with clothes of all shapes, sizes, brands and colours all mixed up together like ribbons in a blender, there was just no visible pattern to the layout. There were board handles and tins of wax on one wall, in another aisle there were various boots and shoes, in another aisle there were leg garments for various species of alien and again the colours were excessive.

It was a surf shop that catered for the masses, and the masses were of every shape and size you could imagine. The only thing that did not look right in the shop was a segregated section, that housed the engines that connected to some of the boards. The engines themselves were not much bigger than a large thermos flask and varied only slightly in shape but had different branding on them.

The most varied thing were the exhaust systems that connected to the various engines, they were of all manner of shape, size and design. The variation in pipe colours, form, magnitude and overall arrangement was actually quite mesmerizing and the two humans could not help but stare.

The second most varied thing that Jack and Claire finally noticed was the boards themselves, these varied so much from your basic plank to balls, wheels, boomerang shapes and back again that at first they did not even recognize them for what they were.

Next to the engine and exhaust section was a curtained off room, which to Jack looked like a photo booth, if it was a photo booth it was very large and could have housed a small yacht.

The various foreign words emanating from behind the curtain were all probably quite rude, because of the inflection and tone. Then there came the tearing sound of fur and glue being removed from a body, involving the forced separation of the two, followed by a tiny whimper like scream.

The curtain was yanked back and out strode a shark, both humans jumped behind the nearest clothes island. Peaking through a shirt sleeve designed for a mini mountain, with colouring from the drunken rainbow collection, Jack watched as the shark like alien hugged the Commander quite vigorously with an open jaw of serrated white teeth. The grey sleek killing machine was a full head shorter than the Commander, but still easily picked him up for an all embracing crocodile hug.

"The only thing missing is the death roll!" said Jack as the creature bounced around with his captive.

Claire snorted and tried not to laugh to loud and then asked "do you think he needs help?"

Looking at the Commanders stiff face, red with anger glowing through the fur, Jack said "oh I don't know, maybe we should leave them alone for a bit, there getting on so well!"

Eventually the creature put the Commander down in front of the clothing island, leaving them with just an occasional glimpse of shark like skin but in some humanoid form. As the Commander and the alien talked in muffled tones, through the fabric, Jack eventually got a look at the creature and it was not quite as scary as he had first thought. Its head was indeed shark shaped and it did have an awful lot of very white, sharp and pointy teeth that ran all around the inside of its mouth. It stood a little shorter than the average human but was very human in shape, with beaver fin like hands, clawed feet and grey blue skin like a shark. The thing that stood out the most though was its mouth, its smile was over three quarters of its head with a massively thick neck, presumably to support the weight of all its teeth. On its short neck were what looked like gills on either side, they flapped and waved as it breathed like a torn flag. When it talked though it only opened the front of its mouth, talking with its tiny lips, this did nothing to help Jack and Claire's worries as it still flashed an awful lot of needle sharp white teeth. It was wearing a long dusty white robe over its sleek shoulders, with a silvery white tail of pony like hair sprouting out if its head and down its back. There was also a crocodile like tail protruding from behind, that it was quite successfully managing to hide, by curling up its back.

After a while the Commander noticed that he was stood alone in the shop and turned around looking for the humans.
"Your friends are hiding over there" said the alien pointing to where the two humans were hidden, behind some more loudly coloured shirts.
The Commander saw there feet poking out from underneath the huge shirt rack and waved them out irritably, when they did not come right away he apologized to the alien "well, I'm sorry Ron, I'll go get them out."
"No worries mate."
The Commander walked over to the rack and said "well your embarrassing me, here I am trying to get a deal on the gear we need and your skulking in the background like a couple of thieving rodents!"
"He's a Shark!" whispered Claire "with millions of teeth" finished Jack.
"Well, a Shark?" asked the Commander.
"Sea dwelling killer" said Jack.
"Well I admit he likes water, but I've never seen him kill anything, apart from the occasional beer and thieving rodents!" said the Commander meaningfully.
In thought for a moment the Commander then added "well actually there is one thing I've seen him kill regularly."
"What's that then?" asked Jack worriedly.
"Well, someone else's profit ha ha ha" laughed the Commander "the only thing I've known the Gekk hunt, is profit" he finished.

Looking at the two humans faces, peaking out from behind the shirts, he could see they still looked worried so added "well you really shouldn't worry, unless your wanting a refund of course."

"Now that's not very nice" said Ron walking up and resting his arms on the nearest rack of clothing before continuing "probably accurate mind" he mused with a toothy smile from gill to gill.

Jack and Claire slowly stepped out from the inside of the lurid coloured shirt rack, to there surprise the Gekk jumped back and ran off towards his curtain with a shout of "humans!"
The Commander looked just as confused at Ron's reaction to the two humans, as the two humans hiding from Ron in the first place.

A short while later the curtain was pulled apart and out stepped the Gekk again. Before he had been wearing a long flowing dusky white robe and now he was wearing a T-shirt, shorts and sandles. The T-shirt had pointy eared cheeky goblin like creatures printed all over it, doing things with surfboards of the 'you can't do that with a board, for legal reasons' variety. The colouring of the T-shirt was from the vigorous colour design division of Fluorescent Rainbow Incorporated Systems. The final touches were blue denim shorts, brown sandles with white socks, sunglasses balanced on the top of his head and an two inch diameter golden coloured ring, holding the ponytail in place on the top of his skull. He was also carrying a small speaker in his hand, which was currently blaring out a surf related song from a well known sand and young man named group. He was also trying to move in time to the music, which was rather like watching how you would imagine your dad would dance if he were a robot standing on marbles, all timing was elsewhere and short stop start movements.

In the other hand he was carrying a Quellz, which as soon as he was close enough to the two humans he quickly dove forward and took a picture of all three of them.
He then stepped away looking at the picture on his Quellz and said in general "dude, they'd never believe I'd met you and humans today!"
Looking up at the Commander Ron asked "why didn't you say you were with humans?"
"Well I didn't know it would make a difference?" asked the Commander.
The Gekk threw his arms up in the air and said "haven't you seen any Hypew?" he pronounced Hypew, 'Hi Poo'.
"Well we've stayed away from any Hypew" the Commander also said it like 'Hi Poo' "why, what's on it?" he asked in a resigned tone.
"The destruction of there home planet for a starters. Followed by them being put on the endangered species list, with various members of the council saying they weren't consulted, so the Commander must've been following his own agenda …" Ron's voice trailed off as he worked something out.
"You were in Command of the fleet weren't you!" said Ron shaking his head.
"Well, yes" replied the Commander simply.
"I would go into hiding if I were you, your names got more crup stuck to it than a ball-of-glue in a sewer!"
"Well, that's one of many things we're aiming to undo" said the Commander nodding his head.
"With a hover-board?" asked Ron in an sarcastic tone.

"Well, not just any hover-board, one of your special surfboards, cloud-boards, sky-surfers, split-runners, gap-bangers, cloud-skimmers, the best one you've got to win the SUD C!"

"No doubt you'd like it on credit! I'm afraid that ain't happening, it's crowns or frowns for you!"

Jack mouthed to Claire 'crowns or frowns' which the Commander saw and said "well you pay for it or you don't get it and get a frown instead."

"There really from Earth?" asked Ron curiously.

"Well, yes they are, were" snapped the Commander.

"Okay, okay. Just get your Quellz out and we'll see if your credit is good?"

The Commander did not hold out much hope for having any credit any more, as he would have imagined his accounts having been frozen, for his supposed war crime of blowing up a planet without authorization

As he looked at his Quellz, some Hypew News scrolled across the front with various captions saying 'ordered not to destroy Earth' and similar titles. The Commander still had the orders on his Quellz and was tempted to post them off to the leading news agencies flashing across the screen. After all, he had been ordered to destroy the Earth as soon as he arrived in the system by the council, but he had hesitated. The council were also no doubt the ones who would have frozen his accounts by now, for destroying a planet they wanted destroyed. Why they had to tell everyone though, that they had given explicit orders not to destroy the planet in the first place was odd, if you looked at it. Surely it would make more sense to order the destruction, rather than tell someone not to destroy something which they would not have destroyed in the first place, unless they were ordered to.

Sighing at the politics they all had to play the Commander held his Quellz out towards Ron's, they briefly touched and Ron typed some figures in his. The Commander looked at his own display as Ron typed and then a few seconds later there was a loud klaxon like noise from the two Quellz, accompanied by the red flashing letters N and E on both devices.

"Sorry mate, no equity" said Ron.

The Commander sighed heavily and threw his Quellz in the air, which Ron deftly caught with his spare hand.

"If you haven't any credit, maybe one of these two have" said Ron passing the Quellz to Claire.

"Well why would they have any credit?" asked the Commander.

"I've got my own Quellz thank you" said Claire primly, handing the Commanders Quellz over to a surprised Jack.

Jack took the Quellz and looked at it closely, as soon as he had it in his hand it just turned itself off and now looked like a very expensive black glossy plastic business card with nothing on it. The corners were all slightly rounded, there was a slight bulge to the back of the device and Jack could just make out two slightly blacker discs on the front. As he held it in his hand it actually felt quite heavy for something that looked like a large credit card. With the way it was designed and the weight, Jack found he felt the need to spin it up the other way in his hand. The larger of the two black discs was now at the top facing him and the smaller at the bottom.

The Commander then put his curly thumb on the top black disc, the screen turned on with a small 'pling' like noise "well I'm going to make you second primary on my Quellz" said the Commander looking directly at Jack.

"Okay?" said Jack questioningly, because he had no real idea what that would actually mean.

Hearing his slight confusion Ron interrupted "it means you'll have access to all your accounts when your holding the Quellz and all the contacts you both have."

"Well it will also mean that any communication sent to me will appear whilst you have it, but I won't be registered on it till I take hold of it" said the Commander.

"So I could see the message but not do anything with it?" asked Jack.

"Well yes, the idea being that it should be harder to track me directly, as your now primary because the company that own Quellz don't allow tracking!" said the Commander.

Jack looked a little bit confused as he slowly replied "but aren't I wanted as well, for being the destroyer of civilizations or something?"

"Well ah yes, you are now nearly officially innocent of that crime, so at the moment your on the back burner so to speak and anyway it's the other you there after, not you Jack!" said the Commander.

"Right now that's all sorted" said Ron "let's see if you got any crow?"

Claire looked at her own Quellz and said to the Commander "is ten thousand crowns a lot?"

Also quietly the Commander replied "well yes, yes it is, its roughly equivalent to ten thousand Earth dollars."

Claire looked thoughtful for a moment and then said "so in real money it's about seven and a half thousand pounds?"

"Well ah, no sorry I meant your pound sterling thingy" the Commander paused "why your planet has, sorry, had such a confusing mishmash of monetary systems I'll never know."

"So individual countries can keep track of their currency and therefore finances easier" replied Claire.

"Well yes, but from an interstellar view, that's far too confusing to have hundreds of different currencies and exchange rates, when all you really need is the Crown!" said the Commander proudly.

"Doesn't the value of the Crown vary in value against the same item? For example if I bought a banana for one crown here, would it cost one Crown somewhere else or two?" asked Claire.

"Well it might cost you twenty crowns but they would still be crowns, that's how anyone makes any money through trade" replied the Commander, in such a way as if he were teaching a child the basics of trading.
Claire was all ready to retaliate with some barbed remark when Jack touched her arm and said "is it really worth arguing with a colleague of such awesome intellect, that he's just proven himself wrong?"
"So what's your balance Jack?" asked Claire, who was actually feeling quite proud about having ten thousand pound like Crowns in her bank account, so to speak.

Jack placed his thumb, like Claire had, over the smaller black disc shape on the bottom of his Quellz and the display lit up. On the display above his thumb appeared the usual time date and weather, all of which were wrong. This of course is standard practice for useful electrical devices because, whilst showing you useful information, there is always some small element that is always incorrect to encourage you to upgrade. The time read as quarter past three in the morning and the weather was foggy, with a chance of lightening, with occasional showers to follow later. Possibly the foggy might be right, but since they were not on Earth any more, the rest looked slightly inaccurate for a moon with no atmosphere.

Swiping the display Jack was then presented with several options but the only one he could select, after several seconds of prodding, was 'enquiry'. When he touched it he was then asked to enter in his personal details, after several prods of various options and some degree of frustration at some of the silly questions, why did it need to know his favourite colour was blue?
Jack was finally presented with options he recognized, he was going to ignore the one asking for 'collect contacts?', in the end he tapped it anyway.
Even with future technology Jack was presented with an egg like timer on the display. A little while later a message apologizing 'for the excessive delay' and 'we apologize for the delay', followed by 'error delay', and then finally 'we will work to rectify this issue in the background, please continue to enjoy your new Quellz' floated across the screen.

The screen went blank for a few seconds, making Jack think he had broken it, then it switched back to a rather nice picture of some sandy alien sand-scape, with creatures bobbing in and out of the sand like it was water. There was a faded pulsing star like button in the middle of the screen, which Jack tapped and was presented with a text search box and a picture animation of a toothy mouth surrounding it. Not exactly sure what the mouth was for, Jack tapped the box with 'search' ghosted out in it. A keyboard then appeared projected out from the screen, with the letters floating like an holographic keyboard.
Jack typed in 'my bank balance'.
After a second the screen went white and the 'tJi' logo floated out of the background in pale blue and green, outlined in an red box with rounded off corners.

"Well, what's your balance Jack?" asked the Commander.
"Um, how much does a race ready board cost?" asked Jack looking up briefly to see Ron answer.

As soon as the question was asked Ron's blue and grey skin changed colour, so slowly at first that Jack was unsure if he had really seen it happen, as it was so subtle. It faded to very rosy red and then to a dark blue, the colour changes all happened over several seconds and left the two humans looking on curiously with mouths open.
"Well, defence response" said the Commander quietly.
"Why? We're not threatening him, are we?" asked Claire.
"Well, only his profits if he gets the price wrong" the Commander said smugly and then looked at there confused faces "too expensive and you'll leave his shop, too cheap and he'll lose any profit."
"Fight or flight" mused Jack.
"Well black or bleak" said the Commander.
Ron then asked with a gulp "you want a price for the complete set up?" Ron looked worried, Jack guessed there was quite a price difference between novice 'surfy' bits (read 'noob' wanting to look special) and professional (read 'special' wanting to look cool) so he said "a basic package price and the top oh-the-line maxed out version please?" asked Jack.
With a sigh of relief and his skin spinning back to its shiny fishy grey and blue, Ron then replied "the most basic board and suit setup would be ten thousand Crowns. The most expensive has no limit but the winner last year, there setup cost one hundred thousand Crowns!" Ron said in hope, whilst rubbing his fin like webbed hands together.
Jack looked back down at the display on his Quellz, looked up and said "I'll take a sixty thousand Crown setup please."

Ron clapped his hands together at an angle and smile swam across his face; as he did so Jack noticed he had no thumb so to speak, there was a talon like claw thing that poked out from the underside of his wrist and into his webbed palm. For some reason this made Jack shudder slightly, mainly because it made Ron look more alien than the shark like head on his shoulders ever did. The head could have been a mask after all, but the claw and talon like thing poking into the palm of his hand and no thumb, made him look very alien. It made him look more like a streamlined killing machine to Jack for some reason, probably because the claw like knife looked like it had been dipped in someone else's blood, whom probably was not a willing volunteer.

Ron ran off with a muffled "I'll just get some board measurements" being called over his shoulder as he almost dived behind a counter. Then he could be heard rummaging about behind the desk counter, sounding like a hungry squirrel in a nut flavoured spanner factory.

The Commander turned to Jack, pulled his wrist round so he could see the display on the Quellz Jack was holding, he whistled through his teeth in surprise. Claire then grabbed at Jack's wrist, looked at the display and asked "what does that mean then Jack?"

Jack looked back down at the display, looked up and said "I have no idea?" whilst turning to look at the Commander.
"Well hey, it's your bank balance" said the Commander.
"Yes, yes it is" replied Jack "but I must admit I wasn't expecting to have any balance of any description?"
"Well it's compensation for, you know, previous events."
Jack looked lost for a moment and then asked with realization dawning "previous events, you mean the blowing up of our home planet?"
"Well, yes" replied the Commander sounding quite guilty.
"So why does Claire have an actual balance and I have no balance whatsoever?" asked Jack, with Claire stood just behind him looking quite smug.
"It's a shame you don't have as much as me" said Claire "and I'm sorry but I would lend you some cash, but I'm afraid I don't have sixty thousand to spare!" finished Claire with a slightly pleased giggle to her voice.
The Commander looked at Claire with disapproval, before he could reply Jack was looking again at his Quellz and asked of anyone who might be listening "so, what does 'illimitable' mean?"
Claire was actually smiling even more, beaming might be a better description as she answered "no balance whatsoever?"
"Well, actually it means unlimited or infinite might be a better description" replied the Commander.
Claire's mouth dropped open in shock, like a castles drawbridge falling down after having its chains dissolved.
Jack's mouth was also hanging open but rather than being in shock, it was more in understanding "so your saying I can buy anything?"
Nodding the Commander replied "well yes, pretty much."
      Before Claire or Jack could ask anything else Ron came bounding across the shop floor from his counter, brandishing a silvery pistol shaped device with strangely curled antennas at the normally dangerous end of such a shiny pistol shaped device.
"Right, just stand still for a few seconds whilst I get some measurements" said Ron pointing the device at Jack.
The Commander and Claire quickly left Jack's side as soon as the Gekk had started to point the device at Jack, like crabs sidling along a beach. He was left stood alone on the shop floor, as various coloured lights scanned up and down his body. The Gekk was stood slowly waving the device up and down in front of Jack, and tapping at a little floating screen that had popped up from the back of the device.
"Won't be minute" said Ron staring intently at the device.
Jack stood still as the lights played up and down his body, the only downside of this measurement process was the urge to scratch. It was as if feathers were titillating his body in all manner of places, the urge to have a good itch and runaway was nearly unbearable, like watching daytime television.
"All done!" announced Ron "I'll have your board knocked up in a few hours, in the mean time you'll need to enter the Accumulator."

Jack was suddenly free of the daytime torture and feeling the need to brush his teeth, which he duly did with a finger.

"What's a cumulator?" asked Claire.

"An Accumulator" corrected Ron "it's over there and in simple terms it takes every possible measurement to find the best suit for surfing" he was pointing at what amounted to a large cardboard looking box, with greenish mould on the outside. It had been hiding behind a rack of surfboards arranged like candles on a centenarians birthday cake.

   As Jack approached the box a doorway dissolved its way into view, the inside was well lit, in fact Jack would go so far as to say excessively. It was a similar brightness and whiteness to the Armourist room, from what felt like months ago but was only a really a few days.

"Just step inside, you'll get suited and booted and I'll get the board sorted" said Ron in a sing-song like fashion.

Jack stepped inside the opening and the doorway started to dissolve its way back into place with a slow 'swooshing' noise. Just before it shut completely, Claire saw a sea green metallic sphere like object start to rise up from the white coloured raised plinth and a slightly digital voice say in a tone of mild despair "what do you want this time?"

Chapter 27 : Coffee Break.

With the box now sealed, Ron made some excuses about 'preparing Jack's board' and quickly moved off back behind his curtains. Where almost immediately he started to swear in various languages again and bang something made of wood with something else made of wood.

The Commander indicated a bench for Claire to sit on, then he walked over to a tall metal cylinder that was a only a few steps away from the surprisingly soft bench.
"Well, coffee?" asked the Commander turning to Claire.
"Yes please" replied Claire, whom after a second or two of hearing bubbling sounds and the smell of freshly brewed coffee wafting towards her, had to ask "where did you get coffee from?"
The Commander turned round and handed her a black cup of steaming white coffee, shrugged and said "well, from the machine."
She spun the black cup around in her hand, noticing 'Fabup' was written in shadowy lettering all over the receptacle and then she worked out what the Commander had just said.
Claire gave him a look that a teacher would give to a smart mouthed child with too quick a wit than was required to answer the question "that's an overly simple answer?" she said.
"Well, true nonetheless" said the Commander sitting down with his own coffee.
Claire looked at him in disbelief "you actually fobbed me off?"
"Well don't get angry with me, I just asked the machine over there for two white coffee's and some sugar."
"But where did the coffee come from, I mean I know where coffee comes from on Earth or rather it did. So where does this coffee come from and it tastes like coffee to?"
"Well really! You want to talk about where coffee comes from, rather than about Jack and what a mammoth task he has ahead of him?"
Folding her arms, which as most human males know, means 'imminent explosion, go cautiously' Claire said in an very reasonable tone of voice "yes."
The Commander sighed and missed the other male clue as Claire uncrossed and crossed her legs, tightening her hands on her arms as she did so.
"Well, it's a berry seed that's picked and processed into a bean, which is mixed with hot water to make coffee" replied the Commander simply.
Claire had been expecting some flippant answer, so had been struck mildly dumb with an accurate answer and yet not the answer she was looking for.
After a moment she asked "what I actually meant was, where is the coffee bean grown, where did it come from?"

The Commander opened his mouth to speak, Claire jumped in before he could give another correct but inaccurate answer "and you can't say on a planet in a field."
"Well, it is actually grown on several hundred planets, so there is no one place it comes from."
"Okay the question I'm really trying to ask I guess is, did the coffee bean originally come from my Earth?"
The Commander was just about to give a sharp reply but caught himself and looked towards where Jack had walked into the accumulator. Carefully the Commander slowly replied, with ever growing surprise as he realized something for the first time "well, two seeds were introduced centuries ago and the market exploded" Claire was listening curiously her anger forgotten "the story is documented as two warm planets being the perfect growing environments for the plant, and the creation of a new drink was born. But the seeds didn't come from there respective planets, they were planted by a new company called 'tJi'."
"So the question still stands, is the coffee from Earth?"
"Well I would guess that originally it was more than likely seeded from Earth. Because tJi has some affiliation with your home planet, just after the company was created tea and then coffee hit the mouths of the Universe. But now most planets have coffee growing facilities of there own, under license."
"What about tea?" asked Claire.
"Well, tea?" questioned the Commander.
"Yes tea, you know mildly crushed leaves with hot water strained through them to make a light beverage?"
"Well we've had tea longer than coffee because ..." the Commanders voice trailed off, as once again he looked at where Jack had walked into the box.
With a little frustration in her voice creeping in Claire tried to get the Commander to finish his sentence with "because?"
"Well, a tea plant was found on a planet years before coffee came to exist, it was used for its healing abilities, then its taste and finally as a light pick me up."
"So I could have had tea instead of coffee then?"
"Well hmm, oh yes" mused the Commander lost in thought staring at the mouldy looking green box Jack was in and rubbing his hairy chin in thought.

      Claire got up and walked over to the metal cylinder, it was about two meters tall, half a meter wide and shaped like a rounded fence post. As she stood in front of it wondering how to get it to work, a screen lit up on the front and simply displayed on it were the words 'speak your drink?' Claire asked for two tea's and then was presented with several million options, after several minutes she walked back to the Commander carrying two tea's, in light green coloured 'Fabup' disposable cups and almost collapsed down next to him on the bench in mock fatigue.
The Commander looked at her and said "well, now you know why I asked for coffee's."

Claire actually looked quite exhausted but replied in mild shock "I never knew there were so many blends, I mean I thought it would have been easy to order a tea, you just ask for tea generally where I come from and get what your given!"

They sat in silence drinking there cups of tea and after several slurps the Commander said "well, you know I think this is the best tea I've ever tasted. What did you order?"

"Tea of course but in its own little bag with an English blend, milk and half a sugar lump."

The Commander made a mental note to try that in the future, if there was a future of course.

Claire then asked "so what does 'illimitable' mean then?"

"Well I assume your talking about Jack's bank balance" Claire nodded "in simple terms, there weren't enough numbers to show the balance."

Claire frowned at him and asked "what does that mean?"

"Well, the number was too big to fit on the display."

"So he got more compensation than me then?" moaned Claire.

"Well no, he just already had a bank account with Crowns in it" replied the Commander simply.

Claire sat frowning to herself, wondering how Jack had an intergalactic bank account and judging by his face, he had been wondering something similar as he had looked at his bank balance. Asking Jack about it would be useless then, mainly because he could not even remember a four month old invasion. The Commander had also just used a curious tone, leading Claire to believe that any question she asked him would result in another accurate but wholly useless answer, again.

The mouldy green looking cardboard box then opened and Jack seemed to be almost pushed out by some invisible force. He had an confused expression on his face, like he was being ejected from a bar for drinking. He was now also wearing a suit.

As he stumbled towards to the two of them, they could see the suit was double breasted, dark grey in colour, with shiny white trainer shoes and a white shirt with a blue tie. They both were now stood looking at Jack with mouths open but for two very different reasons.

Claire had always liked the way Jack looked in a suit, but was reluctant to ever admit it out loud and so stood staring with a pleased smile on her face. The Commander on the other hand was stood with his mouth open, a look of outrage and an ever increasing temper starting to boil over his features.

As Jack looked at the Commander he noticed how angry looking he was and found he was imagining steam frothing from his furry ears.

Hissing in anger the Commander said "well, your supposed to be lying low, you know, incognito."

Jack looked down at his clothing "what's wrong?" he asked curiously, pulling at an lapel.

"Well, your going to stand out!" said the Commander.

"I think he looks very nice" said Claire.

"Well nice" said the Commander almost shouting "he'll be the only one in a suit!"
"We've seen others in suits!" retorted Claire.
"Well yes, yes we have" replied the Commander "but not SPACESUITS!"
"I don't get what you mean?" asked Claire.
The Commander shook his head in disbelief and replied "well, when in space you need to wear a spacesuit, generally they LOOK like spacesuits or flexible armour, NOT actual suits."
Claire looked closely at Jack and his clothing and noticed that it did look a little odd for a suit, in that it appeared to be made from one dark grey piece, the collar of the white shirt and suit were thicker than normal too. There was also what looked like a zip, hidden behind a flap covering over what would have been buttons on a normal shirt and a thick blue tie around his neck dropping into the jacket. The top of the trousers were hidden by the grey jacket, with the bottom of the trousers somehow flexibly attached to some very shiny black leather looking, smooth, lace-less shoes. As she looked closer Claire could see that the shoes had thicker soles than normal, like boots. Nonetheless Jack did look very smart indeed.
"Well, in the box, what did you ask for?" asked the Commander of Jack with a stern look on his foxy jawed face.
"A space suit" replied Jack.
"Well really!"
"What I actually asked for, was, 'a suit for space'."
Raising his arms in frustration the Commander said angrily "well it'll certainly be crucking unique."

     The two humans spent the next few hours wandering around the shops in the area, flicking there eye wear on and off as they wandered about. It was a rabbit warren of alleys and open spaces but at no time did they feel they were lost. The whole place was exceptionally well designed for walking or taking the small pedestrian transporters that they saw everywhere. The shops were all similar to the first board shop they had visited, in that the front window showed there wares like any normal retailer. On entering the shop though, the windows now looking out showed vistas relevant to the products in the shop. There was also the telltale noise reduction and electric shiver that ran up through there entire bodies every time they entered a shop, which was at least half of them that used a suspension field. Every time this happened it set Jack's teeth on edge, like finding long forgotten bits of pepper or spice in the gaps and experiencing a taste explosion, making you wince.
     Jack was getting annoyed with the fog like atmosphere too, it stopped you from seeing very far, he had tried taking off his sunglasses but the continuous bright advertising made everything look surreal. Not that the this whole adventure was not down right silly to Jack's mind. Outside a shop Claire then took off her blinkers and Jack saw her sigh with relief, so he took off his sunglasses. Strangely he felt better for being able to see her brown eyes and kept reminding himself not to look up, which in his mind was also down and the wrong way up.

Later they were sat in a tower at the opposite end of the cavern to where they arrived on the moon. Jack was blankly staring out of the continuous window, at what he thought of as a massive shopping mall. They were sat in a coffee shop near the middle of the building, which would be the top if you were at either base, in the middle of the tube like space. The tower seemed to be wedged in the tunnel like gap, like a support beam holding the faces of the cavern interior apart. They were sat equal distance from both the bottom and the top, with the glass like tower not really being a tower as such, more of a skyscraper that had two bottoms and two tops.

Jack felt a strange vibration in his pocket and then a strange noise, like a cow bellowing out Happy Birthday, he put his hand in his pocket and pulled out the Quellz. On the front was a message from the surf and board shop, informing him that his board was ready to test and collect at his convenience but NOW.

The three of them made there way down to the base of the tower, by the use of one of the many lifts. Jack was very thankful that they were just like normal lifts back on Earth, with buttons and corners and most importantly of all, bottoms.
When they stepped outside the Avacor Joan was sat astride a hovering trike "get on, you haven't got much time" she chirped at them quickly.
"Well, much time for what?" asked the Commander.
"Some Mercs arrived a few minutes ago."
"So?" asked Claire.
"They are looking for you" said Joan simply looking at Jack with a pointed expression, which was quite a good description because of her pointed beak.
"Why?" asked Jack.
"Who knows, but normally when the Mercs are looking for someone, it's to remove them from the living."

Jack stared first at Joan and then at the bright red hovering trike, it looked like a curvaceous convertible three wheeled car, minus the wheels. The trike was bulbously shaped at the front leading to two smaller pods on either side, which flared out at the back like large overpowered engines, which they were. Joan was sat partially inside the front pod, astride its interior like she were riding an angry mean motorbike. She sat behind a curved wind shield, covered in bug splats and dust scars, she kept waving her smaller feathered arms at them to get in the back. They clambered in the back between the two pods, finding three padded seats to sit astride, shaped like skinny pears bent in the middle to make a back rest. There was a seat belt pulled across from the underside of each seat, which Jack applied without even thinking, he was still slightly on edge from watching the Commander bend his knees in the opposite direction to his own as he sat down. Jack shuddered as he moved his bits about on the motorbike like padded red leathered seat.
"I'm sorry inconspicuous this is not, but it is quick" said Joan.
"That's okay, I've always liked red and white flame decals, especially as they flicker" said Jack.

Sniffing Joan replied "no need to be sarcastic."

    The trike lifted off from a few inches above the ground to twenty feet in a second, it left Jack with an open mouth as he tried to explain he was not being sarcastic. Then Joan twisted the throttle on the curved handlebars, the acceleration was fantastic; Jack then appreciated why the seats were so thick and soft, as he lost his voice entirely in one gulp of force.

    Surphon flashed by at such a rate that Jack nearly forgot to breath, when he did breath, he expected to be gulping air because of the speed, like a skydiver but without the benefit of a parachute. As it happened the air felt quite normal on the trike, right up to the point where Jack stretched out a hand as an experiment and it left the safety of the vehicle. The air nearly removed his arm by the method of dragging it off with air burn, like grabbing at a handle on a passing bus, which Jack of course had never done for obvious health and safety reasons. Still, it felt very similar he thought. Jack cringed back in pain holding his shoulder and elbow, the Commander and Claire both shook there heads, although Claire not quite so much as she had been thinking the same thing. Jack had just beaten her to it was all.

"So why are you helping us?" asked Claire of the Avacor.

The Commander replied before Joan could say anything "well because we're still on her card."

"Card?" asked Claire.

"Well yes, her shop assistant work card. Basically we're her responsibility until we leave here, although why she's helping us to evade the Mercs I'm not quite sure?" asked the Commander leaning towards Joan.

    The trike then made several sharp turns between buildings and came to a stop outside the board shop. The three of them jumped out and Joan said "don't be too long please."

Jack replied "okay, thank you" and the three of them undid there belts and clambered out the side of the trike.

    The shop looked the same, rather it looked too much the same, it seemed to be identical in every single way and yet something felt wrong to Jack and Claire. The Commander turned back when he was halfway across the pavement realizing he was not being followed. Both Jack and Claire were stood staring at the building, as the Commander took a few steps towards them and opened his mouth to tell them to hurry up, they both reached into there pockets and put on there respective eye wear. There mouths dropped open in shock at exactly the same time and so the Commander wordlessly stood next to them and did the same.

After a few seconds with the Commander lifting his blinkers up and down in front of his eyes, he had to ask "well, where is it?"

"You know, I really don't know but I thought you might?" asked Jack.

While wearing blinkers or in Jack's case sunglasses, where the shop had been there was just a metal frame holding the Laser Identifying Camera Kit, projecting the image of the shop for all to see, just no actual shop behind it. Behind the frame was a gap and a hole in the floor with extra dust.

With some relief in his voice Jack said "no shop, no board, no surf competition?"

"Why do you sound relieved Jack?" asked Claire.

"Why do you think, we get to go home!"

"No we don't, there's no Earth to go home to!" growled Claire.

Jack shook his head, starting to smile the more he talked "this is all some elaborate hoax, involving, alcohol, drugs and probably rock and roll. We'll wake up in a minute, and none of this will have happened and it'll all be some daft dream."

"Why do you say that?" asked Claire looking around carefully.

"It has to be, because without a board this is all pointless!" Jack shouted the last word and waved his arms about, attracting the attention of a few passing multi-limbed aliens.

Next door there was an alley way between two buildings, a head poked round the corner, it looked first one way and then the other as if it were trying to get its bearings. The Commander was the first to spot the head and then the others, it was trying to look inconspicuous as it first swung one way and the other but because of its size and shark like design it stood no chance.

Jack groaned inwardly and then slightly outwardly as he recognized the head as "Ron!" said Jack with the Commander turning to smile at him and then striding off to say hello. They walked over to the corner of the alley, first the Commander disappeared round the corner then Claire and finally Jack.

When Jack stepped around the corner he was surprised to find he was now in the shop, in its entirety. No hole, no damage it was just there and he was stood just inside the front door. Spinning round Jack could see the shop but not the door he had supposedly walked through, there was also now no front window to look out of, just a large mirror along the entire length of the shop. In front of him was Ron holding and leaning on a surfboard with a red and white flame decal on the underside, he spun it around and on the upper side were autumnal coloured tree leaves in a wind swept design that actually seemed to be moving of there own accord. The board was three meters long, ten centimeters thick in the middle and a meter and a half wide. The front was angled to a point and slightly pointing up, the base had angled ridges that ran from one end to the other and met with three fins at the back.

It really did look like a surfboard, apart from the chunky bottom where the engine lived, the many side vents, the three large exhaust thrust ports, streamlined and pointing out the back. Ron was holding, spinning the board and also smiling broadly.

Outside the shop front under the central walkway sat Joan on her trike, she glanced around looking at the shop and then up and down the shops. There was no sign of her passengers and no sign of the alleyway they had walked into any more, it had simply gone back to being the side of another shop. Then three figures dressed in black dropped down from there own multicoloured hover pod bike hybrids, right in front of the board shop. They stood like angry Raifoon but with knees facing the other way, observed Joan, they looked ready to jump to the attack at any moment. The three black cloaked figures strode up and down the shop front, with there cape like cloaks flapping around as they stomped up and down. These must be the Mercs thought Joan, what actually gave it away was the name embroidered on there right shoulder sleeves and on there left breast in bright white italics, the last letter was italic and squirely like anyway. Being that generally they removed people on sight, it was kind of funny and amusing to see them strutting up and down in front of the shop, like little lost chicks. Joan looked hard again at the shop, it was there in all its advertising glory, so why then had she briefly glimpsed a massive hole? She slowly reached round for her blinkers and nearly fell off the trike when she saw the lack of shop.

"Where are we?" asked Claire.
"In my shop" replied Ron.
"The one that's in a hole, in the wall?"
"Looks aren't everything you know."
"You aren't gonna explain that are you?" asked Claire.
"I would have thought it was obvious" said Jack.
Claire looked round in fury at Jack, because of the know-it-all tone he had used, ready to verbally thump him but on seeing his face she realized he was not being deliberately annoying.
Between only slightly gritted teeth she asked "obvious, how?"
"It's a bluff or more correctly a double bluff of a hole" said Jack as he worked out the explanation for himself.
"Your right of course" said Ron "the shop was always a hole."
"I don't understand" said Claire "if it was always a hole then how are we in it?"
"We are in the hole but in a very, very small part of it" said Ron.
Claire looked at Jack and said "a suspension field?"
"Yep, a really big one" Ron looked quite proud of himself.
"So can't anyone just walk in here now?" asked Claire.
"Not unless they know the door code, or open the door from the inside."
"But there is no door there's just a hole!" said Claire.
"The Commander here knew the code for the doorway, otherwise it's just a closed shop" replied Ron.
Claire did one of those shrugs that said 'I give up' and then asked "so we're safe in here?"
"Only until they get out there high density blinkers out."
"High density blinkers?" asked Jack.

"Well think of them as X-Ray glasses, they can see anything at nearly any level. There basically high grade military blinkers that are designed to search and find the target you require" said the Commander.
"Just out of interest, how do we know there looking for us?" asked Jack.
Ron pulled out his Quellz from some rear pocket, on the display was a three dimensional image of each of them, with various prices on display. 'Presumably for each body part that was turned in' thought Jack.
"As soon as they landed they issued a bounty prize for each of you" said Ron.
Both Jack and Claire were looking at there own Quellz but were unable to find there respective bounties, Jack looked up at Ron and was surprised to see sympathy written on his face or at least the closest a shark like face could manage.
"You need the reward Pass" said Ron simply.
"Can we not download it from somewhere?" asked Claire.
"You can only get it if your ex-military, a Merc or a reward hunter".
Claire and Jack were disappointed but at nearly the same time they both turned to the Commander and Claire said "that means you can download it?"
"Well me!" exclaimed the Commander.
"Yes you, your now ex-military aren't you?" said Claire.
"Well yes, I suppose I am" said the Commander with a certain amount of disappointment in his voice "but as soon as I activate my Quellz they'll know where we are now."
"Before all that though we need to get out of here" said Ron.
"We?" asked Jack.
"Oh didn't I say?"
"No, you didn't!"
"I've been added to the bounty as your associate."
"Which means what?" asked Jack.
"All my neighbours will be after me for a start, it's a cut-throat business retail you know!"
	Indicating that Ron should lead the way, the Commander waved an arm at him, before they went anywhere he left the board standing upright on its own and walked forward towards Jack purposely.
"First though I need payment for the board" said Ron in a threatening tone.
"Really! Have we got time for this?" asked Jack.
"We'll make time, business is business after all."
Ron showed his Quellz to Jack, on it the display was split into two, the bottom half facing Ron had the final balance and the customer name. The other half faced Jack and had the final balance and the vendors name. Jack pulled out his own Quellz, after being directed by the Commander and held it in his hand facing Ron's Quellz.
Jack looked at his display, it now to had the same figure work as Ron's, after the Commander stroked the screen a few times, then Jack asked "three hundred thousand seems a lot to me?"
"Well how much!" exclaimed the Commander glancing at the display in shock.

"Calm down your buying me and all my services!"
Before the Commander could bargain for anything the Quellz made a pleasant dinging noise and Ron looked down "thank you very much" he said to Jack with an incredibly toothy grin.
Jack had to ask something though, as he looked up and down from Ron to the vendors name written on his Quellz "hmm 'Getta GRIP shopping', Gary is your first name?"
With a slight rumble of annoyance in his voice Ron replied "it's just Ron thanks."

      Trying not to smile too much, Jack looked down at his Quellz balance and the business he had just completed with Ron, the final balance still read as 'illimitable', whatever that actually meant Jack was still not really sure.

Chapter 28 : Hosiery Escape.

There was a rumble and a thumping like noise from somewhere outside the shop "it's really time to go" said Ron. The shop keeper almost seemed to run across the shop floor towards the back, with fin like protrusions starting to poke out from the sides of his legs as he ran. The three of them briskly walked after him, Ron directed them through some heavily draped curtain at the rear of the shop. The three of them then stood in what looked like to Jack to be a fairly large, pink cloud influenced changing room. It would have been quite a large changing room but with two humans and a Raifoon crowded into it, it was decidedly cosy and compact. This was also the first time Jack and Claire had been in quite so close a proximity to the Commanders arm pits, one on either side, they both stood for a second looking very surprised and then they started to gag a little.

"Hasn't your species developed deodorant?" asked Claire holding the back of her hand to her face.

The Commander looked down at Claire with some disdain, then Ron came through the curtain behind them and the changing room was most definitely full. Being squashed under each of the Commanders arms, with something dribbling over them, both Claire and Jack prayed for salvation as they gasped for clean air.

Then the plastic back panel they were pressed up against gave way with several plop like sounds and a small but continuous tearing sound. It reminded Jack of the sound of ripping jeans for some reason, something he had only experienced once involving a plank, a stage and some parallel bars. The four of them then tumbled out of the tiny room, with arms and legs thrown in several directions, finishing up like a pile of spaghetti slapped on a plate.

Feeling slightly dizzy they slowly picked themselves up and looked around.

"We're in a hosiery shop?" asked Jack staring around in chocked surprise "I don't know why, but I wouldn't have thought you lot would have needed undergarments! And I don't know why I thought that at all!" he finished after realizing how foolish he now sounded.

Jack walked through the shop following along behind everyone else, gazing around in a mixture of shock and awe, there was anything and everything on display here. It ranged from plastic looking bedtime aids, to frilly things and things without any frills that probably provided thrills of one description or another.

By the time he reached the front of the shop Ron and the Commander were cautiously peering out of the front window, with Jack having seen enough undergarments to last several life times. The occasional flash of naked alien flesh had not helped his mental state, at the best of times he was a frightened and cautious person but this visit had added whole new depths to his vision of underwear shopping and horror.

"Stop staring around like a child in a chocolate cottage" said Claire who was leant against an apparent red brick wall behind the Commander. Jack then noticed his mouth was open and a little drool was trying to escape "I'm full" he said automatically in an confused tone.
"That makes a change" said Claire with a smile, which then disappeared as she finished "it's just a shame it had to be lingerie that filled you up!"

Jack crouched down behind Ron and after a few seconds of looking out of the window over his shoulder asked "what are we looking for and where are we?"
Ron's answer was short "two doors down and we're waiting for the Mercs to go away."

Eventually the three Mercs appeared back in the road, there curvy single seat, meaner looking versions of Joan's trike floating down from where they had been parked. The Mercs were still wearing there black capes and almost black cowboy hats, although they were now a little dustier in places, what really stood out were the colours of there hovering bikes. They were exceptionally bright, very much like you would expect an expensive super or hyper car to be excessively coloured, so were these. One was green, another orange and the third was pink, the colours was so riotous that if there were any decals on the bikes you would not be able to see them because of the vividness of the paint.

Across the road they could see Joan sat on her trike, trying to look inconspicuous by looking into the glowing display of her Quellz. The Mercs gave one last scan around, then at exactly the same time swung a leg over there bikes and zipped off with a roar of there engines.

Jack had noticed several things in the short space of time he had been looking out of the window, the first was the way the Mercs moved, like cowboys from a wild western film all swagger and looking for a gun fight. In fact the only thing missing was them spittooning in the street. The second thing he had noticed, was the supposedly concealed weapons they were carrying under there respective capes. There were all kinds of bulges in odd places, with the occasional muzzle and knife edge poking out, this stuck out because nobody else was wearing anything similar anywhere on the moon he had seen. Well apart from there own concealed weapons obviously, the main difference really was that they were only carrying one each, whilst the Mercs appeared to be carrying several each. Thirdly there bikes had looked awesome, sounded even better and they had just looked amazingly cool. The fourth thing Jack had observed and was struggling with, which he was not a hundred percent sure of, probably ninety eight percent sure of, was the fact they looked and acted like humans.
He turned to Claire and asked "did any of those guys remind you of the ones that chased us to the satellite dish, on Earth?"
"You know not really, after all we were running away really fast" said Claire quickly.
"Well Joan's waving at us, so I guess it's time to go" said the Commander standing up and reaching to shake Ron's hand.

"You aren't getting rid of me that easily mate" replied Ron shaking his hand "I'm coming with."

Shaking his head the Commander said "well, no your not."

"Well yes, I'm afraid I am, I mean even if you had picked up the board you'd still need a board engineer and the Mercs went straight to my shop, which isn't good!"

The Commander looked at Jack and said "well, you forgot the board!"

Opening and shutting his mouth a few times, Jack guessed there was no suitable reply apart from nodding, it was one of those situations where words would have just annoyed the questioner.

The Commander stood up and walked out of the ladies, and possibly men's, delicate underwear shop, with the others following closely behind and jumped into the back of the trike. When they were all seated Jack turned round and found Claire stood on the street with arms folded, foot tapping and a look of disgust on her face.

Speaking to Jack who had been the last to climb in the three seater trike, she said "if you think I'm sitting on your lap, you've got another thing coming."

Jack looked to the other two males sat next to him for help, even being of completely different species they had understood the tone of her voice and were choosing to take great interest in the nearest central bridge support, pointing out interesting graffiti and the misspellings on it.

Joan came to Jack's rescue and in a motherly tone said "come on dear, climb on behind me."

After a moments pause to stick her tongue out at Jack, Claire climbed up behind Joan, sat down behind her and tried to wrap her arms around her waist. Joan guided her hands to somewhere within her pinky plumage and then said "I suggest you all hold on now."

"Well, why?" asked the Commander.

"Because I had a feeling the Mercs would be watching" said Joan and then almost to herself "let the games begin".

"Games, what games?" asked Ron in a worried tone.

Joan flicked some hidden switches under the trike display readout in front of her, then various whirring noises of things folding out from the trike could be heard "I've wanted to do this for years!" she said quietly and enthusiastically.

Cocking there heads to one side the four frowning passengers could hear that the engine tone on the trike had not only changed but had possibly had a new engine fitted, one that sounded about four sizes too big for the size of the trike. It was like listening to a loan violinist, then a whole orchestra suddenly waking up and playing, with a rock band thrown in for good measure as the exuberant exhaust system. To Jack it just sounded brutally amazing; after only a few seconds of the low roar and revving they were all smiling like crazed toddlers high on Christmas presents and sugar.

Back down the street behind them there was suddenly a commotion, as various shopping members of the public were knocked down by the Mercs spinning there bike pods quickly around and gunning there engines to give chase. Joan twisted the handlebar to spin the trike round in a circle and let the beast of an engine make even more noise.

If the acceleration had felt harsh before, when Joan had left the tower with them, now it felt bone shattering as she moved her taloned thumb further round to accelerate. Jack caught a glimpse of a loan bike pod coming up the street towards them, knocking random aliens to either side, with the other two dropping down over the top of the buildings behind it performing similar maneuvers Then they were in an alley, zipping between arches, corridors, random clothes lines and boxes.

Jack found the ride not to bad if he kept his eyes facing forward and his hand on his stomach for support. It did occur to him to ask why alien clothing was hanging on lines across the street, surely they would have some other drying system in place, he just did not trust himself to be able to open his mouth without being violently ill. What was really making him feel rough were the rolls, twists and barrel turns Joan was pulling off with the trike.

Eventually his stomach calmed down enough for him to ask through clenched teeth and even tighter clenched buttocks "are we there yet?"

"Are you blind Jack?" shouted Claire over her shoulder "there still shooting at us, we can't go back to the shuttle with them on our tail!"

Jack perked up a little at the word 'shoot', at no point had anyone mentioned being shot at and he was sure he would have seen some effect of them being fired upon. It was at this point he noticed his eyes were shut and to some degree his ears as well. It was like his brain had decided all on its own that whatever was happening outside his skull, should not be filtered inside of his skull. Jack slowly forced himself to listen to what was going on, as he was still struggling to open his eyes more than just a slit, mainly because everything was so blurry going past. The sounds of the chase slowly filtered through, there was the constant rumble of the souped up engine of the trike, with the occasional sound of the engine being gunned to make various tight turns. The turns themselves being up, down or around some statue as they flew past and something red removed its alien head.   Jack saw this statue as a brief glimpse as they entered a large plaza like area, the statue was made from a stone looking material and was easily the size of several buses. What stuck in Jack's mind was the fact it was some alien cross-breed between a shark, fox and a snake sat astride a rearing horse like whale. Even at the high speed they were going it took several seconds to fly around the base wall of the statue, dodging the falling head. Joan then performed some barrel rolling flick with the trike to leave the statue and another red beam of some kind was fired directly at the front of them. The beam went over there ducking heads, forcing the two chasing bikes to separate and veer off to either side behind them. One flew head on into the fallen statues head, leaving a small nuclear bomb like mushroom bloom shortly after. The other bike twisted away pulling back hard to climb up the side of the plaza, with the engine of the bike screaming in protest, which suddenly stopped as the rider was removed from the bike by a clothes line without any clothes on it. The bike carried on up for a few moments, towards the buildings on the other side of the cavern, before just stopping in mid air, like it was waiting for something. The rider was nowhere to be seen, although there was evidence of an new entrance and exit in the side of one of the buildings surrounding the plaza.
The final Mercs rider flew over there heads, pulling a very tight half loop to chase the trike, then they could be seen shaking there head at there colleagues, as they flew past there remains and entered the same alleyway as the trike.

By now Jack had managed to coax his eyes and ears open but in some respects wished he had not, when Claire started to whistle and cheer and then compliment Joan on her flying skills.
The Commander was looking behind them and said worriedly "well we've still got one chasing us I'm afraid."
"I know, don't worry I've got a plan" said Joan.
The way she said 'I've got a plan' worried Jack, it smacked of over confidence to his mind and so he asked "is it a good plan?"
"Yes" she replied quickly "of course, it's one of mine."
Jack sat for a moment in his seat thinking, with the occasional red energy beam flaming its way past and then asked "is there an element of risk?"

"Well, more so than being disintegrated by energy weapons!" replied the Commander sarcastically.

Jack replied after a moments pause "point taken, so we'll go with Joan's plan then."

"Well honestly I don't trust Avacors overly much, but so far she hasn't steered us wrong and she's in the same muck as us" said the Commander quietly.

"We're all yours Joan" said Jack.

"They are aware this isn't a democracy?" said Joan under her breath. Claire clinging on behind her nearly fell off as she laughed at the comment.

"I'm sorry I didn't mean to offend you" said Joan apologetically.

"Don't worry you didn't, it's more of a sexist stereotype really with some political correctness thrown in."

"I don't understand your meaning, surely that's offensive in its self?"

"They were trying to be accommodating to everyone on the trike, that's all, but your the bird whose flying the thing, so it's your decision."

Joan replied simply "thank you, I think."

"Just out of interest though what is your plan, it'll make them feel better, you know if you tell them?" asked Claire with Joan smiling at her own hidden question of worry.

"The Pugs" she replied.

Claire paused in nodding and then asked "Pugs?"

"You would call them the Police, I think."

After a moments though Claire asked "You've got a Police force that are called..."

"Pugs, to be precise."

The Commanders ears pricked up at this and he asked with a slight tinge of worry in his voice "well how long have they been here?"

Joan shrugged whilst dodging another salvo of red death and said "a few years, it was quite a relief to finally have some legal authority."

"Did you not have any before?" asked Claire.

"Yes, we've always had our own force, but with so many interstellar visitors, it became nearly impossible to move without stepping on someone's tradition or offending there right to bear!"

"To bear?" asked Claire.

"Bare anything frankly, I mean we had our own laws to govern us but being that so many foreigners were now here, they argued that they had more rights to everything. So the Pugs were called in."

"Well that's all we need" said the Commander.

"What's all we need?" asked Jack finally seeming to wake up.

"Well Pugs!" replied the Commander.

"Okay, what are Pugs?" asked Claire.

"Well, Public Universal Guard Services" the Commander almost spat the explanation out.

"What's wrong with them?" asked Jack.

"Well they deal with everything from petty theft to the destruction of a planet, if get my meaning!"

"Ah I see where your going with this, your a wanted criminal!" said Jack.

"Well we're wanted Jack, remember" said the Commander "some more than others."
Jack nodded, shivered and brushed his neck like something was tickling it "you've really gotta get that under control you know" said Claire.
"What under control?" asked Jack.
"Your nervous twitching Jack, its really annoying!"
"What twitching?"
"Your forever scratching and brushing yourself and if you don't stop, I'll start slapping you every time you do it!"
Jack with his mouth half open in thought, trying to remember his last twitch, eventually just nodded and said "okay."

      Joan by now had started her plan of action, which did not register on the passengers until they crashed through a check point in a dark tunnel. Whatever the checkpoint was there for, it was a bit late for the passengers to ask as to its purpose. The bright white barrier arm, several meters wide, had been struck by there speeding trike and after being removed from its mounting had snapped in two. One piece had spun round and decapitated the top of the small grey guard room, collapsing it and then sticking in the wall behind. The other part of the arm was stuck in the ceiling of the tunnel, vibrating intensely and making a twanging noise like a plastic ruler being pinged on the edge of a tabletop.
The single remaining chasing Mercs saw the barrier split in two pieces but due to the volume of dust released into the air, that no amount of vacuuming could ever hope to remove in one suction, they did not see exactly where the bits of barrier went. It was only on leaving the checkpoint mess behind them, in hot pursuit with a loud twang resounding in the ears, that they felt a light chill brush there scalp. Touching the top of there helmet it felt a bit odd, airy in fact, they gave a sigh as there was an angled sliced air hole on top.

      One of the three guards from the checkpoint could be heard groaning from under some of the building debris. It had not been a big building but since all three of them had been inside it, they were now finding out that at least it had not been a heavy building. The checkpoint was only really there to give the public peace of mind, it was used mainly just to slow traffic down now as smuggling between areas was pointless. The first guard continued to groan, after a few seconds he was joined in chorus by the other two guards. Pulling bits of building off himself and reaching for his Pugs issued radio Quellz, he noticed something spinning slowly in the middle of the road. It appeared to be a black shiny plate or bowl spinning on its edge, as it slowed down the guard finished untangling his radio and saw that it appeared to be part of a helmet. Shrugging to himself he raised the radio to his helmet, which meant he looked up to the ceiling to see half the barrier arm still vibrating away in the ceiling of the rocky tunnel. He paused for a moment, looked at the Quellz radio for a moment, tapped parts of the screen and laid his head back on the wall behind him to wait.

Jack had been not so much horrified at the destruction but shocked, he and the others were all very silent as they sailed round various corners in the tunnel with red beams of light occasionally spinning past. The tunnel Jack noticed, after awhile, was actually several fallen skyscraper like buildings that connected to a rocky tunnel network. The system appeared to be shaped like a snake that had swallowed a tin of alphabet soup, containing mainly S's.
The constant swinging from side to side, with the occasional barrel roll thrown in, was not doing anything for any of there stomachs.
Jack eventually had to ask "do you think we should go back and help?"
"Who?" asked Claire.
"You know, the guards from the checkpoint."
"You want to go back and help the guards we just ran into, the ones we ran down?"
"We didn't run them down, they were in the building as it collapsed" said Joan.
"That doesn't make it any better!" said Claire.
"Are we gonna be in any trouble for this?" asked Jack.
"I hope so" said Joan.
Claire and Jack exchanged frowns.
There was then a light, joyful ping noise that came from the screen between the handle bars in front of Joan's eye, looking down briefly she smiled to herself.
Claire hanging on behind her felt the change in her body, she seemed to relax slightly "was it a good ping?" asked Claire sarcastically after a few seconds.
"Yes, we're being pursued" said Joan.
"Okay that's good, how exactly?" asked Claire.
Joan looked round at Ron briefly and smiled "no, no I'm not doing it" he replied to her look.
Joan waved a feathered hand in the direction of the next beam of red light, Ron sighed and reached forward to the central pod that linked the trike together. He opened a panel and started to dig around inside "what's he looking for?" asked Claire.
"He's digging out the tracker and we're going to stick it to our pursuer" said Joan.
After a moment thinking about things Jack asked "how and why?"
"Because we want him to be chased by the Pugs for destroying there checkpoint and how, well that's where we need to close the gap and someone needs to apply the tracker."
There was silence on the trike as it sped around the twisty tunnel, after a few turns Jack guessed they were going around in circles inside the fallen building "are we going in circles?" he asked.
"Yes, the tunnel has many links to other tunnels" said Joan.
"So all someone has to do is get off somewhere and wait for him" Jack thumbed over his shoulder "to pass and somehow stick the tracker to him?"

Ron then made a grunting sound and came up holding a small curvy tennis ball sized object. The ball was dull grey in colour and seemed to somehow pulse blue from somewhere deep inside.
Ron handed the ball to Jack and said "you see the little black hole I'm covering with my finger?"
"No, but yes?" hazarded Jack.
"Don't take your finger off it till you throw it."
Joan suddenly pulled over to one side, in one smooth movement Ron had undone Jack's belt and pushed him off the trike head first, Jack did a somersault and landed on his backside in the tunnel. The trike revved like mad, spun off down the tunnel with its jets kicking up copious amounts of dust and shortly after the Mercs bike flew over the top of Jack, showering him in yet more dust.

Jack had his mouth open from the moment he had been given the grey ball, even when he had been kicked off the trike he still had not quite come to terms with what he was supposed to be doing. When the trike had kicked up all the dust he had to shut his mouth and had covered his nose, otherwise he may have drowned on the shear volume of the stuff. Much as he hated the dust, which even now felt like it was in every possible hole in his body, at least there pursuer had not been able to see him because of it.

Jack found a suitable place to stand amongst the fallen millennia old furniture, just as he did so a set of lights came spiraling round the corner in front of him, he had just enough time to draw back his arm and stop. He had no idea if this was the trike or the chasing bike or even if it was someone else entirely. The first set of lights flashed by with Claire leaving an excited scream behind, followed seconds later by a smaller set of lights and no scream. It happened so quickly that Jack had not realized how fast Joan had actually been flying. The next time though Jack would be ready, least that is what he kept telling himself.

His plan was actually quite simple, all he really needed to do was throw the grey ball thing in the air right in front of the bike and he guessed it would attach itself like a magnetic limpet. The only problem he could foresee was being stood in the right place to throw the ball thing in the air in front of the bike.

After moving some of the furniture around, he managed to make a little barricade in the middle of the tunnel, he found a little desk mirror and angled it on top, hoping that Joan would see it in her lights and fly over the top. Then Jack heard the trike bellowing its way down the tunnel again, the trike flew dead centre over the top of Jack, creating another dust plume. Because of the cover the dust created, Jack was able to put on his sun glasses and look directly for the following set of lights. Jack looked at the bikes approaching lights and then at the dull grey ball in his hand.
"Close enough" he said and tossed the ball into the air.

The ball completely missed the bike, having sailed over the top. Milliseconds later as it started to drop back down, all kinds of spikes and rope like dull grey coils came flooding out of the ball. One coil caught a fin on the back of the bike and the ball retracted on it, sticking to it like mud on clean laundry.

Jack paced backwards and forwards across the tunnel, impatiently picking up various little bits of office paraphernalia, they looked familiar but were of the alien assortment. In the end though they appeared to have the same function as other office bits, mainly to make the workers more efficient by forcing them to laugh at themselves whilst working.

Jack saw a mug like object on the floor, on it was written 'you don't have to be mad to work here but you'll be tortured if you aren't'. Just a very direct way of saying your damned if you do and damned if you don't, thought Jack. He picked up the mug, it simply dissolved into yet more dust as he raised it in the air.
"Typical" said Jack coughing slightly.

Chapter 29 : Dustless New Friends.

It felt like he had been waiting hours in this half lit fallen building, Jack was of a mind to start walking back to the ship but he had no idea which way to walk to get there. So he sat and waited and did not play with his Quellz, he took it out of his pocket a few times though, wondering whether to call someone but struggled to make a decision. The problem was, he was not familiar enough with the technology, oh he could use it alright but it was more a question of whether he should. After all he had no idea if it was traceable, or even how it linked to another Quellz, for all he knew it was like a mobile phone which needed relay masts to work or even a satellite phone with access to open sky. Although that last one was a stretch, as he had used it in the surf shop.

Minutes dragged by in the half light of the tunnel, which seemed to be getting darker as time wore on, then eventually and much to Jack's relief a set of three lights came flooding around the corner. Jack used his Quellz as a make shift torch to flag them down and in so doing panicked as he guessed they might not be friendly.

"Are you alright Jack" asked Claire with a smile on her face as the trike pulled up next to him in a dust cloud "you look awfully pale?"

After a second or two Jack managed to regain control of his facial muscles and with a light clearing of his throat said "it's the dust thank you, I'll just climb aboard shall I?"

Jack sat back down in his original seat, Joan pulled away leaving a massive dust plume in the trike's wake and Jack with a strangely bruised ego.

They eventually reached a door which lead to the landing arm, parked and walked across to the shuttle. Jack was still taken aback by the number of landing arms poking out in all directions and the massive faces and bodies carved out of the surrounding buildings. This time he had a proper look at the place and what it reminded him of was a temple. One of the landing spoon arms also had a super sized stone altar at the end, in the shape of an half moon, making it appear more like some form of sacrificial point. The giveaway really was the blood red colour or probably more accurately the stained blood red colour and blade like slices in the stone. The phrase 'duel purpose' sprang to Jack's mind.

There was something else bothering him about the landing bay, which after walking around Surphon he realized was the lack of dust here and even the fact that none of them were dusty. After there chase through the dust bowl of a city, Jack had expected dust everywhere but here there was none. Jack was also dustless, there was no dust on any of there clothing. He looked back over his shoulder and saw a light white fizz as Joan walked through the door onto the landing arm and meandered through the boxes. She shook out feathers after being fizzed and gave Jack a wink, which considering the size of her eye could never be taken as conspiratorial.

They clambered through the shuttles hatch, with Sara and Summer giving Ron and Joan strange questioning glances, which the Commander waved a paw at in answer and sat down waiting for everyone else to take a seat.
Jack had a burning question in his head "what happened to the Merc?" after finally being picked up in the tunnel he had forgotten to ask about there pursuer.
"The local Pugs are chasing him" was the simple reply from Joan.
"How?" asked Jack.
"We stopped at the checkpoint at the other end of the tunnel and when he approached all manner of alarms went off, the Pugs gave chase."
"So where is he now?"
"Not here!" said Claire buckling up a belt.
"Yes I gathered that!" said Jack to the back of Claire's head.

The Commander turned to look at Sara and Summer, whom were both sat tapping there feet together in perfect timing or maybe perfect impatience. Jack always found it difficult to tell with the opposite sex, as to what individual expressions and tapping feet meant. Maybe that was why he struggled so much with the female of the species and had, in his time, received many a slap across the face just because he had read the signals all wrong. Earlier on he had thought Claire quite liked him, which he had found both exciting and confusing and yet now she had answered him quite shortly and was now ignoring him. Well two can play at that game thought Jack, readying himself to curtly ignore anything from Claire.

Claire was thinking something similar, that Jack actually was quite nice, maybe just a little misunderstood. Then she had seen the other females and remembered that she had a position to maintain, which meant she had been quite short with Jack, maybe too short. She turned to look at him over her shoulder with a slight smile starting on her lips. Jack looked straight at her then looked away quickly with a look of disgust on his face. Claire's eyes flared and she thought 'well if he's going to be like that two can play at that game' and decided in her mind to ignore him until he apologized. Jack had just been thinking about what to reply to Claire and had looked away quickly, annoyed with himself for not having a reply ready for when she had turned round.

A short flight later and they were back on the ship with Claire stomping off, later they met in the ships lounge area. Jack could see Claire, Summer, Sara and the Commander sitting in the lounges varied comfy seats and sofa's, discussing recent events.
"I'd leave her alone for a while if I were you" said Ron, stood just behind Jack.
Jack nearly jumped out of his suit for space in surprise, he had forgotten about there new friends.
"What are you two still doing here? Are you coming with us?" asked Jack.
Joan and Ron exchanged a level look at one another and both nodded in unison.

"Why?" asked Jack as they walked further into the ship.

Joan replied "I'm a soldier, or rather I was a soldier, a soldier with out a cause reduced to skimming off the top of sales. So I would appreciate it, if you would let me join your endeavour?"

Joan paused for a moment and then finished before Jack could reply with "actually you have to let me join your crew, I've not had so much fun in years!"

"My crew?"

"It's your ship Jack" pointed out Ron "and I'm your board specialist anyway, so I have to be here and Joan is a language specialist and can get us past any annoying Avacors."

"Thanks" said Joan drily.

"Present company excepted, of course" finished Ron smoothly.

"You mean present company excluded, I think?" said Joan.

"Aren't they the same thing?" asked Ron.

Jack clicked his fingers together on both hands, not really listening to there discussion but thinking about something else "I'd forgotten about the board, I guess you'll have to make another one?"

"Why would I need to do that?" asked Ron curiously.

"Because your shop was destroyed" Jack looked at Ron's smiling face "wasn't it?"

"I turned those advertising lasers to my favour, making the shop look like a hole in the ground."

"When all the time it was still there!" exclaimed Joan "that was brilliant idea, highly illegal, but a brilliant idea."

"Illegal or not it saved our fins didn't it?"

"Yes, yes it did" mused Joan who was thinking about how many other ways there were to misuse the Laser Identifying Camera Kit.

"I thought you said it was always a hole and we were in a big or small field thing?" asked Jack.

"I lied" said Ron simply whilst shrugging, this looked particularly amazing on a creature with in effect no neck to shrug from.

Both aliens stood nodding there heads at one another with Jack looking on impatiently, they obviously had no sense of holding back information so he asked "so where's the board then?"

Sitting down on the opposite side of the lounge coffee table Ron replied, with a toothy smile "hmm, oh that's already on board."

"How do you know?" asked Jack.

Ron pulled out his Quellz, held it nearly flat in his fin like hand and an image appeared above the screen showing a bluey green spreadsheet of figures and words.

"Whilst we were being chased about" Ron pointed at the floating characters "the contractors were loading your ship with my supplies."

Jack looked at the small floating video image above the Quellz, now showing various equipment being loaded onto the ship by the little green men "Drickers?" asked Jack.

"Yep, the most servitude happy species you'll ever meet" said Ron.

Jack looked at the image on display, he was not sure but the ship looked bigger somehow from the outside, like it had almost grown overnight so to speak.

Jack left Joan and Ron sat suspiciously close together still chatting innocently, he had the feeling that there was more to there leaving together than they wanted to admit and so he went to join Summer's little group. He got as far as one step from the sofa and Claire's super steel melting stare met his eyes, she turned sharply away from Jack with a sniff of prepared disdain. Jack looked on for a moment longer trying to determine what the sharp look, the sniff and turn had actually meant. The only thing he could see was that for some reason it was a private conversation about buying the board, although quite why that was private he did not know, he had been there after all! Jack turned away towards the cockpit and gave a little shrug of mild confusion.

Claire was pleased with herself when Jack had turned and walked away, although some of the pleasure was removed when he had shrugged and shook his head like he had expected her to blank him. Claire resolved to try harder next time.

"You should stop that you know" said Summer.
"Stop what?" asked Claire turning back to face Summer.
"Giving him mixed messages."
"Giving who mixed messages?"
"Really! Jack, you stare at him all time until he looks at you, and then look away quickly like he's a worm."
"Is this one of the human mating rituals I've heard about?" asked Joan suddenly looking round for Jack's reply.
"Yes, yes I think it may be, although she better be careful it doesn't bite her in the posterior" said Summer pointedly looking at Claire.
Claire was sat with her mouth open thinking 'why are they picking on me, I'm not the one whose being an idiot. Am I?'

Claire started to go a rosy red, or in her case a peachy red glow with touches of sunspot, as she realized she had been maybe a little silly. It was becoming all the more obvious as the others talked about there own mating rituals, how colour and scent was still used so strongly even after leaving there home worlds. The end result was that they decided there own mating systems, although unreliable in some circumstances, were infinitely better than the human method of 'pot luck' as Sara called it.

"After all who wants to be with another of there own species who isn't ready?" said Joan finally finishing the conversation with "and how do the humans tell?"

They all sat in silence for a moment with Claire finally feeling the tomato colouring starting to fade from her cheeks, right up until Joan said "I see your skin is de-flushing, does that mean your not so ready to mate any more?"

The colour started to come back, she could feel it, then Jack walked back in the lounge from the cockpit and Claire fled before anything could be said to embarrass her further. She jumped out of her seat and made for the cockpit, brushing past Jack, she prayed to whomever was listening that the aliens would keep there mouths shut before she reached the safety of the doorway. The last thing she heard as the door swooshed shut behind her was Joan asking curiously "so how do you tell, when the female of your species is ready then?"

Jack looked up at the door closing, still wondering why they only made a noise when shutting and Ron answered Joan's question with a smile "it's just a question of how tacky the wax is."
"I can't believe you still use wax on a surf or hover-board, what with all this other technology that must be around?" asked Jack curiously hoping to change the subject.
"Really it's just a case of what works the best, you want the grip to be such that you stay on but at the same time able to move around" said Ron.
"I think Jack was referring to the mix of technologies?" asked Sara looking at Jack.
"Yes, because on the street we saw floating bikes right alongside bikes with wheels?" asked Jack after a moments thought.
"It's more a question of what you need and at what price you want to pay, plus some things are more reliable than others" replied Ron.
Musing Jack said "so it's more to do with what works best rather than what's newest."
"To a certain degree but don't forget cost is in there too" said Ron musing over the profit.

The Commander then nudged Summer who showed him her Quellz "well, so we've left then?" asked the Commander slightly surprised "I didn't feel a thing!"
"As soon as the doors were shut" said Jack simply.
"Well it's not so much that we've left Jack, normally there's a jolt when the clamps let go and another when the engines kick in?"
"Dunno, I went to see Beth in the cockpit and she said 'we'd left and not to worry'."
"You look worried Jack?" asked Sara.
"Why was she telling me not to worry as soon as I walked in the cockpit, I only went up to watch the view as we left and she was telling me 'not to worry'?"

The Commander got up slowly and walked into the cockpit, closely followed by Jack and the others. The other thing that Jack had noticed when he had walked in earlier, was the size of the cockpit, it was more the size of what he would call a bridge now. The others did not seem to notice as they tried to subtly get more information out of Beth, who was still sat in the Captains seat with Claire leaning on it. Now there was another thing, before he had thought of it as the pilots seat, now he was thinking of it as the Captains seat.
Meaning that the ship, for whatever reason, was "getting bigger" mused Jack out loud again.

Everyone turned to look at him, obviously whatever they had been discussing, his small outburst had occurred in the quiet bit between thoughts and had been relevant in some way. Looking at there expressions, maybe relevant was not the right word, maybe accurate was a better word to use.
They carried on staring at Jack, he then asked "did I say something wrong?"
Sara cleared her throat slowly and said "we were discussing whether Claire's, ah" she paused trying to find the right word to use for a moment "behind" said Claire through clenched teeth.
Claire was now sat a the corner of the bridge, looking decidedly sullen and a bit moody to Jack's eye.
"Yes, that's the word I was aiming for, her behind was looking any different" finished Sara cautiously.
Jack looked at them a little lost "I thought we came in here to ask Beth 'what we weren't to worry about'?"
They all exchanged looks that said 'he's right you know, we did, whatever happened?'
As Sara turned to Beth and asked "you changed the subject?" Jack made another mental note to stop thinking out loud.
Beth replied "quite smoothly I thought!"
"But why?" asked Sara.
"I thought it would have been obvious?" said Beth still sat in the Captains chair.
"I don't see it?" said Sara starting to get a little angry now.
Beth managed a sigh, as Sara started to tap her booted foot, a sure sign of impatience "simply, so you wouldn't worry" she answered Sara.
"But now we're all worried!" said Claire angrily, she had been prepared to forgive Jack for his earlier looks of disapproval in her direction, now he had said her backside was BIG and getting BIGGER! She was redirecting her anger towards Beth instead of Jack, after all it would not do to slap him in front of the aliens after they had quizzed there mating rituals. It would make her look silly and as if she were pursuing Jack. Under no circumstances did Claire like to look silly, unless of course there was alcohol and a party involved, plus she was not pursuing Jack, if anything he was chasing her! She felt much better after thinking this through.
In Claire's mind Jack had been slowly climbing out of his well of despair, that she had put in him earlier. With the two word 'getting bigger', Jack had managed to drop himself back down the well, to end up neck deep in the mucky thing and cut the rope he had been climbing up.
Basically Claire was of the view that Jack was never going to live down those two little words, ever!
"Please don't be angry with me, Jack was right after all" said Beth.
"Right about what?" asked Sara.
"Getting bigger."
Claire was blushing furiously, glowing might be another way of putting it, as she tried to control a mixture of embarrassment and anger building up in her mind.

Cautiously and carefully not looking at Claire, Sara asked "what's getting bigger?"
"The ship" came Beth's simple reply.
Sara looked at Jack stood behind a bridge rail, he was looking out the curved window into space, then she looked back at Beth and asked "so your saying the ships getting bigger and Jack knew?"
"Jack didn't know, he just worked it out is all."
"Okay, so Jack wasn't commenting on anyone's physique then?" asked Sara carefully.
"He was commenting on the fact the ships getting bigger!" finished Claire, with sudden realization that she had done the mental equivalent of murdering someone, because she had got the wrong end of the conversation. Some of her natural colour started to return to her cheeks as she looked up at Jack, he looked back down at her and simply looked away. Claire thought she had forgiveness in her eyes, he had it shot down by a blatant look of indifference at her. From Jacks point of view he had felt someone staring at him and had turned to find it was Claire. The look she had been giving him had been worrying, like a hungry lioness looking at a gazelle, all hunger and drooling, so he had quickly looked away so he was not eaten alive, again.

    All this was lost on the others, with the Commander finally asking the ultimate question of Beth "well why's the ship getting bigger and how?"
"Because it's a Biological Gene Manipulated Alloy" said Beth with a sigh, knowing a reaction was forthcoming.
"We're in a Bi-loy!" exclaimed Summer with a gulp, followed by several quick steps away from leaning on the back of a chair, then standing like a deer caught in high powered spotlights, having heard something metal being cocked.

    Jack and Claire turned to stare at Summer who was trying with some degree of success not to touch anything on board the ship, even with her feet. There was a shuffle behind them, turning they found the Commander was doing the same thing as Summer, although he was trying to be nonchalant about it, by casually strolling to his own cleared space and continuously checking nothing was in reach, not even the floor if that were possible. Ron and Joan could be seen trying to do the same thing in there own space, which was only possible as the bridge seemed even bigger now since they had walked in, giving Joan actual room now to flap her wings furiously and hover over the deck. Ron was balanced on his crocodile like tail, with his other appendages folded in to make a ball like shape, giving the impression of a spiky red lollipop as his body changed colour.

    Jack, Claire and Sara exchanged looks that could be read as 'what the cruck are they doing?'
Jack leant forward, still holding onto the guard rail, before he could ask what was going on the Commander said in a tone of an hostage negotiator to the kidnapper "well, let go of the guard rail Jack and step away slowly."
Jack let go of the guard rail and curiously asked "why?"

The Commander completely ignored the question, Summer then carried on in the same tone of voice saying "all of you don't touch anything, if you can don't even touch the floor. We'll make our way to the lifeboats and hope for the best, we might make it" she finished in an not too hopeful tone.
"I doubt it" mumbled Ron worriedly moving sideways like a crab, alternating between tail and clawed toes.
      The three humans exchanged more looks of confusion but did not move as the others started to make there way slowly towards the bridge door. Jack looked at the door, before it had been a single panel big enough to just about admit two people through if they were facing one another. Now though it was a double panelled affair and people three abreast looked like they would fit through without a problem.
"Do you want to explain what's going on, please?" asked Sara of anybody.
The four aliens ignored her, they were intent on moving to the doorway as quickly as possible but with touching as little furniture of the bridge as possible.
The one thing that made Sara more angry than anything else in the Universe was being ignored, especially when she knew that they would have heard her. So she simply grabbed at Summer's arm as she stepped carefully past, Summer caught off balance tripped and sprawled in front of Beth sat in the Captains chair.
      Jack looked at Beth, if ever there was a face trying hard not too laugh she was was currently wearing it and doing quite well. She kept gulping small amounts of air and biting her lip, as Summer panicked trying to stand up without touching anything, Beth finally could not hold it in any longer and started to snort laugh. Everyone turned to face her now, Jack suspected that her laughing like a drunken donkey had something to do with the Bi-loy, although he had no idea what it was. When she had calmed down, after moving from snort laughter to near choking and then finally giggling, Jack guessed the worse was over and asked of her "what's a Bi-loy then?"
Beth replied quickly to prevent another laughing donkey movement "it's a Biological Alloy."
"Um, okay" replied Jack.
"Jack, you have no idea what that is do you?" asked Claire accusingly. Jack nodded "yep, not a clue."
By now Joan, Ron and the Commander were all at the exit, leaving only Summer to look round at Jack and say carefully "it's a living metal."
"So?" asked Jack and Claire together.
Almost grinding her teeth together in frustration Summer gave a quick explanation "this ship is made from a Bi-loy or living metal."
"Yep, we got that much" said Claire impatiently.
"It doesn't think, it needs a biological entity to tell it what to do, where and how to grow."
"You know that still doesn't mean anything to us, right?" said Jack.
"Let me finish, when its old sentient brain, so to speak, dies, it goes looking for a new one!"

Jack and Claire still looked confusedly at one another and then back to Summer "you mean one of us?" asked Claire.
"Yes, well normally it would pick an intelligent entity but failing that one of you would do."
"Har har, aren't we funny today" replied Claire.
Jack then asked "surely though it must already have one?"
Everyone stopped in there bid for freedom out the door and Claire asked "what do you mean?"
"The ships been getting bigger ever since we got on it, so Summer just said that it only grows when being controlled, so someone must already be controlling it."
"You know Jack that's actually quite intelligent" mused Claire.
Beth then clapped her hands together in glee, like one of those overly excitable drama teachers who has just seen her class perform Macbeth properly for the first time in years.
"So who is it?" asked Jack "whose controlling the ship?"
Beth put her head on one side and said "Sarah."
"Well, what! The computer we've been talking too?" asked the Commander.
"Not a computer, but an living entity inside the ship" said Beth.
"How long has she been here?" asked Jack of Beth.
"You don't have to talk about me as if I'm not here you know?" said Sarah from above there heads.
Jack looked round at the walls and asked "how long then?"
"Centuries, I've forgotten exactly how long and really I don't want to know."
Curiosity had got the better of everyone and they were by now all standing, not leaning on anything though, in a group on the bridge.
Summer turned and said to the Commander "she's well over her time then."
Jack overheard this and asked Summer "what do you mean she's well over him time?"
"What there saying Jack, is that the average user only lasts ten years or so and then they have to be replaced" Sarah said this in such a dull tone that everyone was looking around worriedly, apart from Jack, Claire and Sara.
"Replaced?" asked Sara.
"Replaced by another user" said Sarah.
"How?"
"You simply step into the case, compatibility is checked and then you become one with the system."
"For ten years?"
"Much longer in my case."
"So why have you lasted so long?" asked Summer.
"I actually don't know, since there is no precedent for anyone lasting longer than ten years, the only assumption I can make is that being human had me at an advantage."
"You were human?" asked Summer shocked.

"Am still thank you very much, I just have to sound computery to everyone else."
"Why are we discussing this now?" asked Jack.
"Because now you all know the facts, you needn't be frightened any more."
"Unless you need replacing?" mused Summer.
"That will not be necessary" said Sarah and then after looking at Summers face finished "because I won't wear out, I've lived much longer than any human ever should after all."
"Were all War Catchers built like this?" asked Joan thoughtfully.
"Yes, that's one of the main reasons you don't see them any more, you need someone to sacrifice themselves to become not just part of the ship but the ship itself" said Sarah.
"For forever?" asked Jack.
"Ten years in most cases" said Sarah.
"Just out of interest, what makes it grow, the ship I mean" asked Claire curiously.
Sarah replied simply "sunlight."
In a slightly shocked voice Summer asked "it's a plant, we're in a plant?"
"So long as its vegetarian then" said Jack.
"The ship will consume pretty much anything that it's told to eat, grow in anyway I choose and only needs sunlight to make it happen. Before you ask, it's a metal based plant life form that if left to its own devices in space, has been known to grow large enough to encompass an entire sun and extinguish its light."
"That's why you don't see many of these ships then, because they've been destroyed because no one wants to become permanently attached to one?" asked Jack.
"Pretty much yes" said Sarah with a verbal shrug.
Jack put his hand on his chin and in thought asked "so how did you end up here?"
"It was an accident, which one day you will remember."
"Your not going to tell me?"
"That would spoil the surprise, wouldn't it?" replied Sarah with a hint of smile in her voice.
"The question is though, do we trust her?" asked Summer.
In surprise Claire asked "your going to ask that in front of her! And yes bizarre as it might sound I do."
"Me too" said Jack after being nudged quite hard by Claire in the ribs.
Sara then agreed and after a few moments of mumbling amongst themselves, the others all agreed by making the Commander the spoke person of there little group who said "well yes, okay, mainly because we haven't been consumed yet."

The Commander turned to Jack and said then "well, I guess it's time you had some actual surf practice."
"Haven't I already done enough of that?" said Jack thinking back to the hours spent in the picture palace.
"Well yes you have but actually not in the gap, have you?"

Jack looked out of the bridge window, which was huge now, staring as the stars blurred into a line and once more they surfaced through the foamy waves of there reality into the split. Jack had the feeling that he could never get tired of seeing this view, knowing that reality was only a wave away in either direction.
"If this is our Universe below, what's the one above?" asked Jack looking at the rippling waves overhead.
"Well, who knows" replied the Commander in an off hand manner "it could be anything up there?"
"What do you mean, anything?" asked Jack curiously.
"Well exactly that, think of any variation on the Universe ... be it gravity reversed, the absence of oxygen or even if ice-cream was never invented!"
Jack looked up in thought and asked "so how do we find out and can we visit?"
"Well you could easier than me and you've visited them regularly anyway."
"But I just can't remember, right?" finished Jack in a frustrated tone.
It was to Jack's mind getting annoying that most things he asked seem to come back as 'you already know, you just need to remember one day.'
Nodding and shaking his head at the same time the Commander replied "well yes to a certain degree but until you actually remember where you are in your sequence of events, we have no idea what we can and can't tell you?"
"Surely telling me something that I already have done won't make any difference?"
"Well in my time line you might have done it, but not for yourself, because in your personal time line it might not have occurred yet."
"I still don't see what difference that would make if I can't remember?"
"Well simply, you would react differently in a given situation, possibly changing the time line."
"But surely not telling me would also change the time line if you should have told me?"
"Well unfortunately there is no way to know what outcome would occur if we told you everything, so we are erring on the side of caution by living in the moment" said the Commander simply and in an annoying tone thought Jack.
After thinking hard for a few seconds, Jack finally nodded to himself and Summer whispered to the Commander "do you really think he'll buy that?"
"Well I hope so, I know I did" whispered the Commander back, remembering a conversation from long ago.
Summer gave the Commander an odd questioning look and he replied by indicating at Jack with his flexible fingers, that they had already had this conversation but in reverse.

The Commander then turned to Jack and invited him to follow him off the bridge, Jack walked slowly after him trying to figure out in his own mind if what he had been told made sense. He kept finding that he was going around in circles in his mind, always coming back to the same argument, that he only needed to know what he needed currently to know whilst he was in or out of the know.

A little while later Beth asked Claire if she would like to come back to the bridge, as she walked onto the bridge she could see exactly what Jack had noticed. The bridge was now four maybe five times bigger than it had been before, the colour scheme had changed from whites and greys to contrasting shiny white surfaces and black edging everywhere. Jane was also now stood on the bridge, staring out of the window.
"Hello Jane, and where have you been?" asked Claire in an accusing tone.
Jane managed to look guilty for a moment as she turned round and slowly pushed her glasses back up her nose, she was still wearing a white laboratory coat but it looked heavier in some way like it was made of some other material. To Claire's eyes she also now looked more confident, more self assured as she stepped down from the window guard rail. She was then reminded that Jane and Sara were also the only humans left, apart from Jack and therefore the competition might be fierce. Which having thought about it for a moment, Claire rallied against the thought of competing for Jack's affections, being that he was the last human male they had access too and therefore the only way of carrying on the species. She was now really hoping this time travel stuff was going to work!
"In engineering, you know this is the most amazing thing to have happened to me ever!" replied Jane.
"What, having your entire home planet blown into tiny little bits?" answered Claire sarcastically.
With only a slight pause before answering Jane replied "obviously not that so much, just that this future and its technology is amazing" she said in a tone of wonder.

Claire could understand where Jane was coming from, because she had always been a 'tech head', someone the underground had needed to be into the technology, scientifically capable but the down side was insensitivity to everything else.
"So what are you doing on the bridge?" asked Claire.
"Oh I've come to watch Jack surf reality waves, although we may see more rescue than surf ha ha."
Jane then turned to the large white table still sat in the middle of the room and asked Beth to show them the rear of the ship.

An image from a rear facing camera gradually arose from the base of the table, showing the churning wake of the ship as it moved through each wave. It was sailing up and down each one like a sailing ship from Earth.
"I didn't realize we were on a boat" remarked Claire with a smile.

Jane replied with a simple question "didn't you see the bow of the ship?"
"To be honest I never really looked."
"Nearly all the ships that travel in the gap or split have a hull shaped like a boat."
"Okay, why?" asked Claire after nothing else was added by Jane.
"So they don't crash through into reality at the wrong point" Jane saw Claire giving her a blank look "previously the hull was just shaped any-old-how. The ships used to quite regularly fall back into our Universe at stupid points, like where a star or black hole might be, which is usually where the biggest waves are. Quite often they would be destroyed, either by being ripped back through the reality waves or crashing into the large object that caused the wave in the first place. Then someone asked why the spaceships didn't have bows like normal ships, to break the waves and ride them up and down. So they tried it and now nearly every ship that travels in space has a bow of one description or another, which they call a Breaker."
"What every ship?" asked Claire.
"Not every ship, some project a Breaker to hide the fact that they have SUDs."

Claire paused in thought, thinking about Jack and his surfboard. The view from the back of the ship showed a lazy blue line being fed out to trail behind, it looked like it was gradually being uncoiled to drag up and down the starry black waves. Occasionally there was a blue and white foam mix in the waves, as the rope like blue line split a blackened crest as it was dragged along behind the ship.
"What's that?" Claire asked pointing at the blue line.
Jane looked at her in frustration with a tinge of impatience 'didn't she read anything!' she mused to herself. Claire asked again and Jane knew she would have to explain it all or she would keep badgering her until she got an answer.
"The cloud-skimmer only uses a tiny SUD engine, the blue line helps the board stay in the gap to within a radius of fifty meters or so. It's what they use in the competition because it also creates a tunnel which the surfers follow around the track."
"So the blue line is like a tow rope?"
Jane toyed with being truthful but went with easy "yes, exactly that." Claire gave Jane a thoughtful look, wondering how she knew all this stuff, eventually putting it down to the fact she loved reading and learning new things.

The view on the table then switched to show Jack being talked to by the Commander, Jack kept looking out the back of the ship through a doorway and back to the Commander. Claire could work out what the Commander was saying by just looking at Jack's reactions, which was along the lines of 'really! You want me to just step out the back then?'

The door out into the gap appeared to have some form of heat haze rippling across the front. Claire watched Jack slowly test it with a gloved hand, swiping his hand backwards and forwards into the gap creating little swirls as he waved, like smoke on water.

The Commander, after a few minutes of inaction on Jack's part, decided to hurry things along a bit by tapping an off white button on the shirt collar of Jack's suit for space. A sleek black suit matching helmet then folded out from the collar around his neck to cover his head, leaving an open gap shaped like a T for his eyes, nose and mouth. The Commander then handed Jack his surfboard, spun him around to face the gap and gave him a single kangaroo like kick to the rump. This sent Jack unceremoniously out into the gap with the Commander pulling on his own bubble eyed blinkers to watch. Claire could be heard laughing throughout the ship, her titters echoing for quite sometime.

Jack panicked, there was no other word to describe the feeling he was getting, apart from several swear words which would be lost in the gap. He had just been quite literally booted into space or the split or the gap, depending on what you wanted to call it and the reason he had not wanted to take the leap of faith? Space!
Jack did not have a fear of open spaces or of space itself, in fact he had never known himself to be properly worried about any type of space. What he was afraid of was the depths, the depths of space and the fact that the depths of space were in all directions, no up, down, left or right, none of that was relative in space which was probably what was so worrying. He liked swimming and that had plenty of depth; he had done it in the open sea, where touching the bottom was only an option while drowning or being caught by a sea animal and dragged to the chilly depths. What he was having a problem with was the never ending in every direction.

All these thoughts passed before his mind as he was pushed by an heavy booted foot out through the hazy doorway into the gap. His helmet clanged shut sealing him against the outside, at least that is what it sounded like to Jack, he also froze for a few seconds as he sailed out the back of the ship tumbling over and over. Then the training he had earlier in the picture palace came back to him, as he slowly pirouetted round. He dragged the board round and pressed a button in the centre, then he pressed a coloured panel that lit up softly on his arm with a gloved finger. He pulled his feet round to touch the board, as it now started to travel down towards the fuzzy blue line being dragged out behind the ship. Much to Jack's relief he felt a form of gravity pulling him towards the board itself and another gentle tug towards the blue line. He then felt the pads in the palm of his gloved hands expand, which made it easier to control the board by using the little jet exhausts from the SUD system to move the board around. The pads were like touch pads, allowing him to move the board in any direction using the exhausts, he also got more movement by changing his body position like a surfer, skier or skateboarder.

As he chased behind the ship, attached to the blue line like a dolphin high on a gasoline fueled ship wake, Jack could see the blue line was following the rise and fall of the waves in the gap. Jack was easily able to follow its progress, twisting and turning, banking and spinning just for the freedom of it, imagining himself like a fish chasing a ship. It was only when he looked down through the white foam of a blackened wave that he was able to see real space zipping past, a star here, some explosion there. He then remembered he had been frightened near stiff by the anything everywhere of space only a few moments ago. Now though actually being so exposed in the gap was actually quite liberating; Jack caught occasional glimpses into the Universe below his feet and was strangely not frightened any more. It was probably due to the surf like foam spraying up from around the board as he twisted, spun and rolled around the waves of reality. It was giving him a sense of place, something he felt he could touch. Above his head was another Universe entirely, according to the Commander and within touching distance it appeared. As Jack stretched to feel the sky, he started to lose his balance on the board, nearly falling off in an heel and toe balancing act. Although admittedly if he did fall off the board he would not be touching anything for a long time, as he would probably fall back into reality somewhere between the stars, unless he was lucky and fell into a sun.

Then in his ear he heard the Commander say "well I'm glad your having fun Jack, yes we heard you 'whooping', in fact most of the Universe probably heard you, but it's time to reel you in now, as your nearly out of line."
Jack had not noticed that he had been making any sound whatsoever, although now he came to think about it his throat did feel a little coarse. In front of Jack he had also not noticed the ship was now a long way a way, he glanced over his shoulder and behind him he could only see maybe twenty or thirty meters of blue line, which was shortening all the time.
With a gulp Jack mumbled "okay."
"Well get ready Jack, because as we slow down in the gap, more objects from reality interfere with the drive, making the gap more … wavy shall we say."
"So what your telling me is, it's going to get rough?"
"Well it'll be more like what you'll experience in the surf competition, with short and maybe sharper drops between the waves. Now put your board speed to about seventy five percent, then when I tell you, put it to the max and you'll surf right into the docking bay."
"Thanks" replied Jack.

As the ship started to slow down in the split, to allow Jack to catch up, it started to shake and vibrate as it neared the reality stability threshold. If they were not careful it would simply drop out of the gap, with several million possible outcomes for the vessel, most of them ending in 'boom.'
"Don't you think surf is a bit of an understatement?" asked Sarah through the vibrating speaker system in the bay.

The Commander nearly jumped out of his fur, then quickly made sure his blinkers were muted before replying "well I didn't want to spoil the surprise."
"Surprise for whom?" asked Sarah.
"Well Jack obviously, who else?"
"Sara, Jane, Claire and Joan may be surprised, Ron will be okay as he's seen this all before, but don't you think some padding would be in order for his landing?"
"Well Jack's got to learn to control the board one way or another."
"You know I actually think your jealous of Jack's surfing ability, I mean you want him to win alright but I get the feeling you also want him to fail and hitting the bulkhead at high speed might be therapeutic in some way" replied Sarah in a smug tone, finishing with "and bruising his ego whilst massaging yours?"
A look of surprise passed over the Commanders face, as he realized he had been psycho analyzed by the ship and that she was probably right. He felt slightly angry but could find no suitable reply. Then he heard Sarah calling out a count down and only worked out why, when he glanced around and saw Jack neatly flying up one wave and splashing down another, drawing ever closer.

The Commander holding onto a grab hold near the doorway, started to give Jack his own count down from his blinkers, after sliding them back over his eyes and then said "well, maximum throttle!"

Through the slight haze on the docking bay door the Commander watched Jack zipping up and down the waves, swinging from side to side and the first thoughts he had were "well, what a crickan" spoken out loud.
"Why did you call him that?" asked Jane through the ships intercom, a speaker like grill on the wall.
Her voice nearly made the Commander jump out of his fur again, after only a second or two to calm himself replied "well because he's being a performer, show-boating, rather than a trainee and he needs to get his bald ass back in here before we crash through to reality ourselves!"

Jack heard this over the communication system and simply answered by saying "I'm just getting the timing right, I'm three waves away and I'll be right with you."

Everyone turned to look out the back of the ship, as Jack scooted up and down the next few waves. On the final one he was carried gently into the back of the ship, through the hazy doorway and stepped off his board onto the shaking docking bay floor. The Commander was stood with his mouth open in surprise, as Jack had landed without any problems, with the ship vibrations lessening as it accelerated back to cruising speed. Everyone else he had ever seen and that included the professionals, had all with out fail fallen off or smashed themselves in some way on there first real ship landing.

Jack stepped off his floating board and strode forward towards the Commander, he was smiling from ear to ear as his helmet retreated back into the collar of his suit for space. The only thing Jack forgot was the dark red tether attaching his ankle to the board, which he then tripped over with his other foot and went sprawling across the floor of the docking bay.
Everyone tried hard not to laugh but it was one of those comedy moments where the single participant had several visible peaks and troughs of thinking 'I'm falling, I'm not gonna fall, I am, I'm not' with much arm waving, followed by the inevitable crash on the floor.

Jack slowly rolled over and sat upright, he looked down at his feet in there shiny black shoes and the thick but flat red ribbon wrapped around them, Jack sighed to himself and began to unravel his bits.
As he did so he kept coming across thick knots in the ribbon every two meters or so, he looked up at the Commander, who had now recovered from laughing and just about had a straight face, and asked "what are the knots for?"
"Well they're there for when you fall off, if you fall off of course."
Jack looked at the knots in the ribbon, he kept calling it a ribbon but it was an odd shaped tether, in one direction it looked rope like and in the other a belt.
"Fall off?" asked Jack, finally unwrapping his feet and taking the tether off his ankle.
"Well yes, how else would you get back on the board if you fell off?"
Jack actually had not considered falling off, if you fell off at sea you simply swam back to the board or dragged it to you and climbed back on it. But out in the depths of space or even the gap, if you fell off you had to have some way of getting back to the board he supposed.
"So what's with the Velcro?" asked Jack.
"Well Veecro?" asked the Commander and Jack pointed at the thing that had been wrapped around his ankle "that's not Veecro that's a magnetic wrap."

Jack just nodded in agreement, he was feeling deliriously happy. He was experiencing the biggest buzz of his life after surfing the unknown, there was not a surfer alive he thought that would, once they tried it, be smiling from ear to ear after surfing the gap.
"Well we've got a few more day's of practice Jack and then we'll be at the qualification table" said the Commander.
"The qualification table?"
"Well, I've got you through the preliminary table on a technicality."
"Technicality?"
"Well, yes, each known species can have two representatives in the pre-race qualifier."
"And the other is?" asked Jack.
"Well, the female we saw in the picture palace, she might have registered herself as human this year."
Jack managed to look slightly blank and the Commander said "well you know, Samantha Orin Shavan."

Jack nodded to himself remembering her golden looks. He also knew he was going to have problems with her because of the way she had looked, attractive was the main problem he was thinking.

Chapter 30 : Coming Home.

Jack woke up with a typical Monday morning headache. The type that you know is going to last beyond three coffees and especially on the long journey of fourteen stops on the train. He still had not moved but something felt a little out of sync. For a start his whole body ached, like someone had implanted him with a diseased tooth in a sugar-aholics mouth. He then opened his eyes, the sun vanished from view out of the oversized window, to be replaced by the rolling hill leading to the sea. He still had not come to grips or even half understood the explanations for what was going on, mainly because they always seemed to come back to his memory or the lack thereof.

Jack sat up and again he felt something odd on the side of his neck, then one of the doors slide open in front of him and Sara strode out wearing two items of clothing. Jack quickly shut his eyes and looked the other way, thinking that his seeing such a beautiful event would no doubt get him some form of punishment.
"Ah, your awake" said Sara with slight surprise in her tone.
Still looking out the window with his eyes half shut Jack replied "am I not supposed to be?"
Sara laughed lightly as he heard the rustling of material against smooth skin, Jack swallowed hard fixing his gaze on the view of a gently scudding cloud with great interest.
"Don't you remember anything about last night Jack?" asked Sara curiously with a hint of humour.
Jack shook his head "that's a shame Jack, you were very good you know" she teased.
Jack looked round sharply at her, forgetting his embarrassment for a moment "good at what exactly?" he asked as she picked at a long tooth.
"Ah, well if you can't remember maybe we should try something else next time" with that she picked up the last of her clothing off the bed, took Jack by the chin and licked the side of his neck.

Jack was so surprised that he could not move and afterwards his first thought was 'that was nice', his second thought was 'why?' and his final thought was 'what is going on with her and me, and is there anything going on?'
Then he heard the door swoosh shut, Jack realized he had his eyes shut again and when he opened them the room was empty. He wandered over to the bathroom to have a wash and use the facilities.

Later when he had eaten in the lounge on his own, he started to wonder where everyone was and then touched the side of his neck where he had woken with an odd feeling. It did feel slightly tender, but that could have been the way he had slept after all. There was nothing there of course, because Sara had licked it clean, just thinking about the licking was making him feel uncomfortable for some reason. It felt like he had done something dirty, although Sara had seemed quite happy about it, glowing in fact. Jack gave himself a little shake as an sudden chill had ran down his back, stood up from the chair, put his plate and mug on the lounge bar and made his way towards the bridge via his apartment like front door.

On his way there he looked around at the ships interior, the one thing you could say for sure was that it was much bigger than it had been a few hours ago. He mused to himself whether that was the actual ship getting bigger or the inside getting smaller, he was not sure.
Jack finally walked through the lounge area, down a short corridor and entered the bridge via a smoothly sliding double door. When he stepped through it seemed to almost casually swing shut behind him with a 'swoosh' sound.

Jack looked round the bridge, at first he could not see if anyone was actually stood on it because the bridge seemed to be in some dark emergency lighting mode. The lighting however highlighted the final finish of the bridge, which was still mostly a ghostly white, with black lines on the edges and corners of things. The white surfaces now looked like they were white metal rather than a glossy plastic, with the black in some respects looking like tape stuck on to mark the edges.

With a small gulp Jack asked quietly "hello?"
As soon as he said it he felt embarrassed, after all he had been told it was his ship, although Beth did seem to be in control and on the message screens in the lounge it did say 'Beth's W.C.' at the top. That was another thing, he was sure there had only been a few screens on the bridge and in the lounge, now they were dotted around like yea-old family pictures from centuries gone by.

Jack then heard some voices, with relief he saw they were all stood right at the front of the viewing window, leaning on the guard rail. Jack walked forward and as he did so he got an impression of smallness or rather the feeling of belittling. He had never felt belittled before and had never understood the word, until he walked further forward and realized what was making him feel so tiny in the Universe. It was the size of the viewing window now. Once you reached a certain point it was all consuming, like stepping out unwittingly onto a glass balcony on the thousandth floor. When he had been surfing outside the ship he had felt small, but there had been the waves of reality to surf up and down the depths. Here looking out of a window, that was all around you and now so big, he felt the sense of scale of the gap between Universes. Which he felt weird about because here and now he felt less exposed than when he was outside the ship. Yet somehow this view felt more belittling, more spacious than being in space, in a suit for space, in a gap in space.

"Well ah your here Jack" said the Commander "just in time to watch our re-entry into reality and hopefully Nerth."

"Nerth?" asked Jack.

"Well technically Nerthet."

Jack raised his hands in frustration and asked "Nerthet?"

Beth replied "Nerth is a home planet and by adding 'et', it becomes the name of the solar system."

"So Earth's system would have been Earthet?" asked Claire who had been listening.

Beth nodded and turned back to look out the all encompassing window, Jack asked her "shouldn't you be flying the ship?"

"Sarah can handle it, I'm only here as a guide."

"But it's your ship, isn't it?" asked Jack.

"I am the Captain, but your the owner."

Jack stood shaking his head, he was not very good at working things out like this and frankly preferred mucking about on his computer at home, which did not exist now of course he reminded himself. Still something else was bothering him, as the ship started to sink beneath the reality waves. It was something only just mentioned and after a few moments he asked the Commander "what do you mean this will hopefully be Nerthet?"

"Well the drives are more precise now but you still have to allow for 'spin'."

"Spin of what, the bottle?" asked Jack frustratedly.

"Well 'spin' of the galaxy!" answered the Commander like a know-it-all teacher speaking to a student that is denser than osmium.

Jack was really getting annoyed now, everyone kept talking at him as if he should know certain things that were elementary to them but he had never been taught.

Beth took pity on Jack, placed a hand on his shoulder and said "you know that planets 'spin', the system there in 'spins', and the galaxy there in 'spins'?"

"Yeah, of course!" said Jack looking from side to side.

"Generally planets spin around a sun or some other gravity distortion, the planet may also be moving closer or further away from the distortion. The system will be doing the same, as will the galaxies" said Beth simply.

"So there all moving towards or away from one another?" hazarded Jack.

"Yes, at different rates and in different directions."

"And this is relevant because?" asked Jack not seeing how it was relevant at all.

"Because if you travel in space from one point to another, you have to adjust your own direction of 'spin' from the place you've come from to the place your going."

"A bit like jumping from one playground roundabout to another?" asked Claire who had been eavesdropping.

Beth paused in thinking about the analogy and said "yes if you like, but imagine one was spinning in one direction and the one your stood on spinning in another direction and the roundabouts were moving around on wheels."

Jack started to frown and asked "I still don't get it."

"When your moving from one roundabout to another you would have to adjust your 'spin', first to catch up with the roundabout, second to stop the contents zipping by when you got there and thirdly so you popped in at the right time."

Claire and Jack exchanged looks of deep concentration that eventually left them frowning hard at one another.

Beth continued after they had time to mull it over with "bear in mind that if you could stand still in the Universe and I mean perfectly still, the contents of the Universe would be traveling past so fast that you would probably not even see it coming, or going!"

"But we're not stood still?" asked Jack carefully, after a moment of painful thought.

"Precisely, everything in the Universe has motion because of the way it started. Traveling in space from one point to another we can adjust our 'spin' to match our destination. When using the Split Universe Drive we're in effect bypassing the local 'spin' and dropping straight into the Universe where our spin could be the total opposite."

"But it isn't?" asked Claire.

"Correct, it becomes the same as the place we're arriving in due to the reality waves washing over the reality bubble and correcting our 'spin'."

"So why is it possible that this won't be Nerth?" asked Claire.

"Because we know where our destination should be but not only is the Universe moving, the gap between Universes moves and we're moving as well! Then there's re-entry through a reality wave, which like a normal wave has its own internal twists and eddies which can land you somewhere" Beth paused "odd."

"This actually all sounds rather like complicated luck?" said Jack.

"Yeah, lucky that you end up even remotely close to where you want to be" said Claire.

"That's why a biological component is used to travel the split. It was found that no matter how many artificial calculations were completed, the accuracy was limited to fifty percent due to spin. But when a biological component was added it rose to ninety nine percent" said Beth.

"Why?" asked Claire.

"Probably because the Universe is biological in some way. Simply put, we know where our destination should be but something else might influence us or it due to ..."

Jack interrupted "your going to say 'spin' aren't you?"

Beth nodded "'spin' is a general term we use to describe every possible speed, direction, twist and turn, rather than expressing every single possible eventuality in every term!" she then smiled and turned away her job complete.

Jack and Claire exchanged looks of mild confusion with Claire finally asking "what about Universe expansion?"

"Not relevant" came Beth's distant reply.

"Because?" asked Claire.

Turning back Beth said "everything is expanding, the only difference is the rate of expansion in certain areas."

Jack felt relieved that one less complication had been explained, even if he did not understand it in anyway-whatsoever, along with Claire who was nodding.

Jack looked out the window at the Universe washing over them, he found he was holding his breath as they seemed to simply drop out of the gap and into reality like a skipping stone landing in a pond. He watched as the black oily waves foamed white around them, with strange shapes and even faces seeming to splash against there bubble of reality, as they sunk further out of the gap. Then suddenly Jack noticed the foam formed a white line below them which quickly encompassed them in a tube of light.

Jack looked more carefully this time around and could see that it was not a pristine white tube with no end. There were other streaks of vibrant colour in the lining, giving the tube an edge. Then there was a slight bump, a lurch and a blurring of the light making up the tube. The things making up the tube Jack could suddenly see were stars and then they were back in normal space apparently.

Jack suddenly felt that every science fiction and even factual question could be asked, anything he wanted to know was at his fingertips and all he had to do was ask Beth. The only problem he could see was what to ask, the possibilities were endless, so the first question was where to start rather than what to ask.

The Commander, Summer, Jane and Beth all gave small sighs of relief as Sarah overlaid the star system map over the window. It showed them that they were indeed in the right galaxy and even in the right system, with names placed above stars and local planets.

"Wow you guys are really relieved to be here aren't you, I mean we can nearly smell your relief!" said Claire in an amused tone, whilst nudging Jack with her elbow and derailing his mental line of questioning.

"Thanks for that!" said Jack in a mildly annoyed tone.

Claire looked like at him like she had caught him trying to pick her pocket and now he was acting all innocent.

They all stared out of the all encompassing window at the view. The ship had turned to face the centre of the system, with the sun blazing away at its centre. There were several planets and moons visible through the window circling the sun, Jack wondered how they were so clear because surely they would be thousands of miles apart and not visible to his eye.

Jack he asked "how can we see the planets?"

"Hyperversal?" asked Claire, who had also been wondering how they could see everything in such clarity.

"The same as in the Picture Palace?" asked Jack.

"Well no, the images are simply enhanced on the window" said the Commander simply.

They turned to look back out the window at the superimposed view and were therefore unprepared for the blacker than black ships that flashed passed the window like fat swallows on a bombing run. Everyone jumped back from the window in surprise, Jack could have sworn he heard a light tinkling laugh coming from Sarah the ship.

"Who are they?" asked Claire worriedly.

"Well, Newmans" said the Commander "our security welcoming committee."

"That can't be good, can it? I mean after all some of us are wanted criminals?" asked Jack waving at the Commander.

"Well not in this system we're not, it's part of the agreement that everyone is innocent here, unless they commit a crime here of course."

"So you could be a mass murdering genocidal freak outside the system, but provided you don't break any laws in here, you can't be arrested?" asked Claire in an incredulous tone.

"Well exactly" said the Commander.

"But doesn't that mean this will be a haven for every criminal under" Claire paused thinking and added "in the Universe?"

"Well I don't quite get your meaning but if your asking whether a lot will be here? Well yes, yes there are."

"Isn't that dangerous?" asked Jack.

"Well surprisingly, no. It's the safest system in the galaxy with many retired business peoples, annexed Kings, prince's, politicians and of course criminal masterminds."

"How?" asked Jack with some exaggerated hand gestures.

"Well everyone obeys the law here for a start, for the simple reasons that if you commit a crime here you're exiled and everyone that lives here is part of the justice system."

"Part of the justice system?" asked Jack.

"Well yes, simply, anyone that lives here has a monitoring system fitted, as do visitors."

Everyone else exchanged looks that said something along the lines of 'they ain't sticking any monitoring thing in me!'

"Why?" asked Jack.

"Well, security, voting and crime prevention."

"You mean citizen monitoring, power and a massive form of big brother?" asked Claire.

The Commander shrugged and replied simply "well this system is the most sort after to live in, so you either put up with it or don't come here."

"Surely there must be smuggling or some form of crime here?" asked Jack who got a sidelong glance from Claire, with a look that could be read as 'why are you asking about criminals, what have you done in the past to warrant that question?'

"Well people always attempt it and have been known to get away with it, at least for a while, but they are always caught and if not they leave the system quickly and on occasion in a casket."

"Always caught?" asked Claire.

"Well if you want to live a life free from crime, then it's in your own interests to help the authorities isn't it, otherwise what's the point in living here?" said the Commander.

"I would imagine some would see it as a challenge?" said Jane.

"Well some have done and when there caught there exiled. Before you ask about the ones that aren't caught, obviously there either really good criminals or like the vast majority they've simply upped and left" finished the Commander.

There ship then swung a course towards a golden coloured moon, with Sarah flying deftly through its various valleys and canyons, with there black darted security entourage chasing along behind.

They then came to an circular sandy looking opening in the ground, with no markings surrounding it to tell you what it was. They slowly descended through the hole, after only a few meters they touched down on a pedestal, looking like an eagle taking pride of place on a totem pole.

The pedestal then lowered itself down through the hole and into a dark cavern, where it eventually stopped on the sandy floor. If Jack could have seen the action of the pedestal, he would have marveled at the way it was made from the golden sand. It had smoothly collected there ship and then deposited it gently on the sandy floor, by simply becoming once again part of the sandy floor.

Jack still stood looking out the bridge window trying to get his stomach under control as the ship settled. He might not have felt the forces at work, as Sarah had flown like a super fighter pilot through the canyons, but his eyes had been glued to the view and his feet stuck to the floor like a toad in a cars head lights. The ride had all the hallmarks of 'motion sickness' he thought, as he tightened his grip on the guard rail. Turning he saw Claire was staring out the window the same as he had been, but with a greenish cast to her face, making Jack wonder if he had the same colouration problem.

Chapter 31 : Electrifying.

The Commander was the first to step out onto the almost glowing golden floor, with Jack close behind who looked at the ground and thought out loud "gold sand?"
"Well goldish really, it's gold's cousin" said the Commander.
"Lead?" asked Jack vaguely, remembering something he had heard in a chemistry lesson.
"So when do we get probed?" asked Claire, giving Jack a quick glance to see his reaction. She was not disappointed as he visibly shuddered and Claire felt a warm glow inside.
"Well we walk through those arches over there and that's it" said the Commander simply.
Claire looked visibly disappointed.
Jack turned to look around, brushing his ears again like something was tickling them, whatever it was, it was getting annoying to Claire.
"Don't look then" said Sara, Claire gave her a look and was about to reply when she continued "we all have habits that the others find annoying, frustrating even, but here, especially in this place it's all about tolerance."
Claire opened and shut her mouth at a loss as to what to say "it's obvious you like him but your not even able to admit that to your yourself, let alone to Jack!" remarked Sara.
Claire still with her mouth open had a sudden need to question, to change the subject a bit "I could never have him could I? After all the bed times you've been spending with him and don't deny it I've seen you sneaking from his door!"
It was Sara's turn to stand open mouthed in surprise, she had been sure that no one had been watching her coming and goings, but then on any ship there were only so many corridors you could walk down after all.
Claire stood in surprise, she after all would never, could never admit to liking Jack in that way, it was just that he was the last human left that she knew and the other two were female. She also now realized that she had admitted to spying on Jack, to nearly stalking him even. She held her hand over her mouth in shock and was therefore surprised that Sara had not noticed, especially when she replied "yes."
Claire looked at her sharply as they filed towards the admittedly very ornate arches and asked "what do you mean yes?"
"Yes I have been" Sara paused to think of a suitable reply "with Jack of a few evenings, but not in the way you think and Jack isn't really aware of what's going on either, so don't be too harsh on him."
Claire looked at her honest expression and said "that's your honest face isn't it? I've seen you use that before and any questions asked afterwards are subtly deflected."
Sara smiled, her blue eyes glowing brightly for a moment and replied "you know me so well" and then in a whisper like voice she said "and I will explain everything to you one day, just not today."

Jack walking slowly along behind Claire and Sara kept hearing snatches of conversation and catching glances at him over there shoulders. He was sure that they were talking about him in some way and endeavoured to catch up casually and have a listen, eves drop if you will.

As Jack got just within mumbling range, he was joined by Joan and Ron. There continuous marveling at everything, or to Jack's ears and more accurately, prattling, was making listening very difficult. They just would not stop chatting at him and over him, it was like they were deliberately trying to stop him from listening in!

In slight frustration Jack turned and looked back at his ship, the War Catcher, much to his surprise he found it had an hood ornament or figurehead proudly sat at the front of it. He was uncertain if it had always been there but on looking at its cool expression and aged features, it must have been there for years if not centuries. As is usually the case with these things, it was female in the vain of an feminine warrior holding a trident and shield, whilst wearing an goldenish crown, a flowing gown like dress, and coloured an evil glossy black. It also appeared to be winking at Jack, which made him shudder and look away. If he had paid more attention, he might have also noticed that the only other real colour on the figurehead, came from an highly detailed flag emblazoned across her shield.

As the crew neared the arches, both Jack and Claire were staring about like tourists who had forgotten there cameras, and were determined to memorize the entire trip. They both could not avoid looking though at the arches in front of them. There were five arches across the path from the ship. The arches themselves were big, actually really big, big enough to handle a double decker bus or some massive dinosaur even. Jack paused in thinking about this, after all the only reason to have arches this big, were if there were alien lifeforms that needed to fit through them in the first place.

Claire also stared at the arches but she was more interested in what they were walking on. The golden sand crunched under there feet like the sound of snow but they hardly sank into it at all, it also appeared to be everywhere. The rounded walls were a long way off, it gave the impression that they were stood in some great sandy cavernous bowl. It was then she saw the sand raise up from under the ship and carry it off to some dark corner, reminding her of a hand moving underneath a tablecloth.

Looking up Claire could see that the only apparent real light came from the hole they had entered by, the sand though seemed to give off its own dull light. It enabled her to see the far walls of the cavern, where ships were parked all around, buried in the walls like animal trophies.

Claire and Jack formed a queue, standing behind Ron and Joan who walked through the central arch holding each others hand like appendages and laughing at some joke. There was a brief flash of electric across the arch as they passed through, looking briefly like snow flashing across the archway.

Behind Jack stood the Commander, Sara, Summer and Jane, Second had decided to stay on the War Catcher, as having been branded a traitor he felt all kinds of guilt. Even though he should be able to walk freely around this system, he was not taking any chances on his celebritism.
Beth had decided that as an Hersatz, she was not going to take any risks either and had some worrying to do of her own.

The Commander looked at the two humans and said "well, we're only looking at the engravings, you can walk straight on through" he finished by waving them briskly forward.

Jack looked up at the silvery metal arch as did Claire. All five arches were big, that was not in doubt, what was actually quite mesmerizing, once you got over the size of the things, was how ornate and intricate the images were on the arches themselves. Each arch was also shaped differently at the top, the central one they were stood looking up at, met like two bent willow canes tied together near the top. The others connected at the top in different ways, fused or welded together, knotted, the final one was heart shaped and barely touching with some yellow electric light ball fizzing away between the legs at the top. Each arch leg was shaped differently, the middle one was rounded, the others were square or hexagons or some other shapes, but all were two meters in diameter.

"Does it matter which one we walk through?" asked Jack cautiously of anyone, whilst still looking at the arches.
"Not at all" replied Sara, also looking at the arches.
"At what point do we get our monitors then?" asked Claire still looking up at the arches in wonder.
"Well, when you step through, don't worry, all you'll get is a Security Hologram Actuated Monitor" said the Commander.
"A what?" asked Claire worriedly.
Jack started to laugh, stopping short when he saw Claire throwing eye related daggers at him and simply said "don't worry, it's a Sham" and then he started to laugh again.
The Commander looked on with disappointment written over his face as he stared at Jack, but answered Claire with barely a whisker twitch "well, basically it's a floating screen that shows your status on your wrist, if your breaking any rules it ceases your motor control and prevents you from escaping the authorities."
"Ah, so that's why there's no security here" said Claire in wonder.
"Well no, but yes" Claire gave the Commander a dirty look, that was one of the few phrases she did actually dislike with a passion.

Jack walked forward and touched the central shiny metal arch leg. It felt warm to the touch, not hot, just warm and when he took his hand away the metal seemed to make a chime like noise. The chiming sound was like a small bell being rung for dinner at an supposedly upper class, but really just an expensive dinner party.

Jack took a few steps back and stared at the images on the arch legs, which were amazingly detailed, they seemed to tell the evolutionary story of one species or maybe many species leading up the arch legs. Some of the images were etched or carved, with some moulded, others did not seem to go all the way up the legs and others nearly reaching the top. The one thing they all had in common, was that they all had the appearance of movement, like they really were living creatures in the images but moving at an incredibly slow speed like a feather through honey.

"Evolutions journey and its limit" came an amused voice from behind one of the arch legs "or limitlessness, depending on your beliefs."

Jack looked round in surprise at the voice, trying to find which arch leg it had come from. Then a human monk like figure stepped out from behind the nearest metal leg, wearing a white hooded cloak with a gold trim around all its edges. Jack took a step back in fright when the hooded figure turned towards him, it was not that he had no face it was just that he had no face! Inside the hood, the man or alien or creature or whatever it was, was wearing a blank creamy white mask that hinted at facial features, whilst at the same time having none whatsoever. Jack looked closer at the supposed face and wondered if that actually was his face, or her face for that matter.

Jack asked "beliefs?" in an high squeaky tone of worry. The only equivalent sound he could of compared his own voice to, would have been an actresses over reaction gulp, from a rusty creaking gate as it opened from a horror movie. He just hoped no one had noticed.

The reply from the masked individual was short, due to the near uncontrollable giggling coming from Claire "yes, beliefs!"

Claire turned to Jack "you sounded like a whoopee cushion" she then dissolved into laughter leaving Jack and walking through the archway. There was a small shock of lightening, a snowy fizz across the arch and through Claire, which Claire did not seem to notice, then she was on the other side. She had been briefly lit up entirely inside and out, all of her body in black and white x-ray form.

Claire was still laughing to herself as she stepped through and waved at Jack to hurry up from the other side of the arch.

She looked back at his open mouth and asked "what?"

Closing his mouth, Jack asked in a worried voice "did you feel anything?"

"A slight tingle, no why?"

"You were lit up like a hundred foot fir tree at a Christmas light convention!"

Claire frowned at Jack and replied "okay then, I'll check you out when you walk through."

Jack very quickly answered "no, no that's okay, I'll be fine."

He was remembering how much of Claire's anatomy he had just seen, after her seeing his, she would realize how much of hers he had actually seen. Then he would be in trouble for having seen everything, which had neither been his fault, intention or actually had wanted to see in the first place, although maybe some of it minus the snowy electrical x-ray bits perhaps. On top of that, she would conveniently forget that she had now also seen his inside and out too. He knew what the argument would be, that he had seen hers first.
"Come on Jack we haven't got all day" said Claire.
The white robed figure waved at Jack to meander through, with Claire crossing her arms on the other side, hip on a tilt and starting to tap her foot in impatience.

Jack looked round for help, Joan and Ron had already gone through, Jane, the Commander, Summer and Sara were all stood admiring the arches. They were all actively ignoring his stare for help. Jack turned to look back at the arches, they were actually quite mesmerizing to look at, they seemed to be actively changing as time marched on.
The two people missing from the group was Sarah, for the obvious reason that she was a ship and Beth, who was basically a robot which may exclude her from entering the golden moon for some reason. Then Second walked forward out of the gloom of the cavern and looked around with slight worry, until he saw the Commander, with relief then passing across his whiskers and jaw. The Commander went to step forward and hesitated, caught in indecision. Summer rushed forward, ducked her head towards Second, mumbling some growly sounding nursery rhyme, which within seconds had Second standing taller and more confident looking.

Jack looked up at the central arch and its willow like legs, the rope cord at the top actually looked quite menacing for some reason, now that he had to cross the threshold.
"Will you come on Jack!" shouted an impatient Claire, still tapping her foot and creating little clouds of golden dust with her incessantly moving foot.

Jack really was not sure whether he wanted to knowingly cross an active defence line, his legs were reminding him how wet they got last time, a result of crossing the last one in an tunnel on Earth. His stomach was also trying to remind him of the after effects, by gurgling at him.

Sara placed a reassuring hand on Jack's shoulder as she passed by, which made Jack jump. The only reason his feet had not left the ground was because Sara was either surprisingly heavy or very strong and had very cold palms. Jack watched as she crossed the arch with only a token lightening thread fleetingly passing through her body, not lighting up any part of her anatomy whatsoever, just like Ron and Joan.

Then Summer and Second stepped passed Jack and walked through the archway, both lit up like Claire had and neither seemed to notice. The only person who seemed to notice the x-ray like flaring was Claire. The look of surprise written across her face slowly disappeared, to be replaced with a thinking frown. Jack watched as realization slowly played across her face, which turned to an angry expression that was directed towards him, with a tapping foot.

Jack sighed to himself, no matter what happened now she was going to watch him like a hawk hunting a heath-land rabbit, followed by silent abuse for at least the next few hours, minimum.

Before Jack could step through, the Commander and Jane walked past and through the archway, both were lit up like a mouse taking cheese from an electrified trap. Again neither seemed to notice the x-ray effect and being that the Commander had been through the arches before, Jack assumed it was because Jane had not. Jack stepped through the arch, trying to appear casual.

"You and electric don't mix do they Jack" said Claire, at least Jack assumed it was Claire through the ringing in his ears. He groaned a short non-committal reply.
"We do most sincerely apologize" that was the voice of the white robed man from earlier, although how much earlier Jack was not sure.

Jack groaned again, levered himself up into a sitting position and looked around. He was lying a hundred feet or so on the other side of the arches "what happened?" he asked.
"Security protocols" said the robed figure.
"Is that what you call it?" asked Claire with anger creeping into her voice "I wasn't aware that visitors were subject to such shocking treatment!" Jack stifled a groan at the forced humour, the white robed figure stood up straight and said "no need to be like that, the system mistook him for someone else is all. Compensation has already been sanctioned."

Jack listened to Claire argue with the white robbed man, he had heard it all before but at least this time he was getting to hear the other side of the conversation. Usually if he walked passed Claire arguing on the phone in reception back in the office on Earth, he would hear her ripping into someone on the other end of the telephone for not completing some task. She was using the same matter of fact tone, pointing out various failures in the system and he knew that next, if she did get what she wanted, she would move onto personal attacks. It was a tried and tested trick that Jack had heard her use many times, even on himself and without him managing to get a word in. It was also a nice change to have someone else in her sights for a change. Jack laughed to himself, immediately wishing he had not made any noise, as Claire turned briefly and gave him a scathing look.

Jack felt okay to stand, now, so he picked himself off the golden sand, realizing he had been lying on a raised platform of sand about three feet off the ground. He swung his feet off the raised bed, as soon as he stood up the sand went back to being flat and sandy again.

As Jack looked around, getting his bearings, he noticed something on the back of his hand, whatever it was, it was glowing a faint blue and red. Jack swiped his other hand across the back of his hand, a floating angled screen appeared showing a general picture of his body, mostly in green, with a Sham rating of seventy two percent. As he listened to Claire not quite shout at the white robed man, the Sham rating started to drop, eventually reaching zero. Jack swiped his hand in the other direction on the back of his wrist, the display screen faded back to a vague blue and red floating thing being hardly visible, like watching a camouflaged celebrity lie still in the undergrowth.

The robed man threw his hands in the air and stalked away from Claire, muttering to himself something about the individual rights of creatures being too strong.

Claire turned round with a satisfied expression on her face and Jack asked again, whilst still catching his breath "what happened to me?" She shrugged and said "as soon as you walked through the archway you got x-rayed, then lightening bolts came out to touch you like they did with Jane. Only this time they picked you off the ground for a few seconds and then threw you to where we are now."

"Do we know why?"

"Something to do with you being an agent of the Furrykin? Honestly I wasn't really sure what he was on about, he had that bureaucracy tone of 'I'm going to hide behind the paperwork' thing, so he got me a little angry and …"

"You shot him down?" finished Jack.

"Sort of, I hate it when people hide behind red tape or any coloured tape for that matter, just so they can get away with not giving any of the answers or compensation."

"But he'd already offered compensation and you hide behind all kinds of red tape when it comes to me, well anyone for that matter, getting stationary!"

"That's not the same" said Claire hotly "I've got a budget to consider after all and pens don't grow on tree's you know!"

Jack gave her a look that said 'and this is different how?'

"And don't you look at me like that, I've got us all an upgraded apartment over looking the race track in compensation" Claire looked very pleased with herself, self congratulating or smug even.

Chapter 32 : Suite Room.

"Awesome, thank you Claire, thank you very much" said Jack sarcastically, over the near continual rushing, roaring sound of revving engines and the whistling of the air being ripped apart. The noise of the rushing traffic seemed to fill the entire room with wall to wall sound.

The flight from the golden sanded moon to the hotel had been not only magnificent but excessively quick for Jack. One minute they had been boarding a Short Hop Orbital Transport, with the word Interplanetary painted over by the word Orbital, and the next they were on the hotel roof, looking back up at the golden moon. Jack had looked out the window at the volumes of sand as he had sat down, the next time he looked up there was blackness and stars, seconds later burning red and white, then a light jerk as they landed on something and he was told they had arrived.

The lift down from the roof had been a blur too, the only odd memorable thing about it had been the cheesy lift music, which seemed to be a constant everywhere in the Universe.

Jack now stood leaning out of an open window looking down at the race track, flinching slightly as some transport or other flashed noisily by. The track looked similar to the one he had seen in the picture palace, which now seemed an age ago, the main difference though was the traffic. What no one had told him, or Claire for that matter, was that the race track, when not in use, appeared to be the busiest road he had ever seen. There were heavy vehicles the size of battleships, some with wheels and others floating along, moving up and down the tarmac looking road.

Then there were the trike's. There appeared to be more trike's here than there had any right to be, they dodged and weaved between the traffic traveling in every conceivable direction. Angled bubble like cars bobbed along like ducks at a bread and pond convention, weaving around and over the super sized cargo carriers and leisure cruisers. There were also the personal white transport bubbles buzzing around the place, although they moved much slower here than on the Ghost Ship and mostly at ground level. Jack guessed that was because if they got a puncture, there was less depth to the occupants fall.

There room was thirty levels above the tarmac road on a ninety degree bend, the hotel was also a hundred meters from the road and facing the majority of traffic. Under normal circumstances that might have been alright, the problem was the height. The traffic was staying within the hundred meter width of the road, but the depth towered over and above the window Jack was looking out of, several hundred meters in fact, seeming to nearly touch the clouds.

Joan was stood next to Jack looking wistfully out of the window at the passing vehicles "looking for red ones with a hint of flaming white are we?" asked Jack heavy with sarcasm.

Joan gave him a reproachful look "I'm sorry, it's just this noise is ridiculous" said Jack waving his arms about as Joan started to object. Jack then paused, looking backwards and forwards out the window, thinking to himself 'it must shut.' The window itself was large and there were dozens of them along the entire length of the room, they hinged at the top, with a barely visible floating yellow line at about waist height. Rolling his hand over the yellow line in one direction shut the window and in the other direction opened it still further. A little wall ran around the entirety of the window, made up of a wide angled steps, at certain angles to the eye they appeared to pass through one another, as they ran around the hotel room. It was like a deliberate attempt at an optical illusion, to keep you from clambering up to the window and presumably out, to fall to your doom. But these tall windows, in there slight silver frames and the optional falling issue, were not what was bothering Jack.

"Why is there any noise at all?" he asked "surely you've advanced beyond the combustion engine, or even found sound proofing?" asked Jack turning towards Joan.
Joan nodded with her head but kept her single eye looking levelly at Jack, it was the oddest thing to be stood in front of and made Jack's stomach turn in motion sickness.
Joan replied "mainly because it's the law, from nine till nine during the day, all vehicles must be heard."
"Really, that loud!" moaned Jack.
"If you don't like it shut the window, you may also have noticed that there are no fumes coming from the vehicles as they go by?" pointed out Joan.
Jack turned back to the open window and pointed "what's that then coming out the back of every single one of them then?"
Joan sighed inwardly and replied "compressed air or gases."
"Compressed air?"
"Used for sound and some degree of thrust and control."
Jack felt a little embarrassed after looking out of the window for a moment longer, because after a minute or two it was actually quite obvious.
"So what happens after nine then?" he asked "what do they use then?"
"They just use the Gravlec."
Jack nodded knowingly "you don't know what that is do you Jack?" asked Claire.
"Not a clue" said Jack with a smile "but I'm getting used to it."
"Just use your blinkers, and find out!" this time it was Claire's turn to moan at Jack.
"Or you could just tell me?" asked Jack "you always like telling me things."

Claire opened and shut her mouth a few times, like a surprised cat finding that there was not one but two goldfish to choose from in the bowl and each one carrying tiny harpoon guns. She could feel the others staring at her, unfortunately any answer she gave could be twisted too make her look silly. In addition she was quite glad Jack had not added 'or telling me what to do', like they were married or something. Now where had that thought come from?

Jack had not asked his question in any other tone, other than curiosity, so he was very surprised to see Claire stamp her foot, growl at him and storm off to hunt down the rest of the hotel apartment.

Joan turned to Ron and whispered not very conspiratorially "what was that all about?"

Ron replied also in a not so conspiratorial whisper "lovers tiff."

Jack looked round at the pair of them and saw they were both smiling broadly.

       The door they had walked through to enter the apartment made a 'knock knock' sound. Jack was sat looking out the window in an raised seat, the seat was so curvy and voluptuous that just looking at it had made him excited. So he had decided to sit on it instead, so he could not see it.

       The door made the 'knock knock' sound again and Jack clambered out of the seat, trying not to touch anything that might be considered untoward. He walked cautiously over to the door as it made the 'knock knock' sound again. Standing just in front of the door as it had made the sound, Jack cocked his head to listen again and saw a tiny grill in the floor, where the sound appeared to be coming from. Jack raised his hand up towards the door, realizing at the last moment that it neither had a spy hole to see who was outside or a door handle to open the door. The door was basically a blank slate. He waved his hand vaguely at the door, which then demisted becoming transparent, showing two human looking men holding hands, dressed in very sharp, thin and grey suits sporting bow ties in white on the other side.

Jack said "hello?"

The two men looked briefly at one another and one of them asked "Mister Junstan?"

Jack sighed, it was the same whenever he went anywhere foreign, outside of his home. No matter how simply it was written or spelled out, everyone got his surname wrong.

"It's Johnstone, pronounced John-stun."

The two men then had the biggest grins on there faces, followed almost immediately by the deepest frowns that Jack had ever seen.

"Could you let us in please, we need to ask you to vacate your room" said one of the men.

"Why, we've only been here" Jack looked on his wrist for a watch, much to his surprise he found a digital readout that looked like a watch on the back of his hand from the Sham "for an hour?"

"Yes, we're well aware of the time" said the other man "but to be quite frank about it we can't afford the security measures."

"Security measures for what?"
The two men exchanged worried expressions, the first one asked cautiously "for the surf competition?"
"Surf competition?" asked Jack feeling confused.
"Yes, we don't usually have any competitors stay here and don't have the security required" said the second man gaining more confidence in what he was saying as he finished the sentence.
Jack shook his head "that's okay then because I don't need any security thank you" and he turned to walk away from the door.
The two men exchanged quick glances and then almost together replied in semi-squeaky voices "but we do!"
"For what?" asked Jack.
"Well the hotel for a start" said the second man.
"The hotel?"
"Look, we need to come in and discuss your relocation" with that they swiped there hands over the front of the doorway and it obediently opened inwards without a sound.
Jack took a step back from the door and tripped over someone's tangled foot behind him. As he toppled over backwards, in apparent slow motion, he saw he had tripped over his own foot. He then attempted to roll to his feet, with something stopping him from performing this simple maneuver, mainly himself.

Lying flat on his back and feeling slightly winded Jack could hear a conversation going on, when he raised his head he could see Ron talking to the two men. Both of them could not stop bowing and genuflecting towards Ron, then both of them turned and still holding hands, they almost seemed to skip out of the door. The door swooshed shut behind them on its hinges.
Ron turned to Jack and said "sorted mate."
"What is?" asked Jack.
"Staying here of course."
"Why would we want to stay here?" asked Jack slowly trying to move himself off the floor, which was surprisingly difficult because randomly he had landed in a slight tilt and groove in the floor. Meaning that the only way out was to roll over backwards. Red faced and feeling slightly light headed, Jack stood up from rolling onto his knees and swayed in front of Ron, he then leant on the back of a chair which spun round. Jack found himself back on the floor again, at least this time he was facing the floor and stood up much more carefully.
Ron looked at Jack and not for the first time wondered 'why?'
"We have to stay here now Jack, as there isn't anywhere else that has any spare rooms" said Ron simply.
"Aren't we still a week away from the competition?" asked Jack.
"No Jack, the competition starts tomorrow. Right out there" said Ron pointing out the window at the traffic zipping by.

Jack followed his gaze out the window, past all the strangely mismatched but matching furniture. From the moment he had entered the room he had been reminded of an ancient farmers home. This room looked like the collection of furniture, that back in its day had been the talk of the village and now looked a bit tired, worn even. It looked like it had outlasted its owners, been passed down through the ages and arrived in this place. Still serviceable but not matched to its neighbour in anyway, which in itself made it the perfect match to its neighbour. It was like being stood in an furniture auction where the pieces had been matched to there neighbour by millennium and not design. It gave the room a strangely homely feel, especially with the rugs from 'foreign parts'. The only thing that let down the rooms cluster of elderly furniture was the white walls, they and the black and white carpet tiled floor just did not quite fit the divans, chairs and lounge furnishings.
"I think we need the walls to be painted" said Jack still looking about in boredom.
"Cream?" came a voice from the speaker by the door.
"Sarah?" asked Jane walking into the room from a far off door.
"Hello" came the cheerful reply from the floor, shortly followed by the walls flickering to cream and the floor turning to a light woody brown finish.
Jack looked down at the floor, it looked almost exactly like the log cabin floor from his blinkers dream back on the stellar vessel with Beth and Summer, although in a carpet tiled way.
Before Jack could ask where the design came from the Commander walked in the front door, gave a cursory look around and made a non-committal sound in the back of his throat. The Commander then waved a long glossy looking postcard thing in Jack's direction.
"Well I hope your ready for this Jack, actually you don't have a choice" said the Commander, passing Jack the glossy card.
Jack reached his hand out to take the card from the Commander, Ron grabbed his arm before he could take hold of it "beware Jack" he said roughly.
"What of exactly! Your slimy grip?"
With a sharp intake of breath Jane said "that's not very nice Jack."
"Accurate mind" said Jack shaking his hand free from Ron's beaver like grey paw, he looked carefully at his wrist checking for any slime dripping off and found he was bone dry.
Ron waved his hand and said "don't worry I've had worse and Jack, as soon as you touch the card, you are accepting the competition terms and conditions."
Jack quickly put his hands behind his back, with the Commander still waving the glossy card at him.
"Well thanks Ron!" said the Commander with mild sarcasm.
"Why didn't you tell me?" asked Jack looking at the Commander curiously.
"Because he needs you to enter the competition to undo his mistake" said Ron.
"Well look, all he has to do is touch the card" said the Commander.

"But you could have just told him it was out of its case and why you were wearing gloves" said Ron "at least give him the choice?"
"Well he doesn't have a choice and neither do I" said the Commander angrily.
"Actually everyone has a choice, so why don't you just ask him, instead of tricking him now?"
The Commander growled at Ron, sat down and said "well he needs to undo this mess and this is the only way I can think of."
"I agree, but tricking him into signing up to the competition without any knowledge of it is wrong."
The Commander nodded his head slowly, then looked up and offered the card to Jack, who was still standing with his hands behind his back.
Jack asked Ron "so what am I signing up for that's so worrying?"
"He hasn't told you anything has he? Typical" said Ron with a throw of his arms "he's got you in the competition by whatever means he had. The only thing is, you have to finish in the top ten of the ten thousand, before you can get to the SUDS competition."
"The ten thousand?" asked Sara curiously, who was eyeing up the Commander as he carefully placed the card on a chequered coffee like table with mischievous looking table legs.
"Yeah, well he couldn't get you in the final forty-two, because thirty-two of those places are taken by the winners from the last five turns."
"Five turns?" asked Jack.
"Well, various SUD Surf competitions from the last five years for the first thirty-two places, the final is in a week with ten places reserved in the rounds for the first ten across the line from the ten thousand" said the Commander.
"When you say 'ten thousand', what do you actually mean?" questioned Jack.
The Commander looked up at Ron who shook his head, sighed and then said "well, basically, essentially, fundamentally, for example ..."
"Yes?" asked Jack and Sara together impatiently.
"Well I thought it would have been obvious, it was very difficult to get you in the group."
"What group?" Jack almost shouted.
"Well, the ten thousand of course" said the Commander sounding slightly offended.
"Ten thousand what's" Jack felt like screaming "meters jogging backwards, hand shakes in an hour, people feeling lost and confused?"
"Well no, obviously ten thousand participants in the race to be one of the first ten across the line" answered the Commander.
Jack thought about this for a few seconds and then slowly picked up the card saying simply "huh, okay then."

      Everyone else stood looking slightly confused at this action, apart from Claire who was stood looking out the window, rolling her eyes and shaking her head. It was obvious to the her that Jack was still swinging from believing this was all happening, to thinking it was just some dream, a game. Nothing she could say or do would persuade him otherwise.

The card made a small happy sounding jingle noise, like bells hanging from a reindeer as it pulled a sleigh through the snow. The card then turned from white to a rosy red, with writing flashing across the front. The words were printed in a very small font, which meant Jack had to look quite closely to read what it actually said.
Jack slowly read out loud "please look here to confirm entry."
He then heard another little jingly noise and the word 'confirmed' appeared in front of his eyes, the word was then read out by what Jack imagined a badger would sound like, if it had false teeth and a lisp. The card then exploded into confetti in his face. As the pieces of multicoloured card fell through the air they made little pops and whistles like fireworks, which disappeared as soon as they touched the floor.
Jack was then left holding what amounted to a ticket stub for a second rate concert in his hand.
"Well done Jack" said Claire sarcastically from somewhere near the windows.
"Why?" he asked.
"You don't even know what the ten thousand really is!"
"Well it's a race, isn't it?" he asked.
"Yes Jack, it's a race, to cull the herd. A race of ten thousand kilometers, with ten thousand racers, through ten thousand hazards taking probably ten thousand minutes."
"How long's that again?" asked Jack.
"Oh only about seven days, give or take" said Claire with more sarcasm.
"Well actually it's three day's not seven" replied the Commander "and it's more like a few million kilometers really, the ten thousand name is for the number of competitors" he finished in an conversational tone.
Claire gave the Commander such a fierce look that he had to look away, finding something astonishingly interesting on one of his finger nails that wrapped around half of his finger.
"It is the most exciting race you'll ever see though" said Joan wistfully.
"Yes, yes I gathered that, because when I looked it up on my Quellz, the viewing statistics were amazing and do you know what else was amazing?" asked Claire looking around the room.
Everyone exchanged glances, apart from the Commander who was still finding things of monumental interest in his finger nails.
Jack asked "no?"
With hand on hip Claire replied "the casualty rate."

Chapter 33 : Plane Trucking.

Outside the hotel, stood on the fifty meters or so of bluey green grass, the group was having an argument about Jack pulling out from the competition. The discussion carried on for quite some time with a lot of arm waving and noise. The only person not actually really involved in the discussion, was the one person who had been man handled out the door by Claire and Jane insisting that he revoke his entry. Sitting on the grass off to one side Jack listened to the arguments traveling first one way and then the other. No matter how much they argued, supposedly on his behalf, in the end it was not going to make any difference in Jack's mind.
"So how's it going?" asked Ron sitting down next Jack with a wet slap.
"It's not really going to make any difference is it really, I have to get this crystal thing so I can go back and stop Earth from being destroyed in the first place. It just so happens that this is the only way to do it."
"Don't worry about it, you'll be fine."
"How can you be sure exactly, I mean Claire showed me the statistics from the last race!"
"Oh you know statistics, they can be manipulated to show you anything!"
Jack pulled out his own Quellz and showed Ron a page.
"Yeah, well that's only a small percentage" answered Ron.
"It's a thirty nine percent casualty rate!"
"The previous race was worse" said Ron defensively.
"Ron, the ten thousand race before had a ten percent higher mortality rate, that's nearly half!"
Ron shrugged and replied "not too bad then. You seriously thinking of trying to back out, after the Commander got you in the competition in the first place?"
Jack shook his head and sighed "no I guess not, it's just that, was it really that hard to get me in this suicide race?"
"You have absolutely no idea, he had to turn in every favour he has ever been owed and it cost him every crown and regal he has!"
Jack started to shake his head in disbelief, after all why would any sensible creature of any intelligence want to enter a race knowing that forty-nine percent, or nearly half in Jack's mind, was 'not going to make it'. Jack though was only human and in his naive way still was of the age that still thought of himself as indestructible, therefore he would of course be in the survivable percentage.
Ron reached round to a pocket in his thick brown rubber belt and pulled out his Quellz, turning to Jack with a forced smile on his needle sharp teethed face he said "you know how we said the ten thousand was tomorrow?"
"Yes?"
"It's been moved up a bit."
"How much is a bit?"

Ron looked at the counter on his Quellz and replied "try, in about four hours."

"Why?" asked Jack choking a bit.

"The weather of course" answered Ron simply.

Then a black and white striped blunt paper aeroplane shaped truck pulled up on the tarmac. Its nine tyres squealing and smoking on the ground as they locked up to stop it, after landing at high speed further down the road.

Jack looked on in amazement at the vehicle, there were four wheels with tyres on either side and one oversized central one at the front. The cab appeared to be perched right on top of this wheel, with the rest of the black and white striped truck tailing off sleekly behind it and then abruptly stopping squarely at the back. The roof of the blunted truck was one odd sized folded paper aeroplane style wing, sat on top with very little over hang.

Almost the entire side panel of the truck then dissolved from view, eight white clad armoured men stomped out of the side of the truck and swept the area with the palm of there hands, like telling someone to stop and desist. Jack could not help laughing at them, to his eyes it looked like they were performing some online sensation music video, the only thing missing was the cheesy pop song. The timing of there hand movements and even there steps was impeccable, like they had trained for years doing these set moves. The armour they wore was mostly white, with the impression of squared off muscle packs seemingly embossed across the surface.

There helmets were white affairs, although Jack was again trying not to laugh at the shaping, as they looked like squashed pears pointing the sharp end away from there chins. The helmets also had black T pieces where the eyes and nose were, leading down to the slightly discoloured pear chin, shaped like a tiny barrel. On either side of the top of the T piece ran a small black line, making it look they were wearing some form of designer sunglasses and nose guard combo. The black line continued around the back of the helmet, to a single black line that ran down the back of the helmet to the neck of each armoured man.

The neck protector appeared to be a scarf of some description, that varied in colour depending on rank but had various designs across the surfaces that seemed to shimmer and shake. At about the half way point, of the foot long dangling neckerchief, was a series of numbers, letters and shapes that must mean something to somebody thought Jack, like rank.

There were black accents at several points on the armour, which included the belt system each one wore. The belts had pouches of several different sizes and were linked by a black cord to a tiny white back pack that each one had on there backs.

There boots ran a few inches above there ankles and were a shiny black with no apparent way of opening them. To Jack they looked like designer Wellington boots, which from his experience were of no use whatsoever. Especially when they actually encountered any actual farm muck, being that they either started to dissolve or even smoke, usually at an untimely moment, as you sunk up to your knees.
There gloved hands were white on the back, black underneath and looked like fabric gloves. As Jack watched them move about, securing the area, he saw that the armour itself was actually some form of shaped fabric. It enabled them to twist and move like they were wearing normal clothes, rather than some heavy thick metal casing, much like his current suit for space outfit. Which he was still wearing, mainly because he had not, as of yet, worked out how to get out of it!

      The two hotel suited men, still holding hands, walked briskly up to the armoured group and could be seen talking to them. Then with brisk spare arm waves in Jack's direction, they seemed to be indicating that he was the cause of all there collective woes.
They then guided the armoured men towards Jack, who asked "why?" as they approached.
"For our and your security" said one of the suited hotel men.
"Okay, but why?" asked Jack again.
"Because the two of you are celebrities" came the reply.
"No we're not" said Ron.
"Not you two but you two" said one of the suited men pointing at Jack and Claire.
"How are we celebrities exactly" asked Claire stepping closer.
"You don't know?" said the second suited man.
"Don't know what?" asked Claire.
"Nobody told you or even hinted?" said the first suited man.
"What?" asked Claire sounding a bit growly.
"We really don't know how to say this … but you are, the last of your species you know!"
Looking at one another Jack and Claire exchanged confused expressions, until Claire pointed out "but your both human!"
"No, we're Newman."
"But you look the same as us?"
"I'm sorry but we are very different thank you and the Pugs here are for your protection, as well as the security of the hotel."
"Well okay then, now that's sorted" said the Commander.
Coughing with mild drama the first hotel man answered "there is just the matter of the bill?"
"For what?" asked Jack.
"The Pugs, of course!"
"But we haven't …" started Jack.

"Well don't worry Jack I've got this covered, well when I say me ..." said the Commander pointing at Joan's Quellz. Jack saw her Quellz was wrapped around her wrist like a bangle, as the Commander then stood rubbing his bendy furry fingers together indicating money. Joan simply pointed at Jack with an shaking feathered digit and a very worried expression on her beaked face.

"You actually mean me don't you and my illimitable bank account?" quizzed Jack.

Both of the hotel men turned to face Jack with there eyes swiveling in there sockets. Presumably the Police or Pugs, did something similar, because almost immediately they moved into a circle surrounding Claire and Jack, shoved the two hotel men out of the way and nodded at one another. There was also suddenly the lack of chattering, before there had been some form of mumbling in the background, as soon as Jack mentioned the words illimitable and bank in the same sentence it had stopped, like the troopers were suddenly more professional somehow.

"Anyway I'm not really sure I want protection like this?" mused Jack.

"Why not, we might actually need it Jack?" asked Claire thinking of how she did not want to be mobbed in anyway, like some famous people she had seen on television.

Jack pointed at the nearest armoured Policeman and said "oh come on Claire, have you seen what's written on the front of there uniforms, let alone the back."

Claire looked at the front of the nearest armoured man and read out loud "Pugs" written in large letters on the left breast and underneath in somewhat smaller text "Back and Backup?" she finished. Still looking slightly lost as to what Jack was meaning she asked "I don't see what your getting at?"

Jack almost threw his hands up in the air, was he the only one to see the similarity "this is the Police right, do you not see the lettering, how close it is to a well known farm animal of the generally pink variety. Which sometimes has a curly tail and likes to wallow in the wet brown stuff, a name unfortunately given to the constabulary back home!"

After a few moments Claire nodded and put her hand over her mouth to stop herself from laughing, still a small squeak escaped, followed by "I think someone must have been having a laugh when they came up with that name."

"And on the back?" asked Jack feeling like he was getting somewhere. Claire looked at the back of one of the Police men, the lettering was the same black text style, just the positioning of the words was quite apt. 'Pugs' was written across there shoulder blades and 'Back and Backup' was written just above the belt line.

There was also just visible in certain light, vaguely printed on every bit of kit, the letters 'tJi' in shadowy italics.

"I've just realized that this was one our longest conversations Jack " mused Claire.

Jack thought about saying 'and you haven't abused me in any way shape or form' but at the last second nodded and said instead "and I didn't even use the word nefarious."

"You have now, and for the love of everything will you stop waving at fairies as well!" said Claire getting annoyed.

Jack stopped himself and wondered not for the first time what was tickling his skin, it was nearly always on the exposed bits and especially around his ears? The problem was that it had become such a habit now that he did not notice it any more and could not remember when it had started. Although a good guess might be when he woke on his sofa, what felt like months ago back on Earth.

They climbed aboard the flying truck, Claire was still laughing to herself, Jack would have been but he was thinking about the race ahead. Many things were playing on his mind.

"Well you look worried Jack?" commented the Commander, Jack nodded "do you want to talk about it?" added the Commander sitting down next to him.

Jack sat back and looked around the truck, the first thought in his mind was 'no, he didn't want to talk about it or even think about it for that matter' everything was moving quickly again. To take his mind off his impending doom Jack inspected the inside of the truck, it was very well upholstered. The seats were all some form of faux white leather, the floor was a black rubber stripe as were the walls and ceiling. The only view of the outside world was up the steps to the cab of the truck, because of the angle all he could actually see was bits of sky and the occasional building flashing by as they moved off.

Jane then walked back out of the front of the cab, down the steps to the passenger seats with an expression of complete distaste on her face.

With his whiskers twitching the Commander turned to question Jane what was bothering her, Jack did not look like he was going to be talking soon and he really needed to get whatever it was out of Jack's system, before he started the race. Maybe quizzing Jane would help Jack talk?

"Well, is there something wrong Jane?" asked the Commander.

Frowning at the Commander Jane replied sharply "actually yes" she paused thinking furiously "I wanted to know how this vehicle worked but all I got was the occasional grunt from the helmeted moron at the front and a set of finger instructions to come sit back here!"

"With the third rate citizens?" asked Jack quietly.

"What do you mean?" asked Jane with only a slight gulp "we're all the same, aren't we?"

"As you well know we're not all the same and ..." Jack paused for what everyone else thought of as dramatic effect, but was actually him finally seeing things clearly and for the first time knowing that this was actually all real.

"We're not all the same and?" asked Claire interrupting his thoughts. Raising his head up from staring at the floor and thinking 'it actually doesn't matter what we say or do, it means nothing to the Universe', Jack smiled.

It was a glassy smile with little humour in it, Claire was expecting a sharp reply, what she actually got was a question "this security detail is for the last two humans, right?" asked Jack finally looking around the truck.
"Yes, so?"
Pointing at Jane and then Sara, Jack asked "isn't she human and Sara too then?"
Claire looked first at Jane and then at Sara, both had expressions that could be read as 'cruck, they've worked it out, now how do I get out of this?'
Jane shrugged and said "I'm sorry Claire, we knew it was coming and I was sent to try and prevent it."
"Prevent what and what are you?"
"I'm a Newman, I thought that would have been obvious. Because of our similarity to your own species we were easily able to visit your planet and simply take in the sights."
"So everything was an act?" asked Claire in a raised voice.
"No, no not at all, I had to also drop off all kinds of technology before I arrived on Earth."
"So what were you sent to prevent?" asked Jack.
"We didn't know it at the time, but we thought you lot were going to blow your own planet up, what with all the various misuse of materials and the depletion of your atmosphere. What we never saw coming was that the idiots at head office were going to do it for you! I had just got myself into a position where I could start to help repair the planet and the warning came down that an invasion was due to start!"
"And you didn't tell anybody?" accused Claire.
"I didn't want to blow my cover did I!" replied Jane sarcastically "honestly I didn't have time, I only just had time to make a mask before the gas arrived and who would have believed me anyway!"
　　　　Throughout Jane's explanation Sara was sat staring at her, finally no longer able to hold it in any longer she started to laugh and laugh.
"What's so funny?" asked Claire feeling like the laughing was aimed at her in some way, like Sara was trying to deliberately offend her with her happy laugh. If she was to try and remember back, it was probably only the third time she had ever heard Sara laugh at all.
"Now I suppose it's time for your explanation? After all you look human too!" asked Claire feeling and sounding actually quite annoyed.
"Weirdly, I'm in the same position as Jane, apart from I wasn't slipped back into the group at the prison cells" replied Sara a bit too confidently for Claire's liking. Jane looked relieved at that, if a little confused, she then turned quickly to a screen panel on the wall and swiped a code in.

The effect was immediate and down right shocking for almost everyone else, the truck was suddenly see though and it was an awful long way down to the streets below. Several hundred feet in fact, with vehicles flying past in all directions. It took a moment for Jack to realize that only the black parts of the truck had become see through and that there was a slight shadow to the view, like they were looking through a really thick pane of glass to the world below. This realization did not however help his bladder in anyway and when he asked if the truck had a 'loo', Jane pointed at the queue of white helmeted and armoured men stood in a line outside a small door at the back of the vehicle.

The flying truck finally landed on an arm of a spoon shaped landing pad, which was one of many arms sticking out of some massive rounded building, that to Jack looked like an upside down saucepan. The truck rolled up the arm of the spoon, inside the building was the size of thousand football stadiums from back on Earth. It was basically a massive hangar, with ships hanging from truly massive looking chains at all angles and even ships that were just hanging with no apparent support whatsoever.

The truck trundled slowly around the metal floor of the hangar, driving over and under various sized ships until it got to somewhere near the back, or 'arse' as Jack thought of it and stopped.

In front of them was parked the most shiny and streamlined three pronged ship that Jack had ever seen. If a pointy stick had ever wanted a love child with another sharp object shaped like a dart, then this was what it would have wanted. It was shaped so acutely that just looking at it made Jack think of a giant scalpel trident for dissecting the stars themselves. It was also highly reflective, anyway you looked at it you nearly saw what was on the other side of it.

When they were all stood on the loading deck, Jack was surprised to hear some tyre wheel spin, they turned round and the truck appeared to be almost racing away from them and out the hangar. Looking around Jack wondered where his supposed Police escort was.
"Don't worry there not required any more" came Sarah's voice from somewhere near his ear, making him jump slightly.
"I thought this might be better" something the size of two clenched fists flashed passed Jack's eyes from his shoulder and hovered in front of the group. It was really just a slightly glossy white ball, as they watched, it changed shape, morphing first into Jack's face and then into Claire's and finally settling into a white rippling orb. To Jack the ripples across its surface made it look like how he would have imagined a water planet might look. Although if it was a water planet, those ripples would be waves so big that they would be stroking the atmosphere!
"Sarah?" asked Claire.
"Yes?" came the reply.
"I thought you were part of the ship?"
"Don't tell anyone, but I can be anywhere and now with this" the orb did a little triumphant shake "you have something to talk too rather than talk at!"

A few looks were exchanged along the lines of 'I dunno?'
"Actually it was Jack's idea" said Sarah.
Jack made gestures with his hands and pulled a face proclaiming his innocence.
"Indirectly" said Sarah.
"I think it's a great idea and gives you a personality, soul, some character even!" Claire paused in thought whilst giving her compliment "not that you didn't have one before" Claire added quickly "or soul and your character is quite lovely too."
Trying to be complimentary whilst not sounding like she was criticizing was very difficult she realized and possibly she had just gone too far. The others turned to look at her and she clamped her mouth shut, there were many things she could say in reply and it was the first time Jack had seen or heard her not reply. The self restraint must have been maddening for her, with Jack imagining steam coming out of her ears and smoke from the grinding of her teeth. The desperation to proclaim her innocence and argue with anyone who disagreed must be driving her wild.
The only problem she had, which fortunately she had worked out, was that no one had said anything in reply and it was all her own doing.
Claire stalked off muttering to herself, standing in the middle of a really big yellow arrow painted on the floor of the hangar.
Jack watched her walk, or was that stamp away, he just knew that at some point this conversation would be his fault and it was not even a conversation!
  A light whistling sound filled the air nearby, which Jack would have ignored were it not for all the actual aliens jumping into battle like positions and drawing any weapon they had to hand or paw or fin or feathered appendage.
The whistle noise was coming from the ship, then a foot ramp lowered itself from underneath the prow of the silvery pronged dart.
  "All aboard" came Sarah's voice, sounding like a railway conductor from the good old days of railway steam. Her white orb then sped towards the nose of the ship and disappeared up the ramp, with the likes of the Commander and company looking around a bit foolishly. Why they jumped so much at the whistling noise was something Jack did not quite understand, there abrupt turn away from everybody spoke volumes. The only problem was which volume of book, page and paragraph they were working from in Jack's opinion?
  Jack was the first to follow Sarah's orb up and found he was in what he would describe as an angled grey bomb bay. There was a grey door facing him and as he approached, it whistled silently open. He stepped though into a crystal white corridor and the door swooshed shut behind him.
Sarah floated in front of him, her orb spinning around "what do you think?" she asked.
Jack looked about "of what exactly?"
"Me, silly!"
"It's nice to have something to talk to ..." Jack paused.

"But?" questioned Sarah with Jack imagining an imaginary foot tapping in the background.

"Don't you think it's a bit … expressionless?" that was not exactly what he had meant to say. Jack could just not bring himself to say out loud to Sarah what had made him so uncomfortable. What it was actually, was about talking to a floating white orb, that left a smokey white trail in the air as it bobbed along. It looked like something from a biology class that you might find under a microscope while talking about fertilization.

Sarah's orb moved towards Jack suddenly, then sped off down the corridor and flew round a corner, dragging its tail behind. Jack stood for a moment wondering where he should go. Then a second later the orb came flying back around the corner and stopped just in front of his face, the smokey white tail seeming to bunch up behind like a coiled white spring.

There was no way to say it other than to say it "err yes, the um, makeup is a vast improvement, Sarah?"

"I thought so" came the reply from the orb. It was still a glossy white ball but now it looked like eye-shadow, cheek rouge, lipstick and even eyeliner had been added quite liberally without any facial features to tie it all together. What made it look quite wrong, was not so much the lack of facial features, after all Jack had seen many boys and girls with troweled on makeup, no it was the way it all moved in sync when she talked. You expected makeup to stay where it was, not move and react when the thing was talking and expressing itself. One thing though, it would certainly make her look "unique even" thought Jack out loud again.

Sarah then did the equivalent of poking her tongue out at him, which looked surprisingly rude on the face of the orb.

Sarah made a sniff like noise and said "I'll sort out the eye's later, when I've decided on what colour I want."

Looking around at the ship as they walked through the interior, Jack had the feeling somehow that he had been onboard before, although he had not recognized the sleek outside at all.

Jack followed Sarah's orb down the corridor, finally he had to ask something that had been bothering him "what's with the colour changes?"

"What colour changes?"

"Well the corridors are white, the bay was grey and the bridge is white with black edges, why aren't they all the same colour?"

"White areas denote general use, dark greys and blues are storage, greys and black are weapons and white and black are secured areas like the bridge. This applies to nearly all of the ships in production today, like an unofficial standard."

Jack nodded in agreement, he knew that he was not going to remember the colour coding and it just sounded like she had made it all up just keep him from asking any more silly questions.

Jack walked onto the bridge, he glanced about and soon noticed something "is this Beth's ship, this is Beth's ship?"

"Ta da" said Beth spinning the central seat round to face Jack and stamping her feet on the deck. Surprisingly Jack was quite pleased to see Beth, at the same time he also felt a little uneasy in her presence. She always looked at him like she was judging him all the time, much like a close relative might glare at the new close 'friend' your introducing to them for the first time. It was that look of disapproving analysis, which might one day just lead to a cordial hello.

The others slowly walked and plodded onto the bridge, until finally Jack asked "so why am I here and not going to the race start?" Beth replied "we've got to get you back to the Golden moon first." Nobody was giving an explanation, so Jack asked "why? Is my board there?"

Ron said "no mate, your boards in the loading bay in my shop if you remember."

"So why do we need to go back to the Goldenish moon?" asked Jack.
"That's where the race starts!"

"Ron, you said the race was going to be outside our hotel window, not in the depths of space?" complained Jack.

"It is, just not the ten thousand" Ron looked at Jack's confused expression.

"The ten thousand is a race across the system and the final is held outside our hotel, didn't you know that?"

Jack shook his head and slowly his mouth started to open in shock, as he worked out that he was once again going to be in the depths of space, with no support this time.

"Anyway it's only a short hop to the moon" said Ron.

"Why aren't we taking a SHOT to get there?" asked Jack, remembering that they had technically parked on the moon.

"I thought you might prefer going up in your own ship, it took a few hours for the ship to clear customs anyway" said Beth.

The passengers looked round at the ship interior, with curious expressions written large on there faces, as it all did look very familiar.

"Which is why it looks like a mirror sharpened to cut the cosmos?" asked Jack.

"Okay yes" Beth admitted looking at Sarah's orb for confirmation "we used the GFG to make the ship look like a Special Customs and Excise Warrantor, to avoid too much investigation. And before you ask the internal systems are near identical to a War Catcher anyway, because..?"

Sudden realization could be seen making its way across Summer and the Commanders snouted faces "well I'll be a Playtor's uncle" said the Commander.

"The customs ship fleet is based on the War Catchers! That explains the sudden drop in smuggling over the last few years" said Summer thoughtfully nodding at the Commander.

The War Catcher, in its Ghost Field silver mirrored, business suit and shiny sheen coat, lifted off the grey floor of the hangar. It sliced its way through the air, the three sharpened prongs twisting to face the barely visible Golden Moon, with its engines spitting forth a mixture of blue and yellow smoked beams. The ship punched a hole through the dusty clouds, lighting up the air around it like a match in an methane chocked chamber or lift.

Chapter 34 : Moon Lounging.

A little while later on the moon, Jack stepped off the ship ramp and onto the golden coloured sand, he was carrying his board under one arm and marveling at how easily he had been thrown into all this. Within a few steps he heard the mild swoosh noise of the ramp starting to raise itself back up and the ships engines twisting the War Catcher back into the air.

Then Ron shouted "here, mate, you'll need this" through the closing gap Ron threw an angled slightly bug eyed helmet at Jack. It bounced and rolled in the sand, ending up at Jack's feet as he turned. It was actually a rather nice white and dark silver bug eyed helmet, with a tribal design flowing over the top in black. It would actually probably look quite good with his designer suit for space he thought. But did his suit not already have a helmet? Jack picked it up anyway.

"Will he be alright?" asked Claire looking through the windowed floor at Jack's receding stick figure, he gave a little wave which was suddenly lost in a sand cloud, as another ship landed where they had left. Beth sighed inwardly, this was only the fifth time Claire had asked about Jack's well being and they could still see him!

Looking around at the inside of this cave on the moon, Claire for the first time noticed how many landing spoons there were. What she could not quite get over was how many ships were flitting backwards and forwards dropping off things.
"There are a lot of ships about today, aren't there?" she asked.
Beth replied "it is the start of the ten thousand" she slowed like she was checking some internal figure "in about an hour" she then finished speeding up again.
"Well that gives us enough time to get a good position for the middle then!" said the Commander enthusiastically.
"The middle, why not the start?" asked Claire.
"Well, we'll watch the start on the Hyper screen, but the middle is where the action will be" the Commander sounded really excited when he said this. When Claire looked around at the others Summer, Jane, Joan, Beth, Second and even Sara, all had expressions of eagerness and excitement on there faces.

Jack watched his ship gently float up and away without any fuss, then almost immediately afterwards there was a loud roar and plume of stinging golden sand was thrown at Jack. After having nearly been blown off his feet by a cloudy sandstorm, Jack was left wondering how much of it was now in his suit, waiting to aggravate him at later date and at a much more inconvenient moment.

When the sand eventually settled back down on the ground with its cousins, Jack found he had nearly been flattened by an giant squashed egg shaped ship. He was so surprised he tried to step backwards, not noticing that from the knees down he was buried in sand. Sitting down sharply he released his board, which then dug in the sand, twisted round and slapped him on the back of the head.

Mildly concussed for a moment, Jack eventually opened his eyes and would have died from shock were it not for the near continuous apologies he had been listening too for the last few seconds.
Right in front of his eyes as he opened them, was another face so hideously malformed that only a zombie octopus might have loved. It looked like a bear had mated with a spider whilst eating a bag of cooked spaghetti. Not only did it look like a predator from Jack's worse nightmare, it smelled like a lost and long forgotten ripe old wedge of green cheese that had remained hidden for months under a car seat, only on careful inspection would it then be discovered to be an ancient and near sentient fruit.
"I'm terribly sorry, really I am, my ship likes to play jokes" the horrible face pulled away from Jack a little "please don't sue me?" it pleaded.
"Okay" mumbled Jack, slowly fingering sand out of his mouth.

Jack found he was up to his knees looking at an smiling octopus, it had the required eight leg limb things, with two bug eyes rotating around on stalks on its head. The only real difference between an earth octopus and this alien, was that it was human sized and had a jelly like central core shaped like a barrel. Its head flowed into the barrel like body with very little in the way of neck but as Jack stared the creature changed its shape, making itself look more human. It could never pass for human, after all having six legs would be a problem, although in some light or the lack thereof, someone might pay for services rendered. The only problem for Jack was the aliens face, with its bear like teeth, saliva dribbling maw and several small claw like arms around its lips to drag food into its mouth. Hanging just behind the eye stalks was its thick spaghetti like hair, which was slimy and wavy looking all at the same time. The creature was also nearly always changing colour, flowing from blues and sea greens to pinks, inside and out. It was basically a free flowing, nearly see through multicoloured jelly.

"Sorry where are my manners, I'm Juice" the creature held out a sucker encrusted arm, as Jack watched the end morphed into a three fingered hand and thumb.
Jack cautiously took hold of the proffered limb not sure what to expect, the one thing he had not expected to find was that it was warm and dry to the touch.
"Are you alright, I mean can you speak?" asked Juice in a caring manner, still not wanting to be sued.
Jack then found himself lifted up and out of the sand by a spare tentacle, all the time still shaking hands with the alien.
When he was finally stood on his own two feet, Jack had recovered enough to say "thank you?"

The creature then turned around, picked up its own surfboard before turning back to Jack and saying "hurry up or we'll miss the bus" and striding away.

Jack felt genuinely lost for a moment before memory came flooding back, he bent quickly, picked up his board and helmet and jogged after Juice.

Within a few steps Jack had caught up with Juice, who had been flowing over the sand with his legs, he wondered how to start a conversation. Was it impolite to just ask something or was there some alien protocol you had to use before striking up a chat. Whilst he was mulling this over Jack was looking around the massive cave they were in, it really was like the inside of some dug out mountain, minus the actual mountain outside. Not only was it massive but considering they had been both dropped off on the opposite side, it should have taken them at least an hour to walk round to the security arches. And yet the arches were getting suspiciously closer by the second, with the air whistling passed his ears. As he walked Jack took notice of the sandy floor for the first time. It was basically a sandy travelator, one of those moving stair cases with out the stairs, that was hurtling them along with every step.

"Escalator" said Jack out loud and clicking his fingers with the glee of recollection of a name.

"Same to you" said Juice turning his head back to face Jack, which just seemed to flow round to face him with no apparent twist or seam in the neck department. Jack somehow managed to trip on the near solid sandy floor, due to probable mild shock and in the process he let go of his helmet, which immediately stuck to the surfboard by what felt like magnetism.

There were ships briefly landing and taking off again all across the inside of the cavern, leaving variously shaped aliens to make there way across the sands to the archways. There was no queuing, rushing or haste, it was like a well spaced happy crowd ambling towards there imminent future. The total opposite of what Jack had been expecting. He had expected a football crowd type rush, with chanting and shoving, followed by screams of woe. Then he remembered they were surfers, in a surf competition and not a riotous crowd of supporting hooligans. He had only ever been to one ball of the foot game, at the age of twelve, the abuse, the chanting and the gestures leveled at the players had left a dirty mark on his soul. Not quite as big a mark as the wound on his leg, he had never been to a game since and would probably never go again.

Another minute and they would be at the arches and Jack still felt he should say something "are you are surfer too?" instantly Jack regretted asking the dumbest single question he had ever asked to someone carrying a surfboard.

Fortunately Juice was not one easily offended "are you sure your okay, I mean you did get quite a bump on your head?"

"Yes I'm fine thanks, it's just I didn't expect to be here" said Jack waving his free arm at the cave.

"You've got to register first."
"I thought that was what the card was for?" asked Jack looking for and eventually finding the ticket stub.
"That only confirmed your entry and this is where you register to race" Juice looked at Jack carefully before asking "you do know about this race don't you?"
Jack replied "just that it's going to be busy at the start, what with ten thousand of us!"
"Yes, yes this is true."
"Oh and there's a mortality rate of thirty nine percent."
"Yes, yes this is also true" said Juice who was reluctant to add 'but?'
As they neared the arch, in the background could be heard "thank you for registering" as each creature passed through the archways, followed by "please proceed to the bus."
Juice cautiously asked "and do you know why that is?"
With confidence Jack started with "oh that'll be people falling out of the gap" on seeing Juice shaking his head slowly, Jack finished with a question "people falling out of the race? People getting lost?" Juice shook his head again "people not starting then?" asked Jack finally.
"Try being, eaten out of the race" replied Juice as they both stepped through the central arch together.
"Thank you for registering, please proceed to the bus" came a voice in the air.
Jack stopped walking on the other side and tried to walk back through the arch. It was like walking into a sponge wall that kept pushing him back towards Juice.
"Thank you for registering" came the voice again, this time though it was a whiny sound "please proceed to the bus."

"I'm sorry you did WHAT?" said Claire shouting at the end.
"Well I entered him in the competition, to win and save us all!" replied the Commander feeling a little offended at her tone.
"Without mentioning the eaten alive part, not once, not at all ... does he know because I very much doubt he knew before hand?" asked a very angry Claire stomping about the bridge of the War Catcher.
"If he didn't, he certainly does now" said Beth with a slight tinge of humour in her voice.
"What do you mean?" asked Claire.
"He's just appeared on the confirmed registration list of the ten thousand. He's going down in history" said Beth in a proud tone.
"You mean going down whole or in bits?" said Claire sarcastically.

"You really didn't know?" asked Juice.

It turned out there were actually several buses, each carrying a thousand competitors. As they had boarded, each one of them had been brushed with something called Filmament, which Jack had been informed was to enhance the viewers pleasure. Walking along the light yellow sandstone coloured corridor, towards the buses, Jack had watched as adverts flitted across the walls. Everything from bodily enhancements, to spaceship augmentation, to world building flashed across the walls. Juice pointed out the most important advert of all, being the advertising revenue he could accrue for surfing heroically, which Jack took to mean dangerously.

As they walked along Juice slipped easily into a human shaped space suit, two arms, two legs and a hole for the head to seep through, putting two bendy limbs in each segment. He would never admit it, but although it was uncomfortable to start with, he always felt so much better in a four limbed suit than his own species starfish like design. Juice always felt his own species design criteria was of one to make them easier targets for some reason, if he had of been human he might have imagined a red target being painted on the back and front for good measure.

Juice again he asked "you really didn't know about the being eaten alive possibility?"

They were all sat facing a window the size and shape of large hot air balloon. In fact the bus itself was the shape of an upside down hot air balloon, although a really big one that was only twenty or so meters deep, a hundred or so wide and easily two hundred meters tall. Jack had been dragged along in a daze by his new friend and had almost gone willingly, especially after Juice pointed out the troops with guns lining the route to the buses as they shuffled aboard.

"No I didn't" said Jack "I thought my look of shock might have given it away, or even my trying to run back through the gate!"
"You signed up for it!" pointed out Juice.
"Yes, yes I did and I shall be having words at some point with a certain Commander" Jack said this with meaning.
"Hmm I think you should listen to the Wire on the way up."
"The wire what?"
"You know, the Surf Radio channel" said Juice.
"How?"
"Through your blinkers or helmet!" said Juice with some annoyance "didn't you get Vowked?"
"It didn't work" said Jack tapping his skull.
"It only works when you wear the blinkers you know. Where are you from anyway?"
"Earth."
"What, the one that they blew up?"
"Yep."
"Sorry, bet that's a bit of a downer."
"It's okay I'm gonna sort it out one day."
"In the mean time at least put on your helmet and select the Wire."

Jack reached around in his seat and pulled his helmet off his board. The ships or buses as they were called, were obviously designed for this type of transport, as each seat had a slot behind it for a surfboard. Jack had been surprised to see so many different types of helmet, the most common one appearing to be a flattened disc like thing that was stuck to most boards like a hub cap. He had seen a couple of aliens pick them up and simply put them on there heads like a hat. The helmet had then simply unfolded down over there features, like a concertina expanding and enveloping the users head. It was obviously some fashionable design, with colour schemes from the drab but cool range.

Jack slipped on his own helmet, the outside clamour disappeared almost completely. The huge variation in aliens that had been staring at him visibly muffled, finally Jack felt alone, he started to relax and shut his eyes.

"I'm gonna talk to him" said Ron.
Whatever Jack was doing, there was obviously some camera pointing at his face, because they could see every expression and then he shut his eyes.
"Ron, don't bother" said Claire.
Ron stopped reaching for a panel on the bridge "why, I was just going to check on him?"
Claire stared at Jack's enlarged face floating above the table "if he can relax on telly he's fine" she said. The image of Jack's face slowly faded out to a view of his silvery bug eyed helmet.

From the outside all anyone could see was the suits occupants head, gently swaying from side to side to some invisible beat as the bus carried on with its journey into space. After awhile Juice leant over and tapped Jack on his helmet, slowly the swaying stopped and an almost look of panic could be seen as Jack grabbed the seat he was in, look around wildly and then some how physically sighed.
Jack touched a panel on the base of the helmets chin, which made the eyes barely visible behind the silver bug eyes, like some really expensive designer shades.
Turning his head Jack asked of Juice a bit testily "yes?"
"You should really tune in to the Wire you know."

Jack looked round at the rows and columns of seated aliens in there white hook seat chairs, nearly all were tapping appendages of one description or another in time to some musical beat. Each seat was attached to a bar that ran the entire width of the ship, by the simple means of a hook on the back of each chair. Most of the aliens were wearing protective head gear of one description or another and some were also bopping there heads in a similar fashion to what Jack had been.

Jack swiped the pad under his chin, all prepared to go back and listen to the radio station calling itself 'Boldies', which was playing an addictive mix of human like music tracks mixed with alien sounding beats, rhythms and sound effects. Judging by everyone else's head, foot and hand tapping a lot of the competitors were listening to the same station.

Jack sighed to himself and asked in the silence of his helmet for "Vowke the Wire."

Nothing happened for a few seconds and then a small television like screen appeared in the bottom left of his vision, as he stared at it, it grew to fill nearly all his vision like his nose was pressed up against a life sized poster of the thing. Sensing his discomfort the image moved away from his face and swam into focus, shortly followed by the sound.

It was exactly like the pre-match build up you got before some big sporting event back on Earth, with the added bonus for Jack of explaining how the race was actually going to work. The one thing everyone had seemed reluctant to explain to him was how it was all going to work and after listening for a few seconds Jack worked out why...

Chapter 35 : The Old Race.

Two presumably old hand Newman sports personalities, were sat next to one another, relaxing over a soft blue grass like table, whilst discussing the upcoming race of the ten thousand. Jack was tuned-in hooked in his seat and Claire was also sat on the edge of her own seat on the bridge of the War Catcher. If they could have seen one another's faces they would quite possibly have marveled at there almost identical opened mouthed expressions of shock and awe, as the two sports pundits sat and chatted away about this years race.

"The ten thousand this year has actually come a day early!" said one man.
"Which is unusual" replied the other man.
"Yes, yes it is Don. The race has always started to coincide with the spawning, which due to the weathered flaring of Newsol, has started a bit early this year."
"For those of you who have been living under Olsol's glare" Don held a hand up to shadow his face briefly from the lights and made the noise of a fake laugh "we'll start with a few race tit-bits, over to you Dun" finishing with a cheesy grin to his co-host and audience.
"Thank you Don" replied Dun with an equally cheesy grin in reply "the 'ten thousand' as its called derives the name from the number of Competitors taking part, for the full list see our Wired Up Selector."

In the corner of Jack's vision an icon appeared with a scrolling list of names and numbers, which he glanced at and then ignored. They were far too many to even think about, probably about ten thousand. Don interjected with "ten thousand then is not the number of deaths in the races history, which has been widely circulated."
"Thanks Don, no the mortality rate is much higher ha ha" the laugh was a forced one, sounding slightly false with both co-hosts grinning and winking each time they passed the conversation back to one another. Dun continued "now normally any moon or satellite like object circulating this close to a sun, Newsol here and Olsol on the other side of the system, would be either a bit runny, super solid or non-existent."
"So we wouldn't have known they were there anyway?"
"That's right Don. In this case we were surprised to find, nearly two hundred and fifty turns ago, that each sun had a satellite orbiting up close and that each satellite actually had life on it!"
"No Dun, really!" said Don with mock surprise, this was obviously some repeat setup conversation that the two must have had multiple times, with Jack able to hear in the background members of an audience gasping, oohing and ahhing. The only thing he thought curious, was whether the background audience was actually real.

"Yes Don. Plant life. What was more surprising was that the day we found the satellites and there plants, was the day the plants opened up. There beautiful petals unfolding from behind there protective leaves and sending forth a barrage of seeds. Which we now know and call the 'spawning'" Dun said the last word with mock dread.
A brief video insert popped up showing hundreds of amazing flowers unfurling. The colours were nothing like Jack had ever seen before and then they were fogged from view, as lots of something's were ejected like a mist from the centre of each flower. There was also no sense of scale either, for all Jack knew they were plants in his mums window box.
"Gosh Dun, not the great dispersal then?"
"No Don. The seeds flung out from both Suns are boys, girls and ambis, hungry missiles of death and destruction."
"Hungry?" asked Don with feigned interest.
"Oh yes Don, these little beasties come fully loaded with chomping teeth, chewing through anything that gets in there way!"
"Like an unfortunate Surfer for example?" Don nodded knowingly at the camera.
"Where do you think those crazy mortality stats come from my friend!" Dun quizzed in a joyful tone.
"The advertisers?" joked Don, whilst pointing down at some banner at the bottom of the screen.
"Just facts my friend. For example if a surfer just ain't fast enough, he'll get eaten out from behind."
Dun leant towards the camera and winked "and if he's too fast, he might just be swallowed from the front" Don leant forward towards the camera and winked.
Dun leant back in his chair and winked again "then there's the great maelstrom" he paused for effect "where the ejected seeds meet in the middle."
"A maelstrom?" asked Don sitting back.
"The great maelstrom, to beat all maelstroms. Not only will the surfers have to contend with being chased by solar flare accelerated hungry seeds, but, there's the same thing coming the other way and where they meet, is absolute mayhem. Now if a lucky surfer manages to stay in front of the seeds he may only have to dodge the ones coming the other way, but being in front means the seeds coming towards him lock on to him."
"Why's that Dun?"
"Well Don, it's because there all preprogrammed to exchange as much material as possible, just in case they miss there intended target and can therefore seed another Sun!"
"Wow ... so how did the surfing start?"
"Those first science ships which discovered these amazing plants, were, well lets not beat around the bush here, they were consumed by the seeds and anything left was dissolved by the solar flares."
"And the surfing?" asked Don.
"Of the sixteen escape pods launched, only three made it away and they were all piloted by surfers in there spare time."

"So Dun, what happened next?"
Dun paused before replying again, giving time for an advertising banner to flash across the bottom of the screen "I'm glad you ask Don. Five turns later they returned with some friends, surfing the seeds and flares from both suns. Which happened to coincide with a small surf competition here on Nerth."
"So now every five turns, competitors that didn't make the last surf rounds, can run the gauntlet of the Ten Thousand to get in?" asked Don.
"Only the lucky few, the ten thousand is always over subscribed by millions of wannabes, with only the first ten to reach Olsol's plant moon, entered into the final" said Dun.
"Sounds like fun" replied Don in a forced joyous tone.
"It does indeed Don, I only wish I were racing this turn" said Dun in an wistful tone of voice.
"No you don't, not five minutes before we came on set you were saying 'I'm so glad I ain't racing this year har har'."
Dun gave Don a very angry look, his face turning red with suppressed rage and horror, which very quickly gave way to a placid expression and a fixed smile, as he remembered they were on Galaxy wide Hyperversal.

    Jack flicked off the broadcast, took off his helmet and tapped Juice on his helmeted head.
"Hmm, yeah?" said Juice slowly lifting the visor of his own helmet. Juice's helmet had an dark orange shaded slot like visor at human eye level, which slid up showing his independent eye's. The vertical mouth piece on the helmet though, opened and shut like an angry lift in an law firm when your money ran out.
"Are we going to die?" asked Jack quietly.

    Claire leant back from staring at the floating images of the two presenters, who were discussing the upcoming massacre like it was an everyday sporting event and asked in wonder "how is this legal?"
Ron looked surprised and replied "anyone can enter, no one is forced."
"But if they can maybe be tricked, that's okay is it?" asked Claire looking at the Commander.
"Well, I will admit I didn't give Jack all the information upfront, but he could have of found out for himself don't you think?" replied the Commander, standing up quite well he thought, under Claire's forceful stare.

    "You'll be fine, just remember the orientation meeting" said Juice.
The view out of the super sized window was sliding by now and had been for sometime, the bus had turned the window away from there destination for some reason. It was like looking out of a really large train window, whilst traveling at night over a sea bridge. The only thing that made it look a bit odd to Jack, was the near continuous red coloured flaring being dragged across the windows leading edges, like it was being warmed up from somewhere.

Jack then repeated in his head what Juice had just said, turning his head to face him he asked "what orientation meeting?"
"The one from last week."
"I wasn't here last week" after a moments thought Jack added thoughtfully "I was watching my home planet getting blown up!"
"Ah, special dispensation then."
"Special" Jack mumbled "more like unique" he finished sullenly.
"Anyway you won't have time to review it now, because what you want to watch is when we spin round the Sun Newsol and head to the start line."
Jack did not reply, so after a minute Juice looked at him and asked "are you alright?"
He replied "I have no idea what I'm doing or where I'm going or even really why? So everything is not alright."
"That's easy, all you have to do is go in a relative straight line and not get eaten on the way. If you run into trouble just follow the beacon for the finish line, if you get really stuck just follow one of the SV's."
"The SV's?"
"Seasoned Veteran, the ones wearing an S and V on there clothing."
Jack looked around and found that there were actually quite a few creatures with the letters attached to there clothing, then he remembered seeing them somewhere else and turned to look at Juice.
"Your a Seasoned Veteran?" Jack quizzed in surprise, pointing at Juices own winged S and V floating high up on his arm.
"Yep, earned my season wings" said Juice proudly.
"How many races is that then, before you become a Veteran?"
"This'll be my forth, but surviving just one race will do."
Jack looked at his new friend in quiet awe, to have survived the statistics alone was amazing, to come back for more was blatantly stupid.
"Why?" asked Jack.
"Why what?" replied Juice.
"Why do you keep coming back?"
Juice actually looked hurt by Jack's tone of question but answered anyway "because I'm good at it" he whispered quickly in reply. Which Jack took to mean it was the only thing he was good at.

    Then an bored looking brown disc like alien floated directly into Jack's vision. The beige circle was about a meter wide and had what looked like a stuffed bulldog head mounted in the centre. It was very flat faced bulldog, that may have been running too quick when it had been caught, it looked exceptionally bored.
"Smile for the record" it said in a tone so mono and level that Jack was not sure if he should but did anyway. Then there was a flash of a camera from four small round things at equidistant space from one another and the thing floated off to face Juice.
It suddenly became all excited, started to shake and seemed to be bouncing up and down in front of him. Juice smiled for the camera flashing, doing little bodybuilder strength poses with his tentacled legs and arms. Then the disc thing moved off to another unwilling victim chained to there hooked seat.

"What was that?" asked Jack.
"A Hack, Hyper Assistive Camera, they were built for recording in dangerous places."
"No, I meant all your posing?"
"Oh that, that was for the audience and my profile" looking at Jack's frowning expression, Juice continued "because I'm a Veteran, they expect me to do well, or at the very least not die. And the more people that view my profile, the more that view the adverts and the more revenue I accrue."

The bus then gave a little giggle as it turned to face the sun. Jack instinctively covered his face but actually found he was not going blind or being fried in anyway whatsoever. He uncowered himself from the seat, finding that his legs and arms had been folded in all kinds of unusual places around his body and face. He also found the Hack brown disc thing floating almost right in front of him, he could just imagine Claire groaning at the sight of him on Galactic television screaming and curling up in panic. He was not wrong in any way.

The bus as it was called, sped directly towards the Sun, seeming to Jack to be heading right for the middle of the fiery ball of death. The ship then almost at the last minute as far as Jack was concerned, veered off to one side and circled the Sun picking up a massive amount of speed in the process. As it started its third lap it suddenly swung out from the Sun and Jack found they were looking at a bright silver disc right in front of the bus.

As they neared the silver thing it started to look to Jack like a scrunched up ball of foil, or what effect a group of ecological warrior teenagers might have on a tin can found in the middle of a rain-forest, crushed does not begin to cover it.

Then they were over and round into the dark side of the shiny moon, now being on the dark side it almost felt cooler and decidedly less shiny, the moon even looked green in colour to Jack's untrained eye.

The bus moved gently round the moon again, always facing the satellite, Jack watched amazed as the thing rotated. As the moon spun around Jack could see that each scrunched up shiny thing was actually a leaf, there appeared to be quite literally thousands of the veiny things across the entire surface of the moon. As each bright reflective leaf started to reach the dark side, as the moon rotated, it would fold over and become a normal green looking Oak leaf. They were rather large looking leaves as they ponderously turned over; with no sense of scale however, it was nearly impossible to guess how big each one was or even how large the moon actually was. The Oak like leaves then turned there silvery sides out again, before they could get singed, as the moon spun around. Jack guessed that it was about a twelve hour day and night cycle, when he asked Juice, all he got was a nod and a snoring sound like a chainsaw eating a toffee.

The big window in front of Jack shimmered with a golden glare and then Don and Dun appeared, standing on either side of the winners trophy, with the shadow of the leafy moon behind them. Jack took off his helmet to listen to there speech, as it might be quite important he felt.
The trophy caught Jack's eye though because a) it was what he needed to go home and b) it looked gaudy. The prize was attached to a small white marble looking block and looked cheap to Jack. It looked like it was made from gold's shinier cousin and layered in slowly dribbling oil, like somehow a slow trickle of golden oil was continually gently flowing down over the surface.
Surprisingly the trophy was not that ornate, there was a multi-limbed human shaped creature leaning forward on a surfboard, riding a foamy wave embossed on the front. Chasing along behind them was a pear. Although as Jack looked he could see it was a rather sharp pear shape, with a toothy smile and fins on the back. All around the rest of the jugged award were variable sized dots or stars as Jack thought of them. As the trophy slowly spun around there was also an embossed plaque on the back, with a list of names and dates slowly scrolling up over the surface, in the same oily gold finish as the entirety of the trophy.
"Hi there Surf buddies" said presumably Dun pointing and smiling at the trophy.
"I thought you'd retired?" asked Don quietly.
The look of anger Dun gave Don could have shot down a meteorite, with spare change for its cousin the comet.
Speaking through clenched teeth, which slowly loosened Dun continued "we're stood here on this auspicious evening on Nerth, next to the SUDS C trophy, which one of you!" he said pointing out of the screen "will take home and show to your friends for the next five turns! This is an unprecedented move by this years sponsor, one Olgas Faid. We thank you, thank you very much" finished Dun with some degree of reverence in his voice.
The camera moved back to include a very ginger looking Raifoon, the camera then zoomed in to just his eyes, filling the entire window as he blinked. It was the biggest blink Jack had ever seen, the eye lids closed from left and right to meet in the middle like sliding blinds in both eyes, with a splash of red as they mashed together. The camera then erratically zoomed back out to a more sensible distance, with Jack having to look at the creature twice, because he did not look quite right for a Raifoon, there was just something off with the alien.

Claire was thinking the same thing, as the alien launched into some prepared speech about harmony in the cosmos and joining the rise against tyranny.
"What's he on about and why doesn't he look right?" asked Claire. Summer looked up at the floating creature and said "because he isn't a Raifoon" as if that explained everything. She then looked back down at her paws, as she cleaned her nails with a very ornate and viciously curved knife.

Jack had just asked Juice the same thing and got the same answer. Both he and Claire then asked what he was then and got the answer "because he's a Furrykin."
Both Jack and Claire asked of there respective informers "I thought they were the enemy?"
"Not here there not, some of them have even retired locally."
"But don't they want to control the Universe or something?"
"They'll come here last" Juice spoke as if this explained everything.
"Why?" asked Jack.
Sighing Juice said "because they have patience."
"Huh?" asked Jack in a mildly confused manner, Juice though had turned away and was looking expectantly at the window where the Furrykin was building to some crescendo in his obviously very preprepared speech. Only he did not get to finish it as a counter suddenly appeared on the screen with a 'bong' like sound, cutting the alien short. The look of annoyance on his face was priceless, like being told he had won humanitarian of the Universe and then being informed that 'sorry, sorry, we meant to give you the booby prize, sorry, sorry.'

    Juice mumbled something like 'finally' under his breath, to Jack he could have been swearing for all he knew because he was not listening. His ears seemed to be filled with a clamouring noise, it was so loud that he felt he might pass out, then he realized for the first time what real panic must feel like, mainly because he was experiencing it.

Chapter 36 : Free Lunched.

The countdown seemed to take forever for Jack, as he watched the spiral like counter slowly unwind. When it got to the last few digits it switched from a depleting spiral like counter to a simple circular bar counting down, to what was in Jack's mind labeled as 'doomsday'. He looked down at his hands and saw he was shaking so hard that the even the seat he was hooked into seemed to be being moved by him.

"Get your board!" shouted Juice to Jack over the clamour of alien voices.

The noise in his head was so loud that Jack missed the first four shouts, reaching around in his seat to touch the board and he found it would not even move. Another level of panic crept into his mind. Jack never thought it possible that he could have been any more worried than he already was, apparently his bowels had a way of persuading him otherwise.

Juice looked over at Jack's frozen and panicking face, leaned over and pulled the cord out of the board and handed it too him, all the time muttering about 'jitters' and 'trainees.'

Through all the training Jack had had, whilst flying to this event, putting the cord around his ankle had become second nature. Jack's hand fortunately had been gripping onto the edge of the board, because as soon as he had flicked the cord around his ankle, like a set of handcuffs going clang in his mind, the board came loose from its seat housing.

The board swung up over and round so quickly that Jack managed to clout both competitors on either side of him, Juice under his chin and the other around the back of the helmeted head. Juice gave Jack a filthy look from under his helmet and then started to laugh as he looked across Jack to the other racer on the other side of him. The seats were all arranged in tiers, ten deep and a hundred wide, Jack and Juice were sat in the fourth row back. Jack looked over at the black suited surfer and saw his Raifoon like form sat in the seat like an unconscious jelly, all wobbly bits and no direction.

Jack leant over to check he was okay, managing to smack him again with his board as it spun round the back of the seat, whilst still being attached to his ankle.

The first thing that went through his mind was how much longer and harder could Juice laugh and the second was why was his board flapping about like confetti at a whirlwind marriage in the first place? Juice managed to grab Jack's loose board through his fits of laughter and said "if you'd been at the orientation meeting, you would know that the Gravlec is turned off a few minutes before we get pushed out, so it's easier to manage your board!" Juice said all this in one sentence laughing again at the end, whilst handing Jack his board and catching his breath.

Jack checked his board for dents and for something to say asked "Gravlect?"
"Gravlec, fake gravity" came the correction and the answer from Juice.
"What, it's not real?"
"Right and might I suggest you put your helmet back on Jack" said Juice with a pointed nod towards the large window.

Jack looked round at the timer on the window, it appeared to be in its last stage as he stared at it, the problem was he did not understand this type of spiral counter. What eventually gave the timing away was the belt releasing Jack from his seat and the loud voice of Dun speaking from the window, saying "bye bye Surf buddies, have fun!"

The window shimmered and then seemed to fizz before disappearing completely, showing how clear and sharp the view of space actually really could be if you were looking at it without any safe guards. The effect of the window suddenly not being there was that everyone was sucked into the depths of space, with Jack looking around wildly for his helmet and then finding it attached to the top of his board again, he ripped it off and forced it quickly down over his ears as he spun with the rest of the surfers out into space.

Each racer spun about for a few moments, orientating themselves until they were facing the plant moon and the bus. Juice boarded over to Jack who was still reeling in his board, when he had his attention he made some wild tentacled movements to indicate what Jack could do with his radio communications.

Jack asked to speak with Juice, who then said "finally, Jack to speak with me in the future just say 'Vowke com, Juice one' and to listen to anything else just put 'com' in first okay?"

Some of the panic had passed through Jack and gone somewhere, he had been in the vacuum of space often enough that whilst it was horrible, he no longer froze in it, so to speak. What was actually worrying him now was the being eaten alive by some alien seed being flung about from star to star. Juice indicated for Jack to spin round to face the bus. Then an option appeared on the inside if his visor reading 'race details' in blue writing, as soon as he looked at it for a time the visor changed. Now was displayed a whole series of lines and vectors in various colours, some pointing back over Jack's shoulder, towards the other glowing sun. The ones in front of him, pointing to the moon behind the bus, which were slowly fading from a bright white to red.

The surfers were all floating around in the shadow of the moon as the sun Newsol suddenly started to flare. Just as it started the leaves all across the dark side of the moon began to open revealing the most varied colour and shaping of flowers that Jack had ever seen. The riot of colouration was so bright and vivid it actually made both Jack and Claire choke, neither of them had seen anything like this before.

Over the radio link Jack could here Juice counting down and on his display he could see another spiral counter gradually moving down. When both reached zero his board came alive with a thump and he heard Juice say quietly "go time."

Jack was still mesmerized by the flowers, he had not noticed nearly all the other surfers had already left. It was only when he saw the flowers spitting forth some tiny little specks of something, that he realized the man eating seeds were on the way. He spun his board round and found not a trace of his surf buddy or any other buddy near by. He could just imagine Claire shouting at him to get a move on, which he was of course right about, just not the volume of colourful language she was currently using on the bridge.

As Jack leaned forward on his board pressing his palm controls to the maximum, he realized he had not been alone in staring at the beautiful flowering moon. Several other riders had been caught by the display, with one human shaped rider appearing next to him, dressed all in black with a familiar looking helmet and standing astride an almost glowing white board. The newcomer was rubbing the back of there head and then waved a gloved hand at Jack, an option for 'proximity com' appeared on Jack's visor. When he had selected the local com, both his own and this new persons visors became opaque, enabling them both to see one another's faces. Although at the current fifty meter gap, the only thing they could actually see was a vaguely pink shady thing.

Sat on the bridge Claire jumped from her seat, when she saw the familiar looking helmeted man flying along next to Jack. The others were all stood around shaking there heads in disbelief.
Claire had to ask "ten thousand competitors spread across the starry expanse of space and one familiar looking uniform, with Mercs even printed on there shoulder!" she exclaimed.
"Well he does seem to get about doesn't he" said the Commander.
"Do you think!" Claire almost shouted and then asked "does Jack know?"
"Well he is talking to him" came the simply reply.
"It's Jack we're talking about here, he once didn't recognize himself in a mirror!" replied Claire.
To be fair to Jack, Claire was being a little restrictive with the truth, after all he had been drunk, dressed up as a purple dwarf and then stood in front of one of those distorted mirrors you could find at any decent fair ground.
"Is there any way of talking to Jack, if only to tell him to watch his back?"
"Well yes" said the Commander carefully.
Claire looked exasperated and said "well, why haven't you told him?"
"Well actually both Sarah and Beth have been trying for the last few minutes" replied the Commander.
Beth exchanged a worried look with Sarah's floating white orb, what the Commander had just said was not strictly true "what?" asked Claire catching the look.
"We've been a bit economic with the truth" said Beth cautiously.
"Meaning?"

"We did struggle to open communications with Jack initially, after all the race cast is encrypted and then edited before general casting and outside communication is not permitted, after we did crack it, we didn't want to interrupt the conversation" said Beth.
Claire stood with her mouth slightly open, clicked it shut and asked resignedly "let's hear it then."

"Hello, Jack" came the rough sounding voice over Jack's helmet speaker.
"Hello?" replied Jack not knowing really what else to say.
"Are you ready?" came the gravelly reply, the voice sounded like it had been dragged across hot coals, applied to a blender and then dragged through a hedge backwards.
The one thing Jack was reluctant to ask, as the they spoke was about the voice, it was such a distinctive sound that before the conversation went any further he just had to ask "what happened to your voice?"

Listening in Claire sighed, sometimes the one thing Jack was not, was delicate. If she were honest it would be most of the time with Jack, it was one of his better features. If he did not know something, rather than sit nodding he would just ask. Sometimes it made him look soft in the head and other times you could see other people in the group, who had been nodding in agreement, suddenly paying attention as they had not been ready to admit to not knowing something.

The growl like reply that Jack received was an actual growl, which took him a few seconds to realize, just because the voice sounded so full of rough hewn pebbles being washed around on a stormy beach. Jack tried asking again "hello?"
"That's your one question before you die then is it?" asked the voice, as they both flew through space.

"Well now we know why he was so persistent" said the Commander listening to the recording.
Turning her head in irritation, Claire asked "and why's that then?"
"Well not only is he a Mercs, but he is also probably a member of the Creed."
"Meaning what?"
"Well they believe in personal assassination, with the assassinee being given one question before they die."

Jack replied "which one question is my one question then and this isn't my one question is it? And why am I getting one question, I mean who gives you one question and then tells you your going to die all in one sentence, whilst still asking you to ask one question? What happens if I don't want to ask a question? Do I continue to go on living or is that the question? Come to that why is there a question at all and what happens if you can't answer the question?"

Claire started to laugh to herself, that was the old Jack she remembered and the one she had pulled unceremoniously into the sewer to save his life.

"I never said I would answer it" came the sand weathered reply. On the recording Jack paused, playing the conversation through his mind and said "true, but why ask then?"
"To give your death purpose, every death has a reason" said the would be killer mildly.
"But why?" asked Jack.
"That's a bit of a general question isn't it?"
"I don't know what you mean."
"The immediate answer is, because I'm being paid to do it."
"And the longer answer is?" came Jack's hope filled reply.
"Because I'm being paid Well to do it" and the figure laughed, sounding like they were gargling with lava.
Then there was a loud 'clump' sound, like something taking a chunk out of something else and the recording stopped.

Claire looked up at Beth's face with a worried expression.
"That's the end of the cast" said Beth simply.
"He's still alive?" asked Claire carefully "and in one piece?" Claire gulped the last question.
Beth looked closely at some statistics that had floated up on the race screen "yes, yes he is" she said with mild surprise.
"Then what was the 'clump' sound?" asked Claire.

Jack had actually frozen in mild horror, as a set of gnashing white teeth had smoothly appeared out of the blackness of the moons shadow and clamped shut on his would be attacker.
The Mercs looking at the visible bits of Jack's face and hearing Jack gulp over the com, were just enough for the would be assassinator to instinctively duck on there board.
The row upon row of sharp pearly ice white teeth clamped shut over the hunters head, leaving a ringing 'clump' like noise banging around in Jack's helmet as the cast was abruptly stopped. Open mouthed Jack watched the seed go slowly past like a tall sailing ship, he half expected to hear the creak of wood, the wash of water and the wind whistling in the rigging.
What he actually got was something shaped like an angled pear, with several key differences to a pear. The seed was quite large about the size of an London bus, it had several missile like fins at the wide rear, with each one having slowly deployed a reverse looking parachute or umbrella. Each parachute was multicoloured, looking like polished copper on the outside facing the sun, on the inside it was as black as the seed, making the things nearly invisible in one direction.

Jack stood astride his board marveling at the colours being reflected in the parachutes, it then occurred to him that being behind the seed was probably safer than being in front of the thing. The problems being that there was more than one seed in the spawning and he had to finish in the top ten, which also meant being in front of the dangerous invisible things.

Trying to not think about it too much Jack pressed his palm controls and slowly started to pass the seed. As he moved along the seed, he noticed that it was not all black, it actually had a liquid silver like collar around what he would have called its neck. It was only when he was just in front of the collar that he saw the mouth start to open and turn to face his direction. Caught on a man sized tooth was a black curved disc that might once have been part of someone's helmet not too long ago. Dropping back behind the collar Jack watched the mouth shut again and not to leave a trace of where it had been. Then out the corner of his eye he caught the briefest of glances of something bright, fiery and moving very fast to get away from the killer seeds.

The hunter watched the seed sail overhead, they felt a little light headed and on touching the top of there helmet, it felt a bit odd, airy in fact. There was a sigh, as there was an angled sliced air hole on top, or at least there would have been were it not for the emergency Kit Internal Suit Seal. The Kit Internal Suit Seal warning was flashing away in the middle of there visor, it was informing them in bright red writing and various screaming bells and whistles in the ears that the suit integrity had been compromised. They were to seek assistance immediately as the seal would only last approximately one hour. Anger filled the Mercs mind but they had the more immediate problem of the seeds and now they also owed Jack some more life. The hunter banged clenched fists on there thighs in frustration for a few seconds, then applied maximum boost to the board, as another seed passed underneath. The fuel would easily last for the three day race if it was used carefully, but in the case of an emergency you could burn it all within a short time.
The hunter blasted out of the range of the spawning seeds to be 'picked' up, the word rescued would never have entered there mind.

"So how's he doing" asked Jane walking on to the bridge and stretching her arms after a good nights sleep and a lazy morning coffee. When Claire did not answer right away she looked closer at her and said "you should go to bed you know, after all there's still at least a day's worth of racing left."
Claire replied quite sharply "how can I go possibly go to sleep knowing Jack is out there risking his life for our home and anyway if he's not sleeping neither am I" she finished with a humph in her voice. She crossed her arms and legs, a sure sign of imminent explosive possibilities if not dealt with carefully.
Jane replied without apparently noticing the warning signs "what makes you think he doesn't sleep?"

Claire waved at the floating race screen depicting the surfers "how can he sleep when he's in a race being chased by man eating seedage?"
"He simply hits the sleep button on his suit and the race system gives him four hours every twelve."
Claire opened and shut her mouth in surprise, the one thing she had never thought of was an automatic sleep system for the racers.
"So how do we know when he's sleeping?"
"It's not called sleeping really, more of a rest period and it's compulsory before the maelstrom anyway!"
Claire managed to look even more angry "there dots turn blue when there sleeping" came the simple reply from Jane.
Looking back at the floating display Jack's dot was currently circled, as he was being watched by Claire, it was also a rather nice tranquil blue colour.
"How long has it been like that?" Claire asked in a tone of annoyance.
She knew there was no need to be angry with Jack, because there was no way for him to talk to her but he could have found some way to tell her he was going to sleep!
"A few hours" said Sarah from her white ball sat on the edge of the table.
Claire made another humph sound, stood up, clicked various bones that had stuck together and started to march roboticaly off the bridge.
"Before you go, make sure you set an alarm for four hours time" said Jane.
"Why's that?" asked Claire over her shoulder in an annoyed and yet sleepy voice.
"Because Jack sensibly waited to use his rest periods, so that he had an hour to wake up before he reached the maelstrom."

Just over three hours later Claire was back on the bridge.
"Did you have a nice rest?" asked Jane.
"No I didn't" said Claire with a barb in her voice.
"Why not?"
"Because although I'm dog tired, once my head hit the pillow I couldn't stop thinking about Jack and this maelstrom thing. Is Jack in front or behind now?" she asked worriedly.
The Commander turned round and gave some information "well he's probably fair to middling."
Claire asked hotly "what in the world does that mean?"
"Well look for your self, he's near the back which is about an hour behind the leaders."
"So how is that fair to middling?"
"Well because the gravity is about to change" the Commander replied in an excited voice "everyone gets excited about this part of the race. More people tune in to watch the great maelstrom than any other event in the galaxy, even the final of Suds C only occasionally beats the viewing figures for the great maelstrom!"
"And the betting" said Summer with a tinge of disappointment in her voice "it's the only time the Nerths allow betting in there system."

"You sound disappointed?" asked Claire.
"It's one of the few things I hate most, betting" Summer almost seemed to spit the last word and Claire decided to wisely not ask anything more.
    Claire turned to the central table and saw the two presenters, Dun and Don floating at one end with the live map of events in the middle and some dramatic shots of Jack zipping around in space at the other. Jack himself appeared to be not steering in the slightest as she looked, it was just the camera moving about dramatically, showing him speeding around space being chased by the shooting seeds.
    The map floated just above the table in the middle, showing what looked like nearly ten thousand competitors coloured dots. Some were still blue, meaning they were resting but the others were a mixture of greens and reds with an amber number off to one side, presumably those were retirees.
Summer walked over to the table and asked Claire "do you mind if I have a look?" Claire nodded not knowing what exactly she meant.
    Summer put a finger from each paw like hand into the floating map and pulled them apart, as she did so the map zoomed out. Claire felt herself gasp, she had thought the map limiting and now she was surprised to find that it was much more flexible than she realized She was tempted to ask how far they could zoom out, but a fear of volume for some reason kicked in and she shut her mouth in the act of asking the question. The shear size of the thing was actually quite scary, now though she had a question that had been bugging her since she had gone off to try and sleep.
"Why isn't the 'Great Maelstrom' happening in the middle?" Claire asked.
"Well, gravity" came the Commanders answer, in an 'it's obvious tone.'
Summer interrupted before an argument could start "Newsol" she pointed at the sun where Jack had started the race "is like your sun from Earth."
Summer took a breath having got Claire's attention "Olsol" she pointed at the glowing mass at the other end of the table "is an older sun with much higher density, a third of the size but three times the pull."
"Is that why it's an orangey red?" asked Claire.
Summer nodded and Claire then started to talk to herself "so it's harder to escape gravity from Olsol, which is why the race started at Newsol and why the maelstrom is two thirds of the way along" Summer nodded again.
Claire looked closely at the floating image on the table, the racers and the sun's were easy to see but for the life of her she could not see the seeds very well or at all for that matter.
Summer saw what she was looking for and made a few adjustments with her hands and suddenly the seeds were visible in white.

Claire jumped back from the table in shock, the volume of seeds spread across the floating three dimensional map was like two sun lamps being turned on. From either end of the table the two seed masses looked like two massive umbrellas coming to meet one another. It reminded her of two suction cups coming together, or even two plungers coming face to face. Summer turned down the whiteness volume on the seeds slightly and Claire looked on worriedly at not only Jack's circled dot but all the other thousands of dots. They would all be, within the next few minutes, wholly inside the all encompassing embrace of the seeds. The plunger shapes she saw heading towards one another, were a good analogy of the kind of mess Jack might very well be in shortly she thought. Either that or they could represent two used public toilets heading towards one another, leaving Jack and the others right down the u-bend without a paddle.

Jack was enjoying the trip so far, after the hunter Mercs had flown off, it had been a simple case for him of flying towards the bright glowy thing in front of him.
After the first few hours of panic had worn off, Jack had found the flying through space being chased by man eating seeds actually quite boring. Sure he had occasionally had to dodge some super accelerated seed from in front or even from behind, like being overtaken by someone whom allegedly had there accelerator stuck to the floor. But most of his time was spent playing with the functions of his 'suit for space' and doing tricks on his board. There appeared to be a million and one functions on his suit, the board and the helmet, so he spent a fair amount of time going through various menus until he found something interesting. It was not that Jack was unintelligent, more a case of searching for what function appeared in what sub-menu, in what sub-genre. It was akin to looking for your rental car at the airport after a long arduous flight, eventually finding it in the truck stop, because it was classed as many wheeled drive. It was only by accident that he discovered his helmet actually had proper 'blinker' commands, all he had to do was ask a question and put the word 'Vowke' in front.

After hours of sailing through space with general worry now somewhere behind him, the one thing Jack really needed was to use the facilities, either public or private he was not bothered. The problem was he could not exactly pull over and find a convenient bush for a quick bit of relief, even if he did find one spinning through space. Then his suit solved the problem for him, by informing him that an excessive pressure had built up around his waist and other parts, as if he did not know. If he wished to use the 'onboard facilities' all he had to do was inVowke lavatory.

The comfort shortly after for Jack was palpable, followed be his first attempt at accidental suicide, by the simple means of stepping off his surfboard in blessed relief.

This was the first time he had fallen off his board in space, he did not think anybody had seen it and hoped no one had heard his high pitched scream either. The board carried on flying straight, dragging Jack along behind twisting, turning and mildly swearing to himself as he slowly climbed back along the cord.

When he eventually got back to the board, the Gravlec had been a taken for granted and forgotten pleasant surprise. As soon as he had stepped off the board, the lack of reasonable gravity in any one direction had come as quite a shock. One second he had felt weightless, the next he had been dragged in one direction and then the next, he had not appreciated how many forces the Gravlec on his surfboard had had to deal with.

Once Jack was properly back on his board, he then discovered in the settings menu how much fuel the Gravlec actually used, which was why his feet were now hooked in pop up loops on the board and the Gravlec had been turned right down but not off. Moving about on the board without the Gravlec being fully on, Jack could now appreciate the waxing that Ron had applied to the surface. In the shop it had appeared very runny on the board, like custard, out here in the coolness of space it was now slightly sticky. It was like walking in socks over day old spilt juice on vinyl, sticky was a word that might not cover it, but was perfect for the wax.

Jack had also decided that he did not want to fall off or step off again and reasoned that if he could feel the waves of gravity washing over him, it would remind him where he was. It might also make it easier to fly around the seeds, if he had a vague idea where they were coming from and going to.

After a while Jack realized that the Gravlec in the board had been canceling out the external pull of gravity, as he was now being first pulled one way and then another. He then wondered if the sensor system might be able to show him, on his visor display, where the waves were coming from and going to.

Jack was sat cross legged on his board with an open mouth, just staring around with a big grin on his face. He looked so relaxed that Claire on the bridge of the War Catcher had to ask, as the floating image flickered slightly "is he actually alright?"

"His vitals are absolutely fine" Summer looked closer at the statistics on screen and frowned, twitching her whiskers "there actually almost too fine" she commented.

"What do you mean?" asked Claire.

"Everything is in the green and nobody else's vitals are in the green, especially as they near the maelstrom!"

They stared at Jack sat on his board, looking like he had not have a care in the Universe.

After a few minutes of staring at him Claire asked "what exactly is he doing?"

"Funny, I was just thinking the same thing" said Sarah as they watched him sway slightly on his board, she had finally settled on a face for her floating orb representative and was quite pleased with the results. Claire turned to face Sarah, because her voice sounded different somehow and found that her orb now had a very attractive female face floating just off its surface. The face reminded Claire of many famous faces from the bygone era of black and white film, partly because of the attractive lighting but mostly because it was black and white.
Sarah noticed Claire looking at her with an expression of mild confusion on her face and replied "colour is so overrated."
"Actually it quite suits you, is that your own face?" asked Claire innocently.
Summer and the Commander looked sharply at one another with Summer then asking Claire "why would that be her own face?"
"Because it looks human and not one of those made up faces you see in a video game."
"Actually it is my face" or rather it was my face thought Sarah, now was not the time to talk about her own problems.

    Claire shrugged to herself, she had a feeling that there was more to Sarah's answer, maybe one day she would find out, she was more worried about Jack at the moment and his care free attitude, which was more than likely going to get him killed rather than finish the race. Turning back to face the table Claire asked again "so what is he watching?" she asked curiously.
"Right I've done it, I've hacked his suit ..." said Sarah happily.
Both Summer and the Commander gasped in shock.
"Don't worry, nobody will know and now we can talk to him properly now and not just listen" said Sarah sounding rather pleased with herself.
Gaining control of there mouths and vocal chords, eventually, the Commander asked "well how, we were always told that was impossible?"
"Is it?" asked Sarah innocently.
"And I don't care" said Claire "before we talk to him, can we see what he's seeing please?"

    The image that appeared floating in front of them over the table at first glance made no sense or nonsense. It looked to be a whole series of mildly waving vague white lines, that occasionally crashed together creating waves, whirlpools and vortexes of spinning circular lines that swung off at all angles and speeds. It was how Claire would have imagined whirlpools meeting in the sea might have looked, if they had been generated by an eighties retro style computer graphics display. The only problem she had with her comparison of whirlpools in the sea, was the fact that water had a top and bottom, whilst space did not, it was a case of anything everywhere and Jack was calmly meandering through the middle of it all.
"What's he watching, exactly?" asked Claire.
"Gravity" said Beth simply.
"Well it appears he's turned the Gravlec sensor system into a graphical display!" said the Commander with a little light awe in his voice.
"Is that legal?" asked Summer.

"Well, apparently no one knows" said the Commander waving his hand at Dun and Don, the two presenters were now both not chatting and sitting open mouthed, staring at the display of Jack's view into space. It appeared that everyone else had been curious at Jack's carefree attitude and more or less at the same time as Claire, asked to see his view.
"There appears to be a lot of discussion across the Hypew right now about it" said Summer looking at a rolling news screen floating just above her own bridge screen.
"How did they get Jack's view?" asked Claire "I mean Sarah had to hack it didn't you?" she asked turning around looking for Sarah's floating orb to address her question to.
"They don't have to hack anything Claire" said Sarah from somewhere near the roof of the bridge "if you remember you were all fitted with Shams and he was brushed with Filmament, there just using that."
"Is that allowed or even legal, I mean isn't that an invasion of privacy or something?" asked Claire with dawning worry.
"Actually in the event of a crime being committed, they can do pretty much anything they want!"
"But he's not committing a crime, is he?"
"Honestly they can do pretty much anything they want anyway, after all this is totalitarian space" said Sarah.
Claire then started to actually look worried and wondered if anybody had been looking at her, looking at herself, whilst looking in the mirror this morning, at herself.
"Don't worry though, they are fair and do inform you of there intentions" finished Sarah.
"Before or after they've viewed the footage?" said Claire whilst shuffling uncomfortably on her seat.
"Whenever, obviously" said Beth "if Jack was worried at all he could have turned the Filmament thing off anyway."

    Claire looked back at the floating display, showing the overlaid images of whitish wavy lines. The whole thing reminded her of some space faring game from back in the eighties. The main difference being that the lines were smoothly animated, clear and frankly a whole lot of them, as far as the eye could see actually.

    She wondered whether this was really the best way of displaying the coming together of various gravitational forces on an helmet visor. After listening for a moment at the surprise in the voices of the two presenters on the Wire surf channel, discussing the legality and the usefulness of being able to see the forces at work. Claire realized that no one had done this before, or at least if they had, they had not used it in a race before. Apparently now the general consensus was that this was a fantastic idea and in no way should "erm, Jack isn't it?" asked Dun, be penalized.

Even if Jack now lost the race, he would be remembered as they slowly talked there way into making his display a requirement for future races, for various reasons. The Quellz lines were then opened to the public to ask whatever they pleased and someone pointed out the health and safety benefits of seeing what you were surfing. Which then sparked a debate about viewing figures dropping, because of the lack of fatalities, until another caller pointed out that it was actually more exciting to see the surfers actually surfing in a surf competition!

Claire half listening heard the debate rage gently on, there was a little statistics screen nearly buried in the lower corner showing viewing figures. The number had grown so big since the start of the discussion, that it no longer fitted in its box and simply read as a zero with an E in the middle.

Chapter 37 : Simply Black.

     Claire returned to Jack's view of the cosmos, watching the ever contracting gravity waves depicted as crinkly white energy lines. They gradually got brighter and thicker as they neared there source, like a series of overlapping balloon like bubbles slowly deflating, creating waves and crests.
"Pretty ain't it" Ron remarked to Claire.
Claire nodded and asked "but what are we actually seeing?"
"Hmm, well really it's a simplified view of gravity" he replied, careful to not put too much tongue between his sharp teeth as he talked.
"Simplified!" said Claire waving a hand through the wavy line display.
"Yep" Ron saw her face was not pleased with his answer, he sighed, took a deep breath through the gill vents on the side of his neck and continued.
"The top of each wave we're seeing is the strongest bit of an ever decreasing sphere, if we reverse the process then it would look like a sun exploding."
"A sun exploding?" asked Claire disbelievingly.
"In reverse, think of it as being like dropping a bucket in water but slowly. The water pours in at the same rate from around the circle, creating slight ripples and waves. Now if you added another bucket to the water nearby, they would react with one another and may eventually even go into orbit around one another. Between the two buckets the water would turn into waves and ripples, with crests and drops. Jack is basically watching and surfing, up and down these massive contracting waves but all around him, in every direction. Now imagine that the bucket starts to rock gently from side to side, caused by the other bucket and its waves, then the water would pour in at different rates creating odd gravitational drift."
"Is that why things spin?" asked Claire slowly.
"I was only putting things in terms you might understand, think of the bucket as a whirlpool, more of as a hole in the ground that everything is falling into, but from every direction at the same rate."
"Like a black hole?" asked Claire.
"No."
"What do you mean no?" said Claire feeling her temper rising.
"Because most 'Black Holes' are actually Sun's" said Ron in a tired tone of voice.
"Sun's?" asked Claire with mild disbelief.
"Yep, they've just got such a strong attractiveness, that not even light can escape, simply black" replied Ron, who then walked away and stared out of the viewing window.
Claire nodded to herself, Ron was wrong in her mind, after all she had watched enough science programs to think that humans had the Universe all worked out, did they not?

Claire turned back to watch the Wire. In the studio Don and Dun now had an external view that was showing Jack surfing up and down the once invisible waves of gravity. He could be seen maneuvering his board around the slower surfers, with there own tiny wave like gravity distortions making little circles in the line like waves as he passed by. The biggest deformation in the wavy lines came as he passed the seeds; if gravity was decided by mass, then these seeds must be super dense and full of materials to make life somewhere else in the cosmos.

It was an amazing thing to watch and was giving Claire goosebumps, as well as the public in general, because now the external recording systems had been updated and slowly they were showing more and more details of the waves. If Jack was not famous before he would certainly be now thought Claire, the only debate she had was whether she was feeling proud or jealous of him.

'M hour' as Jack was calling it, seemed to approach surprisingly slowly, which was a mixture of relief, frustration and worry. The great maelstrom was something that it appeared everyone in the Universe was interested in, with viewing figures reaching ridiculous levels and a number so large on Jack's own display that he was not sure how you even said it.

The view of the waves all around him and from every object, had been not only a massive distraction but a bonus. It had enabled Jack to avoid the super speedy seeds, the ones with too much interest in getting to there destination no matter what the cost, by the simple method of showing him there bow waves. They were of course not really bow waves, in effect it was there mass influencing the background gravity waves criss-crossing space, creating a drag wave and forward thrusting bow like wave.

On Jack's visor display there had been a number that had been slowly counting down from something around the ten thousand mark, occasionally it jumped down several places at a time. Now it was bouncing up and down over the hundred mark, it was only as he was now looking at it, really for the first time, that it enlarged and the words 'race position' flashed up over the top.

There were also several tiny numbers that had just appeared in the lower half of his visor, as he looked at them they read as apparently being distance to targets. One of the numbers was traveling towards zero at a fantastic rate, it was only when various spark like collisions occurred right in front of his eyes that Jack worked out what the counter had been for. The main maelstrom event had started, so to speak.

Out loud Jack said "oh goody" in a slightly sarcastic tone to no one in particular.

Claire watched on the bridge as the various camera angles from the race showed all manner of near misses, explosions, sparks and obliteration's of not only seeds but surfers as well. It was actually as advertised she thought, a real maelstrom.

Generally there was so much going on at this time, that people simply selected the rider they were interested in and let the system follow them along until they could not any more. The camera would simply then move on to there next favourite surfer, continuing the cast as if nothing had happened.

Claire was appalled by the reactions of everyone and even the creatures in front of her that she might loosely call her friends.

"Why doesn't someone do something?" she asked in general anger.

"Well, about what?" asked the Commander curiously.

"The pointless deaths for a start ... do they not get remembered in any way, does no one care?" Claire could feel her anger rising.

"Well everyone who enters knows the risks, I mean everyone watches the ten thousand and even if they don't they know what it is."

"But there dying out there!"

"Well it's there choice to enter" said the Commander.

"But..."

"Well, there are no buts in this race, millions apply to take part and only ten thousand get to race."

Claire eventually saw that she could never make them see the pointlessness of it all, but at the same time was nearly understanding where they were coming from.

It was a distraction from the war somewhere out there in the blackness of space; there had certainly been war made on Earth for long enough and with great enthusiasm towards one another. At least the aliens were fighting aliens and not each other.

Claire had no idea what the life to death ratio was in interstellar war, guessing that the odds were probably much worse than fifty-fifty, like it was in the ten-thousand race.

She was angry with these aliens, at no point had they actually really explained any of this, especially to Jack before the race. Claire stood leaning on the table, trying not to seethe with anger. The only way she found her anger started to diminish was when she concentrated on Jack, who she now really wanted to help, which was an unusual feeling for Claire with regards to Jack.

"Is there no way to help him?" she asked pointing at Jack, who was currently knelt in a bowling like pose, after having thrown a ball down an imaginary alley.

"Well no, not really, we could talk to him I suppose" said the Commander.

"Do it" replied Claire.

"Well we can, but what would you say and additionally the Pugs are probably going to be listening in on him."

The one thing she had not thought of was what she would have said to Jack, really she just wanted him to know that he was not alone.

"But why are they listening in?"

"Well I'm not saying they are, it's just that more than likely that they could be" said the Commander pointing at a surprise news alert that was flashing away across the Wire cast.

Chapter 38 : Seedy Fireworks.

Jack was enjoying himself immensely, there was no other way to describe the way he was feeling right about now. The thrill of being chased was definitely not something he enjoyed, but the thrill of the evasion and near miss was something he never knew he could enjoy, in an imminent death kind of way.

The first few blackened minutes, when the outer edge of the seeded umbrella came together, had been amazing, like cupped hands clapping slowly and sarcastically together. The difference being that the cups were made up of millions of flung seeds, where the seeds brushed or even crashed into one another there were massive coloured sparks sent off into space. It was how he would have imagined fireworks might look like in space, he had moved in slow shock from a bowling pose to sitting on his board enjoying the show. After a while though it did get a bit monotonous, which was something Jack had never thought he would ever have said about any firework display. The main difference here he supposed was the inevitability of it.

Sat on his board enjoying the show it slowly dawned on him, as he watched, that the exciting display was getting closer, much like two lovers meeting for an embrace. Although if this was love, Jack was reluctant to try it.

As he watched the seeds colliding with one another, exchanging there material on the way, Jack could see the occasional burst of smokey light, as surfers used there board thrusters to weave in and around the things. He was still undecided whether it was better to wait for the seeds to finish there clasping movement or simply to try and dive through the middle.

What eventually made up his mind was the shock of Claire whispering in his ear "hi Jack, don't say anything and don't look surprised."

"Too late muttered Jack" for the longest moment Jack looked shocked and Claire sighed inwardly, then he regained his composure a little and asked a bit hesitantly "why?"

"Well, can he get away with that question?" asked the Commander in Jack's ear.

"I actually believe he can, if you would be quiet and let me talk" said an annoyed Claire.

"Well okay, no need to be so surly" replied the Commander in an offended tone.

"Jack listen very carefully, on all the broadcasts here, there's a news alert talking about a hole in the circle of seeds. The only thing is, its right in the centre of the things coming towards you."

Jack nodded, turning around he started to look for a wave going in his direction, eventually finding one that might be the right size and angle.

"Now your thinking how are they able to see it" continued Claire "well they've now got a long range mass distortion viewer" Claire paused, she knew what Jack's next question would be.
"There calling it the Grams, Gravity Ranged Analyzer of Mass and Space" Claire rolled her eyes, even without seeing her face Jack knew what she was doing, just because of the tone of her voice.
"Basically they've stolen your gravity wave distortion viewer, the range on there's is longer though, so you won't see the hole down the middle until your nearly on top of it. If you understand just nod will you?"

Jack dutifully nodded and started to boost his board, aiming carefully for what he approximated for as the middle. Then his speed nearly doubled as he caught a near perfect distortion, that carried him straight at the middle of the traveling seeds.

After what seemed like hours, Jack could finally see the waves created by the seeds in front of him. The wavy lined display some how resembled a sink plughole, mainly because of the twisting mass of seeds distorting space. Occasionally he might see the things as black dots against the sun Olsol, most of the time they were invisible against the blackness of space as they blocked the light, forcing the majority of surfers to slow right down. Unless of course you were behind the seeds, then all you could see of the seeds was a multi-coloured sea of copper reflections, which would have reminded Jack of cottage kitchen utensils hanging from low beams.

Jack had caught up with the last group or was that the first group of surfers, reigning in his bucking surfboard next to a fellow rider; he recognized Juices form.
Juice might have many tentacled arms and legs, he had still put on a human like space suit though, two arms, two legs and so on. But because he was bendy in such ways that no human ever could be, unless they had jelly for bones, he sat with his legs folded across through and around one another, like a knot tied in a rope.

He appeared to be in deep contemplation, which Jack blatantly ignored as he pulled overhead and tapped him on the helmet. Juice jumped and would have left the board were it not for Jack and his board being directly above. Jack spun about for a few moments, then when he had the board back under control again glided over to Juice, along side him this time and not above.

Juices visor became opaque, for the first time Jack saw real anger in someone's eyes, followed by an invite appearing on his own visor.
"What the creator did you do that for?" said an angry Juice, whilst rubbing his helmeted head.
"Sorry I was only saying hello" apologized Jack.
"Why not just use the com, after all that's what's it there for?" said Juice angrily shaking his head.
Jack opened and shut his mouth a few times, honestly he had forgotten how the thing worked, even after Juice explained it again he still did not quite get it.

"In future remember, it's Vowke com, Juice one, okay?"

Jack nodded slowly, he then asked Juice if he had any way of copying his visor settings to his own helmet. After a few short minutes Juice was sat back down on his board again with an open mouthed expression of awe. Juice was staring around the cosmos in wonder, mumbling something about "bums" as far as Jack could make out over the coms.

Juice suddenly shook himself, which was really effective on someone with basically jelly for a body in a space suit.
Turning to Jack, Juice said with a smile on his tentacle enriched face "go time."
The glare on Juice's bear like teeth was blindingly bright, as a gap briefly opened in the surrounding seeds and Olsol shone through, Jack sighed to himself.

Jack and Juice turned to face the final closing of the clam like seed shell all around them and aimed there surfboards for the supposed freedom of the wave reduced centre.

It worked an absolute treat for a minute or so, until the crashing, bashing, rebounding and explosive detonation of the seeds caught up with them and then all bets were off.

Claire had tried using her blinkers for watching the race, the novelty of really nearly being there had worn off quite quickly after being chomped on. It had felt like being used as shark bait somewhere out at sea, close to midnight and that she was the one being fished for.

Claire was sat on a comfy stool on the end of the viewing table, sometimes standing worriedly and other times sitting worriedly. The Commander and Ron sat at the other end, pounding the viewing table on quite a regular basis in excitement, as a selection of near misses or chomps played across the floating images.
Summer stood with Jane quietly, both were looking surprisingly worried, staring out of the viewing window into space together and straining to hear what was going on behind them.
Beth and Sara sat opposite one another, staring intently from the floating images of various racers and then back down to the space map in the central table.
Sarah's little white ball flew slowly from one end of the bridge and back again, like a tennis ball being slowly bounced from one side to the other, whilst leaving a trail of apparent vapour.

Then a final red 'warning' played across the various screens, images and adverts, informing everyone watching that the final big act of the maelstrom was about to start and probably finish to.

Everyone watching across the various galaxies were holding there respective breaths, it was after all what everyone had tuned in to see. Some had likened it to being caught in a 'mincer', whilst others compared it to a 'blender' and then there was Claire's personal favourite, the 'boozer.'

This final word from Dun and Don, before she had to switch them off, was the perfect description she felt, of a drunken bar fight representing the maelstrom. Claire knew that no particular seed wanted a bar fight, there accidentally brushed collisions 'that's my beer your drinking', caused shortened fuses 'thought it tasted like your wife.' Leading to minor explosions 'suck this fist, sucker', with material being thrown off in every direction 'catch my glass chummy.' Shortly followed by the sassy waitress stepping carefully and lightly through the chaotic melee, she represented the bopping, diving and swinging surfers. At least that is how she interpreted Don and Duns raving and waving descriptions anyway.

Jack and Juice with the help of there visor displays, were finding it much easier to dodge and dive through the gaps around the seeds. Although they were still regularly dodging ricocheting seeds and there constituent parts, it was nowhere near as hairy as elsewhere in the cloud of seeds. This was soon picked up by the other surfers, who saw them not swaying about quite so much on there boards, sitting might be a better description and soon maneuvered over to find out why.

Finally after several minutes they exited the main body of flying seeds, there were now only the occasional seeds trying to catch up, others which had run out of puff and some still zipping away. There were still an awful lot of seeds about but at least Jack could now see the stars and there final destination.

The Sun Olsol sat in front of Jack like a shiny orange dinner plate, with a little white box flashing off slightly to its left on his visor. Focusing on the white box brought up a view of the plant moon orbiting Olsol, making Jack jump as it suddenly filled his vision like a custard pie thrown at him by a supposed humorous clown, only for it to stop just before it slapped him in the face.

The plants that had thrown the seeds into space were now showing there full flowers and were a blooming glory to behold. Jack once again felt like his breath had been taken away, he had never been one for flowers or anything green for that matter, especially on his dinner plate, here the flamboyant view was otherworldly. Which of course technically it was.

"Be careful Jack" said Juice in Jack's ears.

There previous conversation whilst in the cloud of seeds had been a mixture of 'look out' and everything else ranging from 'what's the weather like back home' to 'how many girlfriends!' It had been a bonding experience, which Jack had never experienced before, even when he had gone on camping trips with various childhood organizations for that express purpose. To be fair to the organizers of those camping trips, at no point had they put him in a life threatening situation, maybe if they had he would have a friend. Here he was now having befriended a total alien and he found it liberating, like he could tell Juice anything. It then occurred to him that the one thing they had not discussed was there sexuality or even what sex each of them were. Jack was prepared to leave it at that, admittedly it bothered him like no ones business, like having a scratch he could not reach but maybe it was something he did not need to know after all.
"Be careful of what?" asked Jack looking around.
"The race is really on now."
"What do you mean?"
"That white box on your visor?"
Jack nodded after turning back to face Olsol's plant moon, the white box was tiny and in fact really only looked like a square dot, until you focused on it. It hung just in front of the moon, which in turn was slightly over to the left of the sun.
"That's the finish line and before you max out your boards boost, remember this, you might have won once you cross the line but you've got to be alive to claim the prize."
"What does that mean?" asked Jack to the now receding view of Juices board and back.
Juice had closed his coms or chat or whatever it was called and had left Jack high and dry, so to speak.
"So much for bonding" muttered Jack accelerating his board with a mixture of boost and some really big nearly crushing wavy lines of force.

    It looked to Jack that as they neared the star, a mixture of gravitational forces were at work from almost every direction. What they were creating were massive waves of force, which were moving so much like crashing waves as they met that he could almost forget he were in space. He kept looking back over his shoulder, watching the occasional surfer caught in an eddy and thrown away or on one occasion crushed to nothing by the cross forces. It was in one of his look backs that he saw another reason to get on with the race, the seeds that had left Newsol had shed or closed there parachutes and were being pulled faster and faster towards Olsol.

    Jack easily caught up with Juice, who gave him a little wave and a friendly nudge with his board. In front of Jack were several fellow racers that he could see, his race position on his visor was currently reading thirty two.

Within the next few minutes the winners and various losers would be decided, Jack had his fingers crossed that if he did lose today then he would not be in the body bag losers section. Which would probably be quite a small bag, as what would be left, would be mostly ash this close to Olsol.

As they cruised closer a white square gradually revealed itself to be basically a huge net next to the plant moon. Each corner of the net was supported by a small shiny silvery rocket shaped ship of some description, with its rear engine blasting against the pull of Olsol and the moon.

Juice then nudged Jack's board, with a muffled crackle he reconnected the coms and said to Jack "don't be rash in the dash to the finish."

"Because I want to stay alive?" asked Jack sarcastically, thinking 'now he wants to talk!'

"Because although the net is the finish line, the first across ain't the winner, it's the first ten to be in the net when the timer gets to zero."

"When does the timer start?"

"As soon as someone crosses the net."

"And what happens if more than ten people are in the net when the timer runs out?"

"There never has been" replied Juice with a curios tone to his voice.

"And what happens if there are fewer than ten people in the net when the timer runs out?"

Jack appeared to have a knack for asking questions that had never been asked before, maybe that
was why there planet had been blown up thought Juice with a shrug, whilst ignoring Jack's continuous questions.

Juice and Jack were both leaning forward on there respective boards, having in Jack's mind sorted nothing out about the finish, apart from the fact it sounded like a complete fix. Both were now concentrating, trying to gauge speed against stopping within the net finish line. They had also made up several places by now, not by going any faster than they already had been but by just being careful.

Several racers had already been removed or eaten from behind by some of the faster seeds from Newsol, Juice and Jack with there proximity force monitors, or Grams as the Hypernews networks were calling them, were able to simply roll out of the way. Other seeds that had not made it away from Olsol's gravity were in decaying orbits everywhere, it was like trying to fly through a cloud of hungry asteroids with attitude problems. The surfers traveling too fast in front of Jack and even some from behind who zipped passed, had crashed into the near invisible seed belt. When they hit a seed above the liquid silver like neck band, they disappeared from view with an imagined chomp like sound effect in Jack's mind. Crashing behind the neck band though, they disappeared like they had landed in quick sand, slowly disappearing from sight with arms, legs and other appendages waving eventually in suffocating defeat never to be seen again. Some seeds seemed to smile, burp and even expel some form of light gas from somewhere at the back end, providing a short burst of speed in no particular direction after there light meals.

Claire had watched carefully two racers right at the front, they had been so desperate to beat one another to the finish line, that they had been boosting against one another so much that they sailed right through the net. Neither had touched the sides or lines making up the net, both realized at the last moment that they were not going to stop, so both decided to loop around the plant moon. Not so much a bad decision but a short one; with steam pouring off there space suited backs, they started to circle back around the moon.

After releasing there seeds to fly through space, the flowers on both moons had then sent out long colourful jelly fish like tendrils into space. These ridiculously long arms Jack and Claire had thought were just the used ends of the seed hurlers. They were right but when a surfer was within only a few meters of an arm, as they circled the moon, they were grabbed and drawn into the middle of the flower never to be seen again. Jack watching too, imagined a set of jaws chomping up and down on the surfer. Claire saw what actually happened was actually much worse, involving a paralytic, a probe, a glue like substance and lots of stomach like acids bubbling away merrily deep inside.

This was obviously the way the plants on the moon caught there seed bounty, leaving Jack and Claire wondering how many other Sun's had such close orbiting moons.

Juice and Jack slipped in between and through the seed belt, with Jack imagining the seeds screaming at them as they went by, with the occasional jaw snapping at him like it were a kitten chasing after a fly.

Then they were through the belt, with there visor displays showing twelfth and thirteenth positions, Jack wondered how soon before the timer would appear. No sooner had he thought it, then one of the surfers flashed through the net finish line and clipped one of the white lines making up the net. The timer then appeared on the inside of Jack's visor, this time rather than being just a spiral with lines across it and gradually depleting in sections, it also had a number in the centre.
"A hundred and twenty what's is that?" asked Jack out loud.
Jack had not been expecting a reply and nearly jumped off his board when Juice replied "a hundred and twenty seconds to be in the net."
Of course he had forgotten that the coms were still open with Juice, then Juice started to speed ahead urging his board ever faster.
Jack slowly chased after him, neither of them were going that fast, compared to the surfers flying passed them like they were nearly standing still.

    The viewers watching throughout the galaxy were almost as one leaning forward to stare at there respective screens, displays and Vowke systems. This was the most exciting bit of the ten thousand race after all. The last few minutes of the race had the equivalent of the last three days of racing, surfing, madness and tension condensed into two minutes.

    Claire wanted to shout at Jack and did so quite extensively, with language that not even an adult should use to describe a low life criminal or even an high life criminal. The aliens onboard the War Catcher had actually had to look some of the words up to find out there meanings and then had looked suitably shocked afterwards. The reason for her manic outburst was simple, where Jack had nearly been in the top ten, he was now in the lower thirty and dropping faster than a pair of pants at a skinny dipping party.

    Whilst the others had been checking up on her use of language, Claire had been doing her own research on the plants. After a while it had occurred to her that Jack must be going slower for some reason and if it was not to wind her up, after all he could not see her reaction, then it must be for another purpose. Eventually she found it in a small video clip on her Quellz.

    Claire watched carefully as long tendrils threw there charges into space, they then hung around looking like the dangling arms of a jelly fish, rather long ones and rather large.

Initially they were thought to be some form of communication between the two plant moons, then someone pointed out that the plants could neither see one another and did not appear to have any eyes to do the seeing with. The reason for the far reaching legs risking being burned by their sun was the hunt. Each wavy tendril thing was coated in an highly reflective silvery green tinged like substance, with all manner of coloured suckers and spiky bits wobbling around to stay in the shadow of the arm. These snake like arms were used by the plant to catch the seeds sent from its counter part from across the solar system. The only problem being that the tendrils cannot tell the difference between a seed, ship or errant surfer.

An advert had been scrolling across the bottom of the screen and now the clip had ended something about it had sunk in. Claire touched a finger to the scrolling bar and was immediately taken to a video like advert. A man walked up to the camera in a white suit, black shirt and white tie, he had the whitest teeth Claire had ever seen, seeming to reflect all the light in little star effects.
When he spoke it was in an almost heavenly tone "dead? Mortally challenged? Deceased? No problem, you can watch the ten thousand from beyond the wall, simply subscribe to Dead Hype and we'll take care of it for you."
Before he could finish his advertising spiel the Commander swiped his hand slowly over the screen, the Quellz went blank and Claire looked up with tears in her eyes and a seeming question hung in the air.
"Well no, no you can't" Claire made to ask a question of the Commander "and you really don't want to talk to anyone from the other side, ever."
Claire got some control over her mouth and brain, finally asking "can we actually talk to the dead?"
The Commander shook his head in a 'no' fashion and then confused her by saying "well yes."
"Then why can't I do it?" asked Claire with rising anger.
"Because whomever you want to talk to is dead" said Summer gently.
"So?"
"And you would have to be dead to talk to them!"
"That's not what he said in the advert."
"Well no it's not but in order to talk to the deceased you either have to be dead or walk the Wall" said the Commander.
"Walk the wall?" asked Claire feeling exasperated.
"It's the name given to the gap between us and the dead Universes" replied Summer.
"The dead Universes?"
"You know, we flew here using the gap or split?" said Summer slowly.
"Yes?" said Claire feeling confused.
"There are all types of Universes and just as many gaps separating them, the ones the SUDs use are the more reliable ones between Universes but there are an infinite number of others. Some of which are the Universes where the deceased live, but in order to get there you either have to be dead or walk the Wall, or the gap."

Claire looked infuriated and she could see that they were not going to say anything else because either they did not know or would not say. This was something she would have to look up on her own; when she did do a quick search on her Quellz, all it came up with was the advert for 'Dead Hype.'
There was a link at the end of the advert, which lead to an information page which actually had no information on it, like local government really. The page was asking for her personal details without asking why and what she would get out of it. So she put it out of her mind and turned back to follow Jack in the race. If the worse came to the worse she thought, she could always sign up and then ask Jack what happened from the Wall, whatever that was?

Chapter 39 : Painful Timing.

Jack and Juice were not racing along to make up the places, they had calculated the timing for when they would reach the net, and hopefully at the right speed. They were aiming to not flash by and disappear into the blackness of space, or the red of the sun or even be grabbed by a plant to be digested slowly. There was a counter on there screens and visors, telling them how many were sat in the net and even though dozens had flashed by, only two were actually hanging in the net.

Watching the bright white net grow bigger in front of him, Jack could appreciate how big the thing was. Each twisted rope like length of the net was about two meters in diameter and glowing white like something really glowy. The gap between the ropes making up the net was an healthy two meters as well, making the thing look like an ornate very large square paper doily. The other odd thing, rather than being round like a rope, each arm of the net was actually square in shape and looked to be made of thick ropes. The net was easy to see, it also had ample hand holds in the twisted net of square rope, so Jack was wondering how the surfers kept missing it, being how large it was.

It was only when his Gram's display started to show the twists, turns and eddies all around the net that he saw how they kept missing there grip. It was actually a wonder how anyone managed to be in the net when you saw the turbulence all around it. The lines moved around like a sea of twirling ribbon dancers, getting knotted, stretched, pulled and released in all manner of odd shapes and patterns.

They were down to the last ten seconds when Juice and Jack reached the storm like waves of force hanging around the net. It looked to Jack like waves breaking and cresting over rocks on a beach, very very big rocks. Jack though was not going to end up on a beach or rock, but floating with some speed into a sun or even worse being consumed by a plant. If push came to shove, Jack had already mentally prepared himself to aim for the sun; being plant food, no matter how rich a source of food he might be, was not something Jack wanted to experience for any length of time.   Juice and Jack chose to ride in on the same attractive wave, with both aiming to use the crashing forces coming in the opposite direction to help slow them down. They quite literally flew towards the centre of the net, with Jack slightly ahead, reaching out a hand to grab at an edge. At the same time a wave crested around the net, pushing him between the ropes and into the gap. Jack leapt from his board, with arms flailing wildly he grabbed and stroked the rope as he slid around it. Then on an edge he found something to grab and held on to for dear life, which was entirely accurate. There was a loud cracking in his head and a shot of pain in his shoulder so strong that he yelled out. With what felt like gravity pulling him towards the sun through the net, he had his eyes clamped shut and no feeling from his elbow to his fingers. Jack started to worry, the type of worry that involved swearing, cursing and the possibility of escaping bodily fluids. Then the pain somehow increased, as there was another yank across his entire body, from his damaged arm to his ankle cord. It was how Jack would have imagined being on the rack might feel in a torture chamber, if one hand were being stretched against the opposite leg by a smirking servant of the gloom, or a bank.

"Wowee, that was close, thanks Jack" came the joyful tones of Juice, over Jack's helmet comms.

Jack chose not to answer, currently he was trying not to be ill in his helmet, the pain across his body was very intense and showed no signs of diminishing as Juice hung on below. Jack then felt his body being stretched even further, as he looked down he saw Juice had started to clamber up Jack's board and then the cord and finally his leg. Juice looked like a super enthusiastic kitten clawing his way up a trouser leg, chasing after woollen balls.

When Juice was finally holding onto the net, he gave Jack a grateful bang on his helmeted head, which finally forced Jack's fingers to let go of the roped net edge he had been holding onto. Juice grabbed him as he started to be pulled away and yanked him round into the net; suddenly there was something solid under his back and Jack passed out with a thankful sigh.

After what felt like a few seconds to Jack, he opened his eyes and was surprised to see "Claire?" he asked, standing over him. Panic set in for several moments, he sat up in bed looking around wildly; after three days in a space suit and helmet, to suddenly find them gone he started to choke on the fresh fragrant free air.

A female human looking nurse ran into the room, wearing the traditional white garb but tastefully tailored and outlined in blue, she took one look at him and slapped him gently across the cheek.

The look of shock and surprise on Jack's face had robbed Claire of the verbal abuse she had been going to give him for frightening her, now sympathy had set in for him as well as a bright red mark on his face.

Still looking a bit wild around the eyes Jack asked "what happened?"

"What's the last thing you remember?" asked Claire sitting back down in a chair.

The nurse was stood examining a free floating screen, hovering just off to one side as Jack looked at her and the nurse asked "how are you feeling?"

Jack decided to answer the nurse first, after all he had done the mental bodily check, which appeared to show that all the vital limb bits and bodily accessories were in place. Because you never knew if something was damaged beyond repair and had been carefully removed.

Jack did another check, this time using his hands to determine whether all the relevant bits were attached and one very special place had not been damaged.

During his check Claire groaned and said "you don't need to check that Jack, especially in front of me!"

"Maybe not but it's for my peace of mind after all."

"So how do you feel?" asked the nurse again as Claire shook her head.

"Actually I feel fine, a bit achy maybe but other than that I'm okay."

"Good, we'll do one more check and then you can go" said the nurse smiling to herself.

"Right lets get on with it" said Jack with enthusiasm, the one thing he had never liked was hospitals, this was not because they were horrible places, it was just people tended to die in them. At least that was what he had always thought as a child. Now being an apparent adult, he knew they were there to help in an emergency, with staff that were the most caring in the world. Still people went in to them though, generally to die, because obviously they were really ill in the first place.

The nurse pulled out a white Quellz and held it up for Jack to see "I've got to pay for your services?" he asked in disbelief.

"Of course, you didn't think this was free did you? The very thought" and she laughed heartlessly.

Jack was then given his Quellz by Claire, he flicked it around and found his bank details, proffering it towards the nurse. The nurse put her Quellz next to his and after a few seconds he looked at the display which showed a bill for several million crowns.

The figure then changed to display the word Ice, the nurse started to apologize with tears welling up in her eyes, she then made a run for it out the door, with Jack and Claire looking after in surprise.

The Commander was just walking in the door when she ran out, bashing him to one side, with Jack and Claire listening to her make an burbling apology as she ran off.

"Well what did you do to her, tell her you were fugitives?" the Commander laughed at his joke.
"Actually nothing, I went to pay my medical bill and she just ran off!" Jack was still holding his Quellz out, the Commander looked down at it and smiled with his whiskers shaking in mirth.
Jack looked at his Quellz after he saw the Commanders face and asked "what does Ice mean then?"
"Well it means Insurance Care Everywhere."
"So?" asked Claire.
"Well basically if you have, shall we say an accident anywhere in the galaxy, you are covered for anything and everything to do with it."
"And she ran out the room crying because Jack's insured?" asked Claire.
"Well to get that kind of cover you will have to be valuable to the galaxy beyond measure or your richer than crick."
"You know that doesn't mean anything, right?" asked Claire and the Commander just shrugged.

    Jack had not really been listening to the discussion, he had been more interested in checking out the rest of his body and the room. Being that he was in an alien hospital for aliens, he had been expecting something different from what he was actually lying down in.
The room was not white but a pleasant cream, it had an open airy feeling and look to it, with pictures of alien landscapes hanging on the wall and a window that Jack could see the sky out of but nothing else. There did not appear to be a television, screen or any form of cord to pull in the case of an emergency, although there was the floating screen the nurse had used hovering above his head. There were also various plants dotted around the room, presumably they were the ones supplying the pleasant odour.

    Jack asked again, sounding more confused than normal "what happened?"
"What's the last thing you remember?" asked Claire again.
Jack paused for a moment and replied slowly "being stretched and Juice slamming me into the floor."
"Well the floor was the net, the timer had just reached zero, with you the last one to be accepted into the final rounds" said the Commander rubbing his furry hands together and his bendy thumbs doing a little pleasure dance.
"The Commander here had a bet on you being in the final ten" said Claire.
"Well we knew he would be okay and I won the bet didn't I?" said the Commander defensively.
"Yes, we did" said Claire starting to tap her foot on the floor and staring hard at him "you did intend to share your winnings didn't you?" she finished.
The Commander was just about to ask 'why would I do that?' saw her expression and just nodded instead.
Jack looked round the room again and asked "so what happens now?"
"Well the final race was in four days" said the Commander.
"That's not very long" said Jack.

"Well you've been unconscious for nearly three."
"Why?"
"Well body repairs, obviously. We need to get you back out and familiar with the track as soon as possible."
"So how does this work, because I'm sure there are more than ten surfers in the final?"
"Well there are forty two in the final."
"Forty two! Why forty two?" asked Claire.
"Well the first thirty places come from races over the last five turns, ten places are allocated from the ten thousand and the last two places are from the viewers vote" explained the Commander.
"Viewers vote?" asked Jack.
"Well it's a popularity thing that also keeps viewers interested, it also means that anyone from the ten thousand or from the previous five turns of racing can be brought back, by popular demand."

   A slight chill ran down Jack's spine, he had a feeling about someone who might be invited to be in the final race, they generally wore black and had a knack for attempted murder. He just had to hope that there were so many cameras covering the race that nothing would happen.

Chapter 40 : Donna's.

Back at the hotel apartment Jack walked in last with an exaggerated limp, then looked round in disbelief. There were so many bags lying on nearly every surface, that it was more like a spoiled child's shopping spree than an adults room.
"Your limps gone Jack" pointed out Summer as he walked further into the room.
Jack spun round, he had hopped through most of the bags and was just about to stare out the window at the flying traffic, completely forgetting about the sympathy vote he had been aiming for. Thinking quickly he replied "it takes a few seconds to warm up, and then it's fine."
"Nice save" murmured Claire.
Jack had not seen her sat on the sofa, surrounded and almost covered by bags, with a gentle smile playing across her lips.
"Shop much?" asked Jack sarcastically.
"It's just a bit of fun Jack and you honestly would not believe the size of the shopping centre here, it makes London look small!" replied Claire.
Jack shook his head in disbelief, for a start where had his invite been but then he had been out of it for three days. Still, to come back to a room without a bag-less surface in view was quite a shock.
"Well I'm sorry but the girls worked out that if you succeed, this" the Commander waved his hands around at the bags "will not have happened, so they've just been enjoying it."
"But they won't remember it and what happens then if I don't succeed?" asked Jack.
"Well they'll have quite a bill to pay, won't they ha ha ha?"
"And more landfill no doubt" muttered Jack to himself, looking at the near endless supply of bags with clothing and whatever else the women had bought.
On lifting up a bag to find a seat, Jack saw on the bottom of the bag was a green spot, experimentally he pressed the spot and watched the bag turn itself inside out. The contents of the bag, which was a strange mixture of undergarments, were dumped on the floor and the bag collapsed into a white sugar cube sized lump on Jack's hand. Summer came barreling across the room in an attempt to collect the clothing before anyone could see it, to Jack that meant little. Because of her rash action though, the Commander found himself forced to look, then he managed to look embarrassed, he even seemed to turn a rosy red colour as his skin glowed through his fur and he turned abruptly away. Obviously whatever had landed on the floor was slightly provocative in some way to a Raifoon, or maybe even illegal.

Jack inspected the cube and popped it in his mouth, it did actually taste of sugar, just like the one from the picture palace where he had first witnessed the final race. It dissolved just like a sugar lump should in his mouth. Claire was stood in front of him looking on in surprise, she had wondered what the green spot was for and had just thrown the bags in the corner of her room.

Claire recovered quickly and said to Jack "Jack, you really have got to visit The Sall before we leave." Claire was actually tugging on Jack's sleeve with the look of a shopaholics desperation on her face. It was like watching a child having a sugar come down and demanding more without trying to sound desperate and failing miserably.

Jack prepared for his final race by allowing Claire, or more precisely being ear battered into being dragged by Claire to The Sall. She had tried explained how big the shopping place was, it was only as they did the visitors circuit in a flying car above it, which took nearly twenty minutes at high speed, that Jack started to appreciate how big it really was. Initially there had been no design structure that Jack could see, it was only as they flew up into the clouds to gently float back down, that he saw the spiral like design of The Sall shopping centre. It was made up of blocks and squares, with buildings of every shape and colour you could imagine, some appeared to be floating whilst others actually looked like they were moving around slowly, like lazy afternoon boats on a mill pond. The overall shape of the shopping centre though, was of a series of spiral like forms made up of long arms of more spirals. It reminded Jack of the spiral counters that he had seen in the ten thousand race, counting down to the start. He had a feeling that whomever the designer had been, they had some form of fetish for spirals, circles and a Mandelbrot.

There was a guide on his Quellz, which Claire had shown him, it was more like an interactive map showing your position in a county or zip code. Then there was a list of products, services and well everything else you could imagine, with shops listed by type, species and collections. There were areas that just sold footwear, you might then find the same branded shop in another area but selling a bit of everything else. The competition between shops was fierce, with the population generally shopping by companies they liked rather than price, because price was not always everything, with service before, during and after appearing to be important. There did not appear to be any specific layout or plan for the shops, it was like the shops had just opened where they wanted to and by sheer luck the same trades were in the same place.

After four hours of being shown or dragged around, Jack had had enough. The first hour had been amazing, with anything you could think of being for sale, from gloves with mucus pouches to air vented socks. From teleporting technology to growing your own talking shrubs, there was not one thing that these shops did not cover. Jack even saw an advert for a popular fizzy drink from Earth. He did ponder whether this far out from Earth the company actually knew about it, then he started to laugh, after all there was not a lot they could do about it out here. How would they claim copyright infringement or intellectual property damages hundreds of thousands of light years from Earth, when they struggled to do it across borders. Additionally the planet did not exist any more and therefore neither did the company lawyers, which was probably a bonus for everyone concerned.

Jack had always wanted trainers or sneakers, as some shops called them, that were bright red and had a white lightening strike running down the side. When he asked his Quellz if any shops sold such a thing, he had watched the list scroll up the screen for several seconds. There were just so many variations on the product, even when he touched an image of exactly what he wanted, there were still over fifty shops that sold the thing and even then the price variation was within only ten percent. What the shops mainly seemed to advertise was sustainability and service, at least when they were describing themselves.

There was even an option to design your own product with each shop and have it manufactured. Jack got quite excited on finding this possibility, until he scrolled to the bottom, finding the list of Terms and Conditions so long that you would need a life time to read them, let alone understand them. Nothing changes he thought but still it was nice to have the choice.

Then Claire found another clothes shop she had not seen before and disappeared inside, with Joan and Summer being supposedly dragged along behind. They both pantomimed over there shoulders that they did not want to go, but Jack saw there grins in a reflection in the glass door.

He had wondered why Joan and Summer had been so quick to offer support in his hour of need, stepping in to say they would come along and offer advice. Obviously shopping was a universal female trait, at least in Jack's mind it was. The one thing he was curious about though, was where the money to pay for it all was coming from?

"Your lucky there not trying to make you over" came a gravelly voice from behind Jack. He jumped up from sitting on the stone bench and spun round.

The bench he had been sat on, surrounded a flower arrangement that had reminded him of the plant moons orbiting the two stars. There had been several of these flower beds every fifty meters or so, everywhere they had been. It was like the designers knew that the male of the species was going be bored somewhere and might as well be bored sat on a bench surrounding a flower bed rather than stood up.

The voice had come from somewhere on the other side of the exotic looking flowers, Jack cautiously walked round one way whilst the voice apparently walked around the other way saying.
"I bet you can't believe how much there spending, with the excuse that it's something for you when you cross the finish line" the coal tar coated voice carried on talking, always being just the other side of the flower bed, even when Jack stopped and quickly doubled back.
"It makes me wonder if they know the real you, Jack?" said the thorn scraped voice.

Jack stopped chasing round after the voice, there was not a real Jack to know of, as far as he was aware. What you got with him was what you got, an average looking chap with a slightly protruding belly, with the potential for a receding hair line and not much else. So what this person was on about, Jack was at a loss to explain. The voice he was listening too though did sound like his would be murderer from the ten thousand.
"What is it you actually want?" asked Jack, after all if they had wanted Jack dead then there had been plenty of opportunity lately, death by boredom being the favourite at the moment.
"As you may remember I told you every death should have a purpose, a reason if you will."
"And?"
"With each attempt it gets harder for me to get to you, which I find intriguing and annoying in equal measures. It also started me wondering why anyone should want you dead in the first place, so I began my own investigation into my anonymous employers."
"And is this my last question?" asked Jack, it was like the person demanded attention by not quite finishing what they were saying nearly all the time.

There was no reply to Jack's question and no footsteps in either direction around the flower bed, then he would have jumped high enough to reach the golden moon as a feathered hand landed on his shoulder, belonging to Joan.
"Jack you really have got to stop flapping your hands at nothing" said Joan "it seems to drive Claire quite mad for some reason."
"It's a girl thing" muttered Jack just a little bit too loud he noticed, as Claire turned round from staring at the buildings and gave him her 'don't you dare steal my stationary' stare from the office.
Jack was wondering whether he had asked his final question yet of his would be killer, or whether they were genuinely intrigued enough to leave him alone awhile longer.
"Are we all shopped out?" asked Jack, quickly brushing his shoulders again like swiping at dust hugging spiders.
"Yes, but we are here for you" replied Claire in a sweet tone.
"How are we here for me?"
"Isn't there anything you want to buy?"
Jack thought for a few seconds and said "jet boots, invisibility cape, previous lottery numbers maybe, oh and trainers."

"There are shoes here that never go out of fashion!" said Claire excitedly.

Jack was just about to add another item to his list but had to ask "how do they never go out of fashion?"

"Because they can change shape, colour and design."

Jack thought about this for a moment and then asked "so why would I want to buy them, I mean aren't I supposed to go back in time and save the Earth from annihilation not shoemageddon?"

"They wouldn't be for you would they Jack" said Claire pointedly.

After a moment Jack saw where she was coming from and said "but how would I explain them to you, how exactly do I tell you, when I'm back on Earth, that not only am I from the future, past and present but these shoes I'm giving you, for no reason whatsoever, change shape to be fashionable?"

Claire gave Jack an annoyed look, not because he had done anything wrong exactly, more he had just killed the romance of the moment, the excitement of being given something amazing.

Looking around Jack asked "why are there so many shops that sell shoes if you only ever need one pair anyway?"

"Price Jack, price" said Joan.

Jack did the usual thing men do in this situation as realization dawns and made the traditional 'ah' I understand noise and shrugged his shoulders.

"Anyway I couldn't take anything back with me could I?" asked Jack.

Claire looked at him like he was being silly and asked "why not, you could make millions?"

"Apart from anything else I'd have to try and explain, or make up, where the things came from and I would imagine even the simplest thing bought here might have some odd material in it, that isn't available on Earth. Then there's the design and even the construction of it. Don't get me wrong I'd love a pair of jet boots" Jack finished, appearing lost in thought.

"Why not jet under pants too?" asked Claire with mild sarcasm and then answered her own question with "because you go Nomando, don't you Jack?"

Jack looked at her completely lost for a moment and then asked "Nomando?"

"Your telling me you've never heard of Nomando?"

"No, I've never heard of Nomando before!"

"You know, it's Natural Commando?"

Jack paused in answering and then asked "how do you know what I do and don't wear under my clothes?"

"Lucky guess" said Claire quickly and looked away.

Claire's annoyance was starting to fade, after all he was right, anything she bought could not go back with him, it might change the timeline in some drastic way. Mostly though because in there previous relationship dynamic, she would have never accepted a gift from him, under the assumption that it was a trick or bribe of some description. Basically it would have been binned without any thought, still it would not hurt to try.

"Please take me back something" pleaded Claire, doing her best to make her eyes large and soulful, like the last puppy in the basket.

Jack gave in with a sigh "one small item then, that I can fit in a pocket." Claire thought about complaining as she had a whole suitcase or five back at the apartment, but after thinking for a moment she had a brief insight that he might be in a hurry at some point. She reached round to a pocket and pulled out a small case about the size of a pack of cards. The case was a dark grey but quite reflective and engraved with some odd shapes.

Jack took it carefully with a vague recollection of seeing something like it before "a selector, memory box thing?" he asked.

"Yeah I know, you need a pair of blinkers for them to work but I really like the tribal designs on it" said Claire.

Summer turned to stare at the box in Jack's hand and then caught Joan's eye as they both looked at one another in surprise, neither of them could see the tribal engravings.

Jack put it inside his jacket pocket as they walked, after wearing the suite for space for so long he had opted for loose fitted blue jeans, a sky blue t-shirt, white trainers and a black leather effect jacket from his dressing room. There had been all kinds of other stuff offered to him that was supposedly fashionable on this planet, but he wanted something he felt comfortable in, with a touch of the new. Sarah had been quite sarcastic about his choice of clothing, which had of course made him want to wear it even more. The only thing he had never owned before or had the stomach to wear, was a leather effect jacket and so at the first opportunity he had grabbed at it with both hands so to speak. He had been quite self conscious when they had stepped out of the hotel, with maybe a touch of worry hanging on his shoulders.

The vehicle that had sat on the pavement in front them, as they had exited the hotel, had looked to Jack like a black limousine, with some key features missing like wheels and doors. The underside had been rather a smooth looking grey when he had glanced underneath, as they approached there did not appear to be any doors or windows, it just looked like one large car shaped lozenge. Joan had swiped a feathered hand at a panel that had appeared as they approached and two openings had fizzed into view. From Jack's point of view it had looked like one of those really expensive bullet proof vehicles which had just had its doors removed. The interior windows were all darkly shaded with cream coloured seating and panels. As they had stepped inside, with only a slight stoop required for Jack, the seat he chose started to change from a bean bag shape, to a comfortable almost lounge chair as soon as he approached it. He had sat down with a sigh and looked forward to speak to the driver. Of course there was no one there. In the front of the vehicle there were three seats of the blob design with a white boarded black panel, running under the front window. It was all stylishly curved and moulded into the vehicle but was currently blank. After they were all sat down Joan showed Jack how to use the taxi. You simply placed part of your anatomy in the floating green box that appeared in the middle of the cabin and spoke your destination or selected it from a drop down list. Jack had smiled at the any part of your anatomy bit and had been about to make a rude comment but had caught Claire's eye, or had Claire caught his eye, either way he had kept his comment to himself.

Now as they decided to leave the shops, the black limousine almost seemed to just appear on the pavement in front of them. Jack wondered briefly how it had known they wanted to leave but swiped his hand at the panel anyway.

Once they were seated down comfortably inside Claire asked "where to now?"
Jack actually had felt the need for a lie down after being dragged round so many shoe shops, but what he actually wanted was some food.
"Restaurants?" he asked, placing his hand briefly in the floating green box and looking at the girls.
By now Jack actually thought of these creatures as people, with the added bonus that female shopping habits appeared to be the same the Universe over.

The three ladies got into a discussion about what things they could eat and fancied, showing pictures to one another on there Quellz and describing in depth what they tasted like. To Claire this meant little as her only experience of food had been of the self service F-code machines.
The taxi then took off and headed into the bright afternoon sky.
Joan asked "so which restaurant are we going to?"

Jack was looking down through the floor of the taxi, it was like the security detail truck from before the ten thousand race, as soon as it took off the rubber floor and walls had became see through. Jack had been surprised at the lack of flying traffic in the blue sky, he had expected some form of lights or lanes to be floating around in the air. There was nothing and only the occasional vehicle could be seen, he surmised that they must generally stick the roads.
Joan asked again and Jack replied "somewhere called Donna's."
"Donna's?" asked Summer and Joan together in surprise.
"Yes, it had the highest rating, and food I vaguely recognized"
"But, and this is great Jack, but Donna's you have to book months if not years in advance?" asked Summer still talking in an awed tone.
"Dunno, I just asked for a table for eight!" replied Jack simply.

They continued there flight in silence with both Summer and Joan doing furious searches on there respective devices, trying to find out how Jack had got a table at a restaurant that not even the most famous film stars could get into without a reservation booked months in advance.

Jack meanwhile was playing with his Quellz, after watching various aliens using them he had noticed that they could be bent. As he pulled one corner against the other, the thing could be reshaped and sized and slapped around his wrist like a bracelet. After losing his phone, he used the word 'losing' loosely as he thought of Claire, he was curious and rather pleased with his new phone the 'Quellz.'

Donna's was the most revered eatery in the known galaxies, there was only ever one in each system and it was always in or near a shopping centre or mall. It was also always, without fail fully booked, so how Jack had got a table there was anyone's guess. The ladies furiously searched the Hypew to find out how he had done it and for the life of them could not quite work it out. Although Summer did have an inkling, which she was not prepared to share.

There black limousine like taxi floated up through some scudding clouds and swiftly moved towards a traditionally shaped UFO. It floated in all its silver and chrome glory, with a rounded dome and bottom, with a slowly rotating disc splitting the two parts. There was a tiny sliver of a spire linking the Unidentified Floating Object to the ground, which looked quite small but actually had a ten meter diameter at its narrowest point. The taxi flew round once and landed with a gentle slide on the slowly rotating disc, with its doors fizzing from view like a wall mosaic falling apart.

There were vehicles of every possible description parked on the disc, some square shaped, others spherical, right through to paper plane looking and made of clouds. They were taking off and landing all the time, mainly vertically with one occasionally dropping over the side to the shops below, like a swallow. The one thing Jack did notice about all these ships, was that none of them looked cheap. They all had the look of being decidedly expensive in some way, like the difference between a pork chop and glazed pork chop.

As they stepped out of there ship, car flying taxi combination, a soft red carpet slowly rolled towards them from the central dome. As soon as they stood on it the whipping and whistling of the wind passed to a gentle summer breeze. Jack stepped on and off the red carpet several times, experimenting with being half on and half off near the end. The effect was like standing half in and half out of an aeroplane at three thousand feet, being cold, exhilarating and scary, all at the same time. Eventually Claire turned round and pulled him along, moving after Joan and Summer.

They had themselves wandered slowly down the carpet, having never been in a Donna's but heard about it almost in wonder from friends who had been. It was almost with reverence that they stood waiting where the red carpet met the entrance, waiting patiently for Jack and staring at the doors.

For some reason this worried Claire, Summer was always in a hurry with Jack, either pushing him along as he stared about like a tourist, or sighing as she had to explain something to him yet again. So to have her wait for him without a glare, tap of foot or rude word was a bit of a surprise. Then again even Claire found she was looking with slight wonder at her surroundings. The weird thing was, so far they had only seen the outside of the restaurant and even she felt awe at being at such a place. It was like the feeling you might have got on walking into a church, then noticing that it was actually a cathedral of such size, design, beauty and mainly coloured glass that you were lost in marveling at it. It seemed to ooze contentment some how.

When all four of them were stood by the doors, it suddenly dawned on Jack and Claire that these were proper doors. These were the sort you had back on Earth, the ones with handles and hinges. They were big grey double doors that matched the colour and design of the floating restaurant.

Jack looked at Joan and Summer just stood in front of the doors, they looked like they were waiting for something, so Jack took hold of a handle and opened a door for Claire.

Claire walked through and said "thank you" to Jack, he then waved the two other ladies through, who just gave him a funny look. All the doors they had come across so far had opened either automatically as you walked towards them or required the touch of a panel to slide, fizz, melt there way open. Jack had a smile to himself as they walked past him, obviously these two had not come across a normal door for a long time, if ever. It did make him wonder why, who or what had designed and built this floating restaurant.

As they stepped inside they were met by a wooden pedestal with a leather bound ledger sat open across the top. Behind the ledger stood a bow tie wearing black suited man, with a twirling moustache, slick backed hair and probably the obligatory shiny shoes hiding behind the wood thought Jack. When he opened his mouth to greet them he sounded like he was talking down to them with lofty disdain from a great height, with a tone that also suggested they were not worthy to enter his establishment, let alone eat in it. He had a smile that appeared to be stuck to his face rather than glowing from within, which struggled anyway to be seen behind his waxed moustache. So far he had only glanced briefly up from the ledger, after allegedly greeting them.

Jack peeked over the top of the pedestal, the man had a Quellz resting in the ledger, with some holographic game being played above the screen, it looked like a cross between chess pieces made from rocky boulders and a Go board. The exception was that that they appeared to bleed green goo as they battled for control over the board with axes, swords and hammers.

The man then asked in his oily accented English and a bored tone "reservation?"

Claire replied "yes" in a tone that suggested imminent pain if not answered.

Apparently this man understood her hidden warning immediately and looked up sharply but asked in the same bored and oily voice "hand?"

The two actual humans exchanged questioning looks, until the stuffy man pointed at a green box like panel in the ledger.

Jack made one of those 'oh I see' noises and placed his hand over the panel.

The reaction from the oily man stood behind the ledger was immediate, he stood straight up from his stooped position, like someone had put an iron rod up his back with quite some force. Then he seemed unable to talk for a moment and gestured furiously for them to follow, as he smartly stepped away. He actually seemed to be almost running from them, whilst burbling madly into his Quellz at someone.

The walk through the restaurant was pretty much as Jack and Claire would have expected in any expensive place back home, the only real differences were the clientele and the interior.

Aliens of any and every possible description were sat, floating, standing or lying down in there own heat haze like bubble. When Jack asked Joan what the bubbles were for, she said something about the bubbles being the perfect environment copy for the individual species to eat in.

Then there was the interior itself, it was a complex mix of American diner, traditional British village pub and vaulted cathedral. There was no place like it that Jack or Claire had ever seen, how it was all blended together in so much wood and masonry was anyone's guess.

The ledger man eventually led them to a large spiral glass staircase in the middle of the room, as they stepped onto it each step moved slowly upwards, like river flowing in reverse, you could stand and ascend slowly or step up and go quicker. Jack of course experimented going in both directions, with the step he was stood on going in the direction he moved but only that section, he stopped after getting some stern looks of disapproval from Claire.

At the top of the stairs the bow tied man directed them hastily towards a table in a raised barred off area, with the potential for curtains on a ring on either side. What caught Jack's attention though was the view out of the window, the restaurant floated just above the clouds, giving the impression that you could go outside and have a fluffy candyfloss walk across the sky.

They all sat down on the wooden looking chairs and were all pleasantly surprised when the things started to mould to there various postures. Then a Gekk appeared chaperoned by some members of the Green Army or Tree Pixies as Jack thought of them, they happened to all stand about four foot tall. Then some of the green Drickers appeared bustling around the table, wiping surfaces, checking under the wooden table and other general cleanliness bits and bobs.
The Gekk moved one of its four fingered slate grey hands in a graceful arc towards the table and the two legged Tree Pixies stepped forward, presenting an actual cardboard like menu to each of them.

Jack had not realized how hungry he actually was, it was amazing how being dragged from shop pillar to shop post took it out of you and as far as he could see they only had a couple of bags between them. As he looked at the menu he heard a set of familiar voices, they actually seemed to be complaining about being in an expensive restaurant for some reason.
"Well thank you for the invite Jack" said the Commander in an sarcastic tone.
Jack managed to look suitably confused, for some reason he had assumed that booking the table for eight would have automatically invited the crew, which it apparently had. So why exactly the Commander was angry he could not quite quantify.
"What invite?" asked Jack smiling.
The Commander waved his hands dramatically "well precisely, you talk yourself into the most expensive and booked restaurant in the known Universe and then invite your friends!"
Summer said "your here now, so why don't you all sit down and we'll have a nice meal together as friends should."
Summer looked carefully at Jack, who was looking surprised at being asked anything and nodded in agreement. The nodding from Jack was mainly because this may very well be there last meal together he thought.

The Commander, Sara, Second and Jane walked onto the raised wooden dais and looked around for seating.

The table had been a wooden carved looking piece of solid Oak, as they started to move round to accommodate the newcomers, the table seemed to flow, like a cross between water rolling over a mossy rock and how you would imagine a tree might look if it was growing really quickly. Then more seating grew out of the wooden floor and they all sat down.

Jack looked round the table at his colleagues, the Commander and Summer were both twirling there tail like thumbs around the printed menus, staring and salivating almost in synchronized drips. Jane and Sara were sat with heads together, discussing quietly what they fancied on the menu. Joan and Claire were also sat chatting and pointing at the menu with Claire occasionally looking over the top of her menu at Jack, who was still staring around with an amazed expression on his face.
"You alright Jack?" asked Claire.
"Hmm, oh yeah I'm fine" came the slightly slow reply.
"Really, only your looking around like you've never seen a restaurant before?"
Jack was still slowly staring around as he replied "it's just that this is how I would have imagined my restaurant would have looked!"
Claire took a moment to look around and replied "really, it just looks like a stylish pub to me!"

The Gekk walked slowly up to the table and asked in a polite voice what everyone would like for a starter, main course and dessert. It was only after Jack heard everyone start making there orders, that he realized they all had tailored menus in there hands.

They sat and chatted about nothing in particular, until they finally got round to discussing the race the next day, with Jack then noticing that Ron was missing. When he asked where he was, he was told that Ron was servicing his board with Beth and Sarah.

The food arrived and not only was it immaculate in every way, like it had been designed to excite there taste buds with an abundance of loving, it also looked, smelled, tasted and agreed with there bodies in every other way possible.
"That was amazing!" said Jack as he licked his dessert bowl clean, when he looked up chocolate dripped slowly from his chin.
"I've never tasted fish and chips quite as good, anywhere, ever!" said Claire, trying to not look at Jack and wiping her own chin clear of chocolate.
"It met with your approval?" asked the Gekk waiter cautiously.
"It most certainly did" said a satisfied Jack.
Coffees then arrived, carried on overly ornate silver looking trays, above the heads of the green coloured Drickers.
"We thank you for your pleasure and hope to see you again soon" they said in unison.
"Well, no bill" asked the Commander "to go with our coffees?" whilst looking at the silver plates for a bill of any description.
"You may see it if you wish?" came the slightly confused reply from the Gekk.
"Well yes that would be nice, before we pay it!"

Looking slightly confused for a moment the Gekk replied "ah, I see a test!"

The Gekk then pulled out from somewhere behind its back a large book sized tablet, when the Gekk swiped the screen it looked to Jack to be just a larger version of a Quellz.

The tablet was placed on the table and a golden glowing number slowly raised itself up from the flat screen, with small fireworks firing off, popping and whistling.

Jack asked slowly "seven thousand crowns, what's that in pounds sterling then?"

Under his breath, the Commander quietly replied "well around seven thousand pounds I think or ten thousand dollars at the previous exchange rates."

Jack gulped and said "I'm not paying that, I mean it was an amazing meal, the drinks were out of this world and the dessert was life changing, but seven thousand crowns for dinner, for the eight of us outrageous!"

The Gekk turned to Jack and asked "was something wrong with the meal?"

"No, no it was fantastic."

"Then I fail to see the problem" then with a slight huff he picked up the tablet and stalked away.

Looking slightly confused Jack asked quietly "is it paid then?"

"Well I don't know, but I think we should leave before any questions are asked, don't you?" the Commander asked of Jack, as he started to stand up.

Everyone nodded trying to be quick but not hasty in there bid to escape the bill.

    Just as they reached the exit Jack felt something tap him on the shoulder and turned round to find the obnoxious ledger man slowly kneeling down in front of him. He spread his arms in an apology, muttering near continually about family and needing the money, pleading to be allowed another chance.

After listening for a moment Jack smiled and said "nope", turned and walked to follow his friends to the door. The door was locked. There was no other way to describe it, it would not open and the main reason for this was the inch thick chain and padlock system sealing the door shut. Then the voice of the Gekk came from behind them as they stared at the door "the exits this way!" came the mildly sarcastic tone.

They all trooped towards the door on the other side of the dining room, passing the other diners smiling in there bubbles of food heaven.

When they got to the other door, the Gekk waiter turned to Jack and said "please don't judge us to harshly, we have been very busy with the staff shortages of late and I would ask that you reflect that in your report?"

"What report?" asked Jack.

"The owners report to the board!"

Jack was then handed a large black tablet Quellz with four questions displayed on the screen, at the top was written 'Owners Recommendations to the Board.'
Followed by four questions:
Were the staff courteous and polite … yes or no.
Was the food excellent … yes or no.
Would you come back … yes or no.
Keep this restaurant open … yes or no.
"Whose the owner?" asked Jack.
"You are, of course. What is this another test?" asked the waiter worriedly.
"Who are you then?"
"The manager" the manager was waiter replied in a tone of annoyance "and your the owner?"
"I own this restaurant?" asked Jack in a squeaky mildly panicked voice, after rereading the top of the super black tablet.
"You own all Donna's restaurants I believe" replied the Gekk
Jack gulped and said in a small voice "do I?"

   Jack had never wanted responsibility, he had wanted the wages that went with it but never the responsibility of owning and looking after the contents, staff and especially customers. It was in some respects his worst nightmare. Some people had bad dreams about monsters eating them from the toes up, pausing only to pick out an errant piece of bone stuck in there blood stained teeth. Jack's worst nightmare was owning something where he was responsible for things, everything's.
"How?" he asked.
"In the normal way I would imagine, now could you see your way to giving us a positive report and some more staff … please?" asked the Gekk.
Jack nodded in shock and pressed 'yes' four times. Strictly speaking he did not on the first question, the manager altered it in there favour, like most businesses do when dealing with people from head office, 'who need results!'

   They were then ushered out of the door and onto another carpet, this time it was coloured a nuclear grassy green, giving Jack the uncomfortable feeling that it was irradiating his nether regions.

   They all stepped into the black limousine taxi, Jack was in such deep thought and worry that he did not notice how the others were looking at him. They all knew Jack in some way, some had even known him for several years but none of them knew that he was an owner. The thought of Jack owning anything was actually quite worrying for most of them, just because of the lack of responsibility he showed at all times. After a few minutes into the flight Jack seemed to shake himself, probably believing it all to be a bad dream and asked "so where are we going?"
"Well back to the hotel, it's the big race tomorrow" said the Commander.
"And then you can tell me when you had time to buy a restaurant?" said Claire with slight anger.

Jack actually managed to look surprised and upset as he replied "I genuinely have no idea!"

"Before you get too angry with him Claire, try to remember that he might not remember. When we probed him back on Earth he had no idea what was going on", 'but filled the data storage' added Jane in her head, whilst exchanging meaningful looks with Sara, who just stared back.

It was not that Claire was really angry or disliked Jack, after thinking about it, she was actually starting to like him after all this time. No it was more that he appeared to have had a life somewhere else and how had he fitted it all in? The only explanation she could think of was a doppelganger or some twin or evil copy running amok with his life. It lead to the question though as too whether this was the real Jack sat in front of her. She looked at him closely, the way he moved and the answers to Joan's gentle questioning seemed to show that this was the real Jack. The same dopey answers and the nodding of incompetence. So if he did not own the restaurant, who did and if there was only the one Jack, how did he own the restaurant and not know it? She knew what the answer from everyone else would be 'it's in the memory probe', so she decided to do her own investigations. The first thing to do was question Jack at the earliest opportunity, which would probably now be after the race.

The hotel apartment was a mess, quite literally, if Jack had thought it messy earlier when he had walked in and found it full of randomly stacked shopping bags, now it looked like a ransacked shop floor after a garage sale. The only thing missing was the rummaging late night shopper looking for a last minute deal and there other halves looking for a way out, please.

There was a collective gasp from the group, followed by a voice saying "hello" in a pleasant tone that seemed to ring in the ear with pleasurable undertones.

Looking up they saw a figure silhouetted standing in the window, it looked like a Raifoon but as it turned to face them the shape subtly shifted. As it walked towards them it slowly changed its gait from a reverse kneed Raifoon, to become a knock kneed human.

The Commander was the first to react, reaching round to pull a very small but mean looking grey three barreled micro shotgun from somewhere up the back of his jacket. He pointed the six inch long device at the figure, which was now standing in the middle of the room amongst the strewn clothing, shoes and bags.

"Oh there's no need for that my friend!" came the imperious sounding reply to the shotgun being pointed at it.

"Well I beg to differ" said the Commander looking down the tiny sights situated on top of the micro shotgun.

The creature sighed heavily to itself, unclasping one of its hands from behind its back, it made a small gesture in the Commanders direction. A small coloured dart flew from the shadows from across the room, passing easily wide of the Commander. As it passed though it fired a small hook, which pierced the micro shotgun and dragged it out of the surprised Commanders hands. The dart then stuck in the wall behind, with the micro shotgun dangling below like the unsure wag of a dogs tail.

"Who are you?" asked Jack curiously.

Waving his hands in a florid gesture and bowing to acknowledge them all, the creature said "I am Olgas Faid and I'm very pleased to make your acquaintance."

"A Furrykin! I thought you lot were banned from Nerth?" asked Summer teasingly.

"Oh we have never been banned from this place, merely asked to obey the rules."

      What followed was an exchange of meaningless arguments, that quite obviously was not going anywhere and carried on for several minutes. First it swung one way and then the other, with Jack soon realizing that neither side was going to give in or prove the other wrong.

      He simply stood back from the situation, more accurately he sat down and looked carefully at this Furrykin. This was the same one from the broadcast or cast he had seen earlier, before the ten thousand race, the one that had an eyeful of camera. The colour appeared to be the same, with reddish brown fur tingeing on the verge of ginger. The main difference he could see, compared to the other aliens he had met, was that the creature seemed able to change its shape at will. As they talked, he could see the creature looking closely at all of them. As the argument went backwards and forwards it seemed to slowly refine its shape, to be more in line with a human but still furry like a Raifoon. It looked like it was trying to appease all parties by finding some common appearance that they would find less threatening. Maybe this was some kind of defence mechanism, or a way to put them at ease, by lulling them into a false sense of security before then snapping there necks. Whatever it was Jack was impressed, the others in the room kept having to fall back on old arguments whilst the Furrykin was able to find new angles to speak from.

      Finally the Commander looked at Jack and asked Olgas Faid "well what do you actually want with us and why did you destroy the room?"

"First of all the room was already like this when I arrived" Jack looked around the room, he had not seen anyone else, the dart had come from the shadows though. Then something tickled his neck again and he swiped at it like brushing aside a cobweb.

"Secondly I'm here to help Jack" Olgas said this with satisfaction, as if a final argumentative point had been made.

"Well help Jack with what exactly?" asked the Commander.

"To win of course!"

"To win what? The race tomorrow? Why would you want that?" asked Summer.
"So many questions and so little time to answer them all, but I am offering my assistance to win the race tomorrow and if not the race at least to gain possession of the trophy."
"Why?" asked Jack.
"Why what?" asked Claire.
"Why does he want me to have possession of the trophy?"
"Well it's to fix there mistake isn't it?" said the Commander with realization, looking with surprise at the Furrykin.
"Actually it's to fix yours and your Councils mistake in destroying the Earth" said Olgas.
"But why would you want to do that" asked Jack "surely you wanted Earth destroyed?"
Olgas managed to look quite shocked and then replied "we never want anyone to die in our name and especially not your species, after all why would we want to destroy a species that has helped us so much?"
The non-humans gave Jack and Claire some dangerous looks, but mainly Jack "we haven't helped you, have we?"
"We thank you very much and that is why I am here to help against the backdrop of other wars" said Olgas.
   "Your having second thoughts about this, aren't you?" whispered Summer to the Commander, as Olgas talked slowly to Jack about the Universe in general and all its wars.
"Well it does make you feel like a pawn on a very big board, in a bag containing all the other boards and being shaken by some very large hands. But no, I'm not having second thoughts because we need the humans and there abilities."
"What abilities are those: to mislead, to be mis-sold and my personal favourite to be stupid?" hissed Summer who was feeling highly annoyed for some reason.
Sounding quite offended the Commander replied "well I don't expect you to understand but I do expect you to follow my command."
"Which technically doesn't exist?" pointed out Summer.
"Well this may be true but I have never steered you wrong and in this case it is better that you don't know all the facts."
Summer made a noise that sounded like someone blowing a raspberry through a tube.
   By now Jack was bored of hearing about the far off wars in the Universe and how the Furrykin could cure them all, mostly by eradication of one form or another. It seemed they had a general view that all wars could be avoided if creatures simply got along better, by believing in there one Universe theory, or else. The trouble was, it was the 'or else' that was the problem for the other inhabitants that lived in the Universe.
"So how are you going to help me win or rather get my hands on the trophy?" asked Jack finally interrupting the monotone war lesson.
"It's probably better that you don't know" said Olgas.
"Plausible deniability?"

"Exactly" replied Olgas, mentally adding a question mark at the end.
"But surely this conversation counters that?"
Olgas Faid stood up from sitting down on his chair, walked to the door, when he got there he turned round and said "what conversation would that be?" and walked out the door.
"Well that went well" said the Commander after the door closed behind Olgas Faid.
"How so?" asked Claire.
"Well, we're all still breathing for a start."

Chapter 41 : Race Much.

"Don't look down" came Juices voice, in a conversational tone to Jack's ear.
"Huh, what?" asked Jack.
"When the blue line appears, don't look down" repeated Juice.
"I've seen the fuzzy blue line before you know" replied Jack thinking back to his earlier lessons in the gap.
"True you might have done, but I'll bet it was in the gap and not running through the middle of a planet!"
"What difference does that make?"
"If you look down you'll find out and then you'll wish you hadn't looked down!"
Jack shook his head in disbelief "so your telling me to not look down at something, that I have to look down at to find out what I'm not to look down at?"
"Precisely!"
"That's got to be the singularly most unhelpful thing I've ever been asked not to do."
"Just don't look down is all I'm saying."
"I've got to now haven't I?"
"Make sure I'm not behind you then when you open your visor then" said Juice.
"Why would I be opening my visor?" asked Jack.
"To let something escape mainly" came the simple answer from Juice, whilst making gagging gestures at Jack.

They had got in early to the stadium and then been given a map of the course for this term. It only varied slightly from the previous races, but different enough that it was a challenge and similar enough that the viewers would recognize different corners and straights.

They were sat in what the race organizers were calling the green room. It was a very big room, with seating almost casually arranged for them to sit on or in and positioned in little groups. The room walls were actually grass green with no visible source of light, the ceiling was one complete mirror and the floor was a whole series of wooden rings. When Jack looked down at the floor, which he found completely mesmerizing, it looked like a series of overlapping and interlocking tree wood rings. It also had depth as you moved your head, like you were looking down at the entire length of each tree, at least at the point from where it had been decapitated anyway.

All forty two of the surfers sat in various states of worry and surprisingly they were no visible camera systems in this room. The smell of worry was everywhere to Jack as he wrinkled his nose, he then felt someone staring at him and was surprised to see Sara Orin Shavan staring at him with open hostility on her face.

It was only as he looked closer at her that he noticed the blonde hair and remembered the name from the Picture Palace, "Samantha Orin Shavan?" said Jack out loud. Instantly he felt regret at opening his mouth once again, not thinking before speaking, it was like a compulsion.
"Nefarious" muttered Jack and instantly put a hand over his mouth to stop anything else from escaping.
    The look on her face could have melted iron as she stared hard at Jack without saying anything. Jack on the other hand felt a compulsion to ask another question "do you have a twin?"
She looked away, leaving an angry feeling in the air.
"She doesn't talk much" said Juice quietly.
"No, I've noticed, it'll be the teeth getting in the way" now why had he said that thought Jack.
    Samantha Orin Shavan turned back to stare at Jack, then stood slowly seeming to unfold from her seat like an angry gymnastic lioness. If he could have Jack would have clambered over the back of his seat as she walked towards him, like he used to do when he was a child having watched too much scary television. The weird thing was that as soon as she had been face to face with Jack, the expression on her face had changed from pure hatred to a look of shock and then surprise.
Her head had then flicked round so fast that Jack was not even sure he had seen it turn at all, as she appeared to look for somewhere to drag Jack off too, for the inevitable kill he thought. She grabbed the front of his suit for space, dragged and then pushed him through a door labeled facilities.
    As soon as they were in the privacy of the white porcelain room and the door had fuzzed shut behind them with a 'swooshing' sound, Jack was let go by his would be assailant.
She then backed off against a wall, lowering her head to look at him like an ravenous predator, she had her hands and a foot placed on the wall behind her, looking ready to pounce at any second.
"I've heard about the likes of you" said Samantha in an oily voice.
Jack replied "all good I hope?" with a slight squeak at the end.
    Samantha turned her head slightly as if eyeing him up for something, judging which bit to start chewing on first went through Jack's mind. As is traditional for men in this situation and where she was looking, Jack had one hand on his privates and the other rubbing his neck carefully.
"What do you want?" asked Jack quickly.
She ignored the question, pushed herself lazily off the wall and slowly walked towards him. She was swaying in an hypnotic fashion as she sashayed towards Jack, sniffing the air as she approached him.
    Placing her hands on either side of his head and leaning against the wall, she leant forward and seemed to be tasting the air around Jack with her tongue. At any other time Jack may have enjoyed this amount of attention and sauciness, in his imagination though there would have been less clothing involved and far less passing of worry.
"Hmm" she said "it looks like you do know my sister."

"Yes, yes I do and she's a lovely person in every way" said Jack quickly hoping that she was of the same mind as Sara. He then added in a panic as he thought about it for too long "maybe not in every way, I mean I haven't experienced her in every way but in many ways she is lovely and probably in the ways I haven't experienced either she is lovely too. Not that I don't want to experience her in any way but I haven't, so I won't, wouldn't, but I might, if get the chance which I won't."
Samantha smiled to herself, listening to the rising panic in Jack's voice, it was cute in some respects how worried he was about offending someone he had only just met.
"Yes she is lovely, but it's not right that she has been keeping you all to herself, sisters should share there things, don't you think?" said Samantha with a pout.
"Yes?" Jack hazarded.
"Good, I'm glad you agree" said Samantha as she slowly leant forward to kiss Jack lightly on his lips.

  Jack had shut his eyes as she had leant forward, when he opened them again Samantha was on the opposite side of the facility, leaning against the wall like someone who had just been given an illegal high.
"That was amazing Jack, no wonder my sister has been hiding you away!" said Samantha, as she sensuously wiped her lips with a finger. She appeared to have considerably more colour in her cheeks Jack noticed, like she had suddenly found some spare rouge from somewhere.

  Along with her bright cheeks, she now had ruby red lips and was staring at his jugular; Jack was feeling oddly uncomfortable under her hungry stare. Jack's neck also felt slightly sensitive, like he had been bitten very gently by an overly friendly puppy, it was not an unpleasant feeling but nonetheless Jack gingerly touched his neck. After inspecting his fingers and checking there was no blood, he looked around the room as if seeing it for the first time.

  Apart from the white porcelain tiling there were three doors in the walls, he walked towards the nearest one and opened it to find a toilet. He had not known what to expect really, here was a loo that looked like any public convenience he might have found back on Earth, albeit infinitely cleaner.

  A few minutes later he came out from the stall and looked around for somewhere to clean his hands, Samantha was still leaning against the wall and pointed at a recess in the wall. Jack stuck his hands in the shoe box sized hole and felt his fingers tingle for a few seconds. Pulling his hands out they were dry and actually quite shiny.
He looked around the room and Samantha asked "what are you looking for?"
"It's just that this wasn't what I was expecting of a toilet?"
"It's a flexi facility!"
"Okay?"
"It adapts too what you expect of a toilet."
After a moments thought Jack asked "so you were expecting this too?"

"Nope, you were just first through the door that's all."

Jack was feeling ever so slightly puzzled as he looked at her, she was obviously not human and yet if memory served she had declared herself human for the purpose of the competition. Then she simply turned away and walked out of the facilities, with a sensual snake like walk, before Jack could even think of asking any more questions.

Back in the room that was mainly green, Jack noticed how the group of surf racers were gathered together. The nine from the ten thousand race were sat in there own little section, with others seeming to be sat in small groups of similar looking species. It appeared that even with all the apparent equality that existed, when left to there own devices, similar races of alien clumped together like bacteria in a Petri dish.

Samantha walked up behind Jack and said to him as she passed "sad isn't it?"

Jack sat down next to Juice and wondered exactly what she had been referring too, as there were so many possibilities, whilst swiping at some invisible tickling spiders on his skin.

Jack sat looking at the race course map on his Quellz, wondering out loud why they did not have any practice laps. Juice had simply replied 'it was all part of the fun.'

How exactly it was fun and for whom was another question that crossed Jack's mind, along with several others, especially the one regarding several parts of the course marked simply as 'danger!'

With there helmets off, Jack also struggled talking to Juice's tentacle enriched face. He found it difficult to ask anything of Juice, whilst looking directly at him. Not only was it the spider like legs around his jaws, but also the tiny creatures peeking out from his wavy spaghetti hair. Jack was sure one of the tiny animals was always waving at him and possibly blowing raspberries.

Jack was left with asking his Quellz, as Juice seemed decidedly unhelpful and uninterested in answering any more questions.

On his Quellz Jack finally found out what the danger signing actually meant. There were certain sections of the track that were a free for all, where anything went. The only rule that Jack could see in these sections, was that the racer had to stay within fifty meters of the floating blue line, whilst members of the public, who had paid a fee or lived on the route, could take pot shots at you, with guns! There were even prizes for the public for near misses and strikes on the racers.

There was even a super expensive 'VIP' section listed, that hinted at RUM's being made possibly available again this year, with much excitement in the text. With a sigh Jack remembered being chased by the Rocket Under Mines, hoping dearly they were too expensive this year. As they were a might difficult to outrun and could follow you anywhere, a bit like a fiery loose smell in an elevator.

When a pale faced Jack asked Juice about the danger zones, he replied with a sigh "don't worry it's only for audience participation, to keep the ratings up. There's even few paid cannons along the route, that people not here can fire for a fee from the comfort of there seat at home. Don't worry, the closest anyone got to hitting someone in the last race was a hole in the tip of there board!"

Then the double doors they had entered through opened and there respective boards were towed into the room by some very sassy looking aliens. Jack turned slowly and then his mouth fell open in apparent surprised horror. The one gently tugging Jack's floating board looked human, Jack guessed it was a Newman, admittedly a hugely attractive slinky swimwear wearing Newman.

Jack though would have preferred a female, especially after the wink he received, in some respects he was relieved to see a normal, if very muscly man, towing his board by a short yellow leash.

The large man walked off, taking the leash with him and walked out of the door with the other board towing aliens.

Jack stepped forward to collect his surfboard, which floated shrink wrapped; as is the case with shrink wrap, if you cannot find an edge then you can not find your item. You can see it all you like but actually getting to touch the real item, is like trying to undress your partner stuck in a latex suit when the zips jam whilst covered in oil. Next to impossible, involves a lot of perspiration, rude words and results occasionally in a visit to the kitchen for a knife or scissors. There were no scissors, knives or kitchens available as far as Jack could see.

Jack folded his arms in frustration, finding he was tapping his own foot very much like Sara and Claire did, he stopped.

Jack heard Juice ripping the shrinked cover off his own board and turned to ask how you got at it, then he saw a flash underneath his own board. There was a tiny near invisible, mildly different slightly faded line of the plastic wrap that ran around the edge of the board. Jack ran his fingers along it, finally he found a slight difference in the texture and started to pick at it. Suddenly he had a piece, an edge of the plastic see through coating in his hands, he would have whooped with joy were it not for suddenly noticing the floating circle in front of him. Rather than being a brown disc like the one at the start of the ten thousand, this one was the exact same green as the walls in the room. Jack wondered how long it had been hiding and recording the events in the room, then he wondered with a shudder if there had been a white one in the porcelain facilities earlier.

Kneeling and staring at the floor in apparent thought, Jack heard a dinner bell like sound played out in the green room, reminding Jack of the lumpy custard he remembered from school dinners. Still with head bowed he gave a shudder as the bell rang again, reminding him not only of the lumps but the skin that used to be allowed to form across the top of the yellow peril. It had been near impenetrable by anything less than a thermic lance, or high powered laser and all he had as a child at his disposal was the obligatory bendy, supposedly metal spoon.

He then felt a gentle punch on his right shoulder, presumably from Juice, when he did not react he felt his left ear pinched roughly and was dragged to his feet in a hurry. When his ear was finally released, Jack stood there rubbing it for a moment, turning to find Samantha stood gesticulating that he should look forward and then she bowed.

Still holding his ear which he imagined was probably redder than beetroot, Jack looked forward into the centre of the green room. In front of him stood a slender grey alien, it was human like in form but with a very thin frame, big bulbous white eyes and stood about five foot tall. On either side of it floated a couple of oversized footballs, one was black and the other a creamy white. The grey alien was wearing a rather regal and heavy looking crown on its angled pear shaped head. Currently it was naked, apart from the crown but Jack was not worried because there was not actually anything to see. The alien was a mix of all the slender grey alien pictures he had seen back on Earth, the only real difference was the height thing. In all the films and pictures back home, they had always shown the grey alien as being short and slightly ungainly in some way. Here was a grey alien, only slightly shorter than he was, when it moved it moved with grace and control.

The tree pixies appeared from the floor, clambering up through various impossible gaps in the wooded floor and clipped clothing to the grey alien. It was like watching an armoured shell being clipped together to make a golden looking gem encrusted "suit for space" said Jack out loud. Then a cape was finally added which seemed to click in place like magnets. The cape attached with a half moon circlet on the back of the suit neck, with a clip on either shoulder forcing a dramatic pose from the wearer. The inside of the cape was white, seeming to reflect back all the brash jewels and golden colouring of the 'suit for space', the back of the cape was a deep luxurious looking red velvet, trimmed on the edges with black flower like patterns.

Samantha said in a quiet voice and with some force to Jack "you don't talk unless spoken to in there presence."
Jack looked from the ridiculous cape and back to her and asked "in whose presence are we anyway and that's a more colourful version of this?" he said pinging a cuff with a finger on his 'suit for space'.
"Just be quiet okay" she almost pleaded, whilst slowly stepping off and away from Jack, distancing herself as quickly and inconspicuously as possible.
She then assumed a bowed posture and Jack noticed that all the other lifeforms in the room were doing exactly the same, in there own way.
"Do you see us as equals?" asked the grey alien of Jack, stopping briefly after each word, like it was taking a short breath between every one.
Jack looked down at the alien as it approached and replied "no."
"Do you see yourself as better?"
"No."
"Do you see yourself as superior?"
"No."

"Then why do you not bow?" asked the alien in that infuriating tone that people use who do think there better than everyone else, in effect they just have a certain degree of power.

"Why do I need to?"

"Respect!"

"Respect of what, an alien I've only just met or the crown of an unknown king I've never heard of?"

"Do you not know who I am?"

"Nope, refreshing isn't it!" replied Jack with slight humour in his tone.

"I fail to see what you find amusing?" asked the grey alien with annoyance creeping further into its voice with every passing paused word and sentence.

"Lot's of things actually, dogs on skateboards, cats falling into fish tanks and my personal favourite, pompous people failing to see there faults!"

"Are you suggesting I have faults" the alien sounded like it had never been told that it had a problem "and that I, am pompous?"

Jack stood in thought for a moment, at least he appeared to be in thought before he answered but really was just enjoying the moment. The little grey man as Jack thought of him was not all that bad actually, but Jack guessed it might be the first time anyone had stood up to him or even said no.

Before Jack could answer 'yes' the alien started to laugh, stepped forward and took Jack in a rough bear hug that caught him completely by surprise. In his ear the alien whispered quickly without pausing between each word "we've missed you Jack welcome back and good luck which you won't need!"

Jack was not only taken aback by the hug and quick sentence but by the reactions of the other aliens in the room, almost as one they had looked up, staring in disbelief at the grey aliens reaction to Jack. Then as soon as the alien let go and started to stand back, the others in the room went immediately back to staring at the floor and bowing again, like naughty school children expecting a canning for looking up teachers skirt in the yard as she swished by.

The first thing to go through Jack's mind was 'does no one want me to lose today!'

Addressing the rest of the room the grey alien said "as you all probably know, I am Prince Ajar of Marcoon" the prince paused for dramatic effect "and I wish everyone bi-quantum luck."

The prince then swept out of the green room, with his heavy hanging cape suddenly seeming to be made of silk as it billowed out behind him. The black and cream balls seemed to swing round to face everyone in the room. Jack stared at them curiously. No matter how he looked at them they looked two dimensional, like blank flat discs stuck on a wall. When they moved and you moved, it looked like you were looking at a picture of two platters added to the image at a later date. The only reason he assumed they were round, was because as they moved away from Jack they became smaller.

Jack felt a headache coming on as he tried to recall an image of the balls as they floated out of the room. After they had gone they seemed to leave very little memory of there presence, so like any normal person he pushed it to the back of his mind. The thing at the front of his mind anyway was the babbling of the other racers. They were all pretty much saying how amazing it was to be blessed by member of the Marcoon Royal family. Jack on the other hand simply remembered a pompous little grey man, who had been trying to make himself appear bigger than he actually was, to improve his stature in some way. Although how hugging Jack had helped him achieve this was lost on him. It did appear though as if another random alien knew him from some previous meeting and in addition, wanted to help him win the race. With all the help so far offered did he even need to enter the race, when he could simply walk up to the trophy and say 'thank you very much' and some how time travel? It would be quicker and safer than flapping through all the danger zones listed on the race map.

"What do you mean, danger zones?" asked Claire with a slight dagger edge to her voice. She was sat lounging in the most comfortable chair she had ever sat in and was finding it hard to concentrate. She stood up from the apartment lounge room chair in frustration, her mind working so sluggishly whilst she was sat in it. Almost as soon as she stood up she felt tired and annoyed for leaving the seat, being human she poked her tongue out at it.

She turned to face the Commander and asked the question again "danger zones?"
"Well yes" replied the Commander "look out the window and tell me what do you see?"
Claire glanced briefly out of the window and its continuous glass fronted view "aliens?" she asked, waving a finger at the various species sat on roof tops, ledges and leaning out of windows in anticipation.
"Well yes and do you know why?"
"To watch the race?" she asked carefully.
"Well yes and because we're in one of the danger zones" the Commander said this with a smattering of pride.
"Dangerous to us?"
"Well no, dangerous to the competitors."
"And this benefits Jack how?" asked Claire with her anger starting to reappear.
"Well you could wave at him" the Commander paused "or take a shot at him, it's entirely up to you really."
Claire paused a little too long in answering the Commander, after all Jack could be very annoying and shooting at him might be quite therapeutic. She shook her head to clear it of mildly dark thoughts, she just could not escape the gleeful thought of taking a pot shot at him.
"What if I hit him?" she mused quietly.
"Well to be honest the chances of that are tiny, minuscule even" replied the Commander.

Claire frowned and then asked questioningly "so why does everybody make such a big thing of the danger zones then?"

"Well because it's audience participation, in the biggest race in the galaxy and some of the audience prizes are outstanding, life changing even!"

"Like what?"

"Well if you manage to hit a board it's a hundred crowns, clip a rider you get a thousand crowns and if you knock a surfer off, you might get a hundred thousand crowns!" said the Commander wistfully.

"What about if a surfer dies?"

"Well that happens quite regularly anyway, but they don't want too many riders shot to death, otherwise there'd be no race would there?"

"So surfers do die in the race then?"

"Well yes" said the Commander matter of factly.

Chapter 42 : Start Your Engines.

Klaxon's sirens and all manner of whirling sounding things assaulted Jack's ears, they were then told to stand up in the green room. Jack the felt something moving gently under his feet, like the way you would imagine grass might grow if you were stood on a lawn for long enough, only much quicker. He looked down and saw a dull grey metal like platform, slowly moving under his feet from somewhere behind him. It was like watching a slow moving guillotine gently flowing across the floor, with Jack thinking that was how the trees below were decapitated and ended up as tree rings in the first place. When the metal sliding floor reached the far wall it did not stop, as with a gentle movement Jack felt himself being dragged along with it, as it continued through the opposite grass covered wall.

Involuntarily Jack tried to step backwards, away from being a bug splat on the wall, admittedly it would be a very slow splat given the speed with which they were moving. Looking down Jack found he could not move his feet, it was like they were glued to the spot and panic started to set in.

As he looked round frantically he saw that the furniture of the room was not moving, it appeared to have been placed so that it would not be in the way of anyone being dragged towards the green wall of doom.

No one else in the room was panicking though, Jack looked around with the green camera disc creatures floating about recording the event, in Jack's case just recording panic.

Then the first competitor reached the wall and simply passed straight through, whilst still talking to its nearest competitor. Jack watched there surfboards travel through next and with out fail not one of them looked worried, or as worried as an alien could look.

Samantha was stood just in front of Jack as they approached the wall, with a mischievous look at him she did a little pantomiming as she passed through the wall. Along the lines of 'no, don't eat me' with a small scream from the back of her throat, which turned into a laugh. The look on Jack's face as he passed through the wall and onto the other side, she would have happily paid to see.

Claire was sat on the edge of her seat, watching a free floating broadcast in the apartment, she groaned as she watched Jack shrink back from the grass covered wall. In fact she had watched Jack and his various panics. Not because she had wanted too, but because it seemed that every camera of any description had been focused on him and his reaction to the floor sliding.

On the other side of the grass wall was a warehouse, loading bay or was it a docking bay for planets? Jack was awe struck as they entered. Above his head the entire place was made of various metals, directly over head was a patch work quilt of gantries and struts, holding a smooth metal ceiling above there heads. Under the metal plate they were stood on there was no ground to speak of, just what looked like to be a lush green and blue planet not too different from Earth. It was like looking down from an high orbit on his home planet, until the platform they were all stood on leveled off from its angled acceleration.

Jack glanced round behind and found he could see directly into the green room they had just come from. It appeared that the platform they were stood on had been moving down at an slight angle, but with no sense of motion and just a light breeze blowing at them, the speed was difficult to work out. Even looking up at the ceiling of metal it was still impossible to tell how fast they were traveling, as there was no sense of scale to the metal, Jack hazarded a guess at big.

He stood routed to the spot, quite literally actually. Jack was trying to work out in his head how a fully functioning planet, above his head, could exist with apparently another planet at its core. As far as he could see, the ceiling of metal continued in every direction, disappearing slowly into the dark. The only source of light was coming from the planet below his feet and Jack wondered where they were actually going.

The others seemed oblivious to what was around them, making comments about how boring the tunnel was they were in and how some paintings on the walls might improve the journey.

Jack was tempted to ask about what they were seeing but managed to stop himself just in time, he noticed that they were all wearing there helmets or a variation on the blinkers. Some were glasses, some looked like cool shades and others were simply something stylish clipped to the side of there heads. He found the blinkers uncomfortable and had left his sunglasses, somewhere, so he slowly picked his helmet off his vertically standing board and put it on. Almost as soon as he put it on, even without closing the visor, he was able to see that they were traveling at quite a speed down a corridor that was white in every way. When he held his helmet in his hand, he was again looking at the network of girders above his head.

The dull metal platform they were stood on then slowly stopped and raised itself up towards the ceiling. Above there heads was a faint green oblong shaped fuzzy line, exactly the same size as the platform. Even now Jack found that he flinched as they had passed through what was obviously some form of hologram again. They passed straight through the ceiling and were then stood in a dark room, the only things highlighted were the racers and there boards. It was probably going to be one of those things he would never get used too, he mused.

The sound then started to filter through. It was like being stood underneath a stadium full of excitable and drunk people, although as he thought about it the sound was too loud and had some odd hoots and whistling. Then a seam of light appeared in front of them, the largest ramp Jack had ever seen started to lower itself from the roof. If the sound before had been loud, now as the ramp opened it was deafening and filled with every sound a creature could make, from the tiniest high pitched whistle to the loudest boom and thump. It was like every animal in the world was shouting at the top of its voice just to be heard.

When the black ramp touched down with a light bump in front of them, Jack could see four human like figures stood in the light, at the base of the ramp facing them. They wore deep cowls and had there heads bowed, just like the monk character he had met on the Golden moon. Jack then felt his feet being released from the floor, he felt the urge to run away but one question remained, where to?

As the each racer started to walk up the ramp they were given a card by the cloaked figures, which they looked at and then stuck somewhere on there body. Most seemed to favour placing it on there upper arm.

Jack approached and saw that the white cowled figures all had there cloaks lined with gold leaf trim, exactly the same as on the Golden moon. They still wore blank white creamy masks under there hoods, which still gave Jack the worries. After all anyone or anything could be behind those covers, assuming of course that they were masks and not there actual faces.

Jack took the card offered to him, it was white and blank right up until he had it in his fingers. Then a slow golden firework display played across the card, eventually showing the number forty two as he walked up the black tarmac ramp staring at it.

Halfway up the ramp he placed the card on his left upper arm, where it stuck, as soon as he did so a thin floating golden line appeared on the black tarmac, directing him to stand in his own little golden box. Just before he stepped inside the box Jack stopped, as he realized something was missing. Turning around slowly he looked at the other competitors, the one thing they all had and he did not, apart from confidence, style and panache, was there respective surfboards. Jack gently jogged back down the ramp and picked up his board, which was hovering balanced on its end.

"Not the best start" whispered Juice to Jack as he trotted back past him, whilst Juice collected his card.
Jack turned and grinned at him as he jogged by, also then imagining Claire groaning and holding her head in her hands, which was entirely accurate.
As he jogged gently back up the ramp, carrying the board under one arm with the helmet stuck to the front, he could hear the crowd chortling to themselves.

Jack's golden box was the last on the grid, as he waited for the others to file by to there respective positions, his surfboard was once again balancing on its end, he looked around the stadium. He was stood on black tarmac, which was easily fifty meters or so wide, roughly fifty meters or so above his head he could see a very faint and fuzzy blue line running around the circuit. In front of him the track disappeared around a bend in the stadium, looking behind it did exactly the same and all around him he was encased in faces. If he looked hard he could just about see individuals in the crowd, what was really giving him the worries was just that everywhere he looked there were creatures. The only gap in the tube of alien beings was directly above his head, where the rolling sides of the stadium seating did not quite meet and blue sky was vaguely visible. It was like being stood between two opposing tsunami waves of riotous fans, making a near complete tube of waving appendages and noise.

Jack had been in competitions before, mostly as a child who did not know any better, but the feeling of expectation he was getting from the crowd here was palpable. It was like the air was full of something, similar to being in an enclosed box like an elevator, with someone having eaten far too many gaseous producing vegetables.

Suddenly the crowd went silent, one of those deadly silences that you only ever really got when something terrible was about to happen. Happily for everyone involved it was merely the crowds surprise at the Prince of Marcoon, Ajar too his friends, appearing on a gantry over the tarmac track and launching into a speech.

Jack was definitely not listening as he was starting to feel the first urges of panic. The sort that blanks everything out, which makes you worry even more in case you miss something, which obviously you will because your not listening. Jack tried to force himself out of his state of anxiety. As he finally looked up from staring at the tarmac, he could see that everyone and everything was staring at him.

Jack nearly said 'what?', then he noticed that every surfer was bowing again towards the Prince. The prince laughed and pointed at Jack with both hands, his three long fingers and there thumbs making the traditional shape of a gun and its hammer ready to fire. If the silence before had been deadly, now it was lifeless, like every living thing, including the trees, were expecting him to perish an indescribable death. The crowd held its respective breaths, as Jack suddenly involuntarily found himself dipping into a deep bow and ending up on one knee.
If anyone could have seen his face as he stared at the dark tarmac with bowed head, they would have seen how really, really angry he was.
"Sorry" came a small voice that Jack was unsure if had been in his head or his ear, but did sound an awful lot like Beth's voice, only slightly metallic a long way away and echoey.

So many things were going through Jack's head that he was starting to feel lost, the only thing he found real was the anger he was feeling to whatever had taken control of his body and forced him to bow. It was not something he had ever experienced before, like everyone else who had lost control of various bodily functions at some point in his life, but to be a passenger in your own body as it did something else entirely! That was not only scary but down right rude.
"Who are you?" asked Jack in an angry voice "and what did you do?"
"We do not have time for this right now, as the race is about to start. Please just see us as your assistants" came the voice.
"And then you'll leave?" asked Jack hopefully, as the voice did appear to be in his head somehow.
"That is not possible at this time" came the tinny Beth voice.
"So what are you?" asked Jack as he started to calm down.
"We are here to help you with this race" came the slightly metallic reply, still sounding a bit like Beth.
Jack groaned inwardly, that was all he needed, another dose of help.

A loud klaxon played out, of the 'we're going to vibrate your colon whether you like it or not variety', throughout the stadium and indeed probably the Universe. As Jack was still bowed over staring at the tarmac, he saw a golden counter of the spiral form appear in front of him on the tarmac, just outside his golden box.
"What's that?" asked Jack thinking for some reason that it was very prettily animated.
"Race countdown" came the metallic sounding Beth's voice, still in his head and not in his ears.
"So how long in real time is it?"
"There is no such thing as real time."
Jack grinded his teeth together and calmly asked "in English minutes and seconds?"
Right before his eyes the counter seemed to melt into the number forty and slowly counted down towards zero.

Still kneeling down Jack placed a hand on the tarmac like surface to push himself up, he was surprised at how smooth and near flawless the surface was to the touch.
Still looking at the black asphalt he heard a sound like 'psst' but spoken as if through a curtain of tentacles, which it was. On turning his head he saw Juice waving at him in tiny gestures, Juice then tapped his helmet and pulled on his cord attached to his board, to indicate it was time to use them. Jack waved back, Juice rolled his eyes and slammed his visor shut.

Jack turned to look for his surfboard and found it attempting to dance behind him, it actually managed to look guilty as he frowned at it. He took his white and dark silver bug eyed helmet off the top of the board, tracing the black tribal design flowing over the back and top with a finger. He then put the helmet on, pulled a green cord from the middle of the board and slapped the end around his ankle, locking it in place. The knots every two meters or so in the ribbon like cord still had Jack worried, as if it was predicting him to fall off and have to climb back up.

Jack pushed his surfboard over to lie in the golden box, jumped on top and then noticed it was facing the wrong way round, he got off, spun it around and climbed back aboard. There was some small amount of tittering from the crowd, which Jack chose to ignore, whilst his fellow competitors turned round to see what all the fuss was about. There was the sound of much tutting, shaking of heads and small hand signals in Jack's direction from the other racers. The red and white flamed picture on the underside of Jack's board was actually being reflected back by the shiny surface of the black asphalt, creating a flame like effect in the air under his board. The once autumnal leaves image, brown with age on the top of his surfboard, was now green and vaguely attached to barely visible branches of some tree waving about. Both sides of the board had a depth, which Jack would under normal circumstances be really excited about. Most of the other boards in the race were full of advertising sponsorship pictures, even they had some form of three dimensional effect on them, making Jack's board look slightly out of place purely because of the lack of actual advertisement.

The final ten second count for the start of the surf race was being counted down by everyone in the stadium and most of the galaxy. Creatures all across the cosmos were counting down in anticipation, with a fair few holding there respective breaths.

Lying down on his board Jack was looking up a tail pipe, it was ten meters away but still it was a tail pipe. The exhaust and propulsion system he was staring out must have been three times the size of his, so he turned and looked down under his shoulder to check. The old mantra 'bigger is not always better' crossed his mind but in this case he was fairly sure it would.

The golden numbers in front of Jack appeared to be slowing down, like they were slowly running out of power. As the number approached zero Jack pressed the button in the centre of the board and immediately he felt some extra weight in his bones, then little joystick controls appeared on the inside of his gloves.

The roar of the surfboard engines as they started was massive, briefly swiping away the noise of the crowd with its volume and jets of vary coloured flame. Then the counter reached zero and all the racers shot forward like soap from a clenched fist in an overly friendly spa.

It was not quite the same acceleration as Jack had experienced, it actually felt slower for some reason, that was probably due to the sound overwhelming everything. As soon as the counter had reached zero the golden box had disappeared, not only could Jack hear the Split Universe Drives of everybody else flaring, but some how the golden box had been holding back most of the noise of the crowd. When the sound struck Jack's ears, even through his helmet, he had actually frozen, it was just so loud it was all consuming, like there was nothing else in the world but that sound. Jack guessed that this might be what it was like if you were really famous, loved and stood in the centre of a stadium being trampled over by worshipful fans. He felt his chest constrict like it was being squashed by invisible hugging teddy bears, his hands tightened on the joysticks in his hands and he shut his eyes for a moment.

When he opened his eyes again he was stopped dead, looking into the eye of the beast, Jack gave a tiny whimper as he jumped back slightly on his board and fell off. It was then he realized he was facing an advertisement hoarding and was stopped dead. The other thing was the lack of sound or rather the lack of roaring, it sounded more like chittering or was it chortling?

Jack clambered back on his board, moved to a sitting position with his feet dangling over either side and looked around. The surrounding stadium alien hoard were laughing, presumably at him, waving banners and flags with various odd names on them and pointing. Jack was floating with his board at the end of the start finish straight, parked in the middle of the bend looking at an advertisement for "the beastly I, that'll have you clean from the inside in the devils time" Jack read. Briefly Jack noticed a counter flash up in the bottom part of his helmet display. When he looked at it, it grew in size quickly and showed his advertising revenue going through the roof, as more and more people were looking at him and therefore the sign he was so impartially parked in front of.

Jack shuffled his board about by pushing off from the hoarding with a boot, leaving a print on its surface and three letters 'tJi'. The board moved gently over the long green gently swaying grass, back towards the tarmac circuit. Jack was trying to use full throttle to get back to the tarmac circuit, after a few seconds of still going frustratingly slowly he worked it out. The grass was somehow used as a form of circuit gravel trap, slowing down would be crashers, or in his case drifters. From memory he had a vague recollection of the grass running along the edges of half the circuit and made a mental note to avoid it, unless he needed to stop, obviously.

Chapter 43 : The Three R's.

Reaching the asphalt once again, the board shot away down the track, with Jack looking like he was holding on for dear life, which he actually was because he forgot to reduce the throttle as he left the grass. Claire groaned at him, not so much as it made him look stupid but because it was tarring the rest of humanity with the same brush. He was the current representative that everyone and everything could see, meaning that whatever he did reflected on her, badly generally.
'So no change there then' she thought shaking her head.
Mistaking her nodding head for worry the Commander said "well don't worry you'll see him in a minute."
Claire looked up into his soft blue eyes, suddenly remembering something and asked "where's the gun?"
The Commander looked round for a moment and said "well, ah you have to buy it and then go sit on the ledge?" he answered in slight confusion.
"Buy it from where?"
"Well the Fabar market place on your Quellz" before the Commander had finished talking Claire had already whipped out her device and was searching through.
She then waved her hands around in frustration and asked "so what am I looking for exactly, there's millions of possibilities here?"
"Well I'd recommend the Rotating Reflector Rifle, but?"
"Don't you dare rebut me" answered Claire angrily.
"Well all I was going to say, was that it might be cheaper from the F-Code machine over there?" said the Commander pointing to a small red curtain on the wall.
It looked to Claire like the type of curtain you got for the opening of plaques on the side of buildings, she pulled the curtains apart with a fair degree of annoyance to reveal an orange box. It looked identical to the one on the War Catchers bridge, so she placed her hand on the clear orange screen and asked for a "Roflector Retating Rifle?"
A message scrolled across the screen under her fingers and Claire replied "obviously and yes."
She then paused and turned to ask the Commander "how big is this gun exactly, I mean this hole isn't really that big?"
"Well it'll come out in pieces won't it and then you'll just have to assemble it" came the simple reply.
The Commander was thinking all the time that Claire must really want to help Jack by shooting at the other competitors, whilst Claire was just really thinking she wanted to shoot something, anything and anyone in fact.

After only a few seconds the machine made a light pinging noise and Claire turned back to find the screen panel open and the stock of a rifle ready to be picked up. After several more pinging noises, Claire had on the table in front of her all the pieces to make some form of rifle. She placed them in what she thought was the right order but could not see how they attached to one another. It was only when she felt her Quellz move in her pocket that she was presented with a bill on the screen, which she nearly chocked at but nonetheless touched to pay. As soon as she paid, the rifle assembled itself right in front of her eyes, with several bits spinning around the correct way and then it was finished sat on its side on the table. It was the meanest looking gun she had ever seen. It also appeared to be made entirely of wood but when she touched it, it was cold to the touch. There was a rotating magazine like on a revolver, sat just in front of the trigger that carried eight projectiles. There was also a wooden case that when she opened it contained sixteen bullets. Claire picked a bullet out of the box. Each one looked like it was made of gold, three inches long, about half an inch wide, what had surprised her the most was the weight. Each round felt like it weighed a kilogram or more.

Claire looked back at the gun lying on the table, wondering with eight bullets in the magazine and the weight of the rifle, whether she would be able to even pick it up? There was only one way to find out, so she picked it up, nearly throwing it over her shoulder as it actually weighed the same as your average feather.

Claire sat confused for a moment, as each piece out of the F-Code machine had weighed about a kilogram and now she was holding the five pieces as one rifle. Still shaking her head she started to slide the heavy ammunition into the rotating chamber on the gun. The others watched her carefully, as a smile grew to play across her face as she put each bullet in place. It was surprisingly therapeutic she found, placing each bullet in its chamber and her smile widened. It was not a very nice smile, more the type of smile you might expect from a tiger, which has just discovered how to open the door on his or her zoo enclosure, whilst visitors eat lunch right outside the cage.

Jack could finally see the trails from the other racers, in the distance he thought he could count at least fifteen or more Sky-Burners. The various banners around the stadium, as he had been turning around on his board, had proclaimed many different names for the surfers and there boards: Air-Breakers, Sky-Burners, Cloud-Skaters, Split-Runners, Gap-Bangers and many more. Jack saw many more signs and banners being waved at him furiously as he sped along, encouraging him to go faster, some were actually quite rude to read as he closed on his rivals. The main thing was, he now knew he was catching up with his fellow competitors, at this rate though it would take several laps to get anywhere near the front. What he needed now was some luck, of a kind.

The other problem, apart from his own lack of understanding, was that he had been enjoying the views. No matter how many times he had practiced in the Picture Palace, it still did not prepare you for the way the tunnel like circuit twisted and rolled through first the city and then the countryside. Now they were heading out to sea, up through the occasional cloud, then the mildly fuzzy blue line dived back down through the clouds and into an actual clear tunnel under the sea.

Jack marveled at the underwater vista, it looked like he could see for miles and maybe even the curvature of the planet through the light blue! The water was so clear so pristine, like no waste of any description had ever been dumped into it by a supposedly intelligent species. There were underwater creatures in every direction, most were staring blankly into the tube, it was only then that Jack realized his mistake. He had been thinking of these sea dwellers as inferior creatures, purely because they were underwater, when in effect they were spectators of the idiots racing in the tube. The give away were the banners they were holding and the flags they waved in the gentle underwater currents.

The tube, twisted banked and rolled under the sea, through watery ruins, chasms and rocks, with the slightly fuzzy blue line ever present in the centre of the tunnel. Then finally the tube started to head back up towards the surface and Jack caught his first proper glimpse of a fellow surfer. The tube then turned sharply, from being nearly vertical to horizontal at ninety degrees as it broke the surface of the sea and headed inland. Jack swung around the ceiling of the tunnel in the turn and found himself flying past two competitors somehow tied up with one another's safety cords, spinning out of the tube into the blue sky.

"Well he's made up two places, at least" remarked the Commander to Claire.
When he did not get a reply he turned to look at her and found her struggling to point the Rotating Reflector Rifle out of the window of the apartment.
She was quite literally trying with all her might to point the gun out of the window, something kept pushing it back to face into the room.
The Commander sighed and was just about to get up when Jane walked forward and snatched the gun from Claire's hands.
"Hey!" said Claire with some anger but not too much.
Jane twisted the gun around in her hands, looking for something and then gave a sigh.
"Give me your Quellz" requested Jane in a mildly resigned tone, whilst holding her hand out and clicking her fingers impatiently.

With only a slight pause Claire reached into her pocket and passed it over curiously. Jane had been like this when they had been in the tunnels underneath the city, hiding out from the invaders, usually when she thought up some mad cap scheme to aid them. Claire almost did not hand over her Quellz as she remembered that technically Jane had been an invader, although why she had been helping them in the first place she had no idea. That was a question for later, after she had shot some bullets!

Jane placed Claire's Quellz on the top of the rifle, where it locked into place just in front of the trigger and above the ammunition bay.

She handed the gun back to Claire, who immediately found that as soon as she looked over the top of the rifle, a targeting sight was projected up from the screen of the Quellz. She had wondered how you would hit a target without a gun sight of any description, so she was only slightly embarrassed when she realized she had made one of those 'ah' now I understand noises when it appeared.

"Well you can stop pointing it into the room now and start pointing it out the window if you like!" said the Commander moving out of the sway of the guns waving barrel.

"Hmm, oh sorry I was just looking" said a bemused Claire.

This time as she looked out of the window with the gun she was not pushed back and felt immediately empowered.

The track or tube came from somewhere far out from the left, turned a sharp right around a building and headed straight towards the hotel apartment, where it then performed a sharp left directly in front of her window and disappeared into the distance to her right. The room was also at precisely the same level as the blue fuzzy line marking the centre of the circuit. Whether this was by design, accident or necessity was anyone's guess but Claire was going to enjoy it immensely, as she sighted down her rifle.

Jack was finally having fun, he had made up several places already and his heads up display was telling him everything he wanted to know. As a smile started to cross his lips inside his helmet, a warning symbol started to flash in the bottom left of his screen '3D'. When he focused on it a depleting counter appeared, then shortly afterwards 'Depleting Danger Dynamic' wandered across the display in blinking red letters. This was shortly followed by the word 'danger', flashing continuously like an electrical short in a light and right across Jack's field of vision.

"I guess this is the danger bit then" mumbled Jack to himself as he tried to swipe away the sign.

When the tube left the water it had become nearly invisible, there was just a slight sheen to the surface as it followed the curve and roll of the soft fuzzy blue line. After swinging around the inside of the tube as he had left the sea, Jack realized that they were actually racing inside a tube of some description, that followed the blue line at its centre. The closer he traveled to the fuzzy blue line, the more stable the board felt and the faster it seemed to go. He assumed the tube was foraminous in some way, as the two racers with there tied cords had spun out the tube boundary and back in again behind him. Now the question was where had Jack ever heard that strange word before 'foraminous', something nefarious was going on and he was using words he did not know.

There were now headed back towards the city in a dead straight line with its spires, blocks, balls and variably shaped buildings, some of which were still standing at impossible angles to Jacks eye. Jack found himself slowing down again as he stared at the city, as soon as he realized, he pressed hard down on the throttle in his palm. He zipped along, around the blue line, finding out that the tube was not quite as straight as he first thought. It was like the fuzzy blue line was not actually fixed, seeming to ebb and flow slightly of its own accord like a skipping rope being waved about.

Then as he approached the city, over the beach and through the trees, he found he was flying through a light pink mist, that seemed to hang in the air. A black wiper like blade then traveled slowly from one side of his helmet, across his nose to the other bug eyed eye and back again. It cleaned everything off in the process, leaving Jack wondering for a moment what it was that needed cleaning off so thoroughly. He then had a really clear view down the rest of the tube, with only the occasional coloured misty deposit, and could see a gaggle of floating racers ahead.

Finally he caught up with the main group of his fellow racers, they had been slowed down by a hail of tiny artillery. They were all hovering at two floating posts with red lights top and bottom flashing away, with the word 'danger' floating in the gap between them. It seemed that nearly all the aliens on surfboards had been hit by some form of projectile, leaving them with various cuts, abrasions, broken bits of board, suits, armour and pride. The various leaking fluids had been sucked out of the clear tube towards the sea, by air flow and gravity, creating a light pink mist for Jack's wipers to remove.
As Jack worked out what the pink mist, with tinges of blue actually was, he felt quite ill.

A few competitors had turned round to come back through the flashing posts, which either showed they were really silly for flying back down the way they had come from, through the firing range, or really intelligent as they waited for something.
Either way Jack was ignoring them all, he crouched down as low as he could on his board and pushed as hard as he dared on the throttle.

Jack zipped by underneath his standing competitors, leaving them bouncing around in his wake, like small white and acrylic balls, in a fast spin washing machine. It was only as his little windscreen wiper blade dutifully made its way across his vision again, that Jack realized the Commander had somehow managed to skip this part of the race, not only in the picture palace replay but also in all his practice runs. Jack ground his teeth together in anger, thinking to himself that if he did survive this unscathed, he was still going to punch the Commander very hard on his cute leathery pink nose.

Claire took another sip of her steaming coffee, which made her twitch slightly, she may not get used to the taste here but by golly was the buzz amazing she thought. She put the drink back down on the window ledge and breathed.
"Well you've got about ten more seconds before the lights go out" said the Commander from behind Claire.
"I think that's enough time to take out one more surfer, don't you?" replied Claire, sighting down her rifle and staring through the Quellz heads up display.
The counter on her Quellz was reading twenty two hits and she was determined to make it twenty three, making her very wealthy in the process.
Claire squeezed the trigger on the rifle gently, watching the light from the bullet sail away from her and towards her next victim.
Jane almost at the same time said, whilst looking at the floating Hypew news screen "wow, Jacks just moved up twenty places!"
Claire stared at the green trace of her bullet and with an open mouth mumbled "oh crick!"

Jack saw something bright green traveling towards him and rolled his board over to one side. Whatever it was sailed slowly under the bottom of his board, with a scream like the sound he imagined an elephant might make if it were tied to a missile.
Before anyone or anything else could get a shot off from the surrounding buildings, the two flashing posts turned green and the waiting surfers surged forward, like a ravenous horde of vultures leaving a vegetarian cruise ship as it docked for the last time. They tumbled over one another in there eagerness to get to the other end before the timer ran out.

"How long has he got?" asked Claire staring at the approaching racers in some relief but with a tinge of annoyance as well.
"Well its a minute timer, on a section of track that's about ninety seconds long" said the Commander carefully.
"Will he make it?" she asked worriedly.
"He should do, as he hit the danger posts at nearly full throttle" replied Jane.

They all stared out of the window as Jack approached on his board and turned to his left, zipping around the building. As he flew by he looked over the edge of his board to see who had shot at him, Claire stood guiltily shaking her head, he gave her the filthiest look she had ever experienced. At least she assumed he did, just because of the way his helmeted head had sprung back to face forwards again with a little shake.

The Commander would not be the only with a sore nose at the end of this thought Jack, as he followed the blue line snaking through, over and around buildings.

Chapter 44 : Racing Lines.

The two announcers were back on the Wire cast, Don and Dun were making there bold predictions and ridiculous comments about all the riders and there boards. The thing that got them most excited though was the danger zone, they just would not give up talking about it and how they both longed to be shooters. They reminisced continually about the one day years ago they had both had a practice with the Rotating Reflector Rifle, both had loved it dearly and wanted to shoot at real targets now please.

"Why do you listen to them, there such idiots?" asked Claire waving a hand at the Hypew news screen.
Displayed on the hovering screen was coverage of the race with an insert showing the two Wire hosts, they were talking animatedly about the race they were commentating on.
"Well they might be complete crickans but you must admit they are funny, I've seen you smirking at there comments, they also have a great deal of knowledge about the race and are genuinely excited by it!" replied the Commander.
"But still, they sound like complete... what did you call them again?"
"Well, crickans?"
"Which means what exactly?"
"Well stupid or idiot I suppose."

Claire gave the Commander a look that would have withered titanium and after only a short time she looked away. It would appear that even aliens could not resist adjusting, altering a new language and making up replacement words. She had done it herself in the past, already she had heard various words that were in English but had no meaning she could understand. That was not strictly true, she supposed, as most of them she had heard appeared to be used to swear in some way, usually at some inanimate object that was not working, like there partner.
Claire had been reluctant to look them up on her Quellz, she had fair idea that they would all be rude. Maybe this was why so many of the aliens she had met, well all of them so far, had spoken English. It was the way the language, like so many back on Earth, could be altered and still have meaning. The only thing she needed was a point of reference for some of the words she had heard in passing.
"You'll want to watch this Claire" said Jane pointing at the floating images over the coffee table.
"Why?" asked Claire still pondering the language.
"Well in some respects it's the most interesting part of the race" said the Commander.
"Why?"
"Well because this is where they enter the split" replied the Commander in a dramatic tone.

Everyone leaned forward, to various degrees of there species. Ron and Joan sat together on a sofa, staring at the huge floating screen on the wall. Jane and Sara were sat together looking at the big screen but also using there Quellz to overlay the Wire cast. The Commander and Summer were sat in Raifoon friendly chairs just behind Claire, who was still sighting out of the window, in hope and anticipation. Second, Beth and Sarah had been tasked with getting the ship prepared for as many eventualities as possible, like a foreign army knife without the foreign or knife aspects.

Jack had made up quite a few places since passing through the danger zone, mainly because he realized his timing had been pretty much perfect as he had passed between the posts. Whether or not on the next lap he would be so lucky, was anyone's guess but if Claire had anything to do with it he felt sure he would be in trouble. Then in front of him he caught a vapour trail twisting round the next corner. As he veered around the bend, he had to twist with a barrel roll over a surfer clambering up there rope cord, trying to get back on there board. Jack now saw the edge of the stadium, after flitting between various buildings, then being taken back out to the countryside and back once again to the city. He had been wondering at what point they would pass back across the start finish line.

The vaguely blue fuzzy line, in the centre of the clear tunnel, was now leading Jack down the centre of what looked like a shopping arcade, with coffee stalls and tea chairs. Various faces looked up as he flew by, some even waved a tentacle or other appendage, whether they were actually waving in support or making rude signs Jack could not make out. The tunnel then curved up slightly, seeming to then twist back down into a hole in the ground in front of the stadium. Then he was back amongst the roaring crowd of the stadium once again, it was like being dropped head first into a pan of boiling water minus the heat, the noise was that oppressive.

Finally there was the last bend in the track and Jack could see the bright white line marking the finish, he felt a sense of relief as he approached the line. There was a ping like noise as he came closer and a light started to flash red in his helmet. Then automatically the Split Universe Drive switched on and Jack was enveloped in a soft bubble.

Jack watched as the Universe very briefly became a white tube, it then seemed like he was almost catapulted up through the reality waves, to then be surfing in the gap. As he emerged it was like ducking out from under a black, white foaming wave in the sea and then being back in the split in space. The only real difference was the colour scheme. Out in space the colour of the gap appeared fairly limited, just because of the strange distance perspectives. Partner that with being sandwiched between two vary coloured realities and the colours had been interesting but at a great distance. Here on a planet with proper bits of his own reality only meters away from him, the colours were like nothing he had ever seen before. It was how he would have imagined surfing a world made up near entirely of rainbows and fireworks might have looked. The only problem being that he could not get a proper look, because the foaming white waves in the split were actually quite choppy. In space you were generally quite a long way from the objects of the Universe, there only effect on you being there colour and gravity creating the waves in the gap. Here so close to objects, the ripples were short sharp and decidedly unfriendly, trying to throw Jack off his board like an angry cow with a spear in its bum. Naturally Jack started to slow down, with the crowd and even the Wire hosts wishing him to go faster, Jack finally worked it out as the waves in the gap got more choppy as he slowed.
Almost as soon as he started to pick up speed the waves became more gentle, easier to ride and above all predictable. The one thing he forgot as he splashed through wave after wave, whilst enjoying the sense of actual surfing, was the bend in the track. At the last moment he saw the green coloured grass filtering through to the gap. The grass was now a deliciously violent looking set of very tall wavy tendrils, that flowed and waved around the corners of the track. Jack swung his board around sharply, timing it to perfection to use a wave to steer round the corner and away from the actual apparently screaming grass. Looking over his shoulder the tendril grass was waving in fury, appearing to have actual mouths with green teeth up and down there stems. Jack gave a shudder as he raced away from the grass, determined to stay in the middle of the track as much as possible and close to the now more distinct blue line showing the circuit.

Jack's revenue was amassing at a fantastic rate, no one in the history of the SUDSC had had so much advertising revenue in the first two laps of a race. Claire was amazed at the speed the two surf jockeys were talking at on the Wire that they could even be understood. The pair of them appeared to be more excited about the advertising revenue, than about the actual race at the moment. It was only as she actually listened to what they were saying that she realized why they were so excited. Mainly it was because Jack was being a crickan, a complete and utter one, some how the idiot was endearing himself to the public in Claire's eyes because of his luck.

First of all he had parked in front of an advertising hoarding, then on each turn in the track he had somehow managed to position his board between the filmaments and it seemed every advertising board. The public thought of it as an amusing twist on the normal way they had adverts thrown at them, whilst Claire suspected it was more Jack being a lucky little crick.

Jack seemed to have a knack in pounding the waves, which Claire reluctantly agreed with the two pundits on the Wire about. He did appear to be a very accomplished surfer, using the rise and fall of each wave in the gap to his advantage.

Claire listened intently to the explanations on the Wire, passing it all through her own mental interpretation and translation system for Jack.

The bubble of reality surrounding Jack and his board was shaped like a wedge of cheese, leaving the curved underside of his board to slice up and down the waves of reality. As he traveled slower the waves became more choppy and splashed with colour, the white foam around his board splashing and crashing as he sliced his way through. As he traveled faster the waves were further apart, with deeper falls and rises in there crests and dips. In the gap there was always a wave catching you up and there was always a wave you were catching up to. If you thought about it too hard you tended to have your mind twist a bit, as that would mean that you were at the centre of a series of waves, like being a twig dipped in and out of a bird bath as the ripples washed back and forth. Basically you were the cause of the waves in the first place, being that you were in the gap creating a dip in spaces reality or bird bath.

In space the waves appeared black, because generally as a rule of thumb space is mostly black due to the lack of light or colour. The foam created by the ships hull or the bottom of a surfboard in the gap, was generally white as basically friction was created in the gap. Here though so close to all these colours and traveling so slowly, the waves were still mostly dark but coloured with speckled light from reality around them. The foam and crests of the waves were still white but coloured by the nearest reality and even the angle you looked at them. Reality viewed from inside the gap looked like it was made up of fuzzy rainbows and fireworks.

Claire was watching, listening and interpreting so intently to the explanations on the Wire, it took the Commander several attempts to get her attention and eventually settled for poking her in the ear with a curly thumb.

"What?" asked Claire mildly annoyed.

"Well you've got about thirty seconds before the leaders reach the danger zone" said the Commander.

"So?"

The Commander pointed at the gun sat on the window sill. After the first round of shots and various reloads Claire had found the gun very heavy to use. It could only be fired whilst pointing out of the window, inside the room it also seemed to weigh next to nothing, whilst pointing it out the window though it suddenly had all of its weight. Claire supposed the weight was because the eight kilograms of ammo held in the magazine was ridiculous, she had then paid for an hunting arm from the F-Code machine. When it had appeared she had thought it a joke, it was basically a rectangular piece of credit card sized shiny metal that stuck like a magnet on the underside of the rifle. As soon as she had placed the thing on the gun however, it had become almost weightless and with just one finger found she could have the gun float in the air in front of her pointing out the window. She had experimented with letting go, the rifle had fallen to the floor like a society lady finding out her daughter is pregnant at an abstinence convention. It had not happened all at once, leading Claire to just stare at it tumble through the air and strike the floor with an almighty bang like a solid metal cell door clanging shut.

Claire pulled herself away from the cast, picked up some more overweight ammunition from the F-Code machine and picked up her gun from the window sill. She had wondered whether or not you could point the thing at anything else other than the surfers, when she had tried the hovering display from her Quellz on the gun had simply disappeared.

She sighted down the circuit straight out of the window and waited.

Finally Jack understood the purpose of the blue line properly. It had appeared to be just a guide to following the track, now Jack realized the track was the blue line, traveling down the centre of the tube like circuit. If he strayed too far from it, the gap outside the tube started to become a crushing torrent of turbulent roiling storms. Outside of the tube on a couple of turns he had strayed a bit too close to the edge and had looked into terror. It had been like looking underwater at smoke being twisted and bent around by thousand mile an hour winds in a tornado. That had just been in one square meter of space. It was only as he stared at it, that he noticed that the particles making up the impossible twisting shapes actually looked like galaxies and they in turn were everywhere he could see. The visual pull to go and experience this external place was massive, it was only when Jack looked away that he felt a massive amount of terror and fear suck at him as he saw how far he had wondered from the blue line. It was the depth beyond the blue line that had scared him the most, Jack did not deal with depths and only on looking back at the circuit did he realize how close he had come to experiencing that depth in the gap for real. Weirdly racing this close to reality and so slowly in the split, made the outside appear to have more worrying depth than being in space.

Whatever the blue line did it was obviously some form of stabilizer, without it, it would be near impossible to use the Split Universe Drive on his space-board.

Chapter 45 : Shooting Out.

When the surfers were in the split there was a slight shift in perspective, like everything was set gently off to the left or even the right, possibly up, maybe down and even brown. Which ever way it was, it made actually hitting or even getting close to striking a surfer with the rifle shots really hard. Claire was never one to shirk a challenge and with each shot she fired, she crept ever closer to striking a racer in the gap. So lost in her mission to actually hit a target, she suddenly remembered that Jack would be in there somewhere amongst the throng and paused to check his position on the track.

After the next gaggle of surfers Jack should come into view. It was then she noticed something. Nobody else appeared to be firing. Before there had been hundreds of creatures firing up and down the kilometer long straight but now there was hardly anything. In fact nothing at all, not a thing, it was so quiet you could hear a pin drop in a padded room.

There was a sharp intake of breath behind Claire followed by an "oh no" from Jane.
"What?" asked Claire.
"Well it looks like someone has put a million crown bounty on Jack" said the Commander.
"What exactly does that mean?" asked Claire after a moments thought.
"Well anyone who hits Jack and stops him from finishing the race, gets a million crowns."
"Is that allowed?"
"Well, only in the danger zone."
"So who put the bounty on him?"
"Well it doesn't have to say but I'll wager it's a Furrykin."
"But don't they want Jack to win?"
"Well not all of them, no" said the Commander.

Claire sighted back out of the window through her Quellz floating display, the next group of surfers sped through the floating posts in the distance.
If Jack was lucky he might get to the posts when it was safe, that was unlikely and knowing Jack, he would just sail straight through trusting to luck. The posts started to flash green, Claire watched on the race monitor as Jack came out from under the sea, pleading to herself that he would wait until they were constant green again. If Jack passed through the posts when the lights were red, he may very well be flying through the equivalent of a lead wall with an occasional air hole.

Jack saw the posts still flashing with there green lights as he came around the corner and just knew they were going to switch off at any moment, like trying to time your driving through town centre traffic lights. The choice was to wait and lose some time, possibly too much, or chance being shot at by Claire again. Jack decided to go with luck, just as he met the posts at the start of the danger zone they flicked over to red with there flashing lights. He sailed through thumbing as much speed as he could from the surfboard and still be in control on each wave. He knew that the faster he went the smoother the waves would be, that would also make it easier for the shooters to aim at him as he would be doing less bobbing about on the waves.

Almost as soon as Jack crossed the posts his world lit up with a rainbow of colours, it appeared that everyone and there pet had opened fire with a multitude of coloured lead. Each bullet fired was a different colour, although most were a variation on gold and most probably not made of lead. The trail from each bullet was a different matter altogether though, with colours from every part of the spectrum and even some that Jack had never seen before.

Up to a point it was a breathless view, until he realized exactly what he was looking at. What he was looking at was in effect a barrage of mini missiles. Fortunately for Jack when they crossed over into and through the gap, they slowed down, almost seeming to stop. When they entered the gap there speed was greatly reduced to almost walking pace, which enabled Jack to easily dodge the first few salvo's. The problem as he looked ahead was the volume, it was like looking up in a thunderstorm and being able to see the individual drops of rain aiming to hit you personally. Which was of course exactly what the launcher intended and what you would expect after having just left the hair salon.

Jack found it relatively easy to dodge the ridiculous number of projectiles coming towards him, after they entered the gap, the only thing he was worried about was whether they might catch up with him from behind. He glanced over his shoulder, weirdly as each bullet left the effect of the tube or struck a wave crest, they basically went 'boom.' Jack turned back to face forward, watching the occasional bullet strike a crest and explode in a fury of coloured sparks. He was quite pleased with this revelation, meaning that a vast majority of the munitions were not actually going to reach him as he surfed. It was only when a piece of shrapnel from a passing explosion scraped the back of his white gloved hand, as he gripped the side of his board as he twisted and rolled, that he was shocked by how easily it cut through the fabric and his top layer of skin. What it left in the gap behind him, as a few drops of blood escaped, could only be described as a ball of lunch. Something small, black and worm shaped leapt from his surfboards wake and gobbled up the errant liquid glob. Whatever this creature was it then burped, leaving a faint cloud of reddish smoke, which attracted more of the worm like creatures from Jack's wake. Jack hurriedly looked away and checked the back of his hand, which now showed what looked like a clear gel covering the minor wound and sealing him from the outside Universe.

At this point Jack finally admitted to himself that this all might be real, mainly because of the pain and the determination of not being eaten by small worm like things. It would probably hurt if you were being eaten continuously by small worm like objects. So he made a mental note to not slow down, dodge the hail of bullets and there resultant and inevitable explosions in the gap, whilst also at the same time riding a hover-board in a gap between Universes.

When he said these things in his head, he thought of himself as going slightly mad.

Claire watched the bullets fly towards Jack through her Quellz rifle scope. It was like watching a thousand fireworks being fired all at once, all aimed down a sewer tunnel at one lone rat. The explosions as each one struck a wave in the gap looked amazing, right up until the point she focused on Jack and saw one bang narrowly miss him, the shrapnel firework explosion looked awesome though.
"Is there anything we can do to help him, it looks like a firework display in a drain pipe out there?" asked Claire.
"Pray" said Summer quietly.
"What do you mean pray?"
"Hmm oh sorry I meant pay."
Claire looked carefully at Summer, she had been dead quiet the entire time Jack had been away. She was having suspicions about Summer and Jack, more so than with Sara. Turning she looked for Sara, finding her quietly sat on a sofa staring at the floating screen. Something was going on, other than the race that Claire was unsure of but it all seemed to revolve around Jack.

Every time Jack completed a lap, passing the hotel apartment, all three ladies tensed and Claire finally felt the need to ask a burning question.
Claire not entirely used to holding a gun in her hand for quite so long had forgotten about it as her finger slipped on the trigger. The slight kick of it firing was a complete surprise to her, as she turned away from the window to speak to Summer and Sara. She stood shocked, watching the green trail of her bullet flying down the tube, just below the blue line.

Jack watched as another barrage of bullets and there coloured vapour trails flowed towards him in the danger zone, once again. He had made up several places already because Ron had done an amazing job on the surfboard and the audience had grown bored of waiting for Jack to appear on every lap. Initially Jack had found the board a bit unwieldy and unresponsive, this had been because of the slight delay of the board reacting to the inputs he put in on the waves. Once he had got used to the mild delay before action, Jack had found it actually quite fun. After catching and overtaking so many other racers, he realized just how good a job Ron had done on his board. It turned better, faster and seemed to be more responsive than everyone else's board.

Having only completed the first lap in real air, Jack was not sure how the board would really handle, as he had spent more time in the gap watching the shadow of the split and reality bang together to make each wave.

Then in one of the middle laps he noticed something start to appear on a roof top in the distance of the danger zone. It appeared to be half a clear bubble, about the size of a small car and after a few seconds it had a long protrusion sticking out the front of it. Whatever it was, it was being constructed quite quickly by a vary coloured vector like graphics matrix.

Quickly line by line it was turning into "a cannon!" said Jack to himself, as he flew past in the danger zone, the now nearly constructed cannon turned to follow him.

Jack turned away and started to dodge, roll and flip over the abundant supply of flying munitions, when out the corner of his eye he saw more cannons nearing completion on several rooftops. In annoyed recollection he suddenly remembered Juice saying something about the 'public firing from afar' and 'audience participation.'

As Jack turned from staring at the nearest cannon, shaking his head, a green streak caught his eye, just a fraction too late he realized it was going to hit him just below the belt line. Jack jumped up off his board, it was the only option. Hither too up to this point Jack had not left his board when it had been moving. So it came as quite a surprise what happened next.

The surfboards Automatic Response System Emancipator kicked in, bringing the board to an abrupt stop in the gap, pretty much in the centre of the danger zone, floating a few meters below the dark ice blue line. Jack on the other hand had not stopped moving and had watched his board disappear behind him, like he had been launched from a catapult or trebuchet. The first thing to cross his vision was a bright red flashing word saying ARSE, his thoughts were pretty much along these lines. Then he remembered the cord attached to his ankle, looking down between his legs he found the knotted rope like ribbon thing gradually growing tauter, as it was reeled out of the back of the board. Jack reached a hand down a fraction too late to grab at the cord on his ankle, it suddenly reached its full stretch and swung him away. He ended up swinging hard and fast around the surfboard, like a man attached to a bungee on a windmills sail.

The circular motion went on for quite sometime, which although vomit inducing for Jack, was quite lucky as he was no longer in the gap. The board had automatically dropped out of the split after a few seconds, once Jack had chosen to leave it, meaning that the rules of the Universe were now being reapplied with some vigour. This also meant that any weapons fired at him now did not have to cross any theoretical thresholds and were traveling at there normal slow rates. Because of Jacks rotating and eventual swinging motion he was a hard target to strike. None of the would be shooters thought about aiming for his board though, as they were all focused on striking him in his pendulum form.

Claire was thinking 'oops' as she sat staring down her rifle at Jack swinging round in the free air and watched as bullet after bullet flew passed his limp body. Eventually with some relief she watched as his hand came from dangling below his upturned head and open the visor on his helmet. Something poured out that took a moment for Claire to work out exactly what it was, then she gagged a little herself as she saw the orangey colour, with optional carrot like chunks falling and eventually splatting on the tarmac a few inches below.
"Well what's he doing, why isn't he climbing back up?" asked the Commander.
"I think he just needed to clear his head first" said Claire feeling a bit ill and turning from the window for a moment.
"Technically you could say he stopped to clean his visor" said Jane, plainly.
"The other way to put it, might be to say he needed to clear his helmet?" asked Sara with a light smile on her lips.
"Is he trying to make himself lighter? So he can race more efficiently?" asked Joan curiously.
Claire gave Joan a look that could be expressed as 'really!' and then she asked "but still, why are they still firing at him, surely they can see he's not well?"
The Commander exchanged a look with Summer who simply shrugged, which on a Raifoon looked especially effective due to there bag of bones like structure and wide frame.
Claire looked angrily at the two Raifoons sat calmly on there adaptive chairs, Summer finally noticed the tap tapping of Claire's foot.
"There still firing at him because they can, which is actually pointless" replied Summer in an effort to stop the tapping.
"Why and why?" asked Claire sounding slightly frustrated.
"Because even in the danger zone there are rules for firing weapons. If you look, you'll see that not one shot has actually hit him, even ones fired directly at him, they'll all be bending around him."
Claire looked back through her rifle and Quellz scope, she nearly pulled the trigger herself just to test what she had been told, she could see the bullets flying in from every direction were simply curving away.
Eventually everyone was going to need to reload or go and get some more ammunition, giving Jack some room to move, without accidentally striking a passing projectile but only if he hurried up she thought.

Jack was swinging backwards and forwards on the cord, he had tried reaching up and taking the cord in his hand but had found that his suit was not flexible enough to allow it. No matter what, he was going to stick to that story until the end of time. He was not quite ready to admit that his mid-drift was more like a bag full of tiny chubby koalas, rather than the flat and sleek look of an ironing board he had always imagined it to be.

The word 'nefarious' crossed his mind with regards to the shooters, plus some other thoughts that would not be printable in any magazine or newspaper, followed by the thought of where was that word coming from?

The swinging motion eventually allowed him to twist up and get a grip on the cord. Then he started the long climb back up the knotted rope, after only a few moments he noticed that he was not so much climbing up the rope, that the rope was coming down to meet him with the board attached. The entire time Jack had been swinging around under the board, the one thing he had not noticed was the descent. He looked down and now saw that he was an inch from the ground, so he let go of the cord and stepped onto the tarmac. The surfboard then quickly lowered itself to ground level, floating just at his feet, like a dog waiting for a treat for being a good boy, after running away for the past half hour.

Jack looked around as he prepared to step aboard, he was basically stood in an shopping arcade, full of tables with plastic looking seating and strangely shaped umbrellas. The track ran straight down the middle of it, with the various food and drink shops on either side having a fuzzy plastic looking layer over the front of them. A great deal of the outside furniture was being damaged by the haze of bullets heading his way and not hitting him. The fuzzy plastic like shield was obviously there to stop stray weapons fire from damaging the area, it just was not designed to take this amount of rain of fire. This was probably why Jack was now stood alone on the ground, as the audience had moved surprisingly quickly away, while the furniture was being dismantled into a confetti like mess.

Jack had wondered how he was going to get back on the board if he fell off, it was something he had hoped he would have to worry about later or maybe not at all.

There was still the worrying zing of bullets flying past his head, though strangely none had hit him and now apparently they had stopped. Jack quickly guessed that they had stopped firing to reload, buy some more ammunition or the lights were now green, so he jumped quickly back on his surfboard. The thumb sticks popped back up in his hands, he found the SUD drive button and pressed hard on the controls, aiming back to the fuzzy blue line.

Jack and his surfboard quickly emerged back into the gap, he gave himself a moment to look at his position in the race and was pleasantly surprised to find he had only lost two places. As he neared the end of dangers straight, he watched the apartment containing Claire and company become clearer through the rainbow haze of the split.

Claire was stood in the window waving slowly, almost apologetically as Jack approached, that was then he remembered the colour of the bullet trail he had leapt from the board for. He ignored her as he sailed by and back through the danger posts exit, mainly because green was Claire's favourite colour but mostly because of the guilty look she had on her face.

It took over four minutes to complete a lap, with the most laps ever recorded standing at fourteen in the hour long race. Currently Jack was in third place, with only a few board lengths separating the top four surfers as they jostled for positions. There had been all kinds of accidents and even some that may not have been accidents, so long as they occurred in the danger zone anything went apparently.

Jack was currently in third place with Juice behind him bobbing along, like only an octopus in a space suit could. The problem for Jack was that although he knew Juice, he was not entirely sure what exactly he was going to do as they neared the end of the race. The other minor concern were the two racers in front. One of them kept looking back over there shoulder at him and giving Jack the impression that they were winking at him.

The visors on the racers helmets all varied, some seemed to be coloured and others see through. It was only when he was checking over his shoulder for Juice, when he hit a particularly curvy wave, that he saw Juice's visor become opaque, draining the milky white colouring from his visor. He assumed it was a smile he got from Juice but due to the excessive wavy bits of facial anatomy, he was not sure if it could have been a grimace instead.

After catching up with the front runners, Jack had decided to stay in the group. There had originally been eight of them but after passing through the danger zone a few times, there numbers had been depleted somewhat.

For whatever reason the public seemed inclined to be continually aiming for Jack and so being in a group cut his odds of being hit. The large cannons he had seen being constructed had each fired several times, the end result of which had looked amazing but not actually very effective at racer removal. They were in actual fact more of a nuisance. Each one could fire once every ten seconds, what they eventually fired was a barrage of what looked like actual fireworks. Each shot initially looked like a huge comical shell that you might find in any good quality cartoon, then when it hit the tube boundary, where the Split Universe Drive gap was, they exploded like a massive multi-rocket firework. It looked amazing from the outside, with various adverts written large in letters and logo's on the outside of the tube, on the inside of the tube it just looked like a supersized bowl of slow moving spaghetti had been lobbed at them.

Each explosion was made up of tiny shrapnel like pieces of brightly coloured metal, spinning wildly around giving the clear shadow of the tube some much needed colour. The racers were in effect playing dodgem, space ball or dodge ball depending on your age. They were forced to slow down but not by a great deal, otherwise you lost control of the waves you were surfing and ended up falling through and being dragged back to reality. The waves themselves followed the contours of the tube, creating a strange effect like looking out of an aquarium in shadow but with occasional bright edges and ridges. There were always waves within waves that could be ridden as you traveled faster or slower, the trick was too move from one to the other without falling off and or being bitten by some random metal.

Chapter 46 : The Final Lap.

The final corner before the start finish line swung into view, as the surfers crossed the line the SUD drives switched off automatically and Jack remembered the Commander saying something about this being the most dangerous part of the race. Considering he had already fallen out of the gap earlier, Jack was unsure how it could be any more dangerous than being shot at in the danger zone whilst hanging upside down by an ankle.

What he had not considered was his fellow racers and the effect they had on the split as they all dropped out of the gap, by the simple means of having there respective drives turned off. Jack could see why surfboards and even starships had angled hulls, so they gently rode up and down the waves in the gap. When the drive was just turned off, it was like trying to ride a three wheeled skateboard round the inside of a large blender, whilst being chased by a bucking bull high on freedom. In short it was a tad rough for a few seconds. The proximity of his fellow surfers did not help, they caused eddies and crests in the waves as they sunk back through into reality again.

Then Jack once again felt the force of friction from the air, it was like being stood up while wearing a cape in front of sand blaster. As soon as the drive had turned off Jack had almost dived flat on to his board, more in panic than forethought.

The two racers in front had known what was coming and were holding on for dear life. The only thing they had not been prepared for was other surfers riding quite so close and the bumpy effect they were having on the wave front as they entered reality.

The leader had fallen off in front of Jack, at such an angle that Jack accidentally caught there cord on his own board fin and the force had swung them around for a moment like a child twirling a baton in a big circle. Jack looked at them as he passed, the surfer ground there helmet on the tarmac twice on there orbit around there own board, finally landing back on the surfboard, more by accident than design.

The fallen racer was facing the wrong way on there board, as they turned to look forward Jack recognized the Mercs clothing. Identification was helped by the top of there helmet being shaved off at angle, leaving the remaining hair follicles to wave around freely in the air.

The person in second place had faired a little better, although they had been pulled off there board like they were wearing a parachute. As Jack swerved down to avoid them, he felt the urge to wave and looked up into the face of Samantha as he swung round underneath her. She did not look all that happy about Jack passing between her legs at high speed.

That left Juice somewhere behind Jack. As he turned to look for him with the air making a tearing sound all around him, he realized that he had turned one of the exhaust ports to face forward and was using it as a form of air splitter. How he had the presence of mind or even had thought of it was another thing entirely. Juice had done something similar and gave Jack a sort of thumbs up from his loose space suit.

As they twisted through various parts of this admittedly amazing looking planet, Jack suddenly felt homesick for Earth. Even for the dead end job in his office and being abused by Claire every morning when he went to work. Jack had never felt sombre or depressed before but this was pretty much how he had imagined it might feel.

As they approached the danger zone, once again zipping out and curving over the inside of the tube, Jack felt the urge to retire, permanently. It was at precisely this point that a voice sounding just like Beth's said in his head in a tone of desperation "will you just look at the tiny little screen in your bottom right!"

Jack looked obediently down in his visor and suddenly his vision was filled with puppies, flowers, sand, sea and endless green vistas, making him feel happy and relaxed. Then it was all gone and the posts of the danger zone loomed in front.

"What was that?" asked Jack curiously.

"Someone is performing a wide spectrum cast of depression and anxiety."

"Why?"

"So you fail of course" said Beth's voice.

Before Jack could ask anything else Juice crossed between the posts in front of him and started to slow down. He then realized that everybody left in the race, he glanced down at the position display which was reading two of thirty two, was experiencing the same melancholy thing Beth's voice had just helped him escape. He just hoped the danger zone was not active, which of course it was. He quickly grabbed one of the grips on the front of Juice's board and dragged him along, all the time making hand signals to Juice to apply more speed as the first bullet slung by at medium velocity.

It was like trying to fly through a sieve, a large one made mostly of slow moving metal, although not as slow as being in the gap. Obviously the tube was slowing down the weapon fire but nowhere near as much as being in the gap did. After only a few seconds Jack happened to glance down at the shopping arcade below them and noticed the various statues.

He made the decision to dive to the edge of the blue lines influence and use the various street furniture as cover. Not so much to hide behind but being so close to the objects might confuse there aiming at him.

Now it was like flying through a plastic confetti convention, as bullet after vary coloured bullet and its trails struck the remaining furniture all around. The only thing he had not seen so far was the cannons firing. He looked up and saw that they had started to dissolve line by line.

The corner at the end of the danger zone seemed to take an age to reach, with the circuit slowly edging up to pass right in front of the apartment, where Claire was staring leaning out of the window waving for Jack to 'just get on with it!'
Behind him Jack could hear screams in various languages, as some of the other racers were now being targeted by the shooters. Then he and Juice banked around the corner, passed through the posts just as they started to turn green again.

Then a pressure seemed to stop suddenly in there heads, it was like suddenly being able to breath properly but in there minds. Juice shook his head several times to clear it, the melancholy broadcast had obviously affected him more than the other racers for some reason. He slowly took control of his board again and gave Jack a thumbs up sign to show he could let go of his board.

They flew through The Sall shopping arcade, with its little twists and turns, down another shopping arcade with aliens sat drinking and waving at them as they passed over head for the last time. Then they dipped down into a black tunnel and entered the stadium for the final time.

Jack assumed that Juice would let him win, mainly because he had saved his life but as they entered the stadium Juice shot ahead after he gave Jack a hefty kick off his board. Jack swung off his board but unlike a pendulum managed to swing back up and land on his board again. He was not entirely sure how he had managed it, the choked silence and then roar from the crowd as he landed back on his surfboard showed there appreciation.

After only a few seconds of chasing Juice, Jack realized that there was no way he was going to catch him before he crossed the line. It was the most frustrating thing he had ever felt, after all the things he had gone through to get to the race, let alone survive it. He was now going to lose because a supposed friend had quite literally given him the boot. Jack had no idea what second prize was, he just knew that he needed that trophy.

Jack managed to get within inches of passing Juice, making sure to stay out of his tentacled booted range, only to have the number '2' flash up on his display as he crossed the line.
He could hear Juice shouting something about how many years he had tried and failed to win this competition. His voice appeared to be cracking as he shouted out with sheer joy.

The rest was a blur for Jack. There were interviews and party invites, with Juice waving around a great big golden coloured trophy, whilst wearing gloves. All Jack really remembered was continuous noise and being shoved from one place to another, feeling quite annoyed with his supposed friend.

Eventually back in the apartment Jack walked in and found Claire stood right in front him glowering. It was a great description of her ground state of being whenever she was in front of Jack, at least Jack thought so anyway. Then she slapped him. It was not a hard slap but it was a surprise and then she shocked him even more by kissing him briefly on the lips and then hugging him. She mumbled something about being pleased to see him again and then stepped quickly back and walked off.

Jack was at a loss to explain Claire, then each of the others came over and paid there condolences finally leaving Jack with the Commander.
"I'm sorry I didn't get the trophy" said Jack.
"Well, that's okay" replied the Commander casually.
Jack looked a bit surprised by his tone and asked curiously "is it?"
Then a bell like sound rang out from the door and Summer walked over, she waved her hand making the door see through in one direction and then waved it open.
Juice walked in a little unsteadily, followed by several men wearing 'suits for space' and looking around anxiously for security threats.
The Commander gave Jack a harsh look and said "well now we know your a fashion faux-pa creator?"

Jack was stood open mouthed as Juice seemed to swagger in, then reach round from behind his back to flourish the trophy at him. Jack really was not listening to the Commander, he felt the urge to punch Juice in his smiling many clawed face. The only thing stopping him was the grinning and waving of the little critters, popping in and out of his wavy hair. This close too they appeared to be tiny copies of Juice himself but so much cuter because they had large friendly eyes and had not, as of yet, developed the numerous claw like limbs for dragging food into there mouths.
Juice saw him staring at his hair and said simply with a shrug "my babies."
"You took babies into the race?" asked Claire in surprise.
"Of course, how else would they learn anything?" replied Juice questioningly.
Claire just shrugged, shook her head and took a step away from them all staring at her Quellz.

Juice was also quite obviously drunk or at least the alien equivalent, he then actually lost his grip on the trophy, juggling with the thing as it spun around in his hands. It flew through the air, then bounced on one of the sofas as he finally lost the battle with his own motor control and gravity. The look on the security men's faces were priceless, like performing a bungee jump and then realizing the bungee bit was not attached and they were definitely going to get wet. They were also all human, of the loaded upside down shaped pyramid variety. They looked like walking wedges of cheese all suited and booted in black, with white shirts and strangely chequered ties for there suits for space.

The only person who had reached or at least tried to move to catch the trophy had been Jack, everyone else in the room had just stood in shock as it spun round and landed safely on the sofa.
Jack reached to pick up the trophy, two guards took hold of each arm and twisted both up behind his back before he even got close to touching it. It was only then that Jack noticed that the guards were all female, they all had there hair tied back or shaved in some way and appeared to be of the heavy set weightlifter competition form, because of there bulk.
It was only being women handled this close to them that he smelled "lily of the valley?"
Instantly Jack regretted opening his mouth again because of the extra twist he received in both of his arms. Both women behind his back exchanged looks for a brief second, letting him go with small frowns, as if they were being given external commands from some hidden earpieces or from there dark glasses.

Juice stepped forward, still wearing his race suit, with a gloved appendage picked up the trophy by one of its handles and said "there actually only looking out for you, after all this is the most dangerous and wanted prize in the galaxy!" He finished with a flourish, standing like he had just committed a star jump.
Juice turned his head to his security detail, whilst still in his star pose and ordered "leave us for five minutes."

The five security women moved slowly, precisely, out of the door, stepping out in perfect unison and timing. When they were all outside the door they lined up in the corridor facing the apartment door and stood to attention. The door then swooshed shut and Jack turned angrily to face Juice, who now stood proffering the trophy to Jack almost in self defence.
Jack reached forward to take the trophy and then had his wrist grabbed by Summer before he could take hold of it "are you sure you want to do this?" she asked.
In frustration Jack replied "isn't this what you lot wanted all along, for me to take hold of this thing and flap back in time?"
"Well, yes but only if your sure?" asked the Commander.

Jack shook his hand free of Summer and snatched the trophy from Juice saying "just give me the thing and lets get this over with."
Juice turned to the Commander, flashing his Quellz at him, the Commander briefly touched the screen and whispered something at the display that sounded like 'well, Peace Blossom'.
Jack stood still for a few seconds, holding the trophy in both hands with his eyes closed and then half peaking through one eye at the trophy said "it's not working?"
"Well, that's because the your not holding the sphere Jack" said the Commander turning from Juice.
"You said the trophy was the sphere?"
"Well, does it look like a ball to you?" said the Commander whilst stepping around the room impatiently.

"No, but if it's like any of the other tech around here it could fold into a beach of a ball at any moment!"

Nothing happened for several more seconds, then Jack turned to the Commander who did actually have a confused expression on his face and asked "you don't know how it works, do you?"

"Well no, not exactly" replied the Commander slowly.

"So why am I holding it at arms length then? It's getting quite heavy yo..." the sparkly golden trophy slipped out of Jacks fingers and fell to the floor. It traveled in apparent slow motion from Jack's hand to the floor, with Jack managing to deftly catch an edge and force it into a ferocious spin towards the table.

It had all the hallmarks of a juggling accident involving a chainsaw, where everyone wanted to help and yet at the same time wanting to jump away, with everyone staring in shocked disbelief at the falling item. The trophy bounced off the side of the table and struck the floor with a surprisingly loud dead sounding 'thunk', like the thing was made from diseased wood rather than some solid and expensive metal. Then there was a light popping sound from the base of the trophy, like a cap being taken off a bottle of fizzy pop.

Looking over the top of the table they found the trophy on its side, with the base facing them. On the bottom a large crack had appeared, which on closer inspection of course resolved itself to be a hidden compartment in the dense blocky base, Jack sighed.

Inside was something that looked like a clear crystal but looked perfectly round rather than having any straight edges. Jack moved to pry open the gap, the door to the apartment swung open behind him, followed by some quick foot steps.

Chapter 47 : The Prize.

"So everyone really wants this trophy then?" said Jack standing up, holding the trophy at arms length and prying at the bottom.
"Well, not so much the trophy now but more the contents that everyone now knows that's in it" answered the Commander.
"But why, it's only a 'time sphere', as it's called?" mused Claire, looking up from her Quellz and the research she had been furiously doing.
"It's not just a Time Sphere or God Ball or Spear of Destiny or even Sphere of Destiny but something that enables all time to be altered" said Olgas Faid having strode into the room briskly and taken the trophy from Jack's surprised hands. He was wearing gloves, black leather looking ones with all manner of metal studs and prickly looking attachments that wound up round his wrists, nearly reaching his apparent Raifoon like elbows.
"You look a bit rough round the edges" commented Jack, looking at his disheveled appearance, it looked like a few million volts had been applied to him and then back combed for effect. Spiky would be the word Jack was looking for, with maybe a touch of clumping.
Olgas Faid gave Jack an angry look, which he just smiled at.
"Well, give it back to Jack then and lets get this over" said the Commander.
"First he needs to know how!" said an annoyed Olgas.
Jack exchanged a look with the Commander that basically said 'what?' The Commander leant forward, twisted his furry ear around to show a disguised flat disc behind it and made to pass Jack an invisible version.
"Surely I just go back in time and hand over the 'data wheel' to the Commander here?" said Jack pointing at the Commander.
Shaking his head Olgas replied "it's not just about to whom you hand over the data wheel but how you do it!"
Jack leant towards the Commander, making to pass back the invisible disc and saying "there you go mate, read at your own leisure, if you know what I mean" he winked knowingly as if he were handing over some form of bare viewing contraband.
"Well thanks" replied the Commander sarcastically.
"That is not what I meant" said Olgas, prizing the ball out of the marble base with a gloved hand and dropping the trophy like a discarded toy on the floor.

It landed heavily on the wood carpet tiled floor, bending in the middle like a soft metal being stood on by an elephant. Juice picked it up quickly, with tears forming in his wavy eyes and held it carefully in a soft embrace against his chest. All his life he had wanted the thing, to show everyone he was special, to show them he was the best and now his prize was dented, bent, distorted but mainly broken. The money was amazing but the prize was the trophy and looking at it now, it seemed to have lost its luster, like the light that had been shining from within it had been turned off. It looked like some cheap metal copy that you might find in the supermarket discount trophy section, ready to be handed out even to last place because 'everyone is a winner.'
Juice was finding himself to be surprisingly angry and regretting the deal he had made with the Commander, even if he was now insanely rich.

Claire was curiously angry too, thinking that Jack seemed to have a knack for either learning some things really quickly or giving the appearance of learning things really quickly. Claire was going with another option of the 'he's faking knowledge' theory.
She was curious as to what a 'data wheel' was to and why Jack had mentioned it, with the others just seeming to agree. Maybe some of his memories were maybe coming back after all, though even she could work out what a 'data wheel' might be, just from the name. The only problem she had was that as far as she knew no one had mentioned a data-wheel before. She was assuming the camouflaged disc was the data-wheel, as to what it did she guessed she would have to wait to find out, as this Olgas the Furrykin looked quite angry, explosive even.

Olgas Faid was stood staring unfocused, shaking, being completely absorbed by the crystal like sphere in his gloved hands. It was like he was looking at everything he had ever wanted, right there in his hands, the temptation to touch it with bare flesh was immense, which was making him very angry. He turned back from studying the orb and handed it to Jack with a truly massive sigh of regret, with a face like a toddler having all his toys taken away by the adult, just because they can.

Olgas composed himself for a few moments and then turning to face Jack said "you could have gone back in time at any point in your journey here."
"What! You mean to say I could have avoided ... well everything that has happened to me, too everyone and gone back at the beginning?" exclaimed Jack.
"No" said Olgas.
Spluttering Jack replied "you better explain yourself, you've just said that this whole thing was a waste of time!"
Olgas Faid suddenly felt tired, he turned and sat down on one of the sofas, it adjusted to his build as he prepared to speak in simple terms.

"You could of, well anyone can, travel back in time using current technology. As you and many others might have noticed if this was the case, then there would be many more reports and sightings of time travelers As it is, this is very rare for several reasons. First of all how would you know that they were a time traveler, as anyone disclosing that they were from the future or even the past would immediately be imprisoned or disposed of. Then there's the added problem of the branches of time. If you were to travel back in time and attempt to alter the future, which we all can do, it may not stick. When you travel backwards in time without a sphere, you are likely to only affect your time line, you could change events but only in one possibility or reality."

"But I only want to change one reality?" asked Jack.

"You misunderstand, all realities are connected and overlap all the time. If you were to say to travel back and kill your grandfather, what would happen to you?"

"I would cease to exist?" hazarded Jack after a moments thought.

"Actually no, because you have not killed all your grandfathers everywhere, you never could."

"But I could with a sphere?" questioned Jack, whilst imagining that he would somehow end up swinging the sphere round at his grandfathers head, striking him down, whom ever he was.

"Again no, not exactly but if you were holding an activated sphere whilst you performed the act, then you would have a chance of killing all of them, forever!"

Jack rolled the sphere around in his hands, the ball was giving off an odd glow and seemed to be pulling him towards something but what exactly he had no idea. It seemed to be trying to move in all directions at once like an aggravated child in a sweet shop, the only thing missing was the screams.

"Okay but what would happen to me then and my grandfather?"

"Everything you and your grandfather had ever have done would cease to be, he would never have existed in the first place and neither would you!"

"So how do I 'activate' this ball then?" asked Jack, rolling it from one hand to the other, with Claire and the others staring at him disbelievingly.

Olgas and the Commander were both looking on transfixed as Jack juggled the jewel like sphere from one hand to the other. Inevitability he messed up rolling it around in his hands, as it fell towards the floor the aliens held there collective breaths and flinched. Jack on the other hand said "oh" and deftly caught it with his foot and flicked it back up into his hands.

"Couldn't do that with the trophy then?" asked Juice sarcastically.

Jack turned and grinned at him.

Olgas was about to shout at him but did not, just in case he dropped the ball in shock. Composing himself again Olgas said "when you get to when you need to be, you must activate the sphere before you perform any action. You will have approximately ninety seconds to complete the task before the sphere becomes unusable and fix the event."
"Unusable?"
"To all intent and purposes yes, it'll take several centuries to recharge."
"Right okay so let me get this straight. Your saying that if I change one event without a sphere it won't effect all of history, just a small part of it. But if I change an event whilst holding an activated sphere it will change everything and every event everywhere?"
"Yes, it will fix that event to all versions of reality."
"So what happens if the sphere isn't activated?"
"You would live out your life in that reality, closed off from all the others most probably."
"That would be bad, right?"
"Yes, no Split Universe Drive, no portals and your Universe would collapse in on its self, eventually."
Jack gulped and looked at the sphere in his hands, the one thing he hated more than anything else was responsibility, therefore having responsibility for an entire wealth of Universes and there occupants resting in his shaking hands was quite scary.
Olgas looked at Jack starting to shake like a bull with a bur up its bum in a china shop and said "you must change an event whilst using one of the spheres to fix that event, that's the reason they are so sought after by so many and why time travel is banned."
"Because with a sphere you can fix any event in time anywhere and everywhere!"
"And it stays fixed" said Olgas in a smug tone.
"Unless you undo it all with another ball of course" mused Jack.
Olgas sighed and was ready to explain everything again when the Commander interrupted "well have we really got time for this, doesn't Jack need to go, before the authorities catch on to what we're doing?"
"Yes, yes it is time" turning to face Jack again Olgas continued "are you ready Jack?"
Pulling himself up straight Jack replied "just tell me what to do?"
Olgas stared at him and blinked slowly with his eye lids blinking shut like patio doors and then asked "you don't know what to do?"
"I know what to do, but I don't know how to do it do I?" replied Jack questioningly.
"Hmm maybe that is why the authorities haven't collected us yet" mused Olgas.
"So it's a good thing Jack has no idea what he's doing?" asked Claire in surprise.
Olgas replied simply and with a shrug "yes."
"Well that's a first!" said Claire crossing and uncrossing her arms and legs.

Olgas Faid then reached round somewhere inside his clothing, pulled out a small black leather looking pouch and threw it at Jack. Looking at it in his hands Jack could see it was a perfect fit for the sphere, he dropped the shiny crystal ball inside, tied the pouch shut and then found it clipped to his belt by some form of elasticated magnetism.

They all stood around in the apartment looking a bit lost, with Juice now sitting in a corner with his trophy, just holding it in his hands, rocking himself slowly and almost seeming to cry. His babies did not seem to mind, as they swung about in his spaghetti like hair, swinging from length to length and then landing on the trophy, then running with there eight arms and legs back up his two suited arms with gay abandon.

After a few minutes of silent thought Jack was bored and asked "so what are we doing?"

"Well it would appear that we're being given the chance to find a solution and I think it might be best to do that in Beth?" suggested the Commander.

Jack choked slightly until he realized the Commander meant the War Catcher space ship.

When they left the apartment Olgas Faid bid his farewells, as soon as they were outside of the building he slipped into a sleek blacked out wheel-less angled limousine and disappeared. Then an extremely white similarly shaped vehicle approached and Juice was bundled in the back of it by the security women who had followed them down. Just before it lifted off Juice rolled out some small backdoor, his body changing shape within the suit to enable his escape.

The lift journey down had been unnaturally cosy, it was a large lift and even with so many creatures in it, it should have been fine. It had just been the number of bags and boxes containing shoes that had been the problem and Claire declaring 'I am not leaving them just lying around for anyone to take!' The set of her jaw had stopped any argument but it did mean that the space in the elevator had been limited. The only good thing was that no one had to carry them, the hotel had provided floating black pallets to tow them around on. The pallets had appeared to actually groan when Claire had finally finished stacking them up.

Now stood on the curb waiting for there transport to arrive, Claire suddenly started to shout and curse. As Jack turned, he saw the last pallet tip its load onto the curbside with the other dropped boxes, the black pallet seemed to strut its way back, joining its companions by the hotel doors. They just seemed to be standing, watching, waiting for Claire's reaction. Jack tried not to smile, it did not work.

Then a super sleek and awfully red supersized trike appeared. At least it looked like a trike. It had a sharply curved front pod, with slightly smaller ones on either side flaring out but slightly twisted to create a wing effect. To Jack it looked like the mating of a whale and an eagle had gone on, then it had been painted a really vivid red, with a bright yellow flame decal by a drunk pelican. So he was not surprised when a door appeared in the side near the front and Joan poked her head out. She scanned her eye from side to side, like a buzzard scanning the horizon for the local corpse. She waved them onboard with her short plumed hand, with Jack all the time thinking 'what's with the redness on everything she uses?'

Inside the vehicle was completely utilitarian, with everything for function and nothing for the aesthetic. Jack thought of it as walking into a aeroplane manufacturing plant just before they added any furnishings whatsoever to the plane.

Joan stared at them with her single eye and gestured for them all to sit down as she almost skipped back towards the cockpit. There was a lot of black inside the ship as Jack thought of it. It was reminding him of a boat or a plane in its design but with an awful lot of dark through out the interior. Nearly the entire thing was black in fact, apart from a silver strip running down the middle like a gang plank.

Claire had been a doting mother over her precious shoe boxes, but as Joan gunned the engines Jack watched as she threw box after bag after shoe-box through the doorway. She was also carefully avoiding Jack's eye, as no one else was apparently willing to help.
Claire stepped through the doorway just as Joan then called out over some internal tannoy system "ready?"

The two humans exchanged looks and both started to ask "for what?" just as all the black surfaces inside the ship became see through. Fortunately for Jack he was sat down as the floor and walls became transparent, sending shivers through his system. He watched as the perfect view of the city zipped by underneath, with Joan performing a slow angled pass over the stadium and the blue lined track. Claire on the other hand had spun around when the floor disappeared from view and quite literally fell into her seat, with her eyes appearing to spin in there sockets as she landed wiping a perspiring brow.

The trike was obviously some form of shuttle, they watched as the world disappeared away underneath them, slicing through the atmosphere and aiming for the Golden Moon.

Chapter 48 : Short Flight.

Remembering his last visit to the moon, Jack was a little cautious about getting off and stepping through any arches. As the red multi-pod shuttle flew into a hangar bay filled to the roof with ships of every size and description, but generally of a shuttle like design. Jack looked round trying to find the War Catcher, absent-mindedly swiping at something on his shoulder.

The shuttle maneuvered around several vessels in the process of taking off and landing, it finally parked next to a large silver dart shaped vessel sending up small plumes of golden dust clouds.

"We're here" said Joan as she walked back through the shuttle and waved at the door to open.

With a sigh she stepped down the ramp like staircase of only a few steps and wandered quickly away from the shuttle. She then turned and appeared to be admiring the red trike shaped shuttle, seeming to scan it with her eye from one end to the other like she was recording it some how. It was then as Jack walked towards her that he noticed a golden rim around her single eye and a coloured band that traveled around the back of her head. The rubber banding was almost perfectly see through and Jack asked "are you wearing blinkers?"

With a smile playing across her beak, Joan replied wistfully "yes, they finally released the military version of the blinker for Avacors."

"And that's good because?"

"Previously they were of limited use because of discomfort and made us growly. These have no lens and project the information into our eye."

"So why are we staring at a red ship?" asked Jack pointing at there transport.

"Because for the first time I can see it how you see it and record it at the same time" Joan looked so happy as she looked at the red coloured ship, that Jack was a little confused as to why she was so happy.

Jack left Joan staring at the shuttle and briefly asked the Commander what was up with her, he was quite surprised when he simply said "well, she really likes the colour red."

Jack stared around looking for the arches, specifically the one that electrocuted innocent people, when he could not find them he asked "so, where are the arches?"

The Commander replied "well there at the entrance, not at the exit. You can always go back through them if you wish and have the Sham removed."

"With electricity" chimed in Claire in an amused tone.

Jack shuddered visibly and strode off towards the silvery dart.

On board the War Catcher, hidden by the Ghost Field Generator dressed as some expensive executives transport ship, they set course for where Earth had been. The entire journey of light years would take only a matter of hours with Jack and Claire staring out of the bridges oddly dipped in chocolate shaped window, as they entered the gap between Universes. It was something that Jack would never get tired of watching as they surfaced into the gap and watched the literal waves of reality pound the hull of the ship. Eventually though the tapping of the Commanders long nails on one of the consoles got to be annoying enough, that Jack turned round and found everyone looking at him expectantly.
"Are you ready?" asked Beth sat in the Captains seat.
"Um, for what exactly?" asked Jack.
"Really, the whole purpose of this... adventure and you still don't know?" said a slightly angry Summer.
"I am ready" replied Jack defensively "it's just I don't really know what for?"
　　　　The Commander pulled a camouflaged disc from behind his ear and jaw, it made a small popping sound as it left the skin, which made Jack shudder for some reason as it sounded organic.
After a few seconds it became a silvery disc in his paw and the Commander said "well, this is a Life Archive Record Device or data-wheel, used in many criminal cases especially in undercover work."
He then reached down to the central console table and placed it on the flat surface, as soon as he let go various images floated up and were projected just above the surface. Jack recognized various moments as they flashed by but from the Commanders perspective. Then just as suddenly the images stopped and sat on the console top was a large white disc, about half an inch thick with a diameter of a golf ball. There were three notches taken out on one side, Jack stared at expecting it to do something, be smaller at least and when nothing happened he asked "so what does it do?"
The Commander picked up the data wheel and handed it to Jack "well if I were to place it on a secure console you could see and hear the images. If you place it on the younger me I'll be able to see the events or simply have them as a memory!"
"But it looks rubbish!" moaned Jack staring at the encased data wheel.
"Do you have any idea what's in that?" asked Summer.
Jack swallowed and said "no, not really."
"Everything the Commander here has seen and done since he put it on."
"Yeah about that, when exactly did you put it on?" asked Jack looking at the Commander.
The Commander made a slightly uncomfortable cough like sound, looked sideways at his Second and said "well, soon after I was made Commander."
"Okay" said Jack slowly "so I'm to travel back in time, meet you on your war ship, get you to place this data-wheel on your younger self and stop the war from ever happening?"
"Well, yes and you can't show anyone else the Lard either."

Jack took a moment to work out what he meant and then asked carefully "why?"

"Because they are technically, maybe a little, only slightly illegal" said Summer.

Jack rolled his eyes and asked again "why?"

"You may have noticed that most technology is external" Jack nodded, Summer continued "that was not always the case, there was a time when most technology was inserted into the body. It worked flawlessly for years, until someone found a way to break into it and ruin everyone's lives."

"So how is this technology illegal, doesn't it sit on the outside of your body?"

"Yes, but it uses the same principals as the broken technology" said Summer.

"Well that's not strictly true" said the Commander.

"Yes it is" retorted Summer.

Jack looked on for a moment as an argument appeared to be about to start and stopped it short by asking the Commander "why's it not true?"

"Well, since the data wheel can only be used by me for me and now only on this console" the Commander tapped the central table on the bridge "it's not illegal."

"It's only illegal if anyone else tries to use it?" asked Jack.

"Well, yes."

Jack picked up the data-wheel, spinning the white thing around in his hand and then after feeling the stares put it in the black pouch on his belt next to the sphere and asked "so what now?"

"Well now we all die!" replied the Commander.

The look on everyone's faces were identical, a mixture of surprise, fear and worry followed by some really sharp breaths.

"Well not literally obviously, we'll just sort of cease to exist" said the Commander.

"That makes us all feel so much better!" replied Claire with heavy sarcasm and a glance around for her shoe-box collection.

"We may also continue to exist anyway, in this time line" mused Jane walking onto the bridge and leaning on the central table.

"What do you mean?" asked Claire.

"It's entirely possible that if Jack goes back and does change things for the better, it may not affect every possible outcome and we could still exist here" Jane waved her hands around to take in the Universe.

    They all looked deep in thought, contemplating the possible eventualities, which there were near infinite possibilities of. Jack on the other hand was thinking it was now or never, before his nerve broke or someone suggested he think about what he was doing.

"So what happens now" asked Jack looking at the Commander.

Sighing the Commander said "well, when we get to your solar system, we'll take the shuttle and go and hide in the asteroid belt, just to make sure that it goes according to plan. Then you'll travel back to before the invasion, pass me the data-wheel and persuade me to stop the attack."

"You make it sound so simple" said Jack.

"Well actually it will be, I've given the ship all the codes and protocols and the disguise to get you onboard the Stellar Attack Vessel" Jack opened his mouth and the Commander stopped him by saying "yes Jack, my War Ship."

"Actually I was going to ask which ship was coming back with me, I thought I was going on my own?"

"Well alone the data-wheel won't get you on the SAV will it?"

Jack stopped his argumentative question from forming, he was only really trying to delay them leaving him alone after all.

But still he did have a few questions "why can't I just land on the War Ship and how exactly am I to travel back in time, that's the one thing you've all been vague about?"

"Well, how exactly are you going to explain appearing on the bridge of my ship and not get shot in the process? No, your best option is to dock with the SAV and be taken too me where I will recognize you and listen to what you have to say. As to traveling back in time, your armour will help out."

"My armour?" Jack questioned looking at his 'suit for space' that he was still wearing. It had become so comfortable that he had forgotten about it and in addition he actually thought it looked cool.

The Commander waved at everyone and Summer started to usher them off the bridge. Several steps later they walked out on to the ship deck of the space station. Jack had been so preoccupied with what he was supposed to be doing he had not even noticed there dropping out of the gap, nor there docking with the ghost ship parked in Earth's solar system, right out on the edge.

Jack trailed along behind as they made there way around the back of the War Catcher, where sat brooding in a corner was his first space transport. Someone had changed the 'O' in shot to an 'I' again, by the simple means of some red paint being applied with an brush.

"You still haven't explained the whole armour thing you know?" asked Jack of the Commander.

"Well, no but that voice you've heard in your head occasionally?"

Jack nodded slowly trying to avoid drawing too much attention to himself, especially from Claire, as hearing voices in your head was generally considered a bad thing.

"Well it's your armour trying to talk you, helping you. So all you have to do is listen to it."

They were now all stood waiting in a little group in front of the shuttle, waiting for Jack to say his goodbye's, he could not bring himself to say anything. Mainly because he did not know really what to say and still was unsure what was supposed to happen. Jack was thinking of his life in terms of a roller-coaster ride; he could see roughly where the track went, he was just not sure exactly what would happen when he got in the buggy that was supposedly going to follow the track.

Joan stepped forward first and enveloped him in her feathered arms and clipped wings, she hugged him fiercely but the only thing Jack remembered about her afterwards was the intense floral smell she left on him.

In turn they all hugged him with Claire trying to hang on to be last, for some reason Beth was hanging around at the back, forcing Claire to step forward early and not hug Jack. She reached forth a hand, Jack shook it slowly, feeling a little confused.
Angrily Claire then lent forward and said "I won't remember this but you will" and gave him a kiss on the lips. She then turned smartly and almost seemed to stalk away, keeping her back as straight as possible.

Jack stood feeling very confused as he watched Claire steadily walk away, with what he thought of as excessive hip sway.
Stood beside Joan and Ron, Claire watched Jack yet again swipe his hand at some invisible spiders and there cobwebs. Claire ground her teeth together, for some reason his unconscious waving at fairies really irritated her.

In front of Jack was the Commander holding paws with Second, Claire stood leaning heavily against the Hot Sho(i)t shuttle behind them. Jane stood holding Sara's hand, with Joan and Ron holding one another's hand like appendages. Jack nearly jumped when he felt a hand touch his shoulder, turning his head he found Summer looking at him with her soulful light brown eyes, this close Jack could see there were flecks of gold in her eyes. She lightly touched his face as she almost seemed to dance round him and then whispered something in his ear that he did not hear or understand at all.

Before he could ask what it was about, Juice walked out of the ship and stumbled over to Jack, still holding his trophy. Considering he was basically a bag of muscly jelly being held in place by his space suit, he did do remarkably well at walking like a normal biped. As he meandered past Jack he suddenly swung the trophy round to try and swipe Jack around the head. Instinctively Jack swayed back, he need not of worried as Juice was pulled up short by Summer dancing around him and catching the trophy mid swing. Setting up a reverse swaying motion, as the force of the swing set Juice into a spin and eventual landing on his bottom.

There followed a heated discussion about causality, the meaning of life and where all the Playtor's went, with Juice finally shaking his head in defeat and walking off to stand near Claire. Jack looked at Summer curiously, who simply shrugged and walked over to join the Commander and the waving off committee.

The only person missing was Beth, after a few awkward moments and tiny waves from everyone involved eventually turning into shooing motions, Jack turned and re-boarded Beth's War Catcher.

Chapter 49 : New Maneuvers.

Jack walked up the long gangway into the back of the ship, he turned one last time to wave goodbye and found the exit had already frosted over with the traditional 'swooshing' sound behind him and therefore presumably the ramp had retracted as well. Once again Jack was looking at a loading bay full of boring grey boxes on pallets, some with wheels, some floating and others simply on the metal looking floor. The thing that was confusing him was that somehow they looked tidier.

As Jack turned and stepped away from the loading door, wondering what happens next, there stood Beth in all her Hersatz glory baring nearly all. Jack tried to look everywhere but at the back of her, she stood stock still facing away from him, with frequent glances in her direction he could see that she was wearing at least some undergarments, they just appeared to be flesh coloured.

As she did not appear to be moving in any way Jack realized why he had thought of her as an Hersatz, walking closer to her Jack could see quite clearly the double spine structure in her back.
"Hello Beth?" asked Jack cautiously with a mixture of relief and worry in his voice.
She made no attempt to reply, Jack walked around to the front of her where she stood with her head slightly tipped to one side, the thing that scared him the most were the eyes. Where before they had been intelligent and bright, now they were a milky white and glassy looking.

Jack poked her with a finger and watched as she started to topple over backwards like a tree being uprooted by a digger. Jack grabbed at her to stop her from falling over, finding suddenly that she was actually really quite well built and somehow his hands were now also stuck to her. They made a slow dance like twist together, as Beth continued her felling. Face to face they slowly toppled to the deck with Jack as a cushion.

Jack landed on his back on the surprisingly soft deck of the hard metal ship, with Beth held at arms length above him. After only a few seconds he was amazed at just how heavy Beth was, with sweat starting to pore from his brow and other places, he strained to do anything with her stiff body pressing down above him. He tried tipping her over to one side or the other but with no effect, it was like she was deliberately counter balancing everything he tried. Eventually he could hold her no longer, she sunk down on top of him like a gangster into wet cement.

It was a few seconds later that Jack realized there was no pressure involved. Because of her shear weight that he had been holding up, he had expected to have his chest crushed and not currently be able to breath. Instead here he was with his eyes shut, arms crossed on his chest and no force being applied to him whatsoever.

Jack carefully opened his eyes, there was no one hanging above him or, as he looked around, no one around whatsoever. Jack pushed himself into a sitting position, with considerable difficulty, at the same time he heard an sucking sound as he moved each limb.

Encircling him was a ring of mostly red coloured bits, there was what looked like metal pipes, coils, string and something that looked quite a lot like an overly large spider crab sat between his legs. There was also a distinct lack of any structure and no Beth.

Jack looked wildly around searching for Beth, until the realization sunk in that he was in fact sat in what was left of Beth. Jack let out a tiny whimper and tried to jump up quickly, which inevitability led to much slipping, sliding and splat like noises. Eventually he resulted to rolling out of the goo and standing up slowly several feet away from the messy puddle. He started to gag slightly as he wiped his mouth and found something salty on his tongue. He looked at his hands and they still had bits of Beth's skin stuck to his palms. Jack found a corner in the cargo bay and emptied the contents of his stomach.

Jack had never felt quite so violated for some reason, there was that time in a hotel room in Bangkok, waking up next to lots of used leather goods. That had been a worry but he had never been quite sure if it had all been a dream, whilst this just looked and smelled plain wrong.

A little while later when he felt in more control of his stomach, he looked once again at the mess on the deck and slowly walked over following his wayward footprints. There were several questions now running through his mind, chief among them was 'what had just happened and where was Beth?'

Jack stood talking to himself, mumbling away for several seconds, eventually giggling, pointing at the mess on the floor and then he simply walked away.

Jack made his way down various corridors, finally arriving at what he thought of as his room, he nearly jumped straight on to his bed but at the last second pulled himself up short, looked at his coloured hands and decided to have a wash.

After over twenty minutes of preening, Jack finally emerged wearing his original blue jeans, white t-shirt and a cream cardigan. The socks were whiter than he remembered, as were his trainers but they all felt comfortable, no that was not the word, normal would be more accurate, after all he was technically going home.

Feeling much cleaner and more confident than he had in weeks Jack made his way to the bridge of the War Catcher, he half expected to see Beth sat in the Captains chair looking over the controls. Instead the bridge was eerily quiet, which Jack found quite unnerving, it was then that he realized he had not been alone or by himself for quite some time. He was not by nature a lonely person, it was just that everyone regardless of who they were, at some point needed some 'me time'.

This really was the first time Jack had felt actually alone, for a few seconds it felt brilliant, right up to the point where he noticed there was no sound from the ship whatsoever. There were no pings, boings or bleeps coming from any console and additionally they all appeared to be turned off. There was no engine hum or vibration of any description. Even when he had been stood on foreign planets and moons there had been some sense of feeling, of motion from his feet or stomach. It was something he had never noticed before because it was always there, so when everything was removed it was like some form of sensory deprivation. Then there was the lighting, it appeared to be on emergency power for some reason, which he had only just noticed as he was now standing in the window. Again he had found himself drawn to the all encompassing viewing window, staring out with a look of wonder and then the panic started to kick in.

It began as shakes, finally turning into trouser worry as he really started to panic about what he was supposed to be doing. He honestly had no idea what he was doing and frankly needed some guidance. Jack called out hesitantly "hello?"

He called out several more times and then turned to look back out the window where the view finally fell into place. In front of him spread as far as the eye could see was a planet debris field. There were occasional bits of human made paraphernalia swooping past the window, chairs, a child's swing, a see-saw in a violent orange, frazzled looking mannequins and then he noticed that they were not all made of plastic, some had faces.

Jack turned from the window, nearly walking into Sarah's glossy white floating ball, currently there was no face present or adornment of any description on it. It was so glossy and white that it had no apparent shadow or shading and actually just looked like a plain white disc.

"Hi" said Jack taking a step back "um, what's going on?"

Sarah's floating ball slowly changed shape into an arrow and pointed out the window at something, Jack turned to look and could just about see a tiny white ship with portal like lights in the distance.

"Are we hiding from that, because it doesn't look that big?" asked Jack pointing.

The ball seemed to sigh and then spoke really quickly "the Stellar Attack Vessel monitored our arrival in the system and we're trying to convince it we're friendly."

Jack started to ask another question and was pulled up by Sarah's ball saying "so shut up as we're trying to run quiet" it hissed.

Jack stared out the window at the SAV and wondered what the problem was, as it was so far away. Sensing he was about to ask another question, an outline of a human appeared on the window in front of Jack and then disappeared to be scaled down next to the ship. Jack looked hard at the image and found that the little man projection was about a millimeter tall. If the Cloven Hoofed Pirate Ghost Ship Vessel thing had been the size of a small moon, then the SAV was a hundredth of its size but still monstrous.

After several minutes Jack was bored of being quiet and finally asked "so how much longer do we have to sit here?" after all how did running silent in space actually work. Eventually he surmised that it must have something to do with the vibration of the hull.

"No longer, we're all done" said Sarah in an joyous tone.

The lights then came back on, Jack felt the deck of the bridge come back to life with vibrations, he turned to face Sarah's ball again and asked "really, what's going on now?"

Jack followed Sarah's floating white ball, which now had her quite attractive face on it, the only problem with the image on the ball was that it was like an optical illusion. It was made by changing the shape on the ball, little hills and valleys, if you looked at it you could not tell whether it was an raised up or a recessed image. Jack actually found it quite hard to look at and was just grateful that she had forgotten to apply any makeup, which had been a troweled on nightmare.

He followed her to the central table in front of the raised Captains chair, where she floated above a two dimensional image of the space they were in.

"When we left the Ghost Ship, it was only a short split jump to where we are now" said Sarah.

"I'm sensing a but?" asked Jack.

"All space is relative and we therefore have to be in a specific place to jump back in time and be in the right space"

"I thought it was just me going back?" asked Jack in a surprised and yet relief soaked tone.

"You don't as of yet have all your faculties Jack, so we've made the decision to assist you."

"Yes about that, who is the 'we' we're talking about and what happened to Beth. I'm mean she's just gone?" Jack shuddered at the thought.

"Don't worry Jack she'll, ah, turn up soon."

"I hope not, because I mean well, there wasn't a whole lot left really" said Jack to himself, trying to not remember too hard the sticky patch on the cargo deck floor.

It was one of those images that would stick in his mind forever, like the time as a small boy he saw a squirrel make a mad dash across a busy road and end up as a furry brown star shape imprinted on the tarmac. He remembered laughing at the time, first of all because it looked like some comedy cartoon sketch, but then as they had driven closer he had seen the after effects of being squashed. It had been a curious, mysterious and deadly thing to see as a young child, mixed with two aggressive emotions in the end, laughter and guilt. This was much the way he had felt when Beth had 'disappeared', with the added nasty bonus image in his head of some version of Beth stalking the dark depths of the ship, looking for revenge and dripping everywhere.

Taking a minute or two to compose himself, Jack asked "so why are we here?"
"Because space is relative Jack."
"Um okay, but still, why are we here?"
Almost seeming to growl as she spoke Sarah replied "we don't have an anchor Jack, there is nothing here to attach the time line too. So if we traveled back at the position where Earth would have been now, we would be months ahead of its position in space!"
Jack took a moment to work this out and then said slowly "so we're in the position where Earth would have been a few months ago?"
"More or less and probably less on the more."

Before Jack could even hope to work that one out Sarah continued with "we're ready."
Jack started to protest leaning on the table, he was going to go along the lines of 'how, where, why?' and 'how long will it take?' He was pulled up short by the whitest white flash he had ever seen or felt and the feeling that he had just been dragged sideways, or was that diagonally. He was then left standing or more precisely swaying, feeling like he had just been on a roller coaster ride through a burning field of opiates.
"What just happened?" asked Jack wheezily.
"Really, your going to ask that after everything we've just discussed!" exclaimed Sarah.
Jack replied quickly "call it nefarious disorientation" then something tickled his ear and he swiped his hand quickly. In surprise he actually hit something, when he tried to find it again it was gone. Jack shook his head to try and clear it, he was still swaying slightly and had some form of ringing in his ears that did not seem to want to move out.

Jack tipped his head to one side and tapped on his skull, trying to relieve what he thought of as a pressure whistle from inside his head. Sarah watching him closely said "all time travelers experience some form of irritation when they move through time, as a normal person moving from day to day its called decay. As someone who has traveled back in time, it could be something you might not notice to anything, but most creatures just here a whistle."
"A whistle, it's more like a steam train continuously blowing its top!" moaned Jack.
"You'll get used to it Jack" said Sarah unsympathetically.

Working a finger round the inside of one ear and then the other he wondered out loud "is this what tinnitus is like?"
"Probably, but we have more immediate concerns."
"Such as?"
"Getting you on board the SAV first and then, when your caught, you must declare yourself as a 'stowaway'."
"Why would I want to be caught?"
"Because all stowaways must be presented to the Captain before..." Sarah paused as she tried to source another more suitable word, one that was a bit less regulation sounding "removal" she finished lamely.
Jack walked over and stood in the window, looking out he felt sure he should be able to see the Earth and its moon, but he guessed they were at the edge of the solar system waiting for the attack fleet to arrive.
"Where's Earth?" asked Jack curiously.
"Actually directly in front of you" replied Sarah.
"On the other side of the Sun?"
"No Jack, this side of the Sun, it's just quite bright and the Earths quite small!"

      Jack carried on looking left and right, squinting, trying to see his home world with little luck. Sarah then swooped forward in front of Jack and did a little spin, a few moments later the Earth swung into view, he watched it gently spin around in front of him, like they were in an high speed orbit.

      Jack looked deep in thought and then he remembered his problem with all this time travel "if we're six months ago?"
"Yes?" Sarah sighed.
"Then am I down there, somewhere?" asked Jack pointing.
"Currently, yes."
"What do you mean currently?"
"Your soon to be, shall we say, extracted."
"Couldn't we stop it then?"
"We could, but then none of this would have happened."
"That would be a good thing, wouldn't it?"
"Right up to the point where we don't exist in this Universe any more, then yes."

      Jack just looked at Sarah's blank expression on her ball, he remembered Olgas' explanation of time travel. Jack wondered if he stopped his own abduction and used the mystic sphere ball thingy he had in a pocket somewhere, whether or not he could stop this all from ever happening. The only thing was, would he still personally still exist afterwards. He was quite fond of existing, as were most humans, with the occasional exception of certain individuals of the hero and nut variety. Self sacrifice was something that happened to other people, as far as he was concerned.
"So what your saying is to leave events as they are?" asked Jack carefully.
"Yes" said Sarah.
"Except one?"
"That is why we're here after all."

"But by preventing my abduction..."
"Who said anything about an abduction?"
"I assumed when you said extracted that you meant I was taken against my will."
"Yes but abduction sounds so, rude."
Jack rolled his eyes, as was the case sometimes when talking to Sarah, you found she was either quite human or quite robotic in her replies.
"Okay so how do we know that giving the Data Wheel to the Commander will prevent Earth's destruction and stopping my abduction won't?" asked Jack.
"We don't precisely, all we have to work with are probabilities."
"Guesses you mean."
"Yes, but very accurate ones. Now shush, your destiny awaits you in three, two, one" as Sarah counted down the view in the window changed to show a blank part of space. It was so blank and uninteresting that Jack wondered whether they were looking in the right direction. Then a white line appeared in the middle of the window, within a few seconds it had turned into a thin foaming torrent, giving the impression of immense forces at work. Within seconds the keel of some immense ship was visible, as it broke through the foaming waves. It was like watching from above some sea monster pushing its way up from the depths of the sea, with strange flighty clouds reflected on the surface as it slowly broached the foaming waves.
Just as suddenly there was then nothing to see of the foamy white line, in its place were a whole lot of vessels that resembled some crazed television remote control designs, all in garish white. The ships wallowed about for a moment adjusting there headings, until they were all lined up together. The lights in the windows then suddenly turned off in a depleting sequence, like a storm blowing down power lines really quickly. The ships then seemed to fade to a dark shade, as they turned to angle the light of the nearest star away from there target, looking as though they had passed through a colour changing car wash.
    Jack turned to Sarah and felt the need to whisper "what happens next?"
"Now we use the Ghost Field Generator to dress as a Shark and we drop you off."
    They circled or as Jack thought of it, sphered about. They watched several small dart shaped craft launch from various exit tubes in the vessel, then followed as they flitted, rolled and played like dolphins high on human drugs in the sea about the solar system. There white hulls and flame decals leading you to think they were playful craft, right up until the moment they had a hand in destroying your home.
"Why are we following them?" asked Jack angrily.
"Because we need to blend in, but mostly so we can hijack the flame design and get the SAV access codes."
"And we need the flame design because?"
"The flame design and colour denotes which ship the Shark came from and the access codes enable us to gain entry to a repair hangar."
"Why do we need a repair hangar?"

"Have you seen the size of the Sharks, do you really think our ship is going to fit inside one if the tube launchers it came from?"

"Um no, but wouldn't they land on a docking platform?"

"There are several ways to dock with a SAV, but unless your damaged you won't get access to the repair dock, which is large enough to accommodate most ships, including us."

After following one of the flighty ships into an asteroid field, Jack was surprised to see a bolt of what looked like lightening leave the War Catcher and strike the Shark. The little ship tumbled around, heading to strike a very large asteroid indeed. Then automatic systems on the Shark fired harpoon like elements from its underside, as it spun pass the rock, slowly it was reeled in and tethered to the rock.

"Don't worry Jack they'll be fine, the system will reset in twenty minutes or so and by that time we should be long gone."

Jack just nodded, stood watching through the bridge window as they made there way towards the Stellar Attack Vessel.

As they approached Jack noticed that they seemed to be listing at angle to the SAV of about thirty degrees and when he asked Sarah, she replied by saying "we are damaged you know, from the asteroid field!"

They were then directed to a large door on the side of the vessel that started to slowly open, shining bright light into space and then it stopped opening.

"Is that wide enough?" asked Jack squinting at the gap.

Growling slightly Sarah replied "for a Shark it is."

"But not us? Why didn't you give us the appearance of more damage so they open the door wider?"

"Because then they would have sent out a recovery craft to tow us in and we're a bit heavier than a Shark!"

"Okay, so what are we going to do?"

"Obviously we can't dock now, so we shall fain a blowout and we'll put you in an escape pod."

"We've got escape pods?"

"No we haven't, but they have."

Sarah blew some air out of a vent, along with some dust like debris and flew along the SAV hull. Occasionally clanging the two ships together, making a sound like large kitchen utensils being banged together by giants.

Jack had been sent down to an airlock by Sarah facing the SAV, he was not really sure how he was going to get on board the ship or even get off the ship he was currently on. There had been a conversation about escape pods, since they did not have any and the Sharks did, maybe Sarah was manufacturing one for him?

He stepped into a waiting doorway that Sarah was indicating with a floating green arrow. The door then made a 'swooshing' noise as it shut behind him and he was presented with a small chamber just big enough to hold eight maybe ten people at a push. It was like most of the rest of the ship, looking like it was made from some durable metal but also quite curvy inside, giving the impression of space without there actually being any.

In a tired voice Sarah said over some slightly tinny tannoy system "turn around Jack."

Jack dutifully turned around, finding his teeth starting to itch as he looked out through a shimmering door at a pear shaped glass blob about twenty meters or so away on the side of the SAV. The room he was stood in, or airlock as Jack now thought of it, was considerably smaller, in fact just his size.

It was then, as he watched the glass screen fold away to one side on the blob, that he worked out exactly what Sarah had in mind.

Jack had not really noticed the slight rainbow shimmering of the energy field in front of him, he certainly did when it was turned off. With a scream that sounded for all of half a second, until there was no more air, he was hurled by decompression into the depths of space. Four seconds later he sank into the protective embrace of the pod, the glass looking screen folded back over without a sound and then air was pumped back in with a hiss. Jack looked out of the full length window at the underside of Sarah's Shark patrol ship, waving a clenched fist at it as it moved smoothly away and then seemed to shimmer taking on some new, dark ghost image.

It was surprisingly comfortable inside the escape pod, considering he had just been in the vacuum of space, Jack was curious and thankful about how he had actually survived without any apparent side effects. Looking around he found he was upright but half sat, half lying down in a fireside red leather effect wing-back style chair. It even had the button and stud detailing in the leather. As Jack was admiring the craftsmanship, the chair slowly spun round on its pedestal to face into the pod, the only things missing were the carved table with the whiskey decanter and the log fire.

After nothing else seemed to be happening he leant forward and walked around the inside of the pod. It was actually quite spacious inside, with seats for four people around a central ribbed white column, with just enough room to walk round the outside and not touch the dull silver panelled walls or a seated occupant. The walls were curved like the inside of a really big pear, with ornate detailing between every square panel of dull silver. The only thing missing was a door. There was obviously the way he had come in, through the window but as that was still currently pointing into space, it was not really an option. Jack sack back down on the red leather chair and ran a hand over the ornate arms. That was when he discovered what felt like a button on the arm of the chair, after careful inspection it appeared to be a blackberry disguised as a button, with a matching one on the other chair arm. Pressing one or the other button made a very satisfying click sound but nothing actually happened.

Jack was just about to press both together when Beth's voice suddenly almost seemed to shout in his head, as if from a long way off and getting closer "don't press anything else Jack."
Jack froze in place, he had wondered when Beth would come back to haunt him and now he was actually hallucinating her voice in his head. Before he could mumble anything about going slightly mad Beth said "don't worry Jack your not going mad."
"Are you reading my thoughts?"
"No, we simply know you very well."
Jack did not reply on the grounds that he did not fancy spending any time in a mental clinic and knew that if kept on listening he might actually have to turn himself into one.
"Just think of us as talking to you by phone" it was as if she were voicing his own concerns.
"But your not, are you?" asked Jack worriedly.
"No, but it'll make it a whole lot easier if you think of us as being on the other end of a phone, won't it?"
"I suppose so" mumbled Jack.
Beth then continued "right now that's sorted" not really thought Jack "let's get you out of here before we run out of time."

Then to Jack's mounting worry about his sanity, Beth seemed to raise herself out of him like a ghost passing through. She turned and smiled at him with her green eyes seeming to glow, her mousy brown hair swaying behind her back and her face captivating him. She was wearing an emerald green coloured evening dress, which accentuated every possible part of her anatomy and Jack felt his jaw drop.

Beth then followed his eyes, seeming to see the dress for the first time "thank you Jack, for the dress" she replied whilst performing a little twirl "but don't you think that it's not really in keeping with the occasion."
"Huh?" said Jack still looking and feeling confused.
"We're on an alien vessel after all, trying to stop armageddon and your sat there being male!"
"Huh?"

"We don't have time for this Jack" growled Beth, who then started to storm about the escape pod and poke her hand, face and even on occasion her sandal strapped foot into the walls. Eventually with her green dress billowing as she suddenly stopped, she stared at just another blank dull silver panel with a blueish tinge, she smiled to herself and called Jack over with a wave.

Jack was feeling conflicted and really confused about his feelings for Beth, she was amazingly attractive to his eye but at the same time she did not appear to be here either. When she waved at him again impatiently, he stood up and walked round to the panel she was leaning against. If he had glanced out of the window as he stood up, he might have seen Earth's moon starting to play into view.

Pointing at the panel Beth made a swiping motion with her hand and then with another hand gesture indicated for Jack to do the same. Jack waved his hand across the blueish silver panel, the ornate carvings around the panel lit up with a yellowish light and next to it a door slid to one side.

Jack stepped out cautiously into the washed out, blast damaged looking white corridor, he then turned slowly and found himself face to face with the muzzle of a big glossy black gun pointing at his nose.

Standing to one side of Jack, Beth said "say stowaway Jack."

"Say stowaway Jack" squeaked Jack.

Beth tipped her head back and rolled her eyes behind his back.

Jack was being marched down a corridor quite smartly, his legs were not quite as long as the Raifoon guards on either side of him and they most definitely did not bend in the same way. His hands were handcuffed together in front of him, with some coil that looked to be the offspring of an amorous snake and a jigsaw. From the cuffs ran a further coil to something encircling his neck, when he had pulled experimentally one way or the other with his hands, the coil around his neck had tightened and breathing had become a bit of an issue.

With each quick marching step they were taking Jack found the tension in his muscles starting to dissipate, with the odd crackle of lightening still playing over his scalp. After putting the gun muzzle in his face, Jack had started to shout 'no,no no' as they had approached him outside the pod with some crackling electrical spurting device in there paws, but to no avail.

When he had finished shaking he had found his neck and hands connected by the coil, with the guards making some amusing comment about Newmans and electricity not mixing.

At some point they had crossed from one part of the ship to another, leaving the damage behind and now they were striding down near perfectly white corridors.

Beth walked beside him, glancing about with what Jack thought of pleasure, as she occasionally skipped along to some invisible beat.

"What do you think your doing?" asked Jack of Beth suddenly wincing, as he received a bang on the back of the head from a bubbly black rifle butt, carried by one of the Raifoons.

Beth smiled at him and skipped ahead, turned to face him and floated in front of his face. Jack looked down at her feet, to find them not moving and drifting about a foot above the corridor.

She bent down to look into his eyes and said "Jack, we're inside your head, so these guards" she waved at the two Raifoons "can't see us or hear us."

"So I am going nuts then" moaned Jack.

"Be quiet" grumbled a guard behind him "unless you want another head slap har har."

"No your not nuts Jack, we told you to think of us as being on the phone, so just think of us as being on a video phone in your head. Before you ask another question out loud, simply try asking it without moving your lips, maybe" advised Beth giving a knowing nod towards the guards.

Jack opened his mouth to speak, wisely shut it and mumbled "so, where are we going?"

Beth replied simply "to see the Captain of course!"

Chapter 50 : The End?

Entering the bridge of the Stellar Attack Vessel was like walking onto a film set, as far as Jack was concerned. There were all manner of shaped seats and raised areas, in the middle was obviously where the Captain of the ship sat, as everything seemed to be angled towards the raised dais. The room was basically a sphere, with gantries and walkways in most directions, with creatures walking on all the surfaces, above, below, behind and in front. Everything was also apparently painted in varying shades of white, as Jack looked he could see black and grey shades being slowly chased away by the whiteness. Except on the edges, the edges and corners still had a black tape looking covering to them, over all the boundaries. All this Jack saw, but what really got his attention was the window, or was it a screen, that covered the opposite wall from where they had walked in.

The window panel took up a good eighth of the entire sphere, with the crew walking around it like it was a large pond. Jack could only really see the top of there heads, he felt like he was spying, looking down on them bobbing around the window. It was quite disconcerting watching the top of peoples heads all around you, walking up and down the sides of the sphere, like it was as normal as walking in the park, there were also gantries, ladders and sidestep lifts. The only other thing to go through Jack's mind, was wondering if bald spot top fuzz spray was a big seller in this part of the galaxy, especially for the hair full Raifoons.

The other thing about the display that got his attention, was the pin sharp image on the screen of Earth, it was slowly rotating away like a hog on a spit waiting to be burned. It was as he looked at the image that Jack saw what was wrong, they were looking at the Earth rotating bottom to top, like they were following a rolling football down a hill. Basically it was defying film convention in Jack's book and because of this made everything feel more real some how.

They stood for what felt like several minutes to Jack, waiting on the raised decking for the Captain to finish whatever he was doing in his seat. He then spun round in his chair, seeming to flow towards Jack, taking the steps down from the dais like he were on a slide. As he drew closer with some relief Jack recognized the Commander or Kraggoors' furry markings, what he did not recognize was the expression on his fox like face.

"So your our?" quizzed the Captain.
"Stowaway?" asked Jack, with a nudged prompt from Beth.
"Good, just checking" turning to the guards the Captain said "you can release him."

With sharp looks at one another the two guards stepped forward, one placed a furry mitt on Jack's shoulder, the other held a Quellz just above the handcuffs and pressed in some code. The coil around his neck and the ones on his wrists retracted into a ten centimeter long oblong, which the guard caught easily as it tumbled away, showing how much practice they had and then slipped it into a belt pouch.

Jack had not moved whilst this was going on and even when he was free was unsure whether he should move. The sound of the coils receding into the jigsaw looking, snake skin shaded oblong box, had sounded like the coils of a snake being rubbed together at high speed. It was unnerving, which was probably the point, with Jack thinking he was glad he had been near unconscious when the coils had been applied, otherwise there may have been another trouser incident.
"Commander" said a voice that Jack recognized as Second, his red nose twitching as he spoke.
With a sigh of relief the now Commander replied "finally."

Jack rubbed his wrists each in turn and wondered what was going to happen to next. To his surprise he was given back, by one of the guards, the small black leather bag he had had magnetically clipped to his multi pouched belt. He checked the contents and after seeing a nod from the Commander, Jack pulled out the data wheel from a belt pocket and the crystal like sphere from the soft black bag.

The Commander put his hand on Jack's shoulder and said "so this data wheel is going to advise us not to invade your planet?" Jack placed it slowly in the Commanders hand.
"Yes?" asked Jack with some surprise, thinking something was wrong some how.
"And in your other hand?" asked the Commander as he stepped back, seeming to be looking for something to hide behind.
In a surprise to Beth, Jack had the presence of mind to not say what the sphere was "oh, it's just a mystic ball."

Jack looked at the crystal ball sitting quite calmly in his hand, for some reason it seemed to have a personality all of its own, almost like it was smiling at him. It then occurred to him that he still had no idea how to activate the thing so he could fix the time line, preventing the Earth from so Earth was never invaded.
Beth stepped in front of Jack, still wearing her emerald green evening dress, then she proceeded to prod and poke the ball with a look of deep concentration on her face.
"You don't know how the thing works, do you?" exclaimed Jack.
Everyone on the bridge turned to looked at him, as he realized that once again he had been talking to Beth out loud and not in his head. Honestly he was not sure which way was worse, but talking out loud certainly felt better than talking in his head, that way madness lie. At least he was fairly sure it was that way, either that or getting answers as well.

After a few seconds there was a light cough, Jack saw the Commander was stood directly in front of him again, looking over Beth's shoulder, with the crew thinking he had been talking to the Commander and not some emerald apparition that only he could see.

The Commander held out his hand, nodding for Jack to place the ball in his gloved mitt, as Jack did so Beth seemed to smirk in satisfaction and the Commander smiled as his eyes flashed.

Jack for a moment looked on in mild surprise, he saw the eyes blink like a shutter from left and right meeting in the middle like lift doors, with a flash of red as they slammed together.

The Commander was a Raifoon and he blinked the same as a human, the only creature Jack had met who blinked like a stage curtain was a Furrykin.

"Olgas Faid!" Jack chocked in a quick whisper, then he disappeared with a small pop, like the sound of someone sucking there lips apart.

The crew stood back in surprise as the Newman vanished, leaving a smokey trail in the air and a dusty black cloud like stain on the bridge floor. There was a two meter wide metallic ring on the deck where Jack had been stood, with what looked like flashing glass crystals every half meter of the circumference.

Olgas Faid placed the Data Wheel on his neck, then swiped to cancel the invasion of Earth on the floating panel in front of him. He was now totally consumed by the silver crystal like orb nestling in his gloved hand. The sphere started to slowly shake as he stared proudly at it, then cracks started to appear over its pristine surface, causing Olgas Faid to frown. Slowly the orb lifted itself out of his hand and floated in front of his confused face.

Olgas Faid made to capture the floating ball, watching with growing worry as his gloved hand passed backwards and forwards through the orb. Then the sphere gave a little shake, exploding with a blinding light and a noise like 'twong.'

The End.

Printed in Great Britain
by Amazon